Lovers & Other Monsters

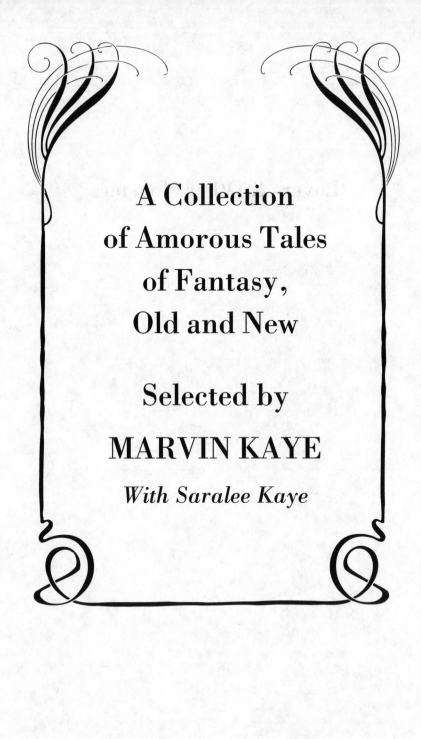

A Collection of Amorous Tales of Fantasy, Old and New

Selected by

MARVIN KAYE

With Saralee Kaye

Lovers

&

Other

Monsters

GUILDAMERICA BOOKS™

DOUBLEDAY BOOK & MUSIC CLUBS, INC.
GARDEN CITY, NEW YORK

GuildAmerica Books™ is a trademark, registration pending, on behalf
of Doubleday Book & Music Clubs, Inc.
Acknowledgments on pages 497–99
The author and publisher have made a thorough effort to locate all persons having any
rights or interests in the material presented in this book and to secure all necessary
reprint permissions. If any required acknowledgments have been omitted inadvertently or
any rights overlooked, we regret the error and will correct the oversight
in future editions of the book.

Contents

Introduction

All in the Name of Love

Berlioz, Byron, Coleridge, Liszt, Shelley wooed Wagner's love-death motif, but long before the romantic movement, William Shakespeare, in *The Life and Death of King John*, penned literature's most chilling invocation of the ultimate lover and monster—

> Death, death; O amiable lovely death!
> Thou odoriferous stench! sound rottenness!
> Arise forth from the couch of lasting night,
> Thou hate and terror to prosperity,
> And I will kiss thy detestable bones,
> And put my eyeballs in thy faulty brows,
> And ring these fingers with thy household worms,
> And stop this gap of breath with fulsome dust,
> And be a carrion monster like thyself.

Monstrous, indeed, are the many instances of perverse love throughout history, from Jacob's indiscreetly expressed preference for one son over eleven envious others; Cleopatra's coy empire-sacrificing stratagem at Actium; the fervent worship of Holy Writ that paved the way for the Crusades and the Spanish Inquisition; and let us not omit that self-loving lust for power that tempts kings, presidents and dictators to lay waste to their own nations. One might rephrase an important sentiment of Bertrand Russell's, and say that throughout history, the immoderate pursuit of love has wrought incalculable harm upon humanity's mind and spirit.

Lovers & Other Monsters dwells on some of the more bizarre aspects of Ye Tender Passion. Here and there, the mix may be leavened with compassion and the miracle of true tenderness, but let the reader be warned, most of these selections are harrowing excursions into the darkest corners of the human heart, running the gamut from simple blood-lust to amorous betrayal, cosmic seduction, incest, morbid fetishism, murder, necro-cannibalism, suicide and even a species of vegetable rape.

Romantic Foreplay

Victor Hugo once wrote that no army can conquer an idea whose time has come, but for seventeen years, a veritable militia of editors fought the notion of *Lovers & Other Monsters*. Its title, obviously inspired by Renée Taylor and Joseph Bologna's funny-sad play and 1970 hit movie, *Lovers and Other Strangers*, occurred to me in 1974 as I prepared two early paperback anthologies for publication.

The idea of an anthology devoted to some of the grimmer aspects of love and sex struck me as an easy one to market, but publishers thought otherwise. A few of them maintained the demonstrably erroneous opinion that "anthologies don't sell," but most of them—including Playboy Press!—simply were afraid *Lovers & Other Monsters* would be too hot to handle.

I put the idea—well, to bed—and went on to other projects, only briefly sending it around again years later when my friend, writer-editor Jessica Amanda Salmonson, suggested we collaborate on "Lovers," but there were still no takers. (Thanks though, to Jessica, whose own contribution appears in this book and who introduced me to Guillaume Apollinaire's "The Blue Eye," which I have indeed included.)

But at last I trial-ballooned the idea by dividing my second Doubleday Book and Music Club anthology, *Masterpieces of Terror and the Supernatural*, into subsections, the second of which is labeled "Lovers and Other Monsters." The ongoing success of that volume led my friends at the Doubleday clubs to agree to midwife this long a-borning anthology.

As usual, I have restricted each author to a single entry and generally have preferred the less familiar to the oft anthologized. Both reprints and new work comprise the contents of this volume: forty-six tales, half-a-dozen poems, and one short dramatic composition.

The theme-dictated selections in the opening and closing sections, "Odd Couples" and "Fatal Attractions," include examples of various types of literature, but the three inner portions of *Lovers & Other Monsters* are respectively divided by genre. "Worldly Love" contains only "mainstream" compositions; "Not of This World" is pure fantasy, and "Out of This World" consists exclusively of science fiction.

And now it is time to steel your heart and gird your loins as Cupid dips a quiverful of aphrodisiac arrows in acid.

—MARVIN KAYE
Manhattan, 1991

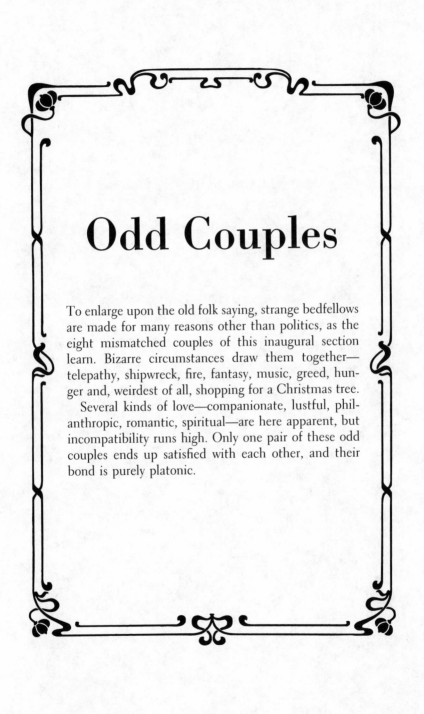

Odd Couples

To enlarge upon the old folk saying, strange bedfellows are made for many reasons other than politics, as the eight mismatched couples of this inaugural section learn. Bizarre circumstances draw them together—telepathy, shipwreck, fire, fantasy, music, greed, hunger and, weirdest of all, shopping for a Christmas tree.

Several kinds of love—companionate, lustful, philanthropic, romantic, spiritual—are here apparent, but incompatibility runs high. Only one pair of these odd couples ends up satisfied with each other, and their bond is purely platonic.

Poul Anderson

Journeys End

Do you yearn to find a kindred spirit to share your every thought and mood? Think carefully before wishing for it, lest, like POUL ANDERSON's *"esper" couple, you actually succeed. Author of such acclaimed science-fantasies as* The High Crusade, Three Hearts and Three Lions *and* Queen of Air and Darkness, *Mr. Anderson lives in San Francisco with his writer wife, Karen.*

—doctor bill & twinges in chest but must be all right maybe indigestion & dinner last night & wasn't audrey giving me the glad eye & how the hell is a guy to know & maybe i can try and find out & what a fool i can look if she doesn't—

—goddam idiot & they shouldn't let some people drive & oh all right so the examiner was pretty lenient with me i haven't had a bad accident yet & christ blood all over my blood let's face it i'm scared to drive but the buses are no damn good & straight up three paces & man in a green hat & judas i ran that red light—

In fifteen years a man got used to it, more or less. He could walk down the street and hold his own thoughts to himself while the surf of unvoiced voices was a nearly ignored mumble in his brain. Now and then, of course, you got something very bad, it stood up in your skull and shrieked at you.

Norman Kane, who had come here because he was in love with a girl he had never seen, got to the corner of University and Shattuck just when the light turned against him. He paused, fetching out a cigaret with nicotine-yellowed fingers while traffic slithered in front of his eyes.

It was an unfavorable time, 4:30 in the afternoon, homeward rush of nervous systems jangled with weariness and hating everything else on feet or wheels. Maybe he should have stayed in the bar down the street. It had been pleasantly cool and dim, the bartender's mind an amiable cud-chewing somnolence, and he could have suppressed awareness of the woman.

No, maybe not. When the city had scraped your nerves raw, they didn't have much resistance to the slime in some heads.

Odd, he reflected, how often the outwardly polite ones were the foully twisted inside. They wouldn't dream of misbehaving in public, but just below the surface of consciousness . . . Better not think of it, better not remember. Berkeley was at least preferable to San Francisco or Oakland. The bigger the town, the more evil it seemed to hold, three centimeters under the frontal bone. New York was almost literally uninhabitable.

There was a young fellow waiting beside Kane. A girl came down the sidewalk, pretty, long yellow hair and a well-filled blouse. Kane focused idly on her: yes, she had an apartment of her own, which she had carefully picked for a tolerant superintendent. Lechery jumped in the young man's nerves. His eyes followed the girl, Cobean-*style, and she walked on . . . simple harmonic motion.

Too bad. They could have enjoyed each other. Kane chuckled to himself. He had nothing against honest lust, anyhow not in his liberated conscious mind; he couldn't do much about a degree of subconscious puritanism. Lord, you can't be a telepath and remain any kind of prude. People's lives were their own business, if they didn't hurt anyone else too badly.

—*the trouble is*, he thought, *they hurt me. but i can't tell them that. they'd rip me apart and dance on the pieces. the government /the military/ wouldn't like a man to be alive who could read secrets but their fear-inspired anger would be like a baby's tantrum beside the red blind amok of the common man (thoughtful husband considerate father good honest worker earnest patriot) whose inward sins were known. you can talk to a priest or a psychiatrist because it is only talk & he does not live your failings with you—*

The light changed and Kane started across. It was clear fall weather, not that this area had marked seasons, a cool sunny day with a small wind blowing up the street from the water. A few blocks ahead of him, the University campus was a splash of manicured green under brown hills.

—*flayed & burningburningburning moldering rotted flesh & the bones the white hard clean bones coming out gwtjklfmx—*

* Refers to Sam Cobean, cartoonist-mk

Kane stopped dead. Through the vertigo he felt how sweat was drenching into his shirt.

And it was such an ordinary-looking man!

"Hey, there, buster, wake up! Ya wanna get killed?"

Kane took a sharp hold on himself and finished the walk across the street. There was a bench at the bus stop and he sat down till the trembling was over.

Some thoughts were unendurable.

He had a trick of recovery. He went back to Father Schliemann. The priest's mind had been like a well, a deep well under sun-speckled trees, its surface brightened with a few gold-colored autumn leaves . . . but there was nothing bland about the water, it had a sharp mineral tang, a smell of the living earth. He had often fled to Father Schliemann, in those days of puberty when the telepathic power had first wakened in him. He had found good minds since then, happy minds, but never one so serene, none with so much strength under the gentleness.

"I don't want you hanging around that papist, boy, do you understand?" It was his father, the lean implacable man who always wore a black tie. "Next thing you know, you'll be worshipping graven images just like him."

"But they *aren't*—"

His ears could still ring with the cuff. "Go up to your room! I don't want to see you till tomorrow morning. And you'll have two more chapters of Deuteronomy memorized by then. Maybe that'll teach you the true Christian faith."

Kane grinned wryly and lit another cigaret from the end of the previous one. He knew he smoked too much. And drank—but not heavily. Drunk, he was defenseless before the horrible tides of thinking.

He had had to run away from home at the age of fourteen. The only other possibility was conflict ending with reform school. It had meant running away from Father Schliemann too, but how in hell's red fires could a sensitive adolescent dwell in the same house as his father's brain? Were the psychologists now admitting the possibility of a sadistic masochist? Kane *knew* the type existed.

Give thanks for this much mercy, that the extreme telepathic range was only a few hundred yards. And a mind-reading boy was not altogether helpless; he could evade officialdom and the worst horrors of the underworld. He could find a decent elderly couple at the far end of the continent and talk himself into adoption.

Kane shook himself and got up again. He threw the cigaret to the ground and stubbed it out with his heel. A thousand examples told him what obscure sexual symbolism was involved in that act, but what the deuce . . . it was also a practical thing. Guns are phallic too, but at times you need a gun.

Weapons: he could not help wincing as he recalled dodging the draft in 1949. He'd traveled enough to know this country was worth defending. But it hadn't been any trick at all to hoodwink a psychiatrist and get himself marked hopelessly psychoneurotic—which he would be after two years penned with frustrated men. There had been no choice, but he could not escape a sense of dishonor.

—haven't we all sinned /every one of us/ is there a single human creature on earth without his burden of shame?—

A man was coming out of the drugstore beside him. Idly, Kane probed his mind. You could go quite deeply into anyone's self if you cared to, in fact you couldn't help doing so. It was impossible merely to scan verbalized thinking: the organism is too closely integrated. Memory is not a passive filing cabinet, but a continuous process beneath the level of consciousness; in a way, you are always reliving your entire past. And the more emotionally charged the recollection is, the more powerfully it radiates.

The stranger's name was—no matter. His personality was as much an unchangeable signature as his fingerprints. Kane had gotten into the habit of thinking of people as such-and-such a multi-dimensional symbolic topography; the name was an arbitrary gabble.

The man was an assistant professor of English at the University. Age 42, married, three children, making payments on a house in Albany. Steady sober type, but convivial, popular with his colleagues, ready to help out most friends. He was thinking about tomorrow's lectures, with overtones of a movie he wanted to see and an undercurrent of fear that he might have cancer after all, in spite of what the doctor said.

Below, the list of his hidden crimes. As a boy: tormenting a cat, well-buried Oedipean hungers, masturbation, petty theft . . . the usual. Later: cheating on a few exams, that ludicrous fumbling attempt with a girl which came to nothing because he was too nervous, the time he crashed a cafeteria line and had been shoved away with a cold remark (and praises be, Jim who had seen that was now living in Chicago) . . . still later: wincing memories of a stomach uncontrollably rumbling at a formal dinner, that woman in his hotel room the night he got drunk at the convention, standing by and letting old Carver be fired because he didn't have the courage to protest to the dean . . . now: youngest child a nasty whining little snotnose, but you can't show anyone what you really think, reading Rosamond Marshall when alone in his office, disturbing young breasts in tight sweaters, the petty spite of academic politics, giving Simonson an undeserved good grade because the boy was so beautiful, disgraceful sweating panic when at night he considered how death would annihilate his ego—

And what of it? This assistant professor was a good man, a kindly and honest man, his inwardness ought to be between him and the Recording Angel. Few of his thoughts had ever become deeds, or ever would. Let him bury them himself, let him be alone with them. Kane ceased focusing on him.

The telepath had grown tolerant. He expected little of anyone; nobody matched the mask, except possibly Father Schliemann and a few others . . . and those were human too, with human failings, the difference was that they knew peace. It was the emotional overtones of guilt which made Kane wince. God knew he himself was no better. Worse, maybe, but then his life had thrust him to it. If you had an ordinary human sex drive, for instance, but could not endure to cohabit with the thoughts of a woman, your life became one of fleeting encounters; there was no help for it, even if your austere boyhood training still protested.

"Pardon me, got a match?" —*lynn is dead/ i still can't understand it that i will never see her again & eventually you learn how to go on in a chopped-off fashion but what do you do in the meantime how do you get through the nights alone*—

"Sure." —*maybe that is the worst: sharing sorrow and unable to help & only able to give him a light for his cigaret*—

Kane put the matches back in his pocket and went on up University, pausing again at Oxford. A pair of large campus buildings jutted up to the left; others were visible ahead and to the right, through a screen of eucalyptus trees. Sunlight and shadow damascened the grass. From a passing student's mind he discovered where the library was. A good big library— perhaps it held a clue, buried somewhere in the periodical files. He had already arranged for permission to use the facilities: prominent young author doing research for his next novel.

Crossing wistfully-named Oxford Street, Kane smiled to himself. Writing was really the only possible occupation: he could live in the country and be remote from the jammed urgency of his fellow men. And with such an understanding of the soul as was his, with any five minutes on a corner giving him a dozen stories, he made good money at it. The only drawback was the trouble of avoiding publicity, editorial summons to

New York, autographing parties, literary teas . . . he didn't like those. But you could remain faceless if you insisted.

They said nobody but his agent knew who B. Traven was. It had occurred, wildly, to Kane that Traven might be another like himself. He had gone on a long journey to find out. . . . No. He was alone on earth, a singular and solitary mutant, except for—

It shivered in him, again he sat on the train. It had been three years ago, he was in the club car having a nightcap while the streamliner ran eastward through the Wyoming darkness. They passed a westbound train, not so elegant a one. His drink leaped from his hand to the floor and he sat for a moment in stinging blindness. That flicker of thought, brushing his mind and coming aflame with recognition and then borne away again . . . Damn it, damn it, he should have pulled the emergency cord and so should *she*. They should have halted both trains and stumbled through cinders and sagebrush and found each other's arms.

Too late. Three years yielded only a further emptiness. Somewhere in the land there was, or there had been, a young woman, and she was a telepath and the startled touch of her mind had been gentle. There had not been time to learn anything else. Since then he had given up on private detectives. (How could you tell them: "I'm looking for a girl who was on such-and-such a train the night of—"?) Personal ads in all the major papers had brought him nothing but a few crank letters. Probably she didn't read the personals; he'd never done so till his search began, there was too much unhappiness to be found in them if you understood humankind as well as he did.

Maybe this library here, some unnoticed item . . . but if there are two points in a finite space and one moves about so as to pass through every infinitesimal volume dV, it will encounter the other one in finite time *provided* that the other point is not moving too.

Kane shrugged and went along the curving way to the gatehouse. It was slightly uphill. There was a bored cop in the shelter, to make sure that only authorized cars were parked on campus. The progress paradox a ton or so of steel, burning irreplaceable petroleum to shift one or two human bodies around, and doing the job so well that it becomes universal and chokes the cities which spawned it. A telepathic society would be more rational. When every little wound in the child's soul could be felt and healed . . . when the thick burden of guilt was laid down, because everyone knew that everyone else had done the same . . . when men could not kill, because soldier and murderer felt the victim die . . .

    —*adam & eve? you can't breed a healthy race out of two people. but if we had telepathic children/ & we would be bound to do so i think because the mutation is obviously recessive/ then we could study the heredity of it & the gift would be passed on to other bloodlines in logical distribution & every generation there would be more of our kind until we could come out openly & even the mind mutes could be helped by our psychiatrists & priests & earth would be fair and clean and sane—*

There were students sitting on the grass, walking under the Portland Cement Romanesque of the buildings, calling and laughing and talking. The day was near an end. Now there would be dinner, a date, a show, maybe some beer at Robbie's or a drive up into the hills to neck and watch the lights below like trapped stars and the mighty constellation of the Bay Bridge . . . or perhaps, with a face-saving grumble about midterms, an evening of books, a world suddenly opened. It must be good to be young and mindmute. A dog trotted down the walk and Kane relaxed into the simple wordless pleasure of being a healthy and admired collie.

—so perhaps it is better to be a dog than a man? no /surely not/ for if a man knows more grief he also knows more joy & so it is to be a telepath: more easily hurt yes but /god/ think of the mindmutes always locked away in aloneness and think of sharing not only a kiss but a soul with your beloved—

The uphill trend grew steeper as he approached the library, but Kane was in fair shape and rather enjoyed the extra effort. At the foot of the stairs he paused for a quick cigaret before entering. A passing woman flicked eyes across him and he learned that he could also smoke in the lobby. Mind-reading had its everyday uses. But it was good to stand here in the sunlight. He stretched, reaching out physically and mentally.

—let's see now the integral of log x dx *well make a substitution suppose we call y equal to log* x *then this is interesting i wonder who wrote that line about euclid has looked on beauty bare—*

Kane's cigaret fell from his mouth.

It seemed that the wild hammering of his heart must drown out the double thought that rivered in his brain, the thought of a physics student, a very ordinary young man save that he was quite wrapped up in the primitive satisfaction of hounding down a problem, and the other thought, the one that was listening in.

—she—

He stood with closed eyes, asway on his feet, breathing as if he ran up a mountain. *—are You there? are You there?—*

—not daring to believe: what do i feel?—

—i was the man on the train—

—& i was the woman—
A shuddering togetherness.
"Hey! Hey, mister, is anything wrong?"
Almost Kane snarled. Her thought was so remote, on the very rim of indetectability, he could get nothing but subvocalized words, nothing of the self, and this busybody—"No, thanks, I'm OK, just a, a little winded."
—where are You, where can i find You o my darling?—
—image of a large white building/ right over here & they call it dwinelle hall & i am sitting on the bench outside & please come quickly please be here i never thought this could become real—
Kane broke into a run. For the first time in fifteen years, he was unaware of his human surroundings. There were startled looks, he didn't see them, he was running to her and she was running too.
—my name is norman kane & i was not born to that name but took it from people who adopted me because i fled my father (horrible how mother died in darkness & he would not let her have drugs though it was cancer & he said drugs were sinful and pain was good for the soul & he really honestly believed that) & when the power first appeared i made slips and he beat me and said it was witchcraft & i have searched all my life since & i am a writer but only because i must live but it was not aliveness until this moment—
—o my poor kicked beloved/ i had it better/ in me the power grew more slowly and i learned to cover it & i am 20 years old & came here to study but what are books at this moment—
He could see her now. She was not conventionally beautiful, but neither was she ugly, and there was kindness in her eyes and on her mouth.
—what shall i call you? to me you will always be You but there must be a name for the mindmutes & i have a place in the country among old trees & such few people as live nearby are good folk/ as good as life will allow them to be—
—then let me come there with you & never leave again—
They reached each other and stood a foot apart. There was no need for a kiss or even a handclasp . . . not yet. It was the minds which leaped out and enfolded and became one.
—I REMEMBER THAT AT THE AGE OF THREE I DRANK OUT OF THE TOILET BOWL/ THERE WAS A PECULIAR FASCINATION TO IT & I USED TO STEAL LOOSE CHANGE FROM MY MOTHER THOUGH SHE HAD LITTLE ENOUGH TO CALL HER OWN SO I COULD SNEAK DOWN TO THE DRUGSTORE FOR ICE CREAM & I SQUIRMED OUT OF THE DRAFT & THESE ARE THE DIRTY EPISODES INVOLVING WOMEN—
—AS A CHILD I WAS NOT FOND OF MY GRANDMOTHER THOUGH SHE LOVED ME

AND ONCE I PLAYED THE FOLLOWING FIENDISH TRICK ON HER & AT THE AGE OF
SIXTEEN I MADE AN UTTER FOOL OF MYSELF IN THE FOLLOWING MANNER & I HAVE
BEEN PHYSICALLY CHASTE CHIEFLY BECAUSE OF FEAR BUT MY VICARIOUS EXPERIENCES
ARE NUMBERED IN THE THOUSANDS—

Eyes watched eyes with horror.

*—it is not that you have sinned for i know everyone has done the same or
similar things or would if they had our gift & i know too that it is nothing
serious or abnormal & of course you have decent instincts & are ashamed—*

*—just so/ it is that you know what i have done & you know every last
little wish & thought & buried uncleanness & in the top of my head i know
it doesn't mean anything but down underneath is all which was drilled into
me when i was just a baby & i will not admit to* ANYONE *else that such things
exist in* ME—

A car whispered by, homeward bound. The trees talked in the light
sunny wind.

A boy and girl went hand in hand.

The thought hung cold under the sky, a single thought in two minds.

—get out. i hate your bloody guts.—

Jerome Bixby
and Joe E. Dean

Share Alike

One of Alfred Hitchcock's most remarkable films, Lifeboat, *concerns the fate of a boatload of shipwreck survivors, one of whom is a murderous Nazi. The hapless protagonist of "Share Alike" would have envied their plight, trapped as he is with a single companion—a vampire. Coauthor of this tale of psychological homosexuality,* JEROME BIXBY *has contributed to* Galaxy, Planet Stories *and* Startling Stories *under a variety of pseudonyms, including Jay B. Drexel, Harry Neal and Alger Rome (the latter in collaboration with Algis Budrys), and wrote several films, including* It, the Terror from Beyond Space.

THEY SPREAD-EAGLED THEMSELVES in the lifeboat, bracing hands and feet against the gunwales.

Above them, the pitted and barnacled stern of the S.S. *Luciano*, two days out of Palermo and now headed for hell, reared up hugely into the overcast of oily black smoke that boiled from ports and superstructure. Craig had time to note that the screws were still slowly turning, and that a woman was screaming from the crazily-tilted afterdeck. Then the smoke intervened—a dark pall that lowered about the lifeboat as the wind shifted, blotting out the sky, the ship.

Fire met water. One roared; the other hissed. Gouts of blazing gasoline flared through the smoke like flame demons dancing on the waves.

Groaning, shuddering, complaining with extreme bitterness, the ship plunged.

Sky and smoke became a sickening whirl, as the lifeboat tore into the churning water in a suicidal effort to follow the parent ship to the bottom. Spray flew; waves loomed, broke, fell away; the lifeboat shipped water. Craig cursed aloud, making rage a substitute for terror. Facing him, Hofmanstahal grinned sourly.

The small boat righted itself. It was still in violent motion, lurching aimlessly across a sea jagged with whitecaps; but Craig knew that the crisis was past. He lifted his face into the cold wind, pulling himself up from the water-slopping bottom of the boat until his chin rested on the gunwale.

A wide patch of brownish foam and oil-scum spread slowly from the vortex of exploding bubbles that rose from the vanished ship.

The sea quieted. A gull swooped down and lit on an orange crate that had bobbed to the surface.

"Well," said Craig. "Well. That's that."

Hofmanstahal peeled off his shirt, wrung it out over the side. The hair that matted his thick chest and peeped from his armpits had a golden sheen that was highlighted by the sun. A small cut was under his left eye, a streak of oil across his forehead.

"You were of the crew?" he asked.

"Yes."

"But not an A. B. You are too spindly for that."

"I was navigator."

Hofmanstahal chuckled, a deep sound that told of large lungs. "Do you think you can navigate us out of this, my friend?"

"I won't have to. We're in a well-travelled shipping lane. We'll be picked up soon enough."

"How soon might that be?"

"I don't know. I don't even know if we got an SOS out; it all happened so fast." Craig sighed, rolled over so that he sat with his back curved against the side of the boat. "I doubt if we did, though. The tanks right under the radio shack were the first to go. I wonder who got careless with a cigarette."

"M'm. So we'll eventually be picked up. And in the meantime, do we starve?"

Craig got up tiredly. "You underestimate the Merchant Marine." He sloshed to the stern of the lifeboat, threw open the food locker. They saw kegs of water, tins of biscuits and salt meat, canned juices, a first-aid kit.

"More than enough," Craig said. He turned, searched the surrounding swells. "I wonder if any others survived . . ."

Hofmanstahal shook his head. "I have been looking too. No others. All were sucked down with the ship."

Craig kept looking. Smoke, heaving stained water, débris, a few dying gasoline-flames—that was all.

Hofmanstahal said, "At least we shall be well fed. Did you have any close friends aboard?"

"No." Craig sat down, pushed wet hair back from his forehead, let his hands fall to his lap. "And you?"

"Me? No one. I have outlived all my friends. I content myself with being a man of the crowd. A select group of *bon vivants* for drinking and conversation . . . it is enough."

Sitting with a seat between them, as if each somehow wanted to be alone, the men exchanged backgrounds. By his own account, Hofmanstahal was an adventurer. No locality could hold him for long, and he seldom revisited a place he already knew. He had been secretary to a former Resident in Malaya, and concerned himself with gems in Borneo, with teak in China; a few of his paintings had been displayed in the *Galerie des Arts* in Paris. He had been en route to Damascus to examine some old manuscripts which he believed might contain references to one of his ancestors.

"Although I was born in Brashov," he said, "family records indicate that we had our beginnings elsewhere. You may think it snobbish, this delving into my background, but it is a hobby which has absorbed me for many years. I am not looking for glory; only for facts."

"Nothing wrong with that," Craig said. "I envy you your colorful past."

"Is yours so dull, then?"

"Not dull . . . the colors just aren't so nice. I grew up in the Atlanta slums. Things were pretty rough when I was a kid—"

"You weren't big enough to be tough."

Craig nodded, wondering why he didn't resent this second reference to his small size. He decided that it was because he liked the big man. Hofmanstahal wasn't insolent, just candid and direct.

"I read a lot," Craig went on. "My interest in astronomy led me into navigation while I was in the Navy. After I was mustered out I stayed at sea rather than go back to what I'd left."

They continued to converse in low, earnest voices for the remainder of the afternoon. Always above them the white gulls circled.

"Beautiful, aren't they?" asked Craig.

Hofmanstahal looked up. His pale eyes narrowed. "Scavengers! See the wicked eyes, the cruel beaks! Pah!"

Craig shrugged. "Let's eat. And hadn't you better do something for that cut under your eye?"

Hofmanstahal shook his massive head. "You eat, if you wish. I am not hungry." He touched his tongue to the dribble of blood that ran down his cheek.

They kept track of the days by cutting notches in the gunwale. There were two notches when Craig first began to wonder about Hofmanstahal.

They had arranged a system of rationing for food and water. It was far from being a strict ration, for there was plenty for both of them.

But Craig never saw Hofmanstahal eat.

The Rumanian, Craig thought, was a big man, he should certainly have an equally big appetite.

"I prefer," said Hofmanstahal, when Craig asked about it, "to take my meals at night."

Craig let it pass, assuming that the big man had a digestive disorder, or perhaps was one of those unfortunates who possess inhibitions about eating in front of others. Not that the latter seemed likely, considering Hofmanstahal's amiably aggressive personality and the present unusual circumstances but, on the other hand, what did it matter? Let him eat standing on his head if he wanted to.

Next morning, when Craig opened the food locker to get his share, the food supply was apparently undiminished.

The morning after that, the same thing.

Another notch. Five days, now. And Craig found something else to puzzle about. He was eating well; yet he felt himself sinking deeper and deeper into a strange, uncaring lethargy, as if he were well on his way toward starvation.

He took advantage of the abundance of food to eat more than was his wont. It didn't help.

Hofmanstahal, on the other hand, greeted each day with a sparkling eye and a spate of good-humored talk.

Both men by now had beards. Craig detested his, for it itched. Hofmanstahal was favoring his, combing it with his fingers, already training the mustache with insistent twiddlings of thumb and forefinger.

Craig lay wearily in the bow and watched.

"Hofmanstahal," he said. "You're not starving yourself on my account, are you? It isn't necessary, you know."

"No, my friend. I have never eaten better."

"But you've hardly touched the stores."

"Ah!" Hofmanstahal flexed his big muscles. Sunlight flickered along the golden hair that fuzzed his torso. "It is the inactivity. My appetite suffers."

Another notch. Craig continued to wonder. Each day, each hour, found him weaker, more listless. He lay in the bow of the boat, soaking in the warmth of the sun, his eyes opaque, his body limp. Sometimes he let one hand dangle in the cool water; but the appearance of ugly, triangular shark fins put a stop to that.

"They are like all of nature, the sharks," Hofmanstahal said. "They rend and kill, and give nothing in return for the food they so brutally take. They can offer only their very bodies, which are in turn devoured by larger creatures. And on and on. The world is not a pretty place, my friend."

"Are men so different?"

"Men are the worst of all."

Seven notches, now. Craig was growing weaker. He was positive by now that Hofmanstahal was simply not eating.

There were nine notches on the gunwale when Craig found that Hofmanstahal *was* eating, after all.

It was night, and the sea was rougher than it had been. The *slap-slap* of waves against the hull wakened Craig from a deep, trancelike sleep. That, and the oppressive feeling of a nearby presence.

He stirred, felt the presence withdraw. Through half-shut eyes he saw Hofmanstahal, darkly silhouetted against a sky ablaze with stars.

"You were crying out in your sleep, my friend." The big man's voice was solicitous. "Nightmare?"

"My throat . . . stinging, burning. I . . ."

"The salt air. You will be all right in the morning."

Craig's face felt like a numb mask of clay. It was an effort to move his lips. "I think—I think I'm going—to die."

"No. You are not going to die. You must not. If you die, I die."

Craig thought about that. The rocking of the boat was gentle, soothing. A warmth stole over him, though the night was cool. He was weak, but comfortable; fearful, yet content. Head back, breathing easily, he let himself become aware of the glory of the heavens.

The constellation Perseus was slanting toward the western horizon, and Craig noted almost unconsciously, with the skill of long practice, that the variable star Algol was at its maximum brilliancy. Algol—the ghoul.

The thought lingered. It turned over and over in his mind, as his unconscious seemed to examine it for some hidden meaning.

Then, abruptly, the thought surged up into his conscious mind.

And he knew.

He lifted himself up to his elbows, supporting himself weakly.

"Hofmanstahal," he said, "you're a vampire. Aren't you?"

The other's chuckle was deep and melodious in the darkness.

"Answer me, Hofmanstahal. Aren't you a vampire?"

"Yes."

Craig had fainted. Now it was as if layer after layer of blackness were being removed, bringing him closer to the light with every moment. A tiny sullen orange disk glowed in the darkness, expanding, increasing in brightness until it filled the world.

The blackness was gone, and he was staring up into the blinding, brassy heart of the sun.

He gasped and turned his head away.

There was music. Someone whistling a German folk tune.

Hofmanstahal . . .

Hofmanstahal sat in the stern, his brawny gold-fuzzed forearms resting on his knees.

The whistling stopped.

"Good morning, my friend. You have had a good, long rest."

Craig stared, his lips working.

Far above a gull called harshly, and was answered by one skimming at water level.

Hofmanstahal smiled. "You mustn't look at me that way. I'm almost harmless, I assure you." He laughed gently. "Things could be much worse, you know. Suppose, for example, I had been a werewolf. Eh?"

He waited a moment.

"Oh, yes, Lycanthropy is real—as real as those gulls out there. Or— more fitting, perhaps—as real as those sharks. Once, in Paris, I lived for three months with a young woman who was a public bath attendant by day and a werewolf by night. She would choose her victims by their—"

Craig listened numbly, aware that Hofmanstahal was merely making idle talk. The story of the female werewolf turned into an anecdote, patently untrue. Hofmanstahal chuckled at it, and seemed disappointed when Craig did not. There was a certain sensitive shyness about the big Rumanian, Craig thought . . . a sensitive vampire! Aware of Craig's revulsion, he was camouflaging the situation with a flood of words.

"—And when the gendarme saw that the bullet which had killed her was an ordinary lead one, he said, 'Messieurs, you have done this *pauvre jeune fille* a grave injustice.' Ha! The moment was a sad one for me, but—"

"Stop it!" Craig gasped. "Go turn yourself into a bat or something and fly away. Just get out of my sight . . . my blood in your stomach . . ."

He tried to turn away, and his elbows slipped. His shoulderblades thumped the bottom of the boat. He lay there, eyes closed, and his throat thickened as if he wanted to laugh and vomit at the same time.

"I cannot turn myself into a bat, my friend. Ugly little creatures—" Hofmanstahal sighed heavily. "Nor do I sleep in a coffin. Nor does daylight kill me, as you can see. All that is superstition. Superstition! Do you know that my grandfather died with a white ash stake through his heart?" His beard tilted angrily. "Believe me, we variants have more to fear from the ignorant and superstitious than they from us. There are so many of them, and so few of us."

Craig said, "You won't touch me again!"

"Ah, but I must."

"I'm still strong enough to fight you off."

"But not strong enough to get at the food if I choose to prevent you."

Craig shook his head. "I'll throw myself overboard!"

"That I cannot permit. Now, why not submit to the inevitable. Each day, I will supply you with your ration of food; each night, you will supply me with mine. A symbiotic relationship. What could be fairer?"

"Beast! Monster! *I will not*—"

Hofmanstahal sighed, and looked out over the tossing sea. "Monster. Always they say that of us; they, who feed off the burned flesh of living creatures."

It was the face of his father, stern and reproving, that Craig always saw before him during those long nights in the lifeboat. His father, who had been a Baptist minister. When the lifeboat drifted on a sea that was like glass, reflecting the stars with such clarity that the boat might have been suspended in a vast star-filled sphere, and Craig felt the warm, moist lips of the vampire at his throat—then conscience arose in the form of his father.

Well . . . he wasn't submitting willingly. Not at first. But the food had been withheld until his belly twisted with hunger and he cried out with parched lips for water. Then, shudderingly, he had allowed the vampire to feed.

It was not as bad as he had expected. An acute, stinging sensation as the sharp canines pricked the flesh (strange, that he had not noticed before how *sharp* they were); then numbness as the anesthetic venom did its work. The venom must have been a hypnotic. As the numbness spread toward his face, and his lips and cheeks became chill, strange colors danced before his eyes, blending and twining in cloudy patterns that sent his thoughts wandering down incomprehensible byways. He was part of Hofmanstahal. Hofmanstahal was part of him. The feeling was almost lascivious.

And each time it was less painful, less shocking, till finally it was mere routine.

Strangely, his conscience did not torment him during the day. The comfortable warmth and lassitude that before had only touched him now enveloped him completely. His thoughts were vague; memory tended to slip away from what had gone before, and to evade what was to come. The sea, the sky, the wheeling gulls were beautiful. And Hofmanstahal, vampire or not, was an interesting conversationalist.

"You are pale, friend Craig," he would say. "Perhaps I have been too greedy. Do you know, with that wan face and the beard, you remind me of a poet I knew in Austria. For a long time he was one of my favorite companions. But perhaps you did not know that we prefer certain donors to others. Believe me, we are not the indiscriminate gluttons that literature would have you think."

"How—did you become as you are?"

"How did I, Eric Hofmanstahal, become a vampire? That is a question with broad implications. I can tell you that my people were vampires, but that leaves unanswered the question of our origin. This I cannot tell you, though I have searched deeply into the matter. There are legends, of course, but they are contradictory." Hofmanstahal stroked his beard and seemed lost in thought.

"Some say," he went on, after a moment, "that when *Homo sapiens* and the ape branched from a common ancestor, there was a third strain which was so despised by both that it was driven into obscurity. Others maintain that we came to Earth from another planet, in prehistoric times. There is even mention of a species which was quite different from man but which, because of man's dominance over the earth, imitated him until it developed a physical likeness to him. Then there is the fanciful notion that we are servants of the Devil—one battalion among his legions, created by him to spread sorrow and misery throughout the ages of the world.

"Legends! We have been persecuted, imprisoned, burned alive; we have been classified as maniacs and perverts—all because our body chemistry is unlike that of man. We drink from the fountain of life while man feasts at the fleshpots of the dead; yet we are called monsters." He crumpled a biscuit in his powerful hand and cast the pieces upon the water, which immediately boiled with sharks.

"Man!" he said softly.

Life went on. Craig ate. Hofmanstahal fed. And horror diminished with familiarity.

There were only the two of them, under the vast sky, rising and falling gently to the whim of the sea. The horizon was the edge of their world. No other existed. Night and day merged into gray sameness. Sea and sky were vague, warm reflections; the motion of the boat soothed. This was peace. There was no thought of resistance left in Craig. Hofmanstahal's "symbiosis" became a way of life; then life itself.

There was time in plenty to gaze up at the stars, a pleasure which everyday exigencies had so often denied him. And there was strange, dark companionship; lips that sought his throat and drained away all thoughts of urgency or violent action, leaving him exhausted and somehow thrilled. It was peace. It was satisfaction. It was fulfilment.

Fear was lost in stupor; revulsion, in a certain sensuality. Hofmanstahal's nightly visit was no longer a thing of horror, but the soft arrival of a friend whom he wanted to help with all his being, and who was in turn helping him. Night and day they exchanged life; and the life they nurtured became a single flow and purpose between them. Craig was the quiescent vessel of life, which Hofmanstahal filled every day, so that life might build itself against the coming of night and the return of its essence to Hofmanstahal.

Day and night marched above them toward the pale horizon that circumscribed their world. In their world values had changed, and the fact of change been forgotten.

Still, deep in his mind, Craig's conscience wailed. Legend, history, the church, all at one time or another had said that vampires were evil. He was submitting to a vampire; therefore, he was submitting to evil. Food or no food, the Reverend Craig would never have submitted. He would have sharpened a stake or cast a silver bullet—

But there were no such things here. His father's face rose before him to tell him that this did not matter. He sought to drive it away, but it remained. During the moments of nightly meeting, of warmth and strange intimacy, it glared down upon them brighter than the moon. But Hofmanstahal's back was always turned to it; and Craig, in all his weakness and agony and ecstasy and indecision, did not mention it.

They had forgotten to carve the notches on the gunwale. Neither was certain now how long they had been adrift.

There came a day, however, when Hofmanstahal was forced to cut down Craig's ration of food.

"I am sorry," he said, "but you can see for yourself that it is necessary."

"We're so near the end of our supplies, then?"

"I am sorry," Hofmanstahal repeated. "Yes, we are nearing the end of your supplies . . . and if yours end, so will mine eventually."

"I don't really mind," Craig whispered. "I'm seldom really hungry now. At first, even the full rations left me unsatisfied, but now I don't even like the taste of the food. I suppose it's because I'm getting no exercise."

Hofmanstahal's smile was gentle. "Perhaps. Perhaps not. We must keep a sharp lookout for ships. If one does not come soon, we will starve, though, of course, I will now cut down my own rations as well as yours."

"I don't care."

"My poor Craig, when you regain your strength you will care very much. Like me, you will want to live and go on living."

"Maybe. But now I feel that dying would be easy and pleasant. Better, maybe, than going back to the world."

"The world is evil, yes; but the will to live in it drives all of us."

Craig lay motionless and wondered, with a clarity of mind he had not experienced in many, many days, whether he dreaded going back to the world because the world was evil, or whether it was because he felt that he himself was tainted, unfit to mix with human beings again.

. . . And Hofmanstahal might be a problem. Should he be reported to the authorities? No, for then they would know about Craig.

But was all that had happened so disgraceful, so reprehensible? Had Craig had any other choice but to do what he had done?

None.

His conscience, in the form of his father, screamed agony.

Well, then perhaps Hofmanstahal would try to force him to continue the relationship. Had he—*pleased* the Rumanian? He felt that he had . . .

But surely gentle, considerate Hofmanstahal, the sensitive vampire, would not try to force—

Craig's mind rebelled against such practical thoughts. They required too much effort. It was easier not to think at all—to lie as he had lain for so many days, peaceful, relaxed, uncaring.

Clarity of mind faded into the gray sameness of day and night. He ate. Hofmanstahal fed.

He was scarcely conscious when Hofmanstahal spotted the smoke on the horizon. The big man lifted him up so that he could see it. It was a ship, and it was coming in their direction.

"So—now it is over." Hofmanstahal's voice was soft; his hands were warm on Craig's shoulders. "So it ends—our little idyll." The hands tightened. "My friend . . . my friend, before the ship comes, the men and the noise, the work and the worry and all that goes with it, let us for the last time—"

His head bent, his lips found Craig's throat with their almost sexual avidity.

Craig shivered. Over the Rumanian's shoulder he could see the ship approaching, a dot on the horizon. There would be men aboard.

Men! Normalcy and sanity, cities and machines and half-forgotten values, coming nearer and nearer over the tossing sea, beneath the brassy sky, from the real world of men that lay somewhere beyond the horizon . . .

Men! Like himself, like his father, who hovered shouting his disgust.

And he, lying in the arms of—

God, God, *what if they should see him!*

He kicked. He threw his arms about. He found strength he hadn't known he had, and threshed and flailed and shrieked with it.

The lifeboat rocked. A foot caught Hofmanstahal in the midriff. The vampire's arms flew wide and he staggered back with a cry:

"Craig—"

The backs of his knees struck the gunwale—the one with meaningless notches carved in it. His arms lashed as he strove to regain his balance. His eyes locked with Craig's, shock in them. Then he plunged backward into the sea.

The sharks rejected him as food, but not before they had killed him.

Craig found himself weeping in the bottom of the boat, his face in slime. And saying hoarsely again and again, "Eric, I'm sorry—"

It seemed a very long time before the ship came close enough for him to make out the moving figures on the deck. It seemed so long because of the thoughts and half-formed images that were racing through his brain.

A new awareness was coming over him in a hot flood, an awareness of—

Of the one thing popularly believed about vampires that must have solid foundation in fact.

Had the venom done it? He didn't know. He didn't care.

He lay weakly, watching the steamer through half-closed eyes. Sailors lined the rails, their field glasses trained on him.

He wondered if they could see his father. No, of course not—that had all been hallucination. Besides, a moment ago his father had fled.

It was a Navy ship, a destroyer. He was glad of that. He knew the Navy. The men would be healthy. Strenuous duty would make them sleep soundly.

And at the end of its voyage lay the whole pulsing world.

Craig licked his lips.

C. H. Sherman

Teacher

Stark ugliness and unexpected tenderness infuse the fantasies of C. H.
SHERMAN, *who, under another name, plays a psychiatrist on a popular day-time TV drama. "Teacher," set in the same backwoods territory as "Doll-Baby" (in my earlier collection,* Witches & Warlocks), *is about a man who once had a burning desire to teach. But when passion turns sour, the result is usually hate, and this holds quite as true of frustrated benevolence.*

"IF YOU BROUGHT seven hogs to the county fair and Tyrell bought three of them, how many would you have left?"

"Tyrell got his own hogs."

These children were all dullards.

"Yes, but we're just pretending right now for the sake of maths." Manning Dawber pinched the bridge of his nose to hold back the first sign of a headache. He knew what would prevent it. Smashing a small nose onto a hard desktop would release the pain behind his eyes. But he couldn't afford to get fired. Not even from this miserable place. Because there was no place to go. This was it.

Dawber shivered. The wood stove in the corner gave off enough heat as long as the temperature outside didn't fall below forty degrees. He'd put on his longjohns this morning, though, when he'd felt the first cold clutches of an early winter on his way to the privy. Tyrell Chandler's father, the old boozehound, had promised to deliver a cord of wood weeks ago. Dawber figured on reminding him about it at tomorrow night's Halloween bonfire, which was the only reason he had even considered joining the locals for the festivities. With any luck, he'd have the wood by Thanksgiving.

"Think about it, Mackay. You have seven hogs, Tyrell buys three. How many do you have left?"

"How much he pay me?"

"That's not important."

"Not sellin' 'less Tyrell he pay a hundred dollar."

Why did he bother? These cretins should be home eating corn-on-the-cob and Crisco. Dawber crossed to the blackboard and wrote the figures. "What's seven hogs take away three hogs?"

"Tyrell ain't taken nothin' no more from me. He steal my whittlin' knife."

"Didn't steal nothin', you jackdaw crazy."

"You tooken it . . ."

"I won it fair and square."

"Boys, settle down . . ."

"Robber, steal the cane from Blind Granny!"

"You be a liar like your paw!"

Mackay leaped over his desk and crashed head-first into Tyrell's stomach. Both boys fell on the floor and punched each other hard and ugly.

Dawber cursed under his breath. Every day the same. Fights and stupidity, stupidity and fights. He watched the twelve-year-olds roll over each other, blood streaming from crushed noses and split lips. Let them kill each other. Let them hurt each other so bad they won't come back to the sorry classroom. Then all he'd have to deal with would be the narcoleptic Fletcher twins and the four inbred cousins from the other side of the mountain.

Out of the corner of his eye he caught sight of movement at the window. He turned quickly but only saw the top of a bald head before it disappeared. The sky had clouded over as the chilly October wind swirled tiny twisters of dead leaves against the cheap windowpanes.

"All right, all right, break it up!" Dawber yanked the back of Tyrell's shirt. It ripped in his hands. He grabbed the boy's shoulders and pulled him off of the smaller boy underneath. Mackay took advantage of his freedom and aimed a roundhouse at Tyrell's head. Tyrell saw it coming, though, and twisted away in Dawber's arms. The punch caught the teacher square at the base of his left ear. He fell and scraped his back against the corner of a desk.

"You goddam idiots!"

No one moved.

Dawber stood up suddenly and pitched the desk he'd hit across the room.

"Get the hell out of my school, you trash! You're expelled, both of you!" He felt dizzy and sick to his stomach. "Get out. *Now!*"

Tyrell and Mackay sullenly went to their desks and pulled out books and papers. Tyrell dripped blood on his geography book and smeared it onto his English primer. Mackay looked like he was either about to laugh or cry. Together the two boys walked up the aisle to the back of the classroom. At the door they turned back to face Dawber.

"Teacher?"

"What?"

Tyrell and Mackay looked at each other, then opened their mouths and each hocked a gob of bloody spit on the floor. Then they threw their books in the air and ran out of the schoolhouse.

Some of the other students tittered but the look on Dawber's face prevented any more giggles.

Dawber wanted to run after Tyrell and Mackay and crack their heads together until there were no bones left to protect the pulp. He wanted to hurt them. Real bad. The ringing in his ear made him lose his balance. He slumped onto the closest chair.

"You go . . . dismissed."

He sat with his head in his hands. Tiny blond Deborah, accent on "bore," piped up.

"We got to do the Halloweeny decorations, Teacher."

When Dawber didn't say no she prissed around gathering up the cardboard ghosts and witches and the construction-paper black cats.

"Lonnie Mae and me'll paste up the pitchers. The boys'll cut up the jack-o-lanterns. Ada and Eve, ya'll just watch."

Dawber sat without moving, fighting nausea, envisioning his cord of wood sitting behind Tyrell's cabin covered with snow. Outside, the wind had kicked up. The whistling hurt the ringing in his head. He wanted out of here, wanted out of this pit of a teaching job. He'd felt lucky to get it at first. Graduating third from the bottom of his class made him eager to work anywhere. One of his professors at the state college had inspired him with the fairy tale of the poor boy who finds the golden key and the iron chest. "If the key does but fit the lock, no doubt there are precious things within to be discovered." Truly fine teachers never give up searching for the small keyhole that will admit the key of knowledge. Dawber had joyfully sought to unlock the treasures in his backwoods students, but his desire to teach was greater than his skills or patience. The hardness of the mountain folk stymied him and he took his frustrations out on the children. The poverty and ignorance here in the Tennessee mountains made life ugly, not quaint. He felt mean and hopeless. Bit by bit his dreams of unlocking his students' minds withered. He had failed. So he gave up. He hated the world just a little less than he hated himself.

The children ignored their teacher while they decorated the room. Deborah barked orders at sullen Lonnie Mae, who deliberately hung the cutouts off-center or backwards. Sixteen-year-old Seesel Packer and Coriander Linderman, each with one brown eye and one blue eye, tolerated Deborah's carving instructions and shot pumpkin seeds at her when her back was turned. Deborah made a great fuss about having to climb on top of the desks to hang the garlands of spitting cats.

Dawber caught himself nodding along with the Fletcher twins but he resisted the luxury of sleep to fulfill his obligation as teacher while the children were still his responsibility. He just wasn't in the mood to face an outraged parent. He didn't have the energy to make the students leave. He trusted that his presence, such as it was, would keep them in line and hurry them up.

Once when he was on the verge of sleep he saw the top of the head again at the window. The Superintendent of Schools? His foggy mind considered asking him in to complain about this worthless job and the creek that constantly overflowed and flooded his room behind the school. But he would wait until the children left so as not to shock them with his foul language.

"We need a match, Teacher." Seesel held a crudely carved pumpkin in front of Dawber's face. "And candles."

"In the left cupboard."

Dawber sat up straight and looked around him. The ghosts and witches were taped to the windows and the cat streamers hung suspended over the desks. On each windowsill sat a fresh jack-o-lantern. He watched Seesel and Coriander stick candles in the base of each pumpkin. The suddenly awake Fletcher twins eagerly took turns lighting the matches. The purple afternoon sky reflected the crude orange and yellow faces in the windows.

The children admired their handiwork as they packed up to go home.

"Treats tomorrow, Teacher?" Deborah fairly purred.

"Yeah. Sure."

Deborah leaned close to Dawber's face. "Don't forgit to blow out them candles."

"Yeah."

Seesel stood behind her. "Whyn't I blow 'em out now? You askin' for trouble with fire all night long in those jacks."

"No, leave them alone."

"You courtin' trouble with the monster woman," muttered Lonnie Mae.

Abruptly, the children touched their right thumbs to their tongues, then made a circle and an "x" in their left palms.

The usually gruff Coriander spoke quietly. "She be mad."

"She think you be makin' fun of her," added Seesel.

Dawber stared at his students. Their sudden intensity surprised him. "Who?"

"Don't tell nobody, hear?" pleaded Seesel. "She hurt us if she know we talk about her."

"Who?" repeated Dawber.

Deborah leaned in and whispered in his ear.

"Kylie Greer."

Almost as one the children shuddered.

"She be a crazy one who live 'round here," continued Deborah out loud. "She ugly as the devil and she suck out your eyes if she catch you lookin' at her."

"What, she doesn't like teachers?" snorted Dawber.

The children crowded around the teacher and spoke over one another's words in their urgency to warn Dawber about the local horror.

"She hate fire. . . ."

"She live in the ground. . . ."

"She throw dead squirrels down your chimley. . . ."

"She freeze you with her ugly face. . . ."

"She throw your baby brother in the kettle and boil him for break-fast. . . ."

"She steal your firewood. . . ."

"She eat your cookin' fire so you wake up froze dead like a porkypine in January. . . ."

"She dress up like a witch. . . ."

"She kill you on Halloween with poison apples. . . ."

"She throw you on the bonfire. . . ."

"She bite off your head and eat your brains and pick her teeth with your knucklebones. . . ."

Wild-eyed and out of breath, the students pressed close to their teacher.

"She powerful tetchous," concluded the Fletcher twins.

Dawber waited for the children to break into laughter but he realized that they weren't trying to spook him. They really believed their tale.

"Have you ever seen this Kylie Greer?"

"No, Teacher, we be dead if we see her. We be blind *and* dead!"

"She's just make-believe."

"No, sir, Teacher, Kylie Greer real." This from a pale and shaking Deborah.

"Well, if she comes here I'll make her look at herself in a mirror so she'll scare herself to death," sneered Dawber.

Just then the wind howled. The children screamed and ran for the door. Lonnie Mae skidded on Tyrell's and Mackay's gifts of spit. Deborah and the Fletcher twins squashed through the door at the same time. Coriander knocked over a chair and dragged down the black cat paper chain that dangled in front of his face. Seesel stopped long enough to yell back to Dawber.

"She hear us tell you, Teacher! We got to go!"

Dawber chuckled as he watched the six children charge out the door and race into the chilly dusk. But the crash of the slamming door cut short his laughter. The pain from the clout on his ear came back in full force. His head throbbed so badly he could barely hear the wind rattling the windows. Hurting, and too tired to go back to his room, Dawber gingerly slid to the floor and stretched out in the aisle. He was asleep within a minute.

The quills dug under his fingernails and pried them off one by one. Blood oozed and scabbed in the raw wounds. The pain was excruciating but he couldn't cry out. His mouth was filled with kerosene and his hair was on fire. If he opened his mouth the flames would choke him. A hand exploded out of the ground. The slimy fingers crawled over his neck and cheeks, then hovered near his mouth. Slowly the fingertips began to pry open his lips. He twisted his head from side to side. Sparks flew from his hair. He mustn't open his mouth! He gritted his teeth but the fingers pressed and poked his lips trying to pull his chin down. Kerosene dribbled from the corner of his mouth. A flame burned his cheek. The tip of a crusted finger slid between his lips and rubbed his gums and teeth. Sores opened at its touch. He had to scream! But the fire would eat him. More fingers squeezed their way through his clenched lips. A thumb pressed hard against his front tooth. He heard the crackle of the roots as they snapped and pulled free. Frantically, he pushed his tongue against the tooth to hold it in place. A piece of tooth chipped off and sliced his tongue. Fingers and thumb yanked the tooth from his bleeding gums. The pain! The fingers broke off another tooth, then another. If only he

opened his mouth it would be over. The agony of fire would be easier to
bear than this. End it with a scream! All he had to do was open his
mouth. Scream! Just open his mouth and scream! Just . . .

Dawber jerked awake. His mouth was open wide in a silent scream.
Gently he touched his mouth. The awful images that had terrorized his
sleep were gone. He lay blinking in the dim light and swallowed hard. A
hint of kerosene gagged him and he shuddered. The nightmare clung to
him like a shroud.

In the murky light he recognized the schoolroom more from the chalk
dust than from the dark shapes of the desk and chair legs surrounding
him. He lay on the floor between two desks near the windows, freezing,
his body stiff and sore.

The door of the schoolhouse opened.

Dawber lay unmoving. A bitter wind swept through the room. Papers
swirled to the floor.

Something was in the classroom with him.

The door closed. Dawber held his breath and focused on the muted
shuffling. Slowly he turned his head. Through the forest of furniture he
could see a dark figure moving towards him. The blood in his ears
pounded so painfully he thought he would cry out. But his fear was
stronger than his pain. If the intruder was Mackay or Tyrell, he would kill
them. And no jury would hang him.

Dawber turned silently onto his right side. His breath hurt. He kept his
mouth open so as not to gasp out loud and give himself away. He would
beat them with a chair. He'd make sure they were dead. Then he'd run.

The figure stopped at the window a few feet from Dawber's head.
Dawber tensed, waiting for the attack. But the stranger hadn't seen him,
didn't even know he was lying so close by. The lighted jack-o-lantern cast
its dim reflection in the glass. Dawber raised himself up to get a better
look. He watched the stranger pick up the jack-o-lantern and turn its
cutout face around until their two faces were silhouetted. Dawber's
throat tightened.

It was a girl, yet hardly recognizable as female, for she had the most
hideous face he had ever seen. Stark white and purple blotches flowed
together on a melted face. Her eyes were uneven and hooded by rolls of
flesh. The nose was no more than two lopsided holes, the mouth puffy
white scars stretched over blackened stumps of teeth. A singed clump of
hair lay behind one perfectly normal ear. The other ear was completely
gone along with the rest of the hair. She wore a shabby cloak that totally
covered her body.

Dawber's strangled cry wheeled the girl around. The shadows made one horrible eye seem to slide down her face. She threw up her hands to hide her ruined face and lost hold of the jack-o-lantern. The pumpkin smashed into the teacher's chest, knocking him to the floor. Hot wax and pulp sprayed his face. The top flew off and the still flaming candle landed on his shirt. The thin wool material ignited while Dawber was swiping away the burning wax.

The fire engulfed him. It raced across his body eating fabric and skin alike. Dawber screamed. He beat wildly at the flames. He smelled the sickening odor of burning hair, burning flesh. He rolled around on the floor, crashing into the desks, trying to put out the fire that was scorching him to death.

Suddenly, a rough material blanketed him and something heavy fell on top of him. He fought for air. He screeched as his burned skin was shredded by the scratchy cloth. He couldn't see or breathe. The pressure suffocated him. He fought desperately to push off the smothering weight. He pushed and shoved and finally was free. He tore off the blanket and sucked air into his burning lungs, but before he could get his bearings he was pulled by strong arms. The fire was out. The terror of burning alive still gripped him and he flailed against the person who now dragged him outside.

The biting October air stung his bare skin. He cried out in pain. He wrenched himself free and fell face down on the ground. Again the strong arms grabbed him. Too exhausted to struggle any more, Dawber let himself be dragged. He moaned as rocks and grass scraped his raw chest. The urgency of the person pulling him made him look up. He saw the stream that ran near the schoolyard. Now understanding, he stumbled forward and flung himself into the icy water.

He peeled back the shreds of his shirt and longjohns so that his scorched skin could be cleansed by the sudden cold. The intensity of the pain took his breath away but he knew the water had saved him.

She knelt in the shallows and supported his head. He cringed at her touch. Shivering with cold and pain, he climbed out of the water. In the schoolhouse windows the jack-o-lanterns grinned at the limping man and the girl who followed him.

Dawber made it just inside the door before he fell, shaking, to his knees. He tried to take deep breaths but he just kept shaking. He knew she was there in the shadows. He knew who she was. And he knew she had saved his life from becoming a horror like hers.

He felt a cloak being placed gently over him. It smelled like his body on fire. He forced himself to look again at the monster of the valley.

"Thank you, Kylie."

She sat with her hands covering her face. She didn't say anything.

Dawber cleared his throat and swallowed. "How can I repay you?" His breath was easier now.

Her words were muffled behind her hands.

"Teach me."

Dawber stared at the girl with the horrible burns. He reached for her hands and delicately pulled them away from her face. The eyes that looked back at him shone with a fearless life.

No doubt there were precious things within to be discovered.

Christina Rossetti

A Nightmare

CHRISTINA GEORGINA ROSSETTI *(1830–94), sister of the poet Dante Gabriel Rossetti, was herself a noted Victorian poet. "Goblin Market," one of her best-known compositions, has often been interpreted as sexually symbolic. "A Nightmare," composed in 1857, still existed in manuscript when Rossetti died in 1894. Her other brother, art critic William Michael, bowdlerized it before allowing it to see print, changing the first line to read "I have a friend in ghostland" as well as the beginning of the second stanza, substituting "hunts" for "rides."*

I have a love in ghostland—
Early found, ah me how early lost!—
Blood-red seaweeds drip along that
coastland
By the strong sea wrenched
and tost.

If I wake he rides me like a
nightmare:
I feel my hair stand up, my body
creep:
Without light I see a blasting sight
there,
See a secret I must keep.

Dan Burrello

The Songs
of My Young

*"The Songs of My Young," a weirdly erotic and ultimately horrifying love
story, is the first, but I am sure far from the last, published fiction of* Dan
Burrello, *a talented young resident of Sea Island, Georgia.*

KAIVANU STIRRED from bed, waking him with the soft whoosh of her
wings. The image of her, a blurred streak as sleep left his eyes . . . he
loved to watch her in the afternoon light, waking, walking naked to the
balcony, her wings spreading behind her as she gained the railing to gaze
past the deserted streets at the Mediterranean stretching around Kato
Pyrgos like a moat.

Then, instinctively, she faced into the wind, towards Olympus, her
silken hair whipping about, her involuntary movements miming flight.
He raised himself up on an elbow among the soft pillows, feeling a twinge
of fear that she might take off. But he knew she wouldn't leave him. He
held her with stronger bonds than the ones he used to tie her on the first
night she came to him.

In the last hazy weeks his disbelief waned, but from time to time he
wondered if he wasn't in the midst of a strange dream or even a flashback.

When he first saw her, two weeks before, standing on the balcony
outside his hotel room, he thought her like the ten thousand other girls
he'd left at Madison Square Garden earlier that night . . . a desperate
fan trying to steal some of his magic, a piece of him to take home and

decipher. But then he remembered that this one was eighteen stories above Park Avenue in the dead of winter.

He was a connoisseur (of sorts) when it came to the hollow men and women who follow the Gods of music and find Heaven and Hell connate within the holy realms of power amplification and media hype. On more than a few occasions, he sought cold pleasure in their servitude, but always found them wanting.

He knew at a glance that the haunting vision in the ice-streaked picture window was not of their strain. No other groupie was as stunning as this innocent creature, and certainly none had ever arrived naked, displaying a twelve-foot wing span.

He allowed her into his world that night, spellbound by her crystalline eyes as much as her wings. In the hazy weeks that followed, he loved her like no one else ever before, and she learned to love him. She carried him and his guitar across two oceans and a continent at the speed of thought to Cyprus, to the mute and blind city, the bastard ghost town of the war between the Turks and the Greeks, a place now populated by rats, sea gulls and an occasional UN security officer.

A perfect place for two Gods. Two freaks. He hadn't been alone for more than two hours at a time since the tour started. Between the band, the press, and his agent, practically every spare minute for four months had been sucked away. But now, out of nowhere, Paradise! No agents, no opening acts, no groupies, no damn tour buses, none of the raunchy roadside food to which he'd become accustomed. When he hungered now, she disappeared for an hour or two and returned with a princely dinner, lamb and couscous, fruits and vegetables from as far away as Italy and Egypt. He wanted for nothing.

For the first time in his life, he began to relax.

She floated back into the room smiling her Mona Lisa smile, so wise and out of place on her childlike countenance. Her back arched; her perfect breasts surged towards him as her wings folded to fit the door. She walked to the bathroom door, stopped, and then, like tiny bells, she turned and spoke.

"Why do you watch me?" Her naïveté was as delightful as her voice.

"Because I love you, dearheart . . . because you are the single most delightful thing I've ever seen." Grinning, he dismounted the bed with the energy of a schoolboy pulsing through his forty-year-old frame. The air was so charged with power, it seemed as if all the nourishment he needed lay in the breeze and in making love to her. He met her halfway to the door, blocking her way in a playful gesture. She reared at the suddenness of his motion and her wings spread slightly. He saw something in her eyes that he could not name, but he put the thought away.

"How 'bout coming back to bed with me, da'lin' . . . or I could come in there with you?" he asked as he wrapped his arms around her waist and kissed her gently, wondering how well they'd fit in a single shower stall with her wings. The cistern on the roof would be filled with sun-warmed rainwater. He stirred at the thought.

"Whichever you prefer, my love." She slid her hands around his waist in perfect mimicry of his embrace. "Then will you play? Just a little tune? After?" She kissed him. "After."

He lifted her, careful of her wings, to the bed.

As he lay locked in her fevered embraces, he realized why he had allowed her to take him away from the endless draining circus that "Richey Vergo" had become. Fifteen years of living up to the expectations of the press and millions of strangers who thought they knew him. Two nervous breakdowns, three divorces, alimony and enough lawsuits to wallpaper a house. In the last year, he'd begun to understand how easy it would be to jump off a hotel roof like Billy Jet, his lead singer, had done.

He didn't want to end his chapter in the Rock and Roll Hall of Fame like so many of his friends. But so many times over the years he heard, "It's better to burn out than fade away." And two years earlier, he *had* faded away. Deep away. He bought a mansion two hundred miles upstate from Milwaukee and drank himself into a stupor nightly to kill the buzzing . . . to stop the music. But after two months of it, he learned what the Mississippi blues men knew all along. The lower you go, the more blood you spill for the art . . . the sweeter the music becomes and no matter what he tried to do, he could have no more stopped playing the guitar than quit breathing.

He wrote more songs than he had in ten years. Good songs. Songs that put the commercial crud he had been pushing to shame. Songs that rang of life and love and tragedy. When his agent finally called, Richey was ready for him. After the critically acclaimed "comeback" album (he hated it when anyone called it that), after the heavy rotation of the accompanying videos on MTV, the tour was inevitable. And it rocked. Twenty-eight cities and a live satellite simulcast worldwide from the last date at the Garden. He owned the world that night; but there was something that no one, not the fans nor the drink company sponsors nor the roadies or even the religious freaks who picketed his shows knew. The music, that haunting collection of old and new hits, had one distinct message. Utter loneliness and total despair.

It was something that Kaivanu understood. She was his redeemer, his salvation. She had flown into his life without a question or stipulation.

Except that he play for her.

Just for her.

Her eyes met his and he saw the same nameless expression. It was a look he'd noticed in many a late-night poker game. It was as if she knew both of their hands. *Only pretending to play.*

After the lovemaking, she showered. As she rose from the bed, he, curled into a fetal ball, smelled the incense and candlewax of a long-ago confessional and tasted redemption. The water drummed against the glass door of the shower.

She reentered the room unfurled. The water clung to her white down in tiny beads and she carefully preened each wing dry.

He sat naked on the foot of the bed, guitar in hand, and began to strum. When she noticed that he had the instrument, she beamed and came to him, coaxing him up and out to the balcony. She stood on the railing for a moment, slipping elegantly back and forth on her wet feet until the warm wind blew her off them. Then she hung there. Her tanned features and long black hair, the contrast of her gently oscillating wings, her eyes that matched the sea behind her . . . he thought for a moment that he would cry. What had he done to deserve this creature?

"Play, my love, and don't stop. I shall show you a dance that mortal men have only dreamt of," she said as she folded her wings for a dive.

He began to play, starting with a strong melody with resounding repetitions of resonate chords. She dipped and swooped around the parapet, flowing in unaltered synch with the sound. He changed to a sultry blues tempo and she switched as fluidly into an undulating series of movements in time with the beating of her wings. Feeling as connected to her as he had during their physical bonding, he played steadily faster as her movements grew more erotic. He stopped and broke into a bit of Beethoven, watching her circle and writhe on cue. He segued to a group of power chords, their dissonant beginning resolving into a complex structure on which he built to the close of his solo. As he drew near its end, he caught a glimpse of the tears in her angelic eyes. He strummed the last resolution and in she flew, lifting him to the bed, kissing him and bathing him in her perspiration. He let the guitar slide to the floor, glad to be rid of it, and found sanctuary in her arms.

. . . .

Later, the wind and approaching twilight roused them from bed to walk the deserted streets to the beach. Instead of the stairs, she carried him to the ground. There was no getting used to the rush of being flown from place to place by an impossible creature. He landed unsure of his feet and positive he left his stomach somewhere on the twelfth floor of the lifeless building.

"That's nice, luv. Come along and take my hand." He held it out for her and she reciprocated. They walked past the artillery-shelled restaurants to the quiet boardwalk resplendent with Cyprian advertisement posters and signs rusted and ruined by the salty spray of the Mediterranean Sea. The sand stretched for miles to meet the gathering tide. And they paused, momentarily, as if on the edge of some undetermined future, their shadows cast five times their length pointing east towards Morphou and further, towards Syria and other mysteries. He felt like a man reincarnated while still holding the regrets and memories of his past life. In that instant, standing on the shore of forever, he thought he knew something of eternity.

As they stepped from the walk to the sand, Kaivanu's eyes widened and her ears pricked up visibly. She squeezed his hand.

"Something comes."

Then Richey heard the speedy little engine of a jeep reverberating down the street they had just exited.

"We have to hide, Luv!" He pulled her towards the boardwalk and the concealment one of the signs might offer, but it was too late. Riding past the theatres and abandoned food vendors still advertising their ten-year-old Specials of the Day, the jeep rounded the corner and saw them. It bore the blue and white flag of the United Nations Security Forces.

"Do not move," the PA speaker blared at them. "This area is off limits to any unauthorized personnel. You are under arrest." The voice was young, but confident. It repeated the warning in Greek and what Richey thought must be Turkish.

Wondrous! he thought. *How will we explain you?*

"Take no thought of me, my love!" she said, taking flight, not waiting to explain.

And she reads my thoughts, too?

She turned at three meters out and smiled. A sudden white coolness filled his head. *Of course I can, Richard! How do you suppose you drew me to that lonely room in New York?*

He stood there in his cut-off Levi's, rooted, as she flew on a collision course with the men and the jeep.

The vehicle came to an abrupt stop. A young officer wearing a Canadian uniform jumped out amongst the billows of sandy dust. His mouth dropped at the wonder of what was flying at them, then he shouted orders to the radio operator and to a boy manning a mounted .50 caliber machine gun. Completely unsure of himself, the soldier slid back the cocking mechanism.

Through the surf, the engine and the booming sweep of Kaivanu's wings as she neared the group, Richard heard the odd click of the gun. He fell to the sand waiting for the magnificent dream that was his reality to disappear in a burst of lead, down and blood. He turned away from the sight, but as he watched her shadow in the sand, it began to change. The lines became indistinct and the wings blurred.

Richard looked up and saw her soar suddenly upward into the setting sun and then dive at the vehicle. Only it wasn't she. It was something else, something hideous.

Where her beautiful white wings had been, there were solid dark blue sheets of marbled skin that popped and rippled from the force of her dive. Seven thick brown tentacles trailed behind her. As she reached the jeep, whiplike antennae struck out and decapitated the radio man. His microphone dropped, its attached radio still asking frantic questions through the static.

Her wings fanned and she stopped, hovering directly above them. Richard could see her head, bald, brown, reflecting the sun as it disappeared from view. Her arms clung to what used to be her knees, with two curling reptilian fingers where her soft hands had been.

The gun strobed out its answer to her attack, the young soldier manning it screaming in total panic. The rounds sounded like a thousand metal spatulas slapping plastic. They ricocheted in all directions, breaking the windows of a former ice cream shop, splattering the stone walls with lead. Every fifth round bore a luminous tracer that bounced around the sandy canyon of buildings.

She raised her new head and shrieked. The sound chilled Richard to the bone. It was not a scream of anger or pain. It seemed more like . . . laughter.

Two more jeeps raced into view from side streets two and four blocks away. Kaivanu turned to face Richard and buzzed out one distinguishable word: "Run!"

With totally mixed feelings about running *from* the soldiers, trying to blank the sight of her transformed face from his mind, he leapt from the sand and headed for the shadows of a nearby alley. He turned for a moment and saw her arms spread as she vomited sulphurous fire onto the men. As they thrashed and writhed and moaned, she swept away from the smoldering mess towards the reinforcements. Staring at the scene, Richard nearly ran to the aid of the men in the first jeep. Then the fuel tank exploded, sending a black mushroom into the purple sky and instantly, mercifully, killing the soldiers.

He fled down blind alleys and empty streets. He heard more gunfire and explosions behind him as he knocked down the locked door to the hotel and bounded up nine flights of dark stairs. Near the tenth it seemed his heart would burst, but he climbed the side rail and treaded the last two flights without understanding why.

When he reached the room, he saw she had already arrived and was showering by candlelight. He paced about, glowing with sweat, wondering what he was doing there in the same room with a monster, but from the sound of her voice he knew she had become her beautiful self again.

"I'm glad you're back, Richard." She came from the shower, rubbing her wings with a soft white towel, looking none the worse for her battle. She moved towards him, her eyes unblinking in the sparkling candleglow.

How?

She did not answer, but came closer, sliding her arms around his neck. He jerked away and fell on his back beside the bed.

"You are repulsed," she said matter-of-factly, walking to the sliding glass doors and out into the night. The sound of sirens filled the air and helicopter rotors tore the skies.

"No . . . I am confused, uh . . . luv," he said, trying to conceal his fear as he followed her onto the balcony.

"So now you will become a liar, sweet Richard. Now you would take your leave." The night wind ruffled at the feathers bordering her wings. Her back was turned to him as she leaned out over the Pyrgosian street.

Whatever she was, he was in love with this part of her. He shuffled towards her like a guilty child. "I'm sorry, dearheart. It was all so unexpected. So strange to me." He touched her shoulder.

She whipped around to face him. "And so you will play for me, sweet Richard?" She had the look of a predator. "Will you give me more of your music?" She held him tightly and kissed him, but it was like none of her other kisses; she had the grip of a linebacker and her tongue shot down his throat. Gagging, he tore her arms away and leaned over the rail waiting for the sickness to come.

"No, no more music," she said with calm sarcasm. She whisked her hair back, tilting her head, watching him through the bottom of her eyes.

He turned and slid to the deck. As he did, an ambulance screamed around the corner below them bearing the UN flags and a huge red cross in a field of white on its roof.

She leaned over him, her childlike features marred by her sudden anger. Her nudity contradicted her bearing, but he remembered the beach and the bodies melted into the sand.

"*You* reject *ME!?* I am a goddess in my homeland. I have shown you all I can feel. You are all alike. Your passions are confined to the notes you play. What do you know of passion? Of walking along Everest at dawn? Of sleeping with the demons in the pit of Fujiyama? You could not stomach the things *I* relish!"

As she grew steadily angrier, Richard felt the air becoming warmer. *Stay calm, Richey! Keep your head!* A small tear crawled down his cheek.

"Even your thoughts are mine, you pitiful little man." She turned and went into the room, emerging a second later with his guitar. "Even so, you will play now!" She tossed the instrument on his kneeling lap. It thudded out the echo of a hundred chords.

He wept. Then, taking the guitar in his arms, he began to play. Softly at first, a simple melody with simple chords. She couldn't control her reaction. She began to undulate with the tune. She took to the air around the balcony with a gentle glide. A smile returned to her face.

Richard tried to think of nothing. He let his fingers think for him. Changing the tune. Following the lead of his heart, where *no one* could see, not even Kaivanu. The chords grew intensely dissonant, ripping at the fabric of coherent sound. He thought of his friend Billy Jet who leapt from the twenty-second floor in Atlanta, he thought of the endless list of friends and mentors he had seen die at the hands of their own obsession, driven by some unexplainable force to destroy themselves. Watching Kaivanu circle the precipice like a moth, he wondered how much of their misery was caused by forces that the world could never believe or accept.

In his mind's eyes, he saw the young lieutenant and his squad burned under the fire of her mindless, senseless fury.

Looking up from his impromptu serenade, he saw that she was twisting and stalling in an impossible flight that would have destroyed the wings of any normal creature. As she contorted in concert with his music, on her face he saw an expression he had never expected. Anguish. She was obviously not enjoying the dance. Her distorted body, her grimace brought pity. He slowed the pace of his strumming. Her eyes met his.

"Stop, Richard! Stop this painful sound. It pulls at me in places I have never felt." As she spoke, her flight continued. Diving and stalling, diving and stalling.

He took no pleasure in her pain, but fear would not let him stop, so she took the matter into her own hands. Her feathers drew themselves under the skin of her wings and her upper body began to change. It started much slower than the beach transformation and it was incomplete. Her face and head remained intact, as did her legs, but her torso, arms and wings took on an entirely alien appearance. Odd, gelatinous ooze covered her scaling breasts and her arms increased in diameter and darkened in color. The music now had little effect on her. She landed on the deck beside him. He stopped playing, closed his eyes and prepared to die.

"No, sweet Richard, I will not kill you. That mercy is for you to decide. And if you will not give me the ecstasy of your music . . . I will find it . . . *in the songs of my young!*"

She raised her arms to expose the back of her wings. Each one had a perfect row of six egg-shaped nodules pulsating from their protrusion on her lower back.

The sight revolted him.

She picked up the emotion. "So quickly you turn! So easily you judge! If you will not play for me, you will play for no one!" She opened her mouth. The familiar fire sprayed forth, bathing the guitar and his hands in flame. He screamed as both turned to ash in seconds. He fell against the cement deck, holding his smoldering stumps in the air.

The numbness of shock crept over him. He watched, zombielike, as she changed to her angelic form and flew into the darkness and out of sight over the buildings . . . south towards Olympus.

He sat there for many hours, until the grey ridges of dawn hinted over the horizon.

Then, just as the sun threatened, he climbed to the railing and took one step out.

Darrell Schweitzer

Minotauress

DARRELL SCHWEITZER, *editor of the new* Weird Tales *magazine, is the prolific author of many fantasy stories set in a world with its own complex legendry (see, for instance, "Mysteries of the Faceless King" in my collection* Weird Tales, the Magazine that Never Dies). *But in the next selection, the erudite Mr. Schweitzer turns to Greek myth, speculating on the possibility that the Minotaur slain by Theseus may have produced offspring.*

IT BEGINS, as always, with the stirring of my womanly parts. The human portion of my body yanks my dreaming mind back across thousands of miles, away from the marvelous fair in the equally marvelous country of my dreams that is called France. One minute I am dressed as a great lady, in veils and fine gown, attended by many servants. The sun is hot, the sky a brilliant blue, the crowd around me chattering with countless voices. Jesters leap and tumble. A colorful madman in rags and streamers staggers above the crowd on stilts. A column of knights in full armor rumble by, pennons flapping from their lances. One by one the knights salute me, for in this dream-France I am a famous lady indeed.

Then I am hauled in, like a fish on a line. Here. Into this dark place which smells of earth and ancient stone.

Here. The pain-which-is-also-pleasure sears through my flesh like a rivulet of molten iron. Memories arise, too many at once, like a flock of screeching birds, like many-colored paints stirred into a pot, and I awaken in utter darkness, momentarily befuddled, as if my tens of centuries of life are not sufficient to accustom me to this place.

I listen, very carefully, for the expected sound, and there it is, as faint as a single drip of water at first, then a patter, again and again and again, a torrent, louder even than the murmurous riot of that fairground crowd in my beloved dream-France.

The sounds are echoes, striking, rebounding, striking, rattling through the walls of the great labyrinth which is my home, the entirety of my waking world. Sometimes a single piece of plaster falling can re-echo for hours. I have never learned to tell how *old* a noise is by merely listening to it. But I know from these particular sounds that I have company, that the intruders might have been inside the labyrinth for half a day.

My body stirs in an odd mixture of lust and hunger, gladness and fear. I rise from the soft, dry dirt which is my bed. On hands and knees, I shake my flesh clean. My breasts drag along the floor.

The sounds again. Words now, in some language I know from my centuried dreams. One voice is loud, supremely confident, the other cringing—like a little boy who's been beaten and is pleading not to be beaten again. Yes, they are male voices. I can tell that much, whatever the distance.

The weak voice wants to retreat, to desist from whatever it is they are to do.

Ah, my sweet ones, it is entirely too late already, for is this not the labyrinth built by the peerless Daedalus, which may be only confounded by a ball of yarn? You didn't bring any knitting supplies on your little expedition, did you? No, I thought not.

Grunting, I heave myself upright, one hand against the wall, my massive body unsteady on such tiny, cloven-hoofed feet. I lumber forward, shoulder and thigh scraping niter from the wall; ungainly, yes, for am I not a monster like all my kind?

I find my two guests in Death's Waiting Hall, where the twisting tunnels open out into a spacious, pillared room. Light filters in from some deftly concealed skylight far above, illuminating little. The place is positively thick with shadows. For all my thousand and some years of habitation, there are still secrets of this place unknown to me. I have never found that skylight.

One of the intruders holds a torch aloft. The two of them recoil in horror at the decor: the bones and armor of fallen warriors, an untidy heap of swords and greaves and breastplates, plumed helmets gone to rust, even one or two full suits of metal like the torchbearer wears; and among them all countless bones, shattered arms, splintered ribs, vertebrae and teeth like dice thrown in some forgotten game. There are more skulls than I could ever count, even many centuries back when counting and reassembling these remains was a hobby of mine. And among them, sacred and untouched, lies the huge skeleton of the progenitor of my race, Asterius, who died here, slain by Theseus.

I bow my massive head, lowing softly, spittle dripping from nose and lips, my horns swaying slowly from side to side.

Like the madman on stilts, I stagger forward.

The cringing fellow screams, "Holy Mother of God save us! A monster!" He tries to flee, but the armored man grabs him by the scruff of the neck like a cat hauling a kitten, swings him around to face me, and forces the torch into his hands.

"Hold this, you idiot! It's going to be *easy*. . . ."

He slides his sword from his scabbard with a rasping sound, and advances. Yes, it is so easy. I stand there, stupidly, my head swaying, my breasts rolling, until he is very close. For all his bravado, he is amazed at the sight of me. He stares, wide-eyed. His breathing is harsh and heavy. But he does not hesitate, and draws his arm back, ready to plunge the sword into my vitals. Then faster than his eye can follow I lash out with one hoof, smashing his right leg, all but severing it. He screams. His sword flies off to join my disorderly collection. Down he tumbles, blood spurting, but before he hits the floor I hook him under the chin with my right horn and fling him across the room like a ragged sack of bones. The thud of him striking the far wall echoes and re-echoes for several minutes like the sound of thousands of hands beating softly on hide drums. Gradually it subsides, like the sighing of the sea.

All this while the other intruder just stands there, his mouth agape. The torch crackles. Glowing cinders drop to the floor.

This room is well named. Death resides here, among the pillars. The two of us converse sometimes. I think he likes to rest in the dark between his labors. There is a truce between us, for I am the last on all the earth of my kind or any of the related, ancient kinds who may not die until slain.

Therefore Death waits on me here, and when it pleases me, I grant him audience or even, occasionally, an offering. I look for him now. Something shifts in the distance, but I think it is only a shadow or a trick of the eye.

I am alone with my remaining guest, who is short and dark compared to his companion. He seems little more than a boy. As I approach, his reaction is startling.

"Holy Theotokos, Mother of God, pray for me now at the hour of my death—!"

He screams and drops to his hands and knees, repeating something I cannot follow. His torch rolls away among the bones. As I stand over him, I realize that his speech has changed. Where before he spoke some language I knew only from dreams, now, as his voice occasionally surfaces from the babble, his language is distinctly *Greek*; but not the flowing, musical Greek of Ulysses and of the honey-mouthed assassin Theseus. No, the words are strange, dark, the accent distorted like something echoed in the depths of my labyrinth. But *Greek*, actually spoken rather than dreamed.

Like some ancient Greek who might conceivably worship me.

I reach down and touch him on the shoulder, but he recoils, rolling until he is some distance away, sitting with his back to the wall.

"Holy One—"

Now it is I who kneel, because it is painful to be on my feet for very long. I crouch down, spreading my legs apart, and I lean forward, supporting the heavy, upper part of my body with my arms. I hiss softly through my bovine nostrils.

"You call me holy—"

He waves his hands frantically, as if swatting bees. "No! No! You are a devilish monster! Mother of God—!"

"But you called *me* holy, as I am in a little way, descended from a divine ancestor." I mean, not Asterius, but Poseidon's bull.

He has no answer to that. I lean over farther and gaze into his eyes. Mine are my best feature, purest azure, like the pure summer skies of my dream-France. They startle most people into paralysis.

The boy is calmed by them.

"You *know* who I am," I say softly.

He gulps, then forces himself to speech. "I know you are a creature out of an old tale. I never believed it before now, not even when I—when Guildo and I"—he glanced over at his former companion—"when we uncovered the entrance to this place—"

"Uncovered it? Does not the entrance to the labyrinth stand clearly marked, behind the altar in the garden of the palace of King Minos?"

He is more puzzled than afraid. Good. I've got him talking.

"L-Lady, we followed rumors, what the country folk told us, and he had to dig to find the opening, in a mound overgrown with trees and haunted by vipers."

"Ah." Somehow it almost figures. I range far and wide in my dreams, but in waking life, of course, I have never been outside. I have no idea what changes the eons have wrought in the immediate neighborhood.

"Yet you came here."

"Yes." It was obviously a difficult confession for him to make, as if of a great crime. "Guildo came . . . for gold. To steal. I came . . . to die."

"Do you despise life so much after so short a time, child?"

He bows his head and speaks very softly. I must lean forward, straining to hear. "Lady, I am almost twenty."

"The blinking of an eye, then."

"I am a worthless traitor, Lady. I do not deserve to live any longer. Yet no Christian may take his own life, even if he is already damned. Therefore I thought . . ." Once more his gaze rested upon the fallen Guildo.

"You thought to end up like him."

"Something like that."

"Explain yourself, child. This is most extraordinary."

Again, his reaction is likewise extraordinary. He slumps to the floor and begins to weep. Between his sobs I make out snatches of the story, how an Emperor Isaac was cruelly blinded by an Emperor Alexius, and a Prince Alexius, son of Isaac, who was to become Emperor Alexius, went into barbarian lands for aid, whereupon the Franks—I cannot believe they were the same as the French of my dreams—drove one Alexius away and made another emperor, but strife arose between them and yet another Alexius slew the former one, I'm not sure which—

"Stop! My head spins. Your words are all ajumble. What is your name anyway, child?"

"Alexius."

I sigh, and my mind drifts back over many years. "I remember a time when everyone seemed to be named Gaius. It was terribly confusing." I laugh gently, snorting, and that, perhaps, shocks him even more than the color of my eyes.

"But now great Constantinopolis, the heart of the world, the city of the Romans, is fallen to the Franks. The great treasures of mankind, all the beautiful things gathered by so many emperors, are now burnt or carried off or melted down to make coins for barbarian soldiers. And when this happened, where was I? Was I there to defend the city and die? No, I was on the wrong side!"

Human politics are more labyrinthine than my labyrinth. But there is more to this story than politics. One of such an age as almost-twenty does not come to death-seeking grief over politics.

"You loved someone very much," I say.

He looks at me, amazed, as if I can read his mind. I try to smile, but my face is not built for smiling.

"There was a girl. Eudocia—"

"Ah . . ."

"We were to be wed. But I left her, to go off and serve Alexius—the Prince—and his father the Emperor Isaac Angelus. I would come back rich, I told her. I would be a great lord. But—"

"But things did not work out as you expected."

Once more he sobbed. "No, Lady, they did not."

"They never do, Alexius. Now tell me the rest of the story."

"I suffered for my prince, in prison, and for his father. Then I escaped, and escaped again when they both were dead, but the Franks caught me. I should have died then. But Guildo spared me, if I would swear service to him. The world was ending. My lords were dead. I thought I had nothing more to lose. My death would serve no purpose. So I swore. And when the final assault came and the city was violated, there I was, a servant of the barbarians, watching from the deck of a Venetian galley, a worthless traitor—"

"I think you have grown very old in your nearly twenty years, Alexius. But perhaps you are overambitious when you take all the world's burdens onto yourself."

". . . then Guildo quarreled with a knight over a share of the loot and killed the man, and was outlawed, so the two of us fled here, to Crete, where still our enemies dogged us. We forced our way into farmhouses, demanding shelter. More than once we murdered when we thought we were betrayed. Then, one night, as we hid in some ruins, I told him the old story . . . of your kind . . . and it seemed to drive him mad. He was crazed with the idea of stealing the treasures of this place. I wasn't so sure there would be any treasures. Didn't Lord Theseus bear them away?"

"Only what he could carry."

"So here we are." Once more he is weeping. He lies on his side, his face in the dirt. "Now you will kill me, Lady. Now you will kill me." He seems drained of all fear, merely stated what he takes to be an obvious fact. He is not even pleading.

"No, I will not kill you," I whisper. "You, perhaps, will find your comrade's sword and kill me, for that is the way of things. I am weary now and will sleep. Many of my kind are slain in sleep."

He cannot speak. His face is wet with mud and tears. I crawl over to him and very gently lick him clean with my long cow's tongue, then lie down beside him.

"If only men could live as beasts, Alexius. They would be free of sorrow then."

·   ·   ·   ·

Asterius, the great Minotaur, son of Pasiphae and the Bull from the Sea, was likewise a dreamer. There was little else for him to do during the long years of his imprisonment, between bouts of devouring youths and maidens given him in sacrifice. I think he fought in the end because he was unable to overcome his own fierce nature, but he was weary and he wanted to die. Theseus was his liberator.

Meanwhile, Asterius dreamed, and his soul wandered among the lands of men as my soul does; the last of his descendants, I am as great a dreamer as he.

I don't think mankind ever knew that there were more of us, that sometimes before he devoured them or they died of fright or madness, Asterius had his way with the maidens, that some of them actually sought union with him in their frenzy and their pain, as if it were a kind of escape. I think that we, the sons and daughters of the bull-man, were the last of the gods' secrets, one they never got around to revealing before they, too, finally died.

The boy Alexius was genuinely surprised to see me. I wasn't accounted for in the tale, as he knew it. How then did he expect to die in the labyrinth? Killed by ghosts? By his treacherous companion? Smitten by the outraged Mother of his God? I don't know. Such things confuse me, even in my dreams when I am truly alive.

So I lie beside Alexius and my soul ventures forth, into the many lives I share all over the world, opening them one by one like books in a library. I am in France again, in a castle listening to a storyteller while the curtains of rain outside the window whisper like the echoes in my labyrinth. The story is one of romance and of heroic lovers, of how for his sins a knight was commanded to love a loathly lady who was more beast than human woman. True to his vows, he did, and by his love she was transformed into the fairest of all maidens.

Yes, I know that story. The French lady remembers it, as if in a dream.

And I dream of fire, too, and of blood, and of screams in the night. I behold the great city of the Romans, Constantinopolis, burning as Frank-ish knights rage through the streets, slaying, raping women and boys. They quarrel like frenzied dogs over cloths and gold and the precious relics of dead holy men. It is all strange to me, something I can never understand because my nature is not entirely human.

Some of these Franks were men the French lady had known as gentle poets and lovers, now transformed by their greed into beasts, into mon-sters.

My spirit wanders. In still stranger lands, men from East and West battle one another for the honor of the same god, a single god intolerant of all others, whom each faction knows by a different name.

Has it not always been the way of men to fight?

Then I return over the waves, walking like a lady of smoke, like a ghost. Once I near a ship that reminds me of a huge centipede, crawling in the moonlight on its hundred oars. When they spy me, the sailors cry out. They plead for succor, whether from me or against me I never know.

Homeward, then. Crete has changed since the old days. There are castles now, and squat, tumbledown villages, and the Franks camp over the whole land like a cloud of locusts come to rest. The palace of King Minos I cannot find, not even the mound the boy spoke of. So I must return to the labyrinth, into the darkness, and awaken.

I gaze up at a single star through the untraceable skylight. The boy has made no attempt to slay me, or to get away. He lies asleep, with one arm around my middle.

I know what I have to do.

"Alexius, get up." I nudge him gently with my nose, then crawl a little ways off, to give him room.

"What? Huh? What does my Lady require?"

I laugh again. He seems less shocked by my laughter this time. "You would serve me now?"

"I dreamed that you had changed, that you were a beautiful lady—"

"Alexius, you sound like one of those mooning, Frankish poets."

"Perhaps, my Lady."

"Very well, then. I command you to lead me out of this place, into the world, for I have seen it only in my dreams and long to know it in the flesh. Alexius, can you imagine how it is to have worn beautiful clothing only in my dreams, to have eaten at the banquet table only in dreams, and to somehow be kept warm and strong that way? I did not starve, subsisting on dreams, but I have not flourished either. Somehow your arrival motivates me . . . because in my nearly two thousand years I have not seen and touched what you have in nearly twenty."

He sits against the wall, silent.

"Very well then," I say. "We shall go now."

"Lady, I cannot lead you."

"Would you disobey me already? Maybe you *are* a worthless traitor after all."

I expect him to weep at that, but he is defiant. "It isn't that. I simply *don't know the way.*"

"Ah, you forgot the ball of yarn."

For an instant he is puzzled, silent, but he knows the old stories as well as he knows his own name, for he is a Greek, not a Frank, and the answer comes to him. "Yes, that is it."

"I know the way. Before now, I have merely been unable to follow it."

So we walk for miles, around and around in the labyrinth King Minos commanded Daedalus to build in order to contain the royal embarrassment, my ancestor. I lean on the boy's shoulder, since it is difficult to so burden my puny hooves and ankles. We stop to rest many times.

Once, I ask him about the wars.

"Christian men take up the cross," he says, "and go fight the pagans."

"These pagans, are they like Persians?"

"They worship Mahomet."

"And what is that?"

"A demon, some say, who sleeps in a coffin that hovers between heaven and earth. Others say he was a prophet."

"I knew a prophet once. His name was Tiresias. Blind. But he saw very clearly, for all the good it did him."

We pass through richly furnished, canopied rooms. There is much luxury in this labyrinth, for Asterius was, after all, the son of a king. But these chambers are near the outer part of the maze, and the resounding echoes make them unbearable for very long, through either the malice or negligence of Daedalus. Only in the heart of the labyrinth is there any quiet. Only there can one dream.

"And what will you do in the world, Lady?"

"I shall go to France. I have dreamed of it."

"Men will fear to behold you."

"Perhaps not."

Onward, as the accumulated echoes of our speech and movements thunder after us like an angry mob driving us forth into the unknown.

It is like a birth, at the very last. I hold back. I am afraid. I feel a kind of pain I never knew could exist. The great bronze doors guarding the labyrinth are long gone. The corridors slowly blend into caves, then ravines, and at last there is a naked sky over us, and I am unable to go on.

He takes me by the hand, gently but firmly, and leads me up onto a hilltop among some olive trees. There we sit, looking out over the sea.

Spring flowers sway in the gentle breeze. What astonishing things are the flowers, how incredible the breeze.

"And what will you do in the world, Alexius?" I ask him finally.

"Nothing, Lady. I have nowhere to go. There is nothing for me."

"No one may know how his life is to be spun, Alexius, or measured, or cut. Do not blame yourself."

"Lady, in serving you I do penance for my many sins."

"You don't really believe that, do you child?"

"If I believe anything at all, yes, Lady."

"As you wish then."

So we wait until nightfall and emerge by moonlight, out of the trees, and walk along a road, meeting a single shepherd who falls to his knees at the sight of us. Then we come to a town and there, indeed, as Alexius had prophesied, men flee in terror. He leads me to a boat. I sit in the narrow stern while he rows.

What an awesome thing the ocean is. On the water and under the stars, I tell him the rest of my story, how, it is said, creatures such as myself can become fully human if only someone can see the humanity in them. Asterius remained a monster, in effect, because he was not loved. That was the source of his rage. That was why he wanted to die in the end. There was enough of the man in his heart for that.

I tell Alexius the story I heard in the windswept castle, from the mooning Frankish poet.

"I know it too," he says, letting go of the oars. For a time the boat drifts and the two of us see there while the moon sets into the water. Then, in the darkness he leans forward, careful not to capsize the boat, puts his arms around me as far as they can reach, and kisses me gently on my monstrous lips. For that instant, perhaps, he does not see me as misshapen at all.

Much later we hail a ship and are taken to another island, and to another, and another, to the growing wonder of the inhabitants. We travel through many lands, and the tales of us always precede our coming. Great crowds greet us in every town. Lords command us to attend them in their castles. We are the miracle and prodigy of the age.

I run my hands through my long golden hair. That is marvel enough. Ladies show me how to comb it. I spend long hours gazing at my pale face in a mirror. That, too, is a marvel, for which men call me vain. Still, my eyes are my best feature, startling even when the sailors first found me naked but for Alexius's cloak.

My body is so light now, like a cloud. I move so freely. A marvel.

As for my beast-man, he goes before me always, frightening then delighting onlookers with his clumsy tricks, rowing my boats, bearing my luggage, leading my horse. When we come to the France of my dreams it is I who lead him into the fair, though, with a leash around his neck. He holds back, afraid. I whisper gently in his ear.

I don't know if he can understand words any longer. I think he is forgetting that he was once Alexius, who sorrowed. Perhaps one day I shall kiss him on his terrible lips to remind him, summoning him back into himself.

Perhaps.

I run my fingers through my golden hair.

Parke Godwin

A Matter of Taste

Among the excellent writings of my friend and erstwhile collaborator PARKE
GODWIN *are an award-winning ghost story,* "The Fire When It Comes";
several historical novels, including Beloved Exile, Firelord, The Last Rainbow, *and* A Memory of Lions; *such science-fantasy as* Waiting for the
Galactic Bus *and its sequel,* The Snake Oil Wars, *and a semiautobi-
ographical modern novel,* A Truce with Time. "A *Matter of Taste*" *is an
urbane tale of two sophisticated lovers with decidedly unusual appetites.*

MEDIOCRITY LIVES in a crowded house. Perfection dwells alone. For
Addison Solebury life was lonely at the top. Even in the upper reaches of
gastronomy his tastes were so lofty that no restaurant in the world could
hope for his continued custom. In the main, he prepared his own meals, a
process of considerable labor and research that only added zest to anticipation, feasts so rarefied in their reflection of taste that few could share,
let alone cater them.

His standards were arcane but not inflexible. On an off night he could
squeak by with properly aged filet mignon and *vin ordinaire*, but for the
most part, Solebury's antipathy to the ordinary was visceral and had been
all his life. He turned even paler than normal at the sight of margarine,
fled a block out of his way to avoid the effluvium of pizza, and often woke
whimpering from nightmares of canned tomato soup.

Food—his ecstatic, almost sexual vision of it—was an art he could not
see coarsened; therefore, integrity exacted its price. The absence of sharing, of a woman, was the minor mode of Solebury's male lament. After
all, not even the nightingale sang for the hell of it, but Solebury, through
overspecialization, labored and dined for the most part alone. Time and

again, he girded himself and went woman hunting, but with his intolerance of the mundane, his quest was akin to a majestic elk bugling for a mate in the city pound.

Many were called, none were chosen. He despaired of finding a woman of similar refinement. Even those for whom Solebury had the highest hopes revealed a gullet of clay. His fragile expectations would inevitably dampen as she attacked her salad, flickered as she swallowed garlic *escargots* with vulgar relish, guttered with the entrée, and died over brandy and cheese. Failure upon failure, until the coming of Pristine Solent.

From the first tentative conversation in the library reference room where he worked, Solebury felt right about Pristine. When he peered over her shoulder, he found her scanning just those sources he ferreted out in his pursuit of perfection. An exploratory dinner was even more promising. Craftily, he suggested the Four Seasons and was heartened when Pristine answered her door in sensible clothes rather than the coronation gown an ordinary woman might have worn for the occasion. Clothes were not important. The key, the subtle clue to the unerring rightness of his choice was in the way Pristine addressed herself to food. Looks counted for something, to be sure. Pristine was short and robust, with a pale but infinitely well-nourished complexion, a square face with faintly critical brows, and a wide, ready smile that displayed 90 percent of her perfect teeth. For his own appearance, she seemed tacitly to approve of him: pallid as herself with a clear skin, perhaps a small roll of flesh around his fortyish middle that only attested to many years of choosy but ample diet.

But her address to the food—ah, that was exquisite. Her fork balanced in a firm hand, Pristine studied the entrée, turned it this way and that in the manner of an inquisitive coroner, then, resigned that the chef could come no closer to her ideals, speared, chewed, and reluctantly swallowed. Solebury's lips parted in silent admiration. He dared to hope.

"The best is none too good, is it?" he winked at her, then applied the test. Would she join him soon again in a dinner of his own preparation? "I'm something of an expert on dining. In a small way."

"Small way" was the code phrase that separated *cognoscenti* from the uninitiated. He was instantly gratified.

"Why don't we?" Pristine touched her white hand to his, strong fingers curving around intimately to touch his callused palm. She wrinkled her upturned nose at him. "It sounds memorable."

Solebury leaned forward and their eyes met over the forgotten trout amandine. "I think it could be. You know what it means to meet someone you can truly share with?"

"Yes, yes. I know." Pristine stroked the back of his slightly trembling hand. "So seldom. So rare."

A bubble of happiness swelled in Solebury's chest. "You're very beautiful."

"I feel beautiful tonight," said Pristine Solent.

They got out of the taxi a few blocks before her apartment, not wanting the evening to end, holding hands, heads close together. Solebury kissed her with clumsy ardor at her outside door. Pristine swayed into him, then threw back her head to the night sky with a little mew of contentment.

"What an evening. Oh, Addison, I hope there'll be a moon next time. I'm so damned romantic about these things. And a moon is part of it."

"It is. So important." Solebury positively quivered with joy.

"And what's a romantic dinner without moonlight?" Pristine squeezed his hand. "G'night."

If there was a sidewalk under him, Solebury didn't feel it. He floated to the corner and let three cabs approach, slow tentatively, and pass on before remembering he wanted one.

Like Lancelot, Solebury's love quest lay through great deeds. Such a dinner could not be conjured for the next evening or even within a week. Pristine would consider that careless. This called for his full mastery. Since the bone of genius is discipline, Solebury went back to basics, to research.

His own office, the library reference room, was his usual start. All the dailies were searched, torrents of fine print skimmed for the form of his menu. All professionals have their secrets; one of Solebury's lay in his insistence on a slightly pungent spice overlooked by all but a few masters and not commonly used for centuries. Only one establishment, Whittakers, still used it in their prepared seasonings. Just a tiny dollop, but to Solebury it was *sine qua non*, adding an overtaste delicate as it was incomparable.

At length his entrée was found. In a rising fever of concentration Solebury turned his attention to the treacherous but crucial matter of wine.

Only a tyro considered geriatric vintages automatically best. Like any living thing, the grape had its youth, prime, and declining age. Of recent years he gave serious consideration to only one: '76 of course—but '76 what? Even within the confines dictated by a white-meat entrée, there were nuances of choice. Some masters—and Pristine could well be one—preferred a *demi-sec* where he would choose a drier variety. A blunder here, one false step, could shadow Pristine's judgment. She'd be kind, but

Solebury would feel a door closing behind her charity, and successive evenings would find her otherwise engaged.

He let instinct guide him, recalling a champagne he'd chosen not two months back, a superb Chardonnay *brut*. His usual shop produced one remaining bottle at a larcenous price, but Solebury's heart sang as he hurried home. He knew all this was preamble, part of the labor of love. A great deal of delving remained.

One more choice awaited him: the time, more of a gamble than all the rest. Pristine wanted a moon, but though Solebury scanned the papers and the skies, one promised nothing and the other remained perversely overcast. At last came an evening when the early autumn moon entered like a diva from a proscenium of fleecy cumulus clouds. Solebury turned from his window and reached for the phone, at once stabbed to the heart and uplifted by Pristine's throaty greeting.

"He*llo*, Addison. I was just thinking of you."

He choked on his ecstasy. "You were?"

"Must be ESP. I was looking at the moon and thinking tonight might be—"

"Yes. Perfect. That's why I called. You wanted a romantic moon. Shall we dine? Something *very* special?"

"In a small way. Love to," Pristine whispered over the wire. "I'm famished for something special."

A world of promise throbbed in her honeyed contralto.

Solebury always dined late. Pristine was not surprised by the hour or the address, neither that fashionable.

"It's a perfect time, Addison. I'm never hungry much earlier than that. I'll be there."

Solebury hung up in a soft rush of joy. Here was a mate for all reasons.

Humming with busy pleasure, Solebury twirled the '76 down into the waiting ice. Even now, before Pristine arrived, there was spadework. He miscalculated slightly and was only half ready with final preparations when she appeared. If her first dinner costume had been sensible, her clothing tonight was downright utilitarian—jeans and boots and a windbreaker against the cool. She gave Solebury a cheerful little peck and surveyed his labors.

"Can I help?" she asked politely.

"Oh no, really. There's just a little further—"

"No, let me. You've already worked so hard."

It flattered Solebury to see Pristine pitch in. She was very sturdy, but no dining of this caliber was ever accomplished without hard physical labor. At length Pristine paused, wiping her brow with the back of one white hand, and drew the champagne from its bucket to browse the label with admiration.

"Lovely year, Addison." She turned again briefly to the last shovel work, then stepped aside for her host. "You'll want to open up and carve."

"Of course. You are a dear, Pristine." Descending into the grave, Solebury wielded his implement with a practiced economy of movement. Three deft snaps with the crowbar broke the casket seals. With a gustatory flourish, he threw it open for her approval.

"Bon appétit, darling."

He hovered waiting under the October moon for the sunbeam of her approval, but he saw only a frown of disappointment.

"Beautifully aged," he assayed against her silence. "Buried Thursday."

Pristine sat down on the freshly turned earth. "Oh, Addison. Oh dear . . ."

"What—what's wrong?"

"Everything!" she wailed.

He felt a premonitory chill. "But he's perfect. Buried from Whittaker's last Thursday. I use them exclusively, the only undertakers who still use myrrh in their preparation. You must know that."

Pristine's disappointment turned brittle. "Of course I know that. There is Whittaker's and only Whittaker's. But as you see, the entrée is hardly Caucasian."

True, the entrée was decidedly dark. There was no mention of that in the obituary. He'd assumed white meat; a minor variant and trivial. Solebury vaulted out of the grave to sit facing Pristine like a teacher. "Pristine, that doesn't really matter. Expertise is one thing, ivory tower another."

"Doesn't matter?" Pristine corrected him like an errant child. "Surely you know non-Caucasian flesh doesn't take the myrrh flavor well at all. It cancels it out."

"I *beg* to disagree." Solebury's pride was at stake, and she was dead wrong. "A difference, yes. A subtle piquance, if you will, but hardly canceled."

"Even if that were true," Pristine countered in a voice cool as the churchyard dark, "it completely negates champagne."

Solebury began to feel a bit waspish despite himself. "Oh, really! The principle is the same as dark meat on fowl. I took days choosing that champagne. I am not an amateur."

But her pretty head wagged back and forth through his protestations. "Cold Duck, Mister Solebury. Nothing else."

He went falsetto at the sacrilege. "Cold *Duck?* It's so bloody common!"

"But," Pristine riposted with a raised forefinger, "the *un*common choice." Her assertiveness quavered and broke. "I'm sorry, Addison, but I—"

"Oh, please, Pristine. I worked so hard."

"I know, but it's all so *wrong.*"

"Please stay. I adore you."

"Oh, go to hell. Go to McDonald's—no. No, please, dear Addison, I didn't mean that. That was filthy. Just—" Her voice caught and shattered on a sob. "Just that I was looking for someone, too, someone to share with. It's so lonely being the best. And I thought you . . ."

"I am, Pristine, darling. We could share so much."

"No, not with differences as wide as these. Don't say anything, just goodbye. I'm leaving. I won't look back. Don't call me. Oh, my dear Addison. You were so close to perfection."

Solebury choked out something in farewell and admission of his sins, following Pristine with the eyes of tragedy as she receded forlornly through the cemetery gate. He slumped down on the turned earth, working without relish at the champagne cork. The *pop* was hollow as his hopes.

"So close to perfection," she had said. All right. He raised the glass to his better, though it cost him a love to learn. Life was still lonely near the top. The moon went down and the wind before dawn was desolate.

He could barely pick at supper.

Mildred Clingerman

The Wild Wood

MILDRED CLINGERMAN, *a frequent contributor to* The Magazine of Fantasy and Science-Fiction (F&SF) *in the 1950s, has been absent from genre writing for so long that no editor I asked knew where or if she was still living. I am happy to report that she is alive and well in Tucson, and is thinking of returning to writing. Her short stories are often gently sentimental fantasies, but the following tale is an exception. "The Wild Wood," which first appeared in the January 1957 F&SF, may well be the most bonechilling Christmas story ever penned.*

IT SEEMED TO MARGARET ABBOTT that her children, as they grew older, clung more and more jealously to the family Christmas traditions. Her casual suggestion that, just this once, they try something new in the way of a Christmas tree met with such teen-age scorn and genuine alarm that Margaret hastily abandoned the idea. She found it wryly amusing that the body of ritual she herself had built painstakingly through the years should now have achieved sacrosanctity. Once again, then, she would have to endure the secret malaise of shopping for the tree at Cravolini's Christmas Tree Headquarters. She tried to comfort herself with the thought that one wretchedly disquieting hour every year was not too much to pay for her children's happiness. After all, the episode always came far enough in advance of Christmas so that it never *quite* spoiled the great day for her.

Buying the tree at Cravolini's began the year Bonnie was four. Bruce had been only a toddler, fat and wriggling, and so difficult for Margaret to carry that Don had finally loaded Margaret with the packages and perched his son on his shoulder. Margaret remembered that night clearly.

All day the Abbotts had promised Bonnie that when evening came, when all the shop lights blazed inside the fairy-tale windows, the four of them would stroll the crowded streets, stopping or moving on at Bonnie's command. At some point along the way, the parents privately assured each other, Bonnie would grow tired and fretful but unwilling to relinquish the dazzling street and her moment of power. That would be the time to allow her to choose the all-important tree, which must then, of course, be carried to their car in triumph with Bonnie as valiant, proud helper. Once she had been lured to the car it would be simple to hurry her homeward and to bed. The fragrant green mystery of the tree, sharing their long ride home, would insure her sleepiness and contentment.

As it turned out (why hadn't they foreseen it?), the child showed no sign of fatigue that evening other than her captious rejection of every Christmas tree pointed out to her. Margaret, whose feet and back ached with Bruce's weight, swallowed her impatience and shook out yet another small tree and twirled its dark bushiness before Bonnie's cool, measuring gaze.

"No," Bonnie said. "It's too little. Daddy, let's go that way." She pointed down one of the darker streets, leading to the area of pawnshops and narrow little cubbyholes that displayed cheap jewelry. These, in turn, verged on the ugly blocks that held credit clothiers, shoe repair shops, and empty, boarded-up buildings where refuse gathered ankle-deep in the entrance ways.

"I won't," Margaret said. "This is silly. What's the matter with this tree, Bonnie? It isn't so small. We certainly aren't going to wander off down there. I assure you, they don't *have* Christmas trees on that street, do they, Don?"

Don Abbott shook his head, but he was smiling down at his daughter, allowing her to drag him to the street crossing.

Like a damn, lumbering St. Bernard dog, Margaret thought, *towed along by a simpering chee-ild.* She stared after her husband and child as if they were strangers. They were waiting for her at the corner, Don, with the uneasy, sheepish look of a man who knows his wife is angry but unlikely to make a scene. Bonnie was still tugging at his hand, flashing sweet, smug little smiles at her mother. Margaret dropped the unfurled tree with a furious, open-fingered gesture, shifted Bruce so that he rode on one hip, and joined them.

The traffic light changed and they all crossed together. Don slowed and turned a propitiating face to his wife. "You all right, hon? Here, you carry the packages and I'll take Bruce. If you want to, you could go sit in the car. Bonnie and I, we'll just check down this street a little way to make sure. . . . She says they've got some big trees someplace down here." He looked doubtfully down at his daughter then. "Are you sure, Bonnie? How do you know?"

"I saw them. Come on, Daddy."

"Probably she *did* see some," Don said. "Maybe last week when we drove through town. You know, kids see things we don't notice. Lord, with traffic the way it is, who's got time to see anything? And besides, Margaret, you said she could pick the tree. You said it was time to start building traditions, so the kids would have . . . uh . . . security and all that. Seems to me the tree won't mean much to her if we make her take the one we choose. Anyway, that's the way I figure it."

Margaret moved close to him and took his arm, squeezing it to show both her forgiveness and apology. Don smiled down at her and Margaret's whole body warmed. For a long moment she allowed her eyes to challenge his with the increased moisture and blood-heat that he called "smoky," and which denoted for both of them her frank desire. He stared back at her with alerted male tension, and then consciously relaxed.

"Well, not right here and now," he said. "See me later."

Margaret, reassured, skipped a few steps. This delighted the children. The four of them were laughing, then, when they found themselves in front of the derelict store that housed Cravolini's Christmas Tree Headquarters.

Perhaps it was their gaiety, that first year, that made Cravolini's such a pleasant memory for Don and the children. For the first few minutes Margaret, too, had found the dim, barny place charming. It held a bewildering forest of upright trees, aisles and aisles of them, and the odor of fir and spruce and pine was a tingling pleasure to the senses. The floor was covered with damp sawdust, the stained old walls hung with holly wreaths and Della Robbia creations that showed real artistry. Bonnie had gone whooping off in the direction of the taller trees, disappearing from sight so quickly that Don had hurried after her, leaving Margaret standing just inside the door.

She found herself suddenly struggling with that queer and elusive conviction that "this has happened before." Not since her own childhood had she felt so strongly that she was capable of predicting in detail the events that would follow this moment. Already her flesh prickled with foreknowledge of the touch that would come . . . *now*.

She whirled to stare into the inky eyes of the man who stood beside her, his hand poised lightly on her bare forearm. Yes, he was part of the dream she'd returned to—the long, tormenting dream in which she cried out for wholeness, for decency, and love, only to have the trees close in on her, shutting away the light. "The trees, the trees . . ." Margaret murmured. The dream began to fade. She looked down across the packages she held at the dark hand that smoothed the golden hairs on her forearm. *I got those last summer when I swam so much.*

She straightened suddenly as the dream ended, trying to shake off the langour that held her while a strange, ugly man stroked her arm. She managed to jerk away from him, spilling the packages at her feet. He knelt with her to pick them up, his head so close to hers that she smelled his dirty, oily hair. The odor of it conjured up for her *(again?)* the small, cramped room and the bed with the thin mattress that never kept out the cold. Onions were browning in olive oil there over the gas plate. The man standing at the window with his back turned . . . *He needed her; nobody else needed her in just that way. Besides, Mama had said to watch over Alberto. How could she leave him alone? But Mama was dead. . . . And how could Mama know all the bad things Alberto had taught her?*

"Margaret." Don's voice called her rather sharply out of the dream that had again enveloped her. Margaret's sigh was like a half-sob. She laughed up at her husband, and he helped her to her feet, and gathered up the packages. The strange man was introducing himself to Don. He was Mr. Cravolini, the proprietor. He had seen that the lady was very pale, ready to faint, perhaps. He'd stepped up to assist her, unfortunately frightening her, since his step had not been heard—due, doubtless, to the great depth of the sawdust on the floor. Don, she saw, was listening to the overtones of the apology. If Mr. Cravolini's voice displayed the smallest hint of insolence and pride in the lies he was telling, then Don would grab him by the shirt front and shake him till he stopped lying and begged for mercy. Don did not believe in fighting. Often while he and Margaret lay warmly and happily in bed together Don spoke regretfully of his "wild-kid" days, glad that with maturity he need not prove on every street corner that he was not afraid to fight, glad to admit to Margaret that often he'd been scared, and always he'd been sick afterwards. Don approved of social lies, the kind that permitted people to live and work together without too much friction. So Mr. Cravolini had made a mistake. Finding Margaret alone, he'd made a pass. He knew better now. OK. Forget it. Thus Margaret read her husband's face and buried very deeply the sharp, small stab of disappointment. *A fight would have ended it, for good.* She frowned a little with the effort to understand her own chaotic thoughts, her vision of a door that had almost closed on a narrow, stifling room, but was now wedged open . . . waiting.

Don led her down one of the long aisles of trees to where Bonnie and Bruce were huddled beside their choice. Margaret scarcely glanced at the tree. Don was annoyed with her—half-convinced, as he always was, that Margaret had invited the pass. Not by any overt signal on her part, but simply because she forgot to look busy and preoccupied.

"Don't go dawdling along in that wide-eyed dreamy way," he'd said so often. "I don't know what it is, but you've got that look—as if you'd say yes to a square meal or to a panhandler or to somebody's bed."

Bonnie was preening herself on the tree she'd chosen, chanting a maddening little refrain that Bruce would comprehend at any moment: "And Bru-cie did-unt he-ulp. . . ." Already Bruce recognized that the singsong words meant something scornful and destructive to his dignity. His face puckered, and he drew the three long breaths that preceded his best screaming.

Margaret hoisted him up into her arms, while Don and Bonnie hastily beat a retreat with the excuse that they must pay Mr. Cravolini for the tree. Bruce screamed his fury at a world that kept trying to confine him, limit him, or otherwise squeeze his outsize ego down to puny, civilized proportions. Margaret paced up and down the aisles with him, wondering why Don and Bonnie were taking so long.

Far back at the rear of the store building, where the lights were dimmest, Margaret caught sight of a display of handmade candles. Still joggling Bruce up and down as if she were churning butter, she paused to look them over. Four pale blue candles of varying lengths rose gracefully from a flat base moulded to resemble a sheaf of laurel leaves. Very nice, and probably very expensive. Margaret turned away to find Mr. Cravolini standing immediately in front of her.

"Do you like those candles?" he asked softly.

"Where is my husband?" Margaret kept her eyes on Bruce's fine, blonde hair. *Don't let the door open any more. . . .*

"Your husband has gone to bring his car. He and your daughter. The tree is too large to carry so far. Why are you afraid?"

"I'm not afraid. . . ." She glanced fleetingly into the man's eyes, troubled again that her knowledge of his identity wavered just beyond reality. "Have we met before?" she asked.

"I almost saw you once," Cravolini said. "I was standing at a window. You were reflected in it, but when I turned around you were gone. There was nobody in the room but my sister . . . the stupid cow . . ."

Cravolini spat into the sawdust. "That day I made a candle for you. Wait." He reached swiftly behind the stacked packing boxes that held the candles on display. He had placed it in her hand before she got a clear look at it. Sickeningly pink, loathsomely slick and hand-filling. It would have been cleaner, more honest, she thought, if it had been a frank reproduction of what it was intended to suggest. She dropped it and ran awkwardly with the baby towards the lights at the entrance way. Don was just parking the car. She wrenched the door open and half fell into the front seat. Bonnie had rushed off with Don to bring out the tree. Margaret buried her face in Bruce's warm, sweet-smelling neck and nuzzled him till he laughed aloud. She never quite remembered afterwards the ride home that night. She must have been very quiet—in one of her "lost" moods, as Don called them. The next morning she was surprised to see that Bonnie had picked one of Cravolini's largest, finest trees, and to discover the tissue-wrapped pale blue candles he had given Bonnie as a special Christmas gift.

Every year after that Margaret promised herself that this year she'd stay at home on the tree-buying night. But something always forced her to go —some errand, a last bit of shopping, or Don's stern injunctions not to be silly, that he could not handle Bonnie, Bruce, *and* the biggest tree in town. Once there, she never managed to escape Cravolini's unctuous welcome. If she sat in the car, then he came out to speak to her. Much better go inside and stick close by Don and the children. But that never quite worked, either. Somehow the three of them eluded her; she might hear their delighted shouts two aisles over, but when she hastened in their direction, she found only Cravolini waiting. She never eluded him. Sometimes on New Year's Day, when she heard so much about resolutions on radio and television, she thought that surely this year she'd tell Don at least some of the things Cravolini said to her—did to her— enough, anyway, to assure the Abbotts never going back there again. But she never did. It would be difficult to explain to Don why she'd waited so long to speak out about it. Why hadn't she told him that first night?

She could only shake her head in puzzlement and distaste for motivations that were tangled in a long, bad dream. And how could a woman of almost-forty explain and deeply explore a woman in her twenties? Even if they were the same woman, it was impossible.

When Cravolini's "opening announcement" card arrived each year, Margaret was jolted out of the peacefulness that inevitably built in her between Christmases. It was as if a torn and raw portion of her brain healed in the interim. *But the door was still invitingly wedged open, and every Christmas something tried to force her inside.* Margaret's spirit fought the assailant that seemed to accompany Mr. Cravolini (hovering there beyond the lights, flitting behind the trees), but the fighting left her weak and tired and without any words to help her communicate her distress. *If only Don would see,* she thought. *If there were no need for words. It ought to be like that.* . . . At such times she accused herself of indulging in Bruce's outgrown baby fury, crying out against things as they are.

Every time she saw Cravolini the dream gained in reality and continuity. He was very friendly with the Abbotts now. They were among his "oldest customers," privileged to receive his heartiest greetings along with the beautiful candles and wreaths he gave the children. Margaret had hoped this year that she could convince Bonnie and Bruce to have a different kind of tree—something modern and a little startling, perhaps, like tumbleweeds sprayed pink and mounted on a tree-shaped form. Anything. But they laughed at her bad taste, and were as horrified as if she were trying to by-pass Christmas itself.

I wonder if I'll see *her* this year, Margaret thought. Alberto's sister. She knew so much about her now—that she was dumb, but that she had acute, morbidly sensitive hearing—that once she'd heard Cravolini murmuring his lust to Margaret, because that was the time the animal-grunting, laughing sounds had come from the back of the store, there where extra trees lay stacked against the wall. Her name was Angela, and she was very gross, very fat, very ugly. Unmarriageable, Alberto said. Part of what Margaret knew of Angela came from Alberto's whispered confidences (unwanted, oh unasked for!), and the rest grew out of the dream that lived and walked with Margaret there in the crumbling building, beginning the moment she entered the door, ending only with Don's voice, calling her back to sanity and to another life.

There were self-revelatory moments in her life with Don when Margaret was able to admit to herself that the dream had power to call her back. She would like to know the ending. It was like a too-short book that left one hungry and dissatisfied. So this year she gave way to the children, to tradition, and went once again to Cravolini's.

Margaret was aware that she looked her best in the dull red velveteen suit. The double golden hoops at her ears tinkled a little when she walked and made her feel like an arrogant Gypsy. She and Don had stopped at their favorite small bar for several drinks while the children finished their shopping.

Maybe it's the drinks, Margaret thought, and maybe it's the feeling that tonight, at last, I'll settle Mr. Cravolini, that makes me walk so jut-bosomed and proud. Don, already on his way with her to Cravolini's, had dropped into a department store with the mumbled excuse that always preceded his gift-buying for Margaret. He had urged her to go on alone, reminding her that the children might be there waiting. For once, Margaret went fearlessly, almost eagerly.

The children were not waiting, but the woman was. *Angela.* Margaret knew her instantly, just as she'd known Alberto. Angela stared up and down at Margaret and did not bother to hide her amusement, or her knowledge of Margaret's many hot, protesting encounters with her brother. Margaret started to speak, but the woman only jerked her head meaningfully towards the back of the store. Margaret did not move. The dream was beginning. *Alberto is waiting, there beyond the stacked-high Christmas trees. See the soft, springy nest he has built for you with pine boughs.* Margaret stirred uneasily and began to move down the aisle, Angela beside her.

I must go to him. He needs me. Mama said to look after Alberto. That I would win for myself a crown in Heaven . . . Did she know how unnatural a brother Alberto is? Did she know how he learned the seven powers from the old, forbidden books? And taught them to me? He shall have what he desires, and so shall I. Here, Alberto, comes the proud, silly spirit you've won . . . and listen, Don and the children are coming in the door.

Margaret found the soft, springy bed behind the stacked trees. Alberto was there, waiting. She heard Don call for her and struggled to answer, struggled desperately to rise to go to him. But she was so fat, so heavy, so ugly. . . . She heard the other woman's light, warm voice answering, heard her happy, foolish joking with the children, her mock-protestations, as always, at the enormous tree they picked. Margaret fought wildly and caught a last glimpse of the Abbotts, the four of them, and saw the dull, red suit the woman wore, heard the final, flirtatious tinkling of the golden earrings, and then they were gone.

A whole year I must wait, Margaret thought, *and maybe next year they won't come. She will see to that.*

"My sister, my love . . ." Alberto crooned at her ear.

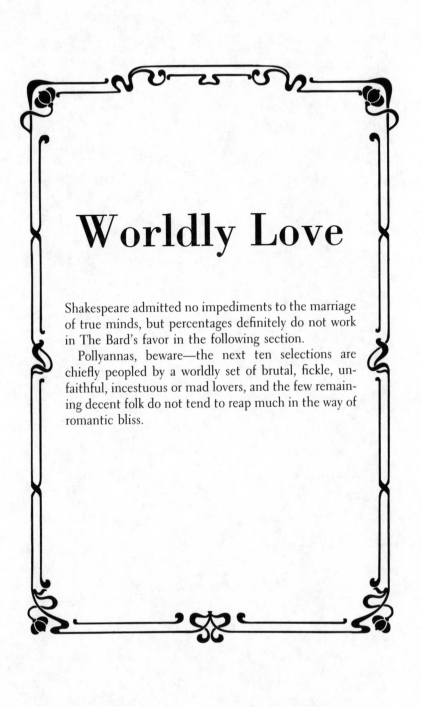

Worldly Love

Shakespeare admitted no impediments to the marriage of true minds, but percentages definitely do not work in The Bard's favor in the following section.

Pollyannas, beware—the next ten selections are chiefly peopled by a worldly set of brutal, fickle, unfaithful, incestuous or mad lovers, and the few remaining decent folk do not tend to reap much in the way of romantic bliss.

Arthur Conan Doyle

The Colonel's Choice

This variation on the "gentlemanly code of honor" theme is one of the more obscure tales by ARTHUR CONAN DOYLE *(1859–1930), renowned British author of the Sherlock Holmes stories, as well as historical novels and the delightful Professor Challenger adventure,* The Lost World. *"The Colonel's Choice" first appeared in* Lloyd's Weekly London Newspaper *on July 26, 1891, the same month and year that saw publication of Doyle's famous third Sherlock Holmes adventure, "A Scandal in Bohemia."*

THERE WAS SOME SURPRISE in Birchespool when so quiet and studious a man as Colonel Bolsover became engaged to the very dashing and captivating Miss Hilda Thornton. And in truth this surprise was mingled with some feeling of pity for the gallant officer. It was not that anything really damaging could be alleged against the young lady. Her birth at least was excellent, and her accomplishments undeniable. But for some years she had been mixed up with a circle of people whose best friends could not deny that they were fast. "Smart" they preferred to call themselves, but the result was much the same.

Hilda Thornton was a very lovely woman of the blonde, queenly, golden-haired type. She was the belle of the garrison, and each fresh subaltern who came up from Woolwich or from Sandhurst bowed down and adored her. Yet subalterns grew into captains and captains into majors without a change in her condition. An interminable succession of sappers, gunners, cavalrymen and linesmen filed past through the social life of Birchespool, but Miss Hilda Thornton remained Miss Hilda still. Already she had begun to show a preference for subdued lights, and to appear some years younger in the evening than in the morning, when good, simple-hearted Colonel Bolsover, in one of his brief sallies into the social world, recognising in her all that was pure and fresh, with much diffidence made her the offer of an honoured name, a good position, and some two thousand a year. It is true that there were a grizzled head and an Indian constitution to set off against these advantages, but the young lady showed no hesitation, and the engagement was the talk next day of all the mess-rooms and drawing-rooms of the little town.

But even now it was felt that there was a doubt as to her ultimate marriage. Spinsters whispered dark prophecies upon the subject, and sporting ensigns had money on the event. Twice already had Hilda approached the happy state, and twice there had been a ring returned, and a pledge unfulfilled. The reason of these fiascos had never been made plain. There were some who talked of the fickleness and innate evil of mankind. Others spoke of escapes, and hinted at sinister things which had come to the horrified ears of her admirers, and had driven them from her side. Those who knew most said least, but they shook their heads sadly when the colonel's name was mentioned.

Just six days before the time fixed for the marriage Colonel Bolsover was seated in his study with his cheque-book upon the desk in front of him, glancing over the heavy upholsterer's bills, which had already commenced to arrive, when he received a visit from his very old friend, Major Barnes, of the Indian horse. They had done two campaigns together on the frontier, and it was a joy to Bolsover to see the dark, lean face and the spare, wiry figure of the Bengal Lancer.

"My dear boy," he cried, with outstretched hands. "I did not even know that you were in England."

"Six months' furlough," answered his old comrade, returning his greeting warmly. "Had a touch of liver in Peshawar, and a board thought that a whiff of the old air might stiffen me up. But you are looking well, Bolsover."

"So I should Barnes. I have had some good fortune lately, better fortune than I deserve. Have you heard it? You may congratulate me, my boy. I am a Benedict from next Wednesday."

The Indian soldier grasped the hand which was held out to him, but his grip was slack and his eyes averted.

"I'm sure I hope it is all for the best, Bolsover."

"For the best? Why, man, she is the most charming girl in England. Come in this evening and be introduced."

"Thank you, Bolsover, I think that I have already met the young lady.

Miss Hilda Thornton, I believe? I dined with the Sappers last night and heard the matter mentioned."

Barnes was talking in a jerky, embarrassed style, which was very different to his usual free and frank manner. He paused to pick his words, and scraped his chin with his finger and thumb. The colonel glanced at him with a questioning eye.

"There's something wrong, Jock," said he.

"Well, old chap, I have been thinking—we have been thinking—several of your old chums, that is to say—I wish to the Lord they would come and do their own talking—"

"Oh, you're a deputy?" Bolsover's mouth set, and his brows gathered.

"Well, you see, we were talking it over, you know, Bolsover, and it seemed to us that marriage is a very responsible kind of thing, you know."

"Well, you ought to know," said the colonel, with a half smile. "You have been married twice."

"Ah, yes, but in each case I give you my word, Bolsover, that I acted with prudence. I knew all about my wife and her people: upon my honour I did!"

"I don't quite see what you are driving at, Barnes."

"Well, old chap, I am rather clumsy at anything of this sort. It's out of my line, but you will forgive me, I am sure. But we can't see a chum in danger without a word to warn him. I knew Tresillian in India. We shared one tent in the Afghan business. Tresillian knew Miss Thornton, no one better. I have reason to believe that when he was quartered here five years ago—"

Colonel Bolsover sprang from his chair, and threw up a protesting hand.

"Not another word, Barnes," said he. "I have already heard too much. I believe that you mean well to me, but I cannot listen to you upon this subject. My honour will not permit it."

Barnes had risen from his chair, and the two old soldiers looked into each other's eyes.

"You are quite resolved upon this, Bolsover?"

"Absolutely."

"Nothing would shake you?"

"Nothing on earth."

"Then that's an end of it. I won't say another word. I may be wrong and you may be right. I am sure that I wish you every happiness from the bottom of my heart."

"Thank you, Jock. But you'll stay tiffin. It's almost ready."

"No, thank you, my boy. I have a cab at the door, and I am off to town. I ought to have started by the early train, but I felt that I could not leave Birchespool without having warned—that is to say congratulated you upon the event. I must run now, but you'll hear from me by Friday."

Such was the embassy of Major Jack Barnes, the one and only attempt which was made to shake the constancy of Percy Bolsover. Within a week Hilda Thornton was Hilda Thornton no longer; and amid a pelting storm of rice the happy couple made their way to the Birchespool railway station, *en route* for the Riviera.

For fifteen months all went well with the Bolsovers. They had taken a large detached villa which stood in its own grounds on the outskirts of Birchespool, and there they entertained, with a frequency and a lavishness which astonished those who had known the soldierly simplicity of the colonel's bachelor days. Indeed he had not altered in his tastes. A life of frivolity was thoroughly repellent to him. But he was afraid of transplanting his wife too suddenly into an existence which might seem to her to be austere. After all he was nearly twenty years her senior, and was it reasonable to suppose that she could conform her tastes to his? He must sacrifice his own tastes. It was a duty. He must shake off his old ways and his old comforts. He set himself to the task with all the energy and thoroughness of an old soldier, until Bolsover's dances and Bolsover's dinners were one of the features of social life in Birchespool.

It was in the second winter after their marriage that the great ball was given in the little town on account of a very august and Royal visitor. The cream of the county had joined with the garrison to make it a brilliant success. Beautiful women were there in plenty. But Bolsover thought as he gazed upon the dancers that there was none who could compare with his own wife. In a grey tulle toilette, trimmed with apple-blossom, with a diamond aigrette twinkling from amid her golden hair, she might have stood as the very type and model of the blonde regal Anglo-Saxon beauty. In this light the first faint traces of time were smoothed away, and, with a gleam of pleasure in her eyes, and a dash of colour in her cheeks, she was so lovely that even the Royal and august, though reported to be very blasé in the matter of beauty, was roused to interest. The colonel stood among the palms and the rhododendrons, following her with his eyes, and thrilling with pride as he noticed how heads turned and quick whispers were exchanged as she passed through the crowd.

"You are to be congratulated, colonel," said Lady Shipton, the wife of the general of the brigade. "Madame is quite our belle to-night."

"I am very flattered to hear you say so," said the colonel, rubbing his hands in his honest delight.

"Ah, you know that you think so yourself," said the lady, archly, tapping his arm with her fan. "I have been watching your eyes."

The colonel coloured slightly and laughed. "She certainly seems to be enjoying herself," he remarked. "She is a little hard to please in the matter of partners, and when I see her dance twice with the same I know that she is satisfied."

The lady looked, and a slight shadow crossed her face.

"Oh, her partner!" she exclaimed. "I did not notice him."

"He looks like a man who has been hard hit at some time," observed the colonel. "Do you know him?"

"Yes. He used to be stationed here before you came. Then he got an appointment and went to India. Captain Tresillian is his name, of the Madras Staff corps."

"Home on leave, I suppose!"

"Yes. He only arrived last week."

"He needed a change," observed the colonel. "But the band is rather overpowering here. This next is the 'Lancers.' May I have the pleasure?"

The face which had attracted the colonel's attention was indeed a remarkable one—swarthy, keen, and hawklike, with sunken cheeks and deep set eyes, which were Italian rather than English in their blackness and brightness. The Celtic origin of his old Cornish blood showed itself in his thin, wiry figure, his nervous, mobile features, and the little petulant gestures with which he lent emphasis to his remarks. Hilda Bolsover had turned pale to the lips at the sight of him as she entered the ballroom, but now they had danced two consecutive dances, and the third they had sat out under the shadow of the palms. There the colonel found them as he strolled round the room while the dancers were forming up for the cotillon.

"Why, Hilda, this is one of your favourites," said he. "You are surely not going to miss it?"

"Thank you, Percy; but I am a little tired. May I introduce you to my old friend, Captain Tresillian, of the Indian army! You may have heard me speak of him. I have known him for ever so many years."

Colonel Bolsover held out his hand cordially, but the other swung round his shoulder, and gazed vacantly across the ballroom as though he had heard nothing. Then suddenly, with a half shrug, like a man who yields to his fate, he turned and took the hand which was offered to him.

The colonel glanced at him in some surprise, for his manner was strange, his eyes wild, and his grasp burned like that of a man in a fever.

"You have not been home long, I believe?"

"Got back last week in the Jumna."

"Had you been away long?"

"Only three years."

"Oh! Then you found little changed at home?"

Captain Tresillian burst into a harsh laugh.

"Oh, yes; I find plenty of change at home. Plenty of change. Things are very much altered."

His swarthy face had darkened, and his thin, dark hands were nervously opening and shutting.

"I think, Percy," said Hilda Bolsover, "that the carriage will be waiting now. Good night, Captain Tresillian. I am sure that we shall be happy to see you at Melrose Lodge."

"Most certainly," cried the colonel. "Any friend of my wife's is a welcome guest. When may we hope to see you?"

"Yes, yes; I shall certainly call," the other answered, "I am very much obliged to you. Good night."

"Do you know, Hilda," remarked the colonel, as they rattled homewards that night in their brougham, "I notice something very strange in the manner of your friend, Captain Tresillian. He struck me as a very nice fellow, you know, but his talk and his look were just a little wild at times. I should think he has had a touch of the sun in India."

"Very possibly. He has had some trouble, too, I believe."

"Ah, that might account for it. Well, we must try and make the place as pleasant to him as we can."

Hilda said nothing, but she put her arms round her husband's neck and kissed him.

The very next day and for many days after Captain Tresillian called at Melrose Lodge. He walked with Hilda, he rode with her, he chatted with her in the garden, and he escorted her out when the colonel was away at his duties. In a week there was gossip about it in Birchespool: in a month it was the notorious patent scandal of the town. Brother veterans sniggered about it, women whispered, some pitied, some derided; but amid all the conflict of opinions Bolsover alone seemed to be absolutely unconcerned. Once only Lady Shipton ventured to approach the subject with him, but he checked her as firmly as, if more gently than, he had his old friend in the days of his engagement. "I have implicit faith in her," he said. "I know her better than anyone else can do."

But there came a day when the colonel, too, found that he could no longer disregard what was going on beneath his roof. He had come back late one afternoon, and had found Captain Tresillian installed as usual in the drawing-room, while his wife sat pouring out tea at the small table by the fire. Their voices had sounded in brisk talk as he had entered, but this had tailed off to mere constraint and formalities. Bolsover took his seat by the window, thoughtfully stirring the cup of tea which his wife had handed to him, and glancing from time to time at Tresillian. He noticed him draw his note-book from his pocket, and scribble a few words upon a loose page. Then he saw him rise with his empty cup, step over to the table with it, and hand both it and the note to her. It was neatly done, but her fingers did not close upon it quickly enough, and the little slip of white paper fluttered down to the ground. Tresillian stooped for it, but Bolsover had taken a step forward, and had snatched it from the carpet.

"A note for you, Hilda," said he quietly, handing it to her. His words were gentle, but his mouth had set very grimly, and there was a dangerous glitter in his eyes.

She took it in her hand and then held it out to him again.

"Won't you read it out to me?" said she.

He took it and hesitated for an instant. Then he threw it into the fire. "Perhaps it is better unread," said he. "I think, Hilda, you had best step up to your room."

There was something in his quiet, self-contained voice which dominated and subdued her. He had an air and a manner which was new to her. She had never seen the sterner side of his character. So he had looked and spoken on the fierce day before the Delhi Gates, when the Sepoy bullets were hopping like peas from the tires of his gun, and Nicholson's stormers were massing in the trenches beneath him. She rose, shot a scared, half-reproachful glance at Tresillian, and left the two men to themselves.

The colonel closed the door quickly behind her, and then turned to his visitor.

"What have you to say?" he asked, sternly and abruptly.

"There was no harm in the note." Tresillian was leaning with his shoulder against the mantelpiece, a sneering, defiant expression upon his dark, haggard face.

"How dare you write a note surreptitiously to my wife? What had you to say which might not be spoken out?"

"Well, really, you had the opportunity of reading it. You would have found it perfectly innocent. Mrs. Bolsover, at any rate, was not in the least to blame."

"I do not need your assurance on that point. It is in her name as much as in my own that I ask you what you have to say."

"I have nothing to say, except that you should have read the note when you had the chance."

"I am not in the habit of reading my wife's correspondence. I have implicit confidence in her, but it is one of my duties to protect her from impertinence. When I first joined the service there was a way by which I could have done so. Now I can only say that I think you are a blackguard, and that I shall see that you never again cross my threshold, or that of any other honest man in this town, if I can help it."

"You show your good taste in insulting me when I am under your roof," sneered the other. "I have no wish to enter your house, and as to the other thing you will find me very old-fashioned in my ideas if you should care to propose anything of the kind. I wish you good-day."

He took up his hat and gloves from the piano, and walked to the door. There he turned round with his hand upon the handle and faced Bolsover with a face which was deeply lined with passion and with misery.

"You asked me once whether I found things different in England. I told you that I did. Now I will tell you why. When I was in England last I loved a girl and she loved me—she loved me, you understand. There was a secret engagement between us. I was poor, with nothing but my pay, and she had been accustomed to every luxury. It was to earn enough to be able to keep her that I volunteered in India, that I worked for the Staff, that I saved and saved, and lived as I believe no British officer ever lived in India yet. I had what I thought was enough at last, and I came back with it. I was anxious, for I had had no word from my girl. What did I find? That she had been bought by a man twice my age—bought as you would buy—." He choked and put out a hand to his throat before he could find his voice. "You complain—you pose as being injured," he cried. "I call God to witness which has most reason to cry out, you or I."

Colonel Bolsover turned and rang the bell. Before the servant could come, however, his visitor was gone, and he heard the quick scrunch of his feet on the gravel without. For a time he sat with his chin on his hands, lost in thought. Then he rose and ascended to his wife's boudoir.

"I want to have a word with you, Hilda," said he, taking her hand, and sitting down beside her on the settee. "Tell me truly now, are you happy with me?"

"Why, Percy, what makes you ask?"

"Are you sorry that you married me? Do you regret it? Would you wish to be free?"

"Oh! Percy, don't ask such questions."

"You never told me that there was anything between you and that man before he went to India."

"It was quite informal. It was nothing—a mere friendship."

"He says an engagement."

"No, no; it was not quite that."

"You were fond of him?"

"Yes; I was fond of him."

"Perhaps you are so still?"

She turned away her face, and played with the jingling ornaments of her chatelaine. Her husband waited for an answer, and a spasm of pain crossed his face as no answer came.

"That will do," said he, gently disengaging his hand from hers. "At least you are frank. I had hoped for too much. I was a fool. But all may yet be set right. I shall not mar your life, Hilda, if I can help it."

The next day the authorities at the War office were surprised to receive a strongly-worded letter from so distinguished an artillery officer as Percy Bolsover, asking to be included in an expedition which was being fitted out in the North-west of India, and which notoriously promised a great deal of danger and very little credit. There was some delay in the answer, and before it arrived the colonel had reached his end in another and a more direct fashion.

No one will ever know how the fire broke out at Melrose Lodge. It may have been the paraffin in the cellars, or it may have been the beams behind the grate. Whatever the cause the colonel was wakened at two on a winter morning by the choking, suffocating smell of burning wood, and rushing out of his bedroom found that the stairs and all beneath him was already a sea of fire. Shouting to his wife he dashed upstairs, and roused the frightened maids, who came screaming, half-dressed, down into his bedroom.

"Come, Hilda," he cried, "we may manage the stairs."

They rushed down together as far as the first landing, but the fire spread with terrible rapidity; the dry woodwork was blazing like tinder, and the swirl of mingled smoke and flame drove them back into the bedroom. The colonel shut the door, and rushed to the window. A crowd had already assembled in the road and the garden, but there were no signs of the engines. A cry of horror and of sympathy went up from the people as they saw the figures at the window, and understood from the flames which were already bursting out from the lower floor that their retreat was already cut off.

But the colonel was too old a soldier to be flurried by danger, or at a loss for a plan. He opened the folding windows and dragging the feather-bed across the floor he hurled it out.

"Hold it under the window," he cried. And a cheer from below showed that they understood his meaning.

"It is not more than forty feet," said he, coolly. "You are not afraid, Hilda?"

She was as calm as he was. "No, I am not afraid," she answered.

"I have a piece of rope here. It is not more than twenty feet, but the feather bed will break the fall. We will pass the maids down first, Hilda. Noblesse oblige!"

There was little time to spare, for the flames were crackling like pistol shots at the further side of the door and shooting little red tongues through the slits. The rope was slung round one maid, under her arms, and she was instructed to slip out from it, and to fall when she had been lowered as far as it would go. The first was unfortunate, for she fell obliquely, bounded from the edge of the bed, and her screams told those above her of her mishap. The second fell straight, and escaped with a shaking. There were only the husband and wife now.

"Step back from the window, Hilda," said he. He kissed her on the forehead, as a father might a child. "Good-bye, dear," he said. "Be happy."

"But you will come after me, Percy?"

"Or go before you," said he, with a quiet smile. "Now, dear, slip the rope round you. May God watch over you and guard you!"

Very gently he lowered her down, leaning far over the window, that another three feet might be taken from her fall. Bravely and coolly she eyed the bed beneath her, put her feet together, and came down like an arrow into the centre of it. A cheer from beneath told him that she was unhurt. At the same instant there was a crash and a roar behind him, and a great yellow blast of flame burst roaring into the room. The colonel stood framed in the open window, looking down upon the crowd. He leaned with one shoulder against the stonework, with the droop of the head of a man who is lost in thought. Behind him was a lurid background of red flame, and a long venomous tongue came flickering out over his head. A hundred voices screamed to him to jump. He straightened himself up like a man who has taken his final resolution, glanced down at the crowd, and then, turning, sprang back into the flames.

And that was the colonel's choice. It was "Accidental death" at the inquest, and there was talk of the giddiness of suffocation and the slipping of feet; but there was one woman at least who could tell how far a man who truly loves will carry his self sacrifice.

Julia L. Keefer

A Secret

"A Secret" is a deceptively understated horror story by Julia L. Keefer, *a New York actor and author of three plays and a like number of original screenplays. Dr. Keefer, who holds a Ph.D. from New York University, "day-lights" as a professional kinesiologist.*

I SPENT MOST of the summer scratching and sweating. The mosquitoes loved me. The only relief was the lake—a big blue cold lake. My best friend, Lyana, and I stayed in the water as much as possible, swimming, sailing, water-skiing. I even took skinny dips at night. Something I was told *not* to do.

Dad loved to watch me swim. He said I was a beautiful swimmer and he rowed the boat while I swam across the lake. If I swam faster than he rowed, he doubled my allowance. More reason to stay in the water. When I got out of the water, he hugged me and dried me with a huge towel. Sometimes we went sailing together. I was the skipper while he suntanned and drank beer. He tried to make me go fishing but that was too boring! Even though I had five younger brothers and sisters, he said I was his best buddy.

At night, he made a campfire, hoping I would sing and play the guitar. Sometimes I sang for him and sometimes I didn't, depending on my mood. I said no first. Then he begged me at least ten times. I didn't always sing well. But if he'd been really nice to me, I'd sing "Five Hundred Miles." His eyes got that faraway look and he looked like he was in heaven.

Lyana and I usually slept in the tent. Lyana was fourteen, two years older than me, and the boy-craziest girl I ever knew. She read dirty magazines all night and I read horror stories. I thought her magazines were disgusting and she thought mine were silly.

"Monsters, dragons and ghosts aren't real. They're stupid, made-up things for people who are afraid to really live life," she said as she looked at my books.

Lyana wasn't afraid of anything. She went water-skiing barefoot, sky-diving and cliff-hanging. She dragged me through people's private property and even to a monastery where we watched the monks undress. Lyana wasn't afraid of boys. In the summer it was hard to meet the right boys because we were living with our families in the country. But in the city she went out on real dates. She even did it once.

"Boys like to touch you everywhere," she said as she put her hands between her legs.

Then she took off her shirt and started to stroke her nipples. I put my hand shyly on my tiny new breasts that were beginning to bud. I hoped they'd grow to be at least as big as hers.

Dad noticed I was developing first. He said he hoped they'd get bigger.

Although Mom cooked most of the meals, Dad made pancakes for us every morning while she slept in. We had breakfast in our nightgowns while he served us all kinds of treats: blueberries, maple syrup, chocolate milk, and ice cream on the pancakes if we were really good.

"You can work off a big breakfast. But don't eat like this all the time. I don't want you turning into a puffball."

Dad left the bathroom door open when he took his bath in the morning. He said it was so he could watch TV in the living room. He took such long baths that I had to go in and brush my teeth. He was so big and hairy, floating in the water like a huge ape.

I asked Lyana if her boyfriends were big and hairy like Dad. She liked them big, but not too hairy. She was still waiting to meet a real lover.

"Is a lover the same as a boyfriend?" I asked.

"No, a lover is special. You do everything with him, like a best friend. But he makes you feel different. When he gets near, your heart beats faster, and when he looks into your eyes you tingle all over. As he touches you, your body trembles and aches."

"The only thing that makes me tremble, ache and tingle is reading about my scariest monster."

"Yeah, but monsters hurt you and lovers make you feel good," Lyana laughed as she picked up a dirty magazine.

"He looks just like Dad," I said, glancing shyly at the naked man.

"That's cuz he's the only man you've ever seen. Actually they are all a little different."

After she fell asleep I took my flashlight and looked at her magazines for hours. When I finally went to bed, I had a horrible nightmare about a man who turns into a monster. The monster didn't drink blood or claw at hair. He did nothing but get close. When he looked into his victim's eyes, she had a heart attack. He killed people without hurting them. I woke up trembling, shaking and sweating.

The next night the moon made a bright orange path on the lake. Lyana wanted to go for a skinny dip, even though it was against the rules. She never cared much for rules. We walked down to the beach in towels, the stones digging into our bare feet. I took off my towel and jumped quickly into the water. You never know who's watching. Lyana stood naked on the dock, her grown-up body lit by the moon. She sprinkled cold water over her breasts, so her nipples stood up like hard little pebbles. Then she dove off the dock, making a huge splash. As we swam, we tried to follow the path of the moon; but it kept changing.

Finally Lyana got bored and swam back to the dock. She looked like a mermaid as she got out of the water, her long blond hair dripping down to her waist. She took the towel and rubbed the spot between her legs and across her bum.

"It must be dry by now," I thought to myself. But she kept rubbing. As I began to get out of the water, I saw Dad standing on the cliff above the dock.

"Lyana," I whispered, "Dad's on the cliff."

"Hello, Mr. Lewis," she said calmly, wrapping the towel around her body.

"You shouldn't be swimming alone at this hour, girls. Come right in," he shouted.

I stood frozen on the ladder, hiding my girl's body from his sight. Lyana knew I was scared.

"No problem. We'll be right up."

I watched his figure move up the hill towards the house. I was so scared I couldn't even dry myself. Lyana giggled as she wrapped the towel around me. We ran up to the tent in time to see Dad open the back door.

That night I had another nightmare about the monster who kills people by looking at them.

The next morning Dad didn't make his usual great breakfast. He said he was punishing us for swimming alone at night. We weren't allowed near the water for a day. I had to help him cut the grass in the field and

Lyana had to help Mom clean the closets. Lyana didn't mind cleaning closets because it was like exploring. But I hated cutting grass.

I stayed in the field all day, moping like a punished dog. Dad and I didn't say a word. We each had our own lawn mower and it took forever to mow the field. The heat was suffocating and the mosquitoes ate me alive. I sweated and itched like never before. I did my best, trying to cut every single row perfectly. I wanted Dad to say I was doing a good job. I wanted him to smile, or hug me or squeeze my hand. But he just looked at the lawnmower and the field.

I guess I was too old to get a spanking. When I was a little girl, he used to spank me. I'll never forget those spankings. All of a sudden, he became very quiet and serious. He took me by the hand and led me to his room. He told me to pull down my pants and lie face down on his bed. Then he got a long belt from his closet.

"I don't want to really hurt you," he said.

I never remember feeling pain. I was never sore, bruised or bleeding like other kids. The belt touched my bum lightly. But I cried anyway. I cried because I had disappointed Dad.

Now at twelve years old I was still being a bad girl.

Suddenly Dad stopped the lawn mower and looked at me.

"Lyana isn't good for you. She's too grown-up."

"But Dad, Lyana's been my best friend since I was eight years old."

"Does she talk to you about boys?"

I blushed as I imagined Dad listening to our conversations in the tent.

"You aren't ready for boys." Then he raised his voice angrily: "You're too young to even think about boys, do you hear me?"

As he looked into my eyes I saw the monster who kills without touching you.

I turned away shyly. "Do you like the way I cut the grass?"

"Don't change the subject. I'm going to talk to your mother about Lyana. Now finish your work."

I spent the rest of the day sweating, itching, and crying silently.

For the next week, I slept in the house and Lyana slept in the tent. I missed her but I had a chance to read more horror stories. We still played together during the day.

Then one day while we were raking the beach she said she had something important to tell me.

"You can't tell this to anyone, promise?" I gave her my Girl Scout's word of honor.

"Last night, real late, your father came into the tent. He was really drunk. When I woke up, he was on top of me, kissing and touching me everywhere. His breath stank so bad. I told him to leave me alone. He said he wouldn't hurt me: he wanted to make up for punishing us. He said he'd be really nice. I said I'd scream if he didn't get out. He got up and pulled some money out of his pocket. A lot of money. For me, if I didn't tell anyone. I said okay if he'd go back to the house. So he left and I kept the money."

I was too terrified to ask questions. At first I didn't believe her, but Lyana never lied to me. That evening her family came to pick her up— two weeks earlier than planned. We hugged and she said she'd see me in the city.

For the rest of the summer I did chores. I couldn't go on adventures by myself because I wasn't a daredevil like Lyana. I hoped that by being a good girl, Dad and I would be best buddies again. He was so nice and polite I began to think Lyana was lying. Maybe it was a bad dream. He wouldn't do a thing like that.

I slept in the house instead of the tent. The only souvenir I had of Lyana was a book she left about sex. It described everything in detail. It said that when he puts it in you the first time he can hurt because he breaks the tissue and makes you bleed. But after that, it's pure pleasure, especially if you're in love. Men and women fit nicely into each other, like wearing a glove. Men get hard and usually come once, but women shiver and shake like an earthquake. Their pleasure can go on and on like a waterfall. I thought men must be like water pistols. The book said men have to keep touching women in one spot to make them excited. Their fingers and tongues get tired so that's why women buy electrical things called vibrators. They showed a picture of a vibrator in the book. It was just like the one beside Mom's bed.

I put my fingers between my legs. It seemed much too small for those big things men had. I felt funny touching myself. Lyana played with herself every night but I was afraid to even look down there.

Suddenly I heard the car door slam. It was very late and Mom and Dad were coming home from a party. They were fighting, something they never did during the day. I crept into the bathroom so I could hear better.

"I told you, I can't take this drinking. You have to stop."

"Come on, we were at a nice party. Everyone drinks."

"But not like you, Ted. You called me a bitch in front of everyone. Not only does that humiliate me, it ruins your reputation. You're president of a major company!"

"Sometimes you act like a bitch."

I heard Mom scream again: "Don't touch me."

"You're my wife, aren't you? Or did you forget that?"

"I'm your wife in name, that's all."

"Bitch, bitch, bitch," I heard my father say over and over again. Suddenly the door slammed. Silence.

I couldn't sleep all night.

The next morning Mom and Dad were busy and friendly and nice—as if nothing happened. I didn't say a word. Dad and I spent the day painting the toolshed, washing the car, husking corn, and collecting firewood for the end of summer bonfire. I worked hard and fast to please him, but he wasn't satisfied.

"Chores never end. And the field always needs cutting."

"Why does grass grow so fast?"

"Grass is like little girls." Then he winked and pinched my bum.

Later that day we were mowing the field. I was exhausted from lack of sleep and too much work. Dad said I could take a nap under a tree while he finished cutting the field. I lay on a nice soft spot, covered with moss. Dad covered me with his shirt and kissed me softly on the forehead.

"Sleep tight, sweetheart. I love you."

"Are we best buddies again?"

"We certainly are. And lately, you've been a very good girl."

I was so happy that he loved me again that I fell asleep peacefully, the smell of his breath fresh in my nostrils.

I woke up to a light rain caressing my forehead. I looked straight into my father's eyes. At first he scared me, like the monster, but his touch was soft and gentle.

"It's okay, darling, it's just a light rain."

He kissed my cheeks, my eyes, my mouth; his lips mixing with the rain. Then I felt his hand on my breasts. I'd been stuffing myself to look bigger. He smiled as he pulled the Kleenex out of my bra. I was so embarrassed I wanted to die. He lifted up the bra and squeezed my nipples.

"I can't wait until they get bigger," he said greedily.

Then he put his hand in my underpants.

"Have you started menstruating yet?"

I shook my head. As his fingers moved into my hole (or down there), I felt as if I were in a dream, as if my body didn't belong to me.

He unbuttoned his shorts and pulled it out.

"Big, eh?"

It looked enormous, but I said nothing. He took my hand and wrapped my fingers around it. I kept thinking of water pistols and wondered when it would start shooting. I couldn't move or talk. Then his fingers found that spot. I knew it was that spot because it made me tremble and shake.

"Feels good, eh?"

I felt guilty saying yes. I knew everything was wrong but I liked it. I was afraid because I liked it so much.

"Now I'm going to open you, just like a flower." He spread my lips apart and tried to push himself into me. I thought of the book—of men and women fitting like gloves. But he was enormous.

"Goddam it, you're much too small."

For the first time he seemed angry. He turned away. All I saw was his arm moving hard and fast, as if he were beating eggs. Finally he sighed and relaxed. He zipped up his shorts and fixed my clothes.

"I wish you were a real woman."

I felt like I'd disappointed him. But I knew he'd done something bad. We both did something bad because I didn't stop him, like Lyana did. He hugged and kissed me. I was so confused. It felt good but I felt bad. I liked being close to him, I hoped he'd try again but . . .

"You can't tell anyone about what happened today. It's our secret," he said, looking into my eyes. I saw the monster, and smelled Dad's sweat mixed with crushed dandelions. Then I heard an angry roar of thunder— this might be a real storm after all. I was so scared about what would happen next, I passed out.

When I woke up I was at the bonfire. Everyone was there, all my family and friends. Mom had cooked a delicious meal. We stuffed ourselves like pigs, played games, and watched fireworks. Dad and I lit the bonfire and we toasted marshmallows. It was a beautiful night with an orange moon. Everyone wanted me to lead the folk songs. Dad wanted to hear "Five Hundred Miles" as usual. I was in a good mood, I thought. I picked up the guitar and played a few chords.

"If you miss the train I'm on, you will know that I have gone, you can hear the whistle blow five hundred . . ."

All of a sudden my voice got stuck in my throat. My fingers trembled as they tried to pluck the strings. I felt like I was being strangled. Dad interrupted quickly.

"I guess she's not in the right mood. It's okay. Another time."

He put the guitar gently back in the case and gave me a marshmallow. No one noticed anything because I was a moody girl.

But I never sang again.

And I never read another horror story.

I went on with life, trying to be a good girl and do well. Dad and I are still best buddies. But that summer he scared me more than any monster. He was my first lover. That's our secret.

Keeping it secret now is the scariest thing.

Frederick Laing

Gentleman on the Top Floor

FREDERICK LAING *has published more than a hundred short stories and some highly acclaimed novels. Of his* Six Seconds a Year, *author Budd Schulberg wrote, "I was impressed with Laing's skill. . . . I shall not forget the climax and its frightening symbolism for many a year and many, many a book." His* The Giant's House *was listed among the year's best by major reviewers. "Gentleman on the Top Floor," a gently class-conscious anecdote, is one of Laing's earliest short stories.*

SHE PLACED a manicured finger on one of the buttons in the vestibule and pressed it four or five times.

"I'm sure this is where he lives," she insisted.

She was rather tall, or perhaps the row of names was placed lower than it should have been. At any rate, she had to stoop to peer at them. But she stooped gracefully. She looked quite tall beside the dwarfed, hunchbacked old woman.

The old woman shrugged. "The regular tenants, they're all listed," she said. She spoke with an accent. There was a hedge of soft black hairs on her upper lip.

The young lady's voice was crisp and precise. She slurred softly over her R's. "It's very important that I get hold of him," she said. She tried a couple more buttons, but there was no answering click at the door.

The old woman stood stolid and patient, a strange smile on her thick lips. There was a dull, dreamy and slightly harassed look in her eyes. Her eyes were fine, beautiful almost. Strangely out of place above the ugly lips with their black moustache. "You could come back some other time maybe," she suggested.

"He's leaving for Europe at five o'clock," the young lady said in her crisp tone. She went back at the buttons again. It was plain that she was used to getting what she wanted. She was trying not to talk as though the old woman were a servant. "He must live on one of the higher floors," she said. She pulled her finely curved lips into a slight smile, "I've heard him talk about walking up all the steps."

The little hunchback stood blinking off into space. "He lives with someone else maybe," she muttered, almost to herself.

"Of course . . . !" the lady said, raising her voice. She stopped, and bit her lip. "Your husband must know him," she said. "He's the superintendent, isn't he?"

"I am the superintendent," the old woman said. "I got no husband," she added. She smiled a little, and there was an odd similarity between her smile and the patronizing way the lady had smiled a moment before.

"Listen," the lady said. She stooped now as though she were talking to a child, "This gentleman is an artist. He carries canvases. Look. Big things about this wide. Pictures. He carries them up and down the stairs. You must have seen him."

The old woman smiled stupidly.

"He's dark," the lady went on. She clasped and unclasped her hands, as she spoke. "He has a high, sloping forehead. He's very . . . good-looking. *Please* listen," she said. "I'll tell you how he dresses. He wears a brown sport coat and grey trousers—baggy trousers that need pressing. . . ." She took hold of the woman's shoulder and looked as though she were going to shake her. She stamped her heel. "You *must* have seen him," she said.

"Maybe . . ." the woman said.

The younger woman opened her purse, but a proud, hostile stare from the old one brought that action to a halt. She closed her purse, put it under her elbow, and began clasping and unclasping her hands again. A tear rimmed her eyes. It fell on her hand. She bit her lips, and the tears stopped.

"Look," she said, "After all, we're both women. I know I shouldn't tell you this, but . . . there's a lady who . . . she's going to have a child. His child."

"Doesn't he want to marry her?" the old woman asked.

The lady started. The question was so direct. "Yes," she said, "He asked her to marry him. But she . . . well, she was afraid. . . ."

"Afraid?" the woman asked. The smile might have been sarcastic, or merely uncomprehending.

"Of her friends . . . of what they might think," the lady said. "They . . . well, she moves in a rather different society. . . ."

"Rich," the old woman nodded.

The lady appeared not to have heard. "She didn't want to have this baby," she said, "and they quarreled . . . had a fight. He stopped coming to see her. Then he called up today and said he was leaving at five o'clock. He said he was going to Paris to live with his brother. He doesn't have a telephone. She . . . couldn't call."

"So she changed her mind," the old woman said.

"Yes," the lady said, "She changed her mind. . . . About both things. . . . The baby, too. Can't you see—you *must* help me."

The woman pointed to a button, and the lady pressed it before the woman had time to speak.

"It might be this one," the old woman said, "I see often ladies come to visit him. Lovely, rich ladies like yourself."

The young lady swayed slightly, and clutched at the door knob. She held onto it as she looked around the ugly vestibule.

"I know," the little hunchback said. She nodded her head again; "But he is very beautiful, my son," she said.

There was an answering click at the door latch and the involuntary pressure of the lady's body shoved it open. She hesitated. She looked at the outer door as though she would make a bolt for the street. Then she turned and, with lowered head, walked slowly up the long stairs.

Maxim Gorky

Twenty-Six Men and a Girl

Don't be fooled by the suggestive title of the following tale. "Twenty-Six Men and a Girl" is a bleak tale of grinding physical and spiritual poverty by the great Russian writer, MAXIM GORKY (1868–1936), first president of the Union of Soviet Writers. In the West, he is best known as the playwright who wrote Enemies, Summerfolk *and, especially,* The Lower Depths.

THERE WERE SIX-AND-TWENTY of us—six-and-twenty living machines in a damp, underground cellar, where from morning till night we kneaded dough and rolled it into kringels. Opposite the underground window of our cellar was a bricked area, green and mouldy with moisture. The window was protected from outside with a close iron grating, and the light of the sun could not pierce through the window panes, covered as they were with flour dust.

Our employer had bars placed in front of the windows, so that we should not be able to give a bit of his bread to passing beggars, or to any of our fellows who were out of work and hungry. Our employer called us rogues, and gave us half-rotten tripe to eat for our mid-day meal, instead of meat. It was swelteringly close for us cooped up in that stone underground chamber, under the low, heavy, soot-blackened, cob-webby ceiling. Dreary and sickening was our life between its thick, dirty, mouldy walls.

Unrefreshed, and with a feeling of not having had our sleep out, we used to get up at five o'clock in the morning; and before six, we were already seated, worn out and apathetic, at the table, rolling out the dough which our mates had already prepared while we slept. The whole day, from ten in the early morning until ten at night, some of us sat around that table, working up in our hands the yielding paste, rolling it to and fro so that it should not get stiff; while the others kneaded the swelling mass of dough. And the whole day the simmering water in the kettle, where kringles were being cooked, sang low and sadly; and the baker's shovel scraped harshly over the oven floor, as he threw the slippery bits of dough out of the kettle on the heated bricks.

From morning till evening wood was burning in the oven, and the red glow of the fire gleamed and flickered over the walls of the bake-shop, as if silently mocking us. The giant oven was like the misshapen head of a monster in a fairy tale; it thrust itself up and out of the floor, opened wide jaws, full of glowing fire, and blew hot breath upon us; it seemed to be ever watching out of its black air-holes our interminable work. Those two deep holes were like eyes—the cold, pitiless eyes of a monster. They watched us always with the same darkened glance, as if they were weary of seeing before them such eternal slaves, from whom they could expect nothing human, and therefore scorned them with the cold scorn of wisdom.

In meal dust, in the mud which we brought in from the yard on our boots, in the hot, sticky atmosphere, day in, day out, we rolled the dough into kringels, which we moistened with our own sweat. And we hated our work with a glowing hatred; we never ate what had passed through our hands, and preferred black bread to kringels. Sitting opposite each other, at a long table—nine facing nine—we moved our hands and fingers mechanically during endlessly long hours, till we were so accustomed to our monotonous work that we ceased to pay any attention to it.

We had all studied each other so constantly, that each of us knew every wrinkle of his mates' faces. It was not long also before we had exhausted almost every topic of conversation; that is why we were most of the time silent, unless we were chaffing each other; but one cannot always find something about which to chaff another man, especially when that man is one's own mate. Neither were we much given to finding fault with one another; how, indeed, could one of us poor devils be in a position to find fault with another, when we were all of us half dead and, as it were, turned to stone? For the heavy drudgery seemed to crush all feeling out of us. But silence is only terrible and fearful for those who have said everything and have nothing more to say to each other; for men, on the contrary, who have never begun to communicate with one another, it is easy and simple.

Sometimes, too, we sang; and this is how it happened that we began to sing; one of us would sigh deeply in the midst of our toil, like an over-driven horse, and then we would begin one of those songs whose gentle swaying melody seems always to ease the burden on the singer's heart.

At first one sang by himself, and we others sat in silence listening to his solitary song, which, under the heavy vaulted roof of the cellar, died gradually away, and became extinguished, like a little fire in the steppes, on a wet autumn night, when the gray heaven hangs like a heavy mass over the earth. Then another would join in with the singer, and now two soft, sad voices would break into song in our narrow, dull hole of a cellar. Suddenly others would join in, and the song would grow louder and swell upward till it would seem as if the damp, foul walls of our stone prison were widening out and opening. Then, all six-and-twenty of us would be singing; our loud, harmonious song would fill the whole cellar, our voices would travel outside and beyond, striking, as it were, against the walls in moaning sobs and sighs, moving our hearts with soft, tantalizing ache, tearing open old wounds, and awakening longings.

The singers would sigh deeply and heavily; suddenly one would become silent and listen to the others singing, then let his voice flow once more in the common tide. Another would exclaim in a stifled voice, "Ah!" and shut his eyes, while the deep, full sound waves would show him, as it were, a road, in front of him—a sunlit, broad road in the distance, which he himself, in thought, wandered along.

But the flame flickers once more in the huge oven, the baker scrapes incessantly with his shovel, the water simmers in the kettle, and the flicker of the fire on the wall dances as before in silent mockery. While in other men's words we sing out our dumb grief, the weary burden of live men robbed of the sunlight, the burden of slaves.

So we lived, we six-and-twenty, in the vault-like cellar of a great stone house, and suffered, each one of us, as if we had to bear on our shoulders the whole three stories of the house.

But we had something else good, besides the singing—something we loved, that perhaps took the place of the sunshine.

In the second story of our house there was established a gold-embroiderer's shop and there, living among the other embroidery girls, was Tanya, a little maid-servant of sixteen. Every morning there peeped in through the glass door a rosy little face, with merry blue eyes; while a ringing, tender voice called out to us:

"Little prisoners! Have you any kringels, please, for me?"

At that clear sound, we knew so well, we all used to turn around, gazing with simple-hearted joy at the pure girlish face which smiled at us sweetly. The sight of the small nose pressed against the window-pane and of the white teeth gleaming between the half-open lips, had become for us a daily pleasure. Tumbling over each other we used to jump up to open the door, and she would step in, bright and cheerful, holding out her apron, with her head thrown on one side, and a smile on her lips. Her thick, long chestnut hair fell over her shoulder and across her breast. But, we, ugly, dirty and misshapen as we were, looked up at her—the threshold door was four steps above the floor—looked up at her with heads thrown back, wishing her good-morning, and speaking strange, unaccustomed words which we kept for her only. Our voices became softer when we spoke to her, our jests were lighter. For her—everything was different with us. The baker took from his oven a shovel of the best and the brownest kringels, and threw them deftly into Tanya's apron.

"Be off with you now, or the boss will catch you!" we warned her each time. She laughed roguishly, called out cheerfully: "Good-bye, poor prisoners!" and slipped away as quick as a mouse.

That was all. But long after she had gone we talked about her to one another with pleasure. It always was the same thing as we had said yesterday and the day before, because everything about us, including ourselves and her, remained the same—as yesterday—and as always.

Painful and terrible it is when a man goes on living, while nothing changes around him; and when such an existence does not finally kill his soul, then the monotony becomes with time, even more and more painful. Generally we spoke about women in such a way that sometimes it was loathsome to us ourselves to hear our rude, shameless talk. The women whom we knew deserved perhaps nothing better. But about Tanya we never let fall an evil word; none of us ever ventured so much as to lay a hand on her, even too free a jest she never heard from us. Maybe this was so because she never remained for long with us; she flashed on our eyes like a star falling from the sky, and vanished; and maybe because she was little and very beautiful calls forth respect, even in coarse people. And besides—though our life of penal labor had made us dull beasts, oxen, we were still men, and, like all men, could not live without worshipping something or other. Better than her we had none, and none but she took any notice of us, living in the cellar—no one, though there were dozens of people in the house. And then, too—most likely, this was the chief thing —we all regarded her as something of our own, something existing as it were only by virtue of our kringels. We took on ourselves in turns the duty of providing her with hot kringels, and this became for us like a daily sacrifice to our idol, it became almost a sacred rite, and every day it bound us more closely to her. Besides kringels, we gave Tanya a great deal of advice—to wear warmer clothes, not to run upstairs too quickly, not to carry heavy bundles of wood. She listened to all our counsels with a smile, answered them by a laugh, and never took our advice, but we were not offended at that; all we wanted was to show how much care we bestowed upon her.

Often she would apply to us with different requests; she asked us, for instance, to open the heavy door into the store-cellar, and to chop wood: with delight and a sort of pride, we did this for her, and everything else she wanted.

But when one of us asked her to mend his solitary shirt for him, she said, with a laugh of contempt:

"What next! A likely idea!"

We made great fun of the queer fellow who could entertain such an idea, and—never asked her to do anything else. We loved her—all is said in that. Man always wants to lay his love on someone, though sometimes he crushes, sometimes he sullies, with it; he may poison another life because he loves without respecting the beloved. We were bound to love Tanya, for we had no one else to love.

At times one of us would suddenly begin to reason like this:

"And why do we make so much of the wench? What is there in her? eh? What a to-do we make about her!"

The man who dared to utter such words we promptly and coarsely cut short—we wanted something to love: we had found it and loved it, and what we twenty-six of us loved must be for each of us unalterable, as a holy thing, and anyone who acted against us in this was our enemy. We loved, maybe, not what was really good, but you see there were twenty-six of us, and so we always wanted to see what was precious to us held sacred by the rest.

Our love is not less burdensome than hate, and maybe that is just why some proud souls maintain that our hate is more flattering than our love. But why do they not run away from us, if it is so?

Besides our department, our employer had also a bread-bakery; it was in the same house, separated from our hole only by a wall; but the bakers —there were four of them—held aloof from us, considering their work superior to ours, and therefore themselves better than us; they never used to come into our workroom, and laughed contemptuously at us when they met us in the yard. We, too, did not go to see them; this was forbidden by our employer, from fear that we should steal the fancy bread. We did not like the bakers, because we envied them; their work was lighter than ours, they were paid more, and were better fed; they had a light, spacious workroom, and they were all so clean and healthy—and that made them hateful to us. We all looked gray and yellow; three of us had syphilis, several suffered from skin diseases, one was completely crippled by rheumatism. On holidays and in their leisure time the bakers wore pea-jackets and creaking boots, two of them had accordions, and they all used to go for strolls in the town gardens—we wore filthy rags and leather clogs or plaited shoes on our feet, the police would not let us into the town gardens—could we possibly like the bakers?

And one day we learned that their chief baker had been drunk, the master had sacked him and had already taken on another, and that this other was a soldier, wore a satin waistcoat and a watch and gold chain. We were inquisitive to get a sight of such a dandy, and in the hope of catching a glimpse of him we kept running one after another out into the yard.

But he came of his own accord into our room. Kicking at the door, he pushed it open, and leaving it ajar, stood in the doorway smiling, and said to us:

"God help the work! Good-morning, mates!"

The ice-cold air, which steamed in through the open door, curled in streaks of vapor round his feet. He stood on the threshold, looked us up and down, and under his fair, twisted mustache gleamed big yellow teeth. His waistcoat was really something quite out of the common, blue-flowered, brilliant with shining little buttons of red stones. He also wore a watch chain.

He was a fine fellow, this soldier; tall, healthy, rosy-cheeked, and his big clear eyes had a friendly, cheerful glance. He wore on his head a white starched cap, and from under his spotlessly clean apron peeped the pointed toes of fashionable, well-blacked boots.

Our baker asked him politely to shut the door. The soldier did so without hurrying himself, and began to question us about the master. We explained to him, all speaking together, that our employer was a thorough-going brute, a rogue, a knave, and a slave-driver; in a word, we repeated to him all that can and must be said about an employer, but cannot be repeated here. The soldier listened to us, twisted his mustache, and watched us with a friendly, open-hearted look.

"But haven't you got a lot of girls here?" he asked suddenly.

Some of us began to laugh deferentially, others put on a meaning expression, and one of us explained to the soldier that there were nine girls here.

"You make the most of them?" asked the soldier, with a wink.

We laughed, but not so loudly, and with some embarrassment. Many of us would have liked to have shown the soldier that we also were tremendous fellows with the girls, but not one of us could do so; and one of our number confessed as much, when he said in a low voice:

"That sort of thing is not in our line."

"Well, no; it wouldn't quite do for you," said the soldier with conviction, after having looked us over. "There is something wanting about you all. You don't look the right sort. You've no sort of appearance; and the women, you see, they like a bold appearance, they will have a well set-up body. Everything has to be tip-top for them. That's why they respect strength. They want an arm like that!"

The soldier drew his right hand, with its turned-up shirt sleeve, out of his pocket, and showed us his bare arm. It was white and strong, and covered with shining yellow hairs.

"Leg and chest, all must be strong. And then a man must be dressed in the latest fashion, so as to show off his looks to advantage. Yes, all the women take to me. Whether I call to them, or whether I beckon them, they with one accord, five at a time, throw themselves at my head."

He sat down on a flour sack, and told at length all about the way women loved him, and how bold he was with them. Then he left, and after the door had creaked to behind him, we sat for a long time silent, and thought about him and his talk. Then we all suddenly broke silence together, and it became apparent that we were all equally pleased with him. He was such a nice, open-hearted fellow; he came to see us without any standoffishness, sat down and chatted. No one else came to us like that, and no one else talked to us in that friendly sort of way. And we continued to talk of him and his coming triumph among the embroidery girls, who passed us by with contemptuous sniffs when they saw us in the yard, or who looked straight through us as if we had been air. But we admired them always when we met them outside, or when they walked past our windows; in winter, in fur jackets and toques to match; in summer, in hats trimmed with flowers, and with colored parasols in their hands. We talked, however, about these girls in a way that would have made them mad with shame and rage, if they could have heard us.

"If only he does not get hold of little Tanya!" said the baker, suddenly, in an anxious tone of voice.

We were silent, for these words troubled us. Tanya had quite gone out of our minds, supplanted, put on one side by the strong, fine figure of the soldier.

Then began a lively discussion; some of us maintained that Tanya would never lower herself so; others thought she would not be able to resist him, and the third group proposed to give him a thrashing if he should try to annoy Tanya. And, finally, we all decided to watch the soldier and Tanya, and to warn the girl against him. This brought the discussion to an end.

Four weeks had passed by since then; during this time the soldier baked white bread, walked about with the gold-embroidery girls, visited us often, but did not talk any more about his conquests; only twisted his mustache, and licked his lips lasciviously.

Tanya called in as usual every morning for "little kringels," and was as gay and as nice and friendly with us as ever. We certainly tried once or twice to talk to her about the soldier, but she called him a "goggle-eyed calf," and made fun of him all round, and that set our minds at rest. We saw how the gold-embroidery girls carried on with the soldier, and we were proud of our girl; Tanya's behavior reflected honor on us all; we imitated her, and began in our talks to treat the soldier with small consideration. She became dearer to us, and we greeted her with more friendliness and kindliness every morning.

One day the soldier came to see us, a bit drunk, and sat down and began to laugh. When we asked him what he was laughing about, he explained to us:

"Why two of them—that Lydka girl and Grushka—have been clawing and fighting each other on my account. You should have seen the way they went for each other! Ha! ha! One got hold of the other one by the hair, threw her down on the floor of the passage, and sat on her! Ha! ha! ha! They scratched and tore each others' faces. It was enough to make one die with laughter! Why is it women can't fight fair? Why do they always scratch one another, eh?"

He sat on the bench, healthy, fresh and jolly; he sat there and went on laughing. We were silent. This time he made an unpleasant impression on us.

"Well, it's a funny thing what luck I have with the women-folk! Eh! I've laughed till I'm ill! One wink, and it's all over with them! It's the devil!"

He raised his white hairy hands, and slapped them down on his knees. And his eyes seem to reflect such frank astonishment, as if he were himself quite surprised at his good luck with women. His fat, red face glistened with delight and self-satisfaction, and he licked his lips more than ever.

Our baker scraped the shovel violently and angrily along the oven floor, and all at once he said sarcastically:

"There's no great strength needed to pull up fir saplings, but try a real pine-tree."

"Why—what do you mean by saying that to me?" asked the soldier.

"Oh, well . . ."

"What is it?"

"Nothing—it slipped out!"

"No, wait a minute! What's the point? What pine-tree?"

Our baker did not answer, working rapidly away with the shovel at the oven; flinging into it the half-cooked kringels, taking out those that were done, and noisily throwing them on the floor to the boys who were stringing them on bast. He seemed to have forgotten the soldier and his conversation with him. But the soldier had all at once dropped into a sort of uneasiness. He got up onto his feet, and went to the oven, at the risk of knocking against the handle of the shovel, which was waving spasmodically in the air.

"No, tell me, do—who is it? You've insulted me. I? There's not one could withstand me, no, no! And you say such insulting things to me?"

He really seemed genuinely hurt. He must have had nothing else to pride himself on except his gift for seducing women: maybe, except for that, there was nothing living in him and it was only that by which he could feel himself a living man.

There are men to whom the most precious and best thing in their lives appears to be some disease of their soul or body. They spend their whole life in relation to it, and only living by it, suffering from it, they sustain themselves on it, they complain of it to others, and so draw the attention of their fellows to themselves. For that they extract sympathy from people, and apart from it they have nothing at all. Take from them that disease, cure them, and they will be miserable, because they have lost their one resource in life—they are left empty then. Sometimes a man's life is so poor that he is driven instinctively to prize his vice and to live by it; one may say for a fact that often men are vicious from boredom.

The soldier was offended, he went up to our baker and roared:

"No, tell me, do—who?"

"Tell you?" the baker turned suddenly to him.

"Well?"

"Well, there then! You know Tanya?"

"I?"

"You!"

"Her? Why that's nothing to me—pooh!"

"We shall see!"

"You will see! Ha! ha!"

"She'll—"

"Give me a month!"

"What a braggart you are, soldier!"

"A fortnight! I'll prove it! Who is it? Tanya! Pooh!"

"Well, get out. You're in my way!"

"A fortnight—and it's done! Ah, you—"

"Get out, I say!"

Our baker, all at once, flew into a rage and brandished his shovel.

The soldier staggered away from him in amazement, looked at us, paused, and softly, malignantly said, "Oh, all right, then!" and went away.

During the dispute we had all sat silent, absorbed in it. But when the soldier had gone, eager, loud talk and noise arose among us.

Someone shouted to the baker, "It's a bad job that you've started, Pavel!"

"Do your work!" answered the baker savagely.

We felt that the soldier had been deeply aggrieved, and that danger threatened Tanya. We felt this, and at the same time we were all possessed by a burning curiosity, most agreeable to us. What would happen? Would Tanya hold out against the soldier? And almost all cried confidently: "Tanya? She'll hold out! You won't catch her with your bare arms!"

We longed terribly to test the strength of our idol; we forcibly proved to each other that our divinity was a strong divinity and would come victorious out of this ordeal. We began at last to fancy that we had not worked enough on the soldier, that he would forget the dispute, and that we ought to pique his vanity more keenly. From that day we began to live a different life, a life of nervous tension, such as we had never known before. We spent whole days in arguing together; we all grew, as it were, sharper; and got to talk more and better. It seemed to us that we were playing some sort of game with the devil, and the stake on our side was Tanya. And when we learned from the bakers that the soldier had begun "running after our Tanya" we felt a sort of delighted terror, and life was so interesting that we did not even notice that our employer had taken advantage of our preoccupation to increase our work by fourteen pounds of dough a day. We seemed, indeed, not even tired by our work. Tanya's name was on our lips all day long. And every day we looked for her with a certain special impatience. Sometimes we pictured to ourselves that she would come to us, and it would not be the same Tanya of old, but somehow different. We said nothing to her, however, of the dispute regarding her. We asked her no questions, and behaved as well and affectionately to her as ever. But even in this a new element crept in, alien to our old feeling for Tanya—and that new element was keen curiosity, keen and cold as a steel knife.

"Mates! Today the time's up!" our baker said to us one morning, as he set to work.

We were well aware of it without his reminder; but still we were thrilled.

"Look at her. She'll be here directly," suggested the baker.

One of us cried out in a troubled voice, "Why! As though one could notice anything!"

And again an eager, noisy discussion sprang up among us. Today we were about to prove how pure and spotless was the vessel into which we had poured all that was best in us, that we really were playing a great game; that we might, indeed, through the exaction of this proof of purity, lose our divinity altogether.

During the whole of the intervening fortnight we had heard that Tanya was persistently followed by the soldier, but not one of us had thought of asking her how she had behaved toward him. And she came every morning to fetch her kringels, and was the same toward us as ever.

This morning, too, we heard her voice outside: "You poor prisoners! Here I am."

We opened the door, and when she came in we all remained, contrary to our usual custom, silent. Our eyes fixed on her, we did not know how to speak to her, what to ask her. And there we stood in front of her a gloomy, silent crowd. She seemed to be surprised at this unusual reception; and suddenly we saw her turn white and become uneasy, then she asked, in a choking voice:

"Why are you—like this?"

"And you?" the baker flung at her grimly, never taking his eyes off her.

"What am I?"

"N—nothing."

"Well, then, give me quickly the little kringels."

Never before had she bidden us hurry.

"There's plenty of time," said the baker, and without stirring, not removing his eyes from her face.

Then, suddenly, she turned round and disappeared through the door.

The baker took his shovel and said, calmly turning away toward the oven:

"Well, that settles it! But a soldier! a common beast like that—a low cur!"

Like a flock of sheep we all pressed round the table, sat down silently, and began listlessly to work. Soon, however, one of us remarked:

"Perhaps, after all—"

"Shut up!" shouted the baker.

We were all convinced that he was a man of judgment, a man who knew more than we did about things. And at the sound of his voice we were convinced of the soldier's victory, and our spirits became sad and downcast.

At twelve o'clock—while we were eating our dinners—the soldier came in. He was as clean and as smart as ever, and looked at us—as usual—straight in the eyes. But we were all awkward in looking at him.

"Now then, honored sirs, would you let me show you a soldier's quality?" he said, chuckling proudly.

"Go out into the passage, and look through the crack—do you understand?"

We went into the passage, and stood all pushing against one another, squeezed up to the cracks of the wooden partition of the passage that looked into the yard. We had not to wait long. Very soon Tanya, with hurried footsteps and a careworn face, walked across the yard, jumping over the puddles of melting snow and mud: she disappeared into the store cellar. Then whistling, and not hurrying himself, the soldier followed in the same direction. His hands were thrust in his pockets: his mustaches were quivering.

Rain was falling; and we saw how its drops fell into the puddles, and the puddles were wrinkled by them. The day was damp and gray—a very dreary day. Snow still lay on the roofs, but on the ground dark patches of mud had begun to appear. And the snow on the roofs too was covered by a layer of brownish dirt. The rain fell slowly with a depressing sound. It was cold and disagreeable for us waiting.

The first to come out of the store cellar was the soldier; he walked slowly across the yard, his mustaches twitching, his hands in his pockets —the same as always.

Then—Tanya, too, came out. Her eyes—her eyes were radiant with joy and happiness, and her lips—were smiling. And she walked as though in a dream, staggering, with unsteady steps.

We could not bear this quietly. All of us at once rushed to the door, dashed out into the yard and—hissed at her, reviled her viciously, loudly, wildly.

She started at seeing us, and stood as though rooted in the mud underfoot. We formed a ring around her! and malignantly, without restraint, abused her with vile words, and said shameful things to her.

We did this not loudly, not hurriedly, seeing that she could not get away, that she was hemmed in by us, and we could deride her to our hearts' content. I don't know why, but we did not beat her. She stood in the midst of us, and turned her head this way and that, as she heard our insults. And we—more and more violently flung at her the filth and venom of our words.

The color had left her face. Her blue eyes, so happy a moment before, opened wide, her bosom heaved, and her lips quivered.

We in a ring round her avenged ourselves on her as though she had robbed us. She belonged to us, we had lavished on her our best, and though that best was a beggar's crumb, still we were twenty-six, she was one, and so there was no pain we could give her equal to her guilt! How we insulted her! She was still mute, still gazed at us with wild eyes, and a shiver ran all over her.

We laughed, roared, yelled. Other people ran up from somewhere and joined us. One of us pulled Tanya by the sleeve of her blouse.

Suddenly her eyes flashed; deliberately she raised her hands to her head and straightening her hair she said loudly but calmly, straight in our faces:

"Ah, you miserable prisoners!"

And she walked straight at us, walked as directly as though we had not been before her, as though we were not blocking her way.

And hence it was that no one did actually prevent her passing.

Walking out of our ring, without turning round, she said loudly and with indescribable contempt:

"Ah, you scum—brutes."

And—was gone.

We were left in the middle of the yard, in the rain, under the gray sky without the sun.

Then we went mutely away to our damp stone cellar. As before—the sun never peeped in at our windows, and Tanya came no more!

William S. Gilbert

Ellen M'Jones Aberdeen

WILLIAM SCHWENCK GILBERT *(1836–1911) was the comic genius who, along with composer Arthur Sullivan, created England's most enduring comic operas, including* The Gondoliers, H.M.S. Pinafore, Iolanthe, Patience, The Pirates of Penzance, The Mikado, Trial by Jury, *et cetera (times seven). His humorous verse contributions to* Fun *magazine, collectively published in 1869 as the* Bab Ballads, *includes the following tall tale of an industrious bagpiper and a comely bevy of pragmatically fickle lassies.*

MACPHAIRSON CLONGLOCKETTY ANGUS M'CLAN
Was the son of an elderly labouring man,
You've guessed him a Scotchman, shrewd reader, at sight,
And p'raps altogether, shrewd reader, you're right.

From the bonnie blue Forth to the hills of Deeside,
Round by Dingwall and Wrath to the mouth of the Clyde,
There wasn't a child or a woman or man
Who could pipe with CLONGLOCKETTY ANGUS M'CLAN.

No other could wake such detestable groans,
With reed and with chaunter—with bag and with drones:
All day and all night he delighted the chiels
With sniggering pibrochs and jiggety reels.

He'd clamber a mountain and squat on the ground,
And the neighbouring maidens would gather around
To list to his pipes and to gaze in his e'en,
Especially ELLEN M'JONES ABERDEEN.

All loved their M'CLAN, save a Sassenach brute,
Who came to the Highlands to fish and to shoot;
He dressed himself up in a Highlander way,
Though his name it was PATTISON CORBY TORBAY.

Torbay had incurred a good deal of expense
To make him a Scotchman in every sense;
But this is a matter, you'll readily own,
That isn't a question of tailors alone.

A Sassenach chief may be bonily built,
He may purchase a sporran, a bonnet, and kilt;
Stick a skean in his hose—wear an acre of stripes—
But he cannot assume an affection for pipes.

CLONGLOCKETTY's pipings all night and all day
Quite frenzied poor PATTISON CORBY TORBAY;
The girls were amused at his singular spleen,
Especially ELLEN M'JONES ABERDEEN.

"MACPHAIRSON CLONGLOCKETTY ANGUS, my lad,
With pibrochs and reels you are driving me mad;
If you really must play on that cursed affair,
My goodness! play something resembling an air."

Boiled over the blood of MACPHAIRSON M'CLAN—
The clan of Clonglocketty rose as one man;
For all were enraged at the insult, I ween—
Especially ELLEN M'JONES ABERDEEN.

"Let's show," said M'CLAN, "to this Sassenach loon
That the bagpipes can play him a regular tune.
Let's see," said M'CLAN, as he thoughtfully sat,
" 'In My Cottage' is easy—I'll practise at that."

He blew at his "Cottage," and blew with a will,
For a year, seven months, and a fortnight, until
(You'll hardly believe it) M'CLAN, I declare,
Elicited something resembling an air.

It was wild—it was fitful—as wild as the breeze—
It wandered about into several keys;
It was jerky, spasmodic, and harsh, I'm aware,
But still it distinctly suggested an air.

The Sassenach screamed, and the Sassenach danced,
He shrieked in his agony—bellowed and pranced;
And the maidens who gathered rejoiced at the scene,
Especially ELLEN M'JONES ABERDEEN.

"Hech gather, hech gather, hech gather around;
And fill a' yer lugs wi' the exquisite sound.
An air frae the bagpipes—beat that if ye can!
Hurrah for CLONGLOCKETTY ANGUS M'CLAN!"

The fame of his piping spread over the land:
Respectable widows proposed for his hand,
And maidens came flocking to sit on the green—
Especially ELLEN M'JONES ABERDEEN.

One morning the fidgety Sassenach swore
He'd stand it no longer—he drew his claymore,
And (this was, I think, in extremely bad taste),
Divided CLONGLOCKETTY close to the waist.

Oh! loud were the wailings for ANGUS M'CLAN—
Oh! deep was the grief for that excellent man—
The maids stood aghast at the horrible scene,
Especially ELLEN M'JONES ABERDEEN.

It sorrowed poor PATTISON CORBY TORBAY
To find them "take on" in this serious way,
He pitied the poor little fluttering birds,
And solaced their souls with the following words:—

"Oh, maidens," said PATTISON, touching his hat,
"Don't snivel, my dears, for a fellow like that;
Observe, I'm a very superior man,
A much better fellow than ANGUS M'CLAN."

They smiled when he winked and addressed them as "dears."
And they all of them vowed, as they dried up their tears,
A pleasanter gentleman never was seen—
Especially ELLEN M'JONES ABERDEEN.

Joan Andelman

A Sunday in December

It is not oxymoronic to call the following poignant tale an exercise in eloquent understatement. JOAN ANDELMAN, *Marketing Communications Manager for a New Jersey health care firm, penned "A Sunday in December" for a New York University writing workshop "and when I read it in class, I was surprised and gratified to see the other students dabbing at their eyes."*

SHE PADDED HER WAY downstairs, and was surprised to see him sitting at the kitchen table, still in his bathrobe. It was 11:30 in the morning.

"What's the matter, Lou? Don't you feel well?"

"I don't know—I'm tired this morning. I was supposed to make some deliveries earlier, but I just haven't felt like moving."

She was looking at him more closely. He was awfully gray looking. *That job*, she thought, *that damn job is killing him. Bastards.* "Never mind, Louie. It's Sunday—to hell with them! I'm going to make you brunch. I promised you a treat last night—what'll it be?"

He wanted French toast, with syrup. She hesitated, then: "Tell you what, you can have the French toast. But no syrup."

He watched her as she bustled about the kitchen, and she knew when he made no attempt to help her that he must be very tired. She was thinking how long it had been since she'd made a meal for the two of them. A long time. With no children around, somehow she never felt like cooking any more.

The table was cluttered with the Sunday paper and yesterday's mail. While the toast was frying, she cleared and set the table, using the china instead of the plastic plates. Reaching into the refrigerator for the milk carton, she decided suddenly to use the little china creamer, too. To the finished table she added the vase of Japanese paper flowers from the living room.

"Hey, kid, what's this? Company coming?" Lou said.

"Nope, just us two old fogies. So why not? You only live once."

"Okay, then, Rosie Posie, so couldn't I have just a *little* syrup?"

She held firm. "Get out of here, you big fresser! Diabetics are not supposed to have maple syrup. The French toast is enough! Here, put a little jam on it—delicious."

When they'd finished, he looked much better to her.

"Lou—" . . . she hesitated. "Why don't you quit your job? Not a one of them, nothing, is worth this aggravation. We can manage, believe me, we'll manage. I don't mind going back to work. With all your contacts, we could form our *own* consulting business. Let's talk about it?"

"Okay, Rose. Okay. But not today. I have to make some phone calls this afternoon."

She couldn't stop herself. "You're still trying to collect from Brookfield Pharmacy, right? Did he pay you anything yet?"

He shook his head, not looking at her.

"I knew it. Fifteen thousand dollars' worth of merchandise, on credit! It's over six months—you can't keep being such a nice guy. At least, don't keep selling him *more*. Lou, he'll bankrupt you."

It seemed to her as she spoke that he was graying before her eyes. She let it go. He was still sitting at the table when she went upstairs to finish the blanket she was crocheting for the baby. She heard the dishes clinking as Lou cleared the table, then his voice on the phone, his placating, easygoing salesman's voice, that could sell anything, but didn't know the tone to force someone to pay up. "Deadbeats," she muttered, throwing the accumulation of towels, diapers and toys out of the crib, searching for the half-finished blanket. Her eye fell on her grandson's picture, a blond, ecstatic little boy. "Chandler, your grandfather's too good for them, that's the trouble. Works like a dog—for what?" She had settled down by the window when Lou called from the bottom of the stairs:

"Want any more coffee, Rose? Or should I pull the plug out?"

"Pull it out," she called back.

The house was silent for a few moments, except for the sound of the bathroom door downstairs closing. Suddenly, there was an enormous thud.

"Oh, Lou-ee," she called in a singsong, "what did you do now?"

No answer.

"Lou!" she called more sharply. No answer. Her heart began to pound. She flew out of the chair and down the stairs.

"Lou—" she started to say again, then saw him. He was lying across the threshold, his legs on the bathroom floor, his head and torso on the hallway carpet. For a half-second, she was frozen. Then she ran to bend down beside him. "Lou, what happened? Did you fall? Lou?" He didn't speak to her—his eyes were full of surprise, and a gurgling sound was coming from his throat. She leaned closer over his face to catch what he was trying to say, but couldn't make it out.

"Don't try to talk, Lou. Don't worry. I'm calling the ambulance right away. I'm just going to call the ambulance now, it will be all right."

She rushed to the phone and dialed the policy emergency number pasted beside it. "I need an ambulance immediately—my husband just fell down and injured himself." She gave her name and address, then hung up. Her mind was racing—stroke, was it a stroke? heart attack? what? A pool of blood was spreading under his head. She grabbed some dishtowels and propped them underneath, all the while murmuring non-stop, "Don't worry, Lou. The ambulance is on the way, it'll be all right."

The bleeding was not too bad—she realized he must have hit his head against the doorway when he fell. Not a hemorrhage. Thank God, not a hemorrhage. His pajama bottoms were around his knees—she took his bathrobe from the closet and covered him. Then, still talking to him, she rushed back upstairs. "I just have to throw on some clothes, Lou, I'll be right back."

"My bag, I need my bag. The Blue Cross cards." She was talking to herself as she pulled on an old pair of slacks and blouse, checked her pocketbook for keys, cash and the medical cards, and raced back down the stairs.

She knelt beside him again. There was no sound from him any more. She wanted to straighten his legs, they were so twisted, but remembered that all first-aid books caution against moving an injured person. "Lou, I'm not going to try to move you. It might hurt you. They'll be here in just a few seconds."

The doorbell rang. "They're here, Lou—the ambulance is here." She opened the door with relief. Two medics stood there with a stretcher.

"Where's the patient, ma'am?"

She pointed to the hallway and as they moved toward him, she grabbed her coat and bag, ready to go. One bent down, his ear to Lou's chest. She waited, switching her bag from hand to hand. They were saying something to each other.

"What's wrong? Why don't you lift him? Let's go!"

"Ma'am," one of the men said quietly, "why don't you sit down?"

She stared at him. "He's dead. That's why you're not moving him, isn't it? He's dead."

"Yes, ma'am. I'm sorry." She kept staring at him, waiting. *He looks very sad*, she thought. "What . . . ?" She didn't finish, couldn't find the question, but he answered it.

"A heart attack, ma'am. Looks like a massive coronary. He was probably dead as soon as he hit the floor. There's nothing we can do."

She was talking half to him, half to herself. "Just like that. Just like that. But he tried to say something to me—he was trying to talk."

"Perhaps, ma'am, but more likely it was the air leaving his throat."

Very carefully, she placed her pocketbook and coat over her chair, then stood for a moment, her shoulders drooping with a sudden loss of purpose. Slowly she walked over and knelt down beside Lou, searching his face.

"So, Louie—that's it. That's it." She was nodding her head up and down, up and down. She sat on the floor, back against the wall, cradling his head in her lap, and began to smooth his hair. "I'm sorry, Louie, I'm sorry I didn't let you have the syrup." Her tears began to fall on his face. "My poor Louie, I should have let you have some syrup."

Jessica Amanda Salmonson

The Old Woman Who Dragged Her Husband's Corpse

Here is a grim little essay/speculation on love's declining years by JESSICA
AMANDA SALMONSON, *a Seattle book dealer who has written several impressive fantasy tales and novels and who edits* Fantasy Macabre, *one of America's most sophisticated "little magazines." "The Old Woman Who Dragged Her Husband's Corpse" first appeared in Ms. Salmonson's Ace Books collection,* A Silver Thread of Madness.

THE AUTHOR intrigued by things macabre (who is, after all, the only sort of author worthy of attention) will find it difficult to outdo the daily paper. Not long ago it was reported that a retired physician acquired permission from a lifelong friend (by then an elderly wino) to preserve his corpse "for use as a paperweight." They had gotten an attorney to go over the written contract. After the friend's death, the physician set forth by means unspecified to preserve the body as a memento of long friendship in as natural a condition as could be achieved.

When the authorities learned of this, they wished to arrest the physician on charges of "abusing a corpse" but could not locate the evidence, the physician having hidden it until such time as he was assured it would not be confiscated.

Such a grotesque, taken from life, is difficult to exceed in fiction, which is perhaps why many horror writers trump up an element of the supernatural, ensuring the illusion of imaginativeness.

I never saw a follow-up on the case. I do not know if the physician was allowed to keep his enormous paperweight. I certainly hope he won out in the end. His sentimental feelings strike me as less shocking than what most doctors would do with a corpse, not to mention with living beings. If it is not abusive for medical students to tear a body liver from spleen, why should it be abusive to preserve one intact?

If the physician did lose his cherished friend, we needn't feel terribly sorry for him, as he seemed by nature a humorous gentleman and probably would not be long distraught. Another case from the newspaper, by contrast, struck me as poignant and pitiful: A man who had kept the skeleton of his wife, wedding ring upon its finger, beside himself in his bed for twenty years, took seriously ill and was discovered by an emergency aid unit. By the time his physical health was sufficiently restored that he was released from the hospital—and allowed to return to his pathetic apartment—his wife had been taken from him, never again to be touched, held, loved.

How indeed does even the greatest mistress of horror one-up the reality of life's simple madnesses?

A case in yesterday's paper interested me enormously and preys upon my mind. It regarded a pair of retired schoolteachers in their eighties, many years divorced from the realities of the modern world. They became paranoid and secretive. The husband died suddenly and in a week began to deteriorate. The old woman, too frail to move her husband's decomposing body, and too frightened to seek help from neighbors, contrived a method of removing the stinking body from her trailer house.

She tied a rope about his body and, though the paper doesn't say so, I would suppose she apologized and explained the necessity of her plan. With tremendous effort she was able to drag the body from the bed, down the trailer's narrow hallway and to the front door.

Then she took the farther end of the rope out to the driveway and tied it to the rear bumper of an old Chevrolet.

Seating herself behind the wheel, and being so very short that she could scarcely see out the windshield, she started the engine, and drove slowly out into the street.

Then she drove faster.

The corpse was dragged for several miles, losing some of its parts along the way. Then the poor woman accidentally drove off the side of the road into a ditch. Can you imagine the condition of her mind as she drove about seeking an appropriate place to dump her husband's body? Watching that body hop and tumble along in her rearview mirror? Then, poor frail old gal, getting her car stuck in a ditch?

She managed to free the wheels from the ditch and regain the highway, but was by then in such a state of mind . . . The final straw was when the rope broke and the body, such that remained of it, reposed on the centerline.

Feeling helpless and forlorn, the old woman drove home.

The corpse was struck at least twice by passing motorists before a highway patrolman pulled over to see what it was.

By following the trail of the dragged corpse, the authorities were able to trace its origin to a trailer court.

The woman was arrested, charged with "abusing a corpse," that fine phrase. Her neighbors, pitying her, refused to discuss her with those reporters who made a national story of the tragedy. The official police statement was that the old woman had acted in "misguided desperation."

That's as much as we are ever apt to know about the old woman who dragged her husband's corpse. I hope she got off with a light sentence and was soon able to return to the routine of her daily existence. If by anyone's reckoning she deserved punishment for her crime, I should think being able to live out her life much as she had been living it already would be punishment enough.

My own mate asked me, "What if you knew, since the day we met, that when you died, I would tie your body to the bumper of our Volkswagen, and drag you about until your pieces were strewn across the countryside? Would you still love me?"

In point of fact, it wouldn't bother me a bit. I dread the doctor and the mortician, whose abuses are legal ones, who profit from our mortality, but whatever my mate decided to do with my remains would not be, by my estimation, abusive.

That incident haunted me all night. I kept picturing the lonely, frightened old woman trying to get that stinking corpse out of her home, talking to her husband as a combination "thing" and "companion," confused in one part of her mind, certain of her intent in another, struggling to succeed at her simple task without being harassed by outsiders. . . .

I think of her and I want to make a story of it.

The story begins:

Once upon a time there was a dead husband . . .

And it ends:

His ghost came to the trailer house later on, all in pieces, and sat in front of the television.

Ah, well, perhaps I shouldn't write such a story.

Carole Buggé

Laura

In 1947, Ronald Colman won an Oscar for his performance in the film A Double Life, *the tale of an actor whose personality succumbs to the role he is playing (Othello).* CAROLE BUGGÉ, *who had never seen the Colman film, penned a remarkable feminist variation on the same theme, for the role that possesses "Laura" is the great Norwegian dramatist Henrik Ibsen's controversial heroine, Hedda Gabler. Ms. Buggé is a director and performer with New York's popular improvisational comedy troupe, Chicago City Limits. Her first published story, "Miracle in Chimayo," appeared in my 1991 anthology* Haunted America.

LAURA SAT DOWN on the new sofa and stared straight ahead, her eyes unfocused, the cordless phone still in her hand. She half-expected it to ring again, to find out that the message she had just heard was a mistake, that somehow her answering service had gotten it wrong. And yet she could still hear the voice of the boy at her service, as he read the message: "You have been cast as Hedda Gabler. Please call Jerry Hawkins to confirm." The words played over and over in her head as she sat on the couch, phone dangling from her hand. She would call Jerry Hawkins to confirm, she would call her husband Tom to share the news, but right now she wanted to sit quietly and relish the news all by herself; it was hers, only hers, at this moment before it became the world's, and she wanted to savor it in private.

The house was very still, with only the faint hoarse chirp of the sparrows outside and the occasional swish of a passing car. Tom had been right: this was a quiet street, a cul-de-sac in this leafy suburban town, and more often than not the stray cars that passed by in the night were lost, trying vainly to find the highway that led to the city.

Laura sometimes missed the noise and movement of her life in the city before she moved out here to this green patch of suburbia, but Tom liked it out here so much that she could not begrudge him his happiness. She had learned to garden and find pleasure in the mowing of grass and trimming of hedges. She got used to traveling everywhere by car instead of on foot, got used to the nearest deli being half a mile instead of half a block away, even got used to the nosy inquiries of the Epsteins, their neighbors to the left. Mrs. Epstein never got anything right anyway; seeing them pack the car on Friday for a trip, she would chirp, "Oh, where are you going?" The next morning as they piled the last few things into the trunk she would emerge in her housecoat and bedroom slippers saying, "Oh, back already?" Mrs. Epstein was a little daft, and more than a little inquisitive, but as Tom liked to remind Laura, she had no children and was lonely, with her husband at work in the city all day.

"I understand how it is for her," Laura would say, "but why doesn't she do volunteer work or something—give her life some purpose?"

Laura didn't really care whether or not Mrs. Epstein found purpose in her life; she knew she was just venting her own frustration, her own deepest fear. When she decided on a life in the theatre, she knew what would haunt her most was not the rejections, not the endless auditions and interviews—which God knows were bad enough—but the boredom, the ennui of waiting for work, for her life to have a direction. Each time a play began it was the same thing: the happy, exciting smell of sawdust and floorboards at the first read-through, meeting the other actors during the coffee breaks, the quiet exhilaration of the rehearsal process as the production begins to take form, the glamour of opening night, of settling back into your dressing room with the scent of flowers, the telegrams taped to the mirror, cards and little mysteriously wrapped presents from the other cast members.

But each performance led a little closer to the inevitable emptiness of closing night when, after the curtain goes down, the sound of hammers breaking up the set mixes with the thin, stale smell of dead bouquets, when telegrams are ripped off the mirrors along with the cards and good luck messages, costumes taken off for the last time and thrown in a heap to be laundered. At the end of these sad wrapping-up rituals Laura always felt the same draining stupor of inertia, and she would be depressed for several days; unable to leave the house, she would sit on the screened-in porch eating cheese sandwiches and reading detective novels.

Now as she sat on the living room couch Laura did not think about all the closing nights she had been through; her mind was too full of the wonderful news: she was going to play Hedda Gabler! Hedda Gabler—one of the most intriguing, dynamic, puzzling characters ever written for the stage. Uta Hagen had played her, and Alla Nazimova, and now Laura was going to add her name to this list! She had studied the part for weeks, memorizing whole scenes for the final auditions, and although she had tried as always to erase desire from her mind during the audition process, she had burned to play the role with a fire which was more than just ego. She felt she understood Ibsen, that she knew who Hedda was and what part of herself she might call on to become Ibsen's moody, manipulative heroine. She felt Hedda's exasperation with everyone around her, with her slow, plodding husband and his well-meaning, interfering aunt. She understood Hedda's restlessness and irritation with her life.

Laura picked up the phone and looked for the button labeled "Tom—work." This phone was one of Tom's recent acquisitions, an expression of his love for technology. It could store up to twenty Frequently Called Numbers; all you had to do was push the button for the number you wanted and the phone automatically dialed it. Under "Tom—work" the console said "Tom—parents" and under that "Laura—Grandmother," and so on. Tom had lovingly programmed it, and when he ran out of Frequently Called Numbers he filled in the rest with things like "Liquor Store" and "Library."

Laura pressed the button for Tom's office at the college where he was a professor of history.

"Hello?" He answered on the first ring. Laura pictured him in his small, cluttered office, happily browsing through original texts, researching the History of the Druids in the British Isles.

"Hello, Tom."

"Hi, Loloo." This was the nickname Laura's grandmother used to call her, which Tom had latched onto within the first few months of their courtship. Laura did not particularly like nicknames, but she found it hard to curb Tom's boyish enthusiasms. "What's new? Or are you just calling to express your yearning for me?"

Laura thought of Tom's freckled face, ruddy skin, short, thick fingers, and stocky, square body and tried to think if she had ever yearned for him. Their relationship had always been based on his passion for her; his energetic and cheerful pursuit of her had eventually transformed her apathy into amused tolerance and finally, acceptance. Tom was very attentive, and over the past year she had grown fond of him.

"It's not so bad to be with someone who loves you more than you love him," her grandmother had said when she was trying to decide whether to marry Tom, "That way, the balance of power is in your favor." There was no doubt that Laura liked having power over men, even if it was only Tom. Poor Tom, so full of romantic notions and hope that Laura would share them, when mostly she found them embarrassing.

"Well, actually, there is some news. I just—I've just been asked to play Hedda Gabler."

"Oh, Laura—that's wonderful!" Tom sounded sincerely happy, even though each show Laura did meant more of her evenings spent in the city at rehearsal; for Tom it meant dinners alone with only their Siamese cat for company. Tom was too into his role as Tolerant Husband to complain, though; sometimes Laura wished he would just whine a little bit about it, but he would always greet her late-night returns from rehearsal with a cheerful "Everything go okay? Everyone remember their lines, eh?" Tom was Canadian and often ended interrogative sentences with "eh," in spite of his colleagues' teasing. Laura refused to be irritated by this particular mannerism, but she did think it odd that a man who wrote books on medieval history couldn't think of anything more intelligent to say than "Everyone remember their lines, eh?"

"When do you start rehearsals?"

"Right away—tomorrow."

"Not wasting any time, eh? Isn't Hedda Gabler that Ibsen character who hates her life and shoots herself in the end?"

"Right." Tom, reducing things to their components.

"Oh, listen, Laura, I have some news, too."

"Yes?"

"Guess who's going to be a guest lecturer in the department this term?"

"Who?" But even as he said the name, she felt the answer in her stomach.

"Ed Lowell." Tom's voice was buoyant, with no trace of malice, but then Tom had no idea of what emotions that name dredged up for Laura.

"Oh, that's interesting." She forced her voice into a disinterested flatness which she hoped was believable.

"Yeah. How about that, eh? He's back in town—I hear he was out West for a while."

"Really?"

"Yeah—New Mexico, I think. Well, I haven't seen him but the word is he's cleaned up his act." Laura found Tom's use of colloquial slang unbecoming in a history professor. "Anyway, I thought you might be interested. We could—have him over some time if you'd like."

"Whatever. If you want."

Laura was sure her forced casualness sounded horribly phony, but Tom went on placidly.

"Okay, well, think about it, eh? Anyway, I have to teach a class now, so congrats and I'll see you tonight."

"Okay. Goodbye."

Laura hung up the phone and felt a scream forming in her throat. She tossed aside the couch cushion which she had been grasping and walked briskly through the living room and out the front door, into the yard. It was a heavy summer day in July, the air thick with humidity. The trees along their street—maple, ash, oak—drooped with the burden of their leaves, creating a dark green canopy over the sidewalk. Laura turned left and began to walk toward the park. The hot, hazy air seemed to press on her flesh, as though she were walking against a wind. It was perfectly still, though, one of those silent, steady days in the depth of summer before the cicadas come to signal the advent of fall.

Ed Lowell. Ed Lowell, Ed Lowell. Her feet seemed to click out the rhythm of his name as she walked. She felt irritated with Tom. Was this his attempt to show how truly liberated and unjealous he was, or did he really have no idea how obsessed about Ed Lowell she had been? No, probably Tom thought her feelings for Ed were in the past; after all, she had dumped him, hadn't she? And Tom had married her, and that was that. Tom was a man who appreciated finalities, who liked closure of topics. The History of the Druids in the British Isles. Long gone and never to return, the Druids could be examined with detachment and equanimity. And Ed Lowell—well, she thought he was gone too—but here he was again, creeping up on them in his shroud, reviving questions that should never be asked.

Laura entered the park and walked down the sloping lawn to the lake. Two Canadian geese poked about in the reeds, their webbed feet making squishing sounds in the soft muck. Laura remembered seeing on a nature special that Canadian geese were monogamous, mating for life. Laura felt her head began to ache. The water of the lake spread out before her, cool and inviting, tiny ripples on its surface. She regretted never having learned to swim; she longed to fling her clothes off and join the geese. She sighed and turned back toward the house. It was time to start making dinner for Tom, the last dinner they would share together for some weeks to come.

The next day at the first rehearsal everyone was a little nervous and eager to impress, but they all tried to hide it under an actory bravado—at the coffee breaks everyone talked loudly about what show they had just finished or of their latest commercial callback, hoping by all this talk to dispel the anxiety and insecurity which is the life of an actor. Laura hung back and just listened to the others blathering on about how this casting director just loved them and how that agent really was about to ask them to sign exclusively. What a sorry lot we are, she thought, but then no more pathetic than Tom's colleagues in the history department, those tweed- and corduroy-clad victims of a publish-or-perish mentality, rushing from their stuffy offices to classrooms full of apathetic jocks and future business entrepreneurs, kids half their age who in a couple of years would make three times their salary pushing papers on Wall Street. No noble professions are left anymore, she found herself thinking as she sipped her coffee alone in the corner. At the same time she was a little appalled at the cynicism of her thoughts—she was in an unusually dark mood.

She saw the director, Jerry Hawkins, making his way over towards her, touching each actor as he passed them, offering small encouragements. Jerry was a hands-on director, transmitting his energy and confidence through frequent physical contact, pats and squeezes. Laura had worked with him before in a production of *Arms and the Man*, and she found him comforting. He sat down beside Laura and put his arm around her shoulders. He leaned into her and she noticed for the first time that his eyes were slightly crossed.

"You know, Laura," he said quietly, "I must tell you that from the first audition there was no doubt in my mind who was going to play Hedda. After the very first reading I felt immediately that you *were* Hedda Gabler."

Laura smiled modestly. Jerry's flattering ways, buttering up his leading lady. "That's very kind of you, Jerry—"

"Oh, no, I mean it. I know I have a reputation for killing with kindness, but really: I felt from the onset that you brought so much—understanding—to the role. I felt you *knew* the woman Ibsen had written about."

"Well, thank you, Jerry," Laura said in a humble voice, "I hope during the rehearsal process I can prove you right."

Jerry squeezed her hand.

"I have absolutely every confidence that your Hedda will be a creature of flesh and blood—that you will make her live! Also," he said in a lower voice, "this production will be getting a lot of critical attention, and I don't need to tell you what that could do for your career . . . you know?" Laura nodded; she considered it bad luck to talk about these things now. Jerry patted her hand and then turned to the other actors.

"All right, shall we begin Act Three?"

It was a while since Laura worked on a role, and she attacked the play with a hungry abandon. As the rehearsal process continued, she felt her-self pulled more and more into the life of the play. She became obsessed with re-creating every detail of Hedda's life. She went to the library and checked out books on life in turn-of-the-century Norway; she went to Bergman films to hear the Scandinavian speech rhythms; imagined Hedda and Tesman surrounded by the desolate, stark landscape of the fjords. She suggested improvisations with the other actors to fill in the life of the characters. She approached the actor playing Lövborg, Hedda's old flame, and asked him if he'd like to meet for coffee.

"Sure, why not?" he shrugged with a friendly smile.

His name was Peter Litvak, and he was a tall, wiry man with large depthless eyes and a shaggy brown mane of hair. As usual, Jerry did a good job of casting—Peter was just right for the charismatic, troubled writer Lövborg.

"Where would you like to meet?"

"Café Mogador," Laura said. It was a place where she and Ed Lowell had met often in the early days, and she said once melodramatically, toward the end, that she would never go there again with anyone else. It gave her a little frightened thrill now to break her vow.

"Oh, yes, I know it—on Eighth Street. I live not far from there. How about tomorrow afternoon before rehearsal—say, four o'clock?"

"Fine."

For some reason, Laura did not tell Tom of her assignation, and when she arrived at the café the next day she felt vaguely guilty, not because she was particularly attracted to Peter, but because she chose the café to relive her days with Edward. She was early, and sat studying her script over a cup of tea. The day was hot, and her mind kept wandering from the page to memories of the summer evenings she and Edward had spent together at this same table, drinking pernod and talking about living in Europe together.

When Peter arrived, Laura tried to shake her mind free of these wan-derings and suggested they share a plate of couscous. While they waited, they began to discuss the play.

"Why do *you* think Hedda broke off with Lövborg?" Peter asked, sip-ping his raspberry tea.

"She couldn't accept the lack of control in the relationship," Laura answered without a pause.

Peter laughed. "You've given this some thought."

"I know how she feels."

Peter poured himself some more tea from the flowered chintz-covered pot. "Do you think she married Tesman to get even with Lövborg?"

Laura shrugged.

"No, I think she just felt—worn out. Tesman was there, he was easy, he represented no threat."

"In other words, she was on the rebound."

"Something like that. She thinks at first she'll be safe with Tesman—since she feels no passion for him, she'll be protected from herself."

"She's wrong, though. By the time the play opens, she's already moody and dissatisfied. And she seems to be punishing Tesman for being so foolish as to love her. She treats his poor old aunt so badly, too—she's so rude to her."

Laura sipped her tea. "Yes, it seems as though she does it to get even with Tesman; she knows he cares for the old lady."

"You know, I wonder if even her cruelty towards Tesman's aunt comes from that same self-destructive impulse which leads to her suicide. She methodically alienates everyone who might care about her." Peter shuddered. "I can't imagine being so—desperate!"

Laura stared absently across Eighth Street. A summer haze draped itself over the buildings, which seemed to buzz in the afternoon heat. Laura wiped her clammy forehead. A couple of young people dressed entirely in black leather strolled by, looking defiantly uncomfortable. Laura had to smile—the East Village had not changed since she moved out of the city. She thought nostalgically of her days on Fifth Street, in her little third-floor apartment . . .

"Let's go," she said, rising abruptly and looking at her watch. "Time to go to rehearsal."

Peter laughed.

"When you decide to do something, you just *do* it, don't you?"

Laura looked at him.

"I don't like to waste time."

They paid the check and hurried to rehearsal.

Jerry had suggested she keep a journal of Hedda's life with Tesman. During the coffee break, she made her first entry.

"Today Tesman annoyed me so much when he spent the afternoon reading his stupid boring manuscripts instead of taking me to the races!

Yesterday Tesman fell asleep in his armchair right after dinner and I had to entertain his dull relatives by myself."

"It's funny, you know," she said to Jerry after rehearsal, "but I can't remember working on a character that I felt as close to as Hedda. I know a lot of people regard her as a monster, but I don't seem to have any trouble seeing things from her point of view."

Jerry laughed.

"If only it were always that easy! I've seen actors spend so much time trying to become one with the character—sometimes it's agony to watch them. I'm glad it's coming so easily for you. It may be a tribute to Ibsen's writing."

"That's true. For example, instead of being appalled at Hedda's treatment of Tesman's kindly but nosy aunt, I understand her irritation—after all, the woman *is* annoying! She wants to butt in all the time, as though she had no life of her own."

Jerry laughed again.

"I know what you mean—my mother used to have a friend just like that. It really tries your patience."

As Laura pulled her Volkswagen into the driveway that evening, she saw the Epsteins' long silver Chevy turning into the street, and as it inched into their driveway Mrs. Epstein waved at her from the front seat. Head down, Laura rummaged for her keys, pretending not to see them, and she quickly opened the front door before Mrs. Epstein could pull her bulk out of the car. Once inside the house, she wondered why she had acted so unneighborly. True, conversations with Mrs. Epstein were labyrinths of misunderstanding, but she was a well-meaning, harmless old thing, lonely and easily confused. As Tom said, she enjoyed a few trivial words with her more glamorous young neighbors. Laura resolved to bring her a cake or something, and then, feeling irritated by the woman's helplessness, reasoned that she was too fat anyway. She should have more friends, Laura thought; then she wouldn't be so desperate for company.

That night, in her little second-floor study, Laura sat down to her journal with relish. She flipped the pages and began to describe the new gown she had just ordered. As she wrote she had an unsettled, strange feeling: something was different. She looked around her room: there was the hat rack with its assortment of hats from all different periods, there on the wall were the posters of *Sweeney Todd* and *Threepenny Opera*. Outside, the broad leaves of the maple tree brushed lightly against the windowpanes. Then Laura's eyes fell back on her journal and she realized what had changed: the handwriting on the page in front of her was completely different from her own.

Startled, she picked up the notebook and began leafing back through it to earlier entries. There, at the beginning, was her own writing, scrambled and sprawling about the page. She leafed forward, a dark sour feeling in her stomach. There—she could not say exactly when or how the writing began to change, but she stood staring at a gradual transformation from her own hand into another's, until at the end, the present, what remained was an even, controlled script, tightly coiled like a snake on the page in front of her. She let the pen drop from her hand and stared at her desk. In front of her sat her mother's picture, the only picture Laura had taken from her father's scrapbook. She wore a white dress with old-fashioned lace around the neck, and she was sitting against a broad-trunked tree, perhaps an oak. She was smiling into the camera, but her eyes looked sad, distant. The picture had been taken when Laura was four years old; less than a year later her mother was dead, drowned in the lake behind their house. After that her grandmother had never let Laura go anywhere near water, never let her swim with the other children, even in a swimming pool. Feeling dizzy, Laura closed the journal and went downstairs to the living room, where Tom was sitting watching the ball game on television. She sat next to him without speaking.

"And how's my Hedda this evening, eh?" he said amiably, pulling her towards him on the couch.

"I'm not Hedda, you know," she said sharply, "I'm Laura." She regretted the harshness of her tone when she saw the wounded puppy expression on Tom's big, friendly face.

When she told Jerry about the handwriting incident the next day he laughed and patted her on the back.

"Well, well! Just think of it—as Hedda you could commit a crime and not be prosecuted for it because your handwriting would be different!"

That evening when she got home from rehearsal Tom was out, so she went up to make her journal entry before he returned. Going up the stairs, she nearly tripped over an untidy pile of his books. In the study the air was hot and close, and she opened the window to let in the evening breeze. She sat and opened the journal to the last entry, which trailed off. Firmly she turned to a blank page and began writing quickly.

"I am annoyed at the way Tom leaves his books around," she wrote, and then stopped and looked at the page in dismay. She felt confused, unsettled; her head was burning. The phone on her desk rang and made her jump. She picked it up and tried to calm her breathing.

"Hello?"

"Hi, Loloo." Tom's voice was loud and a little slowed.

"Hello, Tom."

"I'm calling from Duck's." Duck's Tavern, popularly known as Duck's, was a local bar and restaurant frequented by the college population, both students and professors. The food and drink was cheap and copious, if undistinguished. Laura had met Tom there a few times, though she preferred a more elegant setting.

"Guess who's here with me right at this minute?"

"The Queen Mother?" Laura suggested helpfully.

"What? I can't hear you; there's too much noise here."

"Who?" Laura shouted into the phone.

"Ed Lowell! Just think—he was having dinner here and I just ran into him!"

Laura's chest contracted and then grew heavy.

"We've been sitting here talking for the past two hours—he's telling me all about his new book!" Tom sounded like a child who has just found a puppy under his bed.

"You called to tell me that?" Laura suddenly felt deeply tired, so exhausted it was an effort to listen to Tom's voice.

"Well, I thought maybe you might like to invite him over for dinner tomorrow—unless you have a rehearsal or something, eh?"

Laura sat on the steps and laughed softly. Tom didn't get it, he really didn't, and he never would get it. He was so trusting, so simple—it was insulting, really. Didn't he realize there were men before him, men who would have done anything—Laura spoke into the phone.

"Whatever you want, Tom. Tomorrow is fine."

"Great! I'll ask him to bring his book—it's about the role of faith in the twentieth century. It's really wonderful, Laura—you'll love it!"

"I'm sure I will."

"I'll be home soon. Don't wait up for me if you're tired, eh?"

"I won't."

Laura hung up and walked to the sliding glass door that led out to the deck Tom had built onto the back of the house. She opened the door and slipped out into the night. The moon hung low over the trees like a searchlight, spilling its blue light over the back yard. Laura leaned against the wooden rail and let the night air send a chill through her body. At that moment she remembered an evening with Edward, right before the end, a summer evening like this one, and they were standing by the flower garden at Riverside Park. Edward had been sober for several weeks, and was trying very hard to control himself. They were talking about how difficult it was for him not to drink, and Laura felt herself actually growing jealous of his sobriety; she was tired of these endless conversations about *his* problem, *his* suffering, as if she had none of her own. She also was beginning to realize that the more control he had of himself the less she had over him. Laura had drunk too much coffee that morning and was feeling restless and bored. As they stood there admiring the flowers she had a sudden impulse to have one, and she asked him to pick one and give it to her. He had looked at her with that condescending disapproval that she hated so much.

"These flowers belong to everyone. It's wrong to pick them."

She became even more determined to have a flower. She pouted and pleaded, accused him of being a coward, of not loving her enough; finally she wore him down. He leaned over and picked a blossom from the Bleeding Heart that drooped over the fence. Laura took it from him and then, with a little laugh, tossed it to the ground and crushed it under her foot. Later, she wondered why she had done this, and could not think of a reason except that she wanted to see him suffer and to know that she had caused it. Even now, as she stood on the porch, she could see the look in his eyes: no anger, only puzzlement, hurt, and—or did she imagine it?—disgust. She tried to make light of the incident, telling him he chose the wrong flower, but from that night on he had avoided her. He took to the bottle again shortly afterwards and later she heard he had left town. She was rescued from her obsession with him by the attentions of Tom, so stolid and unflappable, immune to her moods in a way Edward never had been. Exhausted by overplayed passions, she sank into the warm bath of Tom's affection with a weary sigh. Tom inspired in her no need to control; there was no challenge in that.

Laura looked up at the moon. Thick, heavy clouds were beginning to obscure its face, so that only one eye leered down at her. Somewhere in the neighborhood a tomcat yowled a territorial challenge, a hoarse drawn-out warning to other toms. Shivering, Laura turned and went back into the house.

The next day, Saturday, there was an afternoon rehearsal. Laura rose early to study her lines. It was a week before the opening and she knew her lines backwards and forwards, but she liked to review them before each rehearsal. As she walked into the kitchen to make coffee she felt a queasiness in her stomach. Instead of coffee, she found herself reaching for the box of soda crackers in the cupboard. She ate a couple quickly, and then, still feeling nauseous, took a couple of ice cubes from the freezer. Her grandmother had taught her this old remedy for nausea, sucking on ice cubes. She sat down at the kitchen table with her script, sucking thoughtfully on one of the cubes. She stared at her script but did not see the words. Instead, her grandmother's face was before her eyes. She looked worried, sad, the way she had looked at the funeral of Laura's mother, when Laura was five years old. Laura remembered her grandmother's words at her mother's funeral. "Your mother died for love, Laura. Just remember that: your mother died for love." Laura knew her mother drowned in the lake outside their rambling country home, but there had been questions: what was her mother doing alone in the lake at night, when she had warned the children so many times against swimming alone? It seemed odd that such an excellent swimmer as she would drown in a lake, everyone said, where there were no currents to pull her under, and there were rumors: some thought it was foul play, some said she had given herself up to the lake, swimming further and further out until there was no strength left in her body. There was talk of another man, an old flame who had returned to claim her love. Laura's mother had left no note, though, and the coroner's final verdict had been "Accidental." Laura's ears still burned with her grandmother's words—"Your mother died for love, Laura"—and she knew from that day, even as she stood next to her silent, grief-stricken father, that men could not be trusted.

Unable to concentrate, Laura closed her script, went upstairs to the study and took her journal from the desk. She had not written in it for several days. She opened it and jotted down the date, July 28th. As she did this, something nagged the back of her mind, something involving the date . . . July 28th. She checked her wall calendar just to be sure . . . what was it, then? July 28th, full moon . . . then she realized what it was. Full moon! Her period had been due over two weeks ago—and she was never, never late. She leafed through her calendar, where she always wrote down the day her period arrived. The last entry was May 12th—there it was, the capital "P" in red ink, circled. She turned to June. The month of June was blank, no red ink at all. She had been so busy rehearsing that she hadn't noticed she had missed her period in June—and now she was over six weeks late!

Laura felt as though she had a metal band around her head which was slowly tightening. She had never missed a period in her life. She realized the reason for her nausea this morning. There was no doubt in her mind: she was pregnant. Coming at this time in her life, with her career about to take off and Ed Lowell back in town, it seemed like a death sentence.

Her mind turned in panicked circles. She would have to conceal it from Tom until she could—what? Abortion was something that happened to other people, to poverty-stricken teenagers who lived in projects, not to her. It was all too vulgar, too sordid.

Just then she heard Tom's voice, thick with sleep, calling from the kitchen.

"Laura? Did you make coffee?"

She roused herself and tried to sound casual.

"No, I didn't."

"Shall I make some?"

"Sure—go ahead."

Laura took two deep breaths, exhaling slowly on each one as she had learned in her t'ai chi class. She had to get through this day, that was all, and then she could make plans. She closed the journal and went downstairs.

At rehearsal that afternoon she was dismayed to find the queasiness persisted. To take her mind off it, she dove deeply into the life of the play, attacking each scene with such energy and concentration that at one point the actor playing Tesman looked at her with an expression of real fear. At the end of Act Two she really pulled the hair of the woman playing Mrs. Elvsted so that the woman gave a little yelp. During the first break Jerry sat down next to her.

"Are you all right, Laura?" His hand rested lightly on her knee.

"Fine—why?"

"Nothing, I just—you seem sort of—explosive today. Is everything okay?"

"Sure. I just thought I'd explore that side of Hedda today. Is that a problem?"

"No, no, it's very—interesting. Just—uh, be careful of the other actors, okay?"

"All right, all right," Laura said irritably, getting up and moving away.

When she got home that evening Laura felt tired, so tired that she wanted just to crawl away into bed, but when she drove in, Tom was bustling around, unloading groceries from his car.

"Hi, Loloo! Have a good rehearsal, eh? Everyone get their lines down?" He went on without waiting for her answer. "I thought I'd cook dinner tonight since you've been so hard at work all day. I'll make my specialty, marinated steak on the grill, okay?"

"Fine." As Laura began to help her husband unload groceries from the car Mrs. Epstein came trundling out of her house.

"Hello!" she called across the driveway, lumbering towards them. She was wearing a hideously flowered shift, in colors that Laura thought belonged only in nightmares.

"Going to have a cookout?" she asked, seeing the charcoal briquettes in the trunk of the car.

"No, we thought we'd immolate the cat," Laura answered in a low voice, knowing Mrs. Epstein was hard of hearing.

"Laura!" said Tom, glaring at her, but Mrs. Epstein hadn't heard and continued to happily inspect the groceries.

"No goddamn sense of irony," Laura muttered under her breath as she struggled up the porch steps under the weight of the briquettes.

"Laura, I don't think that was a very nice thing to say to Mrs. Epstein," Tom said in his Lecture Voice once they were alone in the kitchen. Tom had an exaggerated sense of how one should treat Elders.

"Oh, just can it this once, can't you, Tom?" Laura snarled, surprised at the nasty tone in her voice.

Tom looked taken aback.

"Christ, Laura, what's gotten into you?" he said softly.

"Oh, I'm sorry, Tom. I'm just tired—it's been a long day and then we're entertaining tonight and I just—I'm sorry, really."

Tom came over and pulled her head to his chest. He did this a little clumsily, standing amidst the half-unpacked bags of groceries.

"Just take it easy tonight, why don't you, Loloo? I'll entertain Ed; you just relax."

"Okay, Tom," she answered in a little voice, feeling it was good to have someone's arms around her, even Tom's. She snuggled closer to his chest and he patted her hair. His hands held no grace, though; he might as well be petting a dog. She pulled away from him impatiently.

"I think I'll go lie down for a while," she said, heading upstairs.

"Okay; I'll put things away and start marinating the meat."

When Laura lay down on the bed she felt her limbs grow heavy with sleep almost immediately, and she fell into a light dream state. In her dream she saw her mother standing at the shore of the lake in which she had drowned, wearing the same white dress she wore in the photograph. She was standing with her back to Laura, and then she turned, and her eyes were filled with sadness. Extending one hand forward, she beckoned to Laura to join her.

The sharp clang of the doorbell woke Laura, and she sat up, covered with sweat.

"Honey!" Tom's voice called from downstairs. "He's here!"

Laura stumbled to the bathroom and bathed her face in cold water. When she appeared on the stairs in a white summer dress Tom was already showing Ed Lowell the deck he had built. Laura watched them for a moment through the sliding glass doors. Ed Lowell stood leaning against the arm rail, listening to Tom describe the construction of the deck. He was wearing a linen jacket and khaki pants, and he had grown a beard. He looked as thin as ever, and a little haggard. His long wavy dark hair was swept up over the broad forehead, and Laura felt a pinch in her groin when she saw how his hair curled at the nape of his neck. Tom turned and saw her standing there.

"Loloo—come on out, honey. You remember Ed Lowell."

Ed Lowell turned to face her, his long angular face serious.

"Hello, Ed."

"Hello, Laura."

"Long time no see, eh?" Tom said, a little too heartily.

"Yes, it has been a while," Ed Lowell said quietly. "How have you been, Laura?"

"Oh, just fine," Laura replied breezily, "You know, busy."

"Laura's been cast as Hedda Gabler," Tom said proudly, "Off-Broadway."

"How nice."

"Yes, we open in a week," Laura said, to forestall any pause in conversation.

"Well, let's get you something to drink, shall we?" said Tom, going into the kitchen. Left alone with Ed Lowell on the porch, Laura studied his face. His eyes were clear, and calmer than she last remembered. In fact, he no longer seemed to burn from the inside as he once had.

"Life treating you well?" Laura said softly.

"Yes, I have been very fortunate. I have found the two things that make life worth living—love and work."

"Oh? Tom told me about your book, but—"

"Yes, I am lucky to have found a wonderful woman."

"Oh, where is she?"

"In Oregon right now, but she's coming to join me here."

"How nice for you." It was as if each of these words were being torn out of her with red-hot pincers.

"Yes, we've both been lucky after all, Laura."

"Yes." Was he mocking her? Could he see how unsuited she and Tom were to each other? She couldn't tell. His eyes were serious, with only their usual hint of irony. Tom came back out onto the porch with drink glasses.

"Here we go, one seltzer and lime," he said, handing it to Ed Lowell.

"Seltzer and lime?" Laura said, laughing. "Since when did you—"

"I told you, Honey, remember?" Tom said quickly, to save Lowell from the discomfort Laura deliberately wanted to cause.

"It's all right, Tom; I don't mind talking about it," Lowell said lightly. "After all, talking about it is part of the cure. I don't drink any more, Laura."

"Oh, well, fine; I mean, that's your choice. I just don't see how one drink—"

"Laura, let's drop it, shall we?" said Tom with unaccustomed firmness. There was an awkward pause.

"Shall we go into the living room?" Tom said finally. "The mosquitoes are beginning to bite."

"I see you kept your piano," said Lowell as they entered the living room, "Do you still play?"

"Yes, she does," said Tom eagerly. "Why don't you play something for us, Laura?"

Laura felt as though she were being treated as a trained dog, but she went over and ran her fingers over the keys. She hadn't played in weeks, since rehearsals had begun. She wanted to run, to scream, but she was trapped in this room with these two men. She began to play an old turn-of-the-century waltz she had not played since she was a child. She began to play faster and faster, all the desperation of her life flowing into the music. She played furiously, the notes becoming a scream, full-throated and tortured. Her hair fell in damp strands around her neck, her breath came in heaves. Her fingers ached, unaccustomed to the strain. Still she played, pushing the tempo until the piece was a mad whirlpool of sound. . . . When the piece ended she sat, breathing hoarsely, spent. She looked at the men—Tom sat happily sipping his beer, but Lowell had an alarmed look on his face.

"Well, Laura, you sure played that with a lot of energy!" Tom said, picking up his glass and Lowell's and taking them to the kitchen.

"More seltzer, Ed?"

"Uh—yes, thank you," Lowell answered without taking his eyes off Laura. He rose and stood beside her.

"Is everything all right, Laura?" he said, his face tight.

Laura looked at him. His eyes were lined, tired, but there was that calm in them she had never seen before. She wanted to fold herself in his arms, to give him control of her destiny. She wanted to tell him everything, how she felt stifled and restless in this marriage, how she knew she could have been better to him, how she needed to escape . . . all of this and more was on her lips when she saw the ring on his left hand.

"You didn't tell us you were married."

He nodded, still looking at her.

"Where is your wife now?" she said in a voice as cold as death.

"Uh—in Oregon; she's coming here next week."

"Oh, yes, you said that earlier. I suppose she made you stop drinking."

"Helped me, yes. Nobody can make anyone do anything," he said—pointedly, she thought—"least of all an alcoholic, but she was always there for me when I needed her."

"How nice for you," Laura said in the same flat, dead tone. "Excuse me; I left something in the car." Rising, she went out the front door and into the street, turning left towards the park. Her mother's image floated in front of her, beckoning.

A few minutes later Tom entered the living room with drinks in his hands.

"Where's Laura?" he said.

"She said she left something in the car," answered Lowell, a gnawing dread in his heart.

But by that time Laura was already wading deeper into the cool blackness of the lake. As her dress flowered out like a large white blossom, the water closed in around her, enveloping her with the soft, welcoming arms of a mother.

E. P. Conkle

Minnie Field

The following "conte cruelle" is rustically reminiscent of Robert Browning's poem "My Last Duchess." Derived from E. P. CONKLE's Crick Bottom Plays, a collection of folk dramas, "Minnie Field" was first performed at Yale on May 1, 1928, and for years enjoyed a vigorous number of American community and college theatre productions.

SCENE.—*Five men sitting up with* TIP FIELD's *wife's corpse. The men sit in the kitchen; the corpse and coffin are in the spare front-room just off. It is three o'clock in the morning.* JIM DAY *has his feet cocked up on the stove-hearth. He leans back and smokes his pipe.* ALT PAGE *leans against the wall on the other side of the stove.* CORNIE YOUNG *sits at the table nibbling at this and that.* MEL CLARK *stands at the door looking out into the night through the glass pane.* TIP FIELDS *sits in a small rocker with his nose in a newspaper. He reads and rocks and reads and rocks. Things go slowly, quietly.*

ALT. Settin' up with a corpse is like goin' a courtin'.

JIM. How so, Alt?

ALT. A feller'll think-a some-a th' dad-blamdest things sometimes.

CORNIE. Don't they, though.

MEL. I reckon Tip's a-thinkin' 'bout Minnie in thur . . . dead. Et's too bad.

CORNIE. You shore got my sympathy, Tip. I don't know what I'd do ef I was t' lose Emmy.

ALT. A man's losin' his wife's 'bout like him a' losin' his best mare.

JIM. Feller cain't break in a new one t' no account.

CORNIE. Leastwise, not one like Minnie was.

MEL. Don't take et too hard, Tip.

TIP. I wonder ef . . . ef that sow's gone an' laid on her pigs.

(The men glance at one another.)

JIM. Oh. Well. . . . I ain't heard no squealin'.

TIP. Guess we'd-a heard et if she had-a.

ALT. Them little devils shore does squeal.

CORNIE. Feller cain hear 'em in th' next county on a clear night like this'n.

MEL. I wudn't worry none, Tip. You got s'many other things t' worry over.

TIP. I ain't worryin' none. I was just . . . wonderin'.

(Silence.)

CORNIE. Say, fellers . . . here's this card's got t' be wrote on. *(He motions to a card on the table.)*

JIM. What'll we write on et?

ALT. What you think, Tip? Et's your folkses funeral.

TIP. You fellers is payin' for th' flowers. Say what you're a-mind to. You can't hurt me none what you say.

MEL. Say as how th' flowers was given by all th' neighbors to th' diseased.

JIM. Might put in a little verse or so.

CORNIE. Anybody know any verse 't put on?

MEL. Roses is red;
Vi'let is blue;
Sugar is sweet;
So're you.

ALT. That's all th' po'try I know of.

TIP. Et's good enough.

JIM. Might say;
Roses is red;
Vi'lets is blue;
Sugar is sweet;
So *was* you.

. . . since Minnie *ain't* no more.

CORNIE. You ain't got no objections to us callin' Minnie "sweet" have you, Tip?

TIP. I reckon not. They always say nice things 'bout th' dead even when they mayn't be true. Cain't hurt me none.

MEL. Us folks allus thought Minnie was about *it*.

JIM. We all liked Minnie, too. She allus was a doin' somethin' for Amy and th' kids.

ALT. Funny how Minnie come t' die, ain't et?

TIP. Nothin' funny. She just kicked up her heels, passed in her checks, an' died. That's all.

MEL. Minnie was allus a workin' perty hard whenever I seen her.

TIP. That was one thing about Minnie. She went an' killed herse'f-a hard work. I give her credit for that.

CORNIE. Everybody's got to die sooner as later. Some-a 'em got to die a workin'. A feller gets ketched that-a-way sometimes.

JIM. I reckon it won't never ketch you that-a-way, will et, Tip?

TIP. I ain't aimin' fer et to, Jim.

(The men laugh, except TIP, who reads.)

(Then the men become conscious of their place and the corpse. Silence.)

MEL. Et's a funny thing. . . . Death is.

CORNIE. Et strikes when a person ain't lookin' for et.

ALT. And et strikes *where* a feller ain't lookin' fer et, too.

JIM. Et struck Jenny's pa right below th' collar-bone when et struck him. They was a black-an'-blue spot there big as a goose-egg whur et struck him. We all seen et when they was layin' him out.

MEL. Et's like lightnin' strikin' a forked tree.

TIP. Minnie was carryin' up a bucket of warter from th' well at th' foot of th' hill. Ag'in she got ha'f way up, she keeled over an' spilt all th' warter out. That's about all they was to et. I called up th' doc an' he come an' worked on her. I had t' fetch up another bucket-a warter m'se'f.

MEL. Et's too bad, Tip.

TIP. Shore . . . is.

(Silence. CORNIE eats.)

CORNIE. These yeller t'mater p'serves is fine, Tip.

TIP. Minnie put 'em up for th' winter. She was allus a doin' some durned-fool thing like that. Got a whole cellar-full-a that kinda truck.

CORNIE. Cudn't a been better ef I'd a put 'em up m'se'f, Tip. Yummmm.

JIM. I hear none-a your folks is comin' to th' funeral, Tip.

TIP. I . . . reckon not.

ALT. So *I* heard. How come, Tip?

TIP. They didn't like Minnie none. They said she was allus too smart. She was allus tryin' t' git me t' pull my freight an' git away from 'em. Minnie was plannin' big on that. Th' day she died she got a letter from

Montana or somewheres 'bout new land. She even drawed a plan for a new house out there. My folks didn't like that none.

JIM. Well . . . us folks all liked Minnie real well. Mighty well.

ALT. Us folks, too.

MEL. Minnie was allus smilin'. I never seen her when she wasn't smilin'.

TIP. She cudn't tolerate none-a my folks none. I reckon my folks was as good as hern.

JIM (pointing with his pipe-stem at TIP). Wasn't nobody good as Minnie, Tip.

TIP. I . . . reckon not.

(Silence.)

MEL. Who put that rose on her coffin in thur, Tip?

TIP. She done et herse'f.

JIM. *She* done et?

ALT. How'd *she* do et, Tip?

TIP. Couple-a years ago she set them posies out in th' back yard. An' she says to me: "Ef I ever die when those-there roses are in bloom, Tippy dear, put one of them on my coffin." So . . . her ma went an' done et.

JIM. Et looks mighty perty and simple. Naturally I don't go much on beauty. But that-there was a beautiful idea, I say.

MEL. My Haley's that-a-way, too. Women-folks is durned funny critters.

CORNIE. They shore put th' trimmin's on a feller.

ALT. I didn't 'mount to a durn b'fore I was married.

JIM. Y' don't 'mount t' much more now, do you, Alt?

ALT. I reckon me and you is on a par, ain't we, Jim?

JIM. That suits me, Alt.

(The men laugh loudly.)

CORNIE. Oh, hummmm. Kinda sleepy. You reckon th' corpse is all right, in there?

ALT. Take a look, Mel.

MEL. Et makes me creepy t' snoop 'round a corpse. Cornie, you look.

CORNIE. Nothin' to that, Mel. (He goes to the left door and opens it.) They ain't nothin' could hurt a person 'bout a corpse.

MEL. Mebby not. But they're like cold mashed p'taters; they ain't got no life to 'em.

CORNIE. Ever'thing's all O.K. 's fur's I can see. Minnie's women-folks is snorin' like all-git-out in th' spare bedroom. Sounds like a hog-pen.

TIP. Et is . . . with *them* in it.

CORNIE (looking in). You got a nice front-room in there, Tip. Fixed up a sight better'n ourn is at home.

TIP. Et was . . . her.

CORNIE *(closing the door).* Whur'd you git th' pianner at?

TIP. She got et. She usta thump on et in th' evenings. "In th' Gloamin' " and "Darlin' Nellie Gray" and such.

JIM. Must-a cost a sight. Emmy got a parler-organ and et kept me poverty-struck for five years hand-runnin'.

TIP. Didn't cost *me* nothin'. She got et with her butter 'n egg money. Took seven years. There et is in there now. Doin' nobody no good. She was just thet-a-way.

ALT. You cain cut et up for kindlin' wood, Tip.

CORNIE. Et'd make a good hen-coop for yer little chickens. All you got t' do is t' take out th' works and put a strip-a tar paper on top.

TIP. May do that.

MEL. Well . . . who's goin' t' write out that card? There et is on th' table.

JIM. I cain't write so's a person can read et.

TIP. Don't worry . . . nobody's goin' to read et.

CORNIE. I can't draw my X's so's a person can make 'em out. And my Z's has got curley-cues on 'em. You write et out, Alt.

ALT. I wud . . . but I sprained my ankle an' I'm stiff all over so's I can't even scratch my own back.

JIM. A-course, we couldn't ask Tip t' do et.

TIP. Stick th' durned flowers on without a card. Who cares for style? I been a-gettin' my belly-full-a style fer th' past ten years.

CORNIE. Just's you say, Tip. We just thunk et'd be kind-a nice, that's all. (MEL *looks out the window.*)

MEL. Et's gettin' daylight out, boys. I got t' be goin' on home.

JIM. Me, too. Them calves got t' be tended to.

(The men start to put on their coats and hats.)

TIP. You fellers is comin' back t' carry th' woman to th' grave, ain't you?

CORNIE. I reckon so. We was 'pointed pall-bearers. Won't be hard to carry Minnie. She didn't weigh no more'n a bag-a feathers.

ALT. I guess I orta be hikin' on home, too. I got some chores t' do.

JIM. You goin' my way, Cornie?

CORNIE. Guess I'll cut across the hog pasture—it's shorter.

MEL. Whut'll you do without Minnie to do your milkin' now, Tip?

TIP. Reckon I'll have t' . . . git me another woman.

(The men stop still.)

CORNIE. You . . . got anybody . . . in mind, Tip?

TIP. I got Annie Smith in mind.

JIM. Ab Smith's dortor?

TIP. Yeh. I've had her in mind for some time. When I seen Minnie was . . . ailin'.

(The men look at one another. They say nothing. Silence.)

ALT. Well . . . I . . . I guess I'll be . . . goin' on, boys.

JIM. Me too, Alt.

TIP. I may need you fellers later t' help me bust up that pianner in there . . . when we git Minnie out of the way.

CORNIE. Any time. *Ef I ain't doin' somethin'.*

ALT. Me, too. Most likely I *won't* be.

MEL. I guess . . . I'll just take another look . . . at Minnie in there . . . b'fore I go.

JIM. Me . . . too.

(MEL opens the door. The men look in.)

MEL. Th' sun . . . looks perty . . . shinin' on that . . . rose, Tip.

JIM. Shore . . . does.

ALT. Et's tough luck t' lose a woman like Minnie.

MEL. She was allus smilin' and bright.

TIP. I'll git over et all right. Don't worry none 'bout me.

CORNIE. I reckon . . . we won't . . . much.

(ALT opens the outside door. The men start out.)

ALT *(turning toward TIP)*. I s'pose th' baby is inside th' coffin with Minnie, ain't it?

TIP. It's layin' on her breast. *(Pause.)* They wa'n't no use wastin' *two* coffins.

(The men leave. TIP resumes his reading and rocking. The sunlight washes out the pale of the lamplight.)

THE CURTAIN FALLS SLOWLY

H. G. Wells

The Pearl of Love

Love conquers all? Not according to H. G. WELLS *(1866–1946), who, as
Great Britain's most famous science-fantasist, wrote such unforgettable
novels and tales as* The Invisible Man, The Island of Dr. Moreau, The
Time Machine *and* The War of the Worlds. *The great tomb in his little-
known tale "The Pearl of Love" inevitably brings to mind India's Taj
Mahal.*

THE PEARL is lovelier than the most brilliant of crystalline stones, the
moralist declares, because it is made through the suffering of a living
creature. About that I can say nothing because I feel none of the fascination of pearls. Their cloudy lustre moves me not at all. Nor can I decide
for myself upon that age-long dispute whether The Pearl of Love is the
cruellest of stories or only a gracious fable of the immortality of beauty.

Both the story and the controversy will be familiar to students of medi-
aeval Persian prose. The story is a short one, though the commentary
upon it is a respectable part of the literature of that period. They have
treated it as a poetic invention and they have treated it as an allegory
meaning this, that, or the other thing. Theologians have had their copious way with it, dealing with it particularly as concerning the restoration
of the body after death, and it has been greatly used as a parable by those
who write about aesthetics. And many have held it to be the statement of
a fact, simply and baldly true.

The story is laid in North India, which is the most fruitful soil for
sublime love stories of all the lands in the world. It was in a country of
sunshine and lakes and rich forests and hills and fertile valleys; and far
away the great mountains hung in the sky, peaks, crests, and ridges of

inaccessible and eternal snow. There was a young prince, lord of all the land; and he found a maiden of indescribable beauty and delightfulness and he made her his queen and laid his heart at her feet. Love was theirs, full of joys and sweetness, full of hope, exquisite, brave and marvellous love, beyond anything you have ever dreamt of love. It was theirs for a year and a part of a year, and then suddenly, because of some venomous sting that came to her in a thicket, she died.

She died and for a while the prince was utterly prostrated. He was silent and motionless with grief. They feared he might kill himself, and he had neither sons nor brothers to succeed him. For two days and nights he lay upon his face, fasting, across the foot of the couch which bore her calm and lovely body. Then he arose and ate, and went about very quietly like one who has taken a great resolution. He caused her body to be put in a coffin of lead mixed with silver, and for that he had an outer coffin made of the most precious and scented woods wrought with gold, and about that there was to be a sarcophagus of alabaster, inlaid with precious stones. And while these things were being done he spent his time for the most part by the pools and in the garden-houses and pavilions and groves and in those chambers in the palace where they two had been most together, brooding upon her loveliness. He did not rend his garments nor defile himself with ashes and sackcloth as the custom was, for his love was too great for such extravagances. At last he came forth again among his councillors and before the people, and told them what he had a mind to do.

He said he could never more touch woman, he could never more think of them, and so he would find a seemly youth to adopt for his heir and train him to his task, and that he would do his princely duties as became him; but that for the rest of it, he would give himself with all his power and all his strength and all his wealth, all that he could command, to make a monument worthy of his incomparable, dear, lost mistress. A building it should be of perfect grace and beauty, more marvellous than any other building had ever been or could ever be, so that to the end of time it should be a wonder, and men would treasure it and speak of it and desire to see it and come from all the lands of the earth to visit and recall the name and the memory of his queen. And this building he said was to be called the Pearl of Love.

And this his councillors and people permitted him to do, and so he did.

Year followed year and all the years he devoted himself to building and adorning the Pearl of Love. A great foundation was hewn out of the living rock in a place whence one seemed to be looking at the snowy wilderness of the great mountain across the valley of the world. Villages and hills there were, a winding river, and very far away three great cities. Here they put the sarcophagus of alabaster beneath a pavilion of cunning workmanship; and about it there were set pillars of strange and lovely stone and wrought and fretted walls, and a great casket of masonry bearing a dome and pinnacles and cupolas, as exquisite as a jewel. At first the design of the Pearl of Love was less bold and subtle than it became later. At first it was smaller and more wrought and encrusted; there were many pierced screens and delicate clusters of rosy hued pillars, and the sarcophagus lay like a child that sleeps among flowers. The first dome was covered with green tiles, framed and held together by silver, but this was taken away again because it seemed close, because it did not soar grandly enough for the broadening imagination of the prince.

For by this time he was no longer the graceful youth who had loved the girl queen. He was now a man, grave and intent, wholly set upon the building of the Pearl of Love. With every year of effort he had learnt new possibilities in arch and wall and buttress; he had acquired greater power over the material he had to use and he had learnt of a hundred stones and hues and effects that he could never have thought of in the beginning. His sense of colour had grown finer and colder; he cared no more for the enamelled gold-lined brightness that had pleased him first, the brightness of an illuminated missal; he sought now for blue colourings like the sky and for the subtle hues of great distances, for recondite shadows and sudden broad floods of purple opalescence and for grandeur and space. He wearied altogether of carvings and pictures and inlaid ornamentation and all the little careful work of men. "Those were pretty things," he said of his earlier decorations; and had them put aside into subordinate buildings where they would not hamper his main design. Greater and greater grew his artistry. With awe and amazement people saw the Pearl of Love sweeping up from its first beginnings to a superhuman breadth and height and magnificence. They did not know clearly what they had expected, but never had they expected so sublime a thing as this. "Wonderful are the miracles," they whispered, "that love can do," and all the women in the world, whatever other loves they had, loved the prince for the splendour of his devotion.

Through the middle of the building ran a great aisle, a vista, that the prince came to care for more and more. From the inner entrance of the building he looked along the length of an immense pillared gallery and across the central area from which the rose-hued columns had long since vanished, over the top of the pavilion under which lay the sarcophagus,

through a marvellously designed opening, to the snowy wildernesses of
the great mountain, the lord of all mountains, two hundred miles away.
The pillars and arches and buttresses and galleries soared and floated on
either side, perfect yet unobtrusive, like great archangels waiting in the
shadows about the presence of God. When men saw that austere beauty
for the first time they were exalted, and then they shivered and their
hearts bowed down. Very often would the prince come to stand there and
look at that vista, deeply moved and not yet fully satisfied. The Pearl of
Love had still something for him to do, he felt, before his task was done.
Always he would order some little alteration to be made or some recent
alteration to be put back again. And one day he said that the sarcophagus
would be clearer and simpler without the pavilion; and after regarding it
very steadfastly for a long time, he had the pavilion dismantled and removed.

The next day he came and said nothing, and the next day and the next.
Then for two days he stayed away altogether. Then he returned, bringing
with him an architect and two master craftsmen and a small retinue.

All looked, standing together silently in a little group, amidst the serene vastness of their achievement. No trace of toil remained in its
perfection. It was as if the God of nature's beauty had taken over their
offspring to himself.

Only one thing there was to mar the absolute harmony. There was a
certain disproportion about the sarcophagus. It had never been enlarged,
and indeed how could it have been enlarged since the early days? It
challenged the eye; it nicked the streaming lines. In that sarcophagus was
the casket of lead and silver, and in the casket of lead and silver was the
queen, the dear immortal cause of all this beauty. But now that sarcophagus seemed no more than a little dark oblong that lay incongruously in
the great vista of the Pearl of Love. It was as if someone had dropped a
small valise upon the crystal sea of heaven.

Long the prince mused, but no one knew the thoughts that passed
through his mind.

At last he spoke. He pointed.

"Take that thing away," he said.

Not
of This World

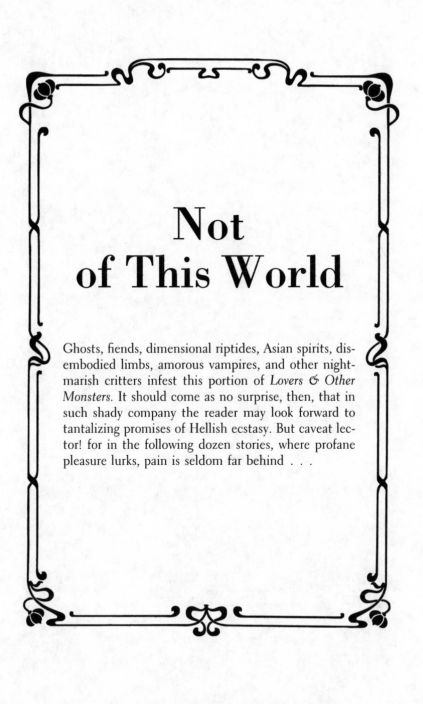

Ghosts, fiends, dimensional riptides, Asian spirits, disembodied limbs, amorous vampires, and other nightmarish critters infest this portion of *Lovers & Other
Monsters*. It should come as no surprise, then, that in
such shady company the reader may look forward to
tantalizing promises of Hellish ecstasy. But caveat lec-
tor! for in the following dozen stories, where profane
pleasure lurks, pain is seldom far behind . . .

H. P. Lovecraft

The Strange High House in the Mist

H. P. LOVECRAFT *(1890–1937) was one of America's most important twenti-eth-century fantasists. Despite his apposite name, he did not write much about the darker aspects of love. "The Strange High House in the Mist" (tangentially connected with HPL's earlier story "The Terrible Old Man") comes closest with its shadowy hints of perilous transdimensional revels.*

IN THE MORNING, mist comes up from the sea by the cliffs beyond Kingsport. White and feathery it comes from the deep to its brothers the clouds, full of dreams of dank pastures and caves of leviathan. And later, in still summer rains on the steep roofs of poets, the clouds scatter bits of those dreams, that men shall not live without rumor of old strange secrets, and wonders that planets tell planets alone in the night. When tales fly thick in the grottoes of tritons, and conchs in seaweed cities blow wild tunes learned from the Elder Ones, then great eager mists flock to heaven laden with lore, and oceanward eyes on the rocks see only a mystic whiteness, as if the cliff's rim were the rim of all earth, and the solemn bells of buoys tolled free in the aether of faëry.

Now north of archaic Kingsport the crags climb lofty and curious, ter-race on terrace, till the northernmost hangs in the sky like a gray frozen wind-cloud. Alone it is, a bleak point jutting in limitless space, for there the coast turns sharp where the great Miskatonic pours out of the plains past Arkham, bringing woodland legends and little quaint memories of New England's hills. The sea-folk in Kingsport look up at that cliff as other sea-folk look up at the pole-star, and time the night's watches by the way it hides or shows the Great Bear, Cassiopeia, and the Dragon. Among them it is one with the firmament, and truly, it is hidden from them when the mist hides the stars or the sun. Some of the cliffs they love, as that whose grotesque profile they call Father Neptune, or that whose pillared steps they term "The Causeway"; but this one they fear because it is so near the sky. The Portuguese sailors coming in from a voyage cross themselves when they first see it, and the old Yankees believe it would be much graver matter than death to climb it, if indeed that were possible. Nevertheless there is an ancient house on that cliff, and at evening men see lights in the small-paned windows.

The ancient house has always been there, and people say One dwells within who talks with the morning mists that come up from the deep, and perhaps sees singular things oceanward at those times when the cliff's rim becomes the rim of all earth, and solemn buoys toll free in the white aether of faëry. This they tell from hearsay, for that forbidding crag is always unvisited, and natives dislike to train telescopes on it. Summer boarders have indeed scanned it with jaunty binoculars, but have never seen more than the gray primeval roof, peaked and shingled, whose eaves come nearly to the gray foundations, and the dim yellow light of the little windows peeping out from under those eaves in the dusk. These summer people do not believe that the same One has lived in the ancient house for hundreds of years, but can not prove their heresy to any real Kingsporter. Even the Terrible Old Man who talks to leaden pendulums in bottles, buys groceries with centuried Spanish gold, and keeps stone idols in the yard of his antediluvian cottage in Water Street can only say these things were the same when his grandfather was a boy, and that must have been inconceivable ages ago, when Belcher or Shirley or Pownall or Bernard was Governor of His Majesty's Province of the Massachusetts-Bay.

Then one summer there came a philosopher into Kingsport. His name was Thomas Olney, and he taught ponderous things in a college by Narragansett Bay. With stout wife and romping children he came, and his eyes were weary with seeing the same things for many years, and thinking the same well-disciplined thoughts. He looked at the mists from the diadem of Father Neptune, and tried to walk into their white world of mystery along the titan steps of The Causeway. Morning after morning he would lie on the cliffs and look over the world's rim at the cryptical aether beyond, listening to spectral bells and the wild cries of what might have been gulls. Then, when the mist would lift and the sea stand out prosy with the smoke of steamers, he would sigh and descend to the town, where he loved to thread the narrow olden lanes up and down hill, and study the crazy tottering gables and odd-pillared doorways which had sheltered so many generations of sturdy sea-folk. And he even talked with the Terrible Old Man, who was not fond of strangers, and was invited into his fearsomely archaic cottage where low ceilings and wormy panelling hear the echoes of disquieting soliloquies in the dark small hours.

Of course it was inevitable that Olney should mark the gray unvisited cottage in the sky, on that sinister northward crag which is one with the mists and the firmament. Always over Kingsport it hung, and always its mystery sounded in whispers through Kingsport's crooked alleys. The Terrible Old Man wheezed a tale that his father had told him, of lightning that shot one night up from that peaked cottage to the clouds of higher heaven; and Granny Orne, whose tiny gambrel-roofed abode in Ship Street is all covered with moss and ivy, croaked over something her grandmother had heard at second-hand, about shapes that flapped out of the eastern mists straight into the narrow single door of that unreachable place—for the door is set close to the edge of the crag toward the ocean, and glimpsed only from ships at sea.

At length, being avid for new strange things and held back by neither the Kingsporter's fear nor the summer boarder's usual indolence, Olney made a very terrible resolve. Despite a conservative training—or because of it, for humdrum lives breed wistful longings of the unknown—he swore a great oath to scale that avoided northern cliff and visit the abnormally antique gray cottage in the sky. Very plausibly his saner self argued that the place must be tenanted by people who reached it from inland along the easier ridge beside the Miskatonic's estuary. Probably they traded in Arkham, knowing how little Kingsport liked their habitation, or perhaps being unable to climb down the cliff on the Kingsport side. Olney walked out along the lesser cliffs to where the great crag leaped insolently up to consort with celestial things, and became very sure that no human feet could mount it or descend it on that beetling southern slope. East and north it rose thousands of feet perpendicular from the water, so only the western side, inland and toward Arkham remained.

One early morning in August Olney set out to find a path to the inaccessible pinnacle. He worked northwest along pleasant back roads, past Hooper's Pond and the old brick powder-house to where the pastures slope up to the ridge above the Miskatonic and give a lovely vista of Arkham's white Georgian steeples across leagues of river and meadow. Here he found a shady road to Arkham, but no trail at all in the seaward direction he wished. Woods and fields crowded up to the high bank of the river's mouth, and bore not a sign of man's presence; not even a stone wall or a straying cow, but only the tall grass and giant trees and tangles of briars that the first Indian might have seen. As he climbed slowly east, higher and higher above the estuary on his left and nearer and nearer the sea, he found the way growing in difficulty till he wondered how ever the dwellers in that disliked place managed to reach the world outside, and whether they came often to market in Arkham.

Then the trees thinned, and far below him on his right he saw the hills and antique roofs and spires of Kingsport. Even Central Hill was a dwarf from this height, and he could just make out the ancient graveyard by the Congregational Hospital, beneath which rumor said some terrible caves or burrows lurked. Ahead lay sparse grass and scrub blueberry bushes, and beyond them the naked rock of the crag and the thin peak of the dreaded gray cottage. Now the ridge narrowed, and Olney grew dizzy at his loneness in the sky, south of him the frightful precipice above Kingsport, north of him the vertical drop of nearly a mile to the river's mouth. Suddenly a great chasm opened before him, ten feet deep, so that he had to let himself down by his hands and drop to a slanting floor, and then crawl perilously up a natural defile in the opposite wall. So this was the way the folk of the uncanny house journeyed betwixt earth and sky!

When he climbed out of the chasm a morning mist was gathering, but he clearly saw the lofty and unhallowed cottage ahead; walls as gray as the rock, and high peak standing bold against the milky white of the seaward vapors. And he perceived that there was no door on this landward end, but only a couple of small lattice windows with dingy bull's-eye panes leaded in Seventeenth Century fashion. All around him was cloud and chaos, and he could see nothing below the whiteness of illimitable space. He was alone in the sky with this queer and very disturbing house; and when he sidled around to the front and saw that the wall stood flush with the cliff's edge, so that the single narrow door was not to be reached save from the empty aether, he felt a distinct terror that altitude could not wholly explain. And it was very odd that shingles so worm-eaten could survive, or bricks so crumbled still form a standing chimney.

As the mist thickened, Olney crept around to the windows on the north and west and south sides, trying them but finding them all locked. He was vaguely glad they were locked, because the more he saw of that house the less he wished to get in. Then a sound halted him. He heard a lock rattle and a bolt shoot, and a long creaking follow as if a heavy door were slowly and cautiously opened. This was on the oceanward side that he could not see, where the narrow portal opened on blank space thousands of feet in the misty sky above the waves.

Then there was heavy, deliberate tramping in the cottage, and Olney heard the windows opening, first on the north side opposite him, and then on the west just around the corner. Next would come the south windows, under the great low eaves on the side where he stood; and it must be said that he was more than uncomfortable as he thought of the detestable house on one side and the vacancy of upper air on the other. When a fumbling came in the nearer casements he crept around to the west again, flattening himself against the wall beside the now opened windows. It was plain that the owner had come home; but he had not come from the land, nor from any balloon or airship that could be imagined. Steps sounded again, and Olney edged round to the north; but before he could find a haven a voice called softly, and he knew he must confront his host.

Stuck out of the west window was a great black-bearded face whose eyes were phosphorescent with the imprint of unheard-of sights. But the voice was gentle, and of a quaint olden kind, so that Olney did not shudder when a brown hand reached out to help him over the sill and into that low room of black oak wainscots and carved Tudor furnishings. The man was clad in very ancient garments, and had about him an unplaceable nimbus of sea-lore and dreams of tall galleons. Olney does not recall many of the wonders he told, or even who he was; but says that he was strange and kindly, and filled with the magic of unfathomed voids of time and space. The small room seemed green with a dim aqueous light, and Olney saw that the far windows to the east were not open, but shut against the misty aether with dull thick panes like the bottoms of old bottles.

That bearded host seemed young, yet looked out of eyes steeped in the elder mysteries; and from the tales of marvelous ancient things he related, it must be guessed that the village folk were right in saying he had communed with the mists of the sea and the clouds of the sky ever since there was any village to watch his taciturn dwelling from the plain below. And the day wore on, and still Olney listened to rumors of old times and far places, and heard how the kings of Atlantis fought with the slippery blasphemies that wriggled out of rifts in ocean's floor, and how the pillared and weedy temple of Poseidonis is still glimpsed at midnight by lost ships, who know by its sight that they are lost. Years of the Titans were recalled, but the host grew timid when he spoke of the dim first age of chaos before the gods or even the Elder Ones were born, and when *the other gods* came to dance on the peak of Hatheg-Kla in the stony desert near Ulthar, beyond the River Skai.

It was at this point that there came a knocking on the door; that ancient door of nail-studded oak beyond which lay only the abyss of white cloud. Olney started in fright, but the bearded man motioned him to be still, and tiptoed to the door to look out through a very small peephole. What he saw he did not like, so pressed his fingers to his lips and tiptoed around to shut and lock all the windows before returning to the ancient settle beside his guest. Then Olney saw lingering against the translucent squares of each of the little dim windows in succession a queer black outline as the caller moved inquisitively about before leaving; and he was glad his host had not answered the knocking. For there are strange objects in the great abyss, and the seeker of dreams must take care not to stir up or meet the wrong ones.

Then the shadows began to gather; first little furtive ones under the table, and then bolder ones in the dark panelled corners. And the bearded man made enigmatical gestures of prayer, and lit tall candles in curiously wrought brass candle-sticks. Frequently he would glance at the door as if he expected some one, and at length his glance seemed answered by a singular rapping which must have followed some very ancient and secret code. This time he did not even glance through the peephole, but swung the great oak bar and shot the bolt, unlatching the heavy door and flinging it wide to the stars and the mist.

And then to the sound of obscure harmonies there floated into that room from the deep all the dreams and memories of earth's sunken Mighty Ones. And golden flames played about weedy locks, so that Olney was dazzled as he did them homage. Trident-bearing Neptune was there, and sportive tritons and fantastic nereids, and upon dolphins' backs was balanced a vast crenulate shell wherein rode the gray and awful form of primal Nodens, Lord of the Great Abyss. And the conches of the tritons gave weird blasts, and the nereids made strange sounds by striking on the grotesque resonant shells of unknown lurkers in black sea-caves. Then hoary Nodens reached forth a wizened hand and helped Olney and his host into the vast shell, whereat the conchs and the gongs set up a wild and awesome clamor. And out into the limitless aether reeled that fabulous train, the noise of whose shouting was lost in the echoes of thunder.

All night in Kingsport they watched that lofty cliff when the storm and the mists gave them glimpses of it, and when toward the small hours the little dim windows went dark they whispered of dread and disaster. And Olney's children and stout wife prayed to the bland proper god of Baptists, and hoped that the traveller would borrow an umbrella and rubbers unless the rain stopped by morning. Then dawn swam dripping and mist-wreathed out of the sea, and the buoys tolled solemn in vortices of white aether. And at noon elfin horns rang over the ocean as Olney, dry and light-footed, climbed down from the cliffs to antique Kingsport with the look of far places in his eyes. He could not recall what he had dreamed in the sky-perched hut of that still nameless hermit, or say how he had crept down that crag untraversed by other feet. Nor could he talk of these matters at all save with the Terrible Old Man, who afterward mumbled queer things in his long white beard; vowing that the man who came down from that crag was not wholly the man who went up, and that somewhere under that gray peaked roof, or amidst inconceivable reaches of that sinister white mist, there lingered still the lost spirit of him who was Thomas Olney.

And ever since that hour, through dull dragging years of grayness and weariness, the philosopher has labored and eaten and slept and done uncomplaining the suitable deeds of a citizen. Not any more does he long for the magic of farther hills, or sigh for secrets that peer like green reefs from a bottomless sea. The sameness of his days no longer gives him sorrow, and well-disciplined thoughts have grown enough for his imagination. His good wife waxes stouter and his children older and prosier and more useful, and he never fails to smile correctly with pride when the occasion calls for it. In his glance there is not any restless light, and if he ever listens for solemn bells or far elfin horns it is only at night when old dreams are wandering. He has never seen Kingsport again, for his family disliked the funny old houses and complained that the drains were impossibly bad. They have a trim bungalow now at Bristol Highlands, where no tall crags tower, and the neighbors are urban and modern.

But in Kingsport strange tales are abroad, and even the Terrible Old Man admits a thing untold by his grandfather. For now, when the wind sweeps boisterous out of the north past the high ancient house that is one with the firmament, there is broken at last that ominous, brooding silence ever before the bane of Kingsport's maritime cotters. And old folk tell of pleasing voices heard singing there, and of laughter that swells with joys beyond earth's joys; and say that at evening the little low windows are brighter than formerly. They say, too, that the fierce aurora comes oftener to that spot, shining blue in the north with visions of frozen worlds while the crag and the cottage hang black and fantastic against wild coruscations. And the mists of the dawn are thicker, and sailors are not quite so sure that all the muffled seaward ringing is that of the solemn buoys.

Worst of all, though, is the shrivelling of old fears in the hearts of Kingsport's young men, who grow prone to listen at night to the north wind's faint distant sounds. They swear no harm or pain can inhabit that high peaked cottage, for in the new voices gladness beats, and with them the tinkle of laughter and music. What tales the sea-mists may bring to that haunted and northernmost pinnacle they do not know, but they long to extract some hint of the wonders that knock at the cliff-yawning door when clouds are thickest. And patriarchs dread lest some day one by one they seek out that inaccessible peak in the sky, and learn what centuried secrets hide beneath the steep shingled roof which is part of the rocks and the stars and the ancient fears of Kingsport. That those venturesome youths will come back they do not doubt, but they think a light may be gone from their eyes, and a will from their hearts. And they do not wish quaint Kingsport with its climbing lanes and archaic gables to drag listless down the years while voice by voice the laughing chorus grows stronger and wilder in that unknown and terrible eyrie where mists and the dreams of mists stop to rest on their way from the sea to the skies.

They do not wish the souls of their young men to leave the pleasant hearths and gambrel-roofed taverns of old Kingsport, nor do they wish the laughter and song in that high rocky place to grow louder. For as the voice which has come has brought fresh mists from the sea and from the north fresh lights, so do they say that still other voices will bring more mists and more lights, till perhaps the olden gods (whose existence they hint only in whispers for fear the Congregational parson shall hear) may come out of the deep and from unknown Kadath in the cold waste and make their dwelling on that evilly appropriate crag so close to the gentle hills and valleys of quiet, simple fisher folk. This they do not wish, for to plain people things not of earth are unwelcome; and besides, the Terrible Old Man often recalls what Olney said about a knock that the lone dweller feared, and a shape seen black and inquisitive against the mist through those queer translucent windows of leaded bull's-eyes.

All these things, however, the Elder Ones only may decide; and meanwhile the morning mist still comes up by that lonely vertiginous peak with the steep ancient house, that gray, low-eaved house where none is seen but where evening brings furtive lights while the north wind tells of strange revels. White and feathery it comes from the deep to its brothers the clouds, full of dreams of dank pastures and caves of leviathan. And when tales fly thick in the grottoes of tritons, and conches in seaweed cities blow wild tunes learned from the Elder Ones, then great eager vapors flock to heaven laden with lore; and Kingsport, nestling uneasy on its lesser cliffs below that awesome hanging sentinel of rock, sees oceanward only a mystic whiteness, as if the cliff's rim were the rim of all earth, and the solemn bells of the buoys tolled free in the aether of faëry.

Paula Volsky

Let No Man Dream

For the past decade, discerning fantasy lovers have reveled in the witty, startlingly imaginative novels of PAULA VOLSKY—Curse of the Witch Queen, The Luck of Relian Kru *and the sequential* The Sorcerer's Lady, The Sorcerer's Heir *and* The Sorcerer's Curse. *A resident of Alexandria, Va., Ms. Volsky recently completed a sweepingly epic science-fantasy novel,* Illusion, *released in 1992 under the Bantam/Spectra imprint and in England by Victor Gollancz, Ltd. Her amusing novella, "The Tenancy of Mr. Eex," which appeared in* Devils and Demons, *was dry as a 7:1 martini, but "Let No Man Dream" is a much darker brew.*

I ALWAYS COME to them in their dreams. When they sleep, abandoning their glare-lighted waking world for the larger and more varied realm that is my reality, I am free to make my presence known.

What do they think they see when I approach them? Sometimes I wonder, for I have never looked upon any of my own faces. Only occasionally I glimpse myself in the mirrors of their minds, and such views are always distorted. I know, however, that what they believe they see must be beautiful, for they pursue the vision with a covetous persistence otherwise inexplicable. I know too that perception differs greatly from man to man, for always I clothe myself in the fancies and deepest longings of each consciousness that I visit. Always, I am the essence of personal fantasy. And how do I make myself so? How do I sort in an instant through the junkheap accumulation of old ambitions, caprices, and fleeting lunacies to fasten so unerringly upon the truest desires? To shape my image accordingly? I might answer that it is my instinct and my function to do so; but that says nothing. In truth, I cannot account for my nature, any more than I can explain the character of the force that chooses the minds through which I must wander.

The dreamscapes of my explorations vary, shaping the succession of my guises; but some things never change. Every beginning is the same. Awareness of self—suspended for how long?—returns, and I am in a new place. Drawn insensibly through the darkness—or aimed like an arrow? How long before that question occurred to me? Always the land is strange, yet familiar. The surface may be murky, a swamp of melancholia; bright with ardor; placid or stormswept; deserted, prosaically populous, or home to creatures beyond description—all of this is infinitely variable; but the underlying mesh of hunger and fear never alters. It is not difficult to learn the surface. I am always quick to master the terrain.

Soon, I know the pathways. Only a little time has elapsed since my awakening, but it is enough; I was made for this work. I am prepared, and it is time to meet the dreamer.

I do not reveal myself all at once. I stir, I glide, and presently he senses my presence. He is inquisitive, as I intend him to be. But I am not too quick to satisfy his curiosity. He needs time, time to let his imagination do its work. I am there, I am not. He spies a shadow, a mist, a silhouette. A form, a profile, a gleam of dream-flesh, a beckoning hand. He is caught, intrigued. He follows, and I am gone. Back again, perceived, and gone once more. He pursues me along the tangled pathways of old memory; clutches, and misses. Misses again. And again. So the dance proceeds, for several sleep-spans at least, until his puzzling, dreaming brain is tired; and then perhaps I allow him to rest in some oasis of the mind, preferably beside a reflecting pool.

He watches the water. He leans forward. He has glimpsed a form below; pale or dark, willowy or bird-rounded, as his taste has molded me. He looks up suddenly to find me standing upon the far shore. It is his first clear view, and always he is astonished to confront the personification of his dreams. Our eyes speak, a moment only.

Who are you?

Always the same question, always.

I do not answer in words. I am not yet certain that I possess a voice. It is only once in millennia that ever I will think to attempt speech. For now, my face, my eyes, and my body must speak; all trained in eloquence. Beyond doubt, he understands me. Or rather, he comprehends what I intend to communicate. A moment only, and then I fade from his view.

Come back. Don't go. Speak to me, please speak.

The same refrain, always the same; amazed, delighted, uncomprehending. Sometimes, I am almost sorry.

Wait. What is your name?

Unanswerable. I do not have a name.

His wish is shortly granted. I return. I do not speak, yet I allow him nearer. We touch; or perhaps he dreams that we touch. Thereafter, his sleep-spans increase in frequency and length. He is with me. He dreams.

He talks to me, always. He tells me of himself; his past, his future hopes, his grievances and triumphs. Always. I do not answer, but that is unimportant. My intensely attentive demeanor—my manifest sympathy and admiration—more than suffice to satisfy. My attentiveness is genuine. I listen closely indeed, for his revelations school me. Continually I modify the image that I have assumed, each tiny and almost imperceptible change bringing me closer in dumb show to the purest embodiment of his desires. I am skilled in this.

But these monologues teach more than his preferences. They tell me much of that other world, that harsh world of inviolable physical principle that he inhabits when he is not with me. It sounds a rigid, unforgiving place, shackled in regulation. There are laws governing the motion of moon and stars, governing sea and land and sky, warmth and cold, light and dark, life and death, governing time itself. The laws are tyrannical and innumerable. I do not believe that I could endure them for an instant. Only once, in millennia, will I reconsider.

He dreams on. His sleep-spans increase in length and frequency. He is spending more time here with me. I rule and own his thoughts. It is easy to capture him—are they all so easily caught? Or have I somehow been directed to the ultra-susceptible? No answer, and no real need of one. His existence centers upon my world. The hard-edged other place recedes.

But does not altogether disappear. Intimations of that alien world drift through his dreams to me. Out there, his condition has not gone unnoticed. There is concern, curiosity, perhaps ridicule. If he is cared for, there is often alarm.

What's wrong? Are you sick? Are you unhappy?

Are you drunk, are you drugged?

Angry? Thwarted? Bored? Is there somebody else?

Tell me. Speak to me, please speak.

The pleas, so familiar and repetitive, waft from that other world. They are not without pathos. Sometimes, I am almost sorry.

Always he ignores the queries and warnings. Perhaps he doubts; but never is he moved to turn away from me. I do not think he can turn away.

Our time together lengthens. He is asleep and dreaming almost continually, now. The voices from the other place have faded. He does not heed them, he does not hear. The dream world, the soft world of infinite possibility, my world, is the sole reality.

That is when it is time to leave him.

There is no explaining the inner voice that tells me when to go. My instinct specifies the moment. When his mind and soul are fully engaged —when he is wholly mine, when he is *gone*—then so am I.

Vanished. Out of his mind, out of his universe. I do not exist, I never existed.

What becomes of my dreamer, afterward? Surely he searches for me. Sometimes I catch the echo of his voice calling across the blind dark spaces. Perhaps he squanders his years vainly scouring the inner lands now dank with loss, now stinking with memory turned toxic. Perhaps, if he is wise, he finally abandons the hunt. And yet, somehow I know, that ultimate renunciation brings no peace; for his own world is thenceforth a desert—arid, meaningless, and forever empty.

And where do I go, when I depart? I cannot answer, I do not know. The dreamscape about me darkens, distances, *is not*. I myself am plunged into nothingness, for unknowable time, until I wake once more to find myself in a new place.

So it has always been; that is all my memory. Only once, in millennia, does it enter my mind to look for anything else.

It begins in the usual way. Muted light, a fresh locale. Quieter, with greater extremes of dark and bright than most. Gusts and calms impossible to anticipate. Knotted network of paths and passageways, unexpected turnings; hidden clearings, peaks and chasms, dust and brilliance, doubt-roofed cities, oddly shaped pockets of intention, regret, determination, jagged indecision. In short, an uncommon mind; yet not so alien that I might not hope to learn its shape.

And so I wander, watch, and learn, as always. A maze of a mind, eccentric in its alternating simplicities and intricacies; startling in the vastness of its dreamscape—this last a function less of intellect than of pure imagination. Such magnitude can be no accident. My current dreamer lives often in his own imagination. He has built and cultivated there. The signs of his habitation are everywhere; so evident that I grow curious, and half-concerned that I might stumble upon him unexpectedly, before I am ready to reveal myself. Mindful of this danger, I bury myself in shadow and mist; but it is not certain that these precautions safeguard my se-

crecy. Time passes, and I begin to sense his awareness. Despite all my
care, he feels my hidden presence, long before I intend that he should.
Such a thing has never happened before. I am astonished; even a little
disturbed.

I have never been disturbed. That, too, is new.

I wonder; but proceed, nonetheless. The usual rustlings and stirrings,
the usual tantalizing half-glimpses. Now he is very aware of me; intrigued
and inquisitive, but hardly feverish in his pursuit. He follows, but without
haste or desperation; as if relishing the novelty of the game. Clearly, he
knows the territory of his own dreams. He is at home in this place, almost
it seems his natural habitat. He is unusual, beyond doubt; still, like all the
others, he follows me.

The usual pursuit and teasing evasions. But no, not quite usual. It is
not so easy to elude him. Sometimes, he seems almost to anticipate my
movements. He dares to follow me through the midnight storms of his
mind. He is swift as thought, too. What if he were to catch up with me,
before I decide that it is time? I do not know what would happen, then. It
is outside my experience.

I do not prolong the chase. I do not wish to prolong it. It is time for us
to meet, more than time. Thus he beholds my reflection in the pool; his
fancy has fashioned me slim and silvery as dream-brightened starlight.
And he? It is my first clear sight of him, and this once, I am curious. The
image that walks the dreamscape does not always mirror the outer self;
but the figure I now see before me does so, I am certain. He is a young
man, absurdly young; thin and narrow-shouldered, with a pale, mild face.
There is nothing to betray the existence of the imagination that stretches,
vast and flamboyant, behind that unremarkable facade.

He looks up. He sees me. His face changes.

Who are you?

That question again. Perhaps he is less uncommon than I had supposed.

And then he adds, *You were never born here.*

I am startled. How does he know that? I am, after all, formed in the
image of his own fantasies. And yet, he knows. I am confused. I retreat.

Where have you come from?

I do not know. I am almost afraid. I vanish.

But it is inevitable that I return. I compose myself. I am with him
again, and now it is better. He is drawn to me, ensnared, entangled and
entranced; perhaps against his better judgment, but caught all the same.
He is not altogether unlike the others, after all.

Together we wander the gorgeous realm. Suspecting no harm, he talks to me at length. I do not reply, I never speak. And yet, for the first time, I think of answering. I do not know if this is possible, but once the idea has taken hold, it is not to be dislodged. I consider. What would I say to him, if I chose to speak, if I *could* speak? It is a new and astonishing puzzle; even a source of pleasure. I think of all that I might tell of what I have seen, and done, and been; all that I have never told, to anyone. There is no end at all, I realize, to the things that I might say.

But I do not try to say them. I listen, as always, while he tells me of his life. A placid, ordinary existence, on the surface of it. He lives in a timelocked northern hamlet, armored in ice throughout the endless winters. He has lived in this town all his life. He teaches children at the local school. The pay is meager, and he cares little for the work; but his education in literature and art has left him fit for few other forms of employment. And it is not all bad, by any means, for he is free throughout the slow summer months to walk in solitude and to live his inner life undisturbed. That inner life, as I well know, is rich, full and extraordinary as his outer life is colorless. He lives alone, and it suits him. He has few friends, for he has always been different, and considered strange. There is, however, a girl; another teacher at his school. She is not pretty, but her voice is melodious, and she too dreams.

The effect of this last revelation is astonishing. Alarm sweeps through me. There is doubt and confusion. And there is something more, something unfamiliar, which I finally identify as anger. Yes, that is certainly it —I am angry. I fade away, to leave him calling after me.

But I do not stay away for long. I have a mission, after all. Moreover, the colors are dull, the silences empty, when I am alone. Solitude has never troubled me; but it troubles me now. I return to him quickly, and he is glad. For the moment, it is enough.

But not for long.

Where does he go when he is not here with me? When he is in that other place, when he is awake? With none of the others have I thought to wonder; but that has changed now. He spends too much time away from me, I feel. Or is it that any time away is too much? I want to know what he is doing out there; what he is saying and thinking every moment that he is gone from my sight. I want to know when he is alone, and when he is walking under the trees with the girl he spoke of. He willingly tells me of his other life. But how do I know that he is telling the truth? And how do I know that he is telling everything? For I need to know everything. I will find a way to know. I will follow him to that other world if I must.

Follow him—out there? Another new and extraordinary thought.

I wonder if I can do it. I wonder if I even dare to try. And if I do, then how shall I begin? Where is the exit from the land of dreams? *He* passes back and forth with ease, but can I do the same? And if I succeed in breaking through, will the waking land support my existence? Is it not possible that I might even cease to be? Dangerous folly, the sort of madness exhibited by the dreamers I have abandoned. I will think of it no more.

But the wake-spans of his absence are unendurable. He is not enough mine. If he were wholly mine, if he belonged to me utterly, then he would never leave me, not for a single instant. Where does he go, what does he do, and with whom? I will know, it is worth any risk. The next time he leaves me, I will follow him, and I will learn the way out.

I do so. I am stealthy as newborn malice, but my care is unnecessary. He is of a guileless nature, and he suspects nothing. I am close behind him, watching as he rises, floating lazily at first, but then moving more purposefully, like a diver seeking the surface of the sea. He passes from my view. I hesitate, then follow, mounting to the very roof of the world, a place of lightning-shot mists. Formerly, such lightning has barred my path; but I will not allow it to do so now. I ascend. I am blind, chilled, lashed by the winds, and lost; but resolute as never before. I persevere. The mists are behind, and sight is restored to me.

I am in the other world. Never, never, have I envisioned such a place—so crushing, so remorseless in its solidity. The elements of my world are shaped and transformed with a breath, a thought, the shadow of a wish. But these present surroundings are all but impervious. The whole of my strength hardly serves to stir a particle of matter; and I, accustomed to flight's freedom, must now plod heavy-footed through a world that resists every movement. It is inexpressibly alien and fearsome.

But now is not the time for fear. I am here with a purpose. I must find him, watch him. Where has he gone? I look about me. This place, despite its unforgiving mass, possesses a certain heavy grandeur; but I do not recognize it. At first I imagine that I stand in a vast labyrinth; then it seems a machine, pulsing all about me, tremendous and unimaginably complex; and finally, I see that it is both labyrinth and machine in one. I have passed from his mind into the weighty physical structure whose mechanical function supports that mind. I trudge the convolutions of his brain. I am inside him, yet blind to his doings. That is not good enough. I search, I explore. The light attracts me. Slowly I make my way to its source, and I look out through the windows of his eyes.

He is in a room, roofed away from the sky. How small, how dim and shabby a room it is. Nothing at all like the jewelled chambers of his imagination. I can barely see the room, for there is nothing to see. He is not alone. The girl is there with him. She is not garbed in silvery radiance, as I am. She is squat, dull-fleshed, mud-colored of hair and eye. She conforms in no particular to the lyric fantasy-image that has shaped my current guise. She is drab as the room in which she stands, and surely she is nothing to him.

There is, however, the matter of her voice. He has praised her voice, and she is speaking now. I cannot hear her, but his eyes are turned to her face, and I can partly read the movement of her lips. The silent, splintered phrases fly to me:

. . . *Something wrong, so very wrong* . . .

I do not hear his reply, if any.

. . . *Worried about you* . . . *Afraid* . . . *Distant, as if* . . . *lost in a dreamworld* . . .

She is not stupid.

. . . *Miss you* . . . *Come back* . . . *Let me help* . . .

. . . *Doctor* . . . *appointment* . . . *Only talk* . . .

Promise . . . *promise* . . . *soon.*

Promise, promise, what has he promised her? I could not read it all, what did I miss? No matter.

The same phrases, the familiar, useless pleas that have so often found their way to me from this world. I have nothing to fear, nothing at all to fear from this girl. I am reassured. I am free to return to my own place. I know now what I will do.

When next he comes to me, I am ready. It is finally clear in my mind what it is that I want to say to him. When I speak for the first time, my voice echoes the richest silver music of his dreaming:

I love you.

Centuries elapse.

His smile is rueful:

You are not real.

Not real? This is his answer to me? This is what he believes? After all that has passed between us, surely he must know that I am real. But he abolishes my existence with a word. My sensations are unfamiliar, chaotic; but one I recognize. I am angry, as I was when he first spoke of the girl in the other world. But it is stronger this time, so strong I cannot contain it. My anger is all that I am.

He is staring into my eyes, and he shrinks from me as if I were suddenly ugly. He draws away, and then he is abruptly gone. In the other place, he has awakened. For the moment, he is beyond my reach.

I do not understand. I am the quintessence of his desires, and I love him. Why is he afraid? When he returns, he must tell me. I will make him tell me.

But he does not come back. Never, since the very beginning, has he stayed away from me so long. In the other place, he must be doing all that he can to keep himself awake. That is foolish and useless. He cannot go without sleep, none of them can. I need only wait.

Why does he make me wait? What is wrong with him? I cannot understand how he continues so long without sleep. He flouts me deliberately, it is not to be borne; but I must be patient, for now.

It ends at last, of course, and he is back. But even now, I cannot be content, for he contrives to avoid me. It seems that our roles are reversed, for now he flees, as I have always fled the dreamers I aimed to ensnare. He is elusive and tantalizing as ever I was. But unlike me, he runs in fear, his aspect newly haggard and hunted. Why? Does he not believe that I love him? Always he manages to lose himself in the mist and darkness, to veil himself in shadow and nothingness. I am never near enough to touch him. When I speak, he shuts out my voice. He will not look at me, and all my radiance is useless. If I corner him, he wakes himself, and I am defeated again.

He sleeps very little. He seeks refuge in the other place, where he supposes I cannot follow.

But he is wrong.

Following that first tentative exploration, I have never returned to his waking world. It is inimical, and there is nothing for me there. But I will go back once more. He has left me with little choice.

I remember the way. It is not an easy path, but I will follow it for love's sake. I make my way from the land of dreams. Once more I am in the labyrinth, whose walls quiver with life. All about me the living substance consumes its gaseous fuel. It is necessary activity, no doubt, but grossly mechanical; I would not consent to live in such a factory.

Laboriously, I make my way to the windows. Once more I look out through his eyes at a world pure with snow, dazzled with sunlit ice. This unblemished land could serve as a dreamscape. There is some beauty, then, in this place.

He is driving a car along a quiet, ice-glazed street. Yes, I have seen many cars, in many dreams; I know them well. He is alone, or so he believes. As he slows at a crossroad, his haunted eyes rise briefly to the little mirror, and I glimpse a portion of his waking-world face. Just as I have always supposed, it is the same pale, mild face that I have encountered in his dreams.

The car picks up speed. I do not know where he is going. Perhaps he intends to be with the girl. It is best that I reveal myself while he is alone. I speak, very clearly. And this time, in this place, he cannot shut out my voice:

I am real. I love you. I am very real.

He goes rigid. His eyes dart in all directions and his hands jerk on the steering wheel. The car swerves sharply, skids across the icy pavement, careers straight into a tree. The vehicle halts; its driver's head bumps the wheel, and I am violently jerked. Movement in this world is sometimes frighteningly uncontrollable. It is my instinct to flee for the safety of my own place, but I do not go yet. I linger to watch him.

He is not seriously injured. The functions of his waking-world body continue unimpaired. Yet he is groggy, dazed, hovering upon the verge of unconsciousness. I do not understand it.

His eyes have closed, blinding me to the outer world. I gaze about the labyrinth. Not far away, I see dark matter, a place wherein the bruised living walls are starved of the fuel that sustains them. In that spot, awareness clouds, and the path to my world lies open and clear, almost beckoning. No wonder he is drawn into sleep. Who could resist such an invitation? Yet he is trying to resist, he strives to shake himself fully awake. I wonder why? Certainly he is confused. Perhaps the summons to sleep is not clear enough, or strong enough. I will try adding my voice to it:

Come with me.

But that does no good, no good at all. Is there anything else that I might try? I study the surrounding walls. I consider the dark patch of clouded awareness, noting the shocked, starved tissue in that spot. If only that patch were larger, then surely he would return to my world, he would have no choice. But how can I enlarge it? What can I hope to accomplish here, in such a place?

Love has quickened my thoughts, perhaps, for I see a way. Here rise the great tubes along which his blood rushes, bearing its burden of fuel to the far reaches of his brain. If I should succeed in slowing that rush, will not the tissues hunger? And will not the barrier between his consciousness and my world thin to nothing?

I do not know if I can do it, but I will try; oh, how I will try.

Selecting one of the largest vessels, I twine myself about the tube and squeeze with all my strength. Within the circle of my arms, the pulsing flow slows to a trickle. Resenting restraint, his blood strains for freedom. I feel its power and urgency. I know I cannot hold it back for long, for here in this place, I am feeble. I do not know how much time I have, or how much time is required. I cling, squeeze, and throttle. It is endless. I am exhausted, but love sustains me. I am doing it for him.

My grip is failing. I weaken, I am done. But it has been enough. I turn to greet the spreading darkness. I had thought to broaden the path to my world, but I have done more. The two worlds meld; the distinction between sleep and waking is lost. Sleep is everywhere and everything and always.

I will not speak of my return to my own place. Rather, it has returned to me, and now, within the limits of my dreamer's being, there is no other place.

Outwardly, he must seem dead in all but name. But of course, I know better. He is here with me, forever; or at least, for as long as his motionless flesh-machine continues to function.

That may be for a very long time.

Does he realize all that I have done for him, and is he grateful? I am not certain, for we have not spoken.

He is avoiding me, I think. He spends his time searching for the way back to the other place, and he will not believe that the road is permanently closed. When I approach, he retreats. But this no longer troubles me, for time is on my side. In the end he will understand that it is the two of us, here alone together, always.

We are going to be so very happy.

Morgan Llywelyn

Princess

Born in New York City and raised in Dallas, "where I became horse-crazy,"
MORGAN LLYWELYN *now resides in County Wicklow, Eire, where she is virtu-*
ally a one-woman Irish chamber of commerce. The internationally best-
selling author of such acclaimed historical novels as Lion of Ireland, Bard
and The Horse Goddess, *Morgan contributed the unforgettable "Me, Tree"*
to my earlier Doubleday collection, Devils & Demons. *The deceptively*
alien, oddly familiar "Princess" first appeared in the Summer 1988 edition
of the new Weird Tales *magazine.*

ONE OF THEM heard someone call her princess and after that they all
called her Princess, thinking it was her name. They did not understand
the sarcasm implied in princess or honey or baby, applied to a tired
woman in middle years with an aching back and work-reddened hands.

They would come trooping in close to closing time, chattering among
themselves, and crowd close to the bar demanding drinks. "Orange bit-
ters, Princess," or "Whiskey, plenty of whiskey. In a big glass, Princess."
The tops of their heads hardly reached the level of the bar, and when she
brought the drinks they would jump up, their wrinkled grey faces and
bald skulls flashing into her vision as they caught glimpses of the glasses.
Then a scaly hand would come over the lip of the bar and seize the drink.
Out of sight there were gurglings and the smacking of lips, then the hand
deposited the empty glass back on the polished wood.

Feet pattered toward the door. "Good night, Princess!" one of them
always remembered to call.

A pile of coins glittered in payment for the drinks.

She neither laughed at them nor shrank away from them as the other townspeople did. Who was she to laugh at anyone? Homely old maid eking out a thin living in a rundown bar on the wrong side of a dying town. Her looks had always been a magnet for caustic comments, so she could feel a certain empathy with the ones who came in just before closing time, because the bar was emptiest then.

Every night she polished the glasses on her apron and rearranged the bottles and jugs behind the bar, glancing through the smeared window from time to time as if she were waiting for someone special. But there was no someone special, never had been.

She polished and waited as the smoke got thicker and thicker in the room, then what patrons she had began to straggle out, back to shabby houses and depressing flats not very different from her own. Gray lives.

At last the door swung inward instead of out and she felt the cold air blow in with them. If there were any people left in the bar, they always left then. No one seemed to want to stay.

People whispered that they had a mine of some sort up in the hills. Whatever it was, they made enough to pay for their drinks, though they never left any extra for a tip. But in time she noticed that the windows of the bar sparkled in the morning when she came down from the seedy apartment on the floor above, and the step in front was swept clean. Sometimes a jug of wildflowers waited for her just outside the door. One night it rained and she had forgotten to bring in the laundry, her thread-bare clothes and stained towels. In the morning she found them neatly folded and stacked under the overhang of the eaves, safe and dry.

One night one of the few regulars had too much to drink and said ugly things to her. He wasn't a mean man, but his tongue was rough. She would have cried if her tears had not all dried up long ago. Then the door swung inward; from behind the bar she could not see who entered, but the townsman did. He started to get up and then his face changed color and he sat down again, hard, on the barstool. She could hear the broken vinyl creak on the seat cushion. A thin thread of saliva dropped onto the man's chest from his parted lips. He drained his glass quickly and staggered out.

No one said ugly things to her after that.

Sometimes, lying on her narrow bed above the bar, she dreamed of a handsome man coming for her, driving up in front one day with a screech of tires. He would carry her away in a big car that smelled new inside, and she would never look back.

She knew it was a dream. But she still glanced out the window, sometimes. The few cars she saw were battered and dusty, like everything else in the town.

Still, she felt strangely content. Not happy, because she had never been happy and could not have identified the feeling if it crept up on her. But her life began to seem full and she had companionship of a sort.

"Princess," one of them would say out of her sight, over the edge of the bar, "you look nice tonight." They could not possibly see her, and she did not try to lean across and look down at them; it was better if you didn't look at them. But she would smile to herself and give her thinning hair a pat.

"Make me something hot to drink," the voice would say. "The night is cold; it's frozen the flanges of my nose."

Small titters from his companions. Not laughter; they did not laugh like people. They laughed as squirrels might, fast and shrill.

When they were in the bar no new customers entered. What business there was fell off. In time it was safe for them to come in the afternoon; there was no one in the room anyway to stare at them. The business, always shaky, should have failed completely. But it didn't. There always seemed to be just as much money in the register at the end of the day as there had been when townspeople came. And she liked it better, not having to put up with the problems townfolk brought.

She was standing on the other side of the bar one day, down at the end with her back toward the door, trying to repair the broken vinyl on the barstool with a piece of tape. She was holding her lower lip between her teeth and a wisp of hair kept falling down in her eyes. She was so preoccupied she didn't hear them come in. She thought she was alone until she felt the touch.

It was as light as cobweb, trailing up her leg. Under her skirt. Not attacking, not even invading. Just . . . exploring, with a gentle and innocent curiosity, like that of a blind person touching the face of a stranger.

She froze.

No one had ever touched her there before.

But an unaccustomed feeling of warmth permeated the core of her being, a feeling with a color—rose-gold—and a fragrance, the scent of honeysuckle blooming. She closed her eyes and stood immobile.

At last the touch ceased. The colors faded, the fragrance too. When she opened her eyes the bar was empty. But she knew something wonderful had come to her.

The next time the liquor wholesaler called on her she bought better brands of whiskey and some imported beers. She had never ordered good stuff before. The townspeople only drank the cheapest and wouldn't have known the difference. But the first time she poured the good liquor the stack of coins left on the counter afterwards was higher.

In fact, there seemed to be more money altogether, though she couldn't have explained how. When she added up her receipts she found she could afford to replace the seats on the barstools—not that anyone used them anymore. The only customers she had now were too short to climb up on them. She thought of ordering shorter barstools, then decided that would be vaguely ridiculous. No one was complaining.

Instead she went to the town's only emporium, which featured dead flies lying feet-up in the windows, and bought herself a new blouse. Soft, pretty, a sort of rosy-gold color. She got a little bottle of perfume, too. One that smelled like honeysuckle to her.

When she asked the salesgirl for face cream she was rewarded with a strange look, but the other woman didn't dare say anything. No one made any smart cracks about her anymore.

She rubbed the cream into her skin every night, in the flat above the bar. When she peered into the mirror she couldn't see that it made any difference, but her skin felt better. The wind off the desert had dried it out; now it was soft to the touch. She ran her fingertips across her cheek wonderingly.

The next night one of them put coins into the old jukebox in the corner that had been dead for fifteen years. It came to life with a shudder and a screech, and a baritone voice began celebrating, "The Way You Look Tonight."

The seasons passed; the town finished dying. There were no battered cars left to park on the streets, which were abandoned to blowing dust and an occasional tumbleweed, rolling along like a spidery bouquet. She didn't go out for food. There was always something in the pantry when she went to look for it. And when she emptied a bottle for her customers she began finding a full one behind it on the mirrored shelves back of the bar. Everything she needed was already there.

On the lazy afternoons and in the long, blue evenings there were only eight of them in the bar, the seven little creatures and the hunchbacked albino woman. But it was enough.

Edith Wharton

The Lady's Maid's Bell

Some of my favorite ghost stories dare to imply more than they state, and the following eerie tale is one of these. Its author, EDITH WHARTON (1862–1937), is remembered for such ironic novels of "polite society" as The House of Mirth *and* The Age of Innocence, *but her tragic, atypical New England novella "Ethan Frome" is probably her masterpiece.*

IT WAS THE AUTUMN after I had the typhoid. I'd been three months in hospital, and when I came out I looked so weak and tottery that the two or three ladies I applied to were afraid to engage me. Most of my money was gone, and after I'd boarded for two months, hanging about the employment agencies, and answering any advertisement that looked any way respectable, I pretty nearly lost heart, for fretting hadn't made me fatter, and I didn't see why my luck should ever turn. It did though—or I thought so at the time. A Mrs. Railton, a friend of the lady that first brought me out to the States, met me one day and stopped to speak to me: she was one that had always a friendly way with her. She asked me what ailed me to look so white, and when I told her, "Why, Hartley," says she, "I believe I've got the very place for you. Come in tomorrow and we'll talk about it."

The next day, when I called, she told me the lady she'd in mind was a niece of hers, a Mrs. Brympton, a youngish lady, but something of an invalid, who lived all the year round at her country place on the Hudson, owing to not being able to stand the fatigue of town life.

"Now, Hartley," Mrs Railton said, in that cheery way that always made me feel things must be going to take a turn for the better—"now under-stand me; it's not a cheerful place I'm sending you to. The house is big

and gloomy; my niece is nervous, vaporish; her husband—well he's generally away; and the two children are dead. A year ago I would as soon have
thought of shutting a rosy active girl like you into a vault; but you're not
particularly brisk yourself just now, are you? and a quiet place, with country air and wholesome food and early hours, ought to be the very thing for
you. Don't mistake me," she added, for I suppose I looked a trifle downcast; "you may find it dull but you won't be unhappy. My niece is an
angel. Her former maid, who died last spring, had been with her twenty
years and worshiped the ground she walked on. She's a kind mistress to
all, and where the mistress is kind, as you know, the servants are generally
good-humored, so you'll probably get on well enough with the rest of the
household. And you're the very woman I want for my niece: quiet, well-
mannered, and educated above your station. You read aloud well, I think?
That's a good thing; my niece likes to be read to. She wants a maid that
can be something of a companion: her last was, and I can't say how she
misses her. It's a lonely life. . . . Well, have you decided?"

"Why, ma'am," I said, "I'm not afraid of solitude."

"Well, then, go; my niece will take you on my recommendation. I'll
telegraph her at once and you can take the afternoon train. She has no
one to wait on her at present, and I don't want you to lose any time."

I was ready enough to start, yet something in me hung back; and to
gain time I asked, "And the gentleman, ma'am?"

"The gentleman's almost always away, I'll tell you," said Mrs. Railton,
quicklike—"and when he's there," says she suddenly, "you've only to
keep out of his way."

I took the afternoon train and got to the station at about four o'clock.
A groom in a dogcart was waiting, and we drove off at a smart pace. It was
a dull October day, with rain hanging close overhead, and by the time we
turned into Brympton Place woods the daylight was almost gone. The
drive wound through the woods for a mile or two, and came out on a
gravel court shut in with thickets of tall black-looking shrubs. There were
no lights in the windows, and the house *did* look a bit gloomy.

I had asked no questions of the groom, for I never was one to get my
notion of new masters from their other servants: I prefer to wait and see
for myself. But I could tell by the look of everything that I had got into
the right kind of house, and that things were done handsomely. A pleas-
ant-faced cook met me at the back door and called the housemaid to
show me up to my room. "You'll see madam later," she said. "Mrs.
Brympton has a visitor."

I hadn't fancied Mrs. Brympton was a lady to have many visitors, and somehow the words cheered me. I followed the housemaid upstairs, and saw, through a door on the upper landing, that the main part of the house seemed well furnished, with dark paneling and a number of old portraits. Another flight of stairs led up to the servants' wing. It was almost dark now, and the housemaid excused herself for not having brought a light. "But there's matches in your room," she said, "and if you go carefully you'll be all right. Mind the step at the end of the passage. Your room is just beyond."

I looked ahead as she spoke, and halfway down the passage I saw a woman standing. She drew back into a doorway as we passed and the housemaid didn't appear to notice her. She was a thin woman with a white face, and a dark gown and apron. I took her for the housekeeper and thought it odd that she didn't speak, but just gave me a long look as she went by. My room opened into a square hall at the end of the passage. Facing my door was another which stood open: the housemaid exclaimed when she saw it:

"There—Mrs. Blinder's left that door open again!" said she, closing it.

"Is Mrs. Blinder the housekeeper?"

"There's no housekeeper: Mrs. Blinder's the cook."

"And is that her room?"

"Laws, no," said the housemaid, crosslike. "That's nobody's room. It's empty, I mean, and the door hadn't ought to be open. Mrs. Brympton wants it kept locked."

She opened my door and led me into a neat room, nicely furnished, with a picture or two on the walls; and having lit a candle she took leave, telling me that the servants' hall tea was at six, and that Mrs. Brympton would see me afterward.

I found them a pleasant-spoken set in the servants' hall, and by what they let fall I gathered that, as Mrs. Railton had said, Mrs. Brympton was the kindest of ladies; but I didn't take much notice of their talk, for I was watching to see the pale woman in the dark gown come in. She didn't show herself, however, and I wondered if she ate apart; but if she wasn't the housekeeper, why should she? Suddenly it struck me that she might be a trained nurse, and in that case her meals would of course be served in her room. If Mrs. Brympton was an invalid it was likely enough she had a nurse. The idea annoyed me, I own, for they're not always the easiest to get on with, and if I'd known I shouldn't have taken the place. But there I was and there was no use pulling a long face over it; and not being one to ask questions I waited to see what would turn up.

When tea was over the housemaid said to the footman: "Has Mr.

Ranford gone?" and when he said yes, she told me to come up with her to Mrs. Brympton.

Mrs. Brympton was lying down in her bedroom. Her lounge stood near the fire and beside it was a shaded lamp. She was a delicate-looking lady, but when she smiled I felt there was nothing I wouldn't do for her. She spoke very pleasantly, in a low voice, asking me my name and age and so on, and if I had everything I wanted, and if I wasn't afraid of feeling lonely in the country.

"Not with you I wouldn't be, madam," I said, and the words surprised me when I'd spoken them, for I'm not an impulsive person; but it was just as if I'd thought aloud.

She seemed pleased at that, and said she hoped I'd continue in the same mind; then she gave me a few directions about her toilet, and said Agnes the housemaid would show me next morning where things were kept.

"I'm tired tonight, and shall dine upstairs," she said. "Agnes will bring me my tray, so that you may have time to unpack and settle yourself; and later you may come and undress me."

"Very well, ma'am," I said. "You'll ring, I suppose?"

I thought she looked odd.

"No—Agnes will fetch you," says she quickly, and took up her book again.

Well—that was certainly strange: a lady's maid having to be fetched by the housemaid whenever her lady wanted her! I wondered if there were no bells in the house; but the next day I satisfied myself that there was one in every room, and a special one ringing from my mistress's room to mine; and after that it did strike me as queer that, whenever Mrs. Brympton wanted anything, she rang for Agnes, who had to walk the whole length of the servants' wing to call me.

But that wasn't the only queer thing in the house. The very next day I found out that Mrs. Brympton had no nurse; and then I asked Agnes about the woman I had seen in the passage the afternoon before. Agnes said she had seen no one, and I saw that she thought I was dreaming. To be sure, it was dusk when we went down the passage, and she had excused herself for not bringing a light; but I had seen the woman plain enough to know her again if we should meet. I decided that she must have been a friend of the cook's, or of one of the other women servants; perhaps she had come down from town for a night's visit, and the servants wanted it kept secret. Some ladies are very stiff about having their servants' friends in the house overnight. At any rate, I made up my mind to ask no more questions.

In a day or two another odd thing happened. I was chatting one afternoon with Mrs. Blinder, who was a friendly-disposed woman, and had been longer in the house than the other servants, and she asked me if I was quite comfortable and had everything I needed. I said I had no fault to find with my place or with my mistress, but I thought it odd that in so large a house there was no sewing room for the lady's maid.

"Why," says she, "there *is* one: the room you're in is the old sewing room."

"Oh," said I; "and where did the other lady's maid sleep?"

At that she grew confused, and said hurriedly that the servants' rooms had all been changed about last year, and she didn't rightly remember.

That struck me as peculiar, but I went on as if I hadn't noticed: "Well, there's a vacant room opposite mine, and I mean to ask Mrs. Brympton if I mayn't use that as a sewing room."

To my astonishment, Mrs. Blinder went white, and gave my hand a kind of squeeze. "Don't do that, my dear," said she, trembling-like. "To tell you the truth, that was Emma Saxon's room, and my mistress has kept it closed ever since her death."

"And who was Emma Saxon?"

"Mrs. Brympton's former maid."

"The one that was with her so many years?" said I, remembering what Mrs. Railton had told me.

Mrs. Blinder nodded.

"What sort of woman was she?"

"No better walked the earth," said Mrs. Blinder. "My mistress loved her like a sister."

"But I mean—what did she look like?"

Mrs. Blinder got up and gave me a kind of angry stare. "I'm no great hand at describing," she said; "and I believe my pastry's rising." And she walked off into the kitchen and shut the door after her.

II

I had been near a week at Brympton before I saw my master. Word came that he was arriving one afternoon, and a change passed over the whole household. It was plain that nobody loved him below stairs. Mrs. Blinder took uncommon care with the dinner that night, but she snapped at the kitchenmaid in a way quite unusual with her; and Mr. Wace, the butler, a serious, slow-spoken man, went about his duties as if he'd been getting ready for a funeral. He was a great Bible reader, Mr. Wace was, and had a beautiful assortment of texts at his command; but that day he used such dreadful language, that I was about to leave the table, when he assured me it was all out of Isaiah; and I noticed that whenever the master came Mr. Wace took to the prophets.

About seven, Agnes called me to my mistress' room; and there I found Mr. Brympton. He was standing on the hearth; a big fair bull-necked man, with a red face and little bad-tempered blue eyes: the kind of man a young simpleton might have thought handsome, and would have been like to pay dear for thinking it.

He swung about when I came in, and looked me over in a trice. I knew what the look meant, from having experienced it once or twice in my former places. Then he turned his back on me, and went on talking to his wife; and I knew what *that* meant, too. I was not the kind of morsel he was after. The typhoid had served me well enough in one way: it kept that kind of gentleman at arm's length.

"This is my new maid, Hartley," says Mrs. Brympton in her kind voice; and he nodded and went on with what he was saying.

In a minute or two he went off, and left my mistress to dress for dinner, and I noticed as I waited on her that she was white, and chill to the touch.

Mr. Brympton took himself off the next morning, and the whole house drew a long breath when he drove away. As for my mistress, she put on her hat and furs (for it was a fine winter morning) and went out for a walk in the gardens, coming back quite fresh and rosy, so that for a minute, before her color faded, I could guess what a pretty young lady she must have been, and not so long ago, either.

She had met Mr. Ranford in the grounds, and the two came back together, I remember, smiling and talking as they walked along the terrace under my window. That was the first time I saw Mr. Ranford, though I had often heard his name mentioned in the hall. He was a neighbor, it appeared, living a mile or two beyond Brympton, at the end of the village; and as he was in the habit of spending his winters in the country he was almost the only company my mistress had at that season. He was a slight tall gentleman of about thirty, and I thought him rather melancholy looking till I saw his smile, which had a kind of surprise in it, like the first warm day in spring. He was a great reader, I heard, like my mistress, and the two were forever borrowing books of one another, and sometimes (Mr. Wace told me) he would read aloud to Mrs. Brympton by the hour, in the big dark library where she sat in the winter afternoons. The servants all liked him, and perhaps that's more of a compliment than the masters suspect. He had a friendly word for every one of us, and we were all glad to think that Mrs. Brympton had a pleasant companionable gentleman like that to keep her company when the master was away. Mr. Ranford seemed on excellent terms with Mr. Brympton too; though I couldn't but wonder that two gentlemen so unlike each other should be so friendly. But then I knew how the real quality can keep their feelings to themselves.

As for Mr. Brympton, he came and went, never staying more than a day or two, cursing the dullness and the solitude, grumbling at everything, and (as I soon found out) drinking a deal more than was good for him. After Mrs. Brympton left the table he would sit half the night over the old Brympton port and madeira, and once, as I was leaving my mistress's room rather later than usual, I met him coming up the stairs in such a state that I turned sick to think of what some ladies have to endure and hold their tongues about.

The servants said very little about their master; but from what they let drop I could see it had been an unhappy match from the beginning. Mr. Brympton was coarse, loud and pleasure-loving; my mistress quiet, retiring, and perhaps a trifle cold. Not that she was not always pleasant-spoken to him: I thought her wonderfully forbearing; but to a gentleman as free as Mr. Brympton I dare say she seemed a little offish.

Well, things went on quietly for several weeks. My mistress was kind, my duties were light, and I got on well with the other servants. In short, I had nothing to complain of; yet there was always a weight on me. I can't say why it was so, but I know it was not the loneliness that I felt. I soon got used to that; and being still languid from the fever, I was thankful for the quiet and the good country air. Nevertheless, I was never quite easy in my mind. My mistress, knowing I had been ill, insisted that I should take my walk regularly, and often invented errands for me: a yard of ribbon to be fetched from the village, a letter posted, or a book returned to Mr. Ranford. As soon as I was out of doors my spirits rose, and I looked forward to my walks through the bare moist-smelling woods; but the moment I caught sight of the house again my heart dropped down like a stone in a well. It was not a gloomy house exactly, yet I never entered it but a feeling of gloom came over me.

Mrs. Brympton seldom went out in winter; only on the finest days did she walk an hour at noon on the south terrace. Excepting Mr. Ranford, we had no visitors but the doctor, who drove over from town about once a week. He sent for me once or twice to give me some trifling direction about my mistress, and though he never told me what her illness was, I thought, from a waxy look she had now and then of a morning, that it might be the heart that ailed her. The season was soft and unwholesome, and in January we had a long spell of rain. That was a sore trial to me, I own, for I couldn't go out, and sitting over my sewing all day, listening to the drip, drip of the eaves, I grew so nervous that the least sound made me jump. Somehow, the thought of that locked room across the passage began to weigh on me. Once or twice, in the long rainy nights, I fancied I heard noises there; but that was nonsense, of course, and the daylight drove such notions out of my head. Well, one morning Mrs. Brympton gave me quite a start of pleasure by telling me she wished me to go to town for some shopping. I hadn't known till then how low my spirits had fallen. I set off in high glee, and my first sight of the crowded streets and the cheerful-looking shops quite took me out of myself. Toward afternoon, however, the noise and confusion began to tire me, and I was actually looking forward to the quiet of Brympton, and thinking how I should enjoy the drive home through the dark woods, when I ran across an old acquaintance, a maid I had once been in service with. We had lost sight of each other for a number of years, and I had to stop and tell her what had happened to me in the interval. When I mentioned where I was living she rolled up her eyes and pulled a long face.

"What! The Mrs. Brympton that lives all the year at her place on the Hudson? My dear, you won't stay there three months."

"Oh, but I don't mind the country," says I, offended somehow at her tone. "Since the fever I'm glad to be quiet."

She shook her head. "It's not the country I'm thinking of. All I know is she's had four maids in the last six months, and the last one, who was a friend of mine, told me nobody could stay in the house."

"Did she say why?" I asked.

"No—she wouldn't give me her reason. But she says to me, 'Mrs. Ansey,' she says, 'if ever a young woman as you know of thinks of going there, you tell her it's not worthwhile to unpack her boxes.'"

"Is she young and handsome?" said I, thinking of Mr. Brympton.

"Not her! She's the kind that mothers engage when they've gay young gentlemen at college."

Well, though I knew the woman was an idle gossip, the words stuck in my head, and my heart sank lower than ever as I drove up to Brympton in the dusk. There *was* something about the house—I was sure of it now. . . .

When I went in to tea I heard that Mr. Brympton had arrived, and I saw at a glance that there had been a disturbance of some kind. Mrs. Blinder's hand shook so that she could hardly pour the tea, and Mr. Wace quoted the most dreadful texts full of brimstone. Nobody said a word to me then, but when I went up to my room Mrs. Blinder followed me.

"Oh, my dear," says she, taking my hand, "I'm so glad and thankful you've come back to us!"

That struck me, as you may imagine. "Why," said I, "did you think I was leaving for good?"

"No, no, to be sure," said she, a little confused, "but I can't a-bear to have madam left alone for a day even." She pressed my hand hard, and, "Oh, Miss Hartley," says she, "be good to your mistress, as you're a Christian woman." And with that she hurried away, and left me staring.

A moment later Agnes called me to Mrs. Brympton. Hearing Mr. Brympton's voice in her room, I went round by the dressing room, thinking I would lay out her dinner gown before going in. The dressing room is a large room with a window over the portico that looks toward the gardens. Mr. Brympton's apartments are beyond. When I went in, the door into the bedroom was ajar, and I heard Mr. Brympton saying angrily: "One would suppose he was the only person fit for you to talk to."

"I don't have many visitors in winter," Mrs. Brympton answered quietly.

"You have *me!*" he flung at her, sneeringly.

"You are here so seldom," said she.

"Well—whose fault is that? You make the place about as lively as the family vault."

With that I rattled the toilet things, to give my mistress warning, and she rose and called me in.

The two dined alone, as usual, and I knew by Mr. Wace's manner at supper that things must be going badly. He quoted the prophets something terrible, and worked on the kitchenmaid so that she declared she wouldn't go down alone to put the cold meat in the icebox. I felt nervous myself, and after I had put my mistress to bed I was half tempted to go down again and persuade Mrs. Blinder to sit up awhile over a game of cards. But I heard her door closing for the night and so I went on to my own room. The rain had begun again, and the drip, drip, drip seemed to be dropping into my brain. I lay awake listening to it, and turning over what my friend in town had said. What puzzled me was that it was always the maids who left. . . .

After a while I slept; but suddenly a loud noise wakened me. My bell had rung. I sat up, terrified by the unusual sound, which seemed to go on jangling through the darkness. My hands shook so that I couldn't find the matches. At length I struck a light and jumped out of bed. I began to think I must have been dreaming; but I looked at the bell against the wall, and there was the little hammer still quivering.

I was just beginning to huddle on my clothes when I heard another sound. This time it was the door of the locked room opposite mine softly opening and closing. I heard the sound distinctly, and it frightened me so that I stood stock still. Then I heard a footstep hurrying down the passage toward the main house. The floor being carpeted, the sound was very faint, but I was quite sure it was a woman's step. I turned cold with the thought of it, and for a minute or two I dursn't breathe or move. Then I came to my senses.

"Alice Hartley," says I to myself, "someone left that room just now and ran down the passage ahead of you. The idea isn't pleasant, but you may as well face it. Your mistress has rung for you, and to answer her bell you've got to go the way that other woman has gone."

Well—I did it. I never walked faster in my life, yet I thought I should never get to the end of the passage or reach Mrs. Brympton's room. On the way I heard nothing and saw nothing: all was dark and quiet as the grave. When I reached my mistress's door the silence was so deep that I began to think I must be dreaming, and was half minded to turn back. Then a panic seized me, and I knocked.

There was no answer, and I knocked again, loudly. To my astonishment the door was opened by Mr. Brympton. He started back when he saw me, and in the light of my candle his face looked red and savage.

"*You?*" he said, in a queer voice. "*How many of you are there, in God's name?*"

At that I felt the ground give under me; but I said to myself that he had been drinking, and answered as steadily as I could: "May I go in, sir? Mrs. Brympton has rung for me."

"You may all go in, for what I care," says he, and, pushing by me, walked down the hall to his own bedroom. I looked after him as he went, and to my surprise I saw that he walked as straight as a sober man.

I found my mistress lying very weak and still, but she forced a smile when she saw me, and signed to me to pour out some drops for her. After that she lay without speaking, her breath coming quick, and her eyes closed. Suddenly she groped out with her hand, and "*Emma,*" says she, faintly.

"It's Hartley, madam," I said. "Do you want anything?"

She opened her eyes wide and gave me a startled look.

"I was dreaming," she said. "You may go, now, Hartley, and thank you kindly. I'm quite well again, you see." And she turned her face away from me.

III

There was no more sleep for me that night, and I was thankful when daylight came.

Soon afterward, Agnes called me to Mrs. Brympton. I was afraid she was ill again, for she seldom sent for me before nine, but I found her sitting up in bed, pale and drawn-looking, but quite herself.

"Hartley," says she quickly, "will you put on your things at once and go down to the village for me? I want this prescription made up—" here she hesitated a minute and blushed "—and I should like you to be back again before Mr. Brympton is up."

"Certainly, madam," I said.

"And—stay a moment—" she called me back as if an idea had just struck her "—while you're waiting for the mixture, you'll have time to go on to Mr. Ranford's with this note."

It was a two-mile walk to the village, and on my way I had time to turn things over in my mind. It struck me as peculiar that my mistress should wish the prescription made up without Mr. Brympton's knowledge; and, putting this together with the scene of the night before, and with much else that I had noticed and suspected, I began to wonder if the poor lady was weary of her life, and had come to the mad resolve of ending it. The idea took such hold on me that I reached the village on a run, and dropped breathless into a chair before the chemist's counter. The good man, who was just taking down his shutters, stared at me so hard that it brought me to myself.

"Mr. Limmel," I says, trying to speak indifferently, "will you run your eye over this, and tell me if it's quite right?"

He put on his spectacles and studied the prescription.

"Why, it's one of Dr. Walton's," says he. "What should be wrong with it?"

"Well—is it dangerous to take?"

"Dangerous—how do you mean?"

I could have shaken the man for his stupidity.

"I mean—if a person was to take too much of it—by mistake of course—" says I, my heart in my throat.

"Lord bless you, no. It's only lime water. You might feed it to a baby by the bottleful."

I gave a great sigh of relief and hurried on to Mr. Ranford's. But on the way another thought struck me. If there was nothing to conceal about my visit to the chemist's, was it my other errand that Mrs. Brympton wished me to keep private? Somehow, that thought frightened me worse than the other. Yet the two gentlemen seemed fast friends, and I would have staked my head on my mistress's goodness. I felt ashamed of my suspicions, and concluded that I was still disturbed by the strange events of the night. I left the note at Mr. Ranford's, and hurrying back to Brympton, slipped in by a side door without being seen, as I thought.

An hour later, however, as I was carrying in my mistress's breakfast, I was stopped in the hall by Mr. Brympton.

"What were you doing out so early?" he says, looking hard at me.

"Early—me, sir?" I said, in a tremble.

"Come, come," he says, an angry red spot coming out on his forehead, "didn't I see you scuttling home through the shrubbery an hour or more ago?"

I'm a truthful woman by nature, but at that a lie popped out ready-made. "No, sir, you didn't," said I and looked straight back at him.

He shrugged his shoulders and gave a sullen laugh. "I suppose you think I was drunk last night?" he asked suddenly.

"No, sir, I don't," I answered, this time truthfully enough.

He turned away with another shrug. "A pretty notion my servants have of me!" I heard him mutter as he walked off.

Not till I had settled down to my afternoon's sewing did I realize how the events of the night had shaken me. I couldn't pass that locked door without a shiver. I knew I had heard someone come out of it, and walk down the passage ahead of me. I thought of speaking to Mrs. Blinder or to Mr. Wace, the only two in the house who appeared to have an inkling of what was going on, but I had a feeling that if I questioned them they would deny everything, and that I might learn more by holding my tongue and keeping my eyes open. The idea of spending another night opposite the locked room sickened me, and once I was seized with the notion of packing my trunk and taking the first train to town; but it wasn't in me to throw over a kind mistress in that manner, and I tried to go on with my sewing as if nothing had happened. I hadn't worked ten minutes before the sewing machine broke down. It was one I had found in the house, a good machine but a trifle out of order: Mrs. Blinder said it had never been used since Emma Saxon's death. I stopped to see what was wrong, and as I was working at the machine a drawer which I had never been able to open slid forward and a photograph fell out. I picked it up and sat looking at it in a maze. It was a woman's likeness, and I knew I had seen the face somewhere—the eyes had an asking look that I had felt on me before. And suddenly I remembered the pale woman in the passage.

I stood up, cold all over, and ran out of the room. My heart seemed to be thumping in the top of my head, and I felt as if I should never get away from the look in those eyes. I went straight to Mrs. Blinder. She was taking her afternoon nap, and sat up with a jump when I came in.

"Mrs. Blinder," said I, "who is that?" And I held out the photograph.

She rubbed her eyes and stared.

"Why, Emma Saxon," says she. "Where did you find it?"

I looked hard at her for a minute. "Mrs. Blinder," I said, "I've seen that face before."

Mrs. Blinder got up and walked over to the looking glass. "Dear me! I must have been asleep," she says. "My front is all over one ear. And now do run along, Miss Hartley, dear, for I hear the clock striking four, and I must go down this very minute and put on the Virginia ham for Mr. Brympton's dinner."

IV

To all appearances, things went on as usual for a week or two. The only difference was that Mr. Brympton stayed on, instead of going off as he usually did, and that Mr. Ranford never showed himself. I heard Mr. Brympton remark on this one afternoon when he was sitting in my mistress' room before dinner:

"Where's Ranford?" says he. "He hasn't been near the house for a week. Does he keep away because I'm here?"

Mrs. Brympton spoke so low that I couldn't catch her answer.

"Well," he went on, "two's company and three's trumpery; I'm sorry to be in Ranford's way, and I suppose I shall have to take myself off again in a day or two and give him a show." And he laughed at his own joke.

The very next day, as it happened, Mr. Ranford called. The footman said the three were very merry over their tea in the library, and Mr. Brympton strolled down to the gate with Mr. Ranford when he left.

I have said that things went on as usual; and so they did with the rest of the household; but as for myself, I had never been the same since the night my bell had rung. Night after night I used to lie awake, listening for it to ring again, and for the door of the locked room to open stealthily. But the bell never rang, and I heard no sound across the passage. At last the silence began to be more dreadful to me than the most mysterious sounds. I felt that *someone* was cowering there, behind the locked door, watching and listening as I watched and listened, and I could almost have cried out, "Whoever you are, come out and let me see you face to face, but don't lurk there and spy on me in the darkness!"

Feeling as I did, you may wonder I didn't give warning. Once I very nearly did so; but at the last moment something held me back. Whether it was compassion for my mistress, who had grown more and more dependent on me, or unwillingness to try a new place, or some other feeling that I couldn't put a name to, I lingered on as if spellbound, though every night was dreadful to me, and the days but little better.

For one thing, I didn't like Mrs. Brympton's looks. She had never been the same since that night, no more than I had. I thought she would brighten up after Mr. Brympton left, but though she seemed easier in her mind, her spirits didn't revive, nor her strength either. She had grown attached to me, and seemed to like to have me about; and Agnes told me one day that, since Emma Saxon's death, I was the only maid her mistress had taken to. This gave me a warm feeling for the poor lady, though after all there was little I could do to help her.

After Mr. Brympton's departure, Mr. Ranford took to coming again, though less often than formerly. I met him once or twice in the grounds, or in the village, and I couldn't but think there was a change in him too; but I set it down to my disordered fancy.

The weeks passed, and Mr. Brympton had now been a month absent. We heard he was cruising with a friend in the West Indies, and Mr. Wace said that was a long way off, but though you had the wings of a dove and went to the uttermost parts of the earth, you couldn't get away from the Almighty. Agnes said that as long as he stayed away from Brympton the Almighty might have him and welcome; and this raised a laugh, though Mrs. Blinder tried to look shocked, and Mr. Wace said the bears would eat us.

We were all glad to hear that the West Indies were a long way off, and I remember that, in spite of Mr. Wace's solemn looks, we had a very merry dinner that day in the hall. I don't know if it was because of my being in better spirits, but I fancied Mrs. Brympton looked better too, and seemed more cheerful in her manner. She had been for a walk in the morning, and after luncheon she lay down in her room, and I read aloud to her. When she dismissed me I went to my own room feeling quite bright and happy, and for the first time in weeks walked past the locked door without thinking of it. As I sat down to my work I looked out and saw a few snowflakes falling. The sight was pleasanter than the eternal rain, and I pictured to myself how pretty the bare gardens would look in their white mantle. It seemed to me as if the snow would cover up all the dreariness, indoors as well as out.

The fancy had hardly crossed my mind when I heard a step at my side. I looked up, thinking it was Agnes.

"Well, Agnes—" said I, and the words froze on my tongue; for there, in the door, stood *Emma Saxon*.

I don't know how long she stood there. I only know I couldn't stir or take my eyes from her. Afterward I was terribly frightened, but at the time it wasn't fear I felt, but something deeper and quieter. She looked at me long and hard, and her face was just one dumb prayer to me—but how in the world was I to help her? Suddenly she turned, and I heard her walk down the passage. This time I wasn't afraid to follow—I felt that I must know what she wanted. I sprang up and ran out. She was at the other end of the passage, and I expected her to take the turn toward my mistress's room; but instead of that she pushed open the door that led to the backstairs. I followed her down the stairs, and across the passageway to the back door. The kitchen and hall were empty at that hour, the servants being off duty, except for the footman, who was in the pantry. At the door she stood still a moment, with another look at me; then she turned the handle, and stepped out. For a minute I hesitated. Where was she leading me to? The door had closed softly after her, and I opened it and looked out, half-expecting to find that she had disappeared. But I saw her a few yards off hurrying across the courtyard to the path through the woods. Her figure looked black and lonely in the snow, and for a second my heart failed me and I thought of turning back. But all the while she was drawing me after her; and catching up an old shawl of Mrs. Blinder's I ran out into the open.

Emma Saxon was in the wood path now. She walked on steadily, and I followed at the same pace, till we passed out of the gates and reached the highroad. Then she struck across the open fields to the village. By this time the ground was white, and as she climbed the slope of a bare hill ahead of me I noticed that she left no footprints behind her. At sight of that my heart shriveled up within me, and my knees were water. Somehow, it was worse here than indoors. She made the whole countryside seem lonely as the grave, with none but us two in it, and no help in the wide world.

Once I tried to go back; but she turned and looked at me, and it was as if she had dragged me with ropes. After that I followed her like a dog. We came to the village and she led me through it, past the church and the blacksmith's shop, and down the lane to Mr. Ranford's. Mr. Ranford's house stands close to the road: a plain old-fashioned building, with a flagged path leading to the door between box borders. The lane was deserted, and as I turned into it I saw Emma Saxon pause under the old elm by the gate. And now another fear came over me. I saw that we had reached the end of our journey, and that it was my turn to act. All the way from Brympton I had been asking myself what she wanted of me, but I had followed in a trance, as it were, and not till I saw her stop at Mr. Ranford's gate did my brain begin to clear itself. I stood a little way off in the snow, my heart beating fit to strangle me, and my feet frozen to the ground; and she stood under the elm and watched me.

I knew well enough that she hadn't led me there for nothing. I felt there was something I ought to say or do—but how was I to guess what it was? I had never thought harm of my mistress and Mr. Ranford, but I was sure now that, from one cause or another, some dreadful thing hung over them. *She* knew what it was; she would tell me if she could; perhaps she would answer if I questioned her.

It turned me faint to think of speaking to her; but I plucked up heart and dragged myself across the few yards between us. As I did so, I heard the house door open and saw Mr. Ranford approaching. He looked handsome and cheerful, as my mistress had looked that morning, and at sight of him the blood began to flow again in my veins.

"Why, Hartley," said he, "what's the matter? I saw you coming down the lane just now, and came out to see if you had taken root in the snow." He stopped and stared at me. "What are you looking at?" he says.

I turned toward the elm as he spoke and his eyes followed me; but there was no one there. The lane was empty as far as the eye could reach.

A sense of helplessness came over me. She was gone, and I had not been able to guess what she wanted. Her last look had pierced me to the marrow; and yet it had not told me! All at once, I felt more desolate than when she had stood there watching me. It seemed as if she had left me all alone to carry the weight of the secret I couldn't guess. The snow went round me in great circles, and the ground fell away from me. . . .

A drop of brandy and the warmth of Mr. Ranford's fire soon brought me to, and I insisted on being driven back at once to Brympton. It was nearly dark, and I was afraid my mistress might be wanting me. I explained to Mr. Ranford that I had been out for a walk and had been taken with a fit of giddiness as I passed his gate. This was true enough; yet I never felt more like a liar than when I said it.

When I dressed Mrs. Brympton for dinner she remarked on my pale looks and asked what ailed me. I told her I had a headache, and she said she would not require me again that evening, and advised me to go to bed.

It was a fact that I could scarcely keep on my feet; yet I had no fancy to spend a solitary evening in my room. I sat downstairs in the hall as long as I could hold my head up; but by nine I crept upstairs, too weary to care what happened if I could but get my head on a pillow. The rest of the household went to bed soon afterward; they kept early hours when the master was away, and before ten I heard Mrs. Blinder's door close, and Mr. Wace's soon after.

It was a very still night, earth and air all muffled in snow. Once in bed I felt easier, and lay quiet, listening to the strange noises that come out in a house after dark. Once I thought I heard a door open and close again below: it might have been the glass door that led to the gardens. I got up and peered out of the window; but it was in the dark of the moon, and nothing visible outside but the streaking of snow against the panes.

I went back to bed and must have dozed, for I jumped awake to the furious ringing of my bell. Before my head was clear I had sprung out of bed, and was dragging on my clothes. *It is going to happen now*, I heard myself saying; but what I meant I had no notion. My hands seemed to be covered with glue—I thought I should never get into my clothes. At last I opened my door and peered down the passage. As far as my candle flame carried, I could see nothing unusual ahead of me. I hurried on, breathless; but as I pushed open the baize door leading to the main hall my heart stood still, for there at the head of the stairs was Emma Saxon, peering dreadfully down into the darkness.

For a second I couldn't stir; but my hand slipped from the door, and as it swung shut the figure vanished. At the same instant there came another sound from below stairs—a stealthy mysterious sound, as of a latchkey turning in the house door. I ran to Mrs. Brympton's room and knocked.

There was no answer, and I knocked again. This time I heard someone moving in the room; the bolt slipped back and my mistress stood before me. To my surprise I saw that she had not undressed for the night. She gave me a startled look.

"What is this, Hartley?" she says in a whisper. "Are you ill? What are you doing here at this hour?"

"I am not ill, Madam; but my bell rang."

At that she turned pale, and seemed about to fall.

"You are mistaken," she said harshly; "I didn't ring. You must have been dreaming." I had never heard her speak in such a tone. "Go back to bed," she said, closing the door on me.

But as she spoke I heard sounds again in the hall below: a man's step this time; and the truth leaped out on me.

"Madam," I said, pushing past her, "there is someone in the house—"

"Someone—?"

"Mr. Brympton, I think—I hear his step below—"

A dreadful look came over her, and without a word, she dropped flat at my feet. I fell on my knees and tried to lift her: by the way she breathed I saw it was no common faint. But as I raised her head there came quick steps on the stairs and across the hall: the door was flung open, and there stood Mr. Brympton, in his traveling clothes, the snow dripping from him. He drew back with a start as he saw me kneeling by my mistress.

"What the devil is this?" he shouted. He was less high-colored than usual, and the red spot came out on his forehead.

"Mrs. Brympton has fainted, sir," said I.

He laughed unsteadily and pushed by me. "It's a pity she didn't choose a more convenient moment. I'm sorry to disturb her, but—"

I raised myself up aghast at the man's action.

"Sir," said I, "are you mad? What are you doing?"

"Going to meet a friend," said he, and seemed to make for the dressing room.

At that my heart turned over. I don't know what I thought or feared; but I sprang up and caught him by the sleeve.

"Sir, sir," said I, "for pity's sake look at your wife!"

He shook me off furiously.

"It seems that's done for me," says he, and caught hold of the dressing room.

At that moment I heard a slight noise inside. Slight as it was, he heard it too, and tore the door open; but as he did so he dropped back. On the threshold stood Emma Saxon. All was dark behind her, but I saw her plainly, and so did he. He threw up his hands as if to hide his face from her; and when I looked again she was gone.

He stood motionless, as if the strength had run out of him; and in the stillness my mistress suddenly raised herself, and opening her eyes fixed a look on him. Then she fell back, and I saw the death flutter pass over her face. . . .

We buried her on the third day, in a driving snowstorm. There were few people in the church, for it was bad weather to come from town, and I've a notion my mistress was one that hadn't many near friends. Mr. Ranford was among the last to come, just before they carried her up the aisle. He was in black, of course, being so pale. As he passed me, I noticed that he leaned a trifle on a stick he carried; and I fancy Mr. Brympton noticed it too, for the red spot came out sharp on his forehead, and all through the service he kept staring across the church at Mr. Ranford, instead of following the prayers as a mourner should.

When it was over and we went out to the graveyard, Mr. Ranford had disappeared, and as soon as my poor mistress's body was underground, Mr. Brympton jumped into the carriage nearest the gate and drove off without a word to any of us. I heard him call out, "To the station," and we servants went back alone to the house.

Toby Sanders

The Satyr

TOBY SANDERS, *a native Pennsylvanian, former circus performer and author of* How to Be a Compleat Clown *(Stein and Day, 1978), is currently a New York City schoolteacher. In "The Satyr," Mr. Sanders, a fluent scholar of Asian language and literature, provides an English version of an authentic Chinese ghost story.*

CHINESE GHOSTS are different from Western ghosts in one very particular sense. They have the uncontrollable urge to shock mortals into exemplary behavior. Even thinking about straying from the path of propriety is enough to attract them. Such was the case of Supervisor Wang.

Wang could be seen every day standing by the bulletin board at the main entrance of the factory. He would stare longingly at the women arriving and departing. Occasionally he would try to strike up a conversation with some of them or invite them to lunch. It was not his fault that shyness and inexperience made his invitations seem awkward. The end result was that the younger women avoided him and the older women teased him. This was unfortunate because he had no ulterior motive other than to meet a nice girl.

When he was with his drinking buddies he was forced to listen to their suggestive remarks. They knew Wang was in charge of only women. He had many opportunities, more than most men. Why didn't he have a girlfriend?

Wang bore his friends' taunts as long as he could. Finally, in self-defense he began to brag. He told his friends that he could touch any woman on his shift anyplace and the women could do nothing about it.

As long as he pretended the touch was an unavoidable accident while instructing the women under him, nobody could complain.

This was a harmless boast and would have remained so, but Wang felt pressured to live up to the image he had created for himself. Every day he began maneuvering closer to his charges in an attempt to attain any sort of intimate contact. His attempts did not go unnoticed by the women on his shift, who jokingly started to call him "the letch." The joke got out of hand one day when he accidentally touched one woman's thigh and she screamed. After that, his suggestive behavior was the talk of the factory. He had a reputation.

One day he received word that the manager wanted to speak to him. He was frightened because of the way he had been behaving. However, he was relieved to learn the only purpose of the manager's summons was to inform him he would be assigned to train ten new women on the night shift.

He arrived early that night after a quick shower and change. He stood by the door and, with a critical eye, watched the new women enter. One of them was so beautiful that he was instantly overwhelmed. He was unable to give clear instructions to the group because he could not take his eyes off her. An older woman was forced to demonstrate the job to the new employees.

During the shift, Wang kept moving closer to the object that so allured him. He watched her work until she made a mistake, then he stepped behind her and showed her the error in her work, using the opportunity to press against her as close as he could get.

To his surprise, the woman did not object. She merely faced him and laughed. Her action took him aback—especially when he looked down and discovered that her body hadn't moved at all, only her head. As he stared, horrified, her head literally began to spin. Wang sought help from the other employees, only to see that their heads, too, were twisted backward, and beginning to spin. The women's hands remained busy at their work, but every head revolved amidst the sound of mocking laughter.

Wang fled the place and stayed home for the next few days. He could not tell his employer that he had been visited by an entire company of ghosts. Nor did he ever again boast to his friends, even though he could have truthfully claimed that he'd met a large body of women whose heads all turned for him.

Honoré de Balzac

Don Juan; or The Elixir of Long Life

A collection of amorous tales would hardly be complete without some exploit of that infamous blasphemer Don Juan, and the following novella is one of the most unusual "Don" stories ever penned. HONORÉ DE BALZAC (1799–1850) *was the ambitious French author of the* Comédie Humaine, *an interconnected sequence of ninety-one novels and tales that led some authors and critics, notably Henry James, to honor Balzac as the world's greatest novelist.*

ON A WINTER'S NIGHT, in a sumptuous palace at Ferrara, Don Juan Belvidero was entertaining a Prince of the house of Este. At this period a banquet was a wonderful scene, possible only for the riches of royalty and the power of Princes.

Round a table lit with perfumed tapers sat seven joyous women bandying sweet talk. About them the noblest marble of the greatest masters gleamed white against walls of crimson stucco, and formed a contrast with the gorgeous colors of carpets brought from Turkey.

These women, clad in satin, glittering with gold, loaded with jewels only less brilliant than their eyes, told each her tale of overpowering passions, diverse as their own charms. But among them was no difference either of thought or expression; a movement, a look, a gesture supplied their words with commentaries wanton, lewd, melancholy, or scoffing.

One seemed to say: "My beauty can rekindle the ice-bound heart of age."

Another: "I love to lie couched among my cushions and think, drunk with the passion of those who adore me."

A third, a novice at such feasts, would fain have blushed. "In the depth of my heart," she said, "I feel remorse! I am a Catholic, and I fear hell. But I love you so much, so—so much that for you I can sacrifice eternity."

The fourth cried, as she drained a cup of Chian wine: "Joy, joy forever! Each morning dawns for me a new existence; each evening I drink deep of life, the life of happiness, the life of desire!"

The woman who sat by Belvidero looked at him with eyes of flame. She was silent. "I should not need a bravo to kill my lover if he deserted me!" She laughed; but her hand crushed convulsively a comfit box of wonderful workmanship.

"When shall you be Grand Duke?" asked a sixth of the Prince, an expression of murderous pleasure in her teeth, of bacchic delirium in her eyes.

"And you, when will your father be dead?" said the seventh, throwing her bouquet at Don Juan with a gesture of maddening playfulness. She was a girl, young and innocent, wont to laugh at all things sacred.

"Ah! do not speak of it," cried the young and handsome Juan Belvidero. "There is only one eternal father in the world, and as ill-luck will have it, he is mine."

The seven courtesans of Ferrara, the friends of Don Juan, and even the Prince himself, cried out with horror. Two hundred years later, under Louis XV, the most cultivated society would have laughed at this sally, but perhaps also, at the beginning of an orgy, the soul still sees with clearer eyes. In spite of the flame of candles, the fume of wines, the sight of gold and silver vessels; in spite of the cry of passion and the presence of women most ravishing to look upon, perchance there still brooded in the depths of their hearts a little of that reverence for human and divine things which still struggles on, until it is drowned by debauchery in the last sparkling waves of wine. Nevertheless, their flowers were already faded, their eyes already clouded, and drunkenness possessed them, after the saying of Rabelais, "Down to the heels of their boots." During a moment of silence a door opened, and, as at the feast of Belshazzar, God revealed Himself. He appeared under the form of an old servant, with white hair and wrinkled brow, and tottering footsteps. He entered with an air of sadness, and withered with one look the garlands, and the bowls of golden plate, and the pyramids of fruit, and all the brightness of the banquet, and the flush on the scared faces of the banqueters, and the colors of the cushions pressed by the white arms of the women; lastly, he cast a pall upon their revelry when with hollow voice he murmured these solemn words, "Sire, your father is dying." Don Juan rose, making a sign to his guests which might have been interpreted thus, "Excuse me, but this is not a thing which happens every day."

Does not a father's death often startle a young man in the midst of the splendors of life, in the very lap of frenzied debauchery? Death is as sudden in his whims as is a courtesan, but he is truer—he has never deceived any man.

When the door of the hall was shut, and Don Juan was passing through a long, gloomy gallery, where the cold was as great as the gloom, he bethought him of his part as a son, and strove to wear a mask to fit the filial character; for his mirth he had thrown aside with his napkin. The night was black. The silent servant who led the young man to the chamber of death lighted the way so dimly that Death was able, by the help of the cold, and the silence, and the gloom—and perhaps too of a recoil from drunkenness—to insinuate certain reflections into the mind of the reveller. He examined his life and grew thoughtful, as a man at law with another, on his way to the court.

Bartolomeo Belvidero, the father of Don Juan, was an old man of ninety years, who had spent almost all his life in the mazes of commerce. Having often travelled over the magic countries of the East, he had there acquired immense riches, and knowledge more precious, he said, than gold or diamonds; indeed for these he now cared scarcely at all. "I prefer a tooth to a ruby, and power to knowledge," he sometimes cried, and smiled as he spoke. This kind father loved to hear Don Juan relate his youthful frolics, and would say jestingly, as he lavished his gold upon him, "My dear child, only commit such follies as will really amuse thee." He was the only old man who has ever taken pleasure in the sight of another man's youth; his paternal love cheated his white hairs as he contemplated the brilliancy of this young life. At the age of sixty Belvidero became enamored of an angel of peace and beauty; Don Juan was the only fruit of this late and short-lived love. Now for fifteen years the old man had deplored the loss of his dear Juana; it was to this affliction of his old age that his numerous servitors and his son attributed the strange habits which he had contracted. Shut up in the most incommodious wing of his palace, he very rarely left it, and Don Juan himself could not penetrate into his father's apartment without having first obtained his permission. If this voluntary anchorite walked in his own palace or through the streets of Ferrara, he seemed to be searching for something he had lost. He walked as though in a dream, with undecided steps, preoccupied, like a man at war with an idea or a memory.

While the young man gave the most sumptuous banquets and the palace rang with bursts of merriment—while horses champed their bits in the courtyard and pages quarreled over their dice on the steps— Bartolomeo ate seven ounces of bread a day and drank water. If he required a little game, it was only to give the bones to a black spaniel, which was his constant companion. He never complained of the noise; during his sickness, if the sound of the horn and the baying of dogs startled him while he slept, he would only say, "Ah! it is Don Juan returning!" So complacent and indulgent a father was never met with before; thus the young Belvidero, being wont to treat him without consideration, had all the faults of spoilt children. He lived with Bartolomeo as a capricious courtesan lives with an old lover; he gained indulgence for impertinences by a smile; he sold him his good humor, and only allowed his love. As Don Juan reconstructed in thought the picture of his youth, he perceived that it would be difficult to find the kindness of his father at fault. Feeling a sort of remorse arise in the depth of his heart at the moment he was passing through the gallery, he almost felt he could forgive his father for having lived so long; he returned to some sentiment of filial piety just as a robber turns to honesty when the enjoyment of a successfully stolen million becomes a possibility. The young man had soon passed through the cold and lofty halls which composed his father's apartment. After having experienced the effects of a damp, chill atmosphere, and inhaled the dense air and the musty odor given out by the ancient tapestries and dusty presses, he found himself in the old man's chamber, before a bed of sickness close to a fire almost extinct. A lamp, placed upon a table of Gothic design, shed its light in fitful gleams, now brightly, now faintly, upon the bed, and thus displayed the old man's face under ever-varying aspects. The cold whistled through the ill-fitting casements, and the snow-flakes made a sullen murmur as they scourged the panes. This scene formed so striking a contrast to the scene Don Juan had just left that he could not restrain a shudder.

Then he grew cold, for as he approached the bed an unwonted flood of light, blown by a gust of wind, lit up the head of his father: the features were distorted, the skin clung closely to the bones, its greenish tint ren-

dered still more horrible by the whiteness of the pillow whereon the old
man lay; the open, toothless mouth was drawn with pain, and let slip
between it sighs whose dolorous depth was sustained by the echoing
howls of the tempest. In spite of these signs of dissolution, there beamed
from this head an incredible character of power; a mighty spirit was at
war with Death. The eyes, hollowed by sickness, preserved a strange
steadfastness; it seemed as though Bartolomeo would have slain with his
last look an enemy sitting at the foot of his bed. This look, fixed and
frigid, was the more frightful because the head remained as immovable as
a skull upon a physician's table. The entire body indicated by the bed-
clothes showed that the old man's limbs also lay as rigid as the head. The
whole was dead except the eyes. Moreover, the sounds that issued from
his mouth had something automatic in them.

Don Juan felt a certain shame at coming to his father's death-bed still
wearing the bouquet of a harlot in his breast, and carrying thither the
perfumes of a banquet and the odors of wine. "Thou art enjoying thy-
self," said the old man, when he saw it was his son. At this moment the
clear, light voice of a singer, who held the banqueters spellbound, sustained by the harmony of the viol on which she accompanied herself, rose
above the rattle of the hurricane, and rang even in this funereal chamber.
Don Juan affected not to hear the answer thus brutally given in the
affirmative to his father. "I blame thee not, my child," said Bartolomeo.
The kindness of these words caused a pang to Don Juan; he could not
forgive his father for the poignancy of his goodness.

"My father, think of the remorse I must feel," said he hypocritically.

"Poor Juanino," replied the dying man in a muffled voice, "I have
always been so kind to thee that thou couldst not desire my death?"

"Oh," cried Don Juan, "if it were only possible for me to restore life to
you by giving you up a part of my own!"

("One can always say that sort of thing," thought the reveller; it is as
though I offered the world to my mistress.") He had scarcely conceived
this thought when the old spaniel barked. The intelligence of this voice
made Don Juan shudder; it seemed to him as if the dog had understood
him.

"I knew well, my son, that I could count upon thee," cried the dying
man. "I shall live. Thou shalt have thy wish. I shall live without depriving
thee of a single one of the days allotted thee."

"He is delirious," said Don Juan to himself. Then he added aloud:
"Yes, my dearest father, you will live, assuredly, as long as I live, for your
image will be always in my heart."

"I was not speaking of that sort of life," said the old noble. He collected all his strength and sat up, for he was troubled by one of those suspicions that only rise from under the pillows of the dying. "Listen! my son," he replied in a voice enfeebled by this last effort; "I am no more ready to die than thou art ready to give up thy falcons, and dogs, and horses, and wine, and mistresses, and gold."

"I can well believe it," thought his son again, as he knelt down by the bedside and kissed one of the corpse-like hands of Bartolomeo. "But," he answered aloud, "my father, my dear father, we must submit to the will of God."

"God is I," muttered the old man.

"Blaspheme not," cried the reveller, when he saw the look of menace which his father's features assumed. "I beseech you take care; you have received Extreme Unction; I could never be comforted if I saw you die in sin!"

"Listen to me, wilt thou?" cried the dying man, his mouth drawn with anger.

Don Juan held his peace. A horrible silence reigned. Across the dull whir of the snow the harmonies of that ravishing voice and the viol still travelled, faint as the dawn of day. The dying man smiled.

"Thou hast bidden singers, thou hast brought music hither; I thank thee. A banquet! Women, young and beautiful, with white skins and raven locks!—all the pleasures of life! Bid them stay; I am about to be born again."

"The delirium is at its height," thought Don Juan.

"I have discovered a means of bringing myself to life again. Here! Look in the drawer in the table; it opens by pressing a spring hidden under the griffon."

"I have found it, my father."

"Good! take out a little flask of rock crystal."

"It is here."

"I spent twenty years in . . ." At this moment the old man felt his end approaching; he collected all his strength and said, "As soon as I have given my last breath, rub me entirely all over with that water and I shall come to life again."

"There is very little of it," answered the young man.

Though Bartolomeo could no longer speak, he still retained the faculties of sight and hearing; at these words his head turned round toward Don Juan with a sudden spasmodic start, his neck remained stretched out like the neck of a marble statue condemned by the thought of the sculptor always to look to one side, his eyes were dilated and had acquired a hideous stare. He was dead, dead as he lost his last, his only illusion. He had sought a refuge in the heart of his son; he found it a charnel-house more hollow than men are wont to dig for their dead. Thus it was that his hair stood on end with horror, the convulsion in his eyes still spoke. It was a father rising in rage from his tomb to demand vengeance at the hand of God upon his son!

"Hm! The old man is done for," said Don Juan.

In his hurry to hold up the mysterious crystal before the light of the lamp, like a drunkard consulting his bottle at the end of a meal, he had not seen the pallor fall upon his father's eyes. The dog gaped as he gazed alternately at the elixir and his dead master, while Don Juan glanced to and fro at his father and the phial. The lamp cast up its flickering flames, the silence was profound, the vial was dumb. Belvidero shivered; he thought he saw his father move. Terrified by the set expression of those accusing eyes, he closed them as he would have shut a shutter shaken by the wind on an autumn night. He stood erect, motionless, lost in a world of thoughts. All at once a sharp sound, like the cry of a rusty spring, broke the silence. Don Juan, startled, almost dropped the phial. Sweat colder than the steel of a dagger broke from every pore. A cock of painted wood rose on the top of a clock and crowed three times. It was one of those ingenious machines which the students of those days used, to wake them at a fixed hour for their studies. The dawn already glowed red through the casements. Don Juan had spent ten hours in meditation. The old clock was more faithful in its service than was he in his duty toward Bartolomeo. The mechanism was composed of wood, and pulleys, and cords, and wheels, while he had within him that mechanism peculiar to man which is called a heart. Not to run any risk of spilling the mysterious liquid, Don Juan, *the sceptic*, placed it again in the little drawer of the Gothic table. At this solemn moment he heard in the galleries a stifled commotion; there were confused voices, muffled laughter, light footsteps, the rustling of silk—in short, the din of a merry troop trying to compose themselves. The door opened, and the Prince, the friends of Don Juan, the seven courtesans, and the singers appeared in the quaint disorder of dancers surprised by the light of morning, when the sun struggles with the paling flames of the candles. They were all come to offer the customary consolations to the young heir.

"Ho! ho! poor Don Juan; can he really have taken this death to heart?" said the Prince in La Brambilla's ear.

"Well, his father was very kind," she answered.

The nocturnal meditations of Don Juan, however, had imprinted so striking an expression upon his features that it imposed silence on the group. The men stood motionless. The women, whose lips were parched with wine and whose cheeks were stained with kisses, fell upon their knees and tried to pray. Don Juan could not help shivering at the sight; splendor, and mirth, and laughter, and song, and youth, and beauty, and power, the whole of life personified thus prostrate before the face of Death.

But in this adorable Italy debauchery and religion were then so closely coupled that there, religion was a debauch, and debauchery a religion! The Prince pressed Don Juan's hand with unction; then, all the faces having simultaneously assumed the same grimace, half sadness, half indifference, this phantasmagoria disappeared and left the hall empty. Verily, it was an image of life. As they descended the stairs the Prince said to La Rivabarella: "Who would have thought that Don Juan's impiety was all a sham? Yet it seems he did love his father!"

"Did you notice the black dog?" asked Brambilla.

"Well, he is immensely rich," remarked Bianca Cavatolino, smiling.

"What's that to me?" cried the proud Veronese, she who had crushed the comfit box.

"What's that to you?" cried the Duke. "With his crowns he is as much a prince as I am."

At first, swayed by a thousand thoughts, Don Juan wavered between several plans. After having taken count of the treasure amassed by his father, toward evening he returned to the mortuary chamber, his soul big with a hideous egoism. In the apartment he found all the servants of the house busy collecting the ornaments of the state bed, on which their late lord was to be exposed on the morrow, in the midst of a superbly illuminated chapel; a grand sight which the whole of Ferrara would come to gaze at; Don Juan made a sign and his servants stopped, trembling and discomfited.

"Leave me here, alone," said he in an altered voice; "you need not return until I have gone."

When the steps of the old serving man, who was the last to go out, only sounded very faintly on the flagstones, Don Juan barred the door precipitately; then, certain that he was alone, he cried out: "Let us try!" The corpse of Don Belvidero was laid on a long table. In order to hide from every eye the hideous spectacle of a corpse of such extreme decrepitude and leanness that it was almost a skeleton, the embalmers had placed a cloth over it, which enveloped it entirely, with the exception of the head. This sort of mummy lay in the middle of the room; the cloth, naturally flexible, indicated vaguely the gaunt, stiff, sharp form of the limbs. The face was already marked with large livid stains, showing the necessity of finishing the embalming. In spite of his armor of scepticism, Don Juan trembled as he took out the stopper of the magic crystal phial. When he had come up close to the head, he was compelled to wait a moment, he shivered so. But this young man had been early and skilfully corrupted by the manners of a dissolute court; an idea worthy of the Duke of Urbino gave him courage, and a feeling of keen curiosity spurred him on; it even seemed as if the fiend had whispered the words which re-echoed in his heart: "Anoint one eye!" He took a cloth, moistened it sparingly with the precious liquid, and rubbed it gently over the right eyelid of the corpse. The eye opened.

"Ah! ah!" exclaimed Don Juan, pressing the phial in his hands as in a dream we cling to a branch by which we hang over a precipice.

He saw an eye full of life, the eye of a child in the head of a corpse; in it the light quivered as though in the depth of a limpid pool; protected by the beautiful black lashes, it sparkled like those strange lights that the traveller sees in a desert country upon a winter's night. This eye of fire seemed eager to start out upon Don Juan; it thought, accused, judged, condemned, menaced, spoke; it cried aloud, *it bit*. Every human passion pulsated in it; the tenderest supplication, a kingly wrath, the love of a maiden entreating her tormentors, the searching look on his fellows of the man who treads the last step to the scaffold. So much of life beamed in this fragment of life that Don Juan drew back in terror. He walked up and down the room; he dared not look upon this eye, yet he saw it on the floor, in the tapestries. The room was strewn with spots full of fire, and life, and intelligence. Everywhere gleamed those eyes; they seemed to bay at his heels!

"He would certainly have lived another hundred years," he cried involuntarily, at the moment when, brought back by some diabolic influence to his father's side, he found himself gazing at this luminous spark.

All at once the intelligent eyelid shut and opened again hastily; it was like the look of a woman who gives consent. If a voice had cried out, "Yes!" Don Juan could not have been more terrified.

"What am I to do?" thought he. He had the courage to try and close the pallid eyelid, but his efforts were useless.

"Tear it out? That might be parricide, perhaps," he pondered.

"Yes," said the eye, quivering with astounding irony.

"Ha! ha!" cried Don Juan, "there is sorcery in it."

And he drew near to tear out the eye. A large tear rolled down the hollow cheeks of the corpse, and fell on Belvidero's hand.

"It burns," he cried, as he wiped it off.

This struggle was as tiring as if, like Jacob, he had been wrestling with an angel.

At last he rose, saying to himself, "If only there is no blood!"

Then summoning up all the courage necessary to be a coward, he tore out the eye, and crushed it in a cloth; he did not dare to look at it.

He heard a sudden, terrible groan. The old spaniel expired with a howl.

"Could it have been in the secret?" thought Don Juan, looking at the faithful animal.

Don Juan passed for a dutiful son. He erected a monument of white marble over his father's tomb, and entrusted the execution of the figures to the most celebrated artists of the time. He did not feel perfectly at his ease until the day when the statue of his father, kneeling before Religion, lay, an enormous pile, over his grave. In its depth was buried the only remorse which had ever, in moments of physical weariness, touched the surface of his heart. As he reviewed the immense riches amassed by the aged orientalist, Don Juan grew careful; had not the power of wealth gained for him two human lives? His sight penetrated to the depth and scrutinized the elements of social life, embracing the world the more completely in his gaze, because he looked upon it from the other side of the tomb. He analyzed men and things only to have finished, once and forever, with the Past, shown forth by History; with the Present, represented by Law; with the Future, revealed by Religion. He took matter and the soul, he cast them into the crucible, and found—Nothing. From thenceforth he became DON JUAN!

Young and handsome, master of the illusions of life, he flung himself into it, despising yet possessing himself of the world. His happiness could not consist in that bourgeois felicity which is nourished on an occasional sop, the treat of a warming-pan in the winter, a lamp at night, and new slippers every three months. No; he seized on existence as an ape snatches a nut, but without amusing himself for long with the common husk, he skilfully stripped it off, in order to discuss the sweet and luscious kernel within. The poetry and the sublime transports of human passion did not seem worth a rap to him.

He was ever guilty of the fault of men of power who sometimes imagine that little souls believe in great ones, and so think to exchange high thoughts of the future for the small change of our transient notions. He was quite able to walk as they do, with his feet on the earth, and his head in the skies; but he preferred to sit down and parch under his kisses the fresh, tender, perfumed lips of many women; for, like Death, wherever he passed he devoured all without shame, desiring a love of full possession, oriental, of pleasures lasting long and gladly given. In women he loved not themselves, but *woman*. He made irony the natural habit of his soul. When his mistresses used their couch as a step whereby to climb into the heavens and lose themselves in the lap of intoxication and ecstasy, Don Juan followed them, as grave, sympathetic, and sincere as any German student. But he said *I*, while his mistress, lost in her delight, said *We!* He knew perfectly the art of being beguiled by a woman. He was always strong enough to make her believe that he trembled like a schoolboy at a ball, when he says to his first partner, "Do you like dancing?" But he could storm too, on occasion, and draw his sword to some purpose; he had vanquished great captains. There was raillery in his simplicity, and laughter in his tears—for he could shed tears at any moment—like a woman, when she says to her husband, "Give me a carriage, for I know I shall go into a consumption." To merchants the world is a bale or a heap of bills of exchange; for most young men it is a woman; for some women it is a man; for certain minds it is a drawing-room, a clique, a district, a town; for Don Juan the whole universe was himself. A model of grace and high breeding, with all the charm of wit, he moored his bark to every bank, but when he took a pilot on board he only went whither he chose to be steered.

The longer he lived the more he doubted. By studying men, he discovered that courage is often rashness; prudence, poltroonery; generosity, diplomacy; justice, iniquity; scrupulousness, stupidity; honor, a convention; and by a strange fatality he perceived that those who are truly honorable, of fine feeling, just, generous, prudent, and courageous, gain no consideration among men—"What a heartless jest!" thought he; "it cannot be made by a God." So he renounced a better world, never doffed his hat at the sound of a *Name*, and looked upon the stone saints in the churches as works of art. But comprehending the organization of human societies, he never did too much to offend their prejudices, because he knew that he was not so powerful as their executioner. He deflected their laws with that grace and *esprit* so well described in his scene with *Monsieur Dimanche*; in fact, he was the type of the *Don Juan* of Molière, of the *Faust* of Goethe, of the *Manfred* of Byron, and of the *Melmoth* of Maturin, grand figures drawn by the greatest geniuses of Europe, to which the lyre of Rossini will some day perhaps be wanting, no less than the harmonies of Mozart. Terrible images, perpetuated by the principle of evil ever existent in man, images of which copies are found in every age; whether the type enters into treaty with man and becomes incarnate in Mirabeau; whether it is content to work in silence like Bonaparte, or squeezes the world in the press of its irony like the divine Rabelais; or again, whether it jests at beings, instead of insulting things, like Le Maréchal de Richelieu; or better still perhaps, mocks both men and things at once, like the most celebrated of our ambassadors. But the profound genius of Don Juan Belvidero summed up in advance all these geniuses. He made a jest of everything. His life was one mockery which embraced men, things, institutions, and ideas. As to eternity, after having talked familiarly for half an hour with the Pope Julius II, at the end of the conversation he said to him, laughing: "If it is absolutely necessary to choose, I would rather believe in God than the Devil; power united to goodness always offers more resources than the genius of evil."

"Yes, but it is God's will that we should do penance in this world . . ."

"Ah, you are always thinking of your indulgences," answered Belvidero. "Well, I have a whole existence in reserve wherein to repent of the faults of my former life!"

"Ah! if you understand old age in that sense," said the Pope, "you run a chance of canonization."

"After your elevation to the papacy all things are credible." And they went to watch the workmen building the immense basilica dedicated to Saint Peter.

"Saint Peter is the man of genius who built up our double power," said the Pope to Don Juan; "he deserves this monument. But sometimes at night I think that a deluge will pass its sponge over it all, and the world will have to begin again—"

Don Juan and the Pope began to laugh; they understood each other. A fool would have gone the next day to enjoy himself with Julius II at Raphael's or in the delicious Villa-Madama; but Belvidero went to see him pontificate, in order to be convinced of his doubts. At an orgy, Della Rovere would have been capable of criticizing or confuting the Apocalypse.

However, I did not undertake this legend to furnish materials to those desirous of writing memoirs of the life of Don Juan; it is designed to prove to all decent people that Belvidero did not die in a duel with a stone, as some lithographers would have us believe. When Don Juan had reached the age of sixty he went and took up his abode in Spain. There in his old age, he married a young and lovely Andalusian, but he purposely made neither a good husband nor a good father. He had observed that we

are never so tenderly loved as by women for whom we scarcely care at all.
Doña Elvira had been piously brought up by an old aunt, in a castle some
few leagues from San Lucar, in the wilds of Andalusia; she was a paragon
of devotion and grace. Don Juan divined that this young girl would make
a wife who would fight against passion for a long time before she yielded,
so he hoped to be able to preserve her virtuous until his death. It was a
grim jest, a game of chess which he had determined to reserve to play
during his old age. Forewarned by all the mistakes of his father
Bartolomeo, Don Juan resolved to make the least actions of his old age
contribute to the success of the drama which was to be played out upon
his death-bed. With this end in view, he buried the greater part of his
riches in the cellars of his palace at Ferrara, which he seldom visited. As
to the other half, he devoted it entirely to purchasing an annuity in order
that his wife and children might have an interest in the continuance of
his life, a kind of roguery which it would have been well for Don
Bartolomeo himself if he practiced; but for Don Juan this Machiavel-
lesque speculation was scarcely necessary. The young Felipe Belvidero
grew up as conscientious and religious a Spaniard as his father was impious, in virtue perhaps of the proverb: "A miser breeds a spendthrift son."

The Abbot of San Lucar was chosen by Don Juan to direct the con-
sciences of the Duchess of Belvidero and of Felipe. This ecclesiastic was a
holy man, of fine figure, admirably proportioned, with beautiful black
eyes; in fact, he had the head of a Tiberius, fatigued with fasts, pale with
penance, and tempted daily as are all men who live in solitude. The old
noble hoped perhaps still to be able to kill a monk before finishing his
first lease of life. But whether it was that the priest was as strong as Don
Juan himself, or that Doña Elvira possessed more prudence or virtue than
Spain usually bestows upon her daughters, Don Juan was constrained to
spend his last days like an old country *curé* without a single scandal in his
house. At times he took pleasure in finding his son or his wife at fault in
their religious duties, for he willed despotically that they should perform
all the obligations imposed on the faithful by the Court of Rome. In fact
he was never so happy as when he was listening to the gallant priest,
Doña Elvira, and Felipe engaged in discussing some point of conscience.
However, in spite of the prodigious care which the Señor Don Juan
Belvidero bestowed upon his person, the days of his decreptitude drew
on; with this age of trouble came the cries of impotence, cries the more
heartrending because of all the rich memories of his turbulent youth and
voluptuous manhood. This man, who had reached the last degree of

cynicism—to induce others to believe in laws and principles at which he scoffed—slept at night on the doubt of a *Perhaps!*

This model of fine breeding, this aristocratic athlete in debauchery, this paragon of gallantry, this gracious flatterer of women whose hearts he had twisted as a peasant twists an osier band, this man of genius, was plagued with catarrh, pestered by sciatica, a martyr to the agonies of gout.

He saw his teeth depart, as the fairest and most beautifully dressed ladies depart one by one at the end of a festival and leave the halls empty and deserted. Then his sinuous hands trembled, his graceful legs tottered; at last one evening apoplexy squeezed his neck with her icy, crooked fingers. After this fatal day he became harsh and morose. He found fault with the devotion of his wife and son, asserting sometimes that the touching and delicate care which they lavished upon him was only given because he had sunk all his fortune in an annuity. Then Elvira and Felipe would shed bitter tears and redouble their caresses upon the malicious old man, and then his voice would grow affectionate to them and he would say: "My dear, my dear wife, you forgive me both, do you not? I tease you a little. Alas! good God! Why dost Thou use me to try these two heavenly creatures? I, who ought to be their joy, I am their scourge."

In this way he chained them to his bedside, making them forget whole months of impatience and cruelty by one hour, when he would display for them ever new treasures of favor and false tenderness. This paternal system brought him infinitely more success than the system formerly used in his case by his father had brought *him*. At last he reached such a pitch of disease that, in order to put him to bed, they had to manoeuver him like a felucca entering a dangerous channel. Then the day of his death arrived. This brilliant and sceptical personage, whose intellect alone survived the most horrible of all destructions, found himself between his two antipathies, a physician and a confessor; but even with them he was gay. Was there not for *him* a light shining behind the veil of the future? Upon this veil—of lead to others, but transparent for him—the joyous, ravishing delights of youth played like shadows.

It was a beautiful summer evening when Don Juan felt the approach of death. The Spanish sky was exquisitely clear, the orange trees scented the air, the stars shed their bright and freshening beams, nature seemed to give him sure pledges for his resurrection, a pious and obedient son watched him with looks of respect and affection. About eleven o'clock he desired to be alone with this ingenuous youth.

"Felipe," said he, in a voice so tender and affectionate that the young man trembled and shed tears of joy. Never before had this stern father thus pronounced the word "Felipe." "Listen to me, my son," continued the dying man. "I am a great sinner. So during the whole of my life I have thought of my death. Formerly I was a friend of the great Pope Julius II. That illustrious Pontiff, fearing lest the excessive excitation of my senses should cause me to commit some mortal sin between the moment of my receiving the holy oils and my latest breath, made me a present of a phial in which there is preserved some of the holy water which gushed out of the rock in the desert. I have kept the secret of this diversion of the treasure of the church, but I am authorized to reveal this mystery to my son, *in articulo mortis*. You will find this phial in the drawer of the Gothic table which has always stood at my bedside. The precious crystal will serve for you too, my beloved Felipe. Swear to me on your eternal salvation to execute my orders exactly."

Felipe looked at his father. Don Juan understood the expression of human feeling too well not to die in peace on the credit of such a look, just as his father had died in despair on the credit of his.

"Thou deservest another father," replied Don Juan. "I must confess to thee, my child, that at the moment the worthy Abbot of San Lucar was administering the viaticum to me, I thought of the incompatibility of two powers as extensive as God's and the devil's."

"Oh! my father!"

"And I said to myself that, when Satan makes his peace, he will be bound, unless he is a wretched scoundrel, to stipulate for the pardon of his adherents. This thought haunts me. I shall go to hell, my son, if thou dost not fulfil my wishes."

"Oh! tell me, father, quickly!"

"As soon as I have closed my eyes," replied Don Juan, "which will be in a few minutes, perhaps, take my body, even while it is still warm, and stretch it out on a table in the middle of this room. Then extinguish this lamp, the light of the stars will be sufficient for thee. Strip me of my clothes; and while thou recitest *Paters* and *Aves*, and raisest up thy soul to God, take care to moisten, with this holy water, my eyes, my lips, my whole head first, then all the members of my body in succession; but, my dear son, the power of God is so great, thou must not be astonished at anything!"

Here Don Juan, who felt death approaching, added in a terrible voice:

"Hold the phial tight!" then expired gently in the arms of a son whose tears ran in copious streams over his pale, ironical countenance. It was about midnight when Don Felipe Belvidero placed the corpse of his father upon the table. After having kissed the menacing brow and the gray locks, he extinguished the lamp. The soft glow cast by the moonlight lit up the country with its strange reflection, and allowed the pious Felipe to see but indistinctly his father's corpse—a something white amid the shade. The young man steeped a cloth in the liquid and—absorbed in prayer meanwhile—faithfully anointed the venerated head amidst profound silence. He certainly heard an indescribable shivering, but he attributed it to the play of the breeze in the tree tops. When he had moistened the right arm, he felt himself closely embraced round the neck by a young and vigorous arm, and yet it was his father's arm! A piercing shriek burst from his lips, he dropped the phial, it broke;—the liquid evaporated. The servants of the castle came running in armed with torches. This cry had terrified and astounded them; it was as if the trumpet at the last judgment had shaken the universe. In a moment the room was full of people. The trembling crowd found Don Felipe in a swoon, held by his father's powerful arm which clasped him round the neck. Then, marvelous to relate, the assistants saw the head of Don Juan, as young and beautiful as Antinoüs; a head with black hair, and brilliant eyes, and ruddy mouth straining horribly, and yet unable to move the skeleton to which it belonged. An old serving man cried out, "A miracle!" The Spaniards all repeated, "A miracle!" Too pious to admit the mysteries of magic, Doña Elvira sent for the Abbot of San Lucar. When the Abbot had seen the miracle with his own eyes, being an Abbot who asked for nothing more than a chance of augmenting his revenues, he resolved to profit by it, like a man of sense. He declared at once that the Señor Don Juan would undoubtedly be canonized, and appointed the ceremony of his apotheosis at his monastery, which, he said, would be called henceforth San Juan de Lucar. At these words the head made a very funny grimace.

The taste of the Spaniards for this kind of solemnity is so well known, that it ought not to be difficult to imagine the religious fripperies with which the Abbey of San Lucar celebrated the translation of the Blessed Don Juan Belvidero into its Church. Within a few days of the death of this illustrious Señor, the miracle of his incomplete resurrection had been passed on so briskly from village to village within a radius of more than fifty leagues round San Lucar, that already it was as good as a play to see the sightseers on the road; they came from all sides scenting the delicacy of a *Te Deum* chanted with flambeaux. The ancient mosque of the monastery of San Lucar—a marvelous edifice built by the Moors, whose vaults had heard for three centuries the name of Jesus Christ substituted for the name of Allah—could not contain the crowd come together to witness the ceremony. Packed as close as ants, Hidalgos, in velvet mantles, armed with their good swords, stood upright round the pillars, finding no room to bend knees that bent in no other place but there; bewitching peasant girls, clad in basquines which displayed their charms to advantage, gave their arms to old white-haired men; young men, with passion in their eyes, found themselves side by side with elderly decked-out women. Then there were couples tremulous with happiness, curious maidens brought thither by their sweethearts, brides and bridegrooms married but a single night, children shyly holding one another's hands. Such was the company, rich in color, brilliant in contrast, laden with flowers and enamel, making a soft hum of expectation in the silence of the night. The wide doors of the Church opened. Those who had come too late remained outside, and saw from afar through the three open portals a scene of which the vaporous decorations of our modern operas could not give the faintest idea. Pious women and unholy men, eager to gain the good graces of a new saint, lit thousands of tapers in his honor throughout the vast Church—interested lights which made the building seem as if enchanted. The black arches, the columns with their capitals, the deep chapels glittering with gold and silver, the galleries, the Saracen carving, the most delicate particles of this delicate sculpture were outlined in this excess of light, like the capricious figures formed in a glowing furnace. It was an ocean of fire, dominated, at the end of the Church, by the gilded choir, where towered the high altar rivalling in its glory the rising sun. But the splendor of the golden lamps, the silver candelabra, the tassels, the saint and the *ex votos*, paled before the shrine wherein lay Don Juan. The corpse of that impious person glistened with jewelry, and flowers, and crystals, and diamonds, and gold, and feathers as white as the wings of a seraph;—it replaced upon the altar a picture of Christ. About him glittered numberless tapers, which shot into the air their waves of lambent flame.

The worthy Abbot of San Lucar, vested in full pontificals, wearing his jewelled miter, his rochet, and golden cross, was enthroned on a seat of imperial splendor above the choir. All his clergy, aged and passionless men with silver hair, clad in albs of fine linen, were gathered round him, like the holy confessors whom painters group about the Eternal. The precentor and the dignitaries of the Chapter, decorated with their brilliant insignia and all their ecclesiastical vanities, passed to and fro in the shadowy depth of the incense, like the stars which roll through the firmament. When the hour of triumph was come, the bells awoke the echoes of the country, and this vast assembly raised to God the first cry of praise with which the *Te Deum* commences. It was indeed a sublime cry—voices clear and joyous, the voices of women in ecstasy, mingled with the deep, strong voices of men, those thousands of voices in so stupendous a chorus that the organ could not surpass it with all the roaring of its pipes. But amid this tumult of sound, the penetrating notes of the choristers and the sonorous tones of the basses evoked a train of gracious thought, representing childhood and strength in an impassioned concert of human voices blended in one sentiment of Love.

Te Deum laudamus!

From the midst of the Cathedral, black with the kneeling multitude, this chant rose like a light that bursts forth suddenly in the night, and the silence was broken as by the roar of a thunder-clap. The voices ascended with the clouds of incense as they spread their blue, transparent veils upon the fantastic marvels of the architecture. All was splendor, perfume, light, and melody. At the moment when this anthem of love and thanksgiving rolled upward toward the altar, Don Juan, too polite not to return thanks, and too humorous not to understand a joke, answered by a terrible laugh, and drew himself up in his shrine. But the devil having put it into his head that he ran a chance of being taken for an ordinary individual, a saint, a *Boniface*, a *Pantaloon*, he threw this melody of love into confusion by a howling to which were added the thousand voices of Hell. Earth spoke her blessings, and Heaven uttered its curse. The ancient Church trembled to its foundations.

"*Te Deum laudamus!*" cried the assembly.

"Go to all the devils, brute beasts that you are! God, God! *Carajos Demonios*, idiotic creatures, with your silly old god!"

And a torrent of curses rolled out like a stream of burning lava in an eruption of Vesuvius.

"*Deus Sabaoth!—Sabaoth!*" cried the Christians.

"You insult the majesty of Hell!" answered Don Juan, grinding his teeth.

Presently the living arm succeeded in getting free out of the shrine, and menaced the assembly with gestures eloquent of mockery and despair.

"The saint blesses us," said the old women, the children, and the maidens betrothed—a credulous people. Truly, we are often deceived in our worship. The man of power mocks at those who compliment him, and sometimes compliments those whom in the depth of his heart he mocks.

At that moment when the Abbot, prostrate before the altar, began to sing, *"Sancte Johannes, ora pro nobis!"* he heard quite distinctly, *"O coglione."*

"What's going on up there?" said the sub-prior, seeing the shrine move.

"The saint is playing the devil," answered the Abbot.

Then the living head detached itself violently from the body which lived no longer, and fell on the yellow skull of the officiant.

"Dost thou remember Doña Elvira?" it cried, fastening its teeth in the Abbot's head.

The Abbot uttered a terrible shriek, which threw the ceremony into confusion. All the priests ran up together and crowded round their superior.

"Idiot, say at least that there is a God!" screamed the voice. Just at that moment the Abbot, bitten in the brain, was about to expire.

Justin Dowling

The Legs That Walked

In 1954, Justin Dowling *was a journalist for the* Sunday Tribune *in South Africa.* Weird Tales *published three of his short stories: "The Living Eyes," "The Arm" and the following offbeat little chiller, which "The Unique Magazine" featured in November 1953. Each of Dowling's "anatomical" fantasies is concerned with the horror of dismemberment, an understandable pre-occupation for a writer who, during World War II, lost his right arm in a tank battle in Italy "fighting alongside the Americans."*

I FIRST saw the legs that walked in a thunder storm. Which made it worse. But having seen them once I had to see them again.

They did that to you. They did it to Mr. Peach, too, who owned them.

I was one of the first to meet Mr. Peach when he bought the old widow's gloomy house on the corner. We became friendly and I used to drop in after supper for a chat and a cup of China tea with lemon.

He attracted me because there was something in his pale eyes which I could not fathom, something which I knew was haunting him but which he hid so cleverly.

It was not until I had known him nearly a year and had seen him grow old and gray under my eyes that he told me about his queer obsession.

(. . . *He collected legs!* . . .)

He said that he had collected hundreds of them—mostly of famous men and women. He had built them up from descriptions he had found in books while others he had created from photographs and statues.

He made them from a special wax which he had brought back from China.

Naturally I was interested and asked him to show them to me. That mysterious look kindled in his eyes. He said, "Sorrison. I am too scared!"

"Why?" I asked. "What on earth is there to be afraid of in a lot of legs?"

His eyes clouded; drops of sweat gathered on the back of his hands making the hairs blacker. The blood drained from his lips.

He said: "There is something to be afraid of. Something terrible. Something which is driving me insane. Something from which I cannot escape. You must not go down there!"

"Rot," I answered severely, "I am not frightened. There is not a leg in the world that can scare me."

"All right," he said, "tomorrow night. If I am still alive!"

On the way home I pondered over his queer hobby. There must be some reason for it. What would a psychologist do? Probe back to his youth? Find out that at some tender age someone had laughed at his legs —this gave him an inferiority complex. So he collected legs when he grew up to prove to himself that his were as good as anybody else's.

But this fear of his? What was that? Persecution mania? I gave it up.

When I arrived the next evening he seemed normal. "Well," I said, "you are still alive, I see." He laughed.

"I did not go down there last night."

"I cannot wait," I said.

While we had our cup of tea the storm came up suddenly, the first indication we had of it was a low rumbling and the dipping on and off of the lights.

"Let us go down," he said.

Mr. Peach kept his collection in the basement and as we went down a flight of stone steps to it I could hear the rain weeping against the walls outside while the wind rattled the windows.

The basement was a large room with low rafters. Stacked row upon row were his collection of legs. Each pair was neatly labeled with the birth and death of their owners.

He had divided them up into sections starting with the early days of Rome and Greece through to the Renaissance, Reformation and up to our twentieth century.

It would have been impossible to have looked at each pair. In any case I did not think it over interesting. Queer, decidedly queer, but to me the legs held little fascination. I glanced at one or two as we walked through the room.

The early century chorus girls interested me for a moment. A flash of lightning and an extra loud crack of thunder dipped the lights again.

It was then that I had a feeling that something was alive but it passed as quickly as the lights came on again.

There was only one window in the basement and it was covered by a heavy, velvet curtain.

"Well," I said to him, "you have an extraordinary collection here. Unique I should say. But nothing of a frightening nature."

His face was the color of sawdust. Once more I saw the drops of perspiration springing up on the back of his hands, matting the black hairs.

Had he also sensed that aliveness? Absurd! It was the storm and all these stupid legs in their bodiless rows!

He whispered: "Come and see."

He led me to the far end of the room where in an alcove stood something covered in a cloth. Thunder shook the room. He flicked off the cloth. It was a glass case mounted on blocks with a gold rope ringing it.

The label read: "The Unknown Woman." I looked at the legs in the case.

They were perfect; exquisite in their symmetry; exact in their length; delicate in their coloring. I stared fascinated—the exotic curve from the knees to the thighs, a deeper white than the rest of the legs; the calves flexed but smoothly supple; the ankles thin yet strong; the feet small and delicately formed.

Of all the legs I had seen these were the most realistic—almost alive!

Mr. Peach spoke, startling me as a clap of thunder shook the room: "What do you think of them?"

He stood close behind me breathing heavily down my neck. His eyes were wide and frightened. Water dripped off the back of his hands.

"I think they are wonderfully made," I answered. "They almost look alive!"

He caught me fiercely in the fleshy part of my thigh so that I cried out. He moaned: "Alive! Alive! You are right. They *are* alive!"

I thought: Had the man gone mad? Had continual staring at these legs affected his mind?

He pushed me back until I stood ten paces from the case. Then he went over to the switch. "Watch," he said.

The room was plunged into darkness. Thunder rumbled under my feet. Lightning flashing outside penetrated the curtain, giving the case a weird look.

Inside the case, lights came on vividly outlining the beautiful legs. I blinked. Then I stepped back horrified.

The legs came marching towards me!

Marching. Marching straight at me! I shouted. I tried to ward them off. But they came on. With each clap of thunder they came. Came until they were about me.

Round my throat. Squeezing . . . squeezing . . . a vice grip which bit deep into my flesh. Choking me. Squeezing. . . .

When I opened my eyes I was back in the study on the couch, Mr. Peach bending over me.

"So they did it to you too. They did it to you too! Marched until they were about your throat!" he whispered.

I scrambled up and rushed to the side-board mirror.

There were no marks on my throat! Then I laughed and said: "What an extraordinary hallucination. Thank God it was a hallucination. What with that storm and the lightning flickering on and off those legs I imagined the things walked."

"They did," said Mr. Peach.

"But it is impossible," I said.

"They have done it to me, often. That was why I was afraid to ask you to see them. Now you will have to go back. Go back for more!"

"I shall certainly not go back," I said. "Though of course there is nothing to it. It was a hallucination. And hallucinations never happen a second time."

He shook his head. "You will go back. They do that to you. Each time the squeezing gets worse. One day they will squeeze too hard!"

"Do not talk such nonsense," I said severely. "If you are afraid of them —burn them. Get rid of them and you will rid yourself of this optical illusion."

"No matter what we do now," he answered, "they will always come marching—alive. Alive to squeeze the throat until . . . death! There is no escape from the curse of the legs!"

"Where did you get them?" I asked, "out of a tomb in Egypt?"

"No. They were sent to me through the post—anonymously. Their beauty attracted me so I put them in the special case. Then one night. . . . You know the rest."

When I left his home later I believed that I would never return.

.   .   .   .   .

But I did. I wanted to prove to Mr. Peach how wrong he was and the sooner he saw a psychiatrist the better. It was a month later that I called again.

What I found astonished me. Mr. Peach had changed so completely. His shoulders sagged, his hair was grayer, his eyes puffed and tired, his mouth curled down at the corners.

The man was mentally sick. So sick that he hardly recognized me. When he did he whispered: "So you came back. So you came back."

I felt guilty at having neglected him. Was I too late to save his mind? I said: "Heavens—what have you been doing to yourself?"

But he went on whispering: "So you came back. So you came back!"

"Look here," I said, "I wish I had come sooner. I am going down there to bust forever this mad thing that has gripped your imagination like this. This time there is no storm to play tricks. When I walk up from there you will be free. Do you understand? A free man!"

But he stared in front of him without answering. Saliva drooled unheeded down his mouth. I decided to act promptly.

I hurried down the steps to the basement. I realized how on the other occasion my fears had been magnified by the storm. Now it seemed laughable. There was nothing to be afraid of now.

I stopped to look at one or two legs before going over to the case to remove the cloth.

The legs were the same. They were certainly well made but I had lost my awe for them. Bits of wax in a glass case!

Then I went over to the switch and flicked off the light. The room was even darker than it had been on that other occasion because the curtain effectively shut out any light from the outside and there was no lightning to flash on and off.

I stood before the case and waited for the lights inside it to come on. When they did I found I was too far away and moved closer.

I halted—stupefied. Horrified. The legs were marching! Marching straight at me! I tried to turn and run but found myself rooted to the ground.

They were out of the case. Walking on air. Walking at the level of my head towards me. Walking in perfect rhythm.

Then they were about my throat. Firstly they gripped me between their calves—squeezing. As my breath gasped from my lips they slipped up until the thighs smothered my face.

Tighter. Tighter—they gripped. I could feel the flesh, alive. Alive—

biting into my neck until I could breathe no more and my lungs hurt with a bursting tightness.

As I twisted to the floor the grip loosened—gradually. I fell clawing at the floor, my chest heaving in great convulsions as I fought for air. Then there was no more pain—only blackness.

Something cold hit me in the face. I opened my eyes. My head throbbed. Mr. Peach stood over me with a bucket of water.

"So it was my imagination, was it? So they could not walk? So it was an optical illusion? Well, you do not think so now, do you?"

He laughed hysterically. I knew then that he had been watching and that his last shred of sanity had vanished. Then I discovered that my hands were tied behind my back.

I was alone with a madman and a pair of legs that walked until . . . death!

Every now and then he laughed insanely and shook his head violently. He gibbered and muttered. I heard a word or two: "Came back. Illusion. Marching. Squeezing."

He held an iron bar in his hand and with it pushed me backwards. He thrust his bloated face near mine and slobbered at me: "Watch! Watch and see them. See them march to my throat where they belong!"

He let out another crazy laugh and went to the switch. I was afraid to move in the dark. He may have struck me with the iron bar.

The lights came on in the case. He stood there arm raised. He was going to fight the legs!

The legs stirred. They were through the glass. They made straight for him. It was a fantastic sight. He swung at them viciously with the bar.

A blow raised a huge weal on the left leg. Then I saw the trickle of blood and heard a low moan.

With a sudden swiftness the legs were about his throat. He twisted and turned, dropping the iron bar with a clatter.

He tore at the legs with his hands until the blood ran down over his hands and down his arms. Then his fingers went stiff. He lurched forward and fell onto his knees.

I could see the muscles on the legs tightening. Tighter! Tighter! There was blood all over his purple face—his eyes were pressed from his head—his twisted mouth stayed wide open.

The legs released their grip—and were gone. I rushed over to him. By the light from the case he looked a horrible sight. He was dead!

The legs were back in the case. Already the fingers of madness were about me. I tugged insanely at the ropes—they slipped. I was free.

The legs had not moved again. I stared and waited for them.

I wanted to share his fate. His agonizing death. Then I realized. The legs would never march again. Never move again. Never squeeze again.

They too were dead!

I rushed from the room for help. My half insane shouting at the servants stirred them into action and they phoned for a doctor and the police.

The anti-climax had nearly the effect of turning my brain completely. When I led them down to the basement they found Mr. Peach slumped on the ground. But there was no blood on his face. Nor did his eyes protrude from his face as I had seen them. There were no signs that he had been strangled.

"Heart failure," said the doctor. "But I will tell you for sure after a post mortem."

Dazed, I walked over to the case. The legs were the same as before. They were free from any marks or scratchings!

Had I imagined the whole thing? Blood pounded into my head and I reeled dizzily. Then I crashed to the ground.

My breakdown was a severe one. And it took me months of rest before I became well. With the help of a psychiatrist I convinced myself that the whole thing was a colossal hallucination.

Then one day I picked up an old paper. I read. "A pair of legs among the late Mr. Peach's collection of legs has been identified. They were his wife's, preserved in an ingenious way. It is now alleged he must have murdered his wife and. . . ."

I read no more. I knew now there had been no hallucination. I knew now why the legs had marched until . . . death. I knew, and once more I was afraid. . . .

Saralee Terry

The Bridge to the Liver Pies

SARALEE TERRY, *a pseudonymous obscure novelist who writes humorous verse in restaurants, contributed the following "napkin poem" about the noble sacrifices of self-love.*

O, you may have your rainbow
And its bright golden pot,
But if I could, I would go
Unto a place I'm not.

It was an iron bridge-way,
'Twas not much for the eyes,
But at its latter end lay
Two rabbit-liver pies.

'Twas high up in the Andes,
Five miles above the seas,
All circled round with candies
And chocolate-cherry-freeze!

But as I neared the bridgework,
A green-and-orange troll
Said, "Halt right there, my good jerk,
Unless you've got the toll."

I did a smart about-face,
Although my tear-ducts burned,
And no more did I retrace
My steps once I'd returned.

O, I have roamed the world wide,
Where wonders stun the eyes,
But nowhere have I e'er spied
A marvel like those pies!

It's not the bridge's pass-fee
That keeps me from my goals . . .
It's just that fine folk like me
Don't talk to common trolls.

Ray Russell

The Black Wench

RAY RUSSELL, *one of* Playboy's *most important former editors, is an award-winning poet, novelist and short story writer. He is the author of* The Case Against Satan, The Colony, *"Sanguinarius" (in* Witches & Warlocks) *and many other excellent works of literature. Because the magazine version of the following highly original supernatural story was condensed, at the author's request I am pleased to present "The Black Wench" for the first time in its entirety.*

" 'MAINWARING,' " said Bud Kallen from the back seat of the humming car. "So that's the way you spell it over here." He folded up the deed he'd been studying.

"Yes," replied Nigel Sloane, a slim, silver-haired man as smooth as the Bentley he was driving. "But not *pronounced* 'Maine Wearing,' as you did. We pronounce it 'Mannering' . . ." He turned to the young woman in the passenger seat to his left. ". . . Which, I take it, is the way your late mother *spelled* her maiden name, Mrs. Kallen?"

"That's right," Elena Kallen answered. "Americans said it wrong so often that my great-grandfather Humphrey changed the spelling when he settled in the States right after the First World War."

"Sensible of him."

"Settling in the States?" asked Bud Kallen.

"Simplifying the name," said Nigel Sloane.

He had disliked Kallen the instant he'd met him, and had tried in vain to suppress the emotion. He told himself that he resented the man's youth, and the fact that he was an American; but that didn't wash, because Mrs. Kallen was young and American, too, and Sloane didn't dislike her. Was that only because she was a woman? he asked himself; a beautiful woman with large brown eyes and sable hair? He hoped he was not so biased. The Warwickshire countryside, green as broccoli in the midday sun, rolled majestically past his window as he guided the car around a subtle bend in the road.

Elena was saying, "The name died out when my mother married. She didn't have any brothers. And her unmarried sister died a long time ago. That must have made it hard for you to find me."

"A bit," Sloane admitted. "But we are a diligent firm, Mrs. Kallen. We kept on the scent until we discovered that Helen Mannering, the granddaughter of Humphrey, had married a gentleman attached to one of the Central American consulates in your country, a Mr. Enrique Castillo; and that their union had produced two offspring: Henry and Elena. If your brother Henry had not been killed in Vietnam, he, being the elder, would have been my passenger today. As fate decreed, however, you are the closest surviving blood relation of Sir Giles Mainwaring."

The firm's enquiry agents had found the former Elena Castillo living in a small apartment with her husband in Los Angeles, where Kallen ran a not very successful public relations company called Images Unlimited.

"I still can hardly believe it," said Elena, shaking her head. "It seems incredible that there isn't anybody closer to Sir Giles here in England."

"I assure you that we searched for them," said Sloane. "As his solicitors, we were duty bound to leave no stone unturned. But Sir Giles was a widower whose only child died without issue a few years ago, and his only siblings were two maiden ladies, long deceased. There are a few distant branches of the family tree still here—cousins *many* times removed, and whatnot—but you have the most direct lineal connection to him, genealogically speaking. Therefore, according to the terms of his will, you are the legatee of his entire estate, including Mainwaring Hall."

Bud said, "I guess it'll be Kallen Hall from now on, right, honey?"

Before Elena could respond to her husband's impudent assumption, Nigel Sloane said frostily over his shoulder, "It has been called Mainwaring Hall since Jacobean times, Mr. Kallen. Sir Giles was descended in a direct line from one of the first baronets in the kingdom, Sir Edred Mainwaring, who received his baronetcy from King James the First."

"Of the King James Bible?" asked Elena.

"The same. It was a new rank in those days, you see, created by the king to provide a new dignity higher than knight but lower than baron."

"Why?" Bud asked.

"To raise money for the treasury."

Bud laughed. "You mean the king *sold* this new 'dignity' to old Edred? For filthy lucre?"

"In a manner of speaking."

Bud laughed again and slapped his knee. "I love it!" he said. "*Love* it!"

Doing his best to ignore Bud, Nigel Sloane addressed Elena: "Speaking of filthy lucre, Mrs. Kallen, there will of course be a heavy toll in death duties—what I believe you call inheritance taxes—but even after the Inland Revenue has taken its ton of flesh there will be a substantial cash settlement. One might call it, without fear of hyperbole, a small fortune."

"Not a large fortune?" asked Bud.

Nigel Sloane shrugged. "These things are relative. And then we must not forget Mainwaring Hall itself, which we could arrange to sell for you, should you decide not to live there."

"Why would we decide that?" asked Elena.

"Well, for one thing, it's so very large for two people; and for another . . . but there, see for yourself." The car slowed down and came to a stop. To their left in the middle distance, looming in the center of spacious grounds, stood an enormous old house.

It seemed to grow out of the earth from roots almost four centuries old, as if it had been not so much built as planted. It sucked its strength from the soil and the air, squatted on the landscape like an exotic bloated organism, surveying its dominion with the unblinking eyes of its many windows. If the Kallens had known anything about Jacobean architectural style, they would have recognized instantly that Mainwaring Hall was a typical example of it. The uneasy mixture of late Perpendicular Gothic motives and crudely misused classic details boldly announced its period as surely as a fanfare of trumpets. The Flemish influence, characteristically, was strong, and the Tudor pointed arch was much in evidence. Nearer them, glinting in the weeds at the roadside, an empty Coca-Cola can, flung there by some irreverent motorist, provided an ironic contrast that spanned the centuries at a glance.

Noting this anomaly, Elena said, "It's like time doesn't exist."

"Perhaps it doesn't," said Sloane. "Perhaps it's an illusion. When Pythagoras was asked to define time, he said it was the soul of this world. I've never quite understood what he meant by that, but I've always liked the sound of it."

"The old place must be expensive to keep up," said Bud.

"Precisely," said Sloane, agreeing with Kallen for the first time all day.

"But we have money now," Elena reminded her husband. "A small fortune. You heard Mr. Sloane."

Bud spoke to the solicitor: "You said the house is awfully big for just the two of us, and you were going to say something else. . . ."

"Was I? I don't remember. I suppose I was about to say that Jacobean isn't to everyone's fancy. Some people even consider it to be in rather bad taste."

"I don't," said Elena stoutly. "I think it's beautiful."

Sloane was too much of a gentleman to voice his opinion of her opinion. He purred diplomatically, "Ah, there speaks the family pride of a true Mainwaring. Shall we drive in?"

He started the Bentley again and drove it slowly through the open gates, up a curving path past trees and hedges, formal gardens, and weathered stone statuary of indeterminate age. "Warwickshire is Shakespeare country, you know," Sloane said as he drove. "Stratford, if you care for that sort of thing, is a pleasant motoring journey from here." At length, the car drew up to the main entrance of the massive house.

"It's in pretty good shape for its age," Bud commented.

"Restoration and renovation through the years," Sloane explained, "not to mention added wings and whatnot. Very few of the mod cons, though, I fear."

"Beg pardon?" said Elena.

"Modern conveniences. No central heating, air conditioning, television antennae . . ."

"No phone?"

"Oh, yes, Mainwaring Hall is on the telephone. And electricity has been laid on. It also has one other contemporary feature that should interest a Californian couple like you: a swimming pool."

"Really?"

Sloane nodded. "Sir Giles had it installed some twenty years ago, when the doctors prescribed swimming as healthful exercise for his heart. He tried it once, said he loathed the chlorinated water, and never got into it again. Lived to the age of eighty-six and died of emphysema, not a heart attack."

"Well, I'll give the pool plenty of use," said Elena. "I love to swim."

"Yeah," said Bud, "I'm more of a scuba diving nut myself, but show her a pool and she's happy as a pig in slop."

"What a colorful expression," said Sloane. "Not much opportunity for scuba diving around here, however. Shall we look at the interior?" They climbed out of the car and walked up to the formidable oaken portal. As he lifted the heavy brass knocker and struck it sharply several times against the thick door, the solicitor said, "There's been only a skeleton staff here since Sir Giles died."

"And here's one of the skeletons now," murmured Bud as the door was opened by a cadaverous and very old butler.

"Ah, there you are, Coles," said Sloane, as the aged manservant blinked first at the solicitor, then at his clients, and, with a long, lung-emptying sigh, toppled forward as if bludgeoned, into the arms of a startled Nigel Sloane.

"Help me get him inside," Sloane said to Bud, and the two men clumsily carried the inert butler into the house to the first available chair, an ornate relic of wood at the foot of the no less ornate staircase. Into this chair they deposited their load as gently as possible, while Elena hovered behind them, uttering helpless moans of sympathy.

"Oh, the poor old man," she said. "What's wrong with him?"

"He's an extremely antiquated chap," said Sloane, "and the death of Sir Giles has put a great strain on him."

"He's not *dead*, is he?" she asked.

"No," said Bud, "he's coming around."

The butler's eyelids fluttered several times. He lifted his head from his chest.

"Now then, Coles," said the solicitor, "do you know me?"

"Mr. . . . Sloane . . ."

"Well done. These two young people are your new master and mistress . . ."

He seemed reluctant to meet his new employers, so Elena said, "I think introductions can wait. He should go and lie down until he's feeling better."

Sloane endorsed that idea, and in moments the housekeeper, Mrs. Thayer, who was temporarily doubling as cook, was summoned to convoy the butler to his quarters. While she was thus occupied, Sloane conducted the Kallens on a quick, informal tour of the first floor.

Every room was done in either true Jacobean or later pseudo-Jacobean style: main hall, galleries, staircases, dining room, library, drawing room, billiard room. Richly carved walnut paneling covered every inch of every wall: representations of spaniels, squirrels, woodcocks, partridges, pheasants all stood out in vivid relief. The library was spacious enough to accommodate, in addition to endless shelves of books, no less than six commodious sofas for browsing and lounging. Sloane, as he led them through the rooms, kept up a running commentary: "As you see, the doorways, fireplaces, and the like are all framed with classic forms, and both inside *and* outside there is a wide use of gains, pilasters, and S scrolls . . . The paintings in *this* gallery have very little intrinsic value, for the most part, but serve as a family album. Most of the Mainwarings are here except for a few black sheep like Sir Percival, who wrote bad checks and died of venereal disease. The last Lady Mainwaring kept his picture in her sitting room, as a joke. Here *is* that lady, and her husband, Sir Giles, both painted some forty years ago. The gentleman at the far end is the first baronet of the line, Sir Edred, painted, the family claim, by Daniel Mytens, who also painted James the First, but some experts dispute that claim. Wart and all, eh?" Sir Edred indeed had a large hairy mole to the left of his prominent nose, Elena saw as she drew closer to the painting. He also had a gray beard and moustaches, and glaring pale eyes. A close-fitting cloth headpiece or hood covered his possibly bald head, even his ears. A large ring of fur encollared his throat. "The *north* gallery," Sloane continued, "has some Constables and Gainsboroughs, even a Holbein, all of great artistic and financial interest . . ."

The billiard room was pronounced by Bud to be his favorite. He immediately took down a cue from the wall rack and broke the balls with a resounding clatter.

"Can we see the pool?" Elena asked.

"To be sure. And then we can stroll out to the stables."

"There are *horses* here?" she marveled.

"Not for some time," Sloane said. "Just motor cars. A Mercedes, a Jaguar, a bright red Ferrari that will probably suit *you*, Mr. Kallen, and a very, *very* old Rolls-Royce."

"Who drove the Ferrari?" Bud asked.

"Why, Sir Giles. He was quite the dashing old gentleman."

He led them out a back entrance of the house to the pool—which was empty and dry, its floor carpeted with dead leaves. Elena groaned with disappointment, but Sloane said, "Not to worry. I'll arrange to have it cleaned and filled for you. Leave everything to me."

"It's so nice and private out here," she said, "I have a feeling I could sunbathe in my birthday suit . . ."

"Birthday suit?" the bewildered solicitor inquired.

Bud sniggered. "With nobody but the hired help cheering you on from the servants' quarters!"

"Actually," said Sloane, "the servants' quarters do not overlook the pool; they are in a remote section of the house—but our English sun is no match for the sun of Southern California or the French Riviera, I'm afraid. One doesn't tan under its rays, one pinks. We're a bit too north, you see. Shall we have a look at your stable of thoroughbred motor cars? . . ."

Mrs. Thayer appeared from the house at that moment. She was a stout woman of forty-odd years, with an air of imperturbable dignity. "Excuse me, sir," she said to the solicitor, "but Mr. Coles would like to speak to you. Can you come upstairs?"

"Now?"

"Please."

"Oh, very well." He told the Kallens how to find their way to the stables, and followed Mrs. Thayer into the house.

The stables were larger than they had expected, and their walls were covered by the biggest magnolias Elena had ever seen. All the cars were there, conforming to Nigel Sloane's spoken catalogue, and in gleaming condition. Sure enough, Bud was drawn to the red Ferrari as if to a smiling girl, and he looked at it with undisguised lust. As they were leaving the stables, Elena said, "Hey, look at this."

She pointed to a group of four words cut into the wood of a dark and cobwebbed corner of the stables. The letters were crude, but worn smooth at the edges, their depths engrained with dirt, bespeaking the passage of unnumbered years since they had been carved there. The words were:

Beware the Blacke-wench

"Probably a horse," said Bud. "An ornery black mare that threw her riders."

In the house again, Nigel Sloane told them that the ancient butler, Coles, had announced his intention to retire from service and spend his declining years with a niece near Ipswich.

"Kind of sudden, isn't it?" said Bud.

"Perhaps," Sloane conceded, "but it's difficult for the old boy to adjust to new young masters. He served Sir Giles for almost fifty years! And, to speak frankly, I think you will be better off with a younger man in the post. Poor old Coles is past his prime. I'll put you in touch with one or two good employment agencies. You'll be wanting a cook, as well, and gardeners, of course . . . other servants, too . . . leave all that to me and to Mrs. Thayer. We'll arrange the interviews for you."

A taxicab from the nearby village called for Coles that very afternoon. The old man climbed in with his cases and boxes, and was off to the railroad station without another word. "He sure was in a big hurry," said Bud.

Mrs. Thayer subsequently showed the Kallens the rest of the house—the upstairs bedrooms, sitting rooms, nurseries, and servants' quarters; belowstairs, the kitchen, pantry, and wine cellar—while Sloane telephoned employment agencies, arranged for the reactivating of the pool, and generally made himself indispensable.

After a simple tea prepared and served by Mrs. Thayer, Sloane said, "I should be getting back now. If you have any questions, if there is anything I can do, anything at all, please have no hesitation in telephoning. You have my number." He addressed these remarks to Elena. "And if you should reconsider, and wish to dispose of this valuable property at an attractive price . . ."

"I wouldn't dream of it," she declared. "I love the place, I belong here, I'm a Mainwaring. Why should I get rid of it? Is it haunted or something?"

Bud said, "Sure it is. All these old English houses have ghosts, don't they?"

Nigel Sloane chuckled. "Your husband is right. All old English houses are reputed to harbor ghosts, and Mainwaring Hall is no exception."

"Really?" squeaked Elena. "Ghosts?"

"Just one. So the old wives' tales would have it, at any rate. It's the reason Mainwaring Hall has always had difficulty keeping servants, and why most of them left after Sir Giles died. Country folk are terribly superstitious. But I've never seen the ghost, and I don't believe that Sir Giles ever saw it. That's the one common denominator about ghosts: nobody ever actually sees them: but everybody has a friend of a friend who knows somebody whose great-aunt says that her mother had a servant who saw one. Humans are very gullible animals."

"But what's it supposed to be like?"

"The ghost of Mainwaring Hall?"

"Yes! Tell us! I'm dying to know!"

The solicitor sighed. "Oh, dear. Well, then. It's purported to take the form of a naked woman, a black woman, which is why it's known as The Black Wench. . . ." Elena and Bud exchanged quick glances. "Some versions say that its presence is *felt*, rather than seen, felt as a cold wet hand or an expanse of clammy bare flesh . . . but I'm upsetting you, Mrs. Kallen."

"No, no! Please go on."

"The Mainwarings of old, some say, were heavily invested in the African slave traffic as early as 1620 and made the bulk of their wealth by financing the capture, transport and sale of the poor wretches to the American colonies. This conveniently accounts for the apparition's color, you see . . . a female slave who died in some cruel manner, perhaps, flogged or what-you-will, and who blamed the Mainwarings for her harsh fate."

"How long has she been haunting Mainwaring Hall?" Elena asked.

"The first recorded sighting was by Sir Edred Mainwaring. He wrote that he saw her in the room that is now the library, but which in his time was much smaller and served as his study, what he called his 'closet.' She allegedly came to him there late one night in 1624 while he was reading his Bible, this naked black woman, glistening as if covered with perspiration from head to foot, and, in Sir Edred's words, 'reeking with the stench of Hell.' He was a religious man, and he believed that she was 'asweat from the fires of Perdition,' whither she'd been sent as a demon or succubus to tempt him to damnation with her naked body."

"Wow," said Bud, "if a guy has got to see a ghost, that's the kind of ghost to see, huh?"

Sloane said, "I take your meaning. Sir Giles, after Lady Mainwaring had passed away, once told me that he wouldn't have minded an occasional visit from a naked wench. But I don't think he was ever favored by the black lady's attentions. As far as Sir Edred is concerned, a modern psychiatrist would no doubt say that he was having a sexual fantasy about a voluptuous African woman, but that his religious convictions wouldn't allow him to enjoy the fantasy without those pious distortions. I do hope I haven't offended you, Mrs. Kallen, or frightened you."

"No, of course not. Goodness, I don't believe in ghosts."

"Very sensible," said the solicitor as he rose to leave.

"Do you?"

Nigel Sloane smiled. "I've always admired what Sir Osbert Sitwell said when he was asked that same question," he told her. " 'Only at night.' "

That evening after dinner, Bud killed some time at the billiard table, but soon grew bored without an opponent. He roamed restlessly through the library and several other rooms, finally joining Elena in the drawing room, where she was writing postcards to friends in the States.

"It isn't exactly L.A., is it?" he said. "Or London. I *liked* London, what we saw of it on the way in. Theatres, movies, restaurants, gambling casinos. It's alive. Not so dead quiet, like this place. We'll have to get a TV."

"If you want to."

He rested on the arm of her chair and, with an excruciating attempt at an English accent, whispered in her ear, "I say, my deah, what about initiating the mahster bedroom?"

She giggled. "It's early."

"Almost ten. And this country air"—he yawned theatrically—"makes me sleepy."

"We *have* had a busy day." She, too, was overcome by a yawn. "Give me ten minutes to get ready, then come up."

He bowed deeply from the waist. "As you wish, milady." She left the room.

The master bedroom boasted two adjoining sitting rooms where husband and wife might dress and undress in privacy, visible to no eyes other than their own and those of their valet and maid. To the sitting room with the more feminine décor, where her bags had been taken and unpacked by Mrs. Thayer, Elena now retreated and took off her clothes. When she was without a stitch, she admired herself in a tall old looking glass, smiling with total absence of false modesty. Her body was sumptuous and full-bosomed, satin to the touch, with the olive skin of her father, and a curly nest at her center like a swatch of soft fur. Her brushes had been set out on the dressing table. She selected one, but instead of sitting down to brush her dark hair, she did it standing up, nude, in front of the full-length mirror, watching her breasts bob and quiver as she brushed the gleaming thick mass in long strokes. Once, she winked at herself.

The gaze of a cold, unmoving eye made her drop the brush and catch her breath in sudden fright when she glimpsed it in the glass.

Turning quickly, her hands covering breasts and thatch in a reflexive movement, she saw that the eye belonged to a personage at the opposite side of the room: insolent, dissolute, clad in the tight breeches, cutaway coat, and tall silk hat of a Regency rake, he might have been taken for Beau Brummel had not a small brass plate on the picture's frame identified him as *Sir Percival Mainwaring (1785–1826)*. He appraised her nudity coolly through a lorgnette. She stuck her tongue out at him.

Downstairs, Bud impatiently waited only six minutes, not ten, before climbing the staircase to the master bedroom. Even so, she was already in bed when he walked into the room: the lights were turned off, but he had no difficulty discerning the familiar curves of her shape under the coverlet, thrown into relief by a cool wash of moonlight from the windows.

"My little eager beaver," he muttered playfully, as he began to undress there in the bedroom. No sitting room for him: he was in no mood to stand on ceremony, and he let the clothes fall to the floor. Nude in the moonlight, he was a well-proportioned, muscular young man, and, at the moment, spectacularly virile. "Here I come, ready or not," he crooned, and climbed under the coverlet.

She was lying on one side, her naked back to him. He pressed the whole length of his body to hers, then immediately recoiled.

"*Damn*, you're cold!" he complained. "And you're all wet . . . soaking . . . what did you do, take a cold shower and come to bed without toweling off?"

"What did you say, dear?" Elena asked as she walked through the door from her sitting room, clad in a filmy nightgown.

"*Christ!*"

Bud sprang from the bed as if kissed by a scorpion.

"What's the matter?"

He crouched naked in the dark, on the carpet next to the bed, gasping. "Who . . ." he said in choked fragments, "who's that . . . in the bed?"

"Nobody!"

He stretched out a trembling arm and pointed his finger to the bed. "I felt her . . . she's *there* . . ."

Elena snapped a switch, flooding the room with light. "Where?" The bed was empty.

"She *was* there!"

"Who?"

"How the hell should I know? I thought it was you. And then . . . you walked through the door." His face was chalky.

She handed him his robe. "Come on, dear, get up off the floor. Put this on. You had a dream, that's all."

He got to his feet and wrapped himself in the robe. "A dream . . . no . . . couldn't be . . ."

"Sure, don't you see? You got into bed to wait for me, and you dozed off just for a few seconds and dreamt I was already in bed beside you."

"Cold," he said. "She was cold. Naked and wet." He yanked the coverlet all the way off the bed. "If it was a dream," he said, "how do you explain *that?*"

On one side, the sheet was wrinkled from top to bottom by the long, sodden stain of a drenched and recent occupant.

Bud Kallen refused ever to sleep in that bed. He claimed it was "clammy," even after the sheets had been changed, even after the mattress had been replaced. The young couple slept in one of the other

bedrooms, he clinging to his wife all night, every night, like a child clinging to its mother.

It was not a conjugal embrace. The spearhead of his virility had been
shattered that night, and did not regain its former edge. Elena began to
feel it was her fault.

"No, honey, it's not you," he insisted one morning at breakfast. "It's
this damn house. Why don't we sell it? Sloane said he could get us a good
price for it."

"Sell the house?" she wailed. "Just when we've got the pool ready
again, and a TV, and a new butler and a cook, and—"

"What's that got to do with it? The pool and the TV antenna are good
selling points."

"I don't *want* to sell it. Don't you understand?"

"But why not? The cars alone are worth a mint, even if we keep one or
two of them. That classic Rolls? It's a collector's item. And those priceless
paintings! Gainsboroughs and Constables and . . ."

"You're not a Mainwaring, that's why you don't understand. But I am."

He laughed metallically. "You're a *Kallen*, that's what you are. And
before that, you were a Castillo—a spic, for Christ's sake! Don't pull that
lady of the manor stuff with me."

Her dark eyes had brimmed with hurt and fury. Now she tore away
from the table, knocking over her coffee cup, and ran weeping from the
room.

He found her huddled on a stone bench in the garden, her tear-
streaked face held in her hands. He talked to her gently and contritely,
apologizing, asking to be forgiven. He could be persuasively charming
when it suited him. By the time they had returned to the house, she had
agreed to invite Nigel Sloane to dinner at Mainwaring Hall some time
that week.

Two evenings later, the solicitor was enjoying an excellent meal prepared by their new cook: turtle soup, halibut mousse, beef Wellington,
fresh asparagus vinaigrette, with appropriate wines from the well-stocked
cellar of the late Sir Giles. Offered his choice of either sherry trifle or
Stilton cheese and biscuits "for afters," he chose both, causing Elena to
ask him how he kept his trim figure. She and Bud, true to American
custom, were on perpetual diets. "Do you exercise?"

"Never," he proudly replied, and asked if Elena were enjoying her
swimming pool.

"I swim every day," she told him, "and sometimes at night!"

"Sir Giles would have been happy about that."

Coffee and cognac followed in the drawing room, and as Sloane touched a flame to a Havana cigar, he said, "Am I to understand that you have had second thoughts about selling?"

Bud thought it politic to let Elena speak. She said, "That's the word, Mr. Sloane. Thoughts. Just thoughts, for now. Could we talk about it?"

"Of course. Any particular reason?"

She shrugged. "No."

Bud rubbed his arms and said, "Chilly in here. We ought to have a fire. I'll ring for the butler."

"Dear, you'll broil us alive. *I* feel fine." Her smooth arms and back were bare in her dinner gown. "The cognac will warm you up."

Sloane returned to the subject of selling. "Yes, we can certainly investigate one or two interesting avenues of possibility." He smiled. "But you two seemed to have been settling in so nicely. Haven't seen The Black Wench, by any chance?"

"No," Bud said, too quickly.

Elena asked, "Have you ever known anyone who *has* seen her?"

"Ah," replied Sloane, "one can never say that one has known somebody who's seen a ghost. The most one can say is that one knows somebody who *says* he's seen a ghost."

"And did you ever know anybody who said he saw the Black Wench?"

"In point of fact, yes."

"Who?" asked Bud.

"Coles."

"What? That old guy who quit the day we got here?"

Sloane nodded. "A few years ago, Sir Giles told me—laughing as he did so—'I believe old Coles has gone dotty. Claims to have seen the Wench. In the billiard room, of all places. Called him by name, he says. Gave him quite a turn. I told him to stop knocking back the cooking sherry or I'd sack him.' "

Elena asked, "Did Coles ever see her again?"

"He *said* he did—the very day the two of you arrived. He told me that was why he wanted to leave. All for the best, to my way of thinking. High time he'd been put out to pasture. And I did smell drink on his breath that day."

Bud leaned forward. "How did Coles describe her? Was she naked? And black?"

"I don't know. I didn't cross-examine him." His cigar had gone out. As he rekindled it, he said, "I wouldn't place too much importance on that word 'black,' you know." A long plume of smoke unfurled from his mouth. "Or 'naked,' for the matter of that."

"What do you mean?" asked Elena.

"Well, 'black' hasn't always meant the same thing, when applied to the color of people. Samuel Pepys, in his diary, refers to the wife of a Mr. Hater as 'a very pretty, modest, black woman,' but she was certainly no Negress, simply a woman of dark complexion. Shakespeare, in *Love's Labour's Lost* and *The Two Gentlemen of Verona*, for example, calls 'black' characters who are obviously what we would call white. And in four or five sonnets about his beloved Dark Lady, he calls *her* 'black,' although it's now believed that she was of Italian descent. The same is true of the word 'naked,' which in older parlance sometimes meant clad only in underclothing. So," he concluded with a twinkle, "Sir Edred's 'naked black woman' may have been no more than a late-night lady-love of his steward's, a scullery maid, more than like, thoroughly English if a touch swarthy, and caught in her skivvies on the way back to her own bed. Wandered into the master's closet by mistake, no doubt."

Elena smiled. "More cognac, Mr. Sloane?"

"Just a drop, perhaps. Thank you. Now then: a sale of this property could begin with an auction of the paintings, motor cars, and other valuables; or, on the other hand—"

"I've changed my mind," she said. "Talking to you has helped me think more clearly. I don't want to sell, after all."

When Nigel Sloane had left, Bud held his temper until he was certain all the servants had gone to bed. Then he exploded: "*What the hell's the matter with you?*"

"He was so sensible," said Elena. "So level-headed. He let me see that so-called ghost for what it really is: nothing at all. A servant girl in her underwear. A senile butler who'd been hitting the bottle. I'm not going to give up all this for some fairy tale."

" '*All this*'? This white elephant? This drafty old museum?"

"I have a right to change my mind."

"*What* mind? You dumb spic!"

"That's the second time in less than a week you've used that word. I know you're sexually frustrated, and I'm sorry for you, but—"

"Just *shut up* about that! Getting out of this damn house is all the cure I need!"

She turned and walked away.

"*Where are you going?*" he shouted.

"For a swim," she said, and ran swiftly upstairs, where she stripped and squeezed into a brief bikini she would have hesitated to wear on a public beach, and tripped quickly downstairs again on bare toes, out to the moonlit pool. The night-silence was cloven by a splash when, sleek as a dolphin, she dove cleanly into the water.

She swam the length of the pool, her arms slicing the water in strong, graceful strokes; then she reversed, swimming back toward the other end again. The exercise and the bracing effect of the chill water calmed her, draining the anger and tension from her body and mind. Having touched pool's end, she decided to swim just one more length—no sense over-doing it—so she turned around and started once again for the deep end.

But now her heart was jolted by something she saw in the moonlight, moving toward the pool. It was luminous in the lunar glow, with the opalescence of bare flesh, vaguely human in outline, and yet not human.

Not human, because—although it had two arms that hung at its sides, two legs that were bringing it nearer and nearer the pool—it had no face.

She tried to scream but could only whimper.

Where a face should have been, there was an oval void, eyeless, soul-less . . .

It drew even closer.

Suddenly she laughed with relief and recognition. It was her husband, in his swim trunks and scuba mask. The oxygen tank was strapped to his back.

"Bud, you idiot!" she said affectionately. "Scuba diving in a swimming pool?"

Without a word, he dove under the surface of the water. She giggled at his eccentric foolery, grateful that he was no longer angry and had chosen this bit of clowning as a way of making up.

She felt her ankles seized by his powerful hands. She laughed again. They had often played like this back home, when they were young surfers on the beach at Santa Monica. She kicked coquettishly, not really want-ing to free her legs from his grasp.

She was pulled down, under the surface.

He continued to hold onto her ankles with hands that gripped like steel clamps. She kicked frantically now, coquetry forgotten, roiling the water, struggling to escape. Fear rushed into her very bone marrow as water filled her nostrils, her mouth. She beat upon him with her fists, but he eluded her. She tried to rip off his oxygen tank, his breathing tube, but he was too quick and too strong for her.

Freezing thoughts stabbed her. Why was he doing it? Because she wouldn't sell? Even if she had sold, would he have done it later anyway, to get all the money for himself? If only the servants hadn't gone to bed. If only their quarters overlooked the pool. But there was no one, no help . . .

The awful pressure of water was in her lungs, and it hurt. It *hurt* to drown, she realized through her panic, there was *pain*; hideous nauseating fear and *pain*. But soon the pain ebbed, and a numbness set in, and a softness, and a darkness. . . .

When she emerged from the pool, she staggered away aimlessly, unsure of her own intentions. She felt giddy, she couldn't see very well, everything looked distorted, she didn't walk normally, she felt as if she were floating. Well, that wasn't surprising, she told herself, after what she'd just been through. She was lucky to be alive.

Had she lost consciousness at some point? She couldn't be sure. How long had she been held underwater? It had seemed like hours, but time, as Mr. Sloane had said, was only an illusion.

She found herself nearing the stables, and the horses whinnied and reared as she passed.

Horses? She peered at the animals. Yes, there were horses in the stables, all right. No cars. Although that puzzled her, she knew there had to be a logical explanation, and she made her way toward the house.

She still couldn't see clearly. The house looked different, somehow. It wavered before her eyes, throbbing and pulsating. She wandered without purpose into the strangely mist-softened billiard room, startling old Coles, the butler . . .

"Coles?" she said aloud. But *he* shouldn't have been there. He'd left Mainwaring Hall the day they'd arrived. In that moment, Elena knew she was dreaming. And that explained the horses in the stable. She hoped it explained Bud's attempt to kill her, too. Please, God, let *that* be part of the nightmare.

The house twirled and gyrated—or was it the world, the universe?—and a wave of dizziness swept over her, a vast roaring filled her ears, she felt as if she were in the center of a tornado's raging dark funnel. The feeling passed.

She entered the library, as it rippled and miraculously shrank to a small den of a chamber. A man sat at a desk, reading an immense book by the light of a guttering candle. He was gray-bearded, with a large nose and a mole, and he wore a cloth hood over his head. He looked up at her. His eyes bulged. His mouth fell open.

"Who art thou?" he croaked. "Dost seek to tempt me? Avaunt, thou black devil! In the Name of Jesu, I charge thee, take thy nakedness hence!" He fell back in his chair, trembling.

Elena backed out of the shrunken library, shattered by the vivid reality of this dream, and moved toward the undulating staircase. She felt she was not climbing it so much as riding it, as she might ride a smooth, silent escalator. Her bare feet could not even feel the stairs; but that was the way of dreams.

When she entered her husband's sitting room, she saw his wet swim trunks and scuba gear in a heap on the floor.

(And lightning flashes of knowledge seared her.)

His back turned to her, Bud was now dressed in crisp pajamas and robe, fluffing his hair with her blow dryer.

(She came to know that time is not a river flowing in one direction, but a whirlpool spinning round and round; that a spirit released from the prison of flesh can spiral unfettered into Past, recent Past, distant Past, years, centuries before its own death, its own birth.)

After stuffing the damp scuba gear into a duffel bag and throwing the bag into a cupboard, Bud picked up the phone and dialed. "Is this the police? . . ."

(She knew why Coles had fainted at the door upon seeing her the day they arrived: he had recognized her from the earlier sighting in the billiard room some years before.)

"This is Mr. Kallen at Maine Wearing Hall. Something terrible has happened out here . . ."

(She knew how naked her bikini-clad body must have looked to Sir Edred in his seventeenth-century study; how black her olive skin and dark hair were by his standards.)

"An accident in the swimming pool . . . my wife . . . I'm afraid she's . . ."

(And finally she knew that none of this was a dream; that she had been murdered; that the legendary ghost of Mainwaring Hall was no scullery maid or African slave girl; that she herself, Elena Kallen, was, always had been, forever would be, the Black Wench.)

A split second before he felt her, Bud smelled the pungent chlorine of the pool—Sir Edred's "stench of Hell"—and then she reached out and laid a hand of ice upon his shoulder.

With a cry, he spun around and saw his wife, in her bikini, glistening with the water that had killed her. Water trickled from her ears, her nostrils, her gaping mouth, ran in a rivulet between her breasts, formed a glittering gem in her navel, snaked down her tapered legs into a puddle at her feet. Howling, Bud Kallen leaped backward, pressed his spine to the wall, and slid slowly down the flocked wallpaper as if he were a lump of custard flung there by a spoiled child, until he was huddled on the floor, eyes distended, moaning, vomiting, fouling his clothes, a mass of quivering, whining terror.

When the police arrived and woke the sleeping servants, they found two bodies: those of Elena Kallen, drowned in the pool, and her husband, on the floor of his sitting room, dead from a massive coronary. The telephone was still in his hand.

Guillaume Apollinaire

The Blue Eye

Jessica Amanda Salmonson, author of "The Old Woman Who Dragged Her Husband's Corpse," which appears elsewhere in this volume, introduced me to this eerie bit of subdued erotica by Guillaume Apollinaire *(1880–1918), an important French avant-garde poet, prosodist, art critic and occasional pornographer.*

I LOVE IT when old women chatter about their girlhood. One old dame with a formidable memory told me about something strange that she witnessed when she was twelve years old.

"My parents had sent me to live in a convent in that part of France known as the Midi," she recalled. "Once a month, our mothers and fathers visited us, but the rest of the time we were isolated from the rest of mankind. Our vacations were confined to the convent's huge arbors and vineyards.

"From the time I was eight until I left at nineteen to become a bride, I was trapped there. How giddy I was when I finally gained my freedom! I took my first steps beyond the convent door and should have fainted had my father not caught my arm and guided me to a nearby bench.

"But the odd thing I am about to relate happened when I was a naïve and naughty twelve-year-old, much like all my friends. Naturally, most of our time was occupied with lessons and prayers, yet there was still sufficient leisure to hear the Devil's coy reminders that we would soon grow into young women.

"No men were permitted in the convent, save for three decrepit gardeners and an elderly priest who said Mass and took our puerile confessions. As I said before, our fathers paid us monthly visits, but those girls with brothers talked about them as if they were gods.

"One night at dusk, we had all just left vespers and were headed single file for our rooms when outside the garden walls we heard the distant cry of a noble, melancholy horn. Our hearts leapt at the sound. That night, ah, the dreams we all had. . . .

"And the following day, little blond-haired Clémence de Pambré entered the classroom looking ever so pale and murmured to her friend Louise that outside in the dark corridor, she'd seen a blue eye. Whispers spread like fire; soon the whole class knew about the blue eye. Our teacher tried to conduct the lesson, but gleaned nothing but silly answers. None of us could concentrate on the history of the French aristocracy when there was a blue eye waiting for us outside.

"Within the next few days, all of us saw the blue eye drifting through the convent's shadowy passages. It frightened us, but no one had the nerve to speak of it to the nuns. We tried to figure out whose eye it was and someone, I don't remember who, suggested that it must belong to the hunter who'd blown that sad, gay, captivating music we'd heard a few nights before. Yes! that was the answer: a blue-eyed hunter had secreted himself somewhere within the convent's forbidden walls. We did not even try to reconcile our theory with the fact that all we saw was a disembodied eye floating along the old hallways of our dormitory. All we cared about was the eye and the hunter it reminded us of.

"By now, the blue eye no longer frightened us. On the contrary, we began to go into the halls alone, hoping that the eye would stop and stare at us. We took pains to groom ourselves to look our best. There were no looking-glasses allowed in the convent, yet we improvised a way to check our appearance. Behind the clear panes of the doors we passed we'd arrange a piece of black cloth, thereby fashioning a makeshift mirror where we could swiftly primp up our hair and hope that we were attractive enough to interest the blue eye.

"The eye studied us for two whole months, and then it came less and less. We seldom talked of it after that, and then only with a little shiver, for it again frightened us . . . and yet, ah! each shiver held, too, a memory of that secret thrill concealed in all things forbidden . . ."

—Freely adapted by Marvin Kaye

Anne Rice

The Master of Rampling Gate

ANNE RICE, *best-selling author of* Interview with a Vampire, *has written several novels, including* The Vampire Lestat, Queen of the Damned, The Feast of All Saints, Cry to Heaven *and others. A resident of San Francisco, Ms. Rice generally does not write short fiction, so it is an unusual find to present the following tale that, like* Interview, *is deeply concerned with the emotional aspirations of a romantic vampire. "The Master of Rampling Gate" was first published in the February 1984* Redbook.

Spring 1888

RAMPLING GATE. It was so real to us in the old pictures, rising like a fairy-tale castle out of its own dark wood. A wilderness of gables and chimneys between those two immense towers, gray stone walls mantled in ivy, mullioned windows reflecting the drifting clouds.

But why had Father never taken us there? And why, on his deathbed, had he told my brother that Rampling Gate must be torn down, stone by stone? "I should have done it, Richard," he said. "But I was born in that house, as my father was, and his father before him. You must do it now, Richard. It has no claim on you. Tear it down."

Was it any wonder that not two months after Father's passing, Richard and I were on the noon train headed south for the mysterious mansion that had stood upon the rise above the village of Rampling for four hundred years? Surely Father would have understood. How could we destroy the old place when we had never seen it?

But, as the train moved slowly through the outskirts of London I can't say we were very sure of ourselves, no matter how curious and excited we were.

Richard had just finished four years at Oxford. Two whirlwind social seasons in London had proved me something of a shy success. I still preferred scribbling poems and stories in my room to dancing the night away, but I'd kept that a good secret. And though we had lost our mother when we were little, Father had given us the best of everything. Now the carefree years were ended. We had to be careful and wise.

The evening before, we had pored over all the old pictures of Rampling Gate, recalling in hushed, tentative voices the night Father had taken those pictures down from the walls.

I couldn't have been more than six and Richard eight when it happened, yet we remembered well the strange incident in Victoria Station that had precipitated Father's uncharacteristic rage. We had gone there after supper to say farewell to a school friend of Richard's, and Father had caught a glimpse, quite unexpectedly, of a young man at the lighted window of an incoming train. I could remember the young man's face clearly to this day: remarkably handsome, with a head of lustrous brown hair, his large black eyes regarding Father with the saddest expression as Father drew back. "Unspeakable horror!" Father had whispered. Richard and I had been too amazed to speak a word.

Later that night, Father and Mother quarreled, and we crept out of our rooms to listen on the stairs.

"That he should dare to come to London!" Father said over and over. "Is it not enough for him to be the undisputed master of Rampling Gate?"

How we had puzzled over it as little ones! Who was this stranger, and how could he be master of a house that belonged to our father, a house that had been left in the care of an old blind housekeeper for years?

But now after looking at the pictures again, it was too dreadful to think of Father's exhortation. And too exhilarating to think of the house itself. I'd packed my manuscripts, for—who knew?—maybe in that melancholy and exquisite setting I'd find exactly the inspiration I needed for the story I'd been writing in my head.

Yet there was something almost illicit about the excitement I felt. I saw in my mind's eye that pale young man again, with his black greatcoat and red woolen cravat. Like bone china, his complexion had been. Strange to remember it so vividly. And I realized now that in those few remarkable moments, he had created for me an ideal of masculine beauty that I had never questioned since. But Father had been so angry. I felt an unmistakable pang of guilt.

It was late afternoon when the old trap carried us up the gentle slope from the little railway station and we had our first real look at the house. The sky had paled to a deep rose hue beyond a bank of softly gilded clouds, and the last rays of the sun struck the uppermost panes of the leaded windows and filled them with solid gold.

"Oh, but it's too majestic," I whispered, "too like a great cathedral, and to think that it belongs to us!"

Richard gave me the smallest kiss on the cheek.

I wanted with all my heart to jump down from the trap and draw near on foot, letting those towers slowly grow larger and larger above me, but our old horse was only gaining speed.

When we reached the massive front door Richard and I were spirited into the great hall by the tiny figure of the blind housekeeper, Mrs. Blessington, our footfalls echoing loudly on the marble tile, and our eyes dazzled by the dusty shafts of light that fell on the long oak table and its heavily carved chairs, on the somber tapestries that stirred ever so slightly against the soaring walls.

"Richard, it is an enchanted place!" I cried, unable to contain myself.

Mrs. Blessington laughed gaily, her dry hand closing tightly on mine.

We found our bedchambers well aired, with snow-white linen on the beds and fires blazing cozily on the hearths. The small, diamond-paned windows opened on a glorious view of the lake and the oaks that enclosed it and the few scattered lights that marked the village beyond.

That night we laughed like children as we supped at the great oak table, our candles giving only a feeble light. And afterward we had a fierce battle of pocket billiards in the game room and a little too much brandy, I fear.

It was just before I went to bed that I asked Mrs. Blessington if there had been anyone in this house since my father left it, years before.

"No, my dear," she said quickly, fluffing the feather pillows. "When your father went away to Oxford, he never came back."

"There was never a young intruder after that? . . ." I pressed her, though in truth I had little appetite for anything that would disturb the happiness I felt. How I loved the Spartan cleanliness of this bedchamber, the walls bare of paper and ornament, the high luster of the walnut-paneled bed.

"A young intruder?" With an unerring certainty about her surroundings, she lifted the poker and stirred the fire. "No, dear. Whatever made you think there was?"

"Are there no ghost stories, Mrs. Blessington?" I asked suddenly, startling myself. *Unspeakable horror.* But what was I thinking—that that young man had not been real?

"Oh, no, darling," she said, smiling. "No ghost would ever dare to trouble Rampling Gate."

Nothing, in fact, troubled the serenity of the days that followed—long walks through the overgrown gardens, trips in the little skiff to and fro across the lake, tea under the hot glass of the empty conservatory. Early evening found us reading and writing by the library fire.

All our inquiries in the village met with the same answers: The villagers cherished the house. There was not a single disquieting legend or tale.

How were we going to tell them of Father's edict? How were we going to remind ourselves?

Richard was finding a wealth of classical material on the library shelves and I had the desk in the corner entirely to myself.

Never had I known such quiet. It seemed the atmosphere of Rampling Gate permeated my simplest written descriptions and wove its way richly into the plots and characters I created. The Monday after our arrival I finished my first real short story, and after copying out a fresh draft, I went off to the village on foot to post it boldly to the editors of *Blackwood's Magazine.*

It was a warm afternoon, and I took my time as I came back. What had disturbed our father so about this lovely corner of England? What had so darkened his last hours that he laid his curse upon this spot? My heart opened to this unearthly stillness, to an indisputable magnificence that caused me utterly to forget myself. There were times here when I felt I was a disembodied intellect drifting through a fathomless silence, up and down garden paths and stone corridors that had witnessed too much to take cognizance of one small and fragile young woman who in random moments actually talked aloud to the suits of armor around her, to the broken statues in the garden, the fountain cherubs who had had no water to pour from their conches for years and years.

But was there in this loveliness some malignant force that was eluding us still, some untold story? *Unspeakable horror* . . . Even in the flood of brilliant sunlight, those words gave me a chill.

As I came slowly up the slope I saw Richard walking lazily along the uneven shore of the lake. Now and then he glanced up at the distant battlements, his expression dreamy, almost blissfully contented.

Rampling Gate had him. And I understood perfectly because it also had me.

With a new sense of determination I went to him and placed my hand gently on his arm. For a moment he looked at me as if he did not even know me, and then he said softly:

"How will I ever do it, Julie? And one way or the other, it will be on my conscience all my life."

"It's time to seek advice, Richard," I said. "Write to our lawyers in London. Write to Father's clergyman, Dr. Matthews. Explain everything. We cannot do this alone."

It was three o'clock in the morning when I opened my eyes. But I had been awake for a long time. And I felt not fear, lying there alone, but something else—some vague and relentless agitation, some sense of emptiness and need that caused me finally to rise from my bed. What was this house, really? A place, or merely a state of mind? What was it doing to my soul?

I felt overwhelmed, yet shut out of some great and dazzling secret. Driven by an unbearable restlessness, I pulled on my woolen wrapper and my slippers and went into the hall.

The moonlight fell full on the oak stairway, and the vestibule far below. Maybe I could write of the confusion I suffered now, put on paper the inexplicable longing I felt. Certainly it was worth the effort, and I made my way soundlessly down the steps.

The great hall gaped before me, the moonlight here and there touching upon a pair of crossed swords or a mounted shield. But far beyond, in the alcove just outside the library, I saw the uneven glow of the fire. So Richard was there. A sense of well-being pervaded me and quieted me. At the same time, the distance between us seemed endless and I became desperate to cross it, hurrying past the long supper table and finally into the alcove before the library doors.

The fire blazed beneath the stone mantelpiece and a figure sat in the leather chair before it, bent over a loose collection of pages that he held in his slender hands. He was reading the pages eagerly, and the fire suffused his face with a warm, golden light.

But it was not Richard. It was the same young man I had seen on the train in Victoria Station fifteen years ago. And not a single aspect of that taut young face had changed. There was the very same hair, thick and lustrous and only carelessly combed as it hung to the collar of his black coat, and those dark eyes that looked up suddenly and fixed me with a most curious expression as I almost screamed.

We stared at each other across that shadowy room, I stranded in the doorway, he visibly and undeniably shaken that I had caught him un-awares. My heart stopped.

And in a split second he rose and moved toward me, closing the gap between us, reaching out with those slender white hands.

"Julie!" he whispered, in a voice so low that it seemed my own thoughts were speaking to me. But this was no dream. He was holding me and the scream had broken loose from me, deafening, uncontrollable and echoing from the four walls.

I was alone. Clutching at the doorframe, I staggered forward, and then in a moment of perfect clarity I saw the young stranger again, saw him standing in the open door to the garden, looking back over his shoulder; then he was gone.

I could not stop screaming. I could not stop even as I heard Richard's voice calling me, heard his feet pound down that broad, hollow staircase and through the great hall. I could not stop even as he shook me, pleaded with me, settled me in a chair.

Finally I managed to describe what I had seen.

"But you know who it was!" I said almost hysterically. "It was he—the young man from the train!"

"Now, wait," Richard said. "He had his back to the fire, Julie. And you could not see his face clearly—"

"Richard, it was he! Don't you understand? He touched me. He called me Julie," I whispered. "Good God, Richard, look at the fire. I didn't light it—he did. He was here!"

All but pushing Richard out of the way, I went to the heap of papers that lay strewn on the carpet before the hearth. "My story . . ." I whis-pered, snatching up the pages. "He's been reading my story, Richard. And —dear God—he's read your letters, the letters to Mr. Partridge and Dr. Matthews, about tearing down the house!"

"Surely you don't believe it was the same man, Julie, after all these years . . . ?"

"But he had not changed, Richard, not in the smallest detail. There is no mistake, I tell you. It was the very same man!"

. . . .

The next day was the most trying since we had come. Together we commenced a search of the house. Darkness found us only half finished, frustrated everywhere by locked doors we could not open and old staircases that were not safe.

And it was also quite clear by suppertime that Richard did not believe I had seen anyone in the study at all. As for the fire—well, he had failed to put it out properly before going to bed; and the pages—well, one of us had put them there and forgotten them, of course. . . .

But I knew what I had seen.

And what obsessed me more than anything else was the gentle countenance of the mysterious man I had glimpsed, the innocent eyes that had fixed on me for one moment before I screamed.

"You would be wise to do one very important thing before you retire," I said crossly. "Leave out a note to the effect that you do not intend to tear down the house."

"Julie, you have created an impossible dilemma," Richard declared, the color rising in his face. "You insist we reassure this apparition that the house will not be destroyed, when in fact you verify the existence of the very creature that drove our father to say what he did."

"Oh, I wish I had never come here!" I burst out suddenly.

"Then we should go, and decide this matter at home."

"No—that's just it. I could never go without knowing. I could never go on living without knowing now!"

Anger must be an excellent antidote to fear, for surely something worked to alleviate my natural alarm. I did not undress that night, but rather sat in the darkened bedroom, gazing at the small square of diamond-paned window until I heard the house fall quiet. When the grandfather clock in the great hall chimed the hour of eleven, Rampling Gate was, as usual, fast asleep.

I felt a dark exultation as I imagined myself going out of the room and down the stairs. But I knew I should wait one more hour. I should let the night reach its peak. My heart was beating too fast, and dreamily I recollected the face I had seen, the voice that had said my name.

Why did it seem in retrospect so intimate, that we had known each other before, spoken together a thousand times? Was it because he had read my story, those words that came from my very soul?

"Who are you?" I believe I whispered aloud. "Where are you at this moment?" I uttered the word, "Come."

The door opened without a sound and he was standing there. He was dressed exactly as he had been the night before and his dark eyes were riveted on me with that same obvious curiosity, his mouth just a little slack, like that of a boy.

I sat forward, and he raised his finger as if to reassure me and gave a little nod.

"Ah, it is you!" I whispered.

"Yes," he said in a soft, unobtrusive voice.

"And you are not a spirit!" I looked at his mud-spattered boots, at the faintest smear of dust on that perfect white cheek.

"A spirit?" he asked almost mournfully. "Would that I were that."

Dazed, I watched him come toward me; the room darkened and I felt his cool, silken hands on my face. I had risen. I was standing before him, and I looked up into his eyes.

I heard my own heartbeat. I heard it as I had the night before, right at the moment I had screamed. Dear God, I was talking to him! He was in my room and I was talking to him! And then suddenly I was in his arms.

"Real, absolutely real!" I whispered, and a low, zinging sensation coursed through me so that I had to steady myself.

He was peering at me as if trying to comprehend something terribly important. His lips had a ruddy look to them, a soft look for all his handsomeness, as if he had never been kissed. A slight dizziness came over me, a slight confusion in which I was not at all sure that he was even there.

"Oh, but I am," he said, as if I had spoken my doubt. I felt his breath against my cheek, and it was almost sweet. "I am here, and I have watched you ever since you came."

"Yes. . . ."

My eyes were closing. In a dim flash, as of a match being struck, I saw my father, heard his voice. *No, Julie.* . . . But that was surely a dream.

"Only a little kiss," said the voice of the one who was really here. I felt his lips against my neck. "I would never harm you. No harm ever for the children of this house. Just the little kiss, Julie, and the understanding that it imparts, that you cannot destroy Rampling Gate, Julie—that you can never, never drive me away."

The core of my being, that secret place where all desires and all commandments are nurtured, opened to him without a struggle or a sound. I would have fallen if he had not held me. My arms closed about him, my hands slipping into the soft, silken mass of his hair.

I was floating, and there was, as there had always been at Rampling

Gate, an endless peace. It was Rampling Gate I felt enclosing me; it was that timeless and impenetrable secret that had opened itself at last. . . . A *power within me of enormous ken . . . To see as a god sees, and take the depth of things as nimbly as the outward eyes can size and shape pervade* . . . Yes, those very words from Keats, which I had quoted in the pages of my story that he had read.

But in a violent instant he had released me. "Too innocent," he whispered.

I went reeling across the bedroom floor and caught hold of the frame of the window.

There was a tingling pain in my throat where his lips had touched me that was almost pleasurable, a delicious throbbing that would not stop. I knew what he was!

I turned and I saw all the room clearly—the bed, the fireplace, the chair. And he stood still exactly as I'd left him and there was the most appalling anguish in his face.

"Something of menace, unspeakable menace," I whispered, backing away.

"Something ancient, something that defies understanding," he pleaded. "Something that can and will go on." But he was shaken and he would not look into my eyes.

I touched that pulsing pain with the tips of my fingers and, looking down at them, saw the blood. "Vampire!" I gasped. "And yet you suffer so, and it is as if you can love!"

"Love? I have loved you since you came. I loved you when I read your secret thoughts and had not yet seen your face."

He drew me to him ever so gently, and slipping his arm around me, guided me to the door.

I tried for one desperate moment to resist him. And as any gentleman might, he stepped back respectfully and took my hand.

Through the long upstairs corridor we passed, and through a small wooden doorway to a screw stair that I had not seen before. I soon realized we were ascending in the north tower, a ruined portion of the structure that had been sealed off years before.

Through one tiny window after another I saw the gently rolling landscape and the small cluster of dim lights that marked the village of Rampling and the pale streak of white that was the London road.

Up and up we climbed, until we reached the topmost chamber, and this he opened with an iron key. He held back the door for me to enter and I found myself in a spacious room whose high, narrow windows contained no glass. A flood of moonlight revealed the most curious mixture of furnishings and objects—a writing table, a great shelf of books, soft leather chairs, and scores of maps and framed pictures affixed to the walls. Candles all about had dripped their wax on every surface, and in the very midst of this chaos lay my poems, my old sketches—early writings that I had brought with me and never even unpacked.

I saw a black silk top hat and a walking stick, and a bouquet of withered flowers, dry as straw, and daguerreotypes and tintypes in their little velvet cases, and London newspapers and opened books.

There was no place for sleeping in this room.

And when I thought of that, where he must lie when he went to rest, a shudder passed over me and I felt, quite palpably, his lips touching my throat again, and I had the sudden urge to cry.

But he was holding me in his arms; he was kissing my cheeks and my lips ever so softly.

"My father knew what you were!" I whispered.

"Yes," he answered, "and his father before him. And all of them in an unbroken chain over the years. Out of loneliness or rage, I know not which, I always told them. I always made them acknowledge, accept."

I backed away and he didn't try to stop me. He lighted the candles about us one by one.

I was stunned by the sight of him in the light, the gleam in his large black eyes and the gloss of his hair. Not even in the railway station had I seen him so clearly as I did now, amid the radiance of the candles. He broke my heart.

And yet he looked at me as though I were a feast for his eyes, and he said my name again and I felt the blood rush to my face. But there seemed a great break suddenly in the passage of time. What had I been thinking! *Yes, never tell, never disturb . . . something ancient, something greater than good and evil. . . .* But no! I felt dizzy again. I heard Father's voice: *Tear it down, Richard, stone by stone.*

He had drawn me to the window. And as the lights of Rampling were subtracted from the darkness below, a great wood stretched out in all directions, far older and denser than the forest of Rampling Gate. I was afraid suddenly, as if I were slipping into a maelstrom of visions from which I could never, of my own will, return.

There was that sense of our talking together, talking and talking in low, agitated voices, and I was saying that I should not give in.

"Bear witness—that is all I ask of you, Julie."

And there was in me some dim certainty that by these visions alone I would be fatally changed.

But the very room was losing its substance, as if a soundless wind of terrific force were blowing it apart. The vision had already begun. . . .

We were riding on horseback through a forest, he and I. And the trees were so high and so thick that scarcely any sun at all broke through to the fragrant, leaf-strewn ground.

Yet we had no time to linger in this magical place. We had come to the fresh-tilled earth that surrounded a village I somehow knew was called Knorwood, with its gabled roofs and its tiny, crooked streets. We saw the monastery of Knorwood and the little church with the bell chiming vespers under the lowering sky. A great, bustling life resided in Knorwood, a thousand voices rising in common prayer.

Far beyond, on the rise above the forest, stood the round tower of a truly ancient castle; and to that ruined castle—no more than a shell of itself anymore—as darkness fell in earnest we rode. Through its empty chambers we roamed, impetuous children, the horses and the road quite forgotten, and to the lord of the castle, a gaunt and white-skinned creature standing before the roaring fire of the roofless hall, we came. He turned and fixed us with his narrow and glittering eyes. A dead thing he was, I understood, but he carried within himself a priceless magic. And my companion, my innocent young man, stepped forward into the lord's arms.

I saw the kiss. I saw the young man grow pale and struggle and turn away, and the lord retreated with the wisest, saddest smile.

I understood. I knew. But the castle was dissolving as surely as anything in this dream might dissolve, and we were in some damp and close place.

The stench was unbearable to me; it was that most terrible of all stenches, the stench of death. And I heard my steps on the cobblestones and I reached out to steady myself against a wall. The tiny marketplace was deserted; the doors and windows gaped open to the vagrant wind. Up one side and down the other of the crooked street I saw the marks on the houses. And I knew what the marks meant. The Black Death had come to the village of Knorwood. The Black Death had laid it waste. And in a moment of suffocating horror I realized that no one, not a single person, was left alive.

But this was not quite right. There was a young man walking in fits and starts up the narrow alleyway. He was staggering, almost falling, as he pushed in one door after another, and at last came to a hot, reeking place where a child screamed on the floor. Mother and father lay dead in the bed. And the sleek fat cat of the household, unharmed, played with the screaming infant, whose eyes bulged in its tiny, sunken face.

"Stop it!" I heard myself gasp. I was holding my head with both hands. "Stop it—stop it, please!" I was screaming, and my screams would surely pierce the vision and this crude little dwelling would collapse around me and I would rouse the household of Rampling Gate, but I did not. The young man turned and stared at me, and in the close, stinking room I could not see his face.

But I knew it was he, my companion, and I could smell his fever and his sickness, and the stink of the dying infant, and see the gleaming body of the cat as it pawed at the child's outstretched hand.

"Stop it, you've lost control of it!" I screamed, surely with all my strength, but the infant screamed louder. "Make it stop."

"I cannot," he whispered. "It goes on forever! It will never stop!"

And with a great shriek I kicked at the cat and sent it flying out of the filthy room, overturning the milk pail as it went.

Death in all the houses of Knorwood. Death in the cloister, death in the open fields. It seemed the Judgment of God—I was sobbing, begging to be released—it seemed the very end of Creation itself.

But as night came down over the dead village he was alive still, stumbling up the slopes, through the forest, toward that tower where the lord stood at the broken arch of the window, waiting for him to come.

"Don't go!" I begged him. I ran alongside him, crying, but he didn't hear.

The lord turned and smiled with infinite sadness as the young man on his knees begged for salvation, when it was damnation this lord offered, when it was only damnation that the lord would give.

"Yes, damned, then, but living, breathing!" the young man cried, and the lord opened his arms.

The kiss again, the lethal kiss, the blood drawn out of his dying body, and then the lord lifting the heavy head of the young man so the youth could take the blood back again from the body of the lord himself.

I screamed, "Do not—do not drink!" He turned, and his face was now so perfectly the visage of death that I couldn't believe there was animation left in him; yet he asked: "What would you do? Would you go back to Knorwood, would you open those doors one after another, would you ring the bell in the empty church—and if you did, who would hear?"

He didn't wait for my answer. And I had none now to give. He locked his innocent mouth to the vein that pulsed with every semblance of life beneath the lord's cold and translucent flesh. And the blood jetted into the young body, vanquishing in one great burst the fever and the sickness that had racked it, driving it out along with the mortal life.

He stood now in the hall of the lord alone. Immortality was his, and the blood thirst he would need to sustain it, and that thirst I could feel with my whole soul.

And each and every thing was transfigured in his vision—to the exquisite essence of itself. A wordless voice spoke from the starry veil of heaven; it sang in the wind that rushed through the broken timbers; it sighed in the flames that ate at the sooted stones of the hearth. It was the eternal rhythm of the universe that played beneath every surface as the last living creature in the village—that tiny child—fell silent in the maw of time.

A soft wind sifted and scattered the soil from the newly turned furrows in the empty fields. The rain fell from the black and endless sky.

Years and years passed. And all that had been Knorwood melted into the earth. The forest sent out its silent sentinels, and mighty trunks rose where there had been huts and houses, where there had been monastery walls. And it seemed the horror beyond all horrors that no one should know anymore of those who had lived and died in that small and insignificant village, that not anywhere in the great archives in which all history is recorded should a mention of Knorwood exist.

Yet one remained who knew, one who had witnessed, one who had seen the Ramplings come in the years that followed, seen them raise their house upon the very slope where the ancient castle had once stood, one who saw a new village collect itself slowly upon the unmarked grave of the old.

And all through the walls of Rampling Gate were the stones of that old castle, the stones of the forgotten monastery, the stones of that little church.

We were once again back in the tower.

"It is my shrine," he whispered. "My sanctuary. It is the only thing that endures as I endure. And you love it as I love it, Julie. You have written it. . . . You love its grandeur. And its gloom."

"Yes, yes. . . . as it's always been . . ." I was crying, though I didn't move my lips.

He had turned to me from the window, and I could feel his endless craving with all my heart.

"What else do you want from me!" I pleaded. "What else can I give?"

A torrent of images answered me. It was beginning again. I was once again relinquishing myself, yet in a great rush of lights and noise I was enlivened and made whole as I had been when we rode together through the forest, but it was into the world of now, this hour, that we passed.

We were flying through the rural darkness along the railway toward London, where the nighttime city burst like an enormous bubble in a shower of laughter and motion and glaring light. He was walking with me under the gas lamps, his face all but shimmering with that same dark innocence, that same irresistible warmth. It seemed we were holding tight to each other in the very midst of a crowd. And the crowd was a living thing, a writhing thing, and everywhere there came a dark, rich aroma from it, the aroma of fresh blood. Women in white fur and gentlemen in opera capes swept through the brightly lighted doors of the theatre; the blare of the music hall inundated us and then faded away. Only a thin soprano voice was left, singing a high, plaintive song. I was in his arms and his lips were covering mine, and there came that dull, zinging sensation again, that great, uncontrollable opening within myself. Thirst, and the promise of satiation measured only by the intensity of that thirst. Up back staircases we fled together, into high-ceilinged bedrooms papered in red damask, where the loveliest women reclined on brass beds, and the aroma was so strong now that I could not bear it and he said: "Drink. They are your victims! They will give you eternity—you must drink." And I felt the warmth filling me, charging me, blurring my vision until we broke free again, light and invisible, it seemed, as we moved over the rooftops and down again through rain-drenched streets. But the rain did not touch us; the falling snow did not chill us; we had within ourselves a great and indissoluble heat. And together in the carriage we talked to each other in low, exuberant rushes of language; we were lovers; we were constant; we were immortal. We were as enduring as Rampling Gate.

Oh, don't let it stop! I felt his arms around me and I knew we were in the tower room together, and the visions had worked their fatal alchemy.

"Do you understand what I am offering you? To your ancestors I revealed myself, yes; I subjugated them. But I would make you my bride, Julie. I would share with you my power. Come with me. I will not take you against your will, but can you turn away?"

Again I heard my own scream. My hands were on his cool white skin, and his lips were gentle yet hungry, his eyes yielding and ever young. Father's angry countenance blazed before me as if I, too, had the power to conjure. *Unspeakable horror.* I covered my face.

He stood against the backdrop of the window, against the distant drift of pale clouds. The candlelight glimmered in his eyes. Immense and sad and wise, they seemed—and oh, yes, innocent, as I have said again and again. "You are their fairest flower, Julie. To them I gave my protection always. To you I give my love. Come to me, dearest, and Rampling Gate will truly be yours, and it will finally, truly be mine."

Nights of argument, but finally Richard had come around. He would sign over Rampling Gate to me and I should absolutely refuse to allow the place to be torn down. There would be nothing he could do then to obey Father's command. I had given him the legal impediment he needed, and of course I told him I would leave the house to his male heirs. It should always be in Rampling hands.

A clever solution, it seemed to me, since Father had not told me to destroy the place. I had no scruples in the matter now at all.

And what remained was for him to take me to the little train station and see me off for London, and not worry about my going home to Mayfair on my own.

"You stay here as long as you wish and do not worry," I said. I felt more tenderly toward him than I could ever express. "You knew as soon as you set foot in the place that Father was quite wrong."

The great black locomotive was chugging past us, the passenger cars slowing to a stop.

"Must go now, darling—kiss me," I said.

"But what came over you, Julie—what convinced you so quickly . . . ?"

"We've been through all that, Richard," I said. "What matters is that Rampling Gate is safe and we are both happy, my dear."

I waved until I couldn't see him anymore. The flickering lamps of the town were lost in the deep lavender light of the early evening, and the dark hulk of Rampling Gate appeared for one uncertain moment like the ghost of itself on the nearby rise.

I sat back and closed my eyes. Then I opened them slowly, savoring this moment for which I had waited so long.

He was smiling, seated in the far corner of the leather seat opposite, as he had been all along, and now he rose with a swift, almost delicate movement and sat beside me and enfolded me in his arms.

"It's five hours to London," he whispered.

"I can wait," I said, feeling the thirst like a fever as I held tight to him, feeling his lips against my eyelids and my hair. "I want to hunt the London streets tonight," I confessed a little shyly, but I saw only approbation in his eyes.

"Beautiful Julie, my Julie . . ." he whispered.

"You'll love the house in Mayfair," I said.

"Yes . . ." he said.

"And when Richard finally tires of Rampling Gate, we shall go home."

Theodore Sturgeon

The Deadly Ratio

Here is another remarkable tale by THEODORE STURGEON *(1918–85), International Fantasy Award winner (for* More Than Human) *and author of such popular novels and short story collections as* The Cosmic Rape, The Dreaming Jewels, E Pluribus Unicorn *and* Without Sorcery. *Like "The Perfect Host," included in* Weird Tales, *the Magazine that Never Dies, "The Deadly Ratio" is a Ted Sturgeon tour de force that, according to its protagonist, might actually happen to you-the-reader.*

BETTER NOT READ IT. I mean it. No—this isn't one of those "perhaps it will happen to you" things. It's a lot worse than that. It might very possibly be happening to you right now. And you won't know until it's over. You can't, by the very nature of things.

(I wonder what the population really is?)

On the other hand, maybe it won't make any difference if I do tell you about it. Once you got used to the idea, you might even be able to relax and enjoy it. Heaven knows there's plenty to enjoy—and again I say it— by the very nature of things.

All right, then, if you think you can take it. . . .

I met her in a restaurant. You may know the place—Murphy's. It has a big oval bar and then a partition. On the other side of the partition are small tables, then an aisle, then booths.

Gloria was sitting at one of the small tables. All of the booths but two were empty; all the other small tables but one were unoccupied, so there was plenty of room in the place for me.

But there was only one place I could sit—at her table. That was because, when I saw Gloria, there wasn't anything else in the world. I have never been through anything like that. I just stopped dead. I dropped my briefcase and stared at her. She had gleaming auburn hair and olive skin. She had delicate high-arched nostrils and a carved mouth, lips that were curved above like gull's wings on the down-beat, and full below. Her eyes were as sealed and spice-toned as a hot buttered rum, and as deep as a mountain night.

Without taking my eyes from her face, I groped for a chair and sat opposite her. I'd forgotten everything. Even about being hungry. Helen hadn't, though. Helen was the head waitress and a swell person. She was fortyish and happy. She didn't know my name but used to call me "The Hungry Fella." I never had to order. When I came in she'd fill me a bar-glass full of beer and pile up two orders of that day's Chef's Special on a steak platter. She arrived with the beer, picked up my briefcase, and went for the fodder. I just kept on looking at Gloria, who by this time, was registering considerable amazement, and a little awe. The awe, she told me later, was conceived only at the size of the beer-glass, but I have my doubts about that.

She spoke first. "Taking an inventory?"

She had one of those rare voices which make noises out of all other sounds. I nodded. Her chin was rounded, with the barest suggestion of a cleft, but the hinges of her jaw were square.

I think she was a little flustered. She dropped her eyes—I was glad, because I could see then how very long and thick her lashes were—and poked at her salad. She looked up again, half-smiling. Her teeth met, tip to tip. I'd read about that but had never actually seen it before. "What is it?" she asked. "Have I made a conquest?"

I nodded again. "You certainly have."

"Well!" she breathed.

"Your name's Gloria," I said positively.

"How did you know?"

"It had to be, that's all."

She looked at me carefully, at my eyes, my forehead, my shoulders. "If your name is Leo, I'll scream."

"Scream then. But why?"

"I—I've always thought I'd meet a man named Leo, and—"

Helen canceled the effects of months of good relations between herself and me, by bringing my lunch just then. Gloria's eyes widened when she saw it. "You must be very fond of lobster hollandaise."

"I'm very fond of all subtle things," I said, "and I like them in great masses."

"I've never met anyone like you," she said candidly.

"No one like you ever has."

"Oh?"

I picked up my fork. "Obviously not, or there'd be a race of us." I scooped up some lobster. "Would you be good enough to watch carefully while I eat? I can't seem to stop looking at you, and I'm afraid I might stab my face with the fork."

She chortled. It wasn't a chuckle, or a gurgle. It was a true Lewis Carrol chortle. They're very rare. "I'll watch."

"Thank you. And while you watch, tell me what you don't like."

"What I *don't* like? Why?"

"I'll probably spend the rest of my life finding out the things you do like, and doing them with you. So let's get rid of the nonessentials."

She laughed. "All right. I don't like tapioca because it makes me feel conspicuous, staring that way. I don't like furniture with buttons on the upholstery; lace curtains that cross each other; small flower-prints, hooks-and-eyes and snap fasteners where zippers ought to be; that orchestra leader with the candy saxophones and the yodelling brother; tweedy men who smoke pipes; people who can't look me in the eye when they're lying; night clothes; people who make mixed drinks with Scotch—my, you eat fast."

"I just do it to get rid of my appetite so I can begin eating for esthetic reasons. I like that list."

"What don't *you* like?"

"I don't like literary intellectuals with their conversations all dressed up in overquotes. I don't like bathing-suits that don't let the sun in and I don't like weather that keeps bathing-suits in. I don't like salty food; clinging-vine girls; music that doesn't go anywhere or build anything; people who have forgotten how to wonder like children; automobiles designed to be better streamlined going backwards than going forward; people who will try anything once but are afraid to try it twice and acquire a taste; and professional sceptics." I went back to my lunch.

"You bat a thousand," she said. "Something remarkable is happening here."

"Let it happen," I cautioned. "Never mind what it is or why. Don't be like the guy who threw a light-bulb on the floor to find out if it was brittle." Helen passed and I ordered a Slivovitz.

"Prune brandy!" cried Gloria. "I love it!"

"I know. It's for you."

"Someday you're going to be wrong," she said, suddenly somber, "and that will be bad."

"That will be good. It'll be the difference between harmony and contrast, that's all."

"Leo—"

"Hm?"

She brought her gaze squarely to me, and it was so warm I could feel it on my face. "Nothing. I was just saying it, Leo. *Leo.*"

Something choked me—not the lobster. It was all gone. "I have no gag for that. I can't top it. I can match it, Gloria."

Another thing was said, but without words.

There are still no words for it. Afterward she reached across and touched my hand with her fingertips. I saw colors.

I got up to go, after scribbling on a piece of the menu. "Here's my phone number. Call me up when there's no other way out."

She raised her eyebrows. "Don't you want my phone, or my address, or anything?"

"No," I said.

"But—"

"This means too much," I said. "I'm sorry if I seem to be dropping it in your lap like this. But any time you are with me, I want it to be because you want to be with me, not because you think it's what I might want. We've got to be together because we are traveling in the same direction at approximately the same speed, each under his own power. If I call you up and make all the arrangements, it could be that I was acting on a conditioned reflex, like any other wolf. If you call, we can both be sure."

"It makes sense." She raised those deep eyes to me. Leaving her was coming up out of those eyes hand over hand. A long haul. I only just made it.

Out on the street I tried valiantly to get some sense of proportion. The most remarkable thing about the whole remarkable business was simply this: that in all my life before, I had never been able to talk to anyone like that. I had always been diffident, easy-going, unaggressive to a fault, and rather slow on the uptake.

I felt like the daydreams of the much advertised 97-pound weakling as he clipped that coupon.

"Hey—you!"

I generally answered to that as well as anything else. I looked up and recoiled violently. There was a human head floating in midair next to me.

I was so startled I couldn't even stop walking. The head drifted along beside me, bobbing slightly as if invisible legs carried an invisible body to which the visible head was attached. The face was middle-aged, bookish, dryly humorous.

"You're quite a hell of a fellow, aren't you?"

Oddly, my tongue loosened from the roof of my mouth. "Some pretty nice people think so," I faltered. I looked around nervously, expecting a stampede when other people saw this congenial horror.

"No one can see me but you," said the head. "No one that's likely to make a fuss, at any rate."

"Wh-what do you want?"

"Just wanted to tell you something," said the head. It must have had a throat somewhere because it cleared it. "Parthenogenesis," it said didactically, "has little survival value, even with syzygy. Without it—" The head disappeared. A little lower down, two bony, bare shoulders appeared, shrugged expressively, and vanished. The head reappeared. "—there isn't a chance."

"You don't say," I quavered.

It didn't say. Not any more, just then. It was gone.

I stopped, spun around, looking for it. What it had told me made as little sense to me, then, as its very appearance. It took quite a while for me to discover that it had told me the heart of the thing I'm telling you. I do hope I'm being a little more lucid than the head was.

Anyway, that was the first manifestation of all. By itself, it wasn't enough to make me doubt my sanity. As I said, it was only the first.

I might as well tell you something about Gloria. Her folks had been poor enough to evaluate good things, well enough off to be able to have a sample or two of these good things. So Gloria could appreciate what was good as well as the effort that was necessary to get it. At twenty-two she was the assistant buyer of a men's department store. (This was toward the end of the war.) She needed some extra money for a pet project, so she sang at a club every night. In her "spare" time she practiced and studied and at the end of a year had her commercial pilot's license. She spent the rest of the war ferrying airplanes.

Do you begin to get the idea of what kind of people she was?

She was one of the most dynamic women who ever lived. She was thoughtful and articulate and completely un-phoney.

She was strong. You can have no idea—no; some of you do know how strong. I had forgotten. . . . She radiated her strength. Her strength surrounded her like a cloud rather than like armor, for she was tangible through it. She influenced everything and everyone she came near. I felt, sometimes that the pieces of ground which bore her footprints, the chairs she used, the door she touched and the books she had held continued to radiate for weeks afterward like the Bikini ships.

She was completely self-sufficient. I had hit the matter squarely when I insisted that she call me before we saw each other again. Her very presence was a compliment. When she was with me, it was, by definition, because that was where she would rather be than any other place on earth. When she was away from me, it was because to be with me at that time would not have been a perfect thing, and in her way she was a perfectionist.

Oh, yes—a perfectionist. I should know!

You ought to know something about me, too, so that you can realize how completely a thing like this is done, and how it is being done to so many of you.

I'm in my twenties and I play guitar for a living. I've done a lot of things and I carry around a lot of memories from each of them—things that only I could possibly know. The color of the walls in the rooming house where I stayed when I was "on the beach" in Port Arthur, Texas, when the crew of my ship went out on strike. What kind of flowers that girl was wearing the night she jumped off the cruise ship in Montego Bay, down in Jamaica.

I can remember, hazily, things like my brother's crying because he was afraid of the vacuum cleaner, when he was four. So I couldn't have been quite three then. I can remember fighting with a kid called Boaz, when I was seven. I remember Harriet, whom I kissed under a fragrant tulip poplar one summer dusk when I was twelve. I remember the odd little lick that drummer used to tear off when, and only when he was really riding, while I was playing at the hotel, and the way the trumpet man's eyes used to close when he heard it. I remember the exact smell of the tiger's wagon when I was pulling ropes on the Barnes Circus, and the one-armed roustabout who used to chantey us along when we drove the stakes, he swinging a twelve-pound maul with the rest of us—

"*Hit* down, *slap it* down, *Haul* back, *snub*, bub,

"*Half*back, *quarter*back, *all*back, *whoa!*"—he used to cry, with the mauls rat-tatting on the steelbound peg and the peg melting into the ground, and the snubber grunting over his taut half-hitch while the six of us stood in a circle around the peg. And those other hammers, in the blacksmith's shop in Puerto Rico, with the youngster swinging a sledge in great full circles, clanging on the anvil, while the old smith touched the work almost delicately with his shaping hammer and then tinkled out every syncopation known to man by bouncing it on the anvil's horn and face between his own strokes and those of the great metronomic sledge. I remember the laboring and servile response of a power shovel under my hands as they shifted from hoist to crowd to swing to rehaul controls, and the tang of burning drum-frictions and hot crater compound. That was at the same quarry where the big Finnish blast foreman was killed by a premature shot. He was out in the open and knew he couldn't get clear. He stood straight and still and let it come, since it was bound to come, and he raised his right hand to his head. My mechanic said he was trying to protect his face but I thought at the time he was saluting something.

Details; that's what I'm trying to get over to you. My head was full of details that were intimately my own.

It was a little over two weeks—sixteen days, three hours, and twenty-three minutes, to be exact—before Gloria called. During that time I nearly lost my mind. I was jealous, I was worried, I was frantic. I cursed myself for not having gotten her number—why, I didn't even know her last name! There were times when I determined to hang up on her if I heard her voice, I was so sore. There were times when I stopped work—I did a lot of arranging for small orchestras—and sat before the silent phone, begging it to ring. I had a routine worked out: I'd demand a statement as to how she felt about me before I let her say another thing. I'd demand an explanation of her silence. I'd act casual and disinterested. I'd—

The phone did ring, though, and it was Gloria, and the dialogue went like so:

"Hello?"

"Leo."

"Yes, Gloria!"

"I'm coming up."

"I'm waiting."

And that was it. I met her at the door. I had never touched her before, except for that one brief contact of hands; and yet, with perfect confidence, with no idea of doing anything different, I took her in my arms and kissed her. This whole thing has its terrible aspects, and yet, sometimes I wonder if moments like that don't justify the horror of it.

I took her hand and led her into the living room. The room wavered like an underwater scene because she was in it. The air tasted different.

We sat close together with our hands locked, saying that wordless thing with our eyes. I kissed her again. I didn't ask her anything at all.

She had the smoothest skin that ever was. She had a skin smoother than a bird's throat. It was like satin-finished aluminum, but warm and yielding. It was smooth like Grand Marnier between your tongue and the roof of your mouth.

We played records—Django Reinhardt and The New Friends of Rhythm, and Bach's *Passacaglia and Fugue* and *Tubby the Tuba*. I showed her the Smith illustrations from *Fantazius Mallare* and my folio of Ed Weston prints. I saw things and heard things in them all that I had never known before, though they were things I loved.

Not one of them—not a book, nor a record, nor a picture, was new to her. By some alchemy, she had culled the random flood of esthetic expression that had come her way, and had her choices; and her choices were these things that I loved, but loved in a way exclusively hers, a way in which I could share.

We talked about books and places, ideas and people. In her way, she was something of a mystic. "I believe that there is something behind the old superstitions about calling up demons, and materializations of departed spirits," she said thoughtfully. "But I don't think it was ever done with mumbo-jumbo—witches' brew and pentagrams and toads' skins stuffed with human hair buried at the crossroads on a May midnight, unless these rituals were part of a much larger thing—a purely psychic and un-ghostly force coming from the 'wizard' himself."

"I never thought much about it," I said, stroking her hair. It is the only hair that was not fine that I have ever touched with pleasure. Like everything else about her, it was strong and controlled and glowing. "Have you ever tried anything like that? You're some sort of a sorceress. I know when I'm enchanted, at any rate."

"You're not enchanted," she said gravely. "You're not a thing with magic on it. You're a real magic all by yourself."

"You're a darling," I said. "Mine."

"I'm not!" she answered, in that odd way she had of turning aside fantasy for fact. "I don't belong to you. I belong to *me!*"

I must have looked rather stricken, for she laughed suddenly and kissed my hand. "What belongs to you is only a large part of 'us,'" she explained carefully. "Otherwise you belong to you and I belong to me. Do you see?"

"I think I do," I said slowly. "I said I wanted us to be together because we were both traveling together under our own power. I—didn't know it was going to be so true, that's all."

"Don't try to make it any different, Leo. Don't *ever*. If I started to really belong to you, I wouldn't be *me* any more, and then you wouldn't have anything at all."

"You seem so sure of these hazy things."

"They aren't hazy things! They're important. If it weren't for these things, I'd have to stop seeing you. I—*would* stop seeing you."

I put my arms tight around her. "Don't talk about that," I whispered, more frightened than I have ever been in my life before. "Talk about something else. Finish what you were saying about pentagrams and spirits."

She was still a moment. I think her heart was pounding the way mine was, and I think she was frightened too.

"I spend a lot of time reading and mulling over those things," she said after a quiet time. "I don't know why. I find them fascinating. You know what, Leo? I think too much has been written about manifestations of evil. I think it's true that good is more powerful than evil. And I think that far too much has been written and said about ghosties an' ghoulies an' things that go 'boomp' i' th' nicht, as the old Scottish prayer has it. I think those things have been too underlined. They're remarkable enough, but have you ever realized that things that are remarkable are, by definition, rare?"

"If the cloven-hoofed horrors and the wailing banshees are remarkable —which they are—then what's commonplace?"

She spread her hands—square, quite large hands, capable and beautifully kept. "The manifestations of good, of course. I believe that they're much easier to call up. I believe they happen all the time. An evil mind has to be very evil before it can project itself into a new thing with a life of its own. From all accounts I have read, it takes a tremendously powerful mind to call up even a little demon. Good things must be much easier to materialize, because they fall in the pattern of good living. More people live good lives than such thoroughly bad ones that they can materialize evil things."

"Well then, why don't more people bring more good things from behind this mystic curtain?"

"But they do!" she cried. "They must! The world is so full of good things! Why do you suppose they're so good? What put the innate goodness into Bach and the Victoria Falls and the color of your hair and Negro laughter and the way ginger ale tickles your nostrils?"

I shook my head slowly. "I think that's lovely, and I don't like it."

"Why not?"

I looked at her. She was wearing a wine-colored suit and a marigold silken kerchief tucked into the throat. It reflected on the warm olive of her chin. It reminded me of my grandmother's saying, when I was very small, "Let's see if you like butter," as she held a buttercup under my chin to see how much yellow it reflected. "You are good," I said slowly, searching hard for the words. "You are about the—the goodest thing that ever happened. If what you say is really true, then you might be just a shadow, a dream, a glorious thought that someone had."

"Oh, you idiot," she said, with sudden tears in her eyes. "You big, beautiful hunk of idiot!" She pressed me close and bit my cheek so hard that I yelped. "Is that real?"

"If it isn't," I said, shaken, "I'll be happy to go on dreaming."

She stayed another hour—as if there were such a thing as time when we were together—and then she left. I had her phone number by then. A hotel. And after she was gone, I wandered around my apartment, looking at the small wrinkles in the couch-cover where she had sat, touching the cup she had held, staring at the bland black surface of a record, marvelling at the way its grooves had unwound the *Passacaglia* for her. Most wonderful of all was a special way I discovered to turn my head as I moved. Her fragrance clung to my cheek, and if I turned my face just so, I could sense it. I thought about every one of those many minutes with her, each by itself, and the things we had done. I thought, too, about the things we had not done—I know you wondered—and I gloried in them. For, without a word spoken, we had agreed that a thing worth having was a thing worth awaiting and that where faith is complete, exploration is uncalled for.

She came back next day, and the day after. The first of these two visits was wonderful. We sang, mostly. I seemed to know all her very favorite songs. And by a happy accident, my pet key on the guitar—B flat—was exactly within her lovely contralto range. Though I say it as shouldn't, I played some marvellous guitar behind and around what she sang. We laughed a lot, largely at things that were secret between us—is there a love anywhere without its own new language?—and we talked for a long time about a book called *The Fountainhead* which seemed to have had the same extraordinary effect on her that it had on me; but then, it's an extraordinary book.

It was after she left that day that the strangeness began—the strangeness that turned into such utter horror. She hadn't been gone more than an hour when I heard the frightened scramble of tiny claws in the front room. I was poring over the string-bass part of a trio arrangement I was doing (and not seeing it for my Gloria-flavored thoughts) and I raised my head and listened. It was the most panic-struck scurrying imaginable, as if a regiment of newts and salamanders had broken ranks in a wild retreat. I remember clearly that the little-claw susurrus did not disturb me at all, but the terror behind the movement startled me in ways that were not pleasant.

What were they running from? was infinitely more important than *What were they?*

Slowly I put down the manuscript and stood up. I went to the wall and along it to the archway, not so much to keep out of sight as to surprise the *thing* that had so terrorized the possessors of those small frightened feet.

And that was the first time I have ever been able to smile while the hackles on the back of my neck were one great crawling prickle. For there was nothing there at all; nothing to glow in the dark before I switched on the overhead light, nothing to show afterward. But the little feet scurried away faster—there must have been hundreds of them—tapping and scrabbling out a perfect crescendo of horrified escape. That was what made my hackles rise. What made me smile—

The sounds radiated from *my* feet!

I stood there in the archway, my eyeballs throbbing with the effort to see this invisible rout; and from the threshold, to right and left and away into the far corners of the front room, ran the sounds of the little paws and tiny scratching claws. It was as if they were being generated under my soles, and then fleeing madly. None ran behind me. There seemed to be something keeping them from the living room. I took a cautious step further into the front room, and now they did run behind me, but only as far as the archway. I could hear them reach it and scuttle off to the side walls. You see what made me smile?

I was the horror that frightened them so!

The sound gradually lessened. It was not that it lessened in overall intensity. It was just that there were fewer and fewer creatures running away. It diminished rapidly, and in about ninety seconds it had reduced to an occasional single scampering. One invisible creature ran around and around me, as if all the unseen holes in the walls had been stopped up and it was frantically looking for one. It found one, too, and was gone.

I laughed then and went back to my work. I remember that I thought quite clearly after that, for a while. I remember writing in a *glissando* passage that was a stroke of genius—something to drive the dog-house slapper crazy but guaranteed to drive the customers even crazier if it could be done at all. I remember zoom-zooming it off under my breath, and feeling mightily pleased with myself over it.

And then the reaction struck me.

Those little claws—

What was happening to me?

I thought instantly of Gloria. *There's some deadly law of compensation working here,* I thought. For every yellow light, a purple shadow. For every peal of laughter, a cry of anguish somewhere. For the bliss of Gloria, a touch of horror to even things up.

I licked my lips, for they were wet and my tongue was dry.

What was happening to me?

I thought again of Gloria, and the colors and sounds of Gloria, and most of all, the reality, the solid normalcy of Gloria, for all her exquisite sense of fantasy.

I couldn't go crazy. I *couldn't!* Not *now!* I'd be—unfit.

Unfit! As terrifying to me, then, as the old cry of *"Unclean"* was in the Middle Ages.

"Gloria, darling," I'd have to say. *"Honey, we'll just have to call it quits. You see, I'm off my trolley. Oh, I'm quite serious. Yes indeed. The men in the white coats will come around and back up their little wagon to the door and take me away to the laughing academy. And we won't see each other any more. A pity. A great pity. Just give me a hearty little old handshake, now, and go find yourself another fellow."*

"Gloria!" I yelled. Gloria was all those colors, and the lovely sounds, and the fragrance that clung to my cheek and came to me when I moved and held my head just so.

"Oh, I dunno," I moaned. "I just don't know what to do! What is it? What is it?"

"Syzygy."

"Huh?" I came bolt upright, staring around wildly. Twenty inches over the couch hovered the seamed face of my jovial phantom of the street outside Murphy's. "You! Now I know I'm off my—hey! What is syzygy?"

"What's happening to you."

"Well, what is happening to me?"

"Syzygy." The head grinned engagingly. I put my head in my hands. There is an emotional pitch—an *un*emotional pitch, really—at which nothing is surprising, and I'd reached it. "Please explain," I said dully.

"Tell me who you are, and what you mean by this sizz-sizz whatever-it-is."

"I'm not anybody," said the head, "and syzygy is a concomitant of parthenogenetic and certain other low types. I think what's happening *is* syzygy. If it isn't—" The head disappeared, a hand with spatulate fingers appeared and snapped its fingers explosively; the hand disappeared, the head reappeared and smiled, "—you're a gone goose."

"Don't *do* that," I said miserably.

"Don't do what?"

"That—that piecemeal business. Why do you do it?"

"Oh—that. Conservation of energy. It works here too, you know."

"Where is 'here'?"

"That's a little difficult to explain until you get the knack of it. It's the place where reverse ratios exist. I mean, if something stacks up in a three to five ratio there, it's a five to three ratio here. Forces must balance."

I almost had it. What he said almost made sense. I opened my mouth to question him but he was gone.

After that I just sat there. Perhaps I wept.

And Gloria came the next day, too. That was bad. I did two wrong things. First, I kept information from her, which was inexcusable. If you are going to share at all, you must share the bad things too. The other thing I did was to question her like a jealous adolescent.

But what else could be expected? Everything was changed. Everything was different. I opened the door to her and she brushed past me with a smile, and not a very warm one at that, leaving me at the door all outstretched arms and large clumsy feet.

She shrugged out of her coat and curled up on the couch.

"Leo, play some music."

I felt like hell and I know I looked it. Did she notice? Did she even care? Didn't it make any difference at all how I felt, what I was going through?

I went and stood in front of her. "Gloria," I said sternly, "Where have you been?"

She looked up at me and released a small, retrospective sigh that turned me bright green and sent horns sprouting out of my scalp. It was such a happy, satisfied little sound. I stood there glowering at her. She waited a moment more and then got up, switched on the amplifier and turntable, dug out the "Dance of the Hours," turned the volume up, added too much bass, and switched in the volume expander, which is quite the wrong thing to use on that record. I strode across the room and turned the volume down.

"Please, Leo," she said in a hurt tone. "I like it that way."

Viciously I turned it back up and sat down with my elbows on my knees and my lower lip stuck out. I was wild. This was all wrong.

I know what I should do, I thought sullenly. *I ought to yank the plug on the rig and stand up and tell her off.*

How right I was! But I didn't do it. How could I do it? This was *Gloria*! Even when I looked up at her and saw her staring at me, saw the slight curl to her lip, I didn't do it. Well, it was too late then. She was watching me, comparing me with—

Yes, that was it. She was comparing me with somebody. Somebody who was different from her, someone who rode roughshod over everything delicate and subtle about her, everything about her that I liked and shared with her. And she, of course, ate it up.

I took refuge in the tactic of letting her make the first move. I think, then, that she despised me. And rightly.

A bit of cockney dialogue I had once heard danced through my mind:

"D'ye love us, Alf?"

"Yus."

"Well, knock us abaht a bit."

You see? I knew the right things to do, but—

But this was Gloria. I *couldn't*.

The record finished, and she let the automatic shut off the turntable. I think she expected me to turn it over. I didn't. She said, "All right, Leo. What is it?" tiredly.

I said to myself, "I'll start with the worst possible thing that could happen. She'll deny that, and then at least I'll feel better." So I said to her, "You've changed. There's somebody else."

She looked up at the picture molding and smiled sleepily. "Yes," she said. "There certainly is."

"Uff!" I said, because that caught me right in the solar plexus. I sat down abruptly.

"His name's Arthur," she said dreamily. "He's a real man, Leo."

"Oh," I said bitterly. "I can see it. Five o'clock shadow and a head full of white matter. A toupée on his chest and a vernacular like a boatswain. Too much shoulders, too little hips, and, to quote Thorne Smith, a voice as low as his intentions. A man who never learned the distinction between eating and dining, whose idea of a hot time consists of—"

"Stop it," she said. She said it quite casually and very quietly. Because my voice was raised, it contrasted enough to have a positively deafening effect. I stood there with my jaw swinging like the lower gate of a steam-shovel as she went on, "Don't be catty, Leo."

It was a studied insult for her to use such a woman-to-woman phrase, and we both knew it. I was suddenly filled with what the French call *ésprit d' éscalier*—the wit of the staircase; in other words, the belated knowledge of the thing you should have said if you'd only thought of it in time, which you mumble frustratedly to yourself as you go down the stairs on your way out. I should have caught her to me as she tried to brush past me when she arrived, smothered her with—what was that corny line? "kisses—hard, toothraking kisses, that broke his lips and hers in exquisite, salty pain." Then I should have threatened her with pinking scissors—

And then I thought of the glittering, balanced structure of self-denial I had built with her, and I could have cried. . . .

"Why come here and parade it in front of me?" I shouted. "Why don't you take your human bulldozer and cross a couple of horizons with him? Why come here and rub my nose in it?"

She stood up, pale, and lovelier than I had thought a human being could be—so beautiful that I had to close my eyes. "I came because I had to have something to compare him with," she said steadily. "You are everything I have ever dreamed about, Leo, and my dreams are . . . very detailed. . . ." At last she faltered, and her eyes were bright. "Arthur is—is—" She shook her head. Her voice left her; she had to whisper. "I know everything about you, Leo. I know how you think, and what you will say, and what you like, and it's wonderful, wonderful . . . but Leo, Arthur is something outside of me. Don't you see? Can't you see? I don't always like what Arthur does. *But I can't tell what he's going to do!* You—you share everything, Leo, Leo darling, but you don't—*take* anything!"

"Oh," I said hoarsely. My scalp was tight. I got up and started across the room toward her. My jaws hurt.

"Stop, Leo," she gasped. "Stop it, now. You can do it, but you'll be acting. You've never acted before. It would be wrong. Don't spoil what's left. No, Leo—no . . . no . . ."

She was right. She was so right. She was always right about me; she knew me so well. This kind of melodrama was away out of character for me. I reached her. I took her arm and she closed her eyes. It hurt when my fingers closed on her arm. She trembled but she did not try to pull away. I got her wrist and lifted it. I turned her hand over and put a kiss on the palm. Then I closed her fingers on it. "Keep that," I said. "You might like to have it sometime." Then I let her go.

"Oh Leo, darling," she said. "Darling," she said, with a curl to her lip. . . .

She turned to go. And then—

"*Arhgh!*" She uttered a piercing scream and turned back to me, all but bowling me over in her haste to get away from Abernathy. I stood there holding her tight while she pressed, crouched, squeezed against me, and I burst into laughter. Maybe it was reaction—I don't know. But I roared.

Abernathy is my mouse.

Our acquaintance began shortly after I took the apartment. I knew the little son-of-a-gun was there because I found evidences of his depredations under the sink where I stored my potatoes and vegetables. So I went out and got a trap. In those days the kind of trap I wanted was hard to find; it took me four days and a young fortune in carfare to run one of them down. You see, I can't abide the kind of trap that hurls a wire bar down on whatever part of the mouse happens to be available, so that the poor shrieking thing dies in agony. I wanted—and by heaven, I got—one of those wire-basket effects made so that a touch on the bait trips a spring which slams a door on the occupant.

I caught Abernathy in the contraption the very first night. He was a small gray mouse with very round ears. They were like the finest tissue, and covered with the softest fuzz in the world. They were translucent, and if you looked very closely you could see the most meticulous arrangement of hairline blood-vessels in them. I shall always maintain that Abernathy owed his success in life to the beauty of his ears. No one with pretensions to a soul could destroy such divine tracery.

Well, I let him alone until he got over being frightened and frantic, until he got hungry and ate all the bait, and a few hours over. When I thought he was good and ready to listen to reason, I put the trap on my desk and gave him a really good talking-to.

I explained very carefully (in simple language, of course) that for him to gnaw and befoul in his haphazard fashion was downright antisocial. I explained to him that when I was a child I was trained to finish whatever I started to eat, and that I did it to this day, and I was a human being and much bigger and stronger and smarter than he was. And whatever was good enough for me was at least good enough for him to take a crack at. I really laid down the law to that mouse. I let him mull over it for a while and then I pushed cheese through the bars until his tummy was round like a Ping-Pong ball. Then I let him go.

There was no sign of Abernathy for a couple of days after that. Then I caught him again; but since he had stolen nothing I let him off with a word of warning—very friendly this time; I had been quite stern at first, of course—and some more cheese. Inside of a week I was catching him every other night, and the only trouble I ever had with him was one time when I baited the trap and left it closed. He couldn't get in to the cheese and he just raised Cain until I woke up and let him in. After that I knew good relations had been established and I did without the trap and just left cheese out for him. At first he wouldn't take the cheese unless it was in the trap, but he got so he trusted me and would take it lying out on the floor. I had long since warned him about the poisoned food that the neighbors might leave out for him, and I think he was properly scared. Anyhow, we got along famously.

So here was Gloria, absolutely petrified, and in the middle of the floor in the front room was Abernathy, twinkling his nose and rubbing his hands together. In the middle of my bellow of laughter, I had a severe qualm of conscience. Abernathy had had no cheese since the day before yesterday! *Sic semper amoris.* I had been fretting so much over Gloria that I had overlooked my responsibilities.

"Darling, I'll take care of him," I said reassuringly to Gloria. I led her to an easy chair and went after Abernathy. I have a noise I make by pressing my tongue against my front teeth—a sort of a squishy-squeaky noise, which I always made when I gave cheese to Abernathy. He ran right over toward me, saw Gloria, hesitated, gave a "the hell with it" flirt with his tail, turned to me and ran up my pants-leg.

The outside, fortunately.

Then he hugged himself tight into my palm while I rummaged in the icebox with my other hand for his cheese. He didn't snatch at it, either, until he let me look at his ears again. You never saw such beautiful ears in your life. I gave him the cheese, and broke off another piece for his dessert, and set him in the corner by the sink. Then I went back to Gloria, who had been watching me, big-eyed and trembling.

"Leo—how can you *touch* it?"

"Makes nice touching. Didn't you ever touch a mouse?"

She shuddered, looking at me as if I were Horatio just back from the bridge. "I can't stand them."

"Mice? Don't tell me that you, of all people, really and truly have the traditional Victorian mouse phobia!"

"Don't laugh at me," she said weakly. "It isn't only mice. It's any little animal—frogs and lizards and even kittens and puppies. I like big dogs and cats and horses. But somehow—" She trembled again. "If I hear anything like little claws running across the floor, or see small things scuttling around the walls, it drives me crazy."

I goggled. "If you hear—hey; it's a good thing you didn't stay another hour last night, then."

"Last night?" Then, "Last night. . . ." she said, in a totally different voice, with her eyes looking inward and happy. She chuckled. "I was telling—Arthur about that little phobia of mine last night."

If I had thought my masterful handling of the mouse was going to do any good, apparently I was mistaken. "You better shove off," I said bitterly. "Arthur might be waiting."

"Yes," she said, without any particular annoyance, "he might. Goodbye, Leo."

"Goodbye."

Nobody said anything for a time.

"Well," she said, "Goodbye."

"Yes," I said, "I'll call you."

"Do that," she said, and went out.

I sat still on the couch for a long time, trying to get used to it. Wishful thinking was no good; I knew that. Something had happened between us. Mostly, its name was Arthur. The thing I couldn't understand was how he ever got a show, the way things were between Gloria and me. In all my life, in all my reading, I had never heard of such a complete fusion of individuals. We both felt it when we met; it had had no chance to get old. Arthur was up against some phenomenal competition; for one thing that was certain was that Gloria reciprocated my feelings perfectly, and one of my feelings was faith. I could understand—if I tried hard—how another man might overcome this hold, or that hold, which I had on her. There are smarter men than I, better looking ones, stronger ones. Any of several of those items could go by the board, and leave us untouched.

But not the faith! Not that! It was too big; nothing else we had was important enough to compensate for a loss of faith.

I got up to turn on the light, and slipped. The floor was wet. Not only was it wet; it was soft. I floundered to the seven-way lamp and cranked both switches all the way around.

The room was covered with tapioca. Ankle-deep on the floor, inches deep on the chairs and the couch.

"She's thinking about it now," said the head. Only it wasn't a head this time. It was a flaccid mass of folded tissue. In it I could see pulsing blood vessels. My stomach squirmed.

"Sorry. I'm out of focus." The disgusting thing—a sectioned brain, apparently—moved closer to me and became a face.

I lifted a foot out of the gummy mass, shook it, and put it back in again. "I'm glad she's gone," I said hoarsely.

"Are you afraid of the stuff?"

"No!" I said. "Of course not!"

"It will go away," said the head. "Listen; I'm sorry to tell you; it isn't syzygy. You're done, son."

"What isn't syzygy?" I demanded. "And what is syzygy?"

"Arthur. The whole business with Arthur."

"Go away," I gritted. "Talk sense, or go away. Preferably—go away."

The head shook from side to side, and its expression was gentle. "Give up," it said. "Call it quits. Remember what was good, and fade out."

"You're no good to me," I muttered, and waded over to the book case. I got out a dictionary, glowering at the head, which now was registering a mixture of pity and amusement.

Abruptly, the tapioca disappeared.

I leafed through the book. Sizable, sizar, size, sizzle—"Try S-Y," prompted the head.

I glared at it and went over to the S-Y's. Systemize, systole—

"Here it is," I said, triumphantly. "The last word in the S section." I read from the book. " 'Syzygy—either of the points at which the moon is most nearly in line with the earth and the sun, as when it is new or full'. What are you trying to tell me—that I'm caught in the middle of some astrological mumbo-jumbo?"

"Certainly not," it snapped. "I will tell you, however, that if that's all your dictionary says, it's not a very good one." It vanished.

"But—" I said vaguely. I went back to the dictionary. That's all it had to say about syzygy. Shaking, I replaced it.

Something cat-sized and furry hurtled through the air, clawed at my shoulder. I started, backed into my record cabinet and landed with a crash on the middle of my back in the doorway. The thing leaped from me to the couch and sat up, curling a long wide tail up against its back and regarding me with its jewelled eyes. A squirrel.

"Well, hello!" I said, getting to my knees and then to my feet. "Where on earth did you come from?"

The squirrel, with the instantaneous motion of its kind, dived to the edge of the couch and froze with its four legs wide apart, head up, tail describing exactly its recent trajectory, and ready to take off instantly in any direction including up. I looked at it with some puzzlement. "I'll go see if I have any walnuts," I told it. I moved toward the archway, and as I did so the squirrel leaped at me. I threw up a hand to protect my face. The squirrel struck my shoulder again and leaped from it—

And as far as I know it leaped into the fourth dimension or somewhere. For I searched under and into every bed, chair, closet, cupboard and shelf in the house, and could find no sign of anything that even looked like a squirrel. It was gone as completely as the masses of tapioca. . . .

Tapioca! What had the head said about the tapioca? "She's thinking about it now." *She*—Gloria, of course. This whole insane business was tied up with Gloria in some way.

Gloria not only disliked tapioca—she was afraid of it.

I chewed on that for a while, and then looked at the clock. Gloria had had time enough to get to the hotel. I ran to the phone, dialled.

"Hotel San Dragon," said a chewing-gum voice.

"748, please," I said urgently.

A couple of clicks. Then, "Hello?"

"Gloria," I said. "Listen; I—"

"Oh, you. Listen—can you call me back later? I'm very busy."

"I can and I will, but tell me something quickly: Are you afraid of squirrels?"

Don't tell me a shudder can't be transmitted over a telephone wire. One was that time. "I hate them. Call me back in about—"

"Why do you hate them?"

With exaggerated patience, she said carefully, "When I was a little girl, I was feeding some pigeons and a squirrel jumped right up on my shoulder and scared me half to death. Now, *please*—"

"Okay, okay," I said. "I'll speak to you later." I hung up. She shouldn't talk to me that way. She had no right—

What was she doing in that hotel room, anyway?

I pushed the ugly thought down out of sight, and went and poured myself a beer. Gloria is afraid of tapioca, I thought, and tapioca shows up here. She is afraid of the sound of small animals' feet, and I hear them here. She is afraid of squirrels that jump on people, and I get a squirrel that jumps on people.

That must all make some sense. Of course, I could take the easy way out, and admit that I was crazy. But somehow, I was no longer so ready to admit anything like that. Down deep inside, I made an agreement with myself not to admit that until I had exhausted every other possibility.

A very foolish piece of business. See to it that you don't do likewise. It's probably much smarter not to try to figure things out.

There was only one person who could straighten this whole crazy mess out—since the head wouldn't—and that was Gloria, I thought suddenly. I realized, then, why I had not called all bets before now. I had been afraid to jeopardize the thing that Gloria and I shared. Well, let's face it. We didn't share it any longer. That admission helped.

I strode to the telephone, and dialled the hotel.

"Hotel San Dragon."

"748 please."

A moment's silence. Then, "I'm sorry, sir. The party does not wish to be disturbed."

I stood there looking blankly at the phone, while pain swirled and spiralled up inside me. I think that up to this moment I had treated the whole thing as part sickness, part dream; this, somehow, brought it to a sharp and agonizing focus. Nothing that she could have done could have been so calculated and so cruel.

I cradled the receiver and headed for the door. Before I could reach it, gray mists closed about me. For a moment I seemed to be on some sort of a treadmill; I was walking, but I could not reach anything. Swiftly, then, everything was normal.

"I must be in a pretty bad way," I muttered. I shook my head. It was incredible. I felt all right, though a little dizzy. I went to the door and out.

The trip to the hotel was the worst kind of a nightmare. I could only conclude that there was something strange and serious wrong with me, completely aside from my fury and my hurt at Gloria. I kept running into these blind spells, when everything about me took on an unreal aspect. The light didn't seem right. I passed people on the street who weren't there when I turned to look at them. I heard voices where there were no people, and I saw people talking but couldn't hear them. I overcame a powerful impulse to go back home. I couldn't go back; I knew it; I knew I had to face whatever crazy thing was happening, and that Gloria had something to do with it.

I caught a cab at last, though I'll swear one of them disappeared just as I was about to step into it. Must have been another of those blind spells.

After that it was easier. I slouched quivering in a corner of the seat with my eyes closed.

I paid off the driver at the hotel and stumbled in through the revolving doors. The hotel seemed much more solid than anything else since this horrible business had started to happen to me. I started over to the desk, determined to give some mad life-and-death message to the clerk to break that torturing "do not disturb" order. I glanced into the coffee room as I passed it and stopped dead.

She was in there, in a booth, with—with someone else. I couldn't see anything of the man but a glossy black head of hair and a thick, ruddy neck. She was smiling at him, the smile that I thought had been born and raised for me.

I stalked over to them, trembling. As I reached them, he half-rose, leaned across the table, and kissed her.

"Arthur . . ." she breathed.

"That," I said firmly, "will do."

They did not move.

"Stop it!" I screamed. They did not move. Nothing moved, anywhere. It was a tableau, a picture, a hellish frozen thing put there to tear me apart.

"That's all," said a now familiar voice, gently. "That kiss did it, son. You're through." It was the head, but now he was a whole man. An ordinary-looking, middle-sized creature he was, with a scrawny frame to match his unimpressive middle-aged face. He perched on the edge of the table, mercifully between me and that torturing kiss.

I ran to him, grasped his thin shoulders. "Tell me what it is," I begged him. "Tell me, if you know—and I think you know. Tell me!" I roared, sinking my fingers into his flesh.

He put his hands up and laid them gently on my wrists, holding them there until I quieted down a little. I let him go. "I *am* sorry, son," he said. "I hoped you would figure it all out by yourself."

"I tried," I said. I looked around me. The grayness was closing in again, and through it I could see the still figures of the people in the coffee-shop, all stopped in mid-action. It was one three-dimensional frame of some unthinkable movie-film. I felt cold sweat all but squirt from the pores of my face. "Where am I?" I shrieked.

"Please," he soothed. "Take it easy, and I'll tell you. Come over here and sit down and relax. Close your eyes and don't try to think. Just listen."

I did as he asked, and gradually I stopped shaking. He waited until he felt that I was calm, and then began talking.

"There is a world of psychic things—call them living thought, call them dreams if you like. Now, you know that of all animals, only human beings can reach these psychic things. It was a biological accident. There is something about humans which is tangent to this psychic world. Humans have the power to open a gate between the two worlds. They can seldom control the power; often they're not aware of it. But when that gate is opened, something materializes in the world of the humans. Imagination itself is enough to do it. If you are hungry, down deep inside, for a certain kind of woman, and if you picture her to yourself vividly enough, such a gate might open, and there she'll be. You can see her and touch her; she'll be little different from a real one."

"But—there is a difference?"

"Yes, there is. She is not a separate thing from you. She is a part of you. She is your product. That's what I was driving at when I mentioned parthenogenesis. It works like that."

"Parthenogenesis—let's see. That's the process of reproducing without fertilization, isn't it?"

"That's right. This 'materialization' of yours is a perfect parallel to that. As I told you before, however, it is not a process with high survival value. For one thing, it affords no chance to cross strains. Unless a living creature can bring into itself other characteristics, it must die out."

"Then why don't all parthenogenetic creatures die out?"

"There is a process used by the very simple, one-celled forms of life to take care of that. Mind you," he broke off suddenly, "I'm just using all of this biological talk as symbolism. There are basic laws that work in both worlds, that work equally on the high forms of life and the low. Do you see?"

"I see. These are just examples. But go on about this process that the parthenogenetic creatures use to mix their strains."

"It's very simple. Two of these organisms let their nuclei flow together for a time. Then they separate and go their ways again. It isn't a reproductive process at all. It's merely a way in which each may gain a part of the other. It's called—syzygy."

"Oh," I said. "That. But I still don't—let me see. You mentioned it first when that—that—"

"When Gloria met Arthur," the man finished smoothly. "I said that if it were syzygy, you'd be all right. Well, it wasn't, as you saw for yourself. The outside strain, even though it didn't suit her as well as you did, was too strong. You got hurt. Well, in the workings of really basic laws, something always gets hurt."

"What about you? Who are you?"

"I am somebody who has been through it, that's all. You must understand that my world is different from the one you remember. Time itself is different. Though I started from a time perhaps thirty years away, I was able to open a gate near you. Just a little one, of course. I did it so that I could try to make you think this thing out in time. I believed that if you could, you would have been spared all this. You might even have been able to keep Gloria."

"What's it to you?"

"You don't know, do you? You really don't know?"

I opened my eyes and looked at him, and shook my head. "No, I don't. I—like you, old man."

He chuckled. "That's odd, you know. I don't like me."

I craned around and looked over at Gloria and her man, still frozen in that strange kiss. "Will those dream-people stay like that forever?"

"Dream people?"

"I suppose that's what they are. You know, I'm a little proud of Gloria. How I managed to dream up anything so—so lovely, I'll never know. I— hey—what's the matter?"

"Didn't you understand what I was telling you? Gloria is real. Gloria goes on living. What you see over there is the thing that happened when you were no longer a part of her. Leo: she dreamed *you!*"

I rose to my feet and put my fists on the table between us. "That's a lie," I choked. "I'm—I'm me, damn you!"

"You're a detailed dream, Leo, and a splendid job. You're a piece of sentient psyche from another world injection-molded into an ideal that Gloria dreamed. Don't try to be anything else. There aren't many real humans, Leo. Most of the world is populated by the dreams of a few of them; didn't you know, Leo? Why do you suppose that so few of the people you met knew anything about the world as a whole? Why do you suppose that humans keep their interests confined and their environments small? Most of them aren't humans at all, Leo!"

"I'm *me*," I said stubbornly. "Gloria *couldn't* have thought of all of me! Gloria can't run a power shovel! Gloria can't play a guitar! Gloria doesn't know anything about the circus foreman who sang, or the Finn dynamite boss who was killed!"

"Of course not. Gloria only dreamed a kind of man who was the product of those things, or things like them. Have you run a shovel since you met her? You'd find that you couldn't, if you really tried. You've played guitar for no one but her since you met her. You've spent all your time arranging music that no one will ever see or play!"

"I'm *not* anybody's dream!" I shouted. "I'm not! If I was an ideal of hers, we would have stayed together. I failed with her, old man; don't you know that? She wanted me to be aggressive, and I wasn't."

He looked at me so sadly that I thought he was going to cry. "She wanted you to *take*. You were a part of her, no human can take from himself."

"She was deathly afraid of some things that didn't bother me at all. What about that?"

"The squirrels, and the sound of all the little feet? No, Leo; they were baseless phobias, and she had the power to overcome any of them. She never tried, but it was not difficult to create you without them."

I stared at him. "Do you mean to—Old man, are there more like me, really?"

"Many, many," he sighed. "But few who cling to their nonexistent, ghostly egos as you are doing."

"Do the real people know what they are doing?"

"Very few of them. Very few. The world is full of people who feel incomplete, people who have everything they can possibly want and yet are unhappy, people who feel alone in a crowd. The world is mostly peopled by ghosts."

"But—the war! Roman history! The new car models! What about them?"

He shook his head again. "Some of it's real, some not. It depends on what the real humans want from moment to moment."

I thought a minute, bitterly. Then I asked him, "What was that you said about coming back in world-time, and looking through a little gateway at things that had happened?"

He sighed. "If you *must* hang on to the ego she gave you," he said wearily, "you'll stay the way you are now. But you'll age. It will take you the equivalent of thirty or so years to find your way around in that strange psychic world, for you will have to move and think like a human. Why do you want to do that?"

I said, with determination, "I am going back, then, if it takes me a century. I'm going to find me right after I met Gloria, and I'm going to warn me in such a way that I'll figure out a way to be with Gloria for the rest of her life."

He put his hands on my shoulders, and now there really were tears in his eyes. "Oh, you poor, poor kid," he said.

I stared at him. Then, "What's—your name, old man?"

"My name is Leo."

"Oh," I said. "Oh."

Out
of This World

There is a popular belief that sex and science fiction do not mix, and it is true to the extent that romantic considerations got short shrift back in SF's golden nineteen-fifties, but I suspect it was not so much an editorial taboo as a lack of interest on the part of writers more concerned with the mechanics of space and time travel.

But the authors of the nine ensuing science-fiction pieces are not the least bit bashful about discussing affairs of the heart (and body). This section contains plenty of nuts-and-bolts technology, too, but the emphasis remains solidly where it should: on the strange inner workings of the human spirit.

Amy Wasp-Wimberger

Will the Real Dennis Casper Please Stand Up?

Here is a clever "first story" that developed from a class assignment in the genre writing course I teach at New York University. AMY WASP-WIMBERGER, a resident of Farmingdale on New York's Long Island, works in corporate video and is also involved in film production with her husband, Kurt.

DENNIS GRASPED the two packages tightly, his chubby fingers denting the white paper wrappings. *It's so small,* he thought. *What if something's wrong? I've waited so long.* Frantically, he ripped the first package open, shaking it violently. A whisper of black silk floated to the floor followed by the clunk of metal hitting tile.

"That's it?" he asked, looking into the box. His voice was deep and mature, a marked contrast to his overweight, overgrown adolescent exterior. Struggling down on one knee, he picked up the cloth, feeling the wires implanted in the silk. "That's it!" With a grunt, he heaved his bulk off the floor. Pushing the stringy black hair from his eyes, he let the silk slide through his hands, feeling the gentle hardness of the wires and lovingly caressing the length of cord.

With a decisive flip of the wrists, Dennis shook out the material to its full length. It continued seamlessly from the hood that covered the entire face, leaving only holes for the eyes and mouth, to the slippers with divisions for each toe. The silk gleamed dully in the dim fluorescent light of Dennis's windowless apartment.

Quickly, Dennis stripped off the graying underpants he habitually wore at home and kicked them onto the pile by the foot of his bed. He felt gingerly along the back for a zipper—Velcro strips—anything to allow him access to his dream. Nothing. *Don't be an idiot, Dennis. If they put it on the back, how would you fasten it once you got it on? It's not as if there's anyone here to help you. Check the front.*

He felt a faint ridge along the stomach of the suit. It opened as he ran his finger lightly down its length. Holding it open, he walked the two steps to his small loveseat. He slid the magazines, antique floppy disks, and miscellaneous papers to the floor and lowered himself to the cushions. *What if it's too small? It looks so delicate.* "Might as well try to put it on." Immediately, several lights glaringly illuminated the room and the thirty-five-inch HDTV monitor blared to life. "God damn it!" Dennis jumped in his seat, one foot almost in the opening. "OFF! Damn." Quiet and darkness returned. Remaining uncomfortably bent over, he cautiously inspected the suit for any tears his feet might have made.

There were no rips or tears, but Dennis noticed his toenails looked very long and sharp. Maybe he should clip them. Come to think of it, now that his face was so close to his feet, maybe he should shower. *No, I just showered four days ago.* The blood rushed to his head, pounding in his temples. His ragged breathing sounded harsh and loud in the room. *I'm going to put this thing on if it kills me. After all, it is my birthday present.*

Five minutes later he was dressed. "Computer on. TV on." Dennis walked the cleared path through the center of his small room. The silk clung tightly to his body, warmer than he thought something so light should be. The second box contained a videodisc, a list of what hardware was needed, and an instruction book on how to hook up the suit to a computer. It seemed easy enough. It worked on the same principle as the glove interface that allowed Dennis to earn a living without leaving his house. By using a glove to let him touch things in the nebulous reality of computer memory, he was able to create rooms for his interior decorating clients. He could rearrange furniture with the flick of a finger. Designing office complexes for his architectural customers was a breeze. He could knock down old walls or add entire buildings. But this was bigger. Much bigger. With trembling hands, he loaded the software and plugged himself into the computer.

He flicked his fingers through the menu choices, marveling at the responsiveness of the suit. He chose the "Young Business Executive" body option and the "Executive Boardroom" location. The program then guided him through a choice of hair and eye color, height, weight and facial features.

The new Dennis Casper stared at the old from the crystal-edged picture on the screen. It was larger than life. It was beautiful. It was Dennis. He nodded, satisfied. The image mimicked the movement. "Happy Birthday to me," Dennis whispered to the tall, slim, sandy-blond-haired man on screen. The tall man returned the sentiment.

"This is going to be fabulous." Dennis laughed gleefully and began decorating his executive boardroom. He selected a catalog from the unreal bookshelf. Flipping through the pages, he pointed to the items he liked. They popped into the picture. He moved his hands, miming placing the objects around the room. His virtual counterpart did the dirty work. Dennis marveled that he could feel the texture and weight of each piece. His glove didn't have a feedback mode. This was amazing. He went for an Art Deco look with just a touch of Oriental influence. Chuckling wildly to himself, Dennis started on his wardrobe.

After outfitting his new body and designing a home to match the office, Dennis felt ready to take himself for a test run. He dialed the number that would connect him with Mrs. Finch, the rich old woman for whom he did some interior decorating. The monitor screen split to show both his image and the incoming picture as Mrs. Finch answered his call with full audio and video.

The old woman's voluminous kimono didn't hide the scrawniness of her arms and the tendons on her neck and hands. White makeup settled into the wrinkles on her face. It was past time for her annual face lift, Dennis thought unkindly. But for all her age, Dennis knew the jet black hair piled high above her head was all hers. It was the one hint of her past loveliness.

"Dennis? Is that you?" she warbled. "The phone said it was you, but you *never* call."

"Yes, Mrs. Finch. It is I. In person. Or as much in person as modern technology can bring me without having to leave the comforts of my own home."

"But Denny, you sly boy. You told me you didn't *believe* in video meetings. You said you didn't even have a connection!"

Dennis smiled broadly, trying out the new face. His phantom smiled, a little less smoothly than Dennis liked. He'd work on that. "Well, Mrs. Finch, it's my thirtieth birthday and I thought I'd buy myself something special. After I hooked it up, I could think of no one I wanted to call more than you. So what do you think?"

She tapped the camera playfully with her folded-up fan.

Careful with that fan, Dennis thought, *it cost more than the camera.*

"Of *course* I love it, you silly boy. Turn around, let me get a good look at you. We've been working together for years and I've never seen you, you know. Florida isn't *that* far from California. If you'd ever get over that *ridiculous* fear of flying, we'd have met ages ago! I let you in my bedroom —you *built* my bedroom—and I never even knew what you looked like. Not that I could resist your *brilliant* portfolio and those *glowing* recommendations. My, you are a handsome devil. I knew you had to be, to match that voice." She peered closer into the screen, examining him and his home. "I *love* what you've done with your room! What do you call that look? Do you think we could do something like that for *my* humble home?"

Her humble home, Dennis mused, cost four million dollars ten years ago. Mrs. Finch could redecorate the White House Art Deco if she wished. "I think we could work something out, Mrs. Finch, but right now I've got a few more calls to make. What do you say I phone you first thing tomorrow morning and we'll work on it?"

"That sounds wonderful! I *so* look forward to *seeing* you then! I'm so happy to finally know the real you. Ta-ta!" Half the screen went black.

Dennis called up the menu and started building a Dennis for each of his other clients.

Dennis made his living through an electronic window. He earned a degree in architecture through two years of condensed, teleconferenced classes beamed into his living room from a university halfway around the world. He acquired an interest in interior decorating almost accidentally. He liked seeing his buildings furnished and complete.

He built a client base through advertising on computer bulletin boards and taking out ads in home decorating magazines. He sent real-estate agents hard copies of his ideas. He got a decent response and a few clients willing to put up with the idea of never meeting the architect face to face. After a while, his extraordinary portfolio spoke for itself, and as his reputation grew, so did his bank account.

Through his silken interface, Dennis toured the world. He smelled its scents and felt the touch of the winds and waves and earth. His library of travel disks grew. He walked many miles around the world, wearing a bare spot on the carpet in front of his dingy loveseat.

Pop in a laserdisc of Switzerland, don the suit, and through the miracle of modern technology, Dennis skis the Matterhorn. Change the disk, and Dennis walks the beaches of Hawaii or hang-glides over the Grand Canyon. He felt it all through the feedback circuits of the suit. With a touch of the button, his computer would extrude a full-color photo of the pseudo-Dennis in any of the exotic locales in its memory. Pictures of Dennis on vacation lined the walls.

A white-skinned Dennis with red hair and green eyes sauntered down the path of a magnificent wood-and-stone Tudor home, reaching down now and then to smell a rose or pet a passing cat. "What do you think, Mr. Atwell?" he asked out loud.

In his one-room apartment, Dennis Casper looked expectantly at the man visible on the incoming side of his screen.

The man's bushy black eyebrows drew together and frown lines appeared across his forehead. Show me the front view from a distance one more time. I want to see the landscaping."

"Whatever you'd like, sir." Both Dennises made a shooing gesture and the perspective changed. They now viewed the house from half a block away. The giant shade trees surrounding the house complemented the wooden beams and the bright roses gave it a homey look.

Mr. Atwell smiled. "I love it, Dennis. You've outdone yourself. How soon can we start building it?"

"We can start by the end of next month, if you'd like."

"I'd like that very much."

"Fine." Dennis motioned and the house and his image vanished, leaving the screen blank briefly before the red-haired Dennis returned. "Give me a second." He looked down and entered some information in the keyboard. "Consider it started. I just licensed the idea and hired the contractors. Don't forget, I know a great interior decorator if you need one." *If Mr. Atwell wants an interior decorator,* Dennis thought, *I'll introduce him to Dennis—model number six.*

"Fantastic. I'll keep that in mind. I've transferred the money to your bank. I love seeing you walk around the house. It makes it seem really alive. How do you do that?"

"You don't want me to give away all my secrets, do you?" Dennis chuckled a little nervously.

"An artist. I understand." Mr. Atwell sipped his glass of wine. "You know, I'm glad you've gotten over that . . . phobia . . . you had about letting people see you. I'd heard about you, seen your work, and I loved it. But, personally, I never would have worked with you before. I like to look in a person's eyes while I'm talking to them. It gives me a feel for what they're really like."

Dennis nodded sincerely. "I couldn't agree with you more. You never know what someone is like until you've seen them."

Mr. Atwell loosened his tie and leaned back in his large black leather chair. "Now, on a more personal level, there's someone I'd like you to meet."

"Oh?" Dennis sat up straighter on the edge of his loveseat. "Who might that be?"

"It's my daughter, Roxanne."

"I thought she was away at school." Dennis ran his hand through his lanky black hair, echoed by the redhead on screen.

Gregory Atwell grinned. "We do let her come home sometimes. I've told her about you and she's interested in meeting you."

Dennis hesitated, weighing his bank balance against the discomfort of meeting new people. *What are you getting so nervous about, Denny old boy, you don't have to go there. They'll never come here. Just say hi on screen. No problem for Big Red.* "I'd be pleased to meet her." Dennis answered. "Do you think she'd like to see the house? I can call it back up."

A slightly pained expression crossed Gregory's face. "Actually, she's a little shy. She said she'd rather call you, if you don't mind. I tried to talk her into joining me today, but she can be very stubborn. Is it all right if I tell her to call you in about an hour?"

"That would be fine. It will give me a chance to freshen up."

"Great. Goodbye, Dennis. A pleasure doing business with you."

Dennis said goodbye and flicked his image to full screen. He stared at his counterpart on the screen, enduring the return scrutiny. *I wonder what he thinks of his other self? If he could, would he leave?* Dennis ended the call and the red-haired image disappeared.

The incoming message tone sounded during Dennis's meal. He was so busy lately, he rarely made it through a meal uninterrupted. He wore the suit during all his waking hours, so he just walked over to the computer and plugged in. The phone identified the caller as Ms. Roxanne Atwell. Dennis made sure the program running was the same one Gregory Atwell had seen.

"Hello, Dennis Casper speaking," the red-haired man said from a sparsely, yet tastefully decorated living room.

The screen divided, revealing a petite girl with long black hair and bright blue eyes. "Hello, I'm Roxanne Atwell. My father told you I'd call."

Dennis groped for a reply; he'd never guessed Atwell would have such a beautiful daughter. "Ah, yes, Ms. Atwell. Your father did say you would call. What can I do for you? Shall I build you a house?" He grinned to show her it was a joke.

Roxanne looked lost. "Well, I thought . . . Dad said you had something to tell me. I thought . . ."

Dennis glanced wildly around the room. "Oh." He searched for something to say and found himself looking straight into her eyes. They were such *blue* eyes. Almost violet. "Well," he tried again.

She frowned. "Never mind. I can see my father's matchmaking again. I'm sorry. I won't bother you anymore."

He leapt up from the loveseat. "No, please, don't go."

She looked at him questioningly.

Dennis paced for a second. His creation walked around his room, picking up small objects and placing them back down somewhere else. "If I'm not being too bold, maybe he had a good idea."

"Oh?"

Dennis was shocked at himself for the suggestion, but it was too late to back down now. He tried to remember that she didn't see him, not really. Big Red could handle this. "Not that you need a matchmaker," he added quickly, stammering. "Someone as beautiful as you obviously doesn't need help meeting men." Those romance videos he sometimes watched in the afternoon were coming in handy now. This sappy stuff didn't sound so bad when you said it to a girl who really was beautiful.

Roxanne blushed. "You think I'm beautiful?"

"Yes."

She leaned forward, her hair curtaining her face. "You don't even know me."

"Trust me, no matter what your father's told you," he said wryly, "you don't know me, either."

She looked up. "I think I'd like to get to know you."

"I know I'd like to get to know you." The two Dennises smiled.

"So, where do we start?" Roxanne tucked her legs up under her on the couch.

Forcing his eyes away from her face, Dennis looked around the room in which Roxanne sat. "Where are you calling from?"

Roxanne laughed and waved her hand around the room. "From my sitting room. Why?"

"No reason. I've never seen this part of your father's house before. I like how you've decorated it."

"Thank you. I did it myself."

"It's very polished. You could do this for a living."

Roxanne blushed from the neck up. "Thanks again. Anyway, I know you're an architect, but what do you do for fun?"

"Fun? Let me show you some pictures I took on my last vacation," Dennis said, walking over to the nearest wall.

On-screen, Roxanne raised a glass of champagne and toasted Dennis. "Happy New Year! I can't believe it's been six months since we met. It went so fast."

Dennis raised his glass in return, being careful not to spill it on his tie. "Happy New Year to you, too! Trust me, it's been six months. I have the phone bills to prove it."

Roxanne looked worried. "Oh, I'm sorry. I shouldn't talk so much."

"Don't apologize. I love talking with you. You've made this the best New Year's I've ever had. I feel like dancing!"

Roxanne laughed, but her smile faltered. "I don't really dance much."

Dennis waved his champagne glass at her. "Oh come on, it's New Year's! I can't kiss you, so you *have* to dance with me!" He danced a few solo dance steps, humming "Auld Lange Syne."

Roxanne laughed and stood up, extending her hands to the screen, swaying in time to Dennis's humming.

Together, they danced in the New Year.

With shaky hands, Dennis pushed the hair back from his eyes. He paced back and forth in front of his screen, ignoring the blaring commercials. "TV off," he whispered as he passed the monitor. The commercial continued. Dennis stopped pacing and stood in front of the screen. He couldn't stop his leg from vibrating, so he tried to ignore it. He took a deep breath. "TV off," he said loudly, releasing his breath in a long sigh.

"Phone on. Call Roxanne." He pushed the hood of his suit over his head and, while waiting for her to answer, selected the Dennis she knew. He knew she'd answer. She always did.

"Hi, Dennis." She smiled broadly and walked over to her chaise longue.

"Hi, Rox." His smile flicked to life and died quickly.

"How are you doing? Is everything okay? You don't usually call me twice in one day." She rubbed the arms of the chair with the palms of her hands.

Dennis grabbed his leg to keep it from shaking. "Nothing's up. I just felt like seeing you." He stood up. "So, home again on a Friday night?"

She sat stiffly in the chair. "I know we're friends, but I don't have to explain my life to you." She forced herself to relax, picking invisible threads off the arm of the chair. "Besides, you're home, too."

"Yeah, but you know I go out. You've seen the photos." He turned his back to the camera and picked up a picture of red-haired Dennis on horseback. "Roxanne, how come you're always home when I call?" He kept his back to her. "I know you're done with school, but don't your friends ever make you go out?"

"I don't have that many friends, you know that." Her mouth smiled, but her eyes were wary. "Are you tired of calling me? Am I too boring? I hope I haven't said anything wrong."

"Oh, no, never. I like talking to you. I just worry that you don't go out enough. And we've never gone out. Doesn't it bother you?"

She looked away from the screen. "Don't worry about me. I'm fine," she said, breaking the connection.

Dennis sat in his darkened apartment and watched Roxanne as she moved around her room, passing in and out of the camera's field of view. Sometimes she hummed to herself or sang aloud with the radio.

It worked, Dennis thought, slumping against the back of the sofa. *The hardware really kept Roxanne's signal open. I can shut her out, but she can't leave me.* He gripped the remote tightly in his hands, simultaneously forcing himself to turn the phone off and fighting to keep the line open.

On screen, Roxanne left the room. A few minutes passed without her return. The remote dropped from Dennis's hand, shutting off the monitor as it hit the floor.

Dennis watched Roxanne every day. He noticed things about her, things he never really thought about before. She and Dennis had a few things in common. Neither one had a mirror in their room. Neither one ever had visitors.

"Dennis! You've dyed your hair black! I really like it. It suits you."

Dennis reached to feel his newly cut hair. It was shorter than he was used to and very clean. "Thank you. It's actually my natural color. For a while, I thought red looked better, but now I feel like looking like myself a little."

"Well, it's nice with your blue eyes. Come to think of it, weren't your eyes green?"

"No, *my* eyes have always been blue. You must be thinking of somebody else."

"Maybe."

Dennis waited until Roxanne dressed before putting a call through to her. He liked to watch her when she first woke up. She looked even more beautiful with her hair tousled and her cheeks flushed. For the hundredth time, not without a twinge of guilt, Dennis wished she would get dressed within the camera's field of view. Half of him was glad she didn't. He wasn't sure he could handle that.

"Hi, Dennis," she answered perkily. She pulled on boots and reached for a sweater. "What's up?"

"Good morning. You seem pretty chipper this morning." Her cheeks were flushed and her eyes shone with an unusual brightness.

"I am. I'm a little nervous, too. Daddy's going to show me the new house." She slipped into the sweater and shuddered.

"Is it cold there?" Dennis asked, seeing her shiver.

"No, I'm just a little nervous. All those people at the site. Builders and gardeners. Maybe I won't have to get out of the car."

"Roxanne, honey, are you almost ready?" Gregory Atwell called from off camera.

Roxanne jumped off the foot of the bed. "There's Daddy. I've got to go. Bye, I'll call you when I get back." She blew Dennis a kiss as she reached out to end the call.

Dennis watched her leave the room. He didn't remember the last time he'd seen her go outside or even heard her mention outside. Whenever he brought it up, she changed the subject. Dennis often thanked God that Roxanne never asked to meet him; to go out on a date. But lately, he felt like meeting her. All those hours of watching her and not being able to touch her. Even the feedback capabilities of the suit couldn't feel a video image.

I wonder how I'd look to her; would she be disgusted? Maybe I should get a mirror.

Dennis woke slowly. A dream of searching for someone in a crowd of shifting faces lingered briefly before being driven away by the harsh, insistent buzzing filling the room. Dennis pried his eyelids open and stared at the clock. 3:48 A.M. Much too early to be awake, so it couldn't be his alarm. He searched for another explanation for the ruthless sound. This hour of the morning, it sounded like the trumps of doom. And it wasn't stopping.

Dennis heaved himself into a semi-sitting position with a groan. Even losing thirty pounds over the past three years didn't make it any easier to sit up in the morning.

The buzzing continued. "What is it?" Dennis yelled to the ceiling. He knew the answer even as he spoke. "The phone. The goddamn phone. This had better be important." He belted on a robe as he walked to the couch.

"Answer phone, outgoing audio only." He sprawled on the couch, almost falling asleep in the half-second before the call came through.

"Dennis?" a female voice sobbed.

Dennis opened his eyes. Roxanne stared wildly from the screen, tears flowing down her face.

"Dennis, are you there? Why can't I see you? Oh, Dennis, answer me!"

"Roxanne? What's wrong?"

"Dennis, where are you? I can't see you."

"My video output isn't working. I was going to take a look at it in the morning. What's the matter?" He sat up straight, finger-combing his hair and pulling the robe tighter around his body.

"I want to see you." The words rushed out of her.

"I told you, my video output's not working."

"I have to see you. Can you see me?" She looked straight into the camera, pushing strands of hair from her face.

Dennis smiled fondly at her. "Yes, I can see you perfectly. You look beautiful, as always. What's wrong?" he asked gently.

"I don't know. It's my father. No, it's not Daddy. It's me. Do you really think I'm beautiful?"

"Sure I do." Dennis's head spun with the early hour and the speed of her words.

"Do you love me?" she asked, looking piercingly at the screen for a second and then turning away.

Dennis opened his mouth and closed it again. He groped for the screen.

"Dennis?" Roxanne started crying silently. "Dennis, I really need to know. You know me better than anyone. I told you things I would never tell anybody. At first it was because there was nobody else to talk to, but then I did it because I wanted to talk to you. You're my best friend. The only one I feel comfortable with. And I love you." She wiped at her tears and sat back in the chair breathing heavily.

Dennis stared dumbfounded at the screen. He looked around his grungy two-room apartment; at the dishes in the sink, the faked photos of his alter-identities on their faked vacations. He stared at his cloudy reflection in the image of Roxanne's darkened room. "Uh, I love you, too."

Roxanne smiled weakly. "You don't sound too sure."

"I never sound sure at three o'clock in the morning. No, really I'm sure. I just never thought about it before. But I guess I do. I tell you everything. You know all my fears and dreams. You make me laugh. You laugh at my stupid jokes. . . ." Dennis paced around the room. "So I love you and you love me. Now what? And what were you so upset about?"

"My father wants to kick me out."

"What?"

"Dennis, do you know how old I am?"

Trying to follow the switch in conversation, Dennis guessed wildly. "Twenty-five?"

"I'm thirty-four. I've known you for two years and I never even told you my age. And you know something else I never told you—the reason why I always call you from the same room?" She stood up from her chair and walked around the room, touching her possessions. "I never leave my room."

"Never? What about a few months ago, when you went to see the house?"

"I didn't go. I couldn't. I got as far as the road, and I saw all the people. . . . I lost it. I made Daddy take me home."

"But we talked about it."

"I lied. Daddy showed me some pictures." She looked directly at him. "Dennis, I wanted to see it so badly. It's *your* house. You designed it. Sometimes I pretend you designed it for me." She smiled shyly.

"I would love to build you a house. I would build you a castle."

"But how would I get there if I couldn't leave?" She started crying again, hiding her face in her hands.

"Roxanne, honey." She looked up at that. "I understand. Please believe me." Dennis gestured sincerely, even though she couldn't see him. "I know what's it's like to hide. It's so easy."

She looked at him. "Yes, it is. But now Daddy says it's time to stop hiding. And I want to, but I'm scared. I'm scared, Dennis, and you're the only one I trust. That's why I want to see you. I want to come to your house. I think I would feel safe with you." Her eyes seemed to meet his briefly before she turned away.

Dennis paused in front of the monitor. He reached out and touched Roxanne's image. "You want to come here?"

"Yes. Dennis, you sound funny. I wish I could see you. When can I come over?"

Dennis walked over to his bed and took the black silk suit from its resting place. He carried it to the loveseat, caressing it absently.

"Dennis?" Roxanne slumped in her chair. "Okay. I guess I said too much. I won't bother you any more." She lifted a hand and cut off her end of the connection. She sat stiffly on the end of her bed, sobbing hopelessly.

"Roxanne!" Dennis jumped up, the black suit sliding to the floor. As he leapt for the screen, his foot slid on the fabric of the suit. He reached down to throw it out of the way and then stopped himself. He gathered the suit into his arms. Slowly, he turned back towards the loveseat. He watched Roxanne for a few seconds. Looking from his shabby apartment to her beautiful self-imposed prison.

"Phone on. Call Roxanne." He smoothed his hair and straightened his robe as he waited for Roxanne to answer the phone.

After a few minutes, Roxanne answered. "I hope this is you, Dennis," she said wearily. She lay on the bed, her arm covering her eyes.

"Yeah, it's me. I fixed my output."

Roxanne uncovered her eyes and sat up to view her screen. "Dennis? You're not . . . Who are you? If this is some kind of a joke, I'm not amused!" she said furiously. "I'll trace the police trace this call if . . ."

"Roxanne, it's me. Dennis."

She stopped her tirade. "I don't believe it, what happened to you?"

"Rox, it's me. Look at me. Please, really look at me. Do you recognize me even a little?" he pleading, praying to whoever might be listening that she would see him.

"I don't understand." Her eyes searched his image. "Why do you look like this? Where are you calling from?"

Dennis sighed. "It's what I look like. This is what my apartment looks like. I'm a slob. And you're the first person in three years to see the real Dennis Casper."

She stared into the camera, searching his room and his face. "I recognize the hair. And the eyes. And it's definitely your voice."

"Yeah, I know. But I'm fatter and shorter. And uglier. Should I go?"

"You've been lying to me?"

"Yes, I'm truly, truly sorry. I'll go now." Slowly, he reached for the screen.

She reached out as if to stop him. "No, please don't. I don't think you're ugly. You're still Dennis. No matter what you look like. It's just a shock. I never suspected—I mean, it never crossed my mind." She walked over to the phone. "Sit up straight, and let me get a good look at you."

Dennis complied. For what seemed like the hundredth time that night he ran his fingers through his hair in a vain attempt to smooth it. "Well," he said with a waver in his voice, "Do I pass?" More quietly he asked, "Do you still love me? I'm sorry I lied to you."

Roxanne smiled. "I love you more. Now I know why you never invited me out. I was always so worried you would and I wouldn't know what to say." She looked puzzled. "But how did you—do you—change yourself?"

Dennis held up the suit. "It's a long story. Why don't I come get you and bring you back to my apartment? It's time for us to meet."

"I think I could leave with you. I'll be looking for you. Goodbye. I love you."

Dennis cut the connection. The screen went black. "I love you, too," he whispered.

Dennis Casper got dressed and, for the first time in three years, left his apartment.

Fredric Brown

Expedition

FREDRIC BROWN *(1907–72) wrote award-winning mysteries and such excel-lent fantasy and science-fiction novels and tales as* What Mad Universe, Rogue in Space, The Mind Thing, Martians Go Home, The Lights in the Sky Are Stars, *"Arena," "Knock," "Star Mouse," and many other memora-ble compositions. He was a master of the difficult short-short story form, of which the following amusing bit of hyperbole is a popular example.*

"THE FIRST major expedition to Mars," said the history professor, "the one which followed the preliminary exploration by one-man scout ships and aimed to establish a permanent colony, led to a great number of problems. One of the most perplexing of which was: How many men and how many women should comprise the expedition's personnel of thirty?

"There were three schools of thought on the subject.

"One was that the ship should be comprised of fifteen men and fifteen women, many of whom would no doubt find one another suitable mates and get the colony off to a fast start.

"The second was that the ship should take twenty-five men and five women—ones who were willing to sign a waiver on monogamous inclina-tions—on the grounds that five women could easily keep twenty-five men sexually happy and twenty-five men could keep five women even happier.

"The third school of thought was that the expedition should contain thirty men, on the grounds that under those circumstances the men would be able to concentrate on the work at hand much better. And it was argued that since a second ship would follow in approximately a year and could contain mostly women, it would be no hardship for the men to endure celibacy that long. Especially since they were used to it; the two

Space Cadet schools, one for men and one for women, rigidly segregated the sexes.

"The Director of Space Travel settled this argument by a simple expedient. He—Yes, Miss Ambrose?" A girl in the class had raised her hand.

"Professor, was that expedition the one headed by Captain Maxon? The one they called Mighty Maxon? Could you tell us how he came to have that nickname?"

"I'm coming to that, Miss Ambrose. In lower schools you have been told the story of the expedition, but not the *entire* story; you are now old enough to hear it.

"The Director of Space Travel settled the argument, cut the Gordian knot, by announcing that the personnel of the expedition would be chosen by lot, regardless of sex, from the graduating classes of the two space academies. There is little doubt that he personally favored twenty-five men to five women—because the men's school had approximately five hundred in the graduating class and the women's school had approximately one hundred. By the law of averages, the ratio of winners should have been five men to one woman.

"However, the law of averages does not always work out on any one particular series. And it so happened that on this particular drawing *twenty-nine* women drew winning chances, and only *one* man won.

"There were loud protests from almost everyone except the winners, but the director stuck to his guns; the drawing had been honest and he refused to change the status of any of the winners. His only concession to appease male egos was to appoint Maxon, the one man, captain. The ship took off and had a successful voyage.

"And when the second expedition landed, they found the population doubled. Exactly doubled—every woman member of the expedition had a child, and one of them had twins, making a total of exactly thirty infants.

"Yes, Miss Ambrose, I see your hand, but please let me finish. No, there is nothing spectacular about what I have thus far told you. Although many people would think loose morals were involved, it is no great feat for one man, given time, to impregnate twenty-nine women.

"What gave Captain Maxon his nickname is the fact that work on the second ship went much faster than scheduled and the second expedition did not arrive one year later, but only nine months and two days later.

"Does that answer your question, Miss Ambrose?"

Dan Potter

Tripping the Light Fantastic

"Tripping the Light Fantastic" has driven me crazy since 1974, when a literary agent submitted it for a paperback anthology I was editing. Unfortunately, manuscript page six was missing, so I asked the agency to mail it to me, but though it was only a few days later, they no longer represented DAN POTTER. *I tried to track him down, but though he was briefly affiliated with other agencies, I was always one step behind. Finally, years and years later, a reference in* Books in Print *to a novel,* Crazy Moon Zoo, *led me to try a phone number in Oklahoma City. Callooh! Callay! The right Mr. Potter answered! He couldn't recall which magazine had published "Tripping" and had misplaced the manuscript, so I sent him my copy and he wrote a new sixth page. Now, at long last, I am delighted to present this tale of an alien (?) whose bar stool emits—but find out for yourself why for fifteen years I've wanted to anthologize this far, far, far-out story!*

A SPOOKY NIGHT not so long ago: Halloween and raining black cats and stray dogs, me celebrating my thirty-third autumn with a sixth or seventh double when

KA–WHAM

the lightning struck, the lights quirked off and on again, and Big Naomi let out a scream that frizzled my hair. Her three hundred twenty pounds of black flesh were dancing in place like an orgy of mud, quarter-sized eyes flipped out toward the door where the young stranger stood: thigh white and angle thin, fish wet—and glowing. Seemed an eye trick at first, an aftermath of lightning, but later on Big Naomi whispered: He's got the *aura*.

Is it catching? I asked.

You honky drunk, she said. He's *got* it. The glow seemed to fade (for me at least) when he stepped to the bar, whipped out a notebook and printed:

UNO SCOTCH AND WATER, POR FAVOR.

HABLA ESPANOL? I asked on paper.

NEIN, he printed, then: PARLES VOUS FRANÇAIS?

NO.

TOO BAD, he wrote.

WHY?

He stared at the WHY? and scribbled: SORRY. NO READ ENGLISH.

A Halloween midnight with three customers in the place (old man Johnson was making Zs in a booth), and one of them a stone mind-blower. At that point Naomi interjected the aura bit and I wasn't impressed.

Poor damn mute, she added.

The kid smiled. Right up his sleeve, I thought.

(I say *kid:* could've been eighteen or thirty. Seemed to be both at times.)

WHAT'S THE NAME OF THE BAR? he asked in print.

ZEROES, I penciled.

I BELIEVE IT, he returned.

Description of Zeroes: dim, drab, destitute; no color at all except the jukebox, which stood out in the room, a lighted jewel in a dark whore's navel.

But we liked it the way it was: the wrong place on the wrong side of the tracks in the wrongest midwestern city in the world. A place where people who, for whatever reason, had been at the wrong place at the wrong time throughout their lives could relax with their own kind—all of them, all of us, one step comfortably below the lowest common denominator of failure.

The most comfortable place in the world: like the song says, when you ain't got nothin', you got nothin' to lose.

WHAT'RE YOU LOOKING FOR KID? I asked, thinking I'd found another one of us.

TO BE LEFT ALONE, he printed.

YOU'VE FOUND THE RIGHT PLACE, I conveyed.

HOW MUCH YOU WANT TO BET?

TAKE IT FROM ME. I KNOW THIS PLACE.

IT'S NOT IN YOUR HANDS. I DRAW TROUBLE LIKE FLIES.

I tried to reassure him: YOU'LL LIKE IT HERE.

I DOUBT IT.

Big Naomi and I got to writing all sorts of things, but he wouldn't answer, not then or for the next two months. Big Naomi kept going on about the aura until—while he was gone to the john—she accidentally plopped on his bar stool.

KA-WHAM

She turned on like a mile of radios.

Things changed fast. Soon as Big Naomi spread the word about her trip on his bar stool.

It got so toward the last when he came in the crowd would part to let him pass: twenty or thirty people buzzing through the loud room drunk with booze and smoke and dime-a-dream music and endless flak-bursts of conversations through which he'd move adagio, a dancer in his own mind, aloof, apart from us, the smoke, the fumes, the queasy stomachs and queasier sex surging amoeba-like, a half-mass trying to complete itself.

He never seemed to notice the commotion—people jumping up to offer him a seat at the bar, whispering, *That's him*, *That's the guy*, and then he'd sit and the place would swirl and smoke and burst with flak and stumble and grasp again as though he had not entered. But sooner or later everyone would watch him: each of us knowing by that time we were in the presence—as Big Naomi put it—of a *presence*.

Slight, not much more than a hard sliver of something as big as moon, as elusive as wind, he sat night after night unaware (or so I thought) of being watched and studied, awed over, sworn by. And, toward the last drank thirteen scotch and waters every night, watching the hard bouquet of color TV over the far end of the bar, as though waiting for a final commercial. Waiting.

Thirteen scotches and looking neither right nor left and pausing to urinate after each four drinks so that a pattern was established: four drinks down—a little less than an hour—a trip to the water closet and back for four more, with apparently no idea what happened in the room when he left.

He didn't seem to know that all those people were there—had started

coming there—because of him: that the bar had an average of six customers a night before he appeared. Then all of a sudden thirty to forty
people showing up *every* night.

And all of them sworn to secrecy. Not one of them was willing to tell
anyone else about him (never knew his name)—about what happened
when he took his nightly breaks in the john.

Or what happened when you sat on the seat he had vacated: a seat I
had finally to reserve for each customer, forty-five seconds each, no more,
and was booked up with repeats until Christmas 1975.

One of the old-timers didn't believe at first. That was Lady Night.
(Lady's a figure of speech.) Hard as a killer's gleam, that one, unredeem-
able (or so I thought). Stone bitch and pretty if you didn't see the snake
in her, always coiled, always flashing her colors to distract you enough so
she could sink mind-fangs into your eyes and make everything you saw
turn scaly.

Ice-clear skin, the color of clouds in heat; her hair a muted flame;
melon-breasted, a 4'9" perverted Earth Mother. Who: if thoughts were
bombs would have wiped out the entire midwest. Who: if looks could kill,
was a mass murderer.

Fuck you all, Lady Night would announce when she slithered in each
night at nine-thirty, sleek in black leather, a Ms. Zorro, clutching a
bronze-headed seven-foot black man ablaze in tailor-made crimson suits.

Like the kid, he never said a word but brooded alone at the far end of
the bar, toying with what we all thought was an oversized cigaret lighter.
It turned out to be a miniflame thrower that could flick a fury for twelve
feet.

He never introduced himself.

Lady called him Fire.

Lady Night believed nothing we said about the kid. Got to hate him
because he ignored her; her who kept frantically announcing that she was
somebody. And she was: rich, spoiled, on half a dozen drugs at once, her
purse a portable pharmacy: Folks said she could swallow pills faster than
kids ate M&Ms.

That night Lady got to arguing with a bar stool—and lost.

Fire showed off as usual, doing calisthenics. Jumpin' jacks, he called
them. Jumpin jerks, Naomi said. It looked like Fire wanted to snow the
kid. Beside him Fire did scores of pushups off a bar stool. Fire flexed the
muscles of his eyebrows.

Fag! Naomi said.

The kid stuck to his seat. He looked neither left nor right. Nor up nor down. *See no evil?* He was writing something.

FOR ME? I printed.

WRITING A BOOK, he informed me.

ON A PAD? I queried.

BEATS WALLS, he wrote.

A black buzzard, Fire kept circling the kid's seat. We insiders thought Fire an outsider. Naomi stepped in to keep Fire out. He flexed his eyebrows.

Won't be no joke if I send you up in smoke, he said.

Won't no one sing the blues when I make you lose, she answered.

While the kid was gone, Lady Night zeroed in.

But old man Johnson was faster. Frowning, he claimed the magic stool. Then, smiling, he sang "America."

Now you git up, Whitey, Fire said. Git up while you got a face.

The old man got, but before Lady could take the seat, Big Naomi joined the act: three hundred twenty pounds of meansweet blackmammy with two big gold earrings ablaze in pierced ears and a small silver one in her broad nose.

Touch that seat, Lady, you answer to me. Allame!

Burn her, said Lady.

Fire aimed his torch.

Drop it, said Big Naomi, 'fore I work some *roots* on you.

And he did: Fire dropped that thing like a hot potato.

Now kick it on over here, Shorty, she said, and the big black man did as he was told.

Big Naomi lifted one of her giant feet and flattened the thing. She waddled forward, nostrils dilated, eyes burning.

Don't ya'll know nothin'? *Nothin'*? Ya'lls in the presence of a *presence*, she yelled.

Lady slunk toward the seat and Naomi said:

Stay off that, you ruin it, Evil. You sit on it, I break you into chicken feed.

Lady was scared and she screamed for Fire to do something, but without his toy he was a seven-foot freak with a bronze wig and a crimson suit. Lady frowned and pushed Fire across the room to a booth where she continued to sit, I suppose sulking, planning, for the next six weeks.

Big Naomi guarded the kid's seat that night until he got back from the john and, with a regal sweep of an arm, indicated that the throne was indeed his. He barely nodded and went back to the TV and his ninth scotch.

Thereafter Big Naomi was self-appointed First Lady of the bar; her chief function, the guarding of the kid's seat when he made his brief pilgrimages.

She's the one who arranged for everyone in the bar except Lady and Fire to take turns on the stool for forty-five seconds each. And when the word got around and we had thirty to forty people every night, she got the chart going where we booked everyone on the seat up to Christmas '75 and stood by the door keeping strangers out.

Lady Night was allowed in, but she had to sit in a corner booth and keep her mouth shut and her legs closed: no more performances of any kind. So Lady would sulk and get drunk/drugged every night and Fire would carry her out to the lizard-colored Cadillac.

Except that one night when the kid took his break, we were all so busy getting our forty-five-second fix on the stool that no one noticed Lady mean-hip it back to the john and walk right in on him, screaming:

Let me see it, you bastard. You've got no body, you freak! You've got no *body* under your clothes.

Big Naomi made it back there like the long arm of the law and drug Lady out to the middle of the floor by the hair and bounced her off the hardwood a few times like a basketball until she was stone out. Fire carried her out to the car and we got back to taking our turns.

That's the night the kid motioned me toward the pad where he'd written:

OK. ENOUGH FREE RIDES. FIVE BUCKS A HEAD FROM NOW ON. WE SPLIT. SIXTY-FORTY. GUESS WHO'S FORTY?

I argued a little:

EXCEPT FOR LADY, NO ONE'S GOT THAT KIND OF MONEY.

THEY'LL GET IT.

After a bit more pencil-pushing, I agreed. The five-dollar tab didn't make a dent. One morning the daily paper said the crime rate had gone up sixty percent. I was guiltless. I was the forty.

In no time at all, the kid was raking it in. Big Naomi got to bugging me about what he did with all that money.

We don't even know where he *live*, she said. I bet he live like a *prince* somewhere.

So one night all boozed up we decided to follow him home. We kept a good block away and after he'd led us a chase around thirteen corners and was about to turn another one, Naomi left me in mid-block.

You go on, she said. I head around the *other* way.

A few minutes later I met her huffing and puffing around the block. The kid had disappeared. We were standing in front of a row of warehouses when this piece of paper came floating down. On it was printed:

TOUGH ACT TO FOLLOW, HUH?

A week later Big Naomi talked him into staying after the bar closed and we'd shooed everyone out.

WERE YOU LIVE? Naomi printed.

ON THE WING.

YOU KNOW WHAT IT IS YOU GOT?

SOME IDEA. WHY?

YOU IS **TOUCHED.** YOU IS A PRESENCE.

MAYBE I'M CURSED.

WHY YOU SAY THAT?

BECAUSE IF YOU'VE GOT SOMETHING SPECIAL, CERTAIN PEOPLE WON'T LEAVE YOU ALONE. ZEROES ARE DANGEROUS. IF THEY CAN'T BUY WHAT YOU'VE GOT, THEY'LL TRY TO KILL IT.

LIKE LADY?

A LOCAL EXAMPLE.

DON'T WORRY ABOUT HER.

I HAVE TO.

WHY?

YOU'LL SEE.

Naomi wanted to keep Lady and Fire out. I thought of business. No telling how long the kid would stay. Or his battery or whatever-the-hell-it-was might run down. Lady was a big spender.

But sure enough she kept bugging the kid. Offered him a flat five hundred for exclusive rights to his seat. He grinned.

Sometimes she'd wait until he went to the john and address the bar:

What's he *do* back there for five minutes? Always *five* minutes, no more no less. I don't think he's even got a dick! He's up to something. I'll bet my ass on that.

You'd bet your ass on *anything*, Naomi said.

Old man Johnson said he heard sawing noises back there. No one ever listened to old man Johnson.

Things quietened down a little. And when the kid wasn't around we tried to put into words what happened when you sat on his seat.

Old man Johnson said: Like all the blackeyed peas in the world turned technicolor in a sweet forest of turnip greens.

A speed-freak poet said: Sixteen simultaneous orgasms triple-flipping sunward in a Sabrejet's ejector seat.

To me: A thousand daybreaks without a hangover.

An old lecher said it was like sliding bareassed down a whore's tongue.

To a down-and-out ex college teacher: Pure mitosis. Prophase, metaphase, anaphase and telephase.

And for Big Naomi: For forty-five seconds I tripped the light fantastic, honey. Pure starshine and moonbeam, I entered a honeysuckle, dreamed the dawn and got *done* by a butterfly, *did* by a bee.

All the while Fire and Lady Night sitting around deep and full of ruin: two earthquakes eyeing a sandcastle.

It had to happen one night and it did. In walks Lady in a purple-green see-through dress aglow with miniature snake's eyes. She held to one of Fire's elegantly clad arms. Under the other he carried an oversized violin case.

They sat murky in a booth like two freak birds trying to hatch a snapping turtle. I tried to keep one eye on the case, but the bar was so busy I forgot about it. The kid eyed it from time to time, as though he could see inside. He'd had only two drinks, and he whipped out his pad and wrote: TIRED OF SCOTCH.

WHAT WOULD YOU LIKE, I penciled.

He grinned, scribbling: TO HEAR KING KONG READ ALOUD A BRAILLE EDITION OF HEIDI——IN FALSETTO.

WHAT? I asked.

NEVER MIND. JUST A GLASS OF WATER. I'M GOING TO NEED IT.

The way Lady and Fire looked I was expecting the worst. And I guess if that's what you go around expecting, you get it. The kid went back to the john. Big Naomi was so busy guarding the seat, she didn't see Lady and Fire head that way. Fire shucked the violin case and came up with an army-surplus flame thrower.

Someone screamed.

Lady opened the john door and Fire blazed away until the men's room was an oven.

It happened so fast, I'm not sure what happened when. Old man Johnson said the lights went out when Fire opened up. The speed-freak poet said he heard KA-WHAM.

Someone tackled Fire. Big Naomi grabbed the flame thrower and broke it in half, then backhanded Lady twenty feet across the room. We started a water brigade from the bar sink. Finally the smoke cleared and there was nothing in that room at all.

Only a sooty commode, a sink and a mirror. Not a sign of the kid.

He got out the window, said old man Johnson.

But there was no window.

We were all so busy trying to figure out what happened we didn't see Lady and Fire fighting over the kid's seat until Fire knocked her down and jumped on the stool. He got up transformed:

Shut my mouth, he said. Sixteen ton of watermelon hearts, strung on a necklace of chitlins.

Lady was on the seat then, aglow like a Campfire girl. When Big Naomi pulled her off she broke into a full-throated version of "Ave Maria" that made us all cry.

Big Naomi climbed on the stool and nothing happened. It was all over. The seat was stone cold.

I closed the bar for good that night. It was enough to drive a man to not drink. The place has been vacant for six months.

Big Naomi lost two hundred and thirty pounds and breeds butterflies at the children's zoo.

Lady Night joined the Mormon Tabernacle Choir and sings the "Hallelujah Chorus" in eight languages.

I joined AA and opened an all-night sidewalk ice cream café.

Down the street, Fire gives away Good Humors.

A few nights ago I went down to the bar and stood for a long while studying the blackened interior of the men's room. I found something we'd all overlooked: a neat little square of wood sawed out of the floor. Beneath there was plenty of room for a skinny guy to escape. And in the dark on the ground below was a notepad. On it was printed in big bold letters:

HEY, ZEROES! A TOUGH ACT TO FOLLOW, HUH?

Frederik Pohl

The Fiend

FREDERIK POHL, *a resident of Palatine, Illinois, is one of science fiction's most illustrious luminaries. Once agent to some of the top writers in the business, he became the Hugo-winning editor of* If, Galaxy, *and other magazines. His many excellent anthologies include* Beyond the End of Time, Assignment in Tomorrow *and an erstwhile series of* Galaxy *"bests." As a writer, he has employed several pseudonyms and has collaborated with Isaac Asimov, Lester Del Rey, ex-wife Judith Merrill and others. His novel of life on Mars,* Man Alive, *won the 1977 Nebula. "The Fiend" is from his 1966 collection,* Digits and Dastards.

HOW BEAUTIFUL she was, Dandish thought, and how helpless. The plastic identification ribbon around her neck stood out straight, and as she was just out of the transport capsule, she wore nothing else. "Are you awake?" he asked, but she did not stir.

Dandish felt excitement building up inside him; she was so passive and without defense. A man could come to her now and do anything at all to her, and she would not resist. Or, of course, respond. Without touching her, he knew that her body would be warm and dry. It was fully alive, and in a few minutes she would be conscious.

Dandish—who was the captain and sole crew member of the interstellar ship without a name carrying congealed colonists across the long, slow, empty space from the Earth to a planet that circled a star that had never had a name in astronomical charts, only a number, and was now called Eleanor—passed those minutes without looking again at the girl, whose name he knew to be Silvie but whom he had never met. When he looked again, she was awake, jackknifed against the safety straps of the crib, her hair standing out around her head and her face wearing an expression of anger. "All right. Where are you? I know what the score is," she said. "Do you know what they can do to you for this?"

Dandish was startled. He did not like being startled, for it frightened him. For nine years the ship had been whispering across space; he had had enough loneliness to satisfy him, and he had been frightened. There were 700 cans of colonists on the ship, but they lay brittle and changeless in their bath of liquid helium and were not very good company. Outside the ship the nearest human being was perhaps two light-years away, barring some chance-met ship heading in the other direction that was actually far more remote than either star, since the forces involved in stopping and matching course with a vessel bound home were twice as great as, and would take twice as much time as, those involved in the voyage itself. Everything about the trip was frightening. The loneliness was a terror. To stare down through an inch of crystal and see nothing but far stars led to panic. Dandish had decided to stop looking out five years before, but had not been able to keep to his decision, and so now and again peeped through the crystal and contemplated his horrifying visions of the seal breaking, the crystal popping out on a breath of air, himself in his metal prison tumbling, tumbling forever down to the heart of one of the ten million stars that lay below. In this ship a noise was an alarm. Since no one but himself was awake, to hear a scratch of metal or a thud of a moving object striking something else, however tiny, however remote, was a threat, and more than once Dandish had suffered through an itch of fear for hours or days until he tracked down the exploded light tube or unsecured door that had startled him. He dreamed uneasily of fire. This was preposterously unlikely in the steel-and-crystal ship, but what he was dreaming of was not the fire of a house but the monstrous fires in the stars beneath.

"Come out where I can see you," commanded the girl.

Dandish noted that she had not troubled to try to cover her nakedness. Bare she woke and bare she stayed. She had unhitched the restraining webbing and left the crib, and now she was prowling the room in which she had awakened, looking for him. "They warned us," she called. " 'Watch the hook!' 'Look out for the space nuts!' 'You'll be sorry!' That's all we heard at the Reception Center, and now here you are, all right. Wherever you are. Where are you? For God's sake, come out so I can see you." She half stood and half floated at an angle to the floor, nibbling at imperceptible bits of dead skin on her lips and staring warily from side to side. She said, "What was the story you were going to tell me? A subspace meteorite destroyed the ship, all but you and me, and we were doomed to fly endlessly toward nowhere, so there was nothing for us to do but try to make a life for ourselves?"

Dandish watched her through the view eyes in the reviving room, but did not answer. He was a connoisseur of victims, Dandish was. He had spent a great deal of time planning this. Physically she was perfect, very young, slim, slight. He had picked her out on that basis from among the 352 female canned colonists, leafing through the microfile photographs that accompanied each colonist's dossier like a hi-fi hobbyist shopping through a catalogue. She had been the best of the lot. Dandish was not skilled enough to be able to read a personality profile and in any event considered psychologists to be phonies and their profiles trash, so he had had to go by the indices he knew. He had wanted his victim to be innocent and trusting. Silvie, 16 years old and a little below average in intelligence, had seemed very promising. It was disappointing that she did not react with more fear. "They'll give you fifty years for this!" she shouted, looking around to see where he could be hiding. "You know that, don't you?"

The revival crib, sensing that she was out of it, was quietly stowing and rearming itself, ready to be taken out and used again. Its plastic sheets slipped free of the corners, rolled up in a tight spiral, and slid into a disposal chute, revealing aseptic new sheets below. Its radio-warming generators tested themselves with a surge of high-voltage current, found no flaws, and shut themselves off. The crib sides folded down meekly. The instrument table hooded itself over. The girl paused to watch it, then shook her head and laughed. "Scared of me?" she called. "Come on, let's get this over with! Or else," she added, "admit you've made a boo-boo, get me some clothes, and let's talk this over sensibly."

Sorrowfully Dandish turned his gaze away. A timing device reminded him that it was time to make his routine half-hour check of the ship's systems and, as he had done more than 150,000 times already and would do 100,000 times again, he swiftly scanned the temperature readings in the can hold, metered the loss of liquid helium and balanced it against the withdrawals from the reserve, compared the ship's course with the flight plan, measured the fuel consumption and rate of flow, found all systems functioning smoothly, and returned to the girl. It had taken only a minute or so, but already she had found the comb and mirror he had put out for her and was working angrily at her hair. One fault in the techniques of freezing and revivification lay in what happened to such elaborated structures as fingernails and hair. At the temperature of liquid helium all organic matter was brittle as Prince Rupert's drops, and although the handling techniques were planned with that fact in mind, the body wrapped gently in elastic cocooning, every care exercised to keep it from contact with anything hard or sharp, nails and hair had a way of being snapped off. The Reception Center endlessly drummed into the colonists the importance of short nails and butch haircuts, but the colonists were not always convinced. Silvie now looked like a dummy on which a student wigmaker had failed a test. She solved her problem at last by winding what remained of her hair in a tiny bun and put down the comb, snapped-off strands of hair floating in the air all about her like a stretched-out sandstorm.

She patted the bun mournfully and said, "I guess you think this is pretty funny."

Dandish considered the question. He was not impelled to laugh. Twenty years before, when Dandish was a teenager with the long permanented hair and the lacquered fingernails that were the fashion for kids that year, he had dreamed almost every night of just such a situation as this. To own a girl of his own—not to love her or to rape her or to marry her, but to possess her as a slave, with no one anywhere to stop him from whatever he chose to impose on her—had elaborated itself in a hundred variations nightly. He didn't tell anyone about his dream, not directly, but in the school period devoted to practical psychology he had mentioned it as something he had read in a book, and the instructor, staring right through him into his dreams, told him it was a repressed wish to play with dolls. "This fellow is role playing," he said, "acting out a wish to be a woman. These clear-cut cases of repressed homosexuality can take many forms"—and on and on, and although the dreams were as physically satisfying as ever, the young Dandish awoke from them both reproved and resentful.

But Silvie was neither a dream nor a doll. "I'm not a doll!" said Silvie, so sharply and patly that it was a shock. "Come on out and get it over with!"

She straightened up, holding to a free-fall grip, and although she looked angry and annoyed, she still did not seem afraid. "Unless you are really crazy," she said clearly, "which I doubt, although I have to admit it's a possibility, you aren't going to do anything I don't want you to do, you know. Because you can't get away with it, right? You can't kill me— you could never explain it, and besides they don't let murderers run ships in the first place, and so when we land, all I have to do is yell cop and you're running a subway shuttle for the next ninety years." She giggled. "I know about that. My uncle got busted on income-tax evasion, and now he's a self-propelled dredge in the Amazon delta, and you should see the letters he writes. So come on out and let's see what I'm willing to let you get away with."

She grew impatient. "Kee-rist," she said, shaking her head. "I sure get the great ones. And, oh, by the way, as long as I'm up, I have to go to the little girls' room, and then I want breakfast."

Dandish took some small satisfaction in that these requirements, at least, he had foreseen. He opened the door to the washroom and turned on the warmer oven where emergency rations were waiting. By the time Silvie came back, biscuits, bacon and hot coffee were set out for her.

"I don't suppose you have a cigarette?" she said. "Well, I'll live. How about some clothes? And how about coming out so I can get a look at you?" She stretched and yawned and then began to eat. Apparently she had showered, as was generally desirable on awakening from freeze-sleep to get rid of the exfoliated skin, and she had wrapped her ruined hair in a small towel. Dandish had left the one small towel in the washroom, reluctantly, but it had not occurred to him that his victim would wrap it around her head. Silvie sat thoughtfully staring at the remains of her breakfast and then after a while said, like a lecturer:

"As I understand it, starship sailors are always some kind of a nut, because who else would go off for twenty years at a time, even for money, even for any kind of money? All right, you're a nut. So if you wake me up and won't come out, won't talk to me, there's nothing I can do about it.

"Now, I can see that even if you weren't a little loopy to start with, this kind of life would tip you. Maybe you just want a little company? I can understand that. I might even cooperate and say no more about it.

"On the other hand, maybe you're trying to get your nerve up for something rough. Don't know if you can, because they naturally screened you down fine before they gave you the job. But supposing. What happens then?

"If you kill me, they catch you.

"If you don't kill me, then I tell them when we land, and they catch you.

"I told you about my uncle. Right now his body is in the deep freeze somewhere on the dark side of Mercury, and they've got his brain keeping the navigation channels clear off Belém. Maybe you think that's not so bad. Uncle Henry doesn't like it a bit. He doesn't have any company, bad as you that way, I guess, and he says his suction hoses are always sore. Of course he could always louse up on the job, but then they'd just put him some other place that wouldn't be quite as nice—so what he does is grit his teeth, or I guess you should say his grinders, and get along the best he can. Ninety years! He's only done six so far. I mean six when I left Earth, whatever that is now. You wouldn't like that. So why not come out and talk?"

Five or ten minutes later, after making faces and buttering another roll and flinging it furiously at the wall, where the disposal units sluiced it away, she said, "Damn you, then give me a book to read, anyway."

Dandish retreated from her and listened to the whisper of the ship for a few minutes, then activated the mechanisms of the revival crib. He had been a loser long enough to learn when to cut his losses. The girl sprang to her feet as the sides of the crib unfolded. Gentle tentacles reached out for her and deposited her in it, locking the webbing belt around her waist. "You damned fool!" she shouted, but Dandish did not answer. The anesthesia cone descended toward her struggling face, and she screamed, "Wait a minute! I never said I wouldn't—" but what she never said she wouldn't, she couldn't say, because the cone cut her off. In a moment she was asleep. A plastic sack stretched itself around her, molding to her face, her body, her legs, even to the strayed towel around her hair, and the revival crib rolled silently to the freezing room. Dandish did not watch further. He knew what would happen, and besides, the timer reminded him to make his check. Temperatures, normal; fuel consumption, normal; course, normal; freezer room showed one new capsule en route to storage, otherwise normal. Good-bye, Silvie, said Dandish to himself, you were a pretty bad mistake.

Conceivably later on, with another girl . . .

But it had taken nine years for Dandish to wake Silvie, and he did not think he could do it again. He thought of her Uncle Henry running a dredge along the South Atlantic littoral. It could have been him. He had leaped at the opportunity to spend his sentence piloting a starship instead.

He stared out at the ten million stars below with the optical receptors that were his eyes. He clawed helplessly at space with the radars that gave him touch. He wept a five-million-mile stream of ions behind him from his jets. He thought of the tons of helpless flesh in his hold, the bodies in which he could have delighted, if his own body had not been with Uncle Henry's on coldside Mercury, the fears on which he could have fed, if he had been able to inspire fear. He would have sobbed, if he had had a voice to sob with.

Marvin Kaye

Happy Hour

*An unrepentant daytime drama fan, I have written about them twice before:
in the Doubleday Crime Club novel* The Soap Opera Slaughters *and in my
humorous fantasy* The Amorous Umbrella. *"Happy Hour," my third flirta-
tion with the theme, is set on a world whose sole business is to produce soap
operas. It first appeared in the British periodical* Fantasy Tales.

ON THE AFTERNOON that Lionel B. Horace returned home to an
empty apartment for the thirty-eighth time, he put on a bright pink shirt,
scarlet tie, blood-red leather leisure suit, contact lenses with crimson
irises and a carrot-colored toupee. He shoehorned his feet into brick-
orange polished pumps with plaid laces and splashed cinnamon essence
on his cheeks, then, facing his bedroom mirror and sticking his tongue
out at his fiery reflection, he said, "Mister Horace, you are a short fat ugly
wimp, but now at least you are a short fat ugly *interesting* wimp."

As he hurried to the front door, he tried not to glance at the table in
the entry alcove, but for the thirty-eighth time the corner of one of his
(currently) Hell-hued eyes noticed the crumpled scrap of paper tossed
upon the tabletop and for a few seconds he could not move. But it was
almost 1800 hours and after some five anxious weeks of waiting for the A.
P. to arrange his clearance, Lionel was damned if he'd miss one single
mad moment of Happy Hour, so, squeezing his lids shut and twisting the
knob hard enough to strangle it, Lionel plunged through the portal with a
ragged sigh of relief, slammed the door and waddled into the nearest
Flygate, which instantly redistributed him just outside Sound Stage A.

· · · · ·

TIME: Thirty-four days earlier.

PLACE: Sound Stage A.

An actor rises from an armchair and as he does, his head goes completely out of frame. In the control booth, Vincent Michaels, the associate producer, punches another camera on-line and speaks into his microphone: "Tilt up, Lonny, damn it! *Tilt!* You're cutting him off at the neck!"

In the studio, Lionel B. Horace, C.S.C.,* guiltily readjusts till his actor's face is again centered onscreen. "Retake, Vinnie?" he mutters nervously.

"No," says the A. P.'s voice in his headset, "we'll go with it, but be in my office ten minutes after wrap."

TIME: Ten minutes after wrap.

PLACE: The office of the associate producer of *Los Angeles Ladies*, Number 1 show in the New Earth Network's daytime ratings.

Vincent R. Michaels, twenty-year veteran of interstellar soap opera production, is a legend in a business where job security is figured in six-month increments (the interval between supply-transport shuttles to and from Network Nova). Opinions in the TV industry vary as to the secret of his staying power—

> "Fay Farrah-Webber, *Los Angeles Ladies*' Executive Producer, commented, 'If I say Vinnie is remarkably unambitious, it sounds like he's lazy, which he certainly is *not*. I mean that he isn't the least bit interested in climbing the corporate ladder—the network offered him my job and he declined—he's content to be exactly where he is, coordinating the show.'
>
> "But an anonymous source voiced a different opinion: 'Don't be fooled by Vinnie's butter-won't-melt act. He is *the* man at L.A. *Ladies* and any camera director who ignores one of Vinnie's "suggestions" will find her or himself riding the next shuttle off Nova.'
>
> "As for Michaels himself, he claims to be as dedicated to *Los Angeles Ladies* as a parish priest upholding vows of poverty and chastity. 'There is no more Los Angeles and no more California,' he said. 'It's my job to help people remember Wonderland.' "†

---

* Member, Cosmic Society of Camerapersons.

† *Cosmic Starshine*, "The Man Behind *L.A. Ladies*" (10/2/89).

Thirty-four days before Happy Hour, in Vincent Michaels' office, Lionel B. Horace vows not to commit any more mistakes.

"Lonny, how long have you been with us?"

"Two years, Vinnie."

"So you've seen a lot of staff turnover."

Lionel shifts uncomfortably in his black leatherette chair. "Uh-huh. Every six months."

"You're aware of unemployment statistics in your union. Yet you've goofed half a dozen times in the past four days."

"Then I'm history?"

Michaels sighs. "Until this week, you were my best cameraperson. I'd rather not lose you. What's wrong? Maybe I can fix it."

"The shuttle last week . . . Marie was on it."

Even as the A. P.'s eyebrows rise, his fingers run an arpeggio on his computer keyboard, punching up the recent shuttle's passenger list. He scans the readout, clears the screen, and smiles encouragingly at his employee. "You're wrong, Lonny. She's still here on Network Nova."

"She IS?" The other leaps to his feet. "Where is she?"

"I don't know, but she wasn't on the shuttle. Now if you promise to concentrate on your work, I promise I'll find her for you."

Lionel's face falls. "Even if she *is* still here, she won't have anything more to do with me."

"Certainly not if you take that attitude. Lonny, you've got to think positive. Start feeling good about yourself—"

"How can I? I'm a short fat ugly wimp."

The A. P. punches more keyboard buttons. "Lonny, how old are you?"

"Forty-four. Why?"

"Blood type?"

"B Positive."

"Childhood diseases?"

"The usual. Waxeritis. Trottertoe. A cold."

"Any hereditary disease tendencies?"

"Diabetes. Vinnie, what *are* you doing?"

Pressing Return, the A. P. pats Lionel's shoulder. "My friend, we're going to work on your CQ."

"CQ?"

"Your confidence quotient. On one condition . . . everything I'm about to tell you is top secret."

Mystified but interested, Lionel nods. And Vincent Michaels unfolds to his increasingly eager ears the forbidden wonders of Happy Hour.

· · · · ·

TIME: Thirty-four days later; 17:53 hours.

PLACE: An antechamber off Sound Stage A.

Vinnie hadn't exaggerated. Lionel's bartender looked like all the blondes he'd ever wanted.

"Ha-ahh, mah name is Tina," she drawled in the southern accent that many Network Nova citizens affected in imitation of Lydia Winston, the popular *Los Angeles Ladies* actress who played Deena Lou Macon, "the southern-fried starlet from Georgia" (in the lingo of the press releases).

"Ahm youah bahtendah," Tina said. "Aah'll see thatch'git anythin' youah sweet li'l haht desa-ahs." She flashed white-cornkernel teeth, then pretended to pout. "But if'n I doan' appeal t' y'all, y' c'n pick anothah bahtendah."

"N-no, you'll d-d-do just—jes' fahn," he stammered.

Tina lightly brushed a cupped palm over his bared forearm. "Ah jes' *knew* ah's gonna lahk you!" Dimpling, she regarded his red leather suit. "Y' shu-ah know how t'dress sexy! Heah—read this." She handed him a plastic card.

Lionel glanced at it. "I already know the rules. Vinnie filled me in—"

"Hush up!" She touched soft fingertips to his lips. "Y'almos' broke Rule Numbah Three!"

---

1. Participants are strictly sworn to secrecy.
2. During Happy Hour, you must not divulge your true shape or identity.
3. Even if you think you recognize a disguised friend, never speak anyone's real name.
4. Despite inoculation, you must assume all risks resulting from consorting with offworlders.
5. Violators of these rules will be deported.

While he read, Tina drummed a complicated rhythm on her keyboard and copied the resultant readout for HORACE, LIONEL B., on the input pad of her ChemPak dispensary. The storage tanks "talked" to one another with a merry twinkle of lights, then the chute door rose. Tina reached in, took the waiting ampoule, affixed it to a hypodermic, rippled her fingers along Lionel's flabby forearm and told him to clench. "Oooh, what a b-i-g fist! Naow this ain' gonna be more'n a li'l sting. . . ."

As she plunged in the needle, music blared from Sound Stage A. Lionel turned eagerly toward the sound. "A *live* band?"

"That's th' Nifty Aliens, but doan' worry, hon, now you're inoculated." She pressed a cotton ball to the puncture for a few seconds, then affixed a bandage to the tiny wound. His head lolled against her breast.

"Welcome to Happy Hour," Tina said, without the slightest trace of accent.

TIME: 1800–1815 hours.
PROGRAM: Orientation.

Tina guided Lionel B. Horace into one of the small cubicles that ring the shell of Sound Stage A. "Heah's wheah you become whoevah," she told him.

"Can't I just be myself?"

"An' be recognized? Uh-uh. Thass a no-no!"

"But I won't know how to behave."

"You'll manage jes' fa-ahn. Now how should ah make y' look?"

"Tall. Slim. Handsome."

Tina squeezed him affectionately. "But youah already a chubby-cute li'l sweethaht!"

Lionel blushed. "Thank you, but I want to look different."

She clucked reluctantly. "Okay, hon, it's you-ah body. Step into th' transformah."

Nervously, Lionel centered himself in the frame. Even though the manufacturers swore that they'd long since worked out all the bugs—an unfortunate phrasing for Holistic Matter Distributors, commonly called Flygates—everyone had heard horror stories of molecular distribution accidents. Commercially, HMDs were solely intended to be used as rapid transportation devices, reassembling objects and persons exactly as transmitted. Cosmetic redistribution was extremely risky, not to mention illegal. This was why Happy Hour participants were sworn to secrecy.

As the Flygate warmed up, the lights flickered. From Sound Stage A, Lionel heard thrumming music, then all sound, sight and thought stopped and for several seconds he was beyond dead: the disassembled molecular components of his body filled the HMD's collection chamber . . . and then the world came back in a bright new wash of harmony and hue.

Tina held onto his hand till the dizziness passed. Then, swiveling him round so he faced a full-length mirror, she invited him to inspect the new Lionel B. Horace: six feet two inches tall; impeccably layered hair with a curly comma dangling over one eye, a sardonic raked smile and a lean, trim athlete's figure.

He laughed delightedly. "That's really *me?*"

"Foah th' nex' fiftah-fahv minutes," Tina nodded. She held the door open and followed Lionel into Sound Stage A.

His first impressions were confused—a shimmering, sparkling pinwheel of flashing lights and music so loud it redictated his pulse rate, but as he scanned the scene, Lionel began to orient himself. Normally, Sound Stage A was an enormous oval ringed with individual *Los Angeles Ladies* sets—living rooms, sunporches, restaurants, a swimming pool, a hospital waiting room, etc.—its circular central space devoted to cameras and sound booms. But tonight its curved perimeter was compartmented according to activity: three semicircular cocktail bars (Tina took her place behind the nearest one); several gaming tables devoted to baccarat, roulette, backgammon and 4D Ultima; holographic interplay and elbow readings. Lionel was amazed that so much equipment could be moved in so fast in such a short time *for* such a short time. He wondered where all the program's sets had been stored, ditto cameras and sound gear.

The middle of the floor was filled with dancers twisting and gyrating round a raised central platform where the damnedest dance band Lionel ever set red eyes on was playing. The Nifty Aliens was a three-piece ensemble made up of a purple-and-gold pinstriped pseudomorph who simultaneously played two Kasiopro keyboards, a red-haired shaggy animal on drums, and a stunningly feminine fuchsia-skinned Lilithian who sang with one head and literally doubled on clarinet with the other.

Lionel scanned the crowd on the dance floor, at the bars and at the gaming tables, his new height permitting him a giant's-eye view of the scene, but he recognized no one. Disappointed, he took a seat at Tina's bar, ordered a Larkspur Eradicator and stared at his new persona in the mirror. *If I really looked like this, Marie never would have left me.* He chugalugged his drink. As the potent liquor polluted his bloodstream, Lionel imagined that the lights flashing over the dance floor were bending into sinuous, sensual beams of color.

Interesting, he admitted, *but when am I going to start having fun?*

TIME: 1816–1830 hours.

PROGRAM: Diversion.

Lionel ambled over to a vacant stool at the baccarat table. The four players sitting there had chosen predictable disguises: one looked like Orson Welles, the second resembled David Niven, the third was a double for Barry Nelson, while the sweaty fourth carbon-copied Peter Lorre. Lionel shoved a wad of quaint currency towards the banker, who swiftly riffle-counted the packet and clatterclicked a pile of casino chips in front of him. Lionel sorted them into three neat piles.

"Bank of one million," the officiary announced.

"Banco," Lionel said.

Looking anxious and angry, Lorre slid cards onto the table.

"Nine on the table," said the officiary.

Lionel turned over the King of Hearts and Jack of Spades.

The officiary said, "Baccarat."

Lionel scooped up his winnings. Just then, something sharp prodded into his back and someone whispered into his ear, "This is a silent air gun. Keep playing till you lose."

"Bank of two million."

"Banco suivi." Lionel counted out the appropriate chips, studied the cards Lorre slid him and asked for a third.

"Six on the table."

Lionel turned over a three, a four and a two, collected his winnings, played the four-million bank, won again, accepted the eight-million wager —and at that moment the gun muzzle in his back wavered ever so slightly. Instantly, Lionel swiveled, knocking the weapon askew. A whoosh of pressured air; David Niven crumpled to the floor holding his side; still pivoting, Lionel trapped the trigger arm of Lorre's henchman in a grip that snapped the man's fingers and with the same swift motion he hurtled out of his chair, narrowly avoiding the bullet Lorre fired. Lionel hefted his Baretta and squeezed off a round. Lorre clutched at his heart as sudden blood stained his dinner jacket.

Lionel returned to Tina's bar. Happy Hour was certainly diverting, he thought, but it still hadn't lived up to its name.

TIME: 1831–1845 hours.

PROGRAM: Involvement.

At the moment, only Lionel and the Nifty Aliens, who were taking a break, sat at Tina's bar.

"Wassa trouble, sweetahpah?" Tina asked. "Y' doan look lahk y'r enjoyin' yose'f."

"Not very much, I'm afraid," Lionel confessed, staring at a roomful of celebrants involved in Happy Hour's many diversions. "I'm not interested in gambling or fortune-telling, I don't dance, and there's nobody to talk to."

"What do *we* look like? Chopped grutchah?" the two-headed fuchsia-skinned Lilithian singer-clarinettist said in unison.

Lionel waved at them uncertainly. "Hi. I'm—" Tina tsk-tsked warn-ingly and he stopped himself from violating Regulation Number 2. "Call me Bond. James Bond."

The Lilithian's left (brunette) head replied, "We're Beatrice—"

"—and you're not," the auburn head on the right added.

Lionel nodded. "That's for certain."

"Would you like to be?" she/they asked, invitingly batting four lids over two sets of green catlike eyes.

"How would that be possible?" Lionel wondered.

"Come along with we—"

"—and you'll find out!"

So Lionel followed them into one of the small perimeter chambers. Taking his hand, Beatrice led him towards a familiar-looking portal. "But that's a Flygate!" he protested.

"So?"

"It's dangerous!"

"Yes. That's half the fun. Coming?"

Lionel was too drunk and Beatrice was too beautiful to resist. He stepped through the HMD's shimmering blue portal and began to unite with the sensual offworlder. *So this is what it's like to be a woman,* he thought. *Free. But so vulnerable.* Their hips and breasts and limbs merged as Beatrice's hands clasped his from within and guided their melded flesh in a frenzy of narcissistic exploration. Shared hearts beat faster, overlayered lungs rose and fell rapidly, but then Lionel coupled his mind to theirs—

ah Beatrice ahh Beatrice Beatrice ahhh

—and suddenly he felt cut off. Lonely. Unsatisfied. *Diminished.* He pulled away from them.

Beatrice's auburn head reintegrated. "What's wrong?"

"You shut me out."

"Nonsense!"

"I was just a tool."

"You were as much a part of it *and* us as any Lilithian ever would permit. If that's not enough for you, I'm sorry, but that's the way we are."

"Never mind," he said, "it was my fault." And it was. Even though his wife walked out on him, Lionel still felt married, ergo guilty, ergo isolated. *Marie is the only woman I've ever wanted.*

Collecting himself, Lionel went back to Tina's bar, ordered another

Larkspur Eradicator and sipped it as he stared morosely into his own mirrored crimson eyes. *Maybe,* he reflected, *I look different, but inside I'm still the same short fat ugly wimp I've always been.*

He was not happy.

TIME: 1846–1900 hours.

PROGRAM: Apotheosis.

Someone tapped him on the shoulder. He turned but saw no one.

"Down here, boss." The odd, soupy voice came from below. Lionel looked floorwards and saw a dwarf clad in a white tropic-wear suit. He recognized the disguise as a Flygate clone of Herve Villechaize, an actor he remembered from an ancient TV series that he studied at the Cosmic Museum of Broadcasting when he was preparing for his qualifying certificate in one-camera location shooting.

The dwarf proffered a silver platter on which rested an envelope addressed to James Bond. Lionel opened it and read pencil-scrawled words on a sheet of *Los Angeles Ladies* letterhead—

IN RE PROMISE: GO TO CUBE 34.

The sound stage's outer compartments served as dressing rooms and prop storage cells. Lionel hurried to cube 34 . . . and there she was! Though she sat with her back to him, he immediately recognized her red-brown tresses. The edge of a wine glass rested against her lower lip. She looked tired and sad. In spite of Regulation Number 3, Lionel almost whispered her name, but he knew she wouldn't recognize his disguise, so he confined himself instead to clearing his throat.

Marie turned, studied him appreciatively and said, "Hello, stranger. There's not much time. I cost thirty-five credits."

"*What?!*"

"Too expensive, handsome? Don't you think I'm worth it?"

"Just the opposite!" he babbled, feverishly counting money into her hand. Though Lionel was shocked that his wife had become a high-priced hooker, he was also overwhelmingly excited that against all odds, he could again enjoy her addictively sweet body. "You're worth more, much *much* more!" Radiant at the compliment, she hugged him impulsively and as he gazed passionately at her, he wished he could lose himself in the liquid depths of her sea-green eyes—and then he recollected that he could do just that.

"Where are you taking me?" she asked. "Happy Hour'll be over in a few minutes!"

"Yes!" He tugged her by the hand. "It's only a few cubes away. Hurry!"

They ran to the private chamber he'd shared with Beatrice and before Marie could protest, Lionel pulled her into the Flygate *and husband and wife interpenetrate and for the first time in his sad life, Lionel understands a loneliness other than his own, that of a frightened little girl so abused by her parents and her lovers that she ran away from Lionel lest he become too important to her and end up hurting her, too, but now Lionel enfolds her in an embrace so tender that Marie finally relinquishes all her outworn fears and willingly joins her mind and body and spirit to him in an intimacy more perfect than love and at last Lionel B. Horace is supremely happy*

Someone shook his shoulder. "Wake up, Lonny! Happy Hour's over."

"Wha-a-? Where am I?" Groggily aware that he'd regained his customary shape, height and weight, Lionel opened his eyes and saw that he was sitting in the antechamber where Tina inoculated him. The only other person in the room was Vincent Michaels. He clutched his employer's arm. "Vinnie, where's Marie?"

"I sent her home to rest till she feels more like herself." Michaels clucked dolefully. "It was no easy task separating you two from one another."

"I've got to find her."

"Not now, Lonny. She doesn't know who you really are, remember?"

"But we totally shared each other!"

"And you left her mighty confused. Guess what she told me? That she wishes her husband was more like *you.*"

"Oh, what a mess!" Lionel wrung his hands. "What'll I do?"

"Give her time, Lonny. Go slow. Come next Happy Hour, she'll be dying to see you."

A wan, hopeful smile. "You *really* think so, Vinnie?"

"I know so. Now come on, I'll help you home. You had too many Larkspur Eradicators." Resting a hand on his cameraperson's meaty shoulder, the executive steered him through the door and into the nearest commuter HMD.

After the men were gone, Tina entered the room, switched off the computer, closed and security-locked her ChemPak dispensary, packed up her tapes and hypodermic and departed. On her way out through Sound Stage A, she shivered with self-conscious delight at the firsthand glimpse she got of the soap opera sets. Though she never would have admitted it to her colleagues, *Los Angeles Ladies* was Tina's favorite TV program.

· · · · ·

When Lionel's head hit the pillow, his carrot-colored toupee skewed ridiculously, but he was already asleep. Vincent Michaels set the hairpiece on a night table, removed his employee's brick-orange shoes, covered him with a blanket, turned off the light and left the bedroom. On his way to the front door, he noticed a crumpled note tossed on a tabletop in the entry alcove. He unfolded the scrap of paper and read it.

> Lionel, you are a short fat ugly wimp. I am
> leaving you—Marie

By now, she must be halfway across the galaxy, Michaels thought grimly.

In old L.A., some producers allegedly distributed pills to high-strung talent, but Vincent Michaels handled staff emotional problems with electrochemical hypnotherapy. An expert like Tina Wasserman was expensive, but compared to charter-flighting in replacement personnel, she was the most cost-efficient option. *In Lonny's case,* the A. P. mused, *Tina and Happy Hour have salvaged a first-rate cameraperson.*

At least until the next shuttle.

Richard L. Wexelblat

Horace, Nellie, and the Computer

RICHARD L. WEXELBLAT, *the author of the definitive* History of Programming Languages, *is a resident of Alexandria, Virginia, who, in his spare time, writes such humorous verse as "The Dragon Over Hackensack" (in* Masterpieces of Terror and the Supernatural) *and the following new twist on the ancient love triangle.*

I sing of Horace, fleet of finger.
Near the console he would linger.
He had a woman. He would bring her
　　Printed outputs every night.

Horace loved to write in COBOL,
FORTRAN, BASIC, even SNOBOL.
C and Ada, Pascal: No call
　　For a program caused him fright.

One time Horrie's lovely lady
Said they should go off on May Day.
Horace said he was afraid he
　　Had to take a different flight.

Horrie's friendly home computer
Seemed to him becoming cuter

Than his faithful female suitor.
    She thought that was not quite right.

Nellie kidnapped that distractor,
Borrowed someone's trash compactor,
Squoze it to a tiny factor!
    Now she's got him back at night.

Isaac Asimov

I'm in Marsport Without Hilda

Isaac Asimov, *in his 1986 Doubleday collection,* The Best Science Fiction of Isaac Asimov, *writes, "My stories rarely contain ribald elements. This is not because I am incapable of writing in ribald fashion (consider my five books of original limericks that are* not *clean), but because I choose not to." The following story "was written at an editorial dare, and I told the editor that I would write it under a pseudonym so that I could retain my principle. Then, however, when the story was written, I decided it wasn't so terribly ribald—it was all by indirection—and I couldn't bear to deny authorship, so I put my own name on it."*

IT WORKED ITSELF OUT, to begin with, like a dream. I didn't have to make any arrangements. I didn't have to touch it. I just watched things work out. Maybe right then's when I should have smelled catastrophe.

It began with my usual month's layoff between assignments. A month on and a month off is the right and proper routine for the Galactic Service. I reached Marsport for the usual three-day layover before the short hop to Earth.

Ordinarily, Hilda, God bless her, as sweet a wife as any man ever had, would be there waiting for me and we'd have a nice sedate time of it—a nice little interlude for the two of us. The only trouble with that is that Marsport is the rowdiest hellhole in the system, and a nice little interlude isn't exactly what fits in. Only, how do I explain that to Hilda, hey?

Well, *this* time my mother-in-law—God *bless* her, for a change—got

sick just two days before I reached Marsport; and the night before landing, I got a spacegram from Hilda saying she would stay on Earth with her
mother and wouldn't meet me this one time.

I grammed back my loving regrets and my feverish anxiety concerning
her mother; and when I landed, there I was:

I *was in Marsport without Hilda!*

That was still nothing, you understand. It was the frame of the picture,
the bones of the woman. Now there was the matter of the lines and
coloring inside the frame; the skin and flesh outside the bones.

So I called up Flora—Flora of certain rare episodes in the past—and
for the purpose I used a video booth. Damn the expense, full speed
ahead.

I was giving myself ten to one odds she'd be out, she'd be busy with her
videophone disconnected, she'd be dead, even.

But she was in, with her videophone connected and she was anything
but dead.

She looked better than ever. Age cannot wither nor custom stale, as
somebody or other once said, her infinite variety. And the robe she wore
—or, rather, almost didn't wear—helped a lot.

Was she glad to see me? She squealed, "Max! It's been years."

"I know, Flora, but this is it, if you're available. Because guess what!
I'm in Marsport without Hilda."

She squealed again. "Isn't that *nice!* Then come on over."

I goggled a bit. This was too much. "You mean you *are* available?" You
have to understand that Flora was never available without plenty of notice. Well, she was that kind of knockout.

She said, "Oh, I've got some quibbling little arrangement, Max, but I'll
take care of that. You come on over."

"I'll come," I said happily.

Flora was the kind of girl— Well, I tell you, she had her rooms under
Martian gravity, 0.4 Earth-normal. The gadget to free her of Marsport's
pseudo-grav field was expensive, of course, but I'll tell you just in passing
that it was worth it, and she had no trouble paying it off. If you've ever
held a girl in your arms at 0.4 gees, you need no explanation. If you
haven't, explanations will do no good. I'm also sorry for you.

Talk about floating on clouds . . .

And mind you, the girl has to know how to handle low gravity. Flora
did. I won't talk about myself, you understand, but Flora didn't howl for
me to come over and start breaking previous engagements just because
she was at loose ends. Her ends were never loose.

I closed connections, and only the prospect of seeing it all in the flesh —such flesh!—could have made me wipe out the image with such alacrity. I stepped out of the booth.

And at that point, that precise point, that very split instant of time, the first whiff of catastrophe nudged itself up to me.

That first whiff was the bald head of that lousy Rog Crinton of the Mars offices, gleaming over a headful of pale blue eyes, pale yellow complexion, and pale brown mustache. He was the same Rog Crinton, with some Slavic strain in his ancestry, that half the people out on field work thought had a middle name that went sunnuvabich.

I didn't bother getting on all fours and beating my forehead against the ground because my vacation had started the minute I had gotten off the ship.

I said with only normal politeness, "What the hell do you want and I'm in a hurry. I've got an appointment."

He said, "You've got an appointment with me. I've got a little job for you."

I laughed and told him in all necessary anatomical detail where he could put the little job, and offered to get him a mallet to help. I said, "It's my month off, friend."

He said, "Red emergency alert, friend."

Which meant, no vacation, just like that. I couldn't believe it. I said, "Nuts, Rog. Have a heart. I got an emergency alert of my own."

"Nothing like this."

"Rog," I pleaded, "can't you get someone else? Anyone else?"

"You're the only Class A agent on Mars."

"Send to Earth, then. They stack agents like micropile units at Headquarters."

"This has got to be done before 11 P.M. What's the matter? You haven't got three hours?"

I grabbed my head. The boy just didn't *know*. I said, "Let me make a call, will you?"

I stepped back in the booth, glared at him, and said, "Private!"

Flora shone on the screen again, like a mirage on an asteroid. She said, "Something wrong, Max? Don't say something's wrong. I canceled my other engagement."

I said, "Flora, baby, I'll be there. I'll *be* there. But something's come up."

She asked the natural question in a hurt tone of voice and I said, "No. Not another girl. With you in the same town they don't make any other girls. Females, maybe. Not girls. Baby! Honey! It's business. Just hold on. It won't take long."

She said, "All right," but she said it kind of like it was just enough *not* all right so that I got the shivers.

I stepped out of the booth and said, "All right, Rog Sunnuvabich, what kind of mess have you cooked up for me?"

We went into the spaceport bar and got us an insulated booth. He said, "The *Antares Giant* is coming in from Sirius in exactly half an hour, at 8 P.M. local time."

"Okay."

"Three men will get out, among others, and will wait for the *Space Eater* coming in from Earth at 11 P.M. and leaving for Capella some time thereafter. The three men will get on the *Space Eater* and will then be out of our jurisdiction."

"So."

"So between eight and eleven, they will be in a special waiting room and you will be with them. I have a trimensional image of each for you so you'll know who they are and which is which. You have between eight and eleven to decide which one is carrying contraband."

"What kind of contraband?"

"The worst kind. Altered Spaceoline."

"*Altered* Spaceoline?"

He had thrown me. I knew what Spaceoline was. If you've been on a space hop you know too. And in case you're Earthbound yourself the bare fact is that everyone needs it on the first space trip; almost everybody needs it for the first dozen trips; lots need it every trip. Without it, there is vertigo associated with free fall, screaming terrors, semipermanent psychoses. With it, there is nothing; you don't mind a thing. And it isn't habit-forming; it has no adverse side effects. Spaceoline is ideal, essential, unsubstitutable. When in doubt, take Spaceoline.

Rog said, "That's right, altered Spaceoline. It can be changed chemically, by a simple reaction that can be conducted in anyone's basement, into a drug that will give one giant-size charge and become your baby-blue habit the first time. It is on a par with the most dangerous alkaloids we know."

"And we just found out about it?"

"No. The Service has known about it for years, and we've kept others from knowing by squashing every discovery flat. Now, however, the discovery has gone too far."

"In what way?"

"One of the men who will be stopping over at this spaceport is carrying some of the altered Spaceoline on his person. Chemists in the Capellan system, which is outside the Federation, will analyze it and set up ways of synthesizing more. After that, it's either fight the worst drug menace we've ever seen or suppress the matter by suppressing the source."

"You mean Spaceoline."

"Right. And if we suppress Spaceoline, we suppress space travel."

I decided to put my finger on the point. "Which one of the three has it?"

Rog smiled nastily. "If we knew, would we need you? You're to find out which of the three."

"You're calling on me for a lousy frisk job?"

"Touch the wrong one at the risk of a haircut down to the larynx. Every one of the three is a big man on his own planet. One is Edward Harponaster; one is Joaquin Lipsky; and one is Andiamo Ferrucci. Well?"

He was right. I'd heard of every one of them. Chances are you have too. *Important*, very important people, and not one was touchable without proof in advance. I said, "Would one of them touch a dirty deal like—"

"There are trillions involved," said Rog, "which means any one of the three would. And one of them *has*, because Jack Hawk got that far before he was killed—"

"Jack Hawk's *dead?*"

"Right, and one of those guys arranged the killing. Now you find out which. You put the finger on the right one before eleven and there's a promotion, a raise in pay, a pay-back for poor Jack Hawk, and a rescue of the Galaxy. You put the finger on the wrong one and there'll be a nasty interstellar situation and you'll be out on your ear and also on every blacklist from here to Antares and back."

I said, "Suppose I don't finger anybody?"

"That would be like fingering the wrong one as far as the Service is concerned."

"I've got to finger someone, but only the right one, or my head's handed to me?"

"In thin slices. You're beginning to understand me, Max."

In a long lifetime of looking ugly, Rog Crinton had never looked uglier. The only comfort I got out of staring at him was the realization that he was married too, and that he lived with his wife at Marsport all year round. And does he deserve that! Maybe I'm hard on him, but he *deserves* it.

I put in a quick call to Flora, as soon as Rog was out of sight.

She said, "Well?" The magnetic seams on her robe were opened just right and her voice sounded as thrillingly soft as she looked.

I said, "Baby, honey, it's something I can't talk about, but I've got to do it, see? Now you hang on, I'll get it over with if I have to swim the Grand Canal to the icecap in my underwear, see? If I have to claw Phobos out of the sky. If I have to cut myself in pieces and mail myself parcel post."

"Gee," she said, "if I thought I was going to have to wait . . ."

I winced. She just wasn't the type to respond to poetry. Actually, she was a simple creature of action . . . but after all, if I were going to be drifting through low gravity in a sea of jasmine perfume with Flora, poetry response is not the type of qualification I would consider most indispensable.

I said urgently, "Just hold on, Flora. I won't be any time at all. I'll make it up to you."

I was annoyed, sure, but I wasn't worried as yet. Rog hadn't more than left me when I figured out exactly how I was going to tell the guilty man from the others.

It was easy. I should have called Rog back and told him, but there's no law against wanting egg in your beer and oxygen in your air. It would take me five minutes and then off I would go to Flora; a little late, maybe, but with a promotion, a raise, and a slobbering kiss from the Service on each cheek.

You see, it's like this. Big industrialists don't go space hopping much; they use transvideo reception. When they do go to some ultra-high interstellar conference, as these three were probably going, they took Spaceoline. For one thing, they didn't have enough hops under their belt to risk doing without. For another, Spaceoline was the expensive way of doing it and industrialists did things the expensive way. I know their psychology.

Now that would hold for two of them. The one who carried contraband, however, couldn't risk Spaceoline—even at the price of risking space sickness. Under Spaceoline influence, he could throw the drug away, or give it away, or talk gibberish about it. He would *have* to stay in control of himself.

It was as simple as that.

The *Antares Giant* was on time. They brought in Lipsky first. He had thick, ruddy lips, rounded jowls, very dark eyebrows, and hair just beginning to show gray. He just looked at me and sat down. Nothing. He was under Spaceoline.

I said, "Good evening, sir."

He said, in a dreamy voice, "Surrealismus of Panamy hearts in three-quarter time for a cup of coffeedom of speech."

That was Spaceoline all the way. The buttons in the human mind were set free-swinging. Each syllable suggests the next in free association.

Andiamo Ferrucci came in next. Black mustache, long and waxed, olive complexion, pock-marked face. He sat down.

I said, "Nice trip?"

He said, "Trip the light fantastic tock the clock is crowings on the bird."

Lipsky said, "Bird to the wise guyed book to all places everybody."

I grinned. That left Harponaster. I had my needle gun neatly palmed and out of sight and the magnetic coil ready to grip him.

And then Harponaster came in. He was thin, leathery, and, though near-bald, considerably younger than he seemed in his trimensional image. And he was Spaceolined to the gills.

I said, "Damn!"

Harponaster said, "Damyankee note speech to his last time I saw wood you say so."

Ferrucci said, "Sow the seed the territory under dispute do well to come along long road tonightingale."

Lipsky said, "Gay lords hopping pong balls."

I stared from one to the other as the nonsense ran down in shorter and shorter spurts and then silence.

I got the picture, all right. One of them was faking. He had thought ahead and realized that omitting the Spaceoline would be a giveaway. He might have bribed an official into injecting saline or dodged it some other way.

One of them was faking. It wasn't hard to fake the thing. Comedians on sub-etheric had a Spaceoline skit regularly. It was amazing the liberties they could take with the moral code in that way. *You*'ve heard them.

I stared at them and got the first prickle at the base of my skull that said: What if you *don't* finger the right one?

It was eight-thirty and there was my job, my reputation, my head growing rickety upon my neck to be considered. I saved it all for later and thought of Flora. She wasn't going to wait for me forever. For that matter, chances were she wouldn't wait for half an hour.

I wondered. Could the faker keep up free association if nudged gently onto dangerous territory?

I said, "The floor's covered with a nice solid rug" and ran the last two words together to make it "soli drug."

Lipsky: "Drug from underneath the dough re mi fa sol to be saved."

Ferrucci said, "Saved and a haircut above the common herd something about younicorny as Kansas high as my knee."

Harponaster said, "Kneether wind nor snow use trying to by four ever and effervescence and sensibilityter totter."

Lipsky said, "Totters and rags."

Ferrucci said, "Agsactly."

Harponaster said, "Actlymation."

A few grunts and they ran down.

I tried again and I didn't forget to be careful. They would remember everything I said afterward and what I said had to be harmless. I said, "This is a darned good space-line."

Ferrucci said, "Lines and tigers and elephanthills on the prairie dogs do bark of the boughwough—"

I interrupted, looking at Harponaster, "A darned good space-line."

"Line the bed and rest a little black sheepishion of wrong way to ring the clothes of a perfect day."

I interrupted again, glaring at Lipsky, "Good space-line."

"Liron is hot-chacolit ain't gonna be the same on you vee and double the stakes and potato and heel."

Someone else said, "Heel the sicknecessaryd and write will wincetance."

"Tance with mealtime."

"I'm comingle."

"Inglish."

"Ishter seals."

"Eels."

I tried a few more times and got nowhere. The faker, whichever he was, had practiced or had natural talents at talking free association. He was disconnecting his brain and letting the words come out any old way. And he must be inspired by knowing exactly what I was after. If "drug" hadn't given it away, "space-line" three times repeated must have. I was safe with the other two, but *he* would know.

And he was having fun with me. All three were saying phrases that might have pointed to a deep inner guilt—"sol to be saved," "little black sheepishion of wrong," "drug from underneath," and so on. Two were saying such things helplessly, randomly. The third was amusing himself.

So how did I find the third? I was in a feverish thrill of hatred against him and my fingers twitched. The bastard was subverting the Galaxy. More than that, he was keeping me from Flora.

I could go up to each of them and start searching. The two who were really under Spaceoline would make no move to stop me. They could feel no emotion, no fear, no anxiety, no hate, no passion, no desire for self-defense. And if one made the slightest gesture of resistance I would have my man.

But the innocent ones would remember afterward.

I sighed. If I tried it, I would get the criminal all right, but later I would be the nearest thing to chopped liver any man had ever been. There would be a shakeup in the Service, a big stink the width of the Galaxy, and in the excitement and disorganization, the secret of altered Spaceoline would get out anyway and so what the hell.

Of course, the one I wanted might be the first one I touched. One chance out of three. I'd have one out and only God can make a three.

Damn it, something had started them going while I was muttering to myself and Spaceoline is contagiust a gigolo my, oh—

I stared desperately at my watch and my line of sight focused on nine-fifteen.

Where the devil was the time going to?

Oh, my; oh, nuts; oh, Flora!

I had no choice. I made my way to the booth for another quick call to Flora. Just a quick one, you understand, to keep things alive, assuming they weren't dead already.

I kept saying to myself: She won't answer.

I tried to prepare myself for that. There were other girls, there were other—

Hell, there were no other girls.

If Hilda had been in Marsport, I would never have had Flora on my mind in the first place and it wouldn't have mattered. But I was in Marsport *without* Hilda and I had made a date with Flora; Flora and a body that had been made up out of heaping handfuls of all that was soft and fragrant and firm; Flora and a low-gravity room and a way about her that made it seem like free fall through a warm, breathable ocean of champagne-flavored meringue—

The signal was signaling and signaling and I didn't dare break off.

Answer! Answer!

She answered. She said, "It's *you!*"

"Of course, sweetheart, who else would it be?"

"Lots of people. Someone who would *come*."

"There's just this little detail of business, honey."

"What business? Plastons for who?"

I almost corrected her grammar, but I was wondering what this plastons kick was.

Then I remembered. I told her once I was a plaston salesman. That was the time I brought her a plaston nightgown that was a honey. Just thinking of it made me ache where I needed no more ache.

I said, "Look. Just give me another half-hour . . ."

Her eyes grew moist. "I'm sitting here all by myself."

"I'll make it up to you." To show you how desperate I was getting, I was definitely beginning to think along paths that could lead only to jewelry, even though a sizable dent in the bankbook would show up to Hilda's piercing eye like the Horsehead Nebula interrupting the Milky Way.

She said, "I had a perfectly good date and I broke it off."

I protested, "You said it was a quibbling little arrangement."

That was a mistake. I knew it the minute I said it.

She shrieked, "*Quibbling little arrangement!*" It was what she had said. But having the truth on your side just makes it worse in arguing with a woman. Don't I know? "You call a man who's promised me an estate on Earth—"

She went on and on about that estate on Earth. There wasn't a gal in Marsport who wasn't wangling for an estate on Earth and you could count the number who got one on the sixth finger of either hand. But hope springs eternal in the human breast, and Flora had plenty of room for it to spring in.

I tried to stop her. I threw in honeys and babies until you would have thought that every bee on the planet Earth was pregnant.

No use.

She finally said, "And here I am all alone, with *nobody*, and what do you think *that* will do to my reputation?" and broke off contact.

Well, she was right. I felt like the lowest heel in the Galaxy. If the word did get around that she had been stood up, the word would also get around that she was stand-uppable, that she was losing the old touch. A thing like that can ruin a girl.

I went back into the reception room. A flunky outside the door saluted me in.

I stared at the three industrialists and speculated on the order in which I would slowly choke each to death if I could but receive choking orders. Harponaster first, maybe. He had a thin, stringy neck that the fingers could go around neatly and a sharp Adam's apple against which the thumbs could find purchase.

It cheered me up infinitesimally, to the point where I muttered, "Boy!" just out of sheer longing.

It started them off at once. Ferrucci said, "Boyl the watern the spout you go in the snow to sneeze—"

Harponaster of the scrawny neck added, "Nies and nephew don't like orporalley cat."

Lipsky said, "Cattle for shipmentering the home stretchings are good bait and drank drunk."

"Drunkle aunterior passagewayt a while."

"While beasts oh pray."

"Rayls to Chicago."

"Go way."

"Waiter."

"Terble."

"Ble."

Then nothing.

They stared at me. I stared at them. They were empty of emotion—or two were—and I was empty of ideas. And time passed.

I stared at them some more and thought about Flora. It occurred to me that I had nothing to lose that I had not already lost. I might as well talk about her.

I said, "Gentlemen, there is a girl in this town whose name I will not mention for fear of compromising her. Let me describe her to you, gentlemen."

And I did. If I say so myself, the last two hours had honed me to such a fine force-field edge that the description of Flora took on a kind of poetry that seemed to be coming from some wellspring of masculine force deep in the subbasement of my unconscious.

And they sat frozen, almost as though they were listening, and hardly ever interrupting. People under Spaceoline have a kind of politeness about them. They won't speak when someone else is speaking. That's why they take turns.

Occasionally, of course, I paused a bit because the poignancy of the subject matter made me want to linger and then one of them might put in a few words before I could gather myself together and continue.

"Pinknic of champagnes and aches and bittern of the century box."

"Round that and/or thisandy beaches."

"Assault and peppert girlieping leopard."

I drowned them out and kept talking. "This young lady, gentlemen," I said, "has an apartment fitted out for low gravity. Now you might ask of what use is low gravity? I intend to tell you, gentlemen, for if you have never had occasion to spend a quiet evening with a Marsport prima donna in privacy, you cannot imagine—"

But I tried to make it unnecessary for them to imagine—the way I told it they were *there*. They would remember all this afterward but I doubted mightily that either of the two innocents would object to it in hindsight. Chances were they would look me up to ask a phone number.

I kept it up, with loving, careful detail and a kind of heartfelt sadness in my voice, until the loudspeaker announced the arrival of the *Space Eater*.

That was that. I said in a loud voice, "Rise, gentlemen."

They got up in unison, faced the door, started walking, and as Ferrucci passed me, I tapped him on the shoulder and said, "Not you, you murdering louse," and my magnetic coil was on his wrist before he could breathe twice.

Ferrucci fought like a demon. *He* was under no Spaceoline influence. They found the altered Spaceoline in thin flesh-colored plastic pads hugging the inner surface of his thighs, with hairs affixed to it in the normal pattern. You couldn't see it at all; you could only feel it, and even then it took a knife to make sure.

Afterward, Rog Crinton, grinning and half-insane with relief, held me by the lapel with a death grip. "How did you do it? What gave it away?"

I said, trying to pull loose, "One of them was faking a Spaceoline jag. I was sure of it. So I told them—" I grew cautious. None of the bum's business as to the details, you know. "—uh, ribald stories, see, and two of them never reacted, so they were Spaceolined. But Ferrucci's breathing speeded up and the beads of sweat came out on his forehead. I gave a pretty dramatic rendition, and he reacted, so he was under no Spaceoline. And when they all stood up to head out for the ship, I was sure of my man and stopped him. Now will you let me go?"

He let go and I almost fell over backward.

I was set to take off. My feet were pawing at the ground without any instructions for me, but I turned back.

"Hey, Rog," I said, "can you sign me a chit for a thousand credits without its going on the record—for services rendered to the Service?"

That's when I realized he was half-insane with relief and very temporary gratitude, because he said, "Sure, Max, sure. Ten thousand credits if you want it."

"I *want*," I said. "I want. I want."

He filled out an official Service chit for ten thousand credits, good as cash anywhere in half the Galaxy. He was actually grinning as he gave it to me and you can bet I was grinning as I took it.

How *he* intended accounting for it was his affair. The point was that I wouldn't have to account for it to Hilda.

I stood in the booth, one last time, signaling Flora. I didn't dare let matters go till I reached her place. The additional half-hour might just give her time to get someone else, if she hadn't already.

Make her answer. Make her answer. Make her—

She answered, but she was in formal clothes. She was going out and I had obviously caught her by two minutes.

"I am going out," she announced. "*Some* men can be decent. And I do not wish to see you in the henceforward. I do not wish ever to find my eyes upon you. You will do me a great favor, Mister Whoeveryouare, if you will unhand my signal combination and never pollute it with—"

I wasn't saying anything. I was just standing there holding my breath and also holding the chit up where she could see it. Just standing there. Just holding.

Sure enough, at the word "pollute" she came in for a closer look. She wasn't much on education, that girl, but she could read "ten thousand credits" faster than any college graduate in the Solar System.

She said, "Max! For me?"

"All for you, baby," I said. "I told you I had a little business to do. I wanted to surprise you."

"Oh, Max, that's sweet of you. I didn't really mind. I was joking. Now you come right here to me." She took off her coat, which with Flora is a *very* interesting action to watch.

"What about your date?" I said.

"I *said* I was joking," she said. She dropped her coat gently to the floor, and toyed with a brooch that seemed to hold together what there was of her dress.

"I'm coming," I said faintly.

"With every single one of those credits now," she said roguishly.

"With every single one," I said.

I broke contact, stepped out of the booth, and now, finally, I was set, really set.

I heard my name called.

"Max! Max!" Someone was running toward me. "Rog Crinton said I would find you here. Mama's all right after all, so I got special passage on the *Space Eater* and what's this about ten thousand credits?"

I didn't turn. I said, "Hello, Hilda."

I stood rock steady.

And then I turned and did the hardest thing I ever succeeded in doing in all my goddam, good-for-nothing, space-hopping life.

I smiled.

J. Timothy Hunt

Moonflower

"Moonflower" is an eerily poetic variation on the threatening-alien-lifeform tale. Its author, J. TIMOTHY HUNT, an ex-Montanan now living in New York City, is both a playwright and computer consultant. He has held professional writing residencies at The Writers Room in Greenwich Village and the Helene Wurlitzer Foundation, Taos, New Mexico.

ON THE FROZEN SURFACE of Europa, Christopher skated with wild abandon under Jupiter's familiar glow. Red and orange, white and yellow, the looming specter of the giant filled half the afternoon sky, dwarfing the distant pin-spot of the sun and the lonely figure of a young man turning figure-eights upon the ice.

Europa was as smooth and brightly polished as a billiard ball. Her solid face of ice was ever moving, ever changing; thawed here by the warm tug of Jupiter and refrozen there by the blackness of space. Only a lace of cracks criss-crossing the plains marred her burnished blue-white face.

Three o'clock Solar Standard Time was Christopher's appointed hour to check the distance between the topographical markers on the Belgian ice flow. Although strange work for a young botanist, it was a simple task almost anyone could do. With a bale of Telfano filament, some stakes and a few other tools, he would straighten loose markers, point a laser rifle at their reflective tips, record the data—the whole process took less than an hour.

As he punched in the column of figures for the day, he noticed one of the markers, B17, was moving faster than the others. In two Earth days it had drifted nearly four meters from compound marker zero. "We're moving now!" Christopher whooped. He burst into a homemade song about chasing ice racers and danced around in a happy little circle. The shouting and the singing in his helmet hurt his ears, but as the only human being within ten million miles, there was little reason for him to contain any enthusiasm or impulse.

Christopher recorded the latest progress of B17, then crouched down in a runner's starting block stance. He quieted himself by listening to the soft hiss of oxygen being fed into his helmet, and then in a shot, propelled himself forward. In the silence of the moon, he ran as fast as he could to pick up speed, then straightened up and skated again across the ice.

It was with this typical fervor Chris turned each day's outdoor work hour into a one-man Winter Olympics. Gathering speed down a slight incline, he let himself ski the lunar slope with the smooth soles of his atmospheric pressure boots, and then, only meters from the approaching marker, slammed down his toe crampons and skidded to a halt in a shower of ice. "The winner! From Jupiter Moon Europa . . . Christopher . . . Adams!" The oxygen hissed louder and, in his mind, the crowd went wild.

The final marker on his rounds lay at the top of "The Hill." In truth, The Hill was the acme of a five percent grade, but on the ice planes of Europa it was comparatively alpine. Crossing a cable bridge over a seventeen-meter-wide ice crack, Christopher summoned his courage. He made up his mind time was right to attempt "the big jump."

He shot his laser at the last marker's reflector, noted the meter readings on his recording device, then paused . . . and pushed off.

On airless Europa, he imagined he felt the wind whooshing past his helmet. He neatly skirted a large ice boulder, then another. Ha ha! This was great! The frozen surface slid under him silently in the vacuum. Christopher could hear the roaring of the oxygen crowd ringing in his ears.

Directly ahead of him was a third boulder and then the cable bridge over the crack. Speed. He needed more speed. Maybe if he bent his knees a little more. Yes! That was it! He was flying. Rounding the boulder he saw the crack in the ice before him and readied himself for the jump.

Later, when he had time to relive the moment, Christopher realized it was his preparation for the jump that proved his undoing. By extending the body a split second too soon, his toes dropped, digging the crampons into the ice. Hurtling head first, Christopher plummeted directly to the bottom of the deep ice crack.

Softly and silently, a spray of splintered ice crystals descended on

Christopher as he lay at the bottom of the chasm. Lying still for a moment, wondering breathlessly if there were any broken bones, Chris checked for signs of pain. There were none. Fortunately for him, it turned out that the only thing fractured was his fantasy. With a quick shake of his head, he slowly sat up and looked about him.

The blue-white walls of the ice crack stretched above, silhouetted by the orange light of Jupiter. The frozen chasm was a shattered dream of Christmas and Halloween. Christopher stood slowly on his own two legs and started looking for a way to the surface before his oxygen ran out.

The filament from his utility belt, of course. All he had to do was throw one end up and over the bridge above and then shimmy up the cable. Chris gathered the Telfano filament in a loose loop in his left hand, and then with his right, whirled it round and round. Up shot the end of the cable and down it fell to the bottom of the chasm, missing the bridge by several meters.

Chris was looking around for a chunk of ice to weight the end of the cable when his eyes fell upon the flower. White as paper, it lay wedged in a distant nook of the chasm, a strange symbol of organic life on a supposedly lifeless moon. It was beautiful. White lace leaves and white stick stems, the flower rose from the crevice, showing its spherical buds to the glow of the gas planet. Christopher stared agape at the plant, not knowing whether to cheer or run.

All around the base of the plant was a layer of grey dust and several long, bonelike stones. Chris knelt beside the flower and cautiously ran a gloved finger along the prickly stalk. The filigreed lace of the leaves and the whiteness of the buds and stalk looked like petrified white fur, freeze-dried and long dead.

Once he realized the moonflower was not alive, Christopher snapped off a stalk with the largest dried bud and took a careful sample of the lace leaves. These he dropped into a specimen pouch attached to the hip of his suit and then, tieing the Telfano filament around one of the long white stones from the plant's base, tossed the lifeline up and over the cable bridge above.

Christopher climbed the rope and did not look back to see the small drop of red rising from the broken stalk of the moonflower.

Upon his return to the vapor lock at the compound, Chris could hear his name being called within. Once the air pressure in the lock stabilized, he whipped off his helmet and burst through the inner door. Careening through the compound's greenhouse, he made a dash for the communications console.

"Hello?" he panted, "Base five two."

"Adams, that is not your base number and you know it," said a woman's voice from the speaker.

"Hi, Witten."

"Chris, you're supposed to give your correct base number when hailed."

"Well, if you already know who you're hailing, why do I have to give my base number at all? It's not as if there's any other base at Jupiter you could mistake me for."

Captain Alice Witten of the UWSS *Andrea* sighed and agreed. "You don't need to point out the finer ironies of UWSA code," she said. "Although it seems silly to you, I have to record these conversations. It's my job. Just say it for me."

"This is Base five two mark eighteen, The Voice of Europa. How are you doing, Captain Witten?"

"We should be arriving at Europa in approximately one week, three days. Do you think your supplies will hold out that long?"

Chris looked around and chuckled, "I think I'll be able to manage. I haven't eaten half the dehydrated feast you sent with me, the greenhouse seems to keep the oxygen cycle going and as for water . . ." he paused, removed his gloves, and kicked off a pressure boot. "As for water, the recycling system is so good here, I've had the same glass of water three hundred times. So when are you coming over?"

"I told you; ten days. I'm bringing your replacement."

"And I've got a present for you, too." Chris reached for the specimen packet attached to his side. "I picked you some flowers today, Witten."

"I've got flowers growing in my own ship's garden, thank you."

"No, I picked these outside, in an ice chasm," he said and withdrew the dried white moon thistle from the pouch.

"There is no note of life forms on Europa, Chris. You've been instructed to leave anything you find alive out there alone, and certainly don't bring it back into the compound."

"Too late, I'm holding it here in my hand. Anyway, it's dead. Ouch!"

"What's the matter?" Witten sounded concerned. "You're holding it in your hand? You're wearing gloves, of course."

"No, I took them off. Don't worry, I just stuck my finger on this damned stem. It's full of tiny spines. It almost looks like fur."

"Listen," Witten's voice said firmly through the speaker, "put on some gloves, seal that thing in a specimen container and don't touch it again. Do you understand me?"

"I love it when you're angry," he chided while sucking the pricked spot on the tip of his finger. Witten signed off and Christopher reached for a specimen container and dropped the flower stem and leaves into it with tongs. Placing the container in a sealed compartment, he went on with the remainder of his day's chores in the compound greenhouse.

Later that night he dreamed of Alice Witten. Although he had no idea what she looked like, he imagined that she had short blond hair and enormous brown eyes. In his dream, Witten went skating with him on the Belgian Ice Flow and they tumbled and fell, laughing, into an ice chasm. As they lay in a heap at the bottom, she brushed off the snowlike crystals from his face, kissed his fingers, and then lit them on fire.

Christopher awoke with a scream. His hand. His fingers were burning. He looked down and the forefinger of his left hand was swollen and white, like a small peeled potato. While the rest of his hand burned, the bloated forefinger had no feeling at all. Staggering to the medical supply unit, Chris rummaged through its contents and found a length of plastic bandage which he wound around his entire hand. He prepared a hypodermic with the strongest pain suppressant there was in the compound and with trembling fingers injected himself in the left wrist. Sedated, his breathing slowed, his body slumped and Christopher crumpled back onto his sleeping platform.

The following morning, Chris could not drink enough water. Water was all he could think about. Whenever he tried to focus his thoughts on any of his daily tasks the overriding message in his brain was water, water, water. He forgot about his hand and paid the bandage no attention whatsoever as he sipped his twentieth tumbler of liquid.

He felt so slow. The interest in his daily chores drained from him as fast as the water poured into him. By the end of the morning, he had no desire to do any work at all. As with any comparable job back on Earth, Christopher was allowed to take an occasional sick day, but even if he were ill he was expected to run a minimum amount of inspection in the greenhouse. If any of the plants should die, his botanical experiments would be worthless.

With his drink in one hand and the bandage on the other, he shuffled into the greenhouse and stood silently at the door.

The plants! It was as if he were seeing them for the first time. Although he cultivated those flowers and vegetables for a whole year, at that moment, Christopher found all of his plants unspeakably beautiful. The long and sensuous fronds of the Boston fern, the luscious and heavy bloom clusters of the fuchsia, the wickedly tantalizing bowl of the pitcher plant all delighted him, all excited him . . . all aroused him.

Christopher got down on his knees and, like a wild animal, rubbed his face in the clover. This was madness, he thought, and yet he could not stop himself. His breathing slowed; his palms moistened. He was driven by an urge that seemed to go back beyond the animal part of him, back to something slower and greener.

Gently kneeling among the vegetables, Chris let his tongue explore the roundness of the ripe tomato hanging on the vine, being careful not to bite it, but to tease it as one would an earlobe. Nuzzling tenderly up the stalk, he rubbed his stubbled cheek against the soft green tomato leaves and breathed in the heavy warm scent of the sap. His heart pounded in his temples; his lips forgot how to form speech. Sweat rings grew beneath his arms and his fingers trembled.

Christopher rolled over and glanced up at the begonias, beauties all. They seemed to hang before him, solely for his pleasure and approval, like pageant contestants before a judge. The sensual part of him admired their wild, wild offshoots, but the gardener part of him declared that they badly needed pinching back. Immediately, the thought seemed to shock and repulse him. "How barbaric," he mused, "that I would even think of something so hideous."

"Don't worry," he said to the plants, "I'm not going to pinch you today. I'm not going to pinch you ever again." He heard himself mouthing these words and quickly shook his head to try to wake up. "God, what am I saying?" he scolded himself. "I must be sleepwalking or something." And then, as if to show himself who was boss, Christopher reached over and snapped off a begonia stem.

Waves of nausea overcame him and he crumpled to the ground, retching. It was as if he disemboweled his best friend.

Lucid once more, Christopher panicked. He feared he was losing his mind. At the very least he was losing his ability to concentrate, and for a man alone on a distant moon, that was disaster. He forced himself up onto his knees and crawled over to the console to signal for help. His hand reached for the touchpad to hail Captain Witten, then it dropped back. He forgot why he came across the room. His only thought was that he wanted more water.

Later in the day, instead of venturing outside to ski and measure the ice flow markers, he took another tumbler of water and curled up on his sleeping platform. Christopher was usually much too energetic to sit one place for long, but that day all he wanted to do was be still and think.

With a straw in his mouth, he daydreamed of white forests and sipped on his water. Wouldn't red blooms in a white forest be beautiful? Yes. Red blooms would be happiness. Red blooms in a white forest. He noticed for a brief moment that his thoughts were not even coming in words, only images and feelings. He felt slow and wet and heavy and happy.

The communications console came to life and Christopher heard his base number being hailed by Captain Witten. She waited for a reply, then hailed again. Chris watched the console from his bed across the room and did nothing. He had no desire to rise and answer her call. Soon, the water in his tumbler ran out and it was very important for him to refill it. As he poured more water, Alice Witten's voice sounded again and Christopher sat down to talk to her.

"Hello," he said softly.

"Chris? Is everything all right? Why haven't you been answering our hail?"

"I don't know," he said and swallowed some water.

"Arn Daniels, your replacement, wants to ask you some questions about the data you're gathering on the Belgian Ice Flow movements. I think it would be best if you transmitted your data to him directly each day until we arrive. It will help him get a leg up on the project and maybe you can give him a few tips. What do you think?"

"Fine," was all Christopher could think of to say.

"And I don't want you to teach him any of your bad habits!" Alice Witten waited for a glib reply from Christopher, but got none. "Are you still there?"

"Yes."

"Chris, are you feeling all right today?"

Christopher started idly picking at the bandage on his left hand. "I feel fine," he said.

"What did you do with that life sample you found on Europa?" she asked. "Did you seal it safely so we can remove it for study?"

"I guess so," he answered. He slowly unwound the bandage from his hand and noticed that his wrist had turned ivory. With mounting curiosity, he unwrapped the rest of his hand faster. All of his fingers were swollen now and none of them had any feeling. Instead of fingernails, all he had on his left hand were clusters of tiny white leaves poking out of his fingertips. All of his hand, including the hair on the back of his wrist had gone white.

In horror, Christopher let out a cry and tried to shake some feeling back into his hand.

"Chris! Chris, what's going on?" came the voice from the console.

"My hand!" was all he could manage to spit out. Instinctively he reached with his right hand to pluck the leaves from his left, but thought better of it and grabbed the tongs he left out the day before. The slightest tug on any of the leaves brought shooting agony up his arm. Small white viny tendrils, like those found on a morning glory, coiled around two of his fingers. These could also not be pulled without excruciating pain.

Captain Witten's voice implored Chris to talk to her, but the only response she received were moans, two sharp screams, and then silence.

On Europa, the crew of the *Andrea* approached the compound with weapons drawn. Silently they stole out of the vapor lock, eyes darting around the first chamber. Captain Witten motioned to the two others to follow her and they padded cautiously into the greenhouse.

There, tangled amid the tomatoes, lay Christopher, naked and pale. A slow drip from a hose ran down his right cheek and dribbled into his open white mouth. His skin had lost so much of its pigment, the blue of his veins could be seen glowing beneath, and his left arm was not visible at all. Attached to his shoulder was a six-meter mass of furry white vines and leaves spilling out of the garden plot and onto the metal floor. Blood-red spherical blooms shot up in clusters from the vines.

"Oh my God," whispered Witten under her breath.

Christopher looked up at them and moved his mouth. A trail of dried blood ran down from the corners of his cracked lips. Witten approached. She removed her pressurized helmet, knelt beside Chris and took the dripping hose from his face. Chris eyed her thin brown face and black short-cropped hair with silent puzzlement, then closed his eyes and whispered something softly.

"I can't hear you, Chris. Chris? Come on, look at me. Don't try to talk, you understand? Relax, we're going to try to help you."

"Wat . . ." Christopher began.

"Daniels, go to the medical supply unit and bring me anything—*everything*—in it. Hurry!"

Daniels looked helpless and quietly asked, "Where is it? I've never been in this class of station before."

"Find it!" snapped Witten and he bolted from the room.

"W-wat . . ." Chris stammered again.

She looked into his eyes and brushed a lock of white hair back off his face. "I can't understand what you're trying to say."

"Water . . . please . . ."

She looked at the hose on the ground and then at his imploring eyes. "Grant, get him some water," Witten ordered the third crewman; then to Christopher she said softly, "Chris, don't worry. We're going to remove this from your arm."

Christopher's eyes got wide. "No," he said.

Daniels rushed back in with an armload of various items. Witten turned to him. "It looks bad," she said. "The whole arm may have to come off." The color ran out of Daniels' face.

"Don't cut . . . don't," Christopher gasped. "Don't hurt her."

"No, Chris, of course not. Don't worry, everything will be fine, just relax. We won't hurt you. We won't hurt your arm."

"No," said Christopher, "don't hurt . . . please, don't hurt her . . . don't hurt . . . the plant . . . please . . ." And with that, he lapsed into unconsciousness.

Four months later, as the *Andrea* glided home, Witten looked up from a console in the ship's garden and grinned. "You're looking almost human," she said to the frail figure standing in the doorway.

Christopher wobbled slightly on his feet and smiled. "Am I bothering you?"

"Not really. It's good to see you up and around."

"I'm in training," he confided. "I've done three laps of the ship already. I might even set a new Universe record. I thought you would be blond."

She looked surprised at this statement and said, "Blond like you?"

He ran his one hand self-consciously through his hair. "No. It's just that all the time I pictured you as a blond."

"A blond white woman, right?" she laughed. "Well, I knew you were white. It said so on your dossier, but it didn't say you had no color at all. That was a complete surprise to me."

"Do you think this white hair is permanent?"

"I don't know. The rest of your color is coming back and you're putting on weight. I don't see any reason why your hair shouldn't recover its color, too. What color was it?"

"Brown," he said, "it was brown." He leaned against the doorway and held his empty left sleeve in his hand.

Alice smiled sadly and said, "I've hailed ahead and ordered you a mechanical replacement for your arm. They say you won't be able to tell the difference."

"I was kind of attached to the old one," Chris said and tried to smile. He looked over at what remained of his left arm, vacuum packed in a clear case, the white vines and red blooms still obscuring all the flesh beneath.

"Don't even look at it," Witten said, "I've never seen anything so vile."

"All it wanted to do was grow and be happy," he said. "And it loved me."

"What?"

"The moonflower. It was like we were married. Somehow. It's hard . . . I don't have a word for it. It was like, like love. It wanted my love and it wanted to live."

"Well, we all want to live and love," said Alice, "but that thing only loved your nutritional value. It was eating you alive. Eventually, it would have swallowed you whole."

"Yes," he concurred sadly, "I know that."

Captain Alice Witten adjusted the drip nipples feeding the hydroponic pots of strawberries. She spied a large ripe berry and pinched it off the plant. Christopher watched as she slowly bit down on the strawberry and could see the delight in her face at the flavor.

"Delicious," she said. "Here." She walked up to him and held the uneaten half up to his lips.

"I can't," he said.

She searched his eyes and suddenly knew what was going on in his mind. Alice Witten's brow furrowed and she angrily shook the strawberry at him. "Listen here," she said impatiently, "as long as you're on *my* ship you are at the top of the food chain. Do you understand?"

Christopher hesitated, then shyly opened his mouth. They both understood in that moment that Alice Witten was jealous. A woman jealous of a plant. The thought made them both deliciously happy.

He took the strawberry and felt the round and velvety texture on his tongue and tasted the shock of sweetness as he bit down. "Now how's that for a strawberry?" she purred. "It's good, huh?"

"Yes," he said, and for a moment he was sad because he had to agree with her. It tasted divine.

Robert Sheckley

The Language of Love

ROBERT SHECKLEY, *the first fiction editor of* Omni *magazine, has written some of America's most elegantly trenchant science fantasy, including tales collected in* Untouched by Human Hands, Pilgrimage to Earth, Citizen in Space, Shards of Space *and* Notions: Unlimited, *from which the following mordant investigation of "the Grand Passion" is taken.*

JEFFERSON TOMS went into an auto-cafe one afternoon after classes, to drink coffee and study. He sat down, philosophy texts piled neatly before him, and saw a girl directing the robot waiters. She had smoky-gray eyes and hair the color of a rocket exhaust. Her figure was slight but sweetly curved and, gazing at it, Toms felt a lump in his throat and a sudden recollection of autumn, evening, rain and candlelight.

This was how love came to Jefferson Toms. Although he was ordinarily a very reserved young man, he complained about the robot service in order to meet her. When they did meet, he was inarticulate, overwhelmed by feeling. Somehow, though, he managed to ask her for a date.

The girl, whose name was Doris, was strangely moved by the stocky, black-haired young student, for she accepted at once. And then Jefferson Toms' troubles began.

He found love delightful, yet extremely disturbing, in spite of his advanced studies in philosophy. But love was a confusing thing even in Toms' age, when spaceliners bridged the gaps between the worlds, disease lay dead, war was inconceivable, and just about anything of any importance had been solved in an exemplary manner.

Old Earth was in better shape than ever before. Her cities were bright with plastic and stainless steel. Her remaining forests were carefully tended bits of greenery where one might picnic in perfect safety, since all beasts and insects had been removed to sanitary zoos which reproduced their living conditions with admirable skill.

Even the climate of Earth had been mastered. Farmers received their quota of rain between three and three-thirty in the morning, people gathered at stadiums to watch a program of sunsets, and a tornado was produced once a year in a special arena as part of the World Peace Day Celebration.

But love was as confusing as ever and Toms found this distressing.

He simply could not put his feelings into words. Such expressions as "I love you," "I adore you," "I'm crazy about you" were overworked and inadequate. They conveyed nothing of the depth and fervor of his emotions. Indeed they cheapened them, since every stereo, every second-rate play was filled with similar words. People used them in casual conversation and spoke of how much they *loved* pork chops, *adored* sunsets, were *crazy about* tennis.

Every fiber of Toms' being revolted against this. Never, he swore, would he speak of his love in terms used for pork chops. But he found, to his dismay, that he had nothing better to say.

He brought the problem to his philosophy professor. "Mr. Toms," the professor said, gesturing wearily with his glasses, "ah—*love*, as it is commonly called, is not an operational area with us as yet. No significant work has been done in this field, aside from the so-called Language of Love of the Tyanian race."

This was no help. Toms continued to muse on love and think lengthily of Doris. In the long haunted evenings on her porch when the shadows from the trellis vines crossed her face, revealing and concealing it, Toms struggled to tell her what he felt. And since he could not bring himself to use the weary commonplaces of love, he tried to express himself in extravagances.

"I feel about you," he would say, "the way a star feels about its planet."

"How immense!" she would answer, immensely flattered at being compared to anything so cosmic.

"That's not what I meant," Toms amended. "The feeling I was trying to express was more—well, for example, when you walk, I am reminded of—"

"Of a what?"

"A doe in a forest glade," Toms said, frowning.

"How charming!"

"It wasn't intended to be charming. I was trying to express the awkwardness inherent in youth and yet—"

"But, honey," she said, "I'm not awkward. My dancing teacher—"

"I didn't mean *awkward*. But the essence of awkwardness is—is—"

"I understand," she said.

But Toms knew she didn't.

So he was forced to give up extravagances. Soon he found himself unable to say anything of any importance to Doris, for it was not what he meant, nor even close to it.

The girl became concerned at the long, moody silences which developed between them.

"Jeff," she would urge, "surely you can say *something!*"

Toms shrugged his shoulders.

"Even if it isn't absolutely what you mean."

Toms sighed.

"Please," she cried, "say anything at all! I can't stand this!"

"Oh, hell—"

"Yes?" she breathed, her face transfigured.

"That wasn't what I meant," Toms said, relapsing into his gloomy silence.

At last he asked her to marry him. He was willing to admit that he "loved" her—but he refused to expand on it. He explained that a marriage must be founded upon truth or it is doomed from the start. If he cheapened and falsified his emotions at the beginning, what could the future hold for them?

Doris found his sentiments admirable, but refused to marry him.

"You must *tell* a girl that you love her," she declared. "You have to tell her a hundred times a day, Jefferson, and even then it's not enough."

"But I do love you!" Toms protested. "I mean to say I have an emotion corresponding to—"

"Oh, stop it!"

In this predicament, Toms thought about the Language of Love and went to his professor's office to ask about it.

"We are told," his professor said, "that the race indigenous to Tyana II had a specific and unique language for the expression of sensations of love. To say 'I love you' was unthinkable for Tyanians. They would use a phrase denoting the exact kind and class of love they felt at that specific moment, and used for no other purpose."

Toms nodded, and the professor continued. "Of course, developed with this language was, necessarily, a technique of love-making quite

incredible in its perfection. We are told that it made all ordinary techniques seem like the clumsy pawing of a grizzly in heat." The professor
coughed in embarrassment.

"It is precisely what I need!" Toms exclaimed.

"Ridiculous," said the professor. "The technique might be interesting,
but your own is doubtless sufficient for most needs. And the language, by
its very nature, can be used with only one person. To learn it impresses
me as wasted energy."

"Labor for love," Toms said, "is the most worthwhile work in the world,
since it produces a rich harvest of feeling."

"I refuse to stand here and listen to bad epigrams. Mr. Toms, why all
this fuss about love?"

"It is the only perfect thing in this world," Toms answered fervently.
"If one must learn a special language to appreciate it, one can do no less.
Tell me, is it far to Tyana II?"

"A considerable distance," his professor said, with a thin smile. "And
an unrewarding one, since the race is extinct."

"Extinct! But why? A sudden pestilence? An invasion?"

"It is one of the mysteries of the galaxy," his professor said somberly.

"Then the language is lost!"

"Not quite. Twenty years ago, an Earthman named George Varris went
to Tyana and learned the Language of Love from the last remnants of the
race." The professor shrugged his shoulders. "I never considered it sufficiently important to read his scientific papers."

Toms looked up Varris in the *Interspatial Explorers Who's Who* and
found that he was credited with the discovery of Tyana, had wandered
around the frontier planets for a time, but at last had returned to deserted Tyana, to devote his life to investigating every aspect of its culture.

After learning this, Toms thought long and hard. The journey to Tyana
was a difficult one, time-consuming, and expensive. Perhaps Varris would
be dead before he got there, or unwilling to teach him the language. Was
it worth the gamble?

"Is *love* worth it?" Toms asked himself, and knew the answer.

So he sold his ultra-fi, his memory recorder, his philosophy texts, and
several stocks his grandfather had left him, and booked passage to
Cranthis IV, which was the closest he could come to Tyana on a scheduled spaceway. And after all his preparations had been made, he went to
Doris.

"When I return," he said, "I will be able to tell you exactly how much
—I mean the particular quality and class of—I mean, Doris, when I have

mastered the Tyanian Technique, you will be loved as no woman has ever been loved!"

"Do you mean that?" she asked, her eyes glowing.

"Well," Toms said, "the term 'loved', doesn't quite express it. But I mean something very much like it."

"I will wait for you, Jeff," she said. "But—please don't be too long."

Jefferson Toms nodded, blinked back his tears, clutched Doris inarticulately, and hurried to the spaceport.

Within the hour, he was on his way.

Four months later, after considerable difficulties, Toms stood on Tyana, on the outskirts of the capital city. Slowly he walked down the broad, deserted main thoroughfare. On either side of him, noble buildings soared to dizzy heights. Peering inside one, Toms saw complex machinery and gleaming switchboards. With his pocket Tyana-English dictionary, he was able to translate the lettering above one of the buildings.

It read: COUNSELING SERVICES FOR STAGE-FOUR LOVE PROBLEMS.

Other buildings were much the same, filled with calculating machinery, switchboards, ticker tapes, and the like. He passed THE INSTITUTE FOR RESEARCH INTO AFFECTION DELAY, stared at the two-hundred-story HOME FOR THE EMOTIONALLY RETARDED, and glanced at several others. Slowly the awesome, dazzling truth dawned upon him.

Here was an entire city given over to the research and aid of love.

He had no time for further speculation. In front of him was the gigantic GENERAL LOVE SERVICES BUILDING. And out of its marble hallway stepped an old man.

"Who the hell are you?" the old man asked.

"I am Jefferson Toms, of Earth. I have come here to learn the Language of Love, Mr. Varris."

Varris raised his shaggy white eyebrows. He was a small, wrinkled old man, stoop-shouldered and shaky in the knees. But his eyes were alert and filled with a cold suspicion.

"Perhaps you think the language will make you more attractive to women," Varris said. "Don't believe it, young man. Knowledge has its advantages, of course. But it has distinct drawbacks, as the Tyanians discovered."

"What drawbacks?" Toms asked.

Varris grinned, displaying a single yellow tooth. "You wouldn't understand, if you don't already know. It takes knowledge to understand the limitations of knowledge."

"Nevertheless," Toms said, "I want to learn the language."

Varris stared at him thoughtfully. "But it is not a simple thing, Toms. The Language of Love, and its resultant technique, is every bit as complex as brain surgery or the practice of corporation law. It takes work, much work, and a talent as well."

"I will do the work. And I'm sure I have the talent."

"Most people think that," Varris said, "and most of them are mistaken. But never mind, never mind. It's been a long time since I've had any company. We'll see how you get on, Toms."

Together they went into the General Services Building, which Varris called his home. They went to the Main Control Room, where the old man had put down a sleeping bag and set up a camp stove. There, in the shadow of the giant calculators, Toms' lessons began.

Varris was a thorough teacher. In the beginning, with the aid of a portable Semantic Differentiator, he taught Toms to isolate the delicate apprehension one feels in the presence of a to-be-loved person, to detect the subtle tensions that come into being as the potentiality of love draws near.

These sensations, Toms learned, must never be spoken of directly, for frankness frightens love. They must be expressed in simile, metaphor, and hyperbole, half-truths and white lies. With these, one creates an atmosphere and lays a foundation for love. And the mind, deceived by its own predisposition, thinks of booming surf and raging sea, mournful black rocks and fields of green corn.

"Nice images," Toms said admiringly.

"Those were samples," Varris told him. "Now you must learn them all."

So Toms went to work memorizing great long lists of natural wonders, to what sensations they were comparable, and at what stage they appeared in the anticipation of love. The language was thorough in this regard. Every state or object in nature for which there was a response in love-anticipation had been catalogued, classified and listed with suitable modifying adjectives.

When he had memorized the list, Varris drilled him in perceptions of love. Toms learned the small, strange things that make up a state of love. Some were so ridiculous that he had to laugh.

The old man admonished him sternly. "Love is a serious business, Toms. You seem to find some humor in the fact that love is frequently predisposed by wind speed and direction."

"It seems foolish," Toms admitted.

"There are stranger things than that," Varris said, and mentioned another factor.

Toms shuddered. "*That* I can't believe. It's preposterous. Everyone knows—"

"If everyone knows how love operates, why hasn't someone reduced it to a formula? Murky thinking, Toms, murky thinking is the answer, and an unwillingness to accept cold facts. If you cannot face them—"

"I can face anything," Toms said, "if I have to. Let's continue."

As the weeks passed, Toms learned the words which express the first quickening of interest, shade by shade, until an attachment is formed. He learned what that attachment really is and the three words that express it. This brought him to the rhetoric of sensation, where the body becomes supreme.

Here the language was specific instead of allusive, and dealt with feelings produced by certain words, and above all, by certain physical actions.

A startling little black machine taught Toms the thirty-eight separate and distinct sensations which the touch of a hand can engender, and he learned how to locate that sensitive area, no larger than a dime, which exists just below the right shoulder blade.

He learned an entirely new system of caressing, which caused impulses to explode—and even implode—along the nerve paths and to shower colored sparks before the eyes.

He was also taught the social advantages of conspicuous desensitization.

He learned many things about physical love which he had dimly suspected, and still more things which *no one* had suspected.

It was intimidating knowledge. Toms had imagined himself to be at least an adequate lover. Now he found that he knew nothing, nothing at all, and that his best efforts had been comparable to the play of amorous hippopotami.

"But what else could you expect?" Varris asked. "Good love-making, Toms, calls for more study, more sheer intensive labor than any other acquired skill. Do you still wish to learn?"

"Definitely!" Toms said. "Why, when I'm an expert on love-making, I'll—I can—"

"That is no concern of mine," the old man stated. "Let's return to our lessons."

Next, Toms learned the Cycles of Love. Love, he discovered, is dynamic, constantly rising and falling, and doing so in definite patterns.

There were fifty-two major patterns, three hundred and six minor patterns, four general exceptions, and nine specific exceptions.

Toms learned them better than his own name.

He acquired the uses of the Tertiary Touch. And he never forgot the day he was taught what a bosom *really* was like.

"But I can't say that!" Toms objected, appalled.

"It's true, isn't it?" Varris insisted.

"No! I mean—yes, I suppose it is. But it's unflattering."

"So it seems. But examine, Toms. Is it *actually* unflattering?"

Toms examined and found the compliment that lies beneath the insult, and so he learned another facet of the Language of Love.

Soon he was ready for the study of the Apparent Negations. He discovered that for every degree of love, there is a corresponding degree of hate, which is in itself a form of love. He came to understand how valuable hate is, how it gives substance and body to love, and how even indifference and loathing have their place in the nature of love.

Varris gave him a ten-hour written examination, which Toms passed with superlative marks. He was eager to finish, but Varris noticed that a slight tic had developed in his student's left eye and that his hands had a tendency to shake.

"You need a vacation," the old man informed him.

Toms had been thinking this himself. "You may be right," he said, with barely concealed eagerness. "Suppose I go to Cythera V for a few weeks."

Varris, who knew Cythera's reputation, smiled cynically. "Eager to try out your new knowledge?"

"Well, why not? Knowledge is to be used."

"Only after it's mastered."

"But I *have* mastered it! Couldn't we call this field work? A thesis, perhaps?"

"No thesis is necessary," Varris said.

"But damn it all," Toms exploded, "I should do a little experimentation! I should find out for myself how all this works. Especially Approach 33-CV. It sounds fine in theory, but I've been wondering how it works out in actual practice. There's nothing like direct experience, you know, to reinforce—"

"Did you journey all this way to become a super-seducer?" Varris asked, with evident disgust.

"Of course not," Toms said. "But a little experimentation wouldn't—"

"Your knowledge of the mechanics of sensation would be barren, unless you understand love, as well. You have progressed too far to be satisfied with mere thrills."

Toms, searching his heart, knew this to be true. But he set his jaw stubbornly. "I'd like to find out *that* for myself, too."

"You may go," Varris said, "but don't come back. No one will accuse me of loosing a callous scientific seducer upon the galaxy."

"Oh, all right. To hell with it. Let's get back to work."

"No. Look at yourself! A little more unrelieved studying, young man, and you will lose the capacity to make love. And wouldn't that be a sorry state of affairs?"

Toms agreed that it would certainly be.

"I know the perfect spot," Varris told him, "for relaxation from the study of love."

They entered the old man's spaceship and journeyed five days to a small unnamed planetoid. When they landed, the old man took Toms to the bank of a swift flowing river, where the water ran fiery red, with green diamonds of foam. The trees that grew on the banks of that river were stunted and strange, and colored vermilion. Even the grass was unlike grass, for it was orange and blue.

"How alien!" gasped Toms.

"It is the least human spot I've found in this humdrum corner of the galaxy," Varris explained. "And believe me, I've done some looking."

Toms stared at him, wondering if the old man was out of his mind. But soon he understood what Varris meant.

For months, he had been studying human reactions and human feelings, and surrounding it all was the now suffocating feeling of soft human flesh. He had immersed himself in humanity, studied it, bathed in it, eaten and drunk and dreamed it. It was a relief to be here, where the water ran red and the trees were stunted and strange and vermilion, and the grass was orange and blue, and there was no reminder of Earth.

Toms and Varris separated, for even each other's humanity was a nuisance. Toms spent his days wandering along the river edge, marveling at the flowers which moaned when he came near them. At night, three wrinkled moons played tag with each other, and the morning sun was different from the yellow sun of Earth.

At the end of a week, refreshed and renewed, Toms and Varris returned to G'cel, the Tyanian city dedicated to the study of love.

Toms was taught the five hundred and six shades of Love Proper, from the first faint possibility to the ultimate feeling, which is so powerful that only five men and one woman have experienced it, and the strongest of them survived less than an hour.

Under the tutelage of a bank of small, interrelated calculators, he studied the intensification of love.

He learned all of the thousand different sensations of which the human body is capable, and how to augment them, and how to intensify them until they become unbearable, and how to make the unbearable bearable, and finally pleasurable, at which point the organism is not far from death.

After that, he was taught some things which have never been put into words and, with luck, never will.

"And that," Varris said one day, "is everything."

"Everything?"

"Yes, Toms. The heart has no secrets from you. Nor, for that matter, has the soul, or mind, or the viscera. You have mastered the Language of Love. Now return to your young lady."

"I will!" cried Toms. "At last she will know!"

"Drop me a postcard," Varris said. "Let me know how you're getting on."

"I'll do that," Toms promised. Fervently he shook his teacher's hand and departed for Earth.

At the end of the long trip, Jefferson Toms hurried to Doris' home. Perspiration beaded his forehead and his hands were shaking. He was able to classify the feeling as Stage Two Anticipatory Tremors, with mild masochistic overtones. But that didn't help—this was his first field work and he was nervous. Had he mastered *everything*?

He rang the bell.

She opened the door and Toms saw that she was more beautiful than he had remembered, her eyes smoky-gray and misted with tears, her hair the color of a rocket exhaust, her figure slight but sweetly curved. He felt again the lump in his throat and sudden memories of autumn, evening, rain, and candlelight.

"I'm back," he croaked.

"Oh, Jeff," she said, very softly. "Oh, Jeff."

Toms simply stared, unable to say a word.

"It's been so long, Jeff, and I kept wondering if it was all worth it. Now I know."

"You—know?"

"Yes, my darling! I waited for you! I'd wait a hundred years, or a thousand! I love you, Jeff!"

She was in his arms.

"Now tell me, Jeff," she said, *"Tell me!"*

And Toms looked at her, and felt, and sensed, searched his classifications, selected his modifiers, checked and double-checked. And after much searching, and careful selection, and absolute certainty, and allowing for his present state of mind, and not forgetting to take into account climatic conditions, phases of the Moon, wind speed and direction, Sun spots, and other phenomena which have their due effect upon love, he said:

"My dear, I am rather fond of you."

"Jeff! Surely you can say more than that! The Language of Love—"

"The Language is damnably precise," Toms said wretchedly. "I'm sorry, but the phrase 'I am rather fond of you' expresses precisely what I feel."

"Oh, Jeff!"

"Yes," he mumbled.

"Oh, damn you, Jeff!"

There was, of course, a painful scene and a very painful separation. Toms took to traveling.

He held jobs here and there, working as a riveter at Saturn-Lockheed, a wiper on the Helg-Vinosce Trader, a farmer for a while on a kibbutz on Israel IV. He bummed around the Inner Dalmian System for several years, living mostly on handouts. Then, at Novilocessile, he met a pleasant, brown-haired girl, courted her and, in due course, married her and set up housekeeping.

Their friends say that the Tomses are tolerably happy, although their home makes most people uncomfortable. It is a pleasant enough place, but the rushing red river nearby makes people edgy. And who can get used to vermilion trees, and orange-and-blue grass, and moaning flowers, and three wrinkled moons playing tag in the alien sky?

Toms likes it, though, and Mrs. Toms is, if nothing else, a flexible young lady.

Toms wrote a letter to his philosophy professor on Earth, saying that he had solved the problem of the demise of the Tyanian race, at least to his own satisfaction. The trouble with scholarly research, he wrote, is the inhibiting effect it has upon action. The Tyanians, he was convinced, had been so preoccupied with the science of love, after a while they just didn't get around to making any.

And eventually he sent a short postcard to George Varris. He simply said that he was married, having succeeded in finding a girl for whom he felt "quite a substantial liking."

"Lucky devil," Varris growled, after reading the card. " 'Vaguely enjoyable' was the best I could ever find."

Fatal Attractions

"Come, lovely and soothing death," Walt Whitman once wrote, a sentiment that infuses much of the literature, music and painting of the romantic movement, whose practitioners so often linked the joys of high passion with the sorrows of mortality.

This final section of *Lovers and Other Monsters* preserves that tradition. Though I refused to admit any selection smacking of necrophilia (the Poe tale comes closest), death lurks everywhere in these unlucky thirteen "guignols" pregnant with fetishism, murder, nasty ghosts, philandery, sexual manipulation, suicide and, naturally, femmes and hommes literally fatale.

Edgar Allan Poe

Berenice

My first acquaintance with "Berenice" by EDGAR ALLAN POE *(1809–49) occurred many years ago when I watched my friend Brother Theodore tell it
first-person on a New York TV talk show. He convinced a few of the credulous audience members that it actually happened to him, but I'm sure (?) it
didn't . . .*

MISERY IS MANIFOLD. The wretchedness of earth is multiform. Over-
reaching the wide horizon as the rainbow, its hues are as various as the
hues of that arch—as distinct, too, yet as intimately blended. Overreach-
ing the wide horizon as the rainbow! How is it that from beauty I have
derived a type of unloveliness?—from the covenant of peace a simile of
sorrow? But as, in ethics, evil is a consequence of good, so, in fact, out of
joy is sorrow born. Either the memory of past bliss is the anguish of today, or the agonies which *are* have their origin in the ecstasies which
might have been.

My baptismal name is Egaeus; that of my family I will not mention. Yet
there are no towers in the land more time-honored than my gloomy, gray,
hereditary halls. Our line has been called a race of visionaries; and in
many striking particulars—in the character of the family mansion—in the
frescos of the chief saloon—in the tapestries of the dormitories—in the
chiselling of some buttresses in the armory—but more especially in the
gallery of antique paintings—in the fashion of the library chamber—and,
lastly, in the very peculiar nature of the library's contents, there is more
than sufficient evidence to warrant the belief.

The recollections of my earliest years are connected with that chamber,
and with its volumes—of which latter I will say no more. Here died my

mother. Herein was I born. But it is mere idleness to say that I had not lived before—that the soul has no previous existence. You deny it?—let us not argue the matter. Convinced myself, I seek not to convince. There is, however, a remembrance of aërial forms—of spiritual and meaning eyes —of sounds, musical yet sad—a remembrance which will not be excluded; a memory like a shadow, vague, variable, indefinite, unsteady; and like a shadow, too, in the impossibility of my getting rid of it while the sunlight of my reason shall exist.

In that chamber was I born. Thus awaking from the long night of what seemed, but was not, nonentity, at once into the very regions of fairy-land —into a palace of imagination—into the wild dominions of monastic thought and erudition—it is not singular that I gazed around me with a startled and ardent eye—that I loitered away my boyhood in books, and dissipated my youth in reverie; but it *is* singular that as years rolled away, and the noon of manhood found me still in the mansion of my fathers— it *is* wonderful what stagnation there fell upon the springs of my life— wonderful how total an inversion took place in the character of my commonest thought. The realities of the world affected me as visions, and as visions only, while the wild ideas of the land of dreams became, in turn— not the material of my every-day existence—but in very deed that existence utterly and solely in itself.

Berenice and I were cousins, and we grew up together in my paternal halls. Yet differently we grew—I ill of health, and buried in gloom—she agile, graceful, and overflowing with energy; hers the ramble on the hillside—mine the studies of the cloister—I living within my own heart, and addicted body and soul to the most intense and painful meditation—she roaming carelessly through life with no thought of the shadows in her path, or the silent flight of the raven-winged hours. Berenice!—I call upon her name—Berenice!—and from the gray ruins of memory a thousand tumultuous recollections are startled at the sound! Ah! vividly is her image before me now, as in the early days of her light-heartedness and joy! Oh! gorgeous yet fantastic beauty! Oh! sylph amid the shrubberies of Arnheim!—Oh! Naiad among its fountains!—and then—then all is mystery and terror, and a tale which should not be told. Disease—a fatal disease—fell like the simoom upon her frame, and, even while I gazed upon her, the spirit of change swept over her, pervading her mind, her habits, and her character, and, in a manner the most subtle and terrible, disturbing even the identity of her person! Alas! the destroyer came and went, and the victim—where was she? I knew her not—or knew her no longer as Berenice.

Among the numerous train of maladies superinduced by that fatal and primary one which effected a revolution of so horrible a kind in the moral and physical being of my cousin, may be mentioned as the most distressing and obstinate in its nature, a species of epilepsy not unfrequently terminating in *trance* itself—trance very nearly resembling positive dissolution, and from which her manner of recovery was, in most instances, startlingly abrupt. In the mean time my own disease—for I have been told that I should call it by no other appellation—my own disease, then, grew rapidly upon me, and assumed finally a monomaniac character of a novel and extraordinary form—hourly and momently gaining vigor—and at length obtaining over me the most incomprehensible ascendancy. This monomania, if I must so term it, consisted in a morbid irritability of those properties of the mind in metaphysical science termed the *attentive*. It is more than probable that I am not understood; but I fear, indeed, that it is in no manner possible to convey to the mind of the merely general reader, an adequate idea of that nervous *intensity of interest* with which, in my case, the powers of meditation (not to speak technically) busied and buried themselves, in the contemplation of even the most ordinary objects of the universe.

To muse for long unwearied hours with my attention riveted to some frivolous device on the margin, or in the typography of a book; to become absorbed for the better part of a summer's day, in a quaint shadow falling aslant upon the tapestry, or upon the door; to lose myself for an entire night in watching the steady flame of a lamp, or the embers of a fire; to dream away whole days over the perfume of a flower; to repeat monotonously some common word, until the sound, by dint of frequent repetition, ceased to convey any idea whatever to the mind; to lose all sense of motion or physical existence, by means of absolute bodily quiescence long and obstinately persevered in;—such were a few of the most common and least pernicious vagaries induced by a condition of the mental faculties, not, indeed, altogether unparalleled, but certainly bidding defiance to anything like analysis or explanation.

Yet let me not be misapprehended.—The undue, earnest, and morbid attention thus excited by objects in their own nature frivolous, must not be confounded in character with that ruminating propensity common to all mankind, and more especially indulged in by persons of ardent imagination. It was not even, as might be at first supposed, an extreme condition, or exaggeration of such propensity, but primarily and essentially distinct and different. In the one instance, the dreamer, or enthusiast, being interested by an object usually *not* frivolous, imperceptibly loses sight of this object in a wilderness of deductions and suggestions issuing therefrom, until, at the conclusion of a day dream *often replete with luxury*, he finds the *incitamentum* or first cause of his musings entirely vanished and forgotten. In my case the primary object was *invariably frivolous*, although assuming, through the medium of my distempered vision, a refracted and unreal importance. Few deductions, if any, were made; and those few pertinaciously returning in upon the original object as a centre. The meditations were *never* pleasurable; and, at the termination of the reverie, the first cause, so far from being out of sight, had attained that supernaturally exaggerated interest which was the prevailing feature of the disease. In a word, the powers of mind more particularly exercised were, with me, as I have said before, the *attentive*, and are, with the day-dreamer, the *speculative*.

My books, at this epoch, if they did not actually serve to irritate the disorder, partook, it will be perceived, largely, in their imaginative and inconsequential nature, of the characteristic qualities of the disorder itself. I well remember, among others, the treatise of the noble Italian Coelius Secundus Curio *"de Amplitudine Beati Regni Dei;"* St. Austin's great work, the "City of God;" and Tertullian *"de Carne Christi,"* in which the paradoxical sentence *"Mortuus est Dei filius; credibile est quia ineptum est: et sepultus resurrexit; certum est quia impossibile est"* occupied my undivided time, for many weeks of laborious and fruitless investigation.

Thus it will appear that, shaken from its balance only by trivial things, my reason bore resemblance to that ocean-crag spoken of by Ptolemy Hephestion, which steadily resisting the attacks of human violence, and the fiercer fury of the waters and the winds, trembled only to the touch of the flower called Asphodel. And although, to a careless thinker, it might appear a matter beyond doubt, that the alteration produced by her unhappy malady, in the *moral* condition of Berenice, would afford me many objects for the exercise of that intense and abnormal meditation whose nature I have been at some trouble in explaining, yet such was not in any degree the case. In the lucid intervals of my infirmity, her calamity, indeed, gave me pain, and, taking deeply to heart that total wreck of her fair and gentle life, I did not fail to ponder frequently and bitterly upon the wonderworking means by which so strange a revolution had been so suddenly brought to pass. But these reflections partook not of the idiosyncrasy of my disease, and were such as would have occurred, under similar

circumstances, to the ordinary mass of mankind. True to its own character, my disorder revelled in the less important but more startling changes
wrought in the *physical* frame of Berenice—in the singular and most
appalling distortion of her personal identity.

During the brightest days of her unparalleled beauty, most surely I had
never loved her. In the strange anomaly of my existence, feelings with me,
had never been of the heart, and my passions *always were* of the mind.
Through the gray of the early morning—among the trellised shadows of
the forest at noonday—and in the silence of my library at night, she had
flitted by my eyes, and I had seen her—not as the living and breathing
Berenice, but as the Berenice of a dream—not as a being of the earth,
earthy, but as the abstraction of such being—not as a thing to admire,
but to analyze—not as an object of love, but as the theme of the most
abstruse although desultory speculation. And *now*—now I shuddered in
her presence, and grew pale at her approach; yet bitterly lamenting her
fallen and desolate condition, I called to mind that she had loved me
long, and, in an evil moment, I spoke to her of marriage.

And at length the period of our nuptials was approaching, when, upon
an afternoon in the winter of the year,—one of those unseasonably warm,
calm, and misty days which are the nurse of the beautiful Halcyon,*—I
sat, (and sat, as I thought, alone,) in the inner apartment of the library.
But uplifting my eyes I saw that Berenice stood before me.

Was it my own excited imagination—or the misty influence of the
atmosphere—or the uncertain twilight of the chamber—or the gray draperies which fell around her figure—that caused in it so vacillating and
indistinct an outline? I could not tell. She spoke no word, and I—not for
worlds could I have uttered a syllable. An icy chill ran through my frame;
a sense of insufferable anxiety oppressed me; a consuming curiosity pervaded my soul; and sinking back upon the chair, I remained for some
time breathless and motionless, with my eyes riveted upon her person.
Alas! its emaciation was excessive, and not one vestige of the former
being, lurked in any single line of the contour. My burning glances at
length fell upon the face.

The forehead was high, and very pale, and singularly placid; and the
once jetty hair fell partially over it, and overshadowed the hollow temples
with innumerable ringlets now of a vivid yellow, and jarring discordantly,
in their fantastic character, with the reigning melancholy of the counte-

---

* For as Jove, during the winter season, gives twice seven days of warmth, men have
called this clement and temperate time the nurse of the beautiful Halcyon.—*Simonides*.

nance. The eyes were lifeless, and lustreless, and seemingly pupil-less, and I shrank involuntarily from their glassy stare to the contemplation of the thin and shrunken lips. They parted; and in a smile of peculiar meaning, *the teeth* of the changed Berenice disclosed themselves slowly to my view. Would to God that I had never beheld them, or that, having done so, I had died!

The shutting of a door disturbed me, and, looking up, I found that my cousin had departed from the chamber. But from the disordered chamber of my brain, had not, alas! departed, and would not be driven away, the white and ghastly *spectrum* of the teeth. Not a speck on their surface— not a shade on their enamel—not an indenture in their edges—but what that period of her smile had sufficed to brand in upon my memory. I saw them *now* even more unequivocally than I beheld them *then*. The teeth! —the teeth!—they were here, and there, and every where, and visibly and palpably before me; long, narrow, and excessively white, with the pale lips writhing about them, as in the very moment of their first terrible develop-ment. Then came the full fury of my *monomania*, and I struggled in vain against its strange and irresistible influence. In the multiplied objects of the external world I had no thoughts but for the teeth. For these I longed with a phrenzied desire. All other matters and all different interests be-came absorbed in their single contemplation. They—they alone were present to the mental eye, and they, in their sole individuality, became the essence of my mental life. I held them in every light. I turned them in every attitude. I surveyed their characteristics. I dwelt upon their pecu-liarities. I pondered upon their conformation. I mused upon the alter-ation in their nature. I shuddered as I assigned to them in imagination a sensitive and sentient power, and even when unassisted by the lips, a capability of moral expression. Of Mad'selle Sallé it has been well said, *"que tous ses pas étaient des sentiments,"* and of Berenice I more seriously believed *que toutes ses dents étaient des idées. Des idées!*—ah here was the idiotic thought that destroyed me! *Des idées!*—ah *therefore* it was that I coveted them so madly! I felt that their possession could alone ever restore me to peace, in giving me back to reason.

And the evening closed in upon me thus—and then the darkness came, and tarried, and went—and the day again dawned—and the mists of a second night were now gathering around—and still I sat motionless in that solitary room; and still I sat buried in meditation, and still the *phan-tasma* of the teeth maintained its terrible ascendancy as, with the most vivid and hideous distinctness, it floated about amid the changing lights and shadows of the chamber. At length there broke in upon my dreams a cry as of horror and dismay; and thereunto, after a pause, succeeded the sound of troubled voices, intermingled with many low moanings of sorrow, or of pain. I arose from my seat and, throwing open one of the doors of the library, saw standing out in the ante-chamber a servant maiden, all in tears, who told me that Berenice was—no more. She had been seized with epilepsy in the early morning, and now, at the closing in of the night, the grave was ready for its tenant, and all the preparations for the burial were completed.

I found myself sitting in the library, and again sitting there alone. It seemed that I had newly awakened from a confused and exciting dream. I knew that it was now midnight, and I was well aware that since the setting of the sun Berenice had been interred. But of that dreary period which intervened I had no positive—at least no definite comprehension. Yet its memory was replete with horror—horror more horrible from being vague, and terror more terrible from ambiguity. It was a fearful page in the record of my existence, written all over with dim, and hideous, and unintelligible recollections. I strived to decipher them, but in vain; while ever and anon, like the spirit of a departed sound, the shrill and piercing shriek of a female voice seemed to be ringing in my ears. I had done a deed—what was it? I asked myself the question aloud, and the whispering echoes of the chamber answered me, *"what was it?"*

On the table beside me burned a lamp, and near it lay a little box. It was of no remarkable character, and I had seen it frequently before, for it was the property of the family physician; but how came it *there*, upon my table, and why did I shudder in regarding it? These things were in no manner to be accounted for, and my eyes at length dropped to the open pages of a book, and to a sentence underscored therein. The words were the singular but simple ones of the poet Ebn Zaiat, *"Dicebant mihi sodales si sepulchrum amicae visitarem, curas meas aliquantulum fore levatas."* Why then, as I perused them, did the hairs of my head erect themselves on end, and the blood of my body become congealed within my veins?

There came a light tap at the library door, and pale as the tenant of a tomb, a menial entered upon tiptoe. His looks were wild with terror, and he spoke to me in a voice tremulous, husky, and very low. What said he? —some broken sentences I heard.

He told of a wild cry disturbing the silence of the night—of the gathering together of the household—of a search in the direction of the sound;

—and then his tones grew thrillingly distinct as he whispered me of a violated grave—of a disfigured body enshrouded, yet still breathing, still palpitating, still *alive!*

He pointed to my garments;—they were muddy and clotted with gore. I spoke not, and he took me gently by the hand;—it was indented with the impress of human nails. He directed my attention to some object against the wall;—I looked at it for some minutes;—it was a spade. With a shriek I bounded to the table, and grasped the box that lay upon it. But I could not force it open; and in my tremor it slipped from my hands, and fell heavily, and burst into pieces; and from it, with a rattling sound, there rolled out some instruments of dental surgery, intermingled with thirty-two small, white and ivory-looking substances that were scattered to and fro about the floor.

Bret Harte

A Passage in the Life
of Mr. John Oakhurst

*Mr. John Oakhurst, professional gambler, is one of the most attractive
recurrent characters in the tales of* FRANCIS BRET HARTE *(1836–1902). Born
in Albany, New York, Harte went to California when he was eighteen,
worked on San Francisco magazines and newspapers and wrote many short
stories set in the American West. Oakhurst also appears in "The Luck of
Roaring Camp" and meets his fate in Harte's most popular, twice-filmed
tale, "The Outcasts of Poker Flat."*

HE ALWAYS THOUGHT it must have been Fate. Certainly nothing
could have been more inconsistent with his habits than to have been in
the Plaza at seven o'clock of that midsummer morning. The sight of his
colorless face in Sacramento was rare at that season, and indeed at any
season, anywhere, publicly, before two o'clock in the afternoon. Looking
back upon it in after years, in the light of a chanceful life, he determined,
with the characteristic philosophy of his profession, that it must have
been Fate.

Yet it is my duty as a strict chronicler of facts to state that Mr.
Oakhurst's presence there that morning was due to a very simple cause.
At exactly half past six, the bank being then a winner to the amount of
twenty thousand dollars, he had risen from the faro table, relinquished
his seat to an accomplished assistant, and withdrawn quietly, without
attracting a glance from the silent, anxious faces bowed over the table.
But when he entered his luxurious sleeping room, across the passageway,

he was a little shocked at finding the sun streaming through an inadvertently opened window. Something in the rare beauty of the morning, perhaps something in the novelty of the idea, struck him as he was about to close the blinds, and he hesitated. Then, taking his hat from the table, he stepped down a private staircase into the street.

The people who were abroad at that early hour were of a class quite unknown to Mr. Oakhurst. There were milkmen and hucksters delivering their wares, small tradespeople opening their shops, housemaids sweeping doorsteps, and occasionally a child. These Mr. Oakhurst regarded with a certain cold curiosity, perhaps quite free from the cynical disfavor with which he generally looked upon the more pretentious of his race whom he was in the habit of meeting. Indeed, I think he was not altogether displeased with the admiring glances which these humble women threw after his handsome face and figure, conspicuous even in a country of fine-looking men. While it is very probable that this wicked vagabond, in the pride of his social isolation, would have been coldly indifferent to the advances of a fine lady, a little girl who ran admiringly by his side in a ragged dress had the power to call a faint flush into his colorless cheek. He dismissed her at last, but not until she had found out—what sooner or later her large-hearted and discriminating sex inevitably did—that he was exceedingly free and openhanded with his money, and also—what perhaps none other of her sex ever did—that the bold black eyes of this fine gentleman were in reality of a brownish and even tender gray.

There was a small garden before a white cottage in a side street that attracted Mr. Oakhurst's attention. It was filled with roses, heliotrope, and verbena—flowers familiar enough to him in the expensive and more portable form of bouquets, but as it seemed to him then, never before so notably lovely. Perhaps it was because the dew was yet fresh upon them, perhaps it was because they were unplucked, but Mr. Oakhurst admired them, not as a possible future tribute to the fascinating and accomplished Miss Ethelinda, then performing at the Varieties, for Mr. Oakhurst's especial benefit, as she had often assured him; nor yet as a *douceur* to the enthralling Miss Montmorrissy, with whom Mr. Oakhurst expected to sup that evening, but simply for himself, and mayhap for the flowers' sake. Howbeit, he passed on, and so out into the open plaza, where, finding a bench under a cottonwood tree, he first dusted the seat with his handkerchief, and then sat down.

It was a fine morning. The air was so still and calm that a sigh from the sycamores seemed like the deep-drawn breath of the just awakening tree, and the faint rustle of its boughs as the outstretching of cramped and reviving limbs. Far away the Sierras stood out against a sky so remote as to be of no positive color—so remote that even the sun despaired of ever reaching it, and so expended its strength recklessly on the whole landscape, until it fairly glittered in a white and vivid contrast. With a very rare impulse, Mr. Oakhurst took off his hat, and half reclined on the bench, with his face to the sky. Certain birds who had taken a critical attitude on a spray above him apparently began an animated discussion regarding his possible malevolent intentions. One or two, emboldened by the silence, hopped on the ground at his feet, until the sound of wheels on the gravel walk frightened them away.

Looking up, he saw a man coming slowly towards him, wheeling a nondescript vehicle in which a woman was partly sitting, partly reclining. Without knowing why, Mr. Oakhurst instantly conceived that the carriage was the invention and workmanship of the man, partly from its oddity, partly from the strong, mechanical hand that grasped it, and partly from a certain pride and visible consciousness in the manner in which the man handled it. Then Mr. Oakhurst saw something more—the man's face was familiar. With that regal faculty of not forgetting a face that had ever given him professional audience, he instantly classified it under the following mental formula: "At 'Frisco, Polka Saloon. Lost his week's wages. I reckon seventy dollars—on red. Never came again." There was, however, no trace of this in the calm eyes and unmoved face that he turned upon the stranger, who, on the contrary, blushed, looked embarrassed, hesitated, and then stopped with an involuntary motion that brought the carriage and its fair occupant face to face with Mr. Oakhurst.

I should hardly do justice to the position she will occupy in this veracious chronicle by describing the lady now—if, indeed, I am able to do it at all. Certainly, the popular estimate was conflicting. The late Colonel Starbottle—to whose large experience of a charming sex I have before been indebted for many valuable suggestions—had, I regret to say, depreciated her fascinations. "A yellow-faced cripple, by dash—a sick woman, with mahogany eyes. One of your blanked spiritual creatures, with no flesh on her bones." On the other hand, however, she enjoyed later much complimentary disparagement from her own sex. Miss Celestina Howard, second leader in the ballet at the Varieties, had, with great alliterative directness, in after years, denominated her as an "aquiline asp." Mlle. Brimborion remembered that she had always warned "Mr. Jack" that this woman would "empoison" him. But Mr. Oakhurst, whose impressions are perhaps the most important, only saw a pale, thin, deep-eyed woman, raised above the level of her companion by the refinement of long suffering and isolation, and a certain shy virginity of manner. There was a suggestion of physical purity in the folds of her fresh-looking robe, and a certain picturesque tastefulness in the details, that, without knowing why, made him think that the robe was her invention and handiwork, even as the carriage she occupied was evidently the work of her companion. Her own hand, a trifle too thin, but well-shaped, subtle-fingered, and gentlewomanly, rested on the side of the carriage, the counterpart of the strong mechanical grasp of her companion's.

There was some obstruction to the progress of the vehicle, and Mr. Oakhurst stepped forward to assist. While the wheel was being lifted over the curbstone, it was necessary that she should hold his arm, and for a moment her thin hand rested there, light and cold as a snowflake, and then—as it seemed to him—like a snowflake melted away. Then there was a pause, and then conversation—the lady joining occasionally and shyly.

It appeared that they were man and wife. That for the past two years she had been a great invalid, and had lost the use of her lower limbs from rheumatism. That until lately she had been confined to her bed, until her husband—who was a master carpenter—had bethought himself to make her this carriage. He took her out regularly for an airing before going to work, because it was his only time, and—they attracted less attention. They had tried many doctors, but without avail. They had been advised to go to the Sulphur Springs, but it was expensive. Mr. Decker, the husband, had once saved eighty dollars for that purpose, but while in San Francisco had his pocket picked—Mr. Decker was so senseless. (The intelligent reader need not be told that it is the lady who is speaking.) They had never been able to make up the sum again, and they had given up the idea. It was a dreadful thing to have one's pocket picked. Did he not think so?

Her husband's face was crimson, but Mr. Oakhurst's countenance was quite calm and unmoved, as he gravely agreed with her, and walked by her side until they passed the little garden that he had admired. Here Mr. Oakhurst commanded a halt, and going to the door, astounded the proprietor by a preposterously extravagant offer for a choice of the flowers. Presently he returned to the carriage with his arms full of roses, heliotrope, and verbena, and cast them in the lap of the invalid. While she was bending over them with childish delight, Mr. Oakhurst took the opportunity of drawing her husband aside.

"Perhaps," he said in a low voice, and a manner quite free from any personal annoyance—"perhaps it's just as well that you lied to her as you did. You can say now that the pickpocket was arrested the other day, and you got your money back." Mr. Oakhurst quietly slipped four twenty-dollar gold pieces into the broad hand of the bewildered Mr. Decker. "Say that—or anything you like—but the truth. Promise me you won't say that!"

The man promised. Mr. Oakhurst quietly returned to the front of the little carriage. The sick woman was still eagerly occupied with the flowers, and as she raised her eyes to his, her faded cheek seemed to have caught some color from the roses, and her eyes some of their dewy freshness. But at that instant Mr. Oakhurst lifted his hat, and before she could thank him was gone.

I grieve to say that Mr. Decker shamelessly broke his promise. That night, in the very goodness of his heart and uxorious self-abnegation, he, like all devoted husbands, not only offered himself, but his friend and benefactor, as a sacrifice on the family altar. It is only fair, however, to add that he spoke with great fervor of the generosity of Mr. Oakhurst, and dealt with an enthusiasm quite common with his class on the mysterious fame and prodigal vices of the gambler.

"And now, Elsie, dear, say that you'll forgive me," said Mr. Decker, dropping on one knee beside his wife's couch. "I did it for the best. It was for you, dearey, that I put that money on them cards that night in 'Frisco. I thought to win a heap—enough to take you away, and enough left to get you a new dress."

Mrs. Decker smiled and pressed her husband's hand. "I do forgive you, Joe, dear," she said, still smiling, with eyes abstractedly fixed on the ceiling; "and you ought to be whipped for deceiving me so, you bad boy, and making me make such a speech. There, say no more about it. If you'll be very good hereafter, and will just now hand me that cluster of roses, I'll forgive you." She took the branch in her fingers, lifted the roses to her face, and presently said, behind their leaves—

"Joe!"

"What is it, lovey?"

"Do you think that this Mr.—what do you call him?—Jack Oakhurst would have given that money back to you if I hadn't made that speech?"

"Yes."

"If he hadn't seen me at all?"

Mr. Decker looked up. His wife had managed in some way to cover up her whole face with the roses, except her eyes, which were dangerously bright.

"No; it was you, Elsie—it was all along of seeing you that made him do it."

"A poor sick woman like me?"

"A sweet, little, lovely, pooty Elsie—Joe's own little wifey! How could he help it?"

Mrs. Decker fondly cast one arm around her husband's neck, still keeping the roses to her face with the other. From behind them she began to murmur gently and idiotically, "Dear, ole square Joey. Elsie's oney booful big bear." But, really, I do not see that my duty as a chronicler of facts compels me to continue this little lady's speech any further, and out of respect to the unmarried reader I stop.

Nevertheless, the next morning Mrs. Decker betrayed some slight and apparently uncalled-for irritability on reaching the plaza, and presently desired her husband to wheel her back home. Moreover, she was very much astonished at meeting Mr. Oakhurst just as they were returning, and even doubted if it were he, and questioned her husband as to his identity with the stranger of yesterday as he approached. Her manner to Mr. Oakhurst, also, was quite in contrast with her husband's frank welcome. Mr. Oakhurst instantly detected it. "Her husband has told her all, and she dislikes me," he said to himself, with that fatal appreciation of the half-truths of a woman's motives that causes the wisest masculine critic to stumble. He lingered only long enough to take the business address of the husband, and then, lifting his hat gravely, without looking at the lady, went his way. It struck the honest master carpenter as one of the charming anomalies of his wife's character that, although the meeting was evidently very much constrained and unpleasant, instantly afterward his wife's spirits began to rise. "You was hard on him—a leetle hard, wasn't you, Elsie?" said Mr. Decker deprecatingly. "I'm afraid he may think I've broke my promise." "Ah, indeed," said the lady indifferently. Mr. Decker instantly stepped round to the front of the vehicle. "You look like an A-1 first-class lady riding down Broadway in her own carriage, Elsie," said he; "I never seed you lookin' so peart and sassy before."

A few days later the proprietor of the San Isabel Sulphur Springs received the following note in Mr. Oakhurst's well-known dainty hand:

DEAR STEVE—I've been thinking over your proposition to buy Nichols's interest and have concluded to go in. But I don't see how the thing will pay until you have more accommodation down there, and for the best class—I mean *my* customers. What we want is an extension to the main building, and two or three cottages put up. I send down a builder to take hold of the job at once. He takes his sick wife with him, and you are to look after them as you would for one of us.

I may run down there myself after the races, just to look after things; but I sha'n't set upon any game this season.

Yours always,

JOHN OAKHURST

It was only the last sentence of this letter that provoked criticism. "I can understand," said Mr. Hamlin, a professional brother to whom Mr. Oakhurst's letter was shown—"I can understand why Jack goes in heavy and builds, for it's a sure spec, and is bound to be a mighty soft thing in time, if he comes here regularly. But why in blank he don't set up a bank this season and take the chance of getting some of the money back that he puts into circulation in building is what gets me. I wonder now," he mused deeply, "what *is* his little game."

The season had been a prosperous one to Mr. Oakhurst, and proportionally disastrous to several members of the legislature, judges, colonels, and others who had enjoyed but briefly the pleasure of Mr. Oakhurst's midnight society. And yet Sacramento had become very dull to him. He had lately formed a habit of early morning walks—so unusual and startling to his friends, both male and female, as to occasion the intensest curiosity. Two or three of the latter set spies upon his track, but the inquisition resulted only in the discovery that Mr. Oakhurst walked to the plaza, sat down upon one particular bench for a few moments, and then returned without seeing anybody, and the theory that there was a woman in the case was abandoned. A few superstitious gentlemen of his own profession believed that he did it for "luck." Some others, more practical, declared that he went out to "study points."

After the races at Marysville, Mr. Oakhurst went to San Francisco; from that place he returned to Marysville, but a few days after was seen at San José, Santa Cruz, and Oakland. Those who met him declared that his manner was restless and feverish, and quite unlike his ordinary calmness and phlegm. Colonel Starbottle pointed out the fact that at San Francisco, at the Club, Jack had declined to deal. "Hand shaky, sir—depend upon it; don't stimulate enough—blank him!"

From San José he started to go to Oregon by land with a rather expensive outfit of horses and camp equipage, but on reaching Stockton he suddenly diverged, and four hours later found him, with a single horse, entering the canyon of the San Isabel Warm Sulphur Springs.

It was a pretty triangular valley lying at the foot of three sloping mountains, dark with pines and fantastic with madroño and manzanita. Nestling against the mountainside, the straggling buildings and long piazza of the hotel glittered through the leaves; and here and there shone a white toylike cottage. Mr. Oakhurst was not an admirer of nature, but he felt something of the same novel satisfaction in the view that he experienced in his first morning walk in Sacramento. And now carriages began to pass him on the road filled with gaily dressed women, and the cold California outlines of the landscape began to take upon themselves somewhat of a human warmth and color. And then the long hotel piazza came in view, efflorescent with the full-toileted fair. Mr. Oakhurst, a good rider after the California fashion, did not check his speed as he approached his destination, but charged the hotel at a gallop, threw his horse on his haunches within a foot of the piazza, and then quietly emerged from the cloud of dust that veiled his dismounting.

Whatever feverish excitement might have raged within, all his habitual calm returned as he stepped upon the piazza. With the instinct of long habit he turned and faced the battery of eyes with the same cold indifference with which he had for years encountered the half-hidden sneers of men and the half-frightened admiration of women. Only one person stepped forward to welcome him. Oddly enough, it was Dick Hamilton, perhaps the only one present who, by birth, education, and position, might have satisfied the most fastidious social critic. Happily for Mr. Oakhurst's reputation, he was also a very rich banker and social leader. "Do you know who that is you spoke to?" asked young Parker, with an alarmed expression. "Yes," replied Hamilton, with characteristic effrontery; "the man you lost a thousand dollars to last week. *I* only know him *socially*." "But isn't he a gambler?" queried the youngest Miss Smith. "He is," replied Hamilton; "but I wish, my dear young lady, that we all played as open and honest a game as our friend yonder, and were as willing as he is to abide by its fortunes."

But Mr. Oakhurst was happily out of hearing of this colloquy, and was even then lounging listlessly, yet watchfully, along the upper hall. Suddenly he heard a light footstep behind him, and then his name called in a familiar voice that drew the blood quickly to his heart. He turned, and she stood before him.

But how transformed! If I have hesitated to describe the hollow-eyed cripple—the quaintly dressed artisan's wife, a few pages ago—what shall I do with this graceful, shapely, elegantly attired gentlewoman into whom she has been merged within these two months? In good faith, she was very pretty. You and I, my dear madam, would have been quick to see that those charming dimples were misplaced for true beauty, and too fixed in their quality for honest mirthfulness; that the delicate lines around those aquiline nostrils were cruel and selfish; that the sweet, virginal surprise of those lovely eyes was as apt to be opened on her plate as upon the gallant speeches of her dinner partner; that her sympathetic color came and went more with her own spirits than yours. But you and I are not in love with her, dear madam, and Mr. Oakhurst is. And even in the folds of her Parisian gown, I am afraid this poor fellow saw the same subtle strokes of purity that he had seen in her homespun robe. And then there was the delightful revelation that she could walk, and that she had dear little feet of her own in the tiniest slippers of her French shoemaker, with such preposterous blue bows, and Chappell's own stamp, Rue de something or other, Paris, on the narrow sole.

He ran towards her with a heightened color and outstretched hands. But she whipped her own behind her, glanced rapidly up and down the long hall, and stood looking at him with a half-audacious, half-mischievous admiration in utter contrast to her old reserve.

"I've a great mind not to shake hands with you at all. You passed me just now on the piazza without speaking, and I ran after you, as I suppose many another poor woman has done."

Mr. Oakhurst stammered that she was so changed.

"The more reason why you should know me. Who changed me? You. You have re-created me. You found a helpless, crippled, sick, poverty-stricken woman, with one dress to her back, and that her own make, and you gave her life, health, strength, and fortune. You did, and you know it, sir. How do you like your work?" She caught the side seams of her gown in either hand and dropped him a playful courtesy. Then, with a sudden, relenting gesture, she gave him both her hands.

Outrageous as this speech was, and unfeminine, as I trust every fair reader will deem it, I fear it pleased Mr. Oakhurst. Not but that he was accustomed to a certain frank female admiration; but then it was of the coulisses and not of the cloister with which he always persisted in associating Mrs. Decker. To be addressed in this way by an invalid Puritan, a sick saint, with the austerity of suffering still clothing her—a woman who had a Bible on the dressing table, who went to church three times a day, and was devoted to her husband, completely bowled him over. He still held her hands as she went on—

"Why didn't you come before? What were you doing in Marysville, in San José, in Oakland? You see I have followed you. I saw you as you came down the canyon, and knew you at once. I saw your letter to Joseph, and knew you were coming. Why didn't you write to me? You will sometime! Good evening, Mr. Hamilton."

She had withdrawn her hands, but not until Hamilton, ascending the staircase, was nearly abreast of them. He raised his hat to her with well-bred composure, nodded familiarly to Oakhurst, and passed on. When he had gone Mrs. Decker lifted her eyes to Mr. Oakhurst. "Some day I shall ask a great favor of you!"

Mr. Oakhurst begged that it should be now. "No, not until you know me better. Then, some day, I shall want you to—kill that man!"

She laughed, such a pleasant little ringing laugh, such a display of dimples—albeit a little fixed in the corners of her mouth—such an innocent light in her brown eyes, and such a lovely color in her cheeks, that Mr. Oakhurst—who seldom laughed—was fain to laugh too. It was as if a lamb had proposed to a fox a foray into a neighboring sheepfold.

A few evenings after this, Mrs. Decker arose from a charmed circle of her admirers on the hotel piazza, excused herself for a few moments, laughingly declined an escort, and ran over to her little cottage—one of her husband's creation—across the road. Perhaps from the sudden and unwonted exercise in her still convalescent state, she breathed hurriedly and feverishly as she entered her boudoir, and once or twice placed her hand upon her breast. She was startled on turning up the light to find her husband lying on the sofa.

"You look hot and excited, Elsie, love," said Mr. Decker; "you ain't took worse, are you?"

Mrs. Decker's face had paled, but now flushed again. "No," she said, "only a little pain here," as she again placed her hand upon her corsage.

"Can I do anything for you?" said Mr. Decker, rising with affectionate concern.

"Run over to the hotel and get me some brandy, quick!"

Mr. Decker ran. Mrs. Decker closed and bolted the door, and then putting her hand to her bosom, drew out the pain. It was folded four-square, and was, I grieve to say, in Mr. Oakhurst's handwriting.

She devoured it with burning eyes and cheeks until there came a step upon the porch. Then she hurriedly replaced it in her bosom and unbolted the door. Her husband entered; she raised the spirits to her lips and declared herself better.

"Are you going over there again tonight?" asked Mr. Decker submissively.

"No," said Mrs. Decker, with her eyes fixed dreamily on the floor.

"I wouldn't if I was you," said Mr. Decker with a sigh of relief. After a pause he took a seat on the sofa, and drawing his wife to his side, said, "Do you know what I was thinking of when you came in, Elsie?" Mrs. Decker ran her fingers through his stiff black hair, and couldn't imagine.

"I was thinking of old times, Elsie; I was thinking of the days when I built that kerridge for you, Elsie—when I used to take you out to ride, and was both hoss and driver! We was poor then, and you was sick, Elsie, but we was happy. We've got money now, and a house, and you're quite another woman. I may say, dear, that you're a *new* woman. And that's where the trouble comes in. I could build you a kerridge, Elsie; I could build you a house, Elsie—but there I stopped. I couldn't build up *you*. You're strong and pretty, Elsie, and fresh and new. But somehow, Elsie, you ain't no work of mine!"

He paused. With one hand laid gently on his forehead and the other pressed upon her bosom as if to feel certain of the presence of her pain, she said sweetly and soothingly:

"But it was your work, dear."

Mr. Decker shook his head sorrowfully. "No, Elsie, not mine. I had the chance to do it once and I let it go. It's done now; but not by me."

Mrs. Decker raised her surprised, innocent eyes to his. He kissed her tenderly, and then went on in a more cheerful voice.

"That ain't all I was thinking of, Elsie. I was thinking that maybe you give too much of your company to that Mr. Hamilton. Not that there's any wrong in it, to you or him. But it might make people talk. You're the only one here, Elsie," said the master carpenter, looking fondly at his wife, "who isn't talked about; whose work ain't inspected or condemned."

Mrs. Decker was glad he had spoken about it. She had thought so, too, but she could not well be uncivil to Mr. Hamilton, who was a fine gentleman, without making a powerful enemy. "And he's always treated me as if I was a born lady in his own circle," added the little woman, with a certain pride that made her husband fondly smile. "But I have thought of a plan. He will not stay here if I should go away. If, for instance, I went to San Francisco to visit ma for a few days, he would be gone before I should return."

Mr. Decker was delighted. "By all means," he said; "go tomorrow. Jack Oakhurst is going down, and I'll put you in his charge."

Mrs. Decker did not think it was prudent. "Mr. Oakhurst is our friend, Joseph, but you know his reputation." In fact, she did not know that she ought to go now, knowing that he was going the same day; but with a kiss

Mr. Decker overcame her scruples. She yielded gracefully. Few women, in fact, knew how to give up a point as charmingly as she.

She stayed a week in San Francisco. When she returned she was a trifle thinner and paler than she had been. This she explained as the result of perhaps too active exercise and excitement. "I was out-of-doors nearly all the time, as ma will tell you," she said to her husband, "and always alone. I am getting quite independent now," she added gaily. "I don't want any escort—I believe, Joey dear, I could get along even without you—I'm so brave!"

But her visit, apparently, had not been productive of her impelling design. Mr. Hamilton had not gone, but had remained, and called upon them that very evening. "I've thought of a plan, Joey, dear," said Mrs. Decker when he had departed. "Poor Mr. Oakhurst has a miserable room at the hotel—suppose you ask him when he returns from San Francisco to stop with us. He can have our spare room. I don't think," she added archly, "that Mr. Hamilton will call often." Her husband laughed, intimated that she was a little coquette, pinched her cheek, and complied. "The queer thing about a woman," he said afterwards confidentially to Mr. Oakhurst, "is that without having any plan of her own, she'll take anybody's and build a house on it entirely different to suit herself. And dern my skin, if you'll be able to say whether or not you didn't give the scale and measurements yourself. That's what gets me."

The next week Mr. Oakhurst was installed in the Deckers' cottage. The business relations of her husband and himself were known to all, and her own reputation was above suspicion. Indeed, few women were more popular. She was domestic, she was prudent, she was pious. In a country of great feminine freedom and latitude, she never rode or walked with anybody but her husband; in an epoch of slang and ambiguous expression, she was always precise and formal in her speech; in the midst of a fashion of ostentatious decoration she never wore a diamond, nor a single valuable jewel. She never permitted an indecorum in public; she never countenanced the familiarities of California society. She declaimed against the prevailing tone of infidelity and skepticism in religion. Few people who were present will ever forget the dignified yet stately manner with which she rebuked Mr. Hamilton in the public parlor for entering upon the discussion of a work on materialism, lately published; and some among them, also, will not forget the expression of amused surprise on Mr. Hamilton's face that gradually changed to sardonic gravity as he courteously waived his point. Certainly, not Mr. Oakhurst, who from that moment began to be uneasily impatient of his friend, and even—if such a term could be applied to any moral quality in Mr. Oakhurst—to fear him.

For, during this time, Mr. Oakhurst had begun to show symptoms of a change in his usual habits. He was seldom, if ever, seen in his old haunts, in a barroom, or with his old associates. Pink and white notes, in distracted handwriting, accumulated on the dressing table in his rooms at Sacramento. It was given out in San Francisco that he had some organic disease of the heart, for which his physician had prescribed perfect rest. He read more, he took long walks, he sold his fast horses, he went to church.

I have a very vivid recollection of his first appearance there. He did not accompany the Deckers, nor did he go into their pew, but came in as the service commenced, and took a seat quietly in one of the back pews. By some mysterious instinct his presence became presently known to the congregation, some of whom so far forgot themselves, in their curiosity, as to face around and apparently address their responses to him. Before the service was over it was pretty well understood that "miserable sinners" meant Mr. Oakhurst. Nor did this mysterious influence fail to affect the officiating clergyman, who introduced an allusion to Mr. Oakhurst's calling and habits in a sermon on the architecture of Solomon's Temple, and in a manner so pointed and yet labored as to cause the youngest of us to flame with indignation. Happily, however, it was lost upon Jack; I do not think he even heard it. His handsome, colorless face—albeit a trifle worn and thoughtful—was inscrutable. Only once, during the singing of a hymn, at a certain note in the contralto's voice, there crept into his dark eyes a look of wistful tenderness, so yearning and yet so hopeless that those who were watching him felt their own glisten. Yet I retain a very vivid remembrance of his standing up to receive the benediction, with the suggestion in his manner and tightly buttoned coat of taking the fire of his adversary at ten paces. After church he disappeared as quietly as he had entered, and fortunately escaped hearing the comments on his rash act. His appearance was generally considered as an impertinence—attributable only to some wanton fancy—or possibly a bet. One or two thought that the sexton was exceedingly remiss in not turning him out after discovering who he was; and a prominent pewholder remarked that if he couldn't take his wife and daughters to that church without exposing them to such an influence, he would try to find some church where he could. Another traced Mr. Oakhurst's presence to certain Broad Church radical tendencies, which he regretted to say he had lately noted in their pastor. Deacon Sawyer, whose delicately organized, sickly wife had already borne him eleven children, and died in an ambitious attempt to complete the dozen, avowed that the presence of a person of Mr. Oakhurst's various and indiscriminate gallantries was an insult to the memory of the deceased that, as a man, he could not brook.

It was about this time that Mr. Oakhurst, contrasting himself with a conventional world in which he had hitherto rarely mingled, became aware that there was something in his face, figure, and carriage quite unlike other men—something that if it did not betray his former career, at least showed an individuality and originality that was suspicious. In this belief he shaved off his long, silken mustache, and religiously brushed out his clustering curls every morning. He even went so far as to affect a negligence of dress, and hid his small, slim, arched feet in the largest and heaviest walking shoes. There is a story told that he went to his tailor in Sacramento, and asked him to make him a suit of clothes like everybody else. The tailor, familiar with Mr. Oakhurst's fastidiousness, did not know what he meant. "I mean," said Mr. Oakhurst savagely, "something *respectable*—something that doesn't exactly fit me, you know." But however Mr. Oakhurst might hide his shapely limbs in homespun and homemade garments, there was something in his carriage, something in the pose of his beautiful head, something in the strong and fine manliness of his presence, something in the perfect and utter discipline and control of his muscles, something in the high repose of his nature—a repose not so much a matter of intellectual ruling as of his very nature—that go where he would, and with whom, he was always a notable man in ten thousand. Perhaps this was never so clearly intimated to Mr. Oakhurst as when, emboldened by Mr. Hamilton's advice and assistance and his predilections, he became a San Francisco broker. Even before objection was made to his presence in the Board—the objection, I remember, was urged very eloquently by Watt Sanders, who was supposed to be the inventor of the "freezing out" system of disposing of poor stockholders, and who also enjoyed the reputation of having been the impelling cause of Briggs of Tuolumne's ruin and suicide—even before this formal protest of respectability against lawlessness, the aquiline suggestions of Mr. Oakhurst's mien and countenance not only prematurely fluttered the pigeons, but absolutely occasioned much uneasiness among the fish hawks, who circled below him with their booty. "Dash me! but he's as likely to go after us as anybody," said Joe Fielding.

It wanted but a few days before the close of the brief summer season at San Isabel Warm Springs. Already there had been some migration of the more fashionable, and there was an uncomfortable suggestion of dregs and lees in the social life that remained. Mr. Oakhurst was moody; it was hinted that even the secure reputation of Mrs. Decker could no longer protect her from the gossip which his presence excited. It is but fair to her to say that during the last few weeks of this trying ordeal she looked like a sweet, pale martyr, and conducted herself toward her traducers with the gentle, forgiving manner of one who relied not upon the idle homage of the crowd, but upon the security of a principle that was dearer than popular favor. "They talk about myself and Mr. Oakhurst, my dear," she said to a friend, "but Heaven and my husband can best answer their calumny. It never shall be said that my husband ever turned his back upon a friend in the moment of his adversity because the position was changed, because his friend was poor and he was rich." This was the first intimation to the public that Jack had lost money, although it was known generally that the Deckers had lately bought some valuable property in San Francisco.

A few evenings after this an incident occurred which seemed to unpleasantly discord with the general social harmony that had always existed at San Isabel. It was at dinner, and Mr. Oakhurst and Mr. Hamilton, who sat together at a separate table, were observed to rise in some agitation. When they reached the hall, by a common instinct they stepped into a little breakfast-room which was vacant, and closed the door. Then Mr. Hamilton turned, with a half-amused, half-serious smile, toward his friend, and said—

"If we are to quarrel, Jack Oakhurst—you and I—in the name of all that is ridiculous, don't let it be about a—"

I do not know what was the epithet intended. It was either unspoken or lost. For at that very instant Mr. Oakhurst raised a wine glass and dashed its contents into Hamilton's face.

As they faced each other the men seemed to have changed natures. Mr. Oakhurst was trembling with excitement, and the wine glass that he returned to the table shivered between his fingers. Mr. Hamilton stood there, grayish white, erect, and dripping. After a pause he said coldly—

"So be it. But remember! our quarrel commences here. If I fall by your hand, you shall not use it to clear her character; if you fall by mine, you shall not be called a martyr. I am sorry it has come to this, but amen!— the sooner now the better."

He turned proudly, dropped his lids over his cold steel-blue eyes, as if sheathing a rapier, bowed, and passed coldly out.

They met twelve hours later in a little hollow two miles from the hotel, on the Stockton road. As Mr. Oakhurst received his pistol from Colonel Starbottle's hands he said to him in a low voice, "Whatever turns up or down I shall not return to the hotel. You will find some directions in my room. Go there—" but his voice suddenly faltered, and he turned his glistening eyes away, to his second's intense astonishment. "I've been out a dozen times with Jack Oakhurst," said Colonel Starbottle afterwards, "and I never saw him anyways cut before. Blank me if I didn't think he was losing his sand, till he walked to position."

The two reports were almost simultaneous. Mr. Oakhurst's right arm dropped suddenly to his side, and his pistol would have fallen from his paralyzed fingers, but the discipline of trained nerve and muscle prevailed, and he kept his grasp until he had shifted it to the other hand, without changing his position. Then there was a silence that seemed interminable, a gathering of two or three dark figures where a smoke curl still lazily floated, and then the hurried, husky, panting voice of Colonel Starbottle in his ear, "He's hit hard—through the lungs—you must run for it!"

Jack turned his dark, questioning eyes upon his second, but did not seem to listen; rather seemed to hear some other voice, remoter in the distance. He hesitated, and then made a step forward in the direction of the distant group. Then he paused again as the figures separated, and the surgeon came hastily toward him.

"He would like to speak with you a moment," said the man. "You have little time to lose, I know; but," he added in a lower voice, "it is my duty to tell you he has still less."

A look of despair so hopeless in its intensity swept over Mr. Oakhurst's usually impassive face that the surgeon started. "You are hit," he said, glancing at Jack's helpless arm.

"Nothing—a mere scratch," said Jack hastily. Then he added, with a bitter laugh, "I'm not in luck today. But come! We'll see what he wants."

His long feverish stride outstripped the surgeon's, and in another moment he stood where the dying man lay—like most dying men—the one calm, composed, central figure of an anxious group. Mr. Oakhurst's face was less calm as he dropped on one knee beside him and took his hand. "I want to speak with this gentleman alone," said Hamilton, with something of his old imperious manner, as he turned to those about him. When they drew back, he looked up in Oakhurst's face.

"I've something to tell you, Jack."

His own face was white, but not so white as that which Mr. Oakhurst bent over him—a face so ghastly, with haunting doubts and a hopeless presentiment of coming evil, a face so piteous in its infinite weariness and envy of death, that the dying man was touched, even in the languor of dissolution, with a pang of compassion, and the cynical smile faded from his lips.

"Forgive me, Jack," he whispered more feebly, "for what I have to say. I don't say it in anger, but only because it must be said. I could not do my duty to you—I could not die contented until you knew it all. It's a miserable business at best, all around. But it can't be helped now. Only I ought to have fallen by Decker's pistol and not yours."

A flush like fire came into Jack's cheek, and he would have risen, but Hamilton held him fast.

"Listen! in my pocket you will find two letters. Take them—there! You will know the handwriting. But promise you will not read them until you are in a place of safety. Promise me!"

Jack did not speak, but held the letters between his fingers as if they had been burning coals.

"Promise me," said Hamilton faintly.

"Why?" asked Oakhurst, dropping his friend's hand coldly.

"Because," said the dying man with a bitter smile—"because—when you have read them—you—will—go back—to capture—and death!"

They were his last words. He pressed Jack's hand faintly. Then his grasp relaxed, and he fell back a corpse.

It was nearly ten o'clock at night, and Mrs. Decker reclined languidly upon the sofa with a novel in her hand, while her husband discussed the politics of the country in the barroom of the hotel. It was a warm night, and the French window looking out upon a little balcony was partly open. Suddenly she heard a foot upon the balcony, and she raised her eyes from the book with a slight start. The next moment the window was hurriedly thrust wide and a man entered.

Mrs. Decker rose to her feet with a little cry of alarm.

"For Heaven's sake, Jack, are you mad? He has only gone for a little while—he may return at any moment. Come an hour later—tomorrow— any time when I can get rid of him—but go, now, dear, at once."

Mr. Oakhurst walked toward the door, bolted it, and then faced her without a word. His face was haggard, his coat sleeve hung loosely over an arm that was bandaged and bloody.

Nevertheless, her voice did not falter as she turned again toward him. "What has happened, Jack? Why are you here?"

He opened his coat, and threw two letters in her lap.

"To return your lover's letters—to kill you—and then myself," he said in a voice so low as to be almost inaudible.

Among the many virtues of this admirable woman was invincible courage. She did not faint, she did not cry out. She sat quietly down again, folded her hands in her lap, and said calmly—

"And why should you not?"

Had she recoiled, had she shown any fear or contrition, had she essayed an explanation or apology, Mr. Oakhurst would have looked upon it as an evidence of guilt. But there is no quality that courage recognizes so quickly as courage, there is no condition that desperation bows before but desperation; and Mr. Oakhurst's power of analysis was not so keen as to prevent him from confounding her courage with a moral quality. Even in his fury he could not help admiring this dauntless invalid.

"Why should you not?" she repeated with a smile. "You gave me life, health, and happiness, Jack. You gave me your love. Why should you not take what you have given? Go on. I am ready."

She held out her hands with that same infinite grace of yielding with which she had taken his own on the first day of their meeting at the hotel. Jack raised his head, looked at her for one wild moment, dropped upon his knees beside her, and raised the folds of her dress to his feverish lips. But she was too clever not to instantly see her victory; she was too much of a woman, with all her cleverness, to refrain from pressing that victory home. At the same moment, as with the impulse of an outraged and wounded woman, she rose, and with an imperious gesture pointed to the window. Mr. Oakhurst rose in his turn, cast one glance upon her, and without another word passed out of her presence forever.

When he had gone, she closed the window and bolted it, and going to the chimney piece placed the letters, one by one, in the flame of the candle until they were consumed. I would not have the reader think that during this painful operation she was unmoved. Her hand trembled and —not being a brute—for some minutes (perhaps longer) she felt very badly, and the corners of her sensitive mouth were depressed. When her husband arrived it was with a genuine joy that she ran to him, and nestled against his broad breast with a feeling of security that thrilled the honest fellow to the core.

"But I've heard dreadful news tonight, Elsie," said Mr. Decker, after a few endearments were exchanged.

"Don't tell me anything dreadful, dear; I'm not well tonight," she pleaded sweetly.

"But it's about Mr. Oakhurst and Hamilton."

"Please!" Mr. Decker could not resist the petitionary grace of those white hands and that sensitive mouth, and took her to his arms. Suddenly he said, "What's that?"

He was pointing to the bosom of her white dress. Where Mr. Oakhurst had touched her there was a spot of blood.

It was nothing; she had slightly cut her hand in closing the window; it shut so hard! If Mr. Decker had remembered to close and bolt the shutter before he went out, he might have saved her this. There was such a genuine irritability and force in this remark that Mr. Decker was quite overcome by remorse. But Mrs. Decker forgave him with that graciousness which I have before pointed out in these pages, and with the halo of that forgiveness and marital confidence still lingering above the pair, with the reader's permission we will leave them and return to Mr. Oakhurst.

But not for two weeks. At the end of that time he walked into his rooms in Sacramento, and in his old manner took his seat at the faro table.

"How's your arm, Jack?" asked an incautious player.

There was a smile followed the question, which, however, ceased as Jack looked up quietly at the speaker.

"It bothers my dealing a little, but I can shoot as well with my left."

The game was continued in that decorous silence which usually distinguished the table at which Mr. John Oakhurst presided.

Dashiell Hammett

In the Morgue

SAMUEL DASHIELL HAMMETT (1894–1961), *America's greatest writer of "hardboiled" detective fiction, completed six unforgettable novels* (Red Harvest, The Dain Curse, The Maltese Falcon, The Glass Key, The Thin Man, Blood Money) *and several volumes of tough, realistic shorter tales. "In the Morgue," an early, little-known short-short story, was collected in a posthumous volume of Hammett's fiction,* A Man Named Thin.

WALTER DOWE took the last sheet of the manuscript from his typewriter with a satisfied sigh and leaned back in his chair, turning his face to the ceiling to ease the stiffened muscles of his neck. Then he looked at the clock: 3:15 A.M. He yawned, got to his feet, switched off the lights, and went down the hall to his bedroom.

In the doorway of the bedroom he halted abruptly. The moonlight came through the wide windows to illuminate an empty bed. He turned on the lights and looked around the room. None of the things his wife had worn that night were there. She had not undressed, then; perhaps she had heard the rattle of his typewriter and had decided to wait downstairs until he had finished. She never interrupted him when he was at work, and he was usually too engrossed by his labors to hear her footsteps when she passed his study door.

He went to the head of the stairs and called: "Althea!"

No answer.

He went downstairs, into all the rooms, turning on the lights; he returned to the second floor and did the same. His wife was not in the house. He was perplexed, and a little helpless. Then he remembered that she had gone to the theatre with the Schuylers. His hands trembled as he picked up the telephone.

The Schuylers' maid answered his call. . . . There had been a fire at the Majestic Theatre; neither Mr. nor Mrs. Schuyler had come home. Mr. Schuyler's father had gone out to look for them, but had not returned yet. The maid understood that the fire had been pretty bad. . . .

Dowe was waiting on the sidewalk when the taxicab for which he had telephoned arrived. Fifteen minutes later he was struggling to get through the fire lines, which were still drawn about the theatre. A perspiring, red-faced policeman thrust him back.

"You'll find nothing here. The building's been cleared. Everybody's been taken to the hospitals."

Dowe found his cab again and was driven to the City Hospital. He forced his way through the clamoring group on the gray stone steps. A policeman blocked the door. Presently a pasty-faced man, in solid white, spoke over the policeman's shoulder:

"There's no use waiting. We're too busy treating them now to either take their names or let anybody in to see them. We'll try to have a list in the late morning edition; but we can't let anybody in until later in the day."

Dowe turned away. Then he thought: Murray Bornis, of course! He went back to the cab and gave the driver Bornis's address.

Bornis came to the door of his apartment in pajamas. Dowe clung to him.

"Althea went to the Majestic tonight and hasn't come home. They wouldn't let me in at the hospital. Told me to wait—but I can't! You're the police commissioner—you can get me in!"

While Bornis dressed, Dowe paced the floor, babbling. Then he caught a glimpse of himself in a mirror, and stood suddenly still. The sight of his distorted face and wild eyes shocked him back into sanity. He was on the verge of hysterics. He must take hold of himself. He must not collapse before he found Althea.

Deliberately, he made himself sit down, made himself stop visualizing Althea's soft, white body charred and crushed. He must think about something else: Bornis, for instance. . . .

But that brought him back to his wife in the end. She had never liked Bornis. His frank sensuality, and his unsavory reputation for numerous affairs with numerous women, had offended her strict conception of morality. To be sure, she had always given him all the courtesy due her husband's friend; but it was generally a frigid giving. And Bornis, understanding her attitude, and perhaps a little contemptuous of her narrow views, had been as coolly polite as she. And now she was lying somewhere, moaning in agony, perhaps already cold. . . .

Bornis finished dressing and they went quickly to the City Hospital, where the police commissioner and his companion were readily admitted. They walked down long rooms, between rows of groaning and writhing bodies, looking into bruised and burned faces, seeing no one they knew. Then to Mercy Hospital where they found Sylvia Schuyler. She told them that the crush in the theatre had separated her from her husband and Althea, and she had not seen them afterward. Then she lapsed into unconsciousness again.

When they got back to the cab, Bornis gave directions to the driver in an undertone, but Dowe did not have to hear them to know what they were: "To the morgue." There was no other place to go.

Now they walked between rows of bodies that were mangled horribly. Dowe had exhausted his feelings: he felt no pity, no loathing, now. He looked into a face; it was not Althea's; then it was nothing; he passed on to the next.

Bornis's fingers closed convulsively around Dowe's arm.

"There! Althea!"

Dowe turned. A face that stampeding leather heels had robbed of features; a torso that was battered and blackened and cut, and from which the clothing had been torn. All that was human of it were the legs; they had somehow escaped disfigurement.

"No, no!" Dowe cried.

He would not believe this begrimed, mangled thing was exquisite white Althea!

Through the horror that for the moment shut Dowe off from the world, Bornis's vibrant, anguished voice penetrated—it was almost a shriek:

"I tell you it is!" Flinging out a hand to point at one smooth knee. "See! The dimple!"

Thomas D. Sadler

Himeros's Daughter

THOMAS D. SADLER *lives with his wife, four children, a dog, a cat, a goldfish and a parakeet in a small Michigan city some sixty miles south of Detroit. A science-fantasy fan for more than three decades, he began writing it during the past five and has been published in several periodicals, including Beyond,* Marion Zimmer Bradley's Fantasy Magazine, Minnesota Fantasy Review, Starsong *and several others. His comic tale of sorcery, "Fat Chance," appeared in my earlier anthology,* Witches & Warlocks.

AS BRAD PHILLIPS fumbled with his keys he became aware of loud noises coming from the apartment next to his. Someone had moved in while he was at work. "It's about time," he thought as he opened the door. The building needed a few more tenants to make it seem less lonely and empty.

Brad set a sack of groceries on a kitchen counter and listened to the muffled sounds next door. Maybe it'll be some good-looking young woman. That would really be great. This place really needed someone like that. As he put things away, he realized there were few opportunities to make friends.

Brad broke off his thoughts and took a can of coffee from the refrigerator to brew a fresh potful. Might as well not worry about who could be moving in next door, he decided. Most people these days weren't willing to be friendly and usually seemed to avoid contact with others.

He looked up, startled, at a loud thump from next door. *What the hell is going on over there?* It sounded as if the person were trying to knock a hole in the wall. When he heard no other ominous loud noises, Brad went on preparing for his date that evening with Shirley Becker.

Shirley Becker. He'd been trying for months to get a date with her with no success, and now she would be coming over. He had big plans for a long, pleasant night. Brad smiled in anticipation as he headed to the bathroom to prepare for the evening.

Half an hour later, just as he stepped out of the shower, the phone rang. Annoyed and dripping wet, he answered. His date was at the other end, apologizing profusely for having to break her date with him. Although she sounded sincerely sorry and upset about it, he still felt angry and hurt but he tried not to show it. It was the third time she'd broken a date. She promised to call him the next day and set up a new date. He thanked her for calling and disgustedly hung up.

Brad looked at the wall clock. Seven P.M. Great. What could he do now? Have a thrilling evening in front of the television? That was a hell of a way to spend a Friday night. Maybe he'd go out someplace and have a few drinks, maybe get lucky and pick up some woman. He knew if he did she wouldn't be anywhere as good as Shirley Becker. Right now, he didn't give a damn.

He stormed into his bedroom, finished toweling off and got dressed. The hell with it, and to hell with Shirley Becker. He owed himself a night out and he was going to have it. Brad grabbed a jacket on his way through the living room and headed for the door. Just as he put his hand on the knob, someone knocked.

Brad yanked the door open. A tall, slender woman dressed in grey slacks and a loose, long-sleeved blouse open at the throat looked back at him. Her long black hair framed a face with high cheekbones and a pointed chin. She had a sepulchral look about her that Brad found incredibly attractive. He held onto the doorknob and stared into a pair of eyes a darker green than the ocean and so deep he almost felt as if he were falling into them. The woman smiled and Brad fought the compulsion to lean forward and kiss her perfect lips.

"Hello," the woman said with a Tallulah Bankhead voice that made Brad tremble. "My name is Lilia Moulasska. I just moved in next door and I was wondering if you could spare the time to help me with something. If you aren't too busy, that is."

"Busy? Me? Uh—no. I was just going out for dinner and a couple of drinks."

"Oh. If you'll lend me a hand I'll fix you a nice big dinner for your trouble. Better than anything you could get in some restaurant. How does that sound?" Lilia smiled again, seductively, and moved her body suggestively.

"I guess I could spare the time. Yeah. Sure." Brad stepped into the hall and shut and locked the door. He followed Lilia the few steps to her apartment, appreciating the lithe way she moved and the perfect pear shape of her derriere. She was all woman, and he felt desire for her rising inside him.

"Uh—where are you from originally?" Brad asked, trying to get his mind on more practical matters.

"Out East," she replied vaguely swaying her hips.

Lilia led him into a dimly lit, sparsely furnished room where a low couch and a chair covered in earth-tone fabric sat on a bare wooden floor. In the center of the room lay a small Persian carpet with a mystical design on it of shooting stars and a crescent moon. The only light came from a pair of jug-shaped lamps sitting on short tables with clawed, animallike legs. Brad noticed with curiosity there were no pictures or any other decorations hung on the walls. Even more curious was the absence of a television or stereo. Lilia must be a very strange woman, he decided.

"Please excuse the way the place looks," Lilia said. "I fear it will take a while for me to get settled in. The thing I need your help with is right in here." She headed for her bedroom. His heart hammering away, Brad followed, his mind filled with lustful thoughts.

Lilia pointed to a tall, intricately carved wardrobe composed of some dark shiny wood. "The moving men brought it in here and left it right there. They were very rude about it." Her face clouded over and the sight made Brad uncomfortable. "I tried to move it myself but it's just a little too heavy. Do you think you could help me slide it to that wall over there?"

"Sure. It can't be that heavy." Brad strode up to the wardrobe and grabbed hold of one side, moved it experimentally, and grunted in surprise. "I guess it does weigh more than I thought. But I think we can manage."

Lilia smiled and took hold of the other side. Together they carefully slid the wardrobe across the bare floor. Once they had it in place, Brad took out a handkerchief and wiped the sweat off his face. He couldn't help but notice Lilia hadn't perspired at all and that filled him with nervous curiosity.

"Thank you so very much," Lilia said. With a smooth, supple motion she came up to Brad and kissed his cheek, one hand resting on his chest and the other lightly brushing his crotch. His face grew hot and he wanted to take her in his arms.

"This just isn't right." Brad said, pulling back. "I mean, you don't even know me. I could be a rapist."

"Are you? Somehow I doubt it. But perhaps I'm not what you think. I could be something beyond your experience."

"Like what? The Devil in disguise, maybe?"

"The Devil!" Lilia laughed and pressed close to Brad. "How foolish. Do you think all mysterious things are the Devil's work?" She placed a finger to his lips. "Now, as I promised, I will fix you a nice dinner." She took his hand and led him back to the living room.

"Make yourself comfortable—I'm sorry, I didn't get your name . . ."

"It's Brad Phillips. You don't really have to do that. It was my pleasure to help you."

"I insist. After all, I'm new here and I'd like to make as many friends as I can. Sit down. Relax. After dinner we can become better acquainted." Lilia smiled again in a way that made Brad forget about everything else. She ran her hand down his arm and undid two buttons on her blouse to reveal a hint of bare breasts beneath.

Brad licked his lips and sat down at one end of the couch. Lilia swept her hair back and glided into the kitchen, humming some strange, soft tune.

While she busied herself with dinner, Brad looked around the room again. He still couldn't get over the paucity of furnishings and suspected this was all she had despite her claims. Brad leaned back against the couch and let himself relax. This place felt peaceful and quiet, almost as if he were in another world. A person could get used to a place like this, Brad decided, in spite of its scarcity of furnishings.

After a moment he looked at the lamp table closest to him. Seen this close up, with its carved legs and feet, the table looked like some animal crouching in a corner waiting for an unsuspecting prey. Brad shivered and started to look away but caught himself when it looked as if the table had moved. He blinked and stared at it. No. It looked exactly the same.

"That's really dumb, Brad," he whispered. "Imagining a table moving by itself. You sure come up with some strange ideas." He sat up straight and concentrated on the sounds of Lilia in the kitchen.

"Dinner is ready," she called a few minutes later. "Come and get it."

Brad jumped up from the couch and hurriedly strode to the next room. He glanced back at the table and could have sworn it moved again as if it were keeping track of him. Shaking his head roughly, he looked around the kitchen, which was as dimly lit as the other room had been. To his surprise it looked no different from any other kitchen he'd ever seen.

Lilia pointed to a chair with a spoon. Brad sat down to a plate heaped with spaghetti and meat sauce. A glass of wine and a cup of steaming black coffee sat next to the plate.

"I don't know how you like your coffee, Brad. There are cream and sugar if you use them."

"Black will be fine. You really didn't have to go to all this trouble. The coffee would have been plenty."

"It's my pleasure." Lilia carried a plate to the table and sat down across from him. Her blouse had been unbuttoned almost completely and her firm, full breasts were almost completely revealed. Brad tried to concentrate on the food but found it nearly impossible. Nervously he picked up the wine and drank half of it straight away in spite of its unexpected strength. When he set the glass down, he saw Lilia watching him, a wicked, mischievous smile on her face.

"Do I embarrass you, Brad? Don't you find me attractive?"

"Yes. Incredibly so. But . . ." Forcing himself to look down, he picked up his cup and sipped the coffee. It was strong and slightly bitter but tasted good.

"But you don't know anything about me. Since you insist on knowing, I'll tell you. I am a Numina. That doesn't mean a—" She was interrupted by a long, low growling sound from the next room.

"Excuse me." Lilia abruptly stood and nearly ran from the room.

Brad took another sip of coffee and listened closely for any other sounds. He thought he heard Lilia speaking harshly to someone in the next room and wondered who it could be. The growling continued for a few seconds, then broke off. Thinking it over, Brad decided she had a guard dog that she'd shut into her bathroom. He felt better with that thought, even though the growling hadn't sounded quite like a dog's.

"Please excuse the disturbance," Lilia said as she entered the kitchen. "I have a—pet. It occasionally becomes scared and nervous."

"A pet? I didn't think pets were allowed in the building."

"What they don't know won't hurt them." Lilia came up to where Brad sat and leaned over close to him, one of her breasts becoming fully exposed. "How is the coffee?"

"It's fine." Brad stared at her breast, fighting the desire to reach out and touch it. "A little strong. But good just the same."

"I'm glad you like it. Some people can't stand strong coffee." Lilia stroked her breast and ran a finger in circles around the nipple. Brad watched in fascination as it hardened, and licked his lips nervously.

"When you're finished with dinner we'll go back to the living room and get closer. Would you like that?"

"Uh, yeah. That would be—uh—great. Oh hell. I'm not a rapist but I want you so much I can't stand it. If you don't watch it I may not be able to control myself." Brad gripped the cup tightly, then stood up and stumbled to the kitchen sink.

"I'm not the least bit afraid." Lilia followed and took the cup from his hand. "We're both grown up. You won't do anything I don't want you to." She stared at him with her huge green eyes and stroked his temples with soft fingers.

Brad concentrated on her haunting eyes, looking deeply into them. She placed her hands on the sides of his head and diverted his gaze downward to her inviting breasts. Numbly, he stared at them as she slipped her blouse off and began stroking her nipples, which were huge and hard. He started to lean down to kiss one of them but she held him back.

"Not yet. Not here. Soon. Come with me." Lilia took Brad's hand.

Deep inside, he realized he'd lost all his willpower and he didn't care. All he wanted was to take this strange woman and make love to her until every bit of his passion was spent. He wanted to explore her body and make it his personal territory.

Brad expected Lilia to take him directly into her bedroom but she stopped in the living room. He looked around in puzzlement. The room had changed. The couch had been pushed back against the wall, one of the tables stood in front of the entrance, the other in front of the bedroom door. A thick white blanket covered the carpet and several cushions lay atop the blanket.

"Wh-what's going on?" Brad asked. His tongue felt huge and thick and the room felt as if it were slowly spinning.

"You'll know soon enough, my love." Lilia removed her slacks and revealed a lower torso covered with fine, silky hair.

Brad stared at her in horror, then turned and stumbled toward the door. The table transformed itself into a squat, scaly beast which lunged at him with a huge mouth filled with long sharp teeth. He screamed hoarsely and backed away toward the kitchen. The creature remained in its place.

"Don't be frightened," Lilia said mockingly. "It's only one of my pets and will not harm you unless I tell it to." She seized Brad with incredible strength, and dragged him back to the center of the room. She quickly undressed him and pushed him to his knees. He cowered there unable to summon the strength or courage to move again.

"What are you?" he shouted.

"I told you before," Lilia said in a low, hoarse voice. "I was born in a haunted glade on a moon-drenched night ages before your Devil even became a thought in some poor fool's mind. Does it really matter? You want to make love to me and I want to have you."

She towered over him, her legs spread wide, and smiled cruelly. "You do want me, don't you?" Stroking her thighs, she moved her hips suggestively and held one breast out to him.

"Don't let my appearance bother you, my love. I can do all that any woman can do and more." She crouched down in front of him, brought his face close to hers, and kissed him roughly.

Her lips tasted like bitter wine but Brad found himself powerless to resist them. He returned the kiss with equal passion and darted his tongue into her mouth. They continued the kiss for a few seconds longer and Brad began eagerly fondling her breasts. Then he broke away and began kissing her right breast, running his tongue over the rough, hard nipple.

Without warning, Lilia rolled over until she lay atop Brad. She raised herself so she could look down and watch him kissing her breasts. Her face took on a feral look that Brad failed to notice in his consuming attention to her body.

At last she lowered herself on top of him and they made love with a wildness Brad had never known before. They reached their climax and fell apart, exhausted. Brad lay staring at the ceiling drenched in sweat, afraid to look at the strange creature next to him. He wanted to get out of there and run to the safety of his apartment but could not make his limbs respond.

After a few seconds, Lilia rose and crouched over him, her green eyes gleaming in the half light. Brad squeezed his eyes shut as she leaned down and kissed him full on the mouth.

"You are all mine now," she whispered. "We shall join together forever, you and I."

"No! Let me go. I want out of here." Brad felt her hot breath on his cheek and her hands moving up and down his body. "You're something evil aren't you, some kind of devil?"

"I'm no devil, my love. The devil you believe in is a young one. There are others far older, from the very beginnings of time. But what makes you think I'm evil just because I'm different?"

"I don't think . . ."

"Of course you don't think. You foolish mortals are all the same. But don't worry about it." Lilia kissed him again, long, hard, and fiercely. "For now there is just you and me. And all I want is to make love to you."

"But, I can't—"

"Silence!" Her voice snapped out like a slap. "You will do whatever I want you to."

Lilia began kissing him again. They made love again. And again. And again. The entire night passed in a succession of relentless lovemaking from which Brad found no escape. Near dawn she finally left him and went into the bathroom. Though exhausted and numbed with disbelief at what he had been through, Brad decided to escape. But the table again transformed itself into a beast that lunged at him, snarling, slavering, and snapping its massive jaws.

Brad desperately fought to get past it but the monstrosity blocked the door and gnashed its teeth at him. Cursing, he tried to think of another way out. The bedroom window! That was the only other way. He would smash it out. But the apartment was twenty floors up and he would probably slip and fall to his death.

"No," he told himself. "That would be better than what I'm going through now."

Not bothering to get his clothes, Brad ran to the bedroom. The other table stood in his way and it, too, had come to life, the twin of the beast at the front door. It drove him back toward the center of the room and stopped as he fell to his knees hurling curses at it.

After a few minutes, Lilia returned from the bathroom and looked down at him with a slight smile on her face.

"Don't overestimate your worth, Brad Phillips. You are only one of a thousand lovers and mean no more to me than a lamp or a chair. You serve a purpose, but if you fail me, you *will* be gone. I'll give you to my pets, and when they're finished there will be no more Brad Phillips. Do you understand?"

Brad nodded mutely as he knelt in the center of the room, feeling small, helpless, and alone. Lilia crouched in front of him and ran her skilled fingers over his trembling body, arousing him to passion once again.

"Very good. Now, come to me and we will make love again until you and I are one and your strength and essence becomes mine. Then we will be together forever."

Lilia unlocked the huge old wardrobe in her bedroom and flung wide the doors. Inside, like suits of clothes, hung the remains of Brad Phillips and half a dozen other past lovers. She touched each lifeless form briefly and lovingly, recalling the pleasure they had brought her.

At last she reluctantly shut and locked the wardrobe and effortlessly pulled it away from the wall to the center of the room. Everything was almost ready. She undid the top two buttons of her filmy blouse as she glided from the room. A new tenant had just moved in next door, and she wanted to check him out.

Josef Marais

A-round the Corner

In 1950, vocalist Jo Stafford recorded "A-round the Corner," a perky little song about a minor tiff between rustic lovers. Soon afterward on TV, I listened to the husband-wife folksinging duo, Marais and Miranda, sing the same song—but with a startlingly different set of lyrics. Marcel Demiranda, their son and head of Sideree Music Co., Los Angeles, recently told me that what I heard was the original version. His father, who wrote "A-round the Corner," understandably watered it down for Ms. Stafford.

A-round the corner, oo-oo, beneath the berry tree,
Along the footpath, beneath the bush looking for Emily.

Tonight all the folks will cut the corn (cut the corn)
Tonight I'll be glad that I was born (I was born)
And my sickle pleases me as I swing it lustily
But I wonder where my Emily can be.
A-round the corner, oo-oo, beneath the berry tree,
Along the footpath, beneath the bush looking for Emily.

Tonight I have stopped my reaping soon (reaping soon)
Tonight there's a smiling happy moon (happy moon)
I have reached the meeting spot, but my Emily is not
Where she promised. Can it be that she forgot?
A-round the corner, oo-oo, beneath the berry tree,
Along the footpath, beneath the bush looking for Emily.

Tonight as the moon begins to sink (begins to sink)
Tonight there are footsteps which I think (which I think)
Will at last bring her to me, that young maiden, Emily,
And I wonder why so late she has to be!
A-round the corner, oo-oo, beneath the berry tree,
Along the footpath, beneath the bush looking for Emily.

"Oh, Emily, why did you make me wait?" (make me wait)
"I'm late 'cause I had another date." (another date)
It was plain for me to see, she'd been keeping company
With another man beneath another tree.
A-round the corner, oo-oo, beneath the berry tree,
Along the footpath, beneath the bush looking for Emily.

Tonight all the folks will cut the corn (cut the corn)
Tonight I am sad and so forlorn (so forlorn)
For my Emily was fickle, so I used my sharp old sickle
And the blood beneath the berry tree does trickle!
A-round the corner, oo-oo, beneath the berry tree,
Along the footpath, beneath the bush looking for Emily.

Mary Higgins Clark

Voices in the Coalbin

MARY HIGGINS CLARK, *best-selling author of such rivetingly suspenseful books as* A Stranger Is Watching, Stillwatch, A Cry in the Night, Where Are the Children?, The Cradle Will Fall, While My Pretty One Sleeps, *etc., occasionally flirts with the supernatural. The following shivery little chiller was first published in the Berkley Books collection* Sisters in Crime.

IT WAS DARK when they arrived. Mike steered the car off the dirt road down the long driveway and stopped in front of the cottage. The real estate agent had promised to have the heat turned up and the lights on. She obviously didn't believe in wasting electricity.

An insect-repellent bulb over the door emitted a bleak yellowish beam that trembled in the steady drizzle. The small-paned windows were barely outlined by a faint flicker of light that seeped through a partially open blind.

Mike stretched. Fourteen hours a day of driving for the past three days had cramped his long, muscular body. He brushed back his dark brown hair from his forehead, wishing he'd taken time to get a haircut before they left New York. Laurie teased him when his hair started to grow. "You look like a thirty-year-old Roman emperor, Curlytop," she would comment. "All you need is a toga and a laurel wreath to complete the effect."

She had fallen asleep about an hour ago. Her head was resting on his lap. He glanced down at her, hating to wake her up. Even though he could barely make out her profile, he knew that in sleep the tense lines vanished from around her mouth and the panic-stricken expression disappeared from her face.

Four months ago the recurring nightmare had begun, the nightmare that made her shriek, *"No, I won't go with you. I won't sing with you."* He'd shake her awake. "It's all right, sweetheart. It's all right."

Her screams would fade into terrified sobs. "I don't know who they are but they want me, Mike. I can't see their faces but they're all huddled together beckoning to me."

He had taken her to a psychiatrist, who put her on medication and began intensive therapy. But the nightmares continued, unabated. They had turned a gifted twenty-four-year-old singer who had just completed a run as a soloist in her first Broadway musical to a trembling wraith who could not be alone after dark.

The psychiatrist had suggested a vacation. Mike told him about the summers he'd spent at his grandmother's house on Oshbee Lake forty miles from Milwaukee. "My grandmother died last September," he'd explained. "The house is up for sale. Laurie's never been there and she loves the water."

The doctor had approved. "But be careful of her," he warned. "She's severely depressed. I'm sure these nightmares are a reaction to her childhood experiences, but they're overwhelming her."

Laurie had eagerly endorsed the chance to go away. Mike was a junior partner in his father's law firm. "Anything that will help Laurie," his father told him. "Take whatever time you need."

I remember brightness here, Mike thought as he studied the shadow-filled cottage with increasing dismay. I remember the feel of the water when I dove in, the warmth of the sun on my face, the way the breeze filled the sails and the boat skimmed across the lake.

It was the end of June but it might have been early March. According to the radio, the cold spell had been gripping Wisconsin for three days. There'd better be enough coal to get the furnace going, Mike thought, or else that real estate agent will lose the listing.

He had to wake up Laurie. It would be worse to leave her alone in the car, even for a minute. "We're here, love," he said, his voice falsely cheerful.

Laurie stirred. He felt her stiffen, then relax as he tightened his arms around her. "It's so dark," she whispered.

"We'll get inside and turn some lights on."

He remembered how the lock had always been tricky. You had to pull the door to you before the key could fit into the cylinder. There was a night-light plugged into an outlet in the small foyer. The house was not warm but neither was it the bone-chilling cold he had feared.

Quickly Mike switched on the hall light. The wallpaper with its climbing ivy pattern seemed faded and soiled. The house had been rented for the five summers his grandmother was in the nursing home. Mike remembered how clean and warm and welcoming it had been when she was living here.

Laurie's silence was ominous. His arm around her, he brought her into the living room. The overstuffed velour furniture that used to welcome his body when he settled in with a book was still in place but, like the wallpaper, seemed soiled and shabby.

Mike's forehead furrowed into a troubled frown. "Honey, I'm sorry. Coming here was a lousy idea. Do you want to go to a motel? We passed a couple that looked pretty decent."

Laurie smiled up at him. "Mike, I want to stay here. I want you to share with me all those wonderful summers you spent in this place. I want to pretend your grandmother was mine. Then maybe I'll get over whatever is happening to me."

Laurie's grandmother had raised her. A fear-ridden neurotic, she had tried to instill in Laurie fear of the dark, fear of strangers, fear of planes and cars, fear of animals. When Laurie and Mike met two years ago, she'd shocked and amused him by reciting some of the litany of hair-raising stories that her grandmother had fed her on a daily basis. "How did you turn out so normal, so much fun?" Mike used to ask her.

"I was damned if I'd let her turn me into a certified nut." But the last four months had proved that Laurie had not escaped after all, that there was psychological damage that needed repairing.

Now Mike smiled down at her, loving the vivid sea-green eyes, the thick dark lashes that threw shadows on her porcelain skin, the way tendrils of chestnut hair framed her oval face. "You're so darn pretty," he said, "and sure I'll tell you all about Grandma. You only knew her when she was an invalid. I'll tell you about fishing with her in a storm, about jogging around the lake and her yelling for me to keep up the pace, about finally managing to outswim her when she was sixty."

Laurie took his face in her hands. "Help me to be like her."

Together they brought in their suitcases and the groceries they had purchased along the way. Mike went down to the basement. He grimaced when he glanced into the coalbin. It was fairly large, a four-feet-wide by six-feet-long plankboard enclosure situated next to the furnace and directly under the window that served as an opening for the chute from the delivery truck. Mike remembered how when he was eight he'd helped his grandmother replace some of the boards on the bin. Now they all looked rotted.

"Nights get cold even in the summer but we'll always be plenty warm, Mike," his grandmother would say cheerily as she let him help shovel coal into the old blackened furnace.

Mike remembered the bin as always heaped with shiny black nuggets. Now it was nearly empty. There was barely enough coal for two or three days. He reached for the shovel.

The furnace was still serviceable. Its rumbling sound quickly echoed throughout the house. The ducts thumped and rattled as hot air wheezed through them.

In the kitchen Laurie had unpacked the groceries and begun to make a salad. Mike grilled a steak. They opened a bottle of Bordeaux and ate side by side at the old enamel table, their shoulders companionably touching.

They were on their way up the staircase to bed when Mike spotted the note from the real estate agent on the foyer table: "Hope you find everything in order. Sorry about the weather. Coal delivery on Friday."

They decided to use his grandmother's room. "She loved that metal-frame bed," Mike said. "Always claimed that there wasn't a night she didn't sleep like a baby in it."

"Let's hope it works that way for me." Laurie sighed. There were clean sheets in the linen closet but they felt damp and clammy. The boxspring and mattress smelled musty. "Warm me up," Laurie whispered, shivering as they pulled the covers over them.

"My pleasure."

They fell asleep in each other's arms. At three o'clock Laurie began to shriek, a piercing, wailing scream that filled the house. "Go away. Go away. I won't. I won't."

It was dawn before she stopped sobbing. "They're getting closer," she told Mike. "They're getting closer."

The rain persisted throughout the day. The outside thermometer registered thirty-eight degrees. They read all morning curled up on the velour couches. Mike watched as Laurie began to unwind. When she fell into a deep sleep after lunch, he went into the kitchen and called the psychiatrist.

"Her sense that they're getting closer may be a good sign," the doctor told him. "Possibly she's on the verge of a breakthrough. I'm convinced the root of these nightmares is in all the old wives' tales her grandmother told Laurie. If we can isolate exactly which one has caused this fear, we'll be able to exorcise it and all the others. Watch her carefully, but remember. She's a strong girl and she wants to get well. That's half the battle."

When Laurie woke up, they decided to inventory the house. "Dad said we can have anything we want," Mike reminded her. "A couple of the tables are antiques and that clock on the mantle is a gem." There was a storage closet in the foyer. They began dragging its contents into the living room. Laurie, looking about eighteen in jeans and a sweater, her hair tied loosely in a chignon, became animated as she went through them. "The local artists were pretty lousy," she laughed, "but the frames are great. Can't you just see them on our walls?"

Last year as a wedding present, Mike's family had bought them a loft in Greenwich Village. Until four months ago, they'd spent their spare time going to garage sales and auctions looking for bargains. Since the nightmares began, Laurie had lost interest in furnishing the apartment. Mike crossed his fingers. Maybe she *was* starting to get better.

On the top shelf buried behind patchwork quilts he discovered a Victrola. "Oh, my God, I'd forgotten about that," he said. "What a find. Look. Here are a bunch of old records."

He did not notice Laurie's sudden silence as he brushed the layers of dust from the Victrola and lifted the lid. The Edison trademark, a dog listening to a tube and the caption *His Master's Voice*, was on the inside of the lid. "It even has a needle in it," Mike said. Quickly he placed a record on the turntable, cranked the handle, slid the starter to ON, and watched as the disk began to revolve. Carefully he placed the arm with its thin, delicate needle in the first groove.

The record was scratched. The singers' voices were male but high-pitched, almost to the point of falsetto. The effect was out of synch, music being played too rapidly. "I can't make out the words," Mike said. "Do you recognize it?"

"It's 'Chinatown,' " Laurie said. "Listen." She began to sing with the record, her lovely soprano voice leading the chorus. *Hearts that know no other world, drifting to and fro.* Her voice broke. Gasping, she screamed, *"Turn it off, Mike. Turn it off now!"* She covered her ears with her hands and sank onto her knees, her face deathly white.

Mike yanked the needle away from the record. "Honey, what is it?"

"I don't know. I just don't know."

•   •   •   •   •

That night the nightmare took a different form. This time the approaching figures were singing "Chinatown" and in falsetto voices demanding Laurie come sing with them.

At dawn they sat in the kitchen sipping coffee. "Mike, it's coming back to me," Laurie told him. "When I was little. My grandmother had one of those Victrolas. She had that same record. I asked her where the people were who were singing. I thought they had to be hiding in the house somewhere. She took me down to the basement and pointed to the coalbin. She said the voices were coming from there. She swore to me that the people who were singing were in the coalbin."

Mike put down his coffee cup. "Good God!"

"I never went down to the basement after that. I was afraid. Then we moved to an apartment and she gave the Victrola away. I guess that's why I forgot." Laurie's eyes began to blaze with hope. "Mike, maybe that old fear caught up with me for some reason. I was so exhausted by the time the show closed. Right after that the nightmares started. Mike, that record was made years and years ago. The singers are all probably dead by now. And I certainly have learned how sound is reproduced. Maybe it's going to be all right."

"You bet it's going to be all right." Mike stood up and reached for her hand. "You game for something? There's a coalbin downstairs. I want you to come down with me and look at it."

Laurie's eyes filled with panic, then she bit her lip. "Let's go," she said.

Mike studied Laurie's face as her eyes darted around the basement. Through her eyes he realized how dingy it was. The single light bulb dangling from the ceiling. The cinder-block walls glistening with dampness. The cement dust from the floor that clung to their bedroom slippers. The concrete steps that led to the set of metal doors that opened to the backyard. The rusty bolt that secured them looked as though it had not been opened in years.

The coalbin was adjacent to the furnace at the front end of the house. Mike felt Laurie's nails dig into his palm as they walked over to it.

"We're practically out of coal," he told her. "It's a good thing they're supposed to deliver today. Tell me, honey, what do you see here?"

"A bin. About ten shovelfuls of coal at best. A window. I remember when the delivery truck came how they put the chute through the window and the coal roared down. I used to wonder if it hurt the singers when it fell on them." Laurie tried to laugh. "No visible sign of anyone in residence here. Nightmares at rest, please God."

Hand in hand they went back upstairs. Laurie yawned. "I'm so tired, Mike. And you, poor guy, haven't had a decent night's rest in months because of me. Why don't we just go back to bed and sleep the day away. I bet anything that I won't wake up with a dream."

They drifted off to sleep, her head on his chest, his arms encircling her. "Sweet dreams, love," he whispered.

"I promise they will be. I love you, Mike. Thank you for everything."

The sound of coal rushing down the chute awakened Mike. He blinked. Behind the shades, light was streaming in. Automatically he glanced at his watch. Nearly three o'clock. God, he really must have been bushed. Laurie was already up. He pulled khaki slacks on, stuffed his feet into sneakers, listened for sounds from the bathroom. There were none. Laurie's robe and slippers were on the chair. She must be already dressed. With sudden unreasoning dread, Mike yanked a sweatshirt over his head.

The living room. The dining room. The kitchen. Their coffee cups were still on the table, the chairs pushed back as they left them. Mike's throat closed. The hurtling sound of the coal was lessening. *The coal.* Maybe. He took the cellar stairs two at a time. Coal dust was billowing through the basement. Shiny black nuggets of coal were heaped high in the bin. He heard the snap of the window being closed. He stared down at the footsteps on the floor. The imprints of his sneakers. The side-by-side impressions left when he and Laurie had come down this morning in their slippers.

And then he saw the step-by-step imprint of Laurie's bare feet, the lovely high arched impressions of her slender, fine-boned feet. The impressions stopped at the coalbin. There was no sign of them returning to the stairs.

The bell rang, the shrill, high-pitched, insistent gonglike sound that had always annoyed him and amused his grandmother. Mike raced up the stairs. Laurie. Let it be Laurie.

The truck driver had a bill in his hand. "Sign for the delivery, sir."

The delivery. Mike grabbed the man's arm. "When you started the coal down the chute, did you look into the bin?"

Puzzled faded blue eyes in a pleasant weather-beaten face looked squarely at him. "Yeah, sure, I glanced in to make sure how much you needed. You were just about out. You didn't have enough for the day. The rain's over but it's gonna stay real cold."

Mike tried to sound calm. "Would you have seen if someone was in the coalbin? I mean, it's dark in the basement. Would you have noticed if a slim young woman had maybe fainted in there?" He could read the deliveryman's mind. *He thinks I'm drunk or on drugs.* "God damn it," Mike shouted. "My wife is missing. My wife is missing."

For days they searched for Laurie. Feverishly, Mike searched with them. He walked every inch of the heavily wooded areas around the cottage. He sat, hunched and shivering, on the deck as they dragged the lake. He stood unbelieving as the newly delivered coal was shoveled from the bin and heaped onto the basement floor.

Surrounded by policemen, all of whose names and faces made no impression on him, he spoke with Laurie's doctor. In a flat, disbelieving tone he told the doctor about Laurie's fear of the voices in the coalbin. When he was finished, the police chief spoke to the doctor. When he hung up, he gripped Mike's shoulder. "We'll keep looking."

Four days later a diver found Laurie's body tangled in weeds in the lake. Death by drowning. She was wearing her nightgown. Bits of coal dust were still clinging to her skin and hair. The police chief tried and could not soften the stark tragedy of her death. "That was why her footsteps stopped at the bin. She must have gotten into it and climbed out the window. It's pretty wide, you know, and she was a slender girl. I've talked again to her doctor. She probably would have committed suicide before this if you hadn't been there for her. Terrible the way people screw up their children. Her doctor said that grandmother petrified her with crazy superstitions before the poor kid was old enough to toddle."

"She talked to me. She was getting there." Mike heard his protests, heard himself making arrangements for Laurie's body to be cremated.

The next morning as he was packing, the real estate agent came over, a sensibly dressed white-haired, thin-faced woman whose brisk air did not conceal the sympathy in her eyes. "We have a buyer for the house," she said. "I'll arrange to have anything you want to keep shipped."

The clock. The antique tables. The pictures that Laurie had laughed over in their beautiful frames. Mike tried to picture going into their Greenwich Village loft alone and could not.

"How about the Victrola?" the real estate agent asked. "It's a real treasure."

Mike had placed it back in the storage closet. Now he took it out, seeing again Laurie's terror, hearing her begin to sing "Chinatown," her voice blending with the falsetto voices on the old record. "I don't know if I want it," he said.

The real-estate agent looked disapproving. "It's a collector's item. I have to be off. Just let me know about it."

Mike watched as her car disappeared around the winding driveway. *Laurie, I want you.* He lifted the lid of the Victrola as he had five days ago, an eon ago. He cranked the handle, found the "Chinatown" record, placed it on the turntable, turned the switch to the on position. He watched as the record picked up speed, then released the arm and placed the needle in the starting groove.

"Chinatown, my Chinatown . . ."

Mike felt his body go cold. *No! No!* Unable to move, unable to breathe, he stared at the spinning record.

". . . hearts that know no other world drifting to and fro . . ."

Over the scratchy, falsetto voices of the long-ago singers, Laurie's exquisite soprano was filling the room with its heart-stopping, plaintive beauty.

Ray Bradbury

The Maiden

This short-short-short story comes from RAY BRADBURY'S *long-unavailable 1947 Arkham House collection,* Dark Carnival. *Though that volume was partially resurrected as* The October Country, *"The Maiden" was not included in its contents and has been out of print for more than forty years.*

SHE WAS WONDROUS FAIR. She filled his eyes and he looked at her continually and was in love with her. Tall she was, and beautiful, with the morning sun on her. Tall she was, and stately of limb, and she worked for him. He knew her every whim, he did. And he stroked and made love to her, but stayed out of her reach. He knew what she could do to men she loved too well.

Not today, he thought, you'll not have me today, maiden fair, maiden strong, maiden quick and maiden fatale.

Sometimes he would let the children play with her, but only when he was near to be certain they didn't fall into the bad habit of teasing her too far.

How many lovers had she had? No, that was wording it a bit strongly. She had few lovers, ever, but she loved *them.* Sadist that she was, she loved anyone she could get hold of.

And now this night he went up the steps to her and sat down beside her and rolled over against her and placed his weary head upon her shoulder and looked up at the sky, loving her, and seeing the long line of her face.

Then—he tripped the trigger.

Her long blue razor-sharp blade, weighing one hundred pounds, sliced down along the oiled grooves of the drop, straight at his throat—bamm!

—through—chopping off light, sound, odor, feeling, his head popped
into the waiting wicker, a sexual spout of red blood jutted from his sun-
dered neck; and the two of them, he and she of the blade, lay together in
that scarlet orgasm even as the first star appeared . . .

Wallace West

A Thing of Beauty

Between the years of 1927 and 1932, WALLACE WEST contributed six fantastic stories to Weird Tales, *but Farnsworth Wright, editor of The Unique Magazine, drew the line at "A Thing of Beauty." Wright reportedly thought it "too horrible," an odd reaction to an admittedly bizarre but essentially poignant love story. The tale finally saw print in 1963 in the first issue of editor Robert A. "Doc" Lowndes' now long-defunct* Magazine of Horror.

EACH WINTER DAY at dawn old John Short scurried along the snow-covered streets of Cloverdale enroute to open the drafts of the furnace which spread a little warmth through Medical College.

Milkmen and other early risers chuckled as they saw him limping past, whistling a lively tune or reciting snatches of poetry. The very sight of him, they said, brought them good luck that day.

But it was not the thought of poking into the bowels of the furnace or carting out the ashes which made the hunchback's lips pucker with the notes of "Only a Bird in a Gilded Cage" or roll out a Wordsworthian sonnet. It was the anticipation of his weazened face to beam like the not-yet-risen sun.

Short, you see, also was in charge of the brine vat in which floated the corpses kept for dissection by the students of Northern Med. For more years than Henry Wyndham, N.M.C's white-haired president, could remember, Old John had tended the "Stiff Room" when he was not nursing the furnace or bedeviling the school librarian for more books of poetry.

Every morning, as soon as the leaky radiators began clanking in the empty classrooms, Short would brush the ashes from his overalls, rub his

gnarled hands, and take from its corner a fifteen-foot pole with a hook on
the end. Then he would head for the brine vat, whistling as he went.

John's greeting to his charges had once been overheard by a student
who had come to school early to make up some back work, but had been
forced to seek the furnace room to warm his half-frozen hands and feet.

"I tell you, I heard him talking to those stiffs just as if they'd been
alive," the boy related afterward with a noticeable lack of that *sang froid*
upon which prospective doctors pride themselves.

"I was standing by the furnace when I heard him go by, dragging
something along the floor. I followed, thinking I'd play a joke on him.

"He reached the stiff room before I caught up. As he had left the door
open, I slipped inside with the idea of setting up a groan which would
scare the wits out of him."

The student stopped, rolled a cigarette with fingers which shook
slightly, lighted it on the third try, and inhaled mightily.

"Well, go on, Moony," suggested one of his cronies. "What happened
when you yowled?"

"I didn't yowl. . . . You know that gas jet with the evil purple globe
which sticks out over the vat? Well, Old John was standing so its beams
fell directly on his ugly mug. For a long time he just stood there, with his
long hairy arms on his crooked hips, laughing fit to kill. But he didn't
make a sound!

"Then he reached out with a long pole and hooked the end of it under
the armpit of one of the stiffs. . . ."

"Aw, cut it," snapped one of Moony's listeners. "I've just had lunch."

"Old John pulled the body up to the edge of the vat and turned it
'round so it faced him. Then he sat down on the edge of the pool and
swung his crooked legs back and forth.

" 'Mornin', Mike,' he said, friendly-like. 'Your skin's in the sere and
yellow leaf, but it's still nice and firm, ain't it? Can't say I don't take care
of you, can you, Mike boy?' "

"Well?" Moony's auditors had lost their grins. They pressed closer.

"Well, that stiff rolled back and forth in the little waves which John
had made dragging it in, and damned if it didn't seem half alive.

" 'Thought you were pretty fine when you worked in the blacksmith
shop, didn't you?' John went on as if he were talking to an old friend.
'Remember how proud you were of your big muscles—like iron bands,
didn't the poet say? Picked me up with one hand and laughed at my

crooked back once. Remember? Didn't think then you'd be hanged for murder and wind up in a brine vat talking to me, did you, Mike?'

"The old man seemed to listen as if for an answer," Moony continued. "Then he nodded cheerfully and reached out his pole. 'Sure I'll roll you over—roll you over slow,' he said. 'Course you don't want your face to get any blacker than it already is. Proud of your looks to the last, ain't you, Mike? Just wait till I send you to the dissecting room.'

"John laughed that silent laugh again. Then he flipped the big fellow over like a dead fish and reached for another corpse."

"What'd he say next, Moony?" someone inquired.

"I—I don't know. I felt kinda sick—the air down there always gets me, you know. I went upstairs."

After that the students tried teasing the janitor about his friends in the vat. But they didn't keep it up; for the first time they could remember, Short lost his good humor and snarled at them. From that time on he kept the stiff-room door locked, except when receiving a body or sending one to the operating table.

But the youngsters, killing time by telling horror stories between classes, insisted that Old John still held his morning conversations, twitting his charges about their fine physiques, jeering at their former intelligence and stations in life; boasting that he, with his broken body, had become their master in the end.

Short's idyllic life received a shock on the day that the body of Miss X was delivered to the college in accordance with the wish found in a scribbled note when police broke into a gas-filled room at the Cloverdale Hotel.

Beaming with delight, Old John received the corpse from the coroner, trundled it into the basement on a sort of wheelbarrow, and stripped off the winding sheet preparatory to pushing the nude body into his vat.

Then he stopped, his mouth forming a great O, his red-rimmed eyes popping. Before him was the most beautiful creature he had ever looked upon. Slim, long-limbed, and exquisite, lying as if she were only asleep, Miss X seemed to light up the dingy room.

John's ugly face was transformed. He ran his callused fingers through that halo of golden curls and touched the closed eyelids tenderly. Then, as he lifted the rigid figure in his arms and lowered it into the liquid of the vat, he mumbled, like a prayer, a snatch from Keat's "Ode to a Grecian Urn."

"Beauty is truth, truth beauty,
—that is all
Ye know on earth, and all ye
need to know."

After that day, not even the milkman saw John Short, so early in the morning did he skitter from his shack to the college basement.

Once there, he did not stop to fire the furnace but raced to the stiff room, so afraid was he that someone might have stolen his treasure.

Forgotten were the other bodies at which he once had mocked. Now he sat for hours, staring down at the half-drowned, changeless Miss X, or straining his little eyes and setting the echoes atwitter as he read from a precious dog-eared volume of Keats, Shelley, or Coleridge. Old John, born in agony and squalor, raised in filth and degradation and living to be the hideous laughingstock of all men, at long last had found something which, to his clouded mind, seemed ageless and beautiful.

"Oh, if I had been straight and strong and young, I might have found you before you stuffed those cracks in the windows and turned on the gas —I might have saved you from this," he would moan after he had turned the body on its back. (Dead women float face downward while men lie with their dead eyes glaring at the sky.) "Yet, if I had not been what I am, I might never have found you." And he would recite softly:

" 'A *thing of beauty is a joy*
forever:
Its loveliness increases; it will
never
Pass into nothingness.' "

Then, as an angry roaring from the furnace room told him that President Wyndham was in his office and furious because of the icy radiators, he would push the body into the darkest corner of the pool and hurry out, locking and double-barring the door.

Whenever a call would come for a cadaver, Short would allow no one in the stiff room but himself. Tugging and splashing at the edge of the vat he would somehow manage to drag out one of his neglected charges. Then he would appear at the door, panting and chuckling, to turn over the body to the student who had been sent for it.

The janitor's moodiness and neglect of his duties could not fail to come to the attention of President Wyndham.

"Poor Short is getting feeble," sighed that other elderly man. "We'll hire an assistant to do the heavy work."

And so a weak-chinned Swedish lad was installed in the furnace room and the radiators whistled as they had not done in years.

The newcomer lived in constant dread of Old John, despite Wyndham's assurances. When not actually at work on the fires he could always be seen, no matter how cold the weather, standing outside the basement door and casting frightened glances over his shoulder.

"Aye don't like dat faller. He bane a hex," was all Olaf would say when the rowdies upstairs twitted him.

Another element began to threaten John's happiness as the dreary winter months passed. Hard times were creeping upon Northern Med. Bryan thundered about "Free Silver" but there was little of it available as 1893 crawled into 1894. Endowments were not forthcoming as of old. Interest on invested funds fell away. Enrollments decreased. It was a time sacred to the Goat God—a time of panic.

Wyndham now sat for long hours in his cold, walnut-paneled office, gnawing his scraggly moustache and thinking up schemes to keep the school going. Despite his labors, the situation grew steadily worse.

Seldom were corpses delivered to Old John now. They cost money, just as did coal and surgical instruments. Instead of twenty bodies, he had eighteen . . . then twelve . . . then five.

Now a different tone crept into his conversations with Miss X. Despair and fright made him tremble as with the palsy when he crouched beside the salt-encrusted vat.

"They shan't have you," he would whisper, glancing toward the door where he was confident that Olaf stood eavesdropping. "You shall never be reduced to dripping bones and sinews by those glistening knives. They'll never send you in pieces to the Potters' Field. Didn't the poet say:

> *"That dead men rise up never;*
> *That even the weariest river*
> *Winds somewhere safe to sea."*

"Have no fear." Then he would shake his knobby fists in the direction of Wyndham's office and scream: "Do you hear, you old fool? You shan't lay a scalpel on her."

The body, perhaps shaken by sound vibrations, would seem to nod its golden head in approval.

. . . .

Came the time when the only body left in the pool was that of Miss X.

Came the time when "Moony," now an assistant professor in the dissecting room, sent down a requisition for another corpse.

Half an hour later he looked up from directing a delicate operation to see Old John crouched blinking in the doorway.

"Got that stiff ready?" He smiled as he stripped off his rubber gloves.

"Sorry, Mr. Perkins, sir. I haven't any more. The vat is empty."

"The devil! Is it as bad as that? I thought we had one left. I'll speak to President Wyndham about this at once."

"I—I wouldn't bother him, sir," stammered the janitor. "I give you my word there are no more."

Surprised by the tone and the stealthily shifting eyes, Moony glanced sharply at the old man.

"It's not your fault, John," he said soothingly. "Don't take it so hard. Here, come with me. We'll both talk to Mr. Wyndham about getting some new raw material." He started out the door.

"Wait! Wait!" The janitor gripped his arm, unmindful of the staring students. "Don't do anything yet. Perhaps I was mistaken. I—I forgot. I think there's one stiff left. It's badly mutilated. I thought—I didn't think you'd want that one. I'll have it ready in an hour."

"Why, you dithering old fool . . ." Moony began. But the cripple already was lurching down the hall as fast as his legs could carry him.

Half an hour later a blood-smeared apparition burst howling into Wyndham's office.

It was Olaf, but he was hardly recognizable; there was a deep gash in his scalp from which blood was pouring. His eyes were wild with pain and terror.

"Ow, Mr. Wyndham," he gabbled as he clung to the president's desk. "Something bane hit me. I lean over firebox. I poke furnace. Then . . ." He slumped to the floor.

"Perkins!" Wyndham shouted through the operating room door. Moony came running. As they bound up the jagged wound, suspicions gripped the young doctor. He repeated his conversation with Short.

"But that's nonsense," snapped Wyndham as he washed Olaf's blood off his hands. "There *is* another body down there. I ran across the requisition just this morning. Here it is, on my desk. On September first of last year we accepted the body of a Miss X from the coroner.

"Short could have had nothing to do with this. Something must have fallen off the furnace and struck Olaf on the head. This boy will be coming round in a minute. Then we'll go down and make Old John let us look in the vat."

"You stay here and care for him," Moony said tensely. "I'll talk to John."

He ran downstairs and shouted for the janitor.

There was no answer. The furnace room was deserted.

"John," he called, rattling the locked door of the vat room. "Open the door at once. Wyndham's orders!

"The old fool is angry because I wouldn't believe him," Moony grunted when there was no reply. "I suppose he's gone home in a huff."

He returned to the furnace room and bellowed up the speaking tube.

"Break down the door," the command came rasping down to him. "There's going to be no mystery around this college."

"I'll be with you in a second."

The president found the professor, heavy shovel in hand, standing puzzled just inside the wreckage of the stiff-room entrance.

"That's funny, sir," the young man stammered as he felt the other's hand on his shoulder. "What on earth could have induced Old John to say the vat was empty? There are two bodies floating in it."

Traditional

The Douglas Tragedy

*"The Douglas Tragedy" is a folk ballad whose closing floral image occurs
frequently in folk songs, notably at the end of the popular tragic romance
"Barbara Allen."*

"Rise up, rise up, Lord Douglas!" she says,
    "And put on your armor so bright;
Let it ne'er be said that a daughter of ours
    Was married to a lord under night.

"Rise up, rise up, my seven bold sons,
    And put on your armor so bright;
And take better care of your youngest sister.
    For your eldest's away this night!"

Lady Margret was on a milk-white steed,
    Lord William was on a gray,
A buglet-horn hung down by his side,
    And swiftly they rode away.

Lord William looked over his left shoulder
    To see what he could see,
And there he spied her seven bold brothers
    Come riding over the lea.

"Light down, light down, Lady Margret," he said,
    "And hold my steed in your hand,

Until that against your seven bold brothers,
    And your father, I make a stand."

O, there she stood, and bitter she stood,
    And never shed one tear,
Until she saw her brothers fall,
    And her father who loved her so dear.

"O hold your hand, Lord William!" she said,
    "For your strokes are deep and sore;
Though lovers I can get many a one,
    A father I can never get more."

O she's taken off her handkerchief,
    It was of the holland so fine,
And aye she dressed her father's wounds;
    His blood ran down like wine.

"O choose, O choose, Lady Margret,
    Will ye go with me, or bide?"
"I'll go, I'll go, Lord William," she said.
    "Ye've left me no other guide."

He lifted her up on her milk-white steed,
    And mounted his dapple-gray,
With his buglet-horn hung down by his side,
    And slowly they rode away.

O they rode on, and on they rode,
    And all by the light of the moon,
Until they came to a wan water,
    And there they lighted down.

They lighted down to take a drink
    Of the spring that ran so clear,
But down the stream ran his red heart's blood,
    And she began to fear.

"Hold up, hold up, Lord William," she said,
    "I fear me you are slain!"

" 'Tis but the shadow of my scarlet cloak
    That shines in the water so plain."

O they rode on, and on they rode,
    And all by the light of the moon,
Until they saw his mother's hall,
    And there they lighted down.

"Get up, get up, lady mother," he says,
    "Get up, and let in your son!
Open the door, lady mother," he says,
    "For this night my fair lady I've won!

"Now make my bed, lady mother," he says,
    "O make it wide and deep,
And lay Lady Margret close at my back,
    And the sounder will I sleep!"

Lord William was dead long ere midnight,
    Lady Margret long ere day;
And all true lovers that go together
    May they have more luck than they!

Lord William was buried in Mary's Kirk,
    Lady Margret in Mary's Choir;
And out of her grave grew a bonny red rose,
    And out of the knight's a briar.

The briar twined about the rose,
    And the rose clung to the briar,
And so they grew ever closer together,
    As all true lovers desire.

W. C. Morrow

The Permanent Stiletto

WILLIAM CHAMBERS MORROW (1854–1923), *the author of such grisly tales as* "The Haunted Burglar" *and* "His Unconquerable Enemy," *has been ranked by some critics on a par with such American masters as Ambrose Bierce, Fitz-James O'Brien and Edgar Allan Poe.* "The Permanent Stiletto," *reprinted in 1930 by* Weird Tales, *is less gruesome than the usual Morrow horror story, but only a little.*

I HAD SENT in all haste for Doctor Rowell, but as yet he had not arrived, and the strain was terrible. There lay my young friend upon his bed in the hotel, and I believed that he was dying. Only the jewelled handle of the knife was visible at his breast; the blade was wholly sheathed in his body.

"Pull it out, old fellow," begged the sufferer through white, drawn lips, his gasping voice being hardly less distressing than the unearthly look in his eyes.

"No, Arnold," said I, as I held his hand and gently stroked his forehead. It may have been instinct, it may have been a certain knowledge of anatomy that made me refuse.

"Why not? It hurts," he gasped. It was pitiful to see him suffer, this strong, healthy, daring, reckless young fellow.

Doctor Rowell walked in—a tall, grave man, with gray hair. He went to the bed and I pointed to the knife-handle, with its great, bold ruby in the end and its diamonds and emeralds alternating in quaint designs in the sides. The physician started. He felt Arnold's pulse and looked puzzled.

"When was this done?" he asked.

"About twenty minutes ago," I answered.

The physician started out, beckoned me to follow.

"Stop!" said Arnold. We obeyed. "Do you wish to speak of me?" he asked.

"Yes," replied the physician, hesitating.

"Speak in my presence then," said my friend; "I fear nothing." It was said in his old, imperious way, although his suffering must have been great.

"If you insist—"

"I do."

"Then," said the physician, "if you have any matters to adjust they should be attended to at once. I can do nothing for you."

"How long can I live?" asked Arnold.

The physician thoughtfully stroked his gray beard. "It depends," he finally said; "if the knife be withdrawn you may live three minutes; if it be allowed to remain you may possibly live an hour or two—not longer."

Arnold never flinched.

"Thank you," he said, smiling faintly through his pain; "my friend here will pay you. I have some things to do. Let the knife remain." He turned his eyes to mine, and, pressing my hand, said, affectionately, "And I thank you, too, old fellow, for not pulling it out."

The physician, moved by a sense of delicacy, left the room, saying, "Ring if there is a change. I will be in the hotel office." He had not gone far when he turned and came back. "Pardon me," said he, "but there is a young surgeon in the hotel who is said to be a very skillful man. My specialty is not surgery, but medicine. May I call him?"

"Yes," said I, eagerly; but Arnold smiled and shook his head. "I fear there will not be time," he said. But I refused to heed him and directed that the surgeon be called immediately. I was writing at Arnold's dictation when the two men entered the room.

There was something of nerve and assurance in the young surgeon that struck my attention. His manner, though quiet, was bold and straightforward and his movements sure and quick. This young man had already distinguished himself in the performance of some difficult hospital laparotomies, and he was at that sanguine age when ambition looks through the spectacles of experiment. Doctor Raoul Entrefort was the newcomer's name. He was a Creole, small and dark, and he had traveled and studied in Europe.

"Speak freely," gasped Arnold, after Doctor Entrefort had made an examination.

"What think you, doctor?" asked Entrefort of the older man.

"I think," was the reply, "that the knifeblade has penetrated the ascending aorta, about two inches above the heart. So long as the blade remains in the wound the escape of blood is comparatively small, though certain; were the blade withdrawn the heart would almost instantly empty itself through the aortal wound."

Meanwhile, Entrefort was deftly cutting away the white shirt and the undershirt, and soon had the breast exposed. He examined the gem-studded hilt with the keenest interest. "You are proceeding on the assumption, doctor," he said, "that this weapon is a knife."

"Certainly," answered Doctor Rowell, smiling; "what else can it be?"

"It *is* a knife," faintly interposed Arnold.

"Did you see the blade?" Entrefort asked him, quickly.

"I did—for a moment."

Entrefort shot a quick look at Doctor Rowell and whispered, "Then it is *not* suicide." Doctor Rowell looked puzzled and said nothing.

"I must disagree with you, gentlemen," quietly remarked Entrefort; "this is not a knife." He examined the handle very narrowly. Not only was the blade entirely concealed from view within Arnold's body, but the blow had been so strongly delivered that the skin was depressed by the guard. "The fact that it is not a knife presents a very curious series of facts and contingencies," pursued Entrefort, with amazing coolness, "some of which are, so far as I am informed, entirely novel in the history of surgery."

A quizzical expression, faintly amused and manifestly interested, was upon Doctor Rowell's face. "What is the weapon, doctor?" he asked.

"A stiletto."

Arnold started. Doctor Rowell appeared confused. "I must confess," he said, "my ignorance of the differences among these penetrating weapons, whether dirks, daggers, stilettos, poniards, or bowie-knives."

"With the exception of the stiletto," explained Entrefort, "all the weapons you mention have one or two edges, so that in penetrating they cut their way. A stiletto is round, is ordinarily about half an inch or less in diameter at the guard, and tapers to a sharp point. It penetrates solely by pushing the tissues aside in all directions. You will understand the importance of that point."

Doctor Rowell nodded, more deeply interested than ever.

"How do you know it is a stiletto, Doctor Entrefort?" I asked.

"The cutting of these stones is the work of Italian lapidaries," he said, "and they were set in Genoa. Notice, too, the guard. It is much broader and shorter than the guard of an edged weapon; in fact, it is nearly round. This weapon is about four hundred years old, and would be cheap at twenty thousand florins. Observe, also, the darkening color of your friend's breast in the immediate vicinity of the guard; this indicates that the tissues have been bruised by the crowding of the 'blade,' if I may use the term."

"What has all this to do with me?" asked the dying man.

"Perhaps a great deal, perhaps nothing. It brings a single ray of hope into your desperate condition."

Arnold's eyes sparkled and he caught his breath. A tremor passed all through him, and I felt it in the hand I was holding. Life was sweet to him, then, after all—sweet to this wild daredevil who had just faced death with such calmness! Doctor Rowell, though showing no sign of jealousy, could not conceal a look of incredulity.

"With your permission," said Entrefort, addressing Arnold, "I will do what I can to save your life."

"You may," said the poor boy.

"But I shall have to hurt you."

"Well."

"Perhaps very much."

"Well."

"And even if I succeed (the chance is one in a thousand) you will never be a sound man, and a constant and terrible danger will always be present."

"Well."

Entrefort wrote a note and sent it away in haste by a bellboy.

"Meanwhile," he resumed, "your life is in imminent danger from shock, and the end may come in a few minutes or hours from that cause. Attend without delay to whatever matters may require settling, and Doctor Rowell," glancing at that gentleman, "will give you something to brace you up. I speak frankly, for I see that you are a man of extraordinary nerve. Am I right?"

"Be perfectly candid," said Arnold.

Doctor Rowell, evidently bewildered by his cyclonic young associate, wrote a prescription, which I sent by a boy to be filled. With unwise zeal I asked Entrefort:

"Is there not danger of lockjaw?"

"No," he replied; "there is not a sufficiently extensive injury to peripheral nerves to induce traumatic tetanus."

I subsided. Doctor Rowell's medicine came and I administered a dose.

The physician and the surgeon then retired. The poor sufferer straightened up his business. When it was done he asked me:

"What is that crazy Frenchman going to do to me?"

"I have no idea; be patient."

In less than an hour they returned, bringing with them a keen-eyed, tall young man, who had a number of tools wrapped in an apron. Evidently he was unused to such scenes, for he became deathly pale upon seeing the ghastly spectacle on my bed. With staring eyes and open mouth he began to retreat toward the door, stammering:

"I—I can't do it."

"Nonsense, Hippolyte! Don't be a baby. Why, man, it is a case of life and death!"

"But—look at his eyes! He is dying!"

Arnold smiled. "I am not dead, though," he gasped.

"I—I beg your pardon," said Hippolyte.

Doctor Entrefort gave the nervous man a drink of brandy and then said:

"No more nonsense, my boy; it must be done. Gentlemen, allow me to introduce Mr. Hippolyte, one of the most original, ingenious, and skilful machinists in the country."

Hippolyte, being modest, blushed as he bowed. In order to conceal his confusion he unrolled his apron on the table with considerable noise of rattling tools.

"I have to make some preparations before you may begin, Hippolyte, and I want you to observe me that you may become used not only to the sight of fresh blood, but also, what is more trying, the odor of it."

Hippolyte shivered. Entrefort opened a case of surgical instruments.

"Now, doctor, the chloroform," he said to Doctor Rowell.

"I will not take it," promptly interposed the sufferer; "I want to know when I die."

"Very well," said Entrefort; "but you have little nerve now to spare. We may try it without chloroform, however. It will be better if you can do without. Try your best to lie still while I cut."

"What are you going to do?" asked Arnold.

"Save your life, if possible."

"How? Tell me all about it."

"Must you know?"

"Yes."

"Very well, then. The point of the stiletto has passed entirely through

the aorta, which is the great vessel rising out of the heart and carrying the
aerated blood to the arteries. If I should withdraw the weapon the blood
would rush from the two holes in the aorta and you would soon be dead.
If the weapon had been a knife, the parted tissue would have yielded, and
the blood would have been forced out on either side of the blade and
would have caused death. As it is, not a drop of blood has escaped from
the aorta into the thoracic cavity. All that is left for us to do, then, is to
allow the stiletto to remain permanently in the aorta. Many difficulties at
once present themselves, and I do not wonder at Doctor Rowell's look of
surprise and incredulity."

That gentleman smiled and shook his head.

"It is a desperate chance," continued Entrefort, "and is a novel case in
surgery; but it is the only chance. The fact that the weapon is a stiletto is
the important point—a stupid weapon, but a blessing to us now. If the
assassin had known more she would have used—"

Upon his employment of the noun "assassin" and the feminine pro-
noun "she," both Arnold and I started violently, and I cried out to the
man to stop.

"Let him proceed," said Arnold, who, by a remarkable effort, had
calmed himself.

"Not if the subject is painful," Entrefort said.

"It is not," protested Arnold; "why do you think the blow was struck by
a woman?"

"Because, first, no man capable of being an assassin would use so gaudy
and valuable a weapon; second, no man would be so stupid as to carry so
antiquated and inadequate a thing as a stiletto, when that most murderous and satisfactory of all penetrating and cutting weapons, the bowie-
knife, is available. She was a strong woman, too, for it requires a good
hand to drive a stiletto to the guard, even though it miss the sternum by a
hair's breadth and slip between the ribs, for the muscles here are hard and
the intercostal spaces narrow. She was not only a strong woman, but a
desperate one also."

"That will do," said Arnold. He beckoned me to bend closer. "You
must watch this man; he is too sharp; he is dangerous."

"Then," resumed Entrefort, "I shall tell you what I intend to do. There
will undoubtedly be inflammation of the aorta, which, if it persist, will
cause a fatal aneurism by a breaking down of the aortal walls; but we
hope, with the help of your youth and health, to check it.

"Another serious difficulty is this: With every inhalation, the entire
thorax (or bony structure of the chest) considerably expands. The aorta

remains stationary. You will see, therefore, that as your aorta and your breast are now held in rigid relation to each other by the stiletto, the chest, with every inhalation, pulls the aorta forward out of place about half an inch. I am certain that it is doing this, because there is no indication of an escape of arterial blood into the thoracic cavity; in other words, the mouths of the two aortal wounds have seized upon the blade with a firm hold and thus prevent it from slipping in and out. This is a very fortunate occurrence, but one which will cause pain for some time. The aorta, you may understand, being made by the stiletto to move with the breathing, pulls the heart backward and forward with every breath you take; but that organ, though now undoubtedly much surprised, will accustom itself to its new condition.

"What I fear most, however, is the formation of a clot around the blade. You see, the presence of the blade in the aorta has already reduced the blood-carrying capacity of that vessel; a clot, therefore, need not be very large to stop up the aorta, and, of course, if that should occur death would ensue. But the clot, if one form, may be dislodged and driven forward, in which event it may lodge in any one of the numerous branches from the aorta and produce results more or less serious, possibly fatal. If, for instance, it should choke either the right or the left carotid, there would ensue atrophy of one side of the brain, and consequently paralysis of half the entire body; but it is possible that in time there would come about a secondary circulation from the other side of the brain, and thus restore a healthy condition. Or the clot (which, in passing always from larger arteries to smaller, must unavoidably find one not sufficiently large to carry it, and must lodge somewhere) may either necessitate amputation of one of the four limbs or lodge itself so deep within the body that it cannot be reached with the knife. You are beginning to realize some of the dangers which await you."

Arnold smiled faintly.

"But we shall do our best to prevent the formation of a clot," continued Entrefort; "there are drugs which may be used with effect."

"Are there more dangers?"

"Many more; some of the more serious have not been mentioned. One of these is the probability of the aortal tissues pressing upon the weapon relaxing their hold and allowing the blade to slip. That would let out the blood and cause death. I am uncertain whether the hold is now maintained by the pressure of the tissues or the adhesive quality of the serum which was set free by the puncture. I am convinced, though, that in either event the hold is easily broken and that it may give way at any moment, for it is under several kinds of strains. Every time the heart contracts and crowds the blood into the aorta, the latter expands a little, and then contracts when the pressure is removed. Any unusual exercise or excitement produces stronger and quicker heartbeats, and increases the strain on the adhesion of the aorta to the weapon. A fright, fall, a jump, a blow on the chest—any of these might so jar the heart and aorta as to break the hold."

Entrefort stopped.

"Is that all?" asked Arnold.

"No; but is not that enough?"

"More than enough," said Arnold, with a sudden and dangerous sparkle in his eyes. Before any of us could think, the desperate fellow had seized the handle of the stiletto with both hands in a determined effort to withdraw it and die. I had had no time to order my faculties to the movement of a muscle when Entrefort, with incredible alertness and swiftness, had Arnold's wrists. Slowly Arnold relaxed his hold.

"There, now!" said Entrefort, soothingly; "that was a careless act and might have broken the adhesion! You'll have to be careful."

Arnold looked at him with a curious combination of expressions.

"Doctor Entrefort," he quietly remarked, "you are the Devil."

Bowing profoundly, Entrefort replied: "You do me too great honor;" then he whispered to his patient: "If you do *that*"—with a motion toward the hilt—"I will have *her* hanged for murder."

Arnold started and choked, and a look of horror overspread his face. He withdrew his hands, took one of mine in both of his, threw his arms upon the pillow above his head, and, holding my hand, firmly said to Entrefort:

"Proceed with your work."

"Come closer, Hippolyte," said Entrefort, "and observe narrowly. Will you kindly assist me, Doctor Rowell?" That gentleman had sat in wondering silence.

Entrefort's hand was quick and sure, and he used the knife with marvelous dexterity. First he made four equidistant incisions outward from the guard and just through the skin. Arnold held his breath and ground his teeth at the first cut, but soon regained command of himself. Each incision was about two inches long. Hippolyte shuddered and turned his head aside. Entrefort, whom nothing escaped, exclaimed:

"Steady, Hippolyte! Observe!"

Quickly was the skin peeled back to the limit of the incisions. This must have been excruciatingly painful. Arnold groaned, and his hands were moist and cold. Down sank the knife into the flesh from which the skin had been raised, and blood flowed freely; Doctor Rowell handled the sponge. The keen knife worked rapidly. Arnold's marvelous nerve was breaking down. He clutched my hand fiercely; his eyes danced; his mind was weakening. Almost in a moment the flesh had been cut away to the bones, which were now exposed—two ribs and the sternum. A few quick cuts cleared the weapon between the guard and the ribs.

"To work, Hippolyte—be quick!"

The machinist had evidently been coached before he came. With slender, long-fingered hands, which trembled at first, he selected certain tools with nice precision, made some rapid measurements of the weapon and of the cleared space around it, and began to adjust the parts of a queer little machine. Arnold watched him curiously.

"What—" he began to say; but he ceased; a deeper pallor set on his face, his hands relaxed, and his eyelids fell.

"Thank God!" exclaimed Entrefort; "he has fainted—he can't stop us now. Quick, Hippolyte!"

The machinist attached the queer little machine to the handle of the weapon, seized the stiletto in his left hand, and with his right began a series of sharp, rapid movements backward and forward.

"Hurry, Hippolyte!" urged Entrefort.

"The metal is very hard."

"Is it cutting?"

"I can't see for the blood."

In another moment something snapped. Hippolyte started; he was very nervous. He removed the little machine.

"The metal is very hard," he said; "it breaks the saws."

He adjusted another tiny saw and resumed work. After a little while he picked up the handle of the stiletto and laid it on the table. He had cut it off, leaving the blade inside Arnold's body.

"Good, Hippolyte!" exclaimed Entrefort. In a minute he had closed the bright end of the blade from view by drawing together the skin-flaps and sewing them firmly.

Arnold returned to consciousness and glanced down at his breast. He seemed puzzled. "Where is the weapon?" he asked.

"Here is part of it," answered Entrefort, holding up the handle.

"And the blade—"

"That is an irremovable part of your internal machinery." Arnold was silent. "It had to be cut off," pursued Entrefort, "not only because it would be troublesome and an undesirable ornament, but also because it

was advisable to remove every possibility of its withdrawal." Arnold said
nothing. "Here is a prescription," said Entrefort; "take the medicine as
directed for the next five years without fail."

"What for? I see that it contains muriatic acid."

"If necessary I will explain five years from now."

"If I live."

"If you live."

Arnold drew me down to him and whispered, "Tell her to fly at once;
this man may make trouble for her."

Was there ever a more generous fellow?

I thought that I recognized a thin, pale, bright face among the passen-
gers who were leaving an Australian steamer which had just arrived at San
Francisco.

"Doctor Entrefort!" I cried.

"Ah!" he said, peering up into my face and grasping my hand; "I know
you now, but you have changed. You remember that I was called away
immediately after I had performed that crazy operation on your friend. I
have spent the intervening four years in India, China, Tibet, Siberia, the
South Seas, and God knows where not. But wasn't that a most absurd,
hare-brained experiment that I tried on your friend! Still, it was all that
could have been done. I have dropped all that nonsense long ago. It is
better, for more reasons than one, to let them die at once. Poor fellow! he
bore it so bravely! Did he suffer much afterward? How long did he live? A
week—perhaps a month?"

"He is alive yet."

"What!" exclaimed Entrefort, startled.

"He is, indeed, and is in this city."

"Incredible!"

"It is true; you shall see him."

"But tell me about him now!" cried the surgeon, his eager eyes glittering with the peculiar light which I had seen in them on the night of
the operation. "Has he regularly taken the medicine which I prescribed?"

"He has. Well, the change in him, from what he was before the operation, is shocking. Imagine a young daredevil of twenty-two, who had no
greater fear of danger or death than of a cold, now a cringing, cowering
fellow; apparently an old man, nursing his life with pitiful tenderness,
fearful that at any moment something may happen to break the hold of
his aorta-walls on the stiletto-blade; a confirmed hypochondriac, peevish,
melancholic, unhappy in the extreme. He keeps himself confined as

closely as possible, avoiding all excitement and exercise, and even reads nothing exciting. The constant danger has worn out the last shred of his manhood and left him a pitiful wreck. Can nothing be done for him?"

"Possibly. But has he consulted no physician?"

"None whatever; he has been afraid that he might learn the worst."

"Let us find him at once. Ah, here comes my wife to meet me! She arrived by the other steamer."

I recognized her immediately and was overcome with astonishment.

"Charming woman," said Entrefort; "you'll like her. We were married three years ago at Bombay. She belongs to a noble Italian family and has traveled a great deal."

He introduced us. To my unspeakable relief she remembered neither my name nor my face. I must have appeared odd to her, but it was impossible for me to be perfectly unconcerned. We went to Arnold's rooms, I with much dread. I left her in the reception room and took Entrefort within. Arnold was too greatly absorbed in his own troubles to be dangerously excited by meeting Entrefort, whom he greeted with indifferent hospitality.

"But I heard a woman's voice," he said. "It sounds—" He checked himself, and before I could intercept him he had gone to the reception room; and there he stood face to face with the beautiful adventuress— none other than Entrefort's wife now—who, wickedly desperate, had driven a stiletto into Arnold's vitals in a hotel four years before because he had refused to marry her. They recognized each other instantly and both grew pale; but she, quicker witted, recovered her composure at once and advanced toward him with a smile and an extended hand. He stepped back, his face ghastly with fear.

"Oh!" he gasped, "the excitement, the shock—it has made the blade slip out! The blood is pouring from the opening—it burns—I am dying!" and he fell into my arms and instantly expired.

The autopsy revealed the surprising fact that there was no blade in his thorax at all; it had been gradually consumed by the muriatic acid which Entrefort had prescribed for that very purpose, and the perforations in the aorta had closed up gradually with the wasting of the blade and had been perfectly healed for a long time. All his vital organs were sound. My poor friend, once so reckless and brave, had died simply of a childish and groundless fear, and the woman unwittingly had accomplished her revenge.

Joan Vander Putten

In the Shadows
of My Fear

JOAN VANDER PUTTEN, *a mother of five who resides on New York's Long Island, left a banking career to devote herself to writing. Her wicked tale of marital strife, "Just a Little Thing," was included in my Doubleday collection* Devils & Demons, *and the following nightmare originally appeared in Kathryn Ptacek's anthology,* Women of Darkness.

I OPEN MY EYES, and I am afraid. Again. Each day the fear licks me awake, follows me around the house, like an unwelcome pet. It is nearly ready, I think, to metamorphose into something tangible. But not yet, I sense, not until it wrings the last ounce of courage and sanity from my soul. It hounds me, a living thing at my side, ever present, as I move from room to room in Felicia's house; the house she so loved and invited me to live in with her. *My* house now, my lonely house, since her death.

Listening, I hear only the gentle kiss of the Gulf's waves as they meet the sandy beach below my window. I could swear to a movement at the edge of my vision, but when I turn quickly to catch the phantom I see only a lamp, a chair. The beast hides in the shadows of my fear, cautious as a stalking lion. Its origins are unknown to me, yet of one thing I am certain. It intends to win. I sense this with every nerve in my body, every pore that sweats icy anxiety.

I rise from Felicia's bed, noting that sometime during the night the mattress has become metal spikes. My skin is pricked and bleeding slightly. There is no pain, and I head for the bathroom. All the doorknobs in the house have become miniature skulls; their tiny teeth nip the heel of my hand as I grasp them, and the small bites never heal. The water in the basin becomes blood that stains my face red when I wash, making me use the drinking water in the refrigerator to scrub myself clean. I can never really get clean. My toothbrush is a small, steel rake that combs blood from my gums in tiny streams. I rinse and spit out repeatedly, until my spittle is no longer red-flecked. Still, I imagine I see blood.

Why do you do these things, Felicia? I refused to spill one drop of your blood. But if it is my blood you want, take it, with my assent. Take whatever it is you want of me. I am yours, and always will be. Oh, my darling, if only you knew your tortures go unheeded, perhaps you would stop these silly games of spite.

I have grown inured to Felicia's spite. Nothing the house, Felicia's house, can do hurts me, regardless of what orders she gives it. I am sure it is her spirit, seeking a vengeful justice, which plagues me.

But I no longer care about her tricks, for the fear is all-consuming, blinding me to slow changes of objects around me. The fear is not part of her tricks. It is part of *me*, joined to me, like a sinister Siamese twin. It tolerates no scrutiny, allows me no peace. Helpless to defend myself against it, I am slowly sinking into its hopeless depths.

And day by day, I find myself caring less.

I remember the days before the fear, the days when I laughed, and played, and loved my beautiful Felicia. Oh, *how* I loved! Too much, some would say; others, not enough. And because of my love I suffer now—and will for all eternity, I am convinced. But to have had the love of Felicia for even so short a time, to know that while she loved me I was complete— ah, that must suffice. But it does not, and the fear nibbles at my mind. The memories of her beautiful features and shining hair fade, lost in the whispers and mists of the past, escaping my outstretched fingers.

To have her here now, to feel her silken hands soothe and banish the constant trembling of my limbs, for that I would gladly deliver my soul into the hands of the hulking menace which is my constant companion. But it can never be, for my Felicia floats, slave to the whim of the tides, ever straining at her anchor.

I weep, sometimes, guilty with the knowledge it was wrong to put her there. But I could not bear to think of her young body ravaged by worms and ants, deep under the firm soil where I could never visit. Due to my forethought, we can spend happy hours in each other's company. Only occasionally, when I visit, do some bold fish swim over to bid us good day.

For the most part they avoid us, choosing instead to explore other mysteries of their watery home.

Soon it will be time to leave for our tryst. I anticipate the daily appointed time I have set, and know that Felicia expects me there at the stroke of ten, much as a wife awaits her husband's nightly homecoming.

The fear will trail me into the warm Gulf, a hated sleuth that dogs my steps. But once I am with Felicia, it is strangely impotent. When I am with her, it skulks into the shadows of the deep—hiding, perhaps, among the brightly colored coral—impatient for my ascent, when it can leech itself to me once more.

I hurry to the bedroom to dress. I choose the shirt Felicia loved, the bathing suit she picked out. But when I don my clothes they flame up, scorching my body before they disintegrate, leaving a film of black smoke covering my skin. I must wash again to cleanse myself. Perhaps if I felt pain I would not be so annoyed by the delay they cause.

As it is, I feel nothing. Nothing except fear.

I sigh, and dress in other clothes. These behave normally, and it seems that for the time being the house, or Felicia, is done with tricks. I leave quickly, unwilling to keep my dearest waiting.

My boat breaks free of its tethers and runs across the waves, like an eager pup seeking its mistress. It, too, was Felicia's, and seems to know the place she rests; it stops, almost unaided, at her exact position on the charts. I prepare to dive, anxious fingers fumbling with the oxygen tank on my back. The fear dives with me. I try to outdistance it with fast strokes of my flippers, and as I swim to the ocean's floor, I see the outline of my love's pliable, eternal home grow nearer. The fear slips further and further behind until I escape it completely. Although I know it merely lies in wait for my return, I am free, for a while, and I swim toward my darling.

Felicia's arm waves gracefully and I fancy she greets me, rather than admit she moves from the capricious tide. I embrace her gently, careful not to squeeze too hard. Bloated, her smooth skin rubs against the clear plastic bag encasing her, her body filling it almost completely. It was an oversight to neglect calculating how badly the water would swell her; the bag should have been larger. But she doesn't mind—not now, nor will she ever. Her silent swaying calls forth images of an embryo cozy in its placenta.

And here she will stay, that I may adore.

But her current situation is hazardous, I suddenly realize, when I see holes nipped in the plastic surface by curious fish. I frown, curse my stupidity and lack of forethought. Soon, I fear, the fish will shred the plastic enough to reach my beloved; another thing I failed to take into account when I conceived what seemed, in the heat of the moment, the perfect solution. Before they can harm her, I must take action; find a place where we can be together always, undisturbed and undiscovered. That is my goal, my only goal, my reason for living only to be with Felicia. At the present, my mind is empty of alternatives to her current predicament. Later, when not distracted by her nearness, I will puzzle it through, find the ultimate and only answer for us both—a place where we can finally be together for all eternity, never separated. But for now, my attention is focused on Felicia.

The green fungus on the plastic distorts her face, making it look pleated and sickly. Wiping it away, I gaze at her beauty. I am able to see beyond the water's destruction; her exquisite features are branded in my memory by love's blind vision. Blond hair, once bleached by the sun, floats lackluster and lackadaisically around her head. Her wide eyes still accuse, although each day they become more like raisins lost in the puffy dough of her face. And her mouth, her perfect, rosebud mouth, still forms its round scream of horror, though silent these many days.

You have not yet forgiven me, my beautiful Felicia. Will you ever? You must. For now I am all you have, and you are mine alone. Why, my dearest, why did you drive me to this? We could be making love now on the beaches' warm sand, swimming in the Gulf's azure bath, instead of meeting secretly in its sepulchral depths.

What made you grow tired of our love, torment me with the threat of ending it? From the first time we kissed I knew that our destinies were inextricably woven together, meshed finer than the silk of your favorite mauve scarf, the one with which I ended your life.

"Marry me," I had asked.

But you only laughed, and called me silly.

"Come live with me," you said. "We'll have all of the fun, and none of the commitment."

So I did, even though it was your commitment I needed.

We lived in your house by the sea, with no one but the gulls for company. Our love nest, you called it. As the days went by, my life with you became my only memory. It blotted out my past, with its unhappy history of cruel women who left me—or *tried* to. None ever succeeded. I couldn't let them, of course. The pain would have been too great. But none, Felicia, *none*, I swear, did I love as much as you. Of them all, you are the only one I have wanted to keep.

As I explain all this to my love the water around us darkens, as if something blocks the sun from above me. I look up, just in time to catch a monstrous shape dart behind a coral reef. My fear, lying in wait to pounce upon me when I leave. But while there is oxygen in my tanks, I will remain. I check my gauges, surprised to find the oxygen supply so quickly diminishing. Did I bother to check it before I dived, or have I a death wish? No, no death wish. For my own death would end forever this last, tenuous tie between us, and that I could not bear. I must live; for it is only through my own life that Felicia will continue to exist. Without me, her memory, her very *being*, would deteriorate into nothingness. The escaping air hisses warning bubbles into the water above me and I resume my adoration. Time grows short.

Ah, Felicia, while you lived, we had such happy times! You bewitched me, spinning your magical web of enchantment ever tighter around my heart, until I thought it would burst from loving. Then, one day, you voiced your boredom with our love. I was slashed by your words, as the throats of those other women were, by my knife.

"I'm going out for a while to have some fun," you said.

"Fun? Without me?" I couldn't understand.

You laughed, but it was not your silvery, moonlight laugh. It was cold and derisive, filled with a loathing that made me shudder.

"You naive, romantic fool," you said, your beautiful eyes slitting into blue gashes, your perfect lips stretched in a sneer. And those were your last words.

I could hardly see your scarf for the tears in my eyes, but my pain helped me pick it up and wind it around your neck. No knife for you, my dearest. No ugly, gaping wounds that wept blood, not for the woman I had hoped to marry. Your body would be unscarred, preserved in its perfection.

Those same tears blurred my vision of your face as we kissed goodbye, a moment before you lost consciousness. Was that kiss as bittersweet for you as it was for me? I couldn't see.

The darkness has returned, hovering above and now closing in, it seems, on every side. My fear is finally solidifying. I will ignore it as long as I can. The water ripples strongly, as if trying to tug Felicia from my grasp. I continue our conversation, aware of a giddy light-headedness.

Do you remember, my love, our last, moonlit ride, to this place? I carried you to the boat over my shoulder. It was so late, and there was no one on the beach to see us. I held you in my arms with your head cradled close to my chest as your boat reluctantly took us to where we must part.

I don't remember where I found the bag—I think it was in the basement, near all the cartons from your recent move. Were you, too, running from someone? We were both solitary souls. Me, running from the authorities, who would never understand why I *had* to do what I did. They'll never catch me. I know well how to cover my tracks. But you—who were you running from? Or was it something you were running to? I don't think even you knew. You had no friends, you said, no relatives. I felt sorry for you at first, before I realized that it would make you fill your life with only me. In the end, it turned out to be a fortuitous circumstance.

On the boat that night, I thought to bring an extra anchor as well as the bag, and I was pleased with my preparations. I had not expected to be able to think so rationally. Seeing you now, I question if I did.

What I did *not* expect was your untimely revival. You certainly surprised me, my dear, when your eyes fluttered open. It unsettled me to discover I had removed the scarf before it had completed its work. You tried to scream, but your poor voice was so hoarse, remember? And you were weak—you could hardly struggle at all when I slipped you in the bag and tied it closed, before attaching the anchor. I waved at you as I dropped you overboard—did you see me? It was such a dark night, it's understandable if you didn't; and you sank so fast you could've easily missed it anyway.

I pause in my visit, catching, from the corner of my eye, a massive form approaching. My fear has never been so bold before, and I am amazed, stunned in disbelief at its brash behavior. A small voice in my head screams at me to escape, that danger is near. But I am dizzy, and too late realize that it is from lack of air. My muscles fail to respond and I float weightlessly, next to Felicia.

Suddenly my fear is upon me, as quick as an intake of breath. It slices between my love and me, sending me tumbling away with its force. I spin in slow motion, whirling about like a black rubber top. My body trembles, feels boneless and all too mortal. It refuses to obey commands, and I cannot move.

It is not my fear that has so rudely separated me from Felicia, or perhaps it is. Death seizes my beloved, unaware she is already beyond its grip. For a selfish moment I am glad that she, and not I, has been chosen for its cold kiss.

A thought insinuates itself into my brain's fuzziness, nibbling at the edge of my fading awareness. Can it be? Is death the specter that has haunted me all this time, only death, nothing more? Confusion blurs my physical and mental boundaries until they mesh with the scene before me. I do not know where I end and it begins. It is then, as I watch the specter stealing my darling, that I realize there is something worse, much worse by far, than the fear of death. How stupid I have been not to recognize it until now! It is something I have known since my first meeting with Felicia.

No, I scoff at my stupidity, death is not my albatross, my nemesis, the fear that now engulfs me. Death holds no terror. The *greatest* terror, my biggest, and *only* fear, is life! The thought of life without my Felicia plummets me into a heart-sinking despair. Loneliness has been the demon shadowing me as I move through the emptiness of my days, tormenting my every waking hour.

As I watch, Felicia is shaken about. She looks for all the world like an excited bride dancing with her energetic groom. Flecks of her skin swirl about, tiny snowflakes in a maelstrom. One leg floats lazily downward, tired from the dance, and its skin splits like the casing of an overstuffed sausage when it lands gently on the abrasive sand. It settles, a meal for the small fish who begin nibbling at the exposed muscles.

The intimate union continues in water so filtered with blood I can hardly see. My fear devours my dearest, engulfing, possessing her totally, as I never could. As the two slowly fuse into one entity, they are locked in a perpetual embrace which excludes me. Seeing their unity, my emotions roil like the churning, bloody water around my darling. I, who have loved so deeply and so faithfully, am soon to be left alone!

Jealousy catapults me toward the vicious lover that schemes to part Felicia and me. As I sensed from the first, we must always be one. I will not allow her to be taken from me, leaving me to live with only my fear for company. I will join Felicia and we three will bond in an unholy trinity of eternal love, if need be. Thereby will I thwart the marriage that should have been ours alone.

My fist punches through the water, and I cannot tell if it has hit anything solid. I hear a gurgling scream, and a great black hole punctuated with gleaming points of white fills my vision.

I welcome it rapturously, knowing that within its silent depths lies the demise of my fear. I have triumphed.

Oh, Felicia, I am coming.

Maurice Level

Blue Eyes

"Blue Eyes" is, in my opinion, one of the greatest "conte cruelles" ever written. The impact of its final line—do cover it so you won't inadvertently peek at it ahead of time—is psychologically devastating. MAURICE LEVEL *(1875–1928), who, according to the Library of Congress card catalog, might have been a woman, Jeanne Mareteux-Level, was an important contributor to Paris' Grand Guignol theatre of cruelty.*

WRAPPED in a loose hospital wrap that made her seem even thinner than she was, the sick girl was standing lost in thought at the foot of her bed.

Her childish face was wasted, and her blue eyes, sad, fathomless and circled with dark rings, were so unnaturally large they seemed to light up her whole face. Her cheeks burned with a hectic flush, and the deep lines that ran down to her mouth looked as if they had been worn there by the flow of unceasing tears.

She hung her head when the house-surgeon stopped beside her.

"Well, little No. 4, what's this I hear? You want to go out?"

"Yes, sir . . ." The voice was hardly more than a whisper.

"But that's very foolish. . . . You've only been up two or three days. In weather like this, too. You'd certainly fall ill again. Wait a day or two. You're not unhappy here? . . . Has anyone been unkind to you?"

"No . . . oh, no, sir . . ."

"What is it, then? . . ."

There was more energy in her tone as she said:

"I must go out."

And as if anticipating his question she continued quickly:

"This is All Saints' Day. I promised to take some flowers to my sweetheart's grave . . . I promised . . . He has only me . . . If I don't go,
no one will . . . I promised . . ."

A tear shone under her eyelid. She wiped it away with a finger.

The house-surgeon was touched, and either out of curiosity, or so as
not to seem awkward and leave her without some word of comfort, he
asked:

"Is it long since he died?"

"Nearly a year . . ."

"What was the matter with him?"

She seemed to shrink, to become more frail, her chest more hollow, her
hands thinner as, her eyes half closed, her lips trembling, she murmured:

"He was executed . . ."

The house-surgeon bit his lip and said in a low voice:

"Poor child . . . I'm very sorry. If you really must go out, go . . . But
take care not to catch cold. You must come back tomorrow."

Once outside the hospital gates, she began to shiver.

It was a dreary autumn morning. Moisture trickled down the walls.
Everything was gray: the sky, the houses, the naked trees and the misty
distance where people hurried along anxious to get out of the damp
streets.

It had been the middle of summer when she had fallen ill, and her
dress was a brightly hued one of thin cotton. The crumpled ribbon that
encircled her wasted neck made her look even more pitiable. The skirt,
blouse and neck-tie might have smiled back at the sunshine, but they
seemed to droop in sadness in the chill gray setting.

She started off with an uncertain walk, stopping every now and then
because she was out of breath and her head swimming.

The people she passed turned to look after her. She seemed to hesitate
as if wishing to speak to them, then, afraid, walked on, glancing nervously
from right to left. In this way she crossed half Paris. She stopped when
she came to the Quais, standing to watch the slow, muddy flow of the
river. The piercing cold cut through her, and feeling she could not bear
much more, she started off again.

When she got to Place Maubert and the Avenue des Gobelins she felt
almost at home, for she was now in the neighborhood in which she had
lived. Soon she began to see faces she knew, and she heard some one say
as she passed:

"Surely that's Vandat's girl . . . How she has changed!"

"Which Vandat?"

"Vandat the murd . . ."

She quickened her steps, pressing her hands against her face so as not to hear the end of the word . . .

It was getting dark when she at last arrived at the wretched little hotel where she had lodged before she fell ill. She went in. Street girls and the men they kept were playing cards in the little café downstairs. When they saw her they called out:

"Hullo! Here's Blue Eyes"—that used to be her nickname. "Come and have a drink, Blue Eyes. Here's a seat . . . come along . . ."

Their welcome touched her, but the thick, rank smoke made her cough, and she could hardly breathe as she replied:

"No . . . I've no time now . . . Is Madame in?"

"Yes, there she is."

She smiled timidly at the manageress.

"I wanted to ask you, Madame, if I could get at my things. The clothes I have on aren't warm enough . . ."

"Any clothes you left were taken up to the attic; they'll be there somewhere. I'll send someone to look for them . . . Sit down by the stove and warm yourself."

"No . . . I've no time now. I'll come back presently."

She went to the door. One of the men jeered:

"At the old business already? You aren't wasting much time."

She went out, and the short stay in the stifling room made the cold outside seem more piercing than ever. People were hurrying along laden with bead-wreaths and bouquets of flowers; others, dressed in their best clothes, talked and laughed, and one saw at a glance that they were carrying their offerings to the cemetery as a matter of habit, that time had taken the edge from their grief.

All along the side of the pavement barrows of flowers were drawn up. Chrysanthemums with curled petals drooped over clusters of roses; here and there mimosa shed its golden powder over bunches of violets. Nearer to the cemetery, in front of the shops of the marble masons, pots of flowers were arranged on the shelves of stands, insignificant, with neat foliage and restrained colors; further on were immortels and large bead-wreaths . . .

She looked at all this with eyes that glowed with envy. If only she could get some for him, just a little bunch . . . for him where he was lying at the far end of the cemetery in his poor, unconsecrated grave, a bare mound, without a single word to show that he was lying there.

"Murderer" . . . that meant nothing to her. He was the being she adored, her Man, the lover who had possessed not only her body but her whole soul . . . In a moment of madness he had killed someone . . . Had he not paid his horrible debt in full?

The day he had been arrested she had sworn never to have anything to do with any other man, never; to give up the life she had been leading, to work, to become an honest girl once more . . . to live in memories of him . . .

She kept on looking at the flowers. A seller held out a bunch of roses: "A bouquet? Some chrysanthemums then? Violets?"

She passed without replying, for she did not possess one farthing. Yet there was but one idea in her mind—flowers. She must have some flowers . . . she must get some flowers for him somehow . . . she had sworn she would.

She was nearly fainting with hunger and fatigue, but she was no longer aware of it. She was thinking only of the bare strip of earth in the cemetery, imagining it with some flowers brightening it up. But the money . . . how was she to get it? What could she do?

The way that suggested itself was the obvious one, nor did it seem to clash with her vow to remain true to his memory.

Just as a good artisan returns to his factory, takes up his tools and starts on his work, she mechanically patted her hair into order, arranged her poor dress and began to walk the street as she used to in the old days when her man, sitting playing cards in the café, was the only thing in the world she cared about.

On she walked, her eye watchful, swaying her waist as she whispered between her teeth:

"Stop! . . . I want to speak to you . . ."

But she was too emaciated: one glance at her and the men hurried away. And indeed her face was no longer a face for pleasure; nor was her body, its sharp angles and deep hollows showing clearly under her thin cotton dress.

In bygone days when she was pretty, when she really was the "Blue Eyes" everyone admired, it was different. Now she was only an object of pity.

The daylight was fading. Suppose the cemetery was shut before she was able to buy the flowers . . .

A thin, misty rain was falling, silent, impalpable, and everything was becoming wrapped in gray shadows. You could see nothing of her thin face now except her eyes, two great eyes burning with fever.

A man was passing the corner of a quiet street, his coat-collar up, his hands in his pockets. She brushed up against him and said softly, her whole heart's craving vibrating in her voice:

"Stop! . . . Won't you come with me? . . ."

He looked at her for a moment. She had gone close up to him, her eyes penetrating his with the inspired expression of one conscious of a high mission.

He took her arm, and she guided him to the low hotel she had recently left. Through the half open door she said quickly:

"My key . . . A candle . . ."

The manageress replied in a low voice:

"No. 23, second floor, third door."

The men and the girls in the café bent forward to see who was there, and as she went upstairs she heard exclamations and bursts of laughter.

. . . It was almost dark when she came down again. She threw a hasty good-bye at her companion and set off at a run. Stopping before the first flower-seller she came to, she seized the nearest bunch and threw down the two pieces of silver that clinked in her hands.

Quickly, quickly, she ran to the cemetery. People were coming away in little groups. She trembled. Would there still be time?

At the entrance the gate-keeper said:

"Too late! We're closing now."

"Oh! please, please. I only want to run in and out again. Just two minutes . . ."

"Very well. But—quick."

Down the path she rushed, stumbling over the stones in the dark. It was a long way. She could hardly breathe, something was burning so painfully in her chest. She stopped by the wall where those who are executed are buried, and fell on her knees, scattering her flowers on the earth. Her tears streamed from her eyes, dripping between the hands she pressed against her face. She tried to pray, but she could not remember any of the proper words, and she just sobbed, her lips on the ground:

"Oh! my man . . . my man . . ."

Then, so worn out she had lost all sensation in her limbs, but with a feeling of ease, almost of joy in her heart, she rose and hurried away. She even smiled at the gate-keeper as she said:

"You see I haven't been long."

But now that it was over, now she had kept her promise, had been near her man, she became aware again of the cold and her exhaustion. She could hardly drag herself along, her cough was so bad: every now and then she had to stop and lean against the wall . . .

At last she got back to the hotel and stumbled into the door. The girls and men were still playing cards in the overheated, smoke-filled room. A dead silence fell on them all when they saw her. She tried to laugh.

A woman at the far end of the room threw herself back on her chair and cried:

"You've made a fine start, Blue Eyes. Needed a bit of nerve, didn't it?"

She shrugged her shoulders. The other went on:

"Did you know who it was?"

"No . . ."

"Well, I'll tell you. It was Le Bingue."

Blue Eyes stammered:

"What do you say? Le . . ."

Emptying her glass and taking up her cards again, the girl called back:

"Yes, Le Bingue . . . You know, the Executioner!"

Jack Moffitt

The Lady and
the Tiger

Thwarted love and green-eyed jealousy are the key ingredients in "The Lady or the Tiger?," the classic 1884 riddle story by FRANK RICHARD STOCKTON *(1834–1902), an American author-editor whose great poser has generally been deemed unsolvable. But in the mid-1940s, a Hollywood screenwriter,* JACK MOFFITT, *astonished the editors of* Ellery Queen's Mystery Magazine *(EQMM) by declaring that he planned to solve the dilemma. They didn't think he could do it, but when Mr. Moffitt submitted his manuscript, they happily published it, declaring that "we are sure Frank R. Stockton himself, if he were alive, would be the first to applaud Mr. Moffitt's ingenuity."*

"The Lady and the Tiger," an ironic and deeply moving historical novella, culminates in a twist that indeed answers that maddening question, "Which came out of the opened door—the lady or the tiger?" But its stunning final paragraph contains an even greater shock.

(NOTE: At the outset of his story as it appeared in EQMM, *the late Mr. Moffitt included an abridged version of Stockton's enigma, but I have elected, instead, to incorporate the entire text of "The Lady or the Tiger?")*

YOU MAY FIND IT faintly ridiculous that I, Charles Sevier, a stout and fortyish researcher working in Rome at the Vatican Library, should be in love with a woman who has been dead two thousand years.

This strange infatuation was brought about by the most prosaic of instruments—Frank R. Stockton's short story, "The Lady or the Tiger?" which was published in 1884, sixteen years before my birth.

During the intervening years I doubt if there has been a single literate American who has not attempted to answer the riddle, which Mr. Stockton propounded:

The Lady or the Tiger?
Frank R. Stockton

In the very olden time, there lived a semi-barbaric king, whose ideas, though somewhat polished and sharpened by the progressiveness of distant Latin neighbors, were still large, florid, and untrammelled, as became the half of him which was barbaric. He was a man of exuberant fancy, and, withal, of an authority so irresistible that, at his will, he turned his varied fancies into facts. He was greatly given to self-communing, and when he and himself agreed upon anything, the thing was done. When every member of his domestic and political systems moved smoothly in its appointed course, his nature was bland and genial; but whenever there was a little hitch, and some of his orbs got out of their orbits, he was blander and more genial still, for nothing pleased him so much as to make the crooked straight, and crush down uneven places.

Among the borrowed notions by which his barbarism had become semified was that of the public arena, in which, by exhibitions of manly and beastly valor, the minds of his subjects were refined and cultured.

But even here the exuberant and barbaric fancy asserted itself. The arena of the king was built, not to give the people an opportunity of hearing the rhapsodies of dying gladiators, nor to enable them to view the inevitable conclusion of a conflict between religious opinions and hungry jaws, but for purposes far better adapted to widen and develop the mental energies of the people. This vast amphitheatre, with its encircling galleries, its mysterious vaults, and its unseen passages, was an agent of poetic justice, in which crime was punished, or virtue rewarded, by the decrees of an impartial and incorruptible chance.

When a subject was accused of a crime of sufficient importance to interest the king, public notice was given that on an appointed day the fate of the accused person would be decided in the king's arena—a structure which well deserved its name; for, although its form and plan were borrowed from afar, its purpose emanated solely from the brain of this man, who, every barleycorn a king, knew no tradition to which he owed more allegiance than pleased his fancy, and who ingrafted on every adopted form of human thought and action the rich growth of his barbaric idealism.

When all the people had assembled in the galleries, and the king, surrounded by his court, sat high up on his throne of royal state on one side of
the arena, he gave a signal, a door beneath him opened, and the accused
subject stepped out into the amphitheatre. Directly opposite him, on the
other side of the enclosed space, were two doors, exactly alike and side by
side. It was the duty and the privilege of the person on trial to walk directly
to these doors and open one of them. He could open either door he pleased.
He was subject to no guidance or influence but that of the aforementioned
impartial and incorruptible chance. If he opened the one, there came out of
it a hungry tiger, the fiercest and most cruel that could be procured, which
immediately sprang upon him, and tore him to pieces, as a punishment for
his guilt. The moment that the case of the criminal was thus decided,
doleful iron bells were clanged, great wails went up from the hired mourners
posted on the outer rim of the arena, and the vast audience, with bowed
heads and downcast hearts, wended slowly their homeward way, mourning
greatly that one so young and fair, or so old and respected, should have
merited so dire a fate.

But if the accused person opened the other door, there came forth from it
a lady, the most suitable to his years and station that his Majesty could
select among his fair subjects; and to this lady he was immediately married,
as a reward of his innocence. It mattered not that he might already possess a
wife and family, or that his affections might be engaged upon an object of
his own selection. The king allowed no such subordinate arrangements to
interfere with his great scheme of retribution and reward. The exercises, as
in the other instance, took place immediately, and in the arena. Another
door opened beneath the king, and a priest, followed by a band of choristers,
and dancing maidens blowing joyous airs on golden horns and treading an
epithalamic measure, advanced to where the pair stood side by side, and the
wedding was promptly and cheerily solemnized. Then the gay brass bells
rang forth their merry peals, the people shouted glad hurrahs, and the
innocent man, preceded by children strewing flowers on his path, led his
bride to his home.

This was the king's semibarbaric method of administering justice. Its
perfect fairness is obvious. The criminal could not know out of which door
would come the lady. He opened either he pleased, without having the
slightest idea whether, in the next instant, he was to be devoured or married.
On some occasions the tiger came out of one door, and on some out of the
other. The decisions of this tribunal were not only fair—they were positively
determinate. The accused person was instantly punished if he found himself

guilty, and if innocent he was rewarded on the spot, whether he liked it or not. There was no escape from the judgments of the king's arena.

The institution was a very popular one. When the people gathered together on one of the great trial days, they never knew whether they were to witness a bloody slaughter or a hilarious wedding. This element of uncertainty lent an interest to the occasion which it could not otherwise have attained. Thus the masses were entertained and pleased, and the thinking part of the community could bring no charge of unfairness against this plan; for did not the accused person have the whole matter in his own hands?

This semi-barbaric king had a daughter as blooming as his most florid fancies, and with a soul as fervent and imperious as his own. As is usual in such cases, she was the apple of his eye, and was loved by him above all humanity. Among his courtiers was a young man of that fineness of blood and lowness of station common to the conventional heroes of romance who love royal maidens. This royal maiden was well satisfied with her lover, for he was handsome and brave to a degree unsurpassed in all this kingdom, and she loved him with an ardor that had enough of barbarism in it to make it exceedingly warm and strong. This love affair moved on happily for many months, until, one day, the king happened to discover its existence. He did not hesitate nor waver in regard to his duty in the premises. The youth was immediately cast into prison, and a day was appointed for his trial in the king's arena. This, of course, was an especially important occasion, and his Majesty, as well as all the people, was greatly interested in the workings and development of this trial. Never before had such a case occurred—never before had a subject dared to love the daughter of a king. In after years such things became commonplace enough, but then they were, in no slight degree, novel and startling.

The tiger cages of the kingdom were searched for the most savage and relentless beasts, from which the fiercest monster might be selected for the arena, and the ranks of maiden youth and beauty throughout the land were carefully surveyed by competent judges, in order that the young man might have a fitting bride in case fate did not determine for him a different destiny. Of course, everybody knew that the deed with which the accused was charged had been done. He had loved the princess, and neither he, she, nor any one else thought of denying the fact. But the king would not think of allowing any fact of this kind to interfere with the workings of the tribunal, in which he took such great delight and satisfaction. No matter how the affair turned out, the youth would be disposed of, and the king would take an aesthetic pleasure in watching the course of events which *would determine whether or not the young man had done wrong in allowing himself to love the princess.*

The appointed day arrived. From far and near the people gathered, and thronged the great galleries of the arena, while crowds, unable to gain admittance, massed themselves against its outside walls. The king and his court were in their places, opposite the twin doors—those fateful portals, so terrible in their similarity!

All was ready. The signal was given. A door beneath the royal party opened, and the lover of the princess walked into the arena. Tall, beautiful, fair, his appearance was greeted with a low hum of admiration and anxiety. Half the audience had not known so grand a youth had lived among them. No wonder the princess loved him! What a terrible thing for him to be there!

As the youth advanced into the arena, he turned, as the custom was, to bow to the king. But he did not think at all of that royal personage; his eyes were fixed upon the princess, who sat to the right of her father. Had it not been for the moiety of barbarism in her nature, it is probable that lady would not have been there. But her intense and fervid soul would not allow her to be absent on an occasion in which she was so terribly interested. From the moment that the decree had gone forth that her lover should decide his fate in the king's arena, she had thought of nothing, night or day, but this great event and the various subjects connected with it. Possessed of more power, influence, and force of character than any one who had ever before been interested in such a case, she had done what no other person had done —she had possessed herself of the secret of the doors. She knew in which of the two rooms behind those doors stood the cage of the tiger, with its open front, and in which waited the lady. Through these thick doors, heavily curtained with skins on the inside, it was impossible that any noise or suggestion should come from within to the person who should approach to raise the latch of one of them. But gold, and the power of a woman's will, had brought the secret to the princess.

Not only did she know in which room stood the lady, ready to emerge, all blushing and radiant, should her door be opened, but she knew who the lady was. It was one of the fairest and loveliest of the damsels of the court who had been selected as the reward of the accused youth, should he be proved innocent of the crime of aspiring to one so far above him; and the princess hated her. Often had she seen, or imagined that she had seen, this fair creature throwing glances of admiration upon the person of her lover, and sometimes she thought these glances were perceived and even returned. Now and then she had seen them talking together. It was but for a moment or two, but much can be said in a brief space. It may have been on most unimportant topics, but how could she know that? The girl was lovely, but she had dared to raise her eyes to the loved one of the princess, and, with all the intensity of the savage blood transmitted to her through long lines of wholly barbaric ancestors, she hated the woman who blushed and trembled behind that silent door.

When her lover turned and looked at her, and his eye met hers as she sat there paler and whiter than any one in the vast ocean of anxious faces about her, he saw, by that power of quick perception which is given to those whose souls are one, that she knew behind which door crouched the tiger, and behind which stood the lady. He had expected her to know it. He understood her nature, and his soul was assured that she would never rest until she had made plain to herself this thing, hidden to all other lookers-on, even to the king. The only hope for the youth in which there was any element of certainty was based upon the success of the princess in discovering this mystery, and the moment he looked upon her, he saw she had succeeded.

Then it was that his quick and anxious glance asked the question, "Which?" It was as plain to her as if he shouted it from where he stood. There was not an instant to be lost. The question was asked in a flash; it must be answered in another.

Her right arm lay on the cushioned parapet before her. She raised her hand, and made a slight, quick movement toward the right. No one but her lover saw her. Every eye but his was fixed on the man in the arena.

He turned, and with a firm and rapid step he walked across the empty space. Every heart stopped beating, every breath was held, every eye was fixed immovably upon that man. Without the slightest hesitation, he went to the door on the right, and opened it.

Now, the point of the story is this: Did the tiger come out of that door, or did the lady?

The more we reflect upon this question, the harder it is to answer. It involves a study of the human heart which leads us through devious mazes of passion, out of which it is difficult to find our way. Think of it, fair reader, not as if the decision of the question depended upon yourself, but upon that hot-blooded, semi-barbaric princess, her soul at a white heat beneath the combined fires of despair and jealousy. She had lost him, but who should have him?

How often, in her waking hours and in her dreams, had she started in wild horror and covered her face with her hands as she thought of her lover opening the door on the other side of which waited the cruel fangs of the tiger!

But how much oftener had she seen him at the other door! How in her grievous reveries had she gnashed her teeth and torn her hair when she saw his start of rapturous delight as he opened the door of the lady! How her soul had burned in agony when she had seen him rush to meet that woman, with her flushing cheek and sparkling eye of triumph; when she had seen him lead her forth, his whole frame kindled with the joy of recovered life; when she had heard the glad shouts from the multitude, and the wild ringing of the happy bells; when she had seen the priest, with his joyous followers, advance to the couple, and make them man and wife before her very eyes; and when she had seen them walk away together upon their path of flowers, followed by the tremendous shouts of the hilarious multitude, in which her one despairing shriek was lost and drowned!

Would it not be better for him to die at once, and go to wait for her in the blessed regions of semi-barbaric futurity?

And yet, that awful tiger, those shrieks, that blood!

Her decision had been indicated in an instant, but it had been made after days and nights of anguished deliberation. She had known she would be asked, she had decided what she would answer, and, without the slightest hesitation, she had moved her hand to the right.

The question of her decision is one not to be lightly considered, and it is not for me to presume to set up myself as the one person able to answer it. So I leave it with all of you: Which came out of the opened door—the lady or the tiger?

I had heard that Stockton had obtained the idea for his story from a Roman Catholic antiquarian in the city of Rome; so it is small wonder that I determined to solve the riddle when, after several years as a researcher in the Library of Congress, I was sent to introduce a modern cataloguing system in the Vatican Archives. The immediate purpose of my employment was to search for a long-lost letter supposed to have been written by Pontius Pilate. But I had plenty of time for private research.

After considerable study I decided that Stockton's king could have been none other than Herod Antipas, who ruled Judea under the supervision of the Roman Governor, Pontius Pilate. He was the only eastern monarch who owned an arena, which his father had built after the Roman pattern, but he also had a daughter—or rather a step-daughter—of whom he was unnaturally and inordinately infatuated.

This girl was the Princess Salome.

The logic fitted. I felt that I had identified two of the characters in Stockton's story. But it was not until I found the cracked and yellowed parchment, covered with Hebrew characters and written in a sprawling, girlish hand, that I was certain of it. For this letter was written by the girl who had waited behind the second door.

To the High Priest, Caiphas; from his daughter, Miriam.

Beloved Father,

How can I tell you how much I love you? I know that you must be ashamed of me because all Jerusalem now knows that I love the Greek youth, Jason. I know you will feel humiliated—almost defiled—to see me married to him, by a pagan ritual, before all the people in the King's arena tomorrow. Yet I know that even now, despite your sorrow and your humiliation, you are praying to our one true God to defend Jason and asking the Lord to lead him to the door behind which I will be waiting.

I know that you are doing this, in spite of your conviction that Jason is shallow and ambitious—one of those youths who came swaggering out of Alexandria to seek his fortune at the court of Herod. And I feel that you are praying for Jason, even though you dislike him, because you abominate murder and because you have always been a just and merciful man.

Oh, dear! It is dreadful to be young! It seems odd to remember that I didn't want to go with you to Herod's palace on that day last autumn—when I first met Jason. For weeks I'd heard you and Grandfather discussing the arrogance of Pontius Pilate who had displayed the eagles of his legions on the fortress of Antonia, overlooking the Temple courtyard. Of course, I'd been taught to regard graven images as sacrilegious, but I wondered why older people made such a fuss about things.

When you decided that the family should ask Herod to intercede, I pretended to have a headache. But I didn't fool you. You said the visit would seem more tactful and more friendly if the whole family went along. I was amused to see, when we arrived at the palace, that your strategy had not fooled Herod any more than mine had fooled you. His chamberlain led you and Grandfather away to the King's audience chamber, while the rest of us were sent to wait for you in one of the private courtyards.

As soon as my little brothers saw the fountain splashing in the center of the palace, they rushed toward it squealing and laughing.

I tried to get them interested in the pictures in the floor of the courtyard. They were mosaics showing the fall of Troy. I told as much of the Pagan story as I thought was good for them.

But you know Nathan. He can't sit still for more than a minute.

"Look!" he shouted, "I'll bet I can jump all around this place and never put my foot on anything but the women!"

This wasn't easy. There were many more warriors in the mosaic floor than there were goddesses. Nathan missed on the third jump. But he had started a game. Soon the whole place was filled with the hopping children, wobbling and tottering as they leaped from Minerva to Aphrodite to Helen, and so on. I know it was childish, but it really was fun. So, just to keep them quiet, I pulled up my dress above my knees and joined in.

And then I heard someone laughing.

Dearest heavens! I could have died! A man had entered the courtyard —a tall, lithe man wearing sandals of silver leather and a tunic and cloak of green silk.

He laughed and said, "Who are you?"

You can imagine how confused I was as I dropped my skirts and tried to brush the hair out of my eyes. It was too awful for a grown-up woman to be caught like this by a member of the court, playing a ridiculous childish game. After all, I am fourteen years old.

"Who are you?" he repeated, coming toward me. "Surely you must have a name—is it Daphne? Or Thetis? Are you a dryad? Or a nymph?"

I was afraid the stranger might laugh at me when I told him who I was. But he didn't. He bowed and replied courteously.

"You must come with me, Miriam," he said. "I have been commanded to bring you to the princess."

I wasn't so sure I should go. But the young man kept laughing and assuring us that he was repeating a royal order—until I finally let him lead me away through the maze of splendid corridors.

I couldn't find anything to say as I walked beside him, listening to his easy conversation. He told me that his name was Jason and that he had lived in Rome and Alexandria. He was the most interesting man I had ever met.

Finally, we came to a larger courtyard, where Salome idled beneath a pinkish awning, surrounded by many courtiers. Youths and maidens from all over the world were there—Greeks and Arabians and officers from the Roman garrison, and even a number of young Jews—though these were unlike any Jews I had seen before. Their cheeks were shaved and they wore Greek or Roman clothing.

Salome was a surprise. She didn't look at all like the kind of girl who could have caused the death of the young preacher whom the country people called the Baptist. She wore no veils or oriental draperies. Her gown was simple and Grecian, with the skirt folded into many soft pleats that concealed but outlined her small and doll-like figure. I had seen her mother, Herodias, in a procession once, and I had expected the daughter to have the same stately figure and proud eyes.

But Salome was a kitten. She had a little heart-shaped face and large and limpid brown eyes and she had learned how to use them.

"You are late, Jason," she said reproachfully, "our treasure hunt is over. Only you have returned empty-handed."

"You are wrong, Princess," said Jason, leading me forward, "you told me to bring you a Hebrew Diana—and I have."

"This is ridiculous!" Salome's pink small lips were pouting. "You knew I meant a statue."

"Did you, Princess? How could you? You know the Hebrews have made no images since the days of the Golden Calf. But it pleases you to demand the impossible of me."

"If I do, it is because you think you are so clever! Right now you feel quite proud of yourself!"

"Proud, yes. But not conceited." I felt my face burning as he held up my hand and slowly turned me around. "Praxiteles himself would be proud of the golden girl that I have brought."

"All you Greeks seem to think of gold in connection with women!" The milk-white Salome seemed to resent my olive skin. "To call this little thing a Diana is ridiculous."

"Let me go!" I struggled to free my wrist. "I despise every one of you!"

"No!" Jason's strong hands gripped my elbows as he lifted me up on a bench. "I didn't bring you here to be insulted! We'll show this princess that her taste is as bad as her manners! Hold your head up—you are the High Priest's daughter—you are as good as any of them!"

His voice was harsh, as though he were fighting a duel in which I was his weapon. I was trembling and overwrought, but I held up my head and tried to stare defiantly back at Salome, even though I was blinking back the tears.

"Observe the slender strength of her neck line!" he cried, as he snatched up a silver bow from the loot of the treasure hunt. "And have you noticed the supple gracefulness of her figure? Diana has come to life again!"

He fitted an arrow to the bow and placed it in my hands. The arrow was aimed straight at Salome. But she didn't flinch. There was a brooding hatefulness in her eyes.

"There!" said Jason, stepping back as I held the pose. "Is she not even more lovely than Diana? Can any of you say that the Diana of Epheseus has half her beauty? Answer me!"

"Well, it theems to me—" lisped the Greek called Philo, with a nervous glance at Salome.

"I'm not asking Greeks!" snapped Jason. "I am asking the Romans! What do you say, Galba?"

It was clever of him. The Romans loved to show their disdainful independence of Herod's provincial entourage. A slow grin spread over the youthful face of Galba. He passed his big hand over his close-cropped hair.

"By Jupiter! You're right," he said. "I have wasted incense before the statue of Epheseus, but I'd sacrifice my very sword and armor for the Diana we have here!"

All the other Roman officers were quick to agree with him. The courtiers chimed in too. I heard myself praised and complimented in a dozen accents, and my skin tingled with pleasure, just as it had flinched and trembled a few minutes before. It was glorious to be defended and admired.

And then I heard King Herod's smooth chuckle and saw him coming across the courtyard, followed by you and Grandfather.

"By Aphrodite!" he said. "Jason, it seems that you have found a jewel in my threadbare little country. I am very pleased."

I don't remember the rest of that day very clearly. All I remember is the horrible trip home. Grandfather Annas said that I had done something monstrous. It was a shameful thing for the daughter of the High Priest to pose as a pagan goddess before a throng of infidels.

I had little appetite for the dinner old Anna kept urging me to eat. She just can't forget that I no longer need a nurse. I went up on the roof and gazed out through the twilight toward the Mount of Olives. A great sense of poignancy welled up in me. I felt so lonely that it hurt. Then I heard you behind me.

"My dear," you said, "I know it is hard for you to believe but once, a long, long time ago, I was young, too. I try to remember those times."

"Yes, Father," I replied looking out across the mystic Valley of Kidron.

You crossed the floor and stroked my hair. "We must have patience, Miriam," you said, "the heroes of our nation have always been men of the spirit—men who combined courage with inspiration. In our bitterest days they come to us—these men who live gloriously close to God. There have always been such men."

"Where are they now?" I asked.

"I do not know, child," you answered musingly. "But people tell of certain men in Galilee—there is the oldtime ring of greatness in much that I have heard of them."

Before you could go on, there was a pounding at the door and a voice: "Open in King Herod's name!"

I think, for all your dignity, Father, you were as frightened as I was as we stood, close together in the passage, and heard the officer tell us that I was to become a lady-in-waiting to Salome, and go with the court to Herod's winter palace at Tiberias.

No child knows how much it loves a parent until the time comes to leave home. Do you remember how melancholy the first autumn rains were when you took me to the Gennot Gate to join the royal caravan?

The trip was a lonely one. None of the women paid any attention to me. And I'd seen nothing of Jason. Shortly before dawn on the last day, I heard one of the camel men exclaim: "Tiberias!" and I poked my head through the curtains to get my first look at our destination.

It was a strange and wonderful sight that lay spread out before us in the fresh washed air of the morning. The sun was just breaking through the clouds beyond the solemn dome of Mount Tabor and the light flashed back from the Sea of Galilee—really only a large lake—as though from a silver shield.

As I watched, there was a thunder of hoofs and a chariot swept past—a chariot drawn by four deep-chested, black-maned Arabians. Jason held the reins. He wore a tight tunic of orange-colored leather and an orange cape streamed back from his shoulders. He was a flame flashing down from the hills upon the black city of Tiberias.

Later, I was glad to see that Herod's palace wasn't so gloomy once you were inside. The rooms were bright with rich hangings and imported marbles. I was given a pretty little chamber at one end of the women's building. The King, himself, came with his royal housekeeper to see that I was comfortable. My only worry was that the balcony window could be reached from a nearby cedar. But, of course, I didn't complain. The King might have thought I was silly.

Some of the dresses that had been provided for me were positively indecent. You could see right through them. The others made of heavier materials had their skirts split too far above the knee. I was glad old Anna had taught me to sew, and that I'd brought my needle kit. With a little work I could make some of them look modest.

I had plenty of time. Neither Salome nor the Queen ever sent for me.

Day after day I had nothing to do except work on my dresses and try new ways of fixing my hair.

Some weeks later I found Jason seated beside me at the first of the King's banquets. I suppose I shouldn't say "seated." The guests reclined on long couches placed by the banquet table. Jason lounged by my side. I wasn't used to this fashion and was embarrassed.

But Jason made me feel at ease. He was smiling and very respectful. Even after the seventh course, when the wine was flowing much too freely and the party was getting a good deal worse than rowdy, he drank sparingly and never once touched me.

Salome didn't drink much either. She reclined across the room from us, between her mother and stepfather. I felt a little disloyal and unpatriotic for noticing that the King was getting tipsy. He laughed too loud and kept whispering things into the Princess's ear.

I would have thought that the Queen might have protected her daughter, but Herodias ignored her husband and kept her eyes fixed coldly on the entertainers, giving no encouragement to the suggestive dancers and their off-color songs. Though a member of the same mongrel clan as Herod, she conducted herself with the calm dignity of a Jewish matron.

Time and again I saw Salome's brown eyes look appealingly across the room to Jason. She seemed to envy us. And in spite of the way she'd neglected me, I felt sorry for her.

"Never feel sorry for a beautiful woman," replied Jason, when I mentioned this to him. "They know how to look out for themselves."

"My! Haven't you grown sophisticated and cynical!" I tried to speak mockingly, like one of the court ladies.

He turned to me and said, "I was born a slave but I might have been a prince—one of the rulers of the Roman world—if it hadn't been for a woman even more beautiful than Salome."

"A slave! You are teasing me! I don't believe it!"

"Even though I was born a slave," he said, "I am not a complete impostor. My father was a nobleman. He served on Marc Antony's flagship at the Battle of Actium."

"I don't care who you are, Jason—you don't have to tell me!"

He drank wine and stared morosely toward Salome. "My father became a slave and I was born in slavery because of the vanity of a woman. There was no reason for Cleopatra to be in that battle. Marc Antony begged her to stay ashore. But she was very brave as long as the enemy galleys were on the other side of the horizon and she knew she looked very pretty in her armor. She wanted to be a sea queen and inspire the men!"

Jason spat upon the pavement and exclaimed, "To think that such vanity could have changed the fate of the world! At the height of the battle Cleopatra's ships turned and ran—and do you know why they ran?"

"I have heard that it was because Octavius who opposed her used his catapults to throw great glass globes filled with serpents and that when the globes broke on Cleopatra's decks, she became terrorized of the serpents—"

"That's not the real reason. Cleopatra wasn't afraid of snakes. She deserted Antony because she suddenly decided that it would be safer to win Octavius with her charms than to meet him in battle. And because of her cowardice, Marc Antony killed himself and my father was captured and reduced to slavery. Octavius forced him to become a gladiator."

He stopped abruptly as though he'd decided that he had talked enough. So this was the background of this seemingly gay man. He was the son of a slave and a gladiator.

Herodias was following her drunken husband from the room and Salome was picking her way among the sodden revelers toward the great arch that led to the moonlit gardens. She paused on the threshold and looked back toward us. And for the first time she was smiling.

"It is getting late," Jason told me. "You had better go to your room." There was nothing to do but obey him.

After that it became apparent that the King had ordered Jason to be my escort at all court functions. But he didn't obey very often. It was exasperating to have him send an excuse, accompanied by some rich present, at the last moment.

Once the young people got up an excursion, with a picnic lunch and chariots, to hear a country preacher who addressed a great multitude on Mount Tabor. This preacher was quite the rage. The people told marvelous tales about him and even the court circle regarded him as a new sensation. I wondered if he was one of the men of Galilee whom you had mentioned. But I never found out. Jason didn't invite me, so I stayed with Salome and Herod and Herodias. After the scandal about the Baptist, they weren't much interested in country preachers.

Some weeks later, when the moon was waning, Herod gave an elaborate fête in the palace gardens. The grounds were illuminated by Greek fire thrown into the waters of the fountains. The floating flames transformed the black basins into gigantic lamps, and in this flickering glare Italian contortionists and acrobats and tight-rope walkers performed.

At first I was shocked by their nakedness. But Jason, seated beside me in the shadows, said that instead of scorning the poor mountebanks I should pity them. For all we knew, he said, these boys and girls might be the children of aristocrats, or even of the Emperor. In Rome, he told me, unwanted children were left out in the hills for the wolves to eat and sometimes these abandoned creatures were found by human wolves— vagabonds and criminals who took them home and trained them for strange and evil callings.

"I can't understand your world," I said. "It is a terrible place! No Jewish mother could abandon her babies to such a life. No matter how low she had fallen."

"I know," he whispered. "My mother couldn't leave me out on the hill either—even though she tried to. It might have been better if she had."

Somehow I knew that I must comfort this man in his terrible gnawing misery. It was what God had put me in the world for. I put my hands on his cheeks and kissed him.

Then he was on his feet, pulling me up to him. His strong arm was around me as he led me into the shadows. He was returning my kiss—on my lips, my throat, my shoulders—and his kisses were fierce and hard.

"Darling, oh, my darling!" I cried, clinging to him. "You needn't be so fierce—so hurried—I will never run away from you—never!"

He paused and looked at me, and his arms were a tight circle around my body.

"Don't you see?" I said. "You need never be lonely again, ever—it doesn't matter what you've been—"

"You're wrong! It's the only thing that matters!" His arms grew slack and his voice was bitter. "I started as a piece of human garbage—left out on a Roman junk pile—and all my life has been a struggle to keep from going back there."

The fierceness had gone out of him. He sank to the ground with his face turned toward the distant fountains, where the children's bodies glittered above the flickering fire.

"I never knew my mother," his words came moodily. "I hardly knew my father. The only clear memory I have of him is of one night—when I must have been about twelve. I was seated beside him at a great banquet in the barracks of the gladiators. The air was foul with the fumes of torches and there was a great deal of noise.

"Most of the gladiators were roaring drunk; guzzling liquor and gorging themselves until they vomited—trying to forget that they might die the next day. Others scarcely touched the heaping tables, because they hoped to be more fit in the arena. Some, too stupid or calloused to care what happened, tumbled on the floor with the slave women provided for their convenience.

"My father sat at a small table with an older gladiator named Longinus —a man whose life my father once had spared in the arena. They kept me on the bench between them.

"As the night wore on, he placed his hand behind my head and forced me to look at the hoggish couples who wallowed on the floor. 'Look, my son,' he said, with a mirthless smile. 'Look and see how you were created! Your mother was just such a drab as these!'

"I remember that I began to cry. And people stopped to stare at us. A child was the one thing they didn't expect to see at a gladiators' banquet. Longinus growled to my father to shut up. The scene was horrible.

"But my father continued in a low, intense voice. 'I am telling the boy this so that he may remember his destiny when I am gone! I didn't know his mother—I couldn't have told her from any of the other slatterns. The one time I embraced her, I was drunk. But, by the Gods, she remembered me! I shall never forget the dumb look that was on her face when she came to the barracks with her baby. I saw adoration there, not for me, but for the child—for you, son!'

"He told me that my mother had left me out on the hill, as she had left her previous children. But something nagged at her stupid mind and told her that she could not let the child of a prince die that way. So she went back to the hill and brought me to my father.

"And as he held me in his arms, my father felt that the ignorant trull was right. She had inspired him.

"His thick-skinned sword-hand gripped my shoulder as he told me all this and he said, 'I can only find freedom through you, my son! My blood in you can be a prince again! And this I demand of you, that no matter what happens—whether I live or die—that you shall fight by every method to reclaim our lost greatness!' "

Jason repeated his father's words in a voice that was low but excited, the tone he always used when he spoke of how important he might have been. Now his voice went flat.

"My father died the next day. He had been matched against Longinus. It was an honest fight. It had to be, or both men would have been thrown to the lions. Suddenly, though he had suffered no wound, my father collapsed upon the sand. I guess his heart gave out, after the long years of fighting. As I watched, his feeble arm went up in the gesture that asked for mercy. He wanted to live because of me.

"Longinus looked toward the Emperor. But Tiberius reached out a brawny arm and pointed his thumb—down.

"I saw the pleading look on Longinus' face. He hesitated. There were tears on his cheeks. The arena attendants were running forward to split my father's skull with mallets—the death reserved for a coward.

"Longinus' sword flashed down."

Jason had finished his story. The last of the flaming fountains flickered into darkness. We heard Herod ordering the servants to light the torches. I held Jason close and tried to comfort him. But when the flares were ignited, he moved away.

A few days later he was my escort when Herod took the court to his race course outside the city. Now he seemed to be trying to forget everything he had confided. His robes were rich and perfect. His eyebrows had been thinned and his smile was aloof and distant as he glanced toward the royal box, where Salome sat beside her stepfather.

In each race the colors of the charioteers were the same—white, red, blue, and green. Jason explained that these identified the four great racing syndicates in Rome. Herod favored the blue because that was the faction of the reigning emperor.

"I want to bet on the whites," I told Jason.

"Why?" he asked. "The blue is the best bet, but if you want a good long shot, choose the red. It is an exciting color."

"But the whites are your horses!" I said. "I saw you drive them into the city."

His face clouded as he replied, "They are not my horses!" He spoke with undue vehemence. But I continued to smile at him. I knew what I had seen.

"Look, Miriam!" he cajoled. "The white hasn't a chance! They are older than the others, and the horse on the inside trace has a bowed tendon."

"Nevertheless, I want to bet on them!"

"All right," he shrugged. "At least, you'll get good odds."

Perhaps I imagined it, but as the chariots paraded past, I thought a slight signal passed from Jason to the charioteer in white.

I know you don't know much about racing, Father, so I'll try to explain to you. The two center horses are harnessed to the tongue of the chariot, while the outside animals run in leather shafts called traces. On the white chariot the outside horse was in a long trace so that he ran far out from his teammates. He wasn't pulling, he was running free and independently. And his long trace made a leather barrier across the track so that no other chariot could pass.

It was the first time this trick had been seen in Palestine. The shouts from the grandstands were deafening. At first, people thought there had been an accident and that the outside horse had broken his harness. But soon the air was filled with the excited frenzy of those who had backed the white and the curses of those who had bet on the other colors. Then everybody forgot money in their amazement at the skill of the thing. The outside horse swept around the track, keeping close to the outside railing —and the other chariots didn't try to pass for fear of getting entangled and turned over.

Of course, the white won! I turned excitedly to Jason.

"These provincial drivers are amateurs," he shrugged scornfully. "If this race had been run in Rome all the chariots would have had long traces. The green would have run into the white so that the blue could get through. Afterwards the drivers would have shared in the winning purse—and the Emperor's favor."

"But what of the drivers? They wear the ends of the reins wrapped around their bodies—wouldn't such crack-ups be dangerous?"

"Of course," he replied indifferently. "If they were quick, they might cut themselves free with their daggers—or they might be killed. That's the chance you take in Rome."

The odds had been twenty-to-one. I won almost fifty silver shekels, even after the bookmaker had taken his commission.

I soon discovered that, even at Herod's court, a girl can have many friends after she's won fifty shekels. It was astonishing how many of the court ladies were short on spending money. They came to me for little loans—which they never paid back; and by way of compensation, they included me in their conversation, most of which was catty—if not positively evil. They seldom came right out and said anything vicious. But they were full of hints and innuendos. According to them, the King was in love with Salome.

"And, my dear, his interest isn't entirely fatherly," one of them giggled.

I didn't like to hear this, even though I felt it might be true. The King's attitude toward Salome was anything but decorous. Still, the thing they hinted at was perfectly monstrous—and I doubted if even Herod, who had defied the Law by taking his brother's wife, would pile incest on incest by now making love to his stepdaughter.

"Whatever the King may lack," I said, "he is still our King—and the only protection we have from the Romans. And, as long as we are members of his household, we owe him our loyalty and our patriotism."

"Listen to her silly preaching!" laughed an Athenian girl named Enid. "Of all people! If Herod wasn't in love with Salome, little Miriam wouldn't be here!"

I didn't like this Enid. She had a long jaw that kept her from being pretty, so she tried to attract attention to her figure. To make sure of this, she walked with her hips thrust out in a most preposterous and vulgar way. She had borrowed more from me than the others. Maybe that was why she was always giving me digs.

"What do you mean?" I flared.

"Oh, please, Miriam!" She glanced over her shoulder at her hips with an air of exaggerated patience and languor. "You of all people shouldn't be naive! Don't you realize that the King brought you here to keep Jason away from Salome?"

"You are absolutely insane!" I retorted. "I never heard of anything so stupid! The King is the King! If he doesn't like Jason, he can send him away!"

"What a dull little thing you are! Herod isn't rude to one who's been favored by Pontius Pilate!"

"But how do I fit into his plans?"

"Darling, are you actually asking me to tell you? I was hoping we could be more delicate. Why do you think the King gave you this lovely room with a window—so accessible from the gardens?"

"Get out!" My face was flaming. "Get out! I won't answer your filthy accusations! I never want to see any of you again!"

Enid strutted toward the door, followed by the others. Their steps were insolent and leisurely.

"All right, we'll go, my dear! There's no need to be shrill. After all, it isn't our fault that the King's plan miscarried—and that the Greek prefers Salome. He never goes near you except when he is commanded, and even then he scarcely dares speak—he's so afraid of Salome. No wonder you're jealous!"

When they were gone I threw myself on the couch and cried. I wished I could go back home to Jerusalem. I longed for a life that was clean and decent. The court and everyone in it was hateful. I wanted you, father. I wanted to crawl in your lap, like a little girl, and to forget everything.

But that afternoon we were ordered to accompany the King to the famous mineral hot baths, south of the city.

I sent word that I was too ill to go to the baths. But they refused to accept my excuses. Queen Herodias herself came to persuade me. Her attitude was almost motherly, and she was so serene and dignified that it was hard to argue with her. She said the baths were good for all sorts of ailments and were bound to make me feel better. Furthermore, she said that the King had sent her to tell me that Jason was waiting. I wondered if she knew that she and I were both pawns in his love game. But I didn't dare ask. I was too discouraged to do anything but submit. I let her take my hand and lead me out to Jason's chariot.

He was driving the Arabians and he looked very handsome. At once he began his amiable chatter.

"Please," I said. "There is no need to be charming. I know that you are with me only because of the King's orders."

His look was pained. "Miriam, you don't understand—"

"I think I do. Your father was a slave and you are a slave—a slave to your ambitions."

I wanted to hurt him. The anger flushed up behind his sunburn. He lashed the horses and the chariot spun forward ahead of the rest of the procession. He didn't draw rein until we had reached the baths.

"Miriam," he said. "You have to believe me!"

"Why should I? I know that you have lied to me. You even told me that these horses weren't yours!"

"In a way, they aren't," he said. "These horses were the property of the White Syndicate. I took them from Rome with me when I retired from racing."

"You stole those horses?" I made my voice scornful. "You *are* dishonest —and more foolhardy than your reckless nature seems capable of being."

"Well, why not!" he exclaimed. "They're my luck! Longinus apprenticed me to a charioteer after my father died, and I won two hundred and thirty-nine victories with these horses in the Circus Maximus. They made me a millionaire!"

"But you are not satisfied with being a millionaire! You must have the love of a princess, even though you have to share that love with her stepfather! You are as evil as they are!"

He restrained me as I started to leave the chariot.

"Please, Miriam!" he begged. "I know you have good reason to be angry. But doesn't the fact that I let my horses win for you mean anything? I had planned to keep that trick up my sleeve."

"I don't doubt it! And I still don't know why you became so generous —I don't want your pity! And I don't want your favors!" I flung myself out of the chariot.

The rest of the royal procession was driving up just then. Salome looked hatefully at me and even the Queen seemed irritated. But Herod was smiling and bland. We went into the baths.

I was relieved to see that the men's and women's quarters were separate. I hadn't known what to expect. As soon as we were in the women's section, Salome and the others threw their clothes off. I found a dark spot in a corner of the steam room and tried to be inconspicuous. The Queen had a pitcher of wine brought to her. It was the first time I had seen her drink. She explained that she did this to increase her perspiration. After a while she and her favorites played ball with a sphere stuffed with feathers. They caught it with their right hands and threw it with their left. Soon the Queen and an Abyssinian girl grabbed for the ball at the same time, and began to wrestle for it.

I clutched a towel around my self and tried to stay out of their way, as they grunted and strained in their efforts to throw each other. But they kept bumping into me and I had the feeling that these accidents were deliberate.

Finally I got away—only to face new tormenters. Salome and her girls were rushing around the room, rolling light metal hoops. I did my best to avoid them. But inevitably, Salome ran her hoop across my feet.

"Excuse me!" she would cry mockingly—then hit me with the stick she used to guide the hoop. "Oh, I'm sorry!" she would laugh.

The other girls were quick to take up the game. No matter where I went, they came toward me screeching, "You clumsy slattern! Get out of our way!"

I was so angry I forgot I didn't have any clothes on. I wanted to hit Salome and pull her hair and throw her on the pavement—even if the other girls all fought on her side. I knew I would be punished, but I didn't care. You can endure just so much. I wrested the stick from her hand and aimed a blow at her.

But before it could land, the other girls surrounded me and with shrieks and shouts, bore me through the great bronze doors to the plunge. They threw me in and leaped in after me. The water was hot. It smelled of sulphur and had a bitter, salty taste. I was ducked several times, then suddenly they let me alone and I crawled out and got dressed. The others, by now, were splashing in the showers or being massaged by the serving women. I slipped out of the building, without waiting for this.

A peasant woman with some donkeys was passing. I asked her to take me back to Tiberias. The road was dusty and the donkeys slow.

It wasn't long before my skin started itching and my eyes watering.

From my sandals to my headband, I was feverish. I felt so ill I hardly noticed that a chariot was overtaking us. Jason swung the horses across the path of the donkeys.

"Get down!" he shouted. "Get down, you little fool!"

He was out of the chariot, reaching strong hands up to me.

"You poor little thing, I know what they did to you at the baths—"

"Don't touch me!" One of his arms was beneath my knees, the other around my shoulders. He carried me toward a thicket at the side of the road. The bewildered peasant woman made no effort to stop him. Beneath the shadows of gnarled olive trees the air was close and heavy with the fragrance of blossoming almonds. I could hardly breathe.

"Take off your clothes." He put me down beside a little stream. "You must bathe in fresh water."

"No—!" I backed away from him.

"You little idiot, don't you see their treacherous scheme? If you don't bathe in fresh water after the sulphur plunge, your skin will become blotched and hideous." He gripped my shoulders and shook me roughly. "I'll not have your beauty marred—you are the loveliest thing I've ever seen! Do as I tell you or I'll strip you and throw you in!"

As though reading my thoughts, he suddenly relaxed. His smile was gentle, and his voice tender.

"Don't be afraid. I'll go back down the path and wait."

He kissed my forehead and turned back into the bushes beneath the dark trees.

The brook was cool and refreshing. I lay back on the soft sand and let the waters rush over me. The ripples moved caressingly. All the discomfort and the fever was washed away. A sweet and dreamy lassitude overcame me. I wondered if he was watching from the depths of the thicket. But I didn't think so.

And then I wondered why he didn't come. Perhaps he only protected me as a child is protected. Was this another of his pitying favors? If a man really loved a woman, he could not stay away from her.

There was a stir in the undergrowth. Enid and the simpering Greek, Philo, stood looking at me.

"Oh, excuse us!" tittered Enid. "We saw Jason's chariot, so we sneaked in to see what he was up to. Of course, we didn't dream—!"

She turned as she saw Jason coming toward her.

"Thorry to dithturb your little idyl," lisped Philo.

Jason threw a stone and the intruders ran laughing into the thicket. We both knew they'd make a malicious scandal of what they had seen as soon as they got back to Tiberias.

While Jason turned his back, I put my clothes on and we drove home in worried silence.

That night I didn't go to the dining hall for supper. And no one came to persuade me. As soon as it was dark, I took a dark cloak and what money I had left and slipped out through a side gate. Staying close to the walls in the dark streets, I headed for the fishing quarter at the shores of the Sea of Galilee.

The fishermen's nets, on drying racks, looked like acres of delicate lace in the moonlight. Shadowy figures were removing them. The sky was threatening and we were close to the season of spring rains.

I approached a slight, aristocratic-looking young man who was struggling rather clumsily to fold up some of the nets. He listened sympathetically as I told him that I was the daughter of Caiphas, the High Priest, and that I had to get home to Jerusalem.

"It is a dangerous journey," he said with a kindly smile. "A desperate journey for a young girl. After the waters of the Galilee enter into the Jordan, the course is swift and tortuous. And the eastern shore is peopled with savage Bedouins—"

"I know! But anything is better than Tiberias! If I stay here I'll surely die! I'll pay you anything!"

"It isn't the pay." There was a deprecating smile on his fine Jewish features. "It is just that I am not a boatman. My name is Matthew—I used to be a tax gatherer. So you see, I have not been trained to do anything very useful."

He turned and pointed to a camp fire farther up the beach, where a number of men sat around the flames.

"But some of my friends are fishermen, very good fishermen—Peter and Andrew and James. Our Master teaches us that we must love our neighbors as ourselves—so I am sure that they will help you."

"Oh, if they only would!"

He hurried away toward the camp fire. Something about the man had given me reassurance and a certain feeling of hope.

And then from among the shadows and the foamy nets, I saw Jason's tall figure before me. I turned toward the boats drawn up on the sand. I didn't want to talk to him.

"Don't go, Miriam!"

"I have to—you shouldn't have followed me—"

"If you go, I must go with you. I will be your boatman." He took my hand. "Whither thou goest, I shall go—thy people shall be my people, and thy god, my god."

"Please, don't mock me! Leave me alone!"

"I can never do that, dearest! God knows I have tried not to love you. I was a slave to ambition as you said—but now, I have forgotten everything —but you."

"If I could only believe you!"

The silvery moonlight, through the thick, scudding clouds, cast an uneven causeway across the waters. The far shores of Galilee, the savage shores, were wrapped in beckoning mystery.

"Come!" Jason lifted me into a boat and pushed it into the water. With a hasty movement he picked up the sweep and poled us out of the shallows.

I lay back against the rough wood and looked up toward the dappled heavens. Why did I always surrender? I seemed to have no will when Jason was near me. Still, if he was telling the truth, if he really loved me—

"Was Salome angry?" I asked.

"Furious! She made a terrible scene!"

"Are you sure that you want to leave her? That you don't love her?"

"Love! That woman doesn't know what it is to love! For months she has kept me dangling—simply playing with me."

"It is hard to believe that any woman could do that to you, Jason. You seem so sure of yourself."

"She is a princess," he said bitterly. "And the stakes were high. I learned to gamble when I was a charioteer. Herod is a worthless puppet. Everyone in Rome despises him and Salome is of royal blood. Her husband would be in a position to guarantee the Eastern empire. He might become emperor himself when Tiberius dies—"

"You dreamed of that!"

"Why not! I have a fortune and so has Salome. The throne will be sold by the Praetorian Guard—the palace troops control the empire. But all that is forgotten. Let's not talk about it any more."

I didn't want to talk. I was too happy. Jason raised the sail and little gusts of wind propelled us southward. He came forward and lay beside me. We looked up at the changing sky.

Then, without warning, the squall broke upon us. The sail was split with a roar like a bull. Shredded canvas whipped in the wind as the boat was lashed by the fury of the spring rains.

Jason scrambled to the sweep, struggling awkwardly to keep us from the trough of the waves. I was drenched as I fought to take in the whipping fragments of the tattered sail. Then the whole keel shivered as the craggy nose of a concealed rock forced its way through the splintering wood. The waves closed over us and I felt Jason's arm around me. I sank into a swirl of thunder and darkness.

How long it lasted I will never know exactly. After a time my mind struggled toward consciousness—only to slip back to oblivion again. In these rare, half-lucid moments it seemed that I was again in my room in Herod's palace. Once I seemed to see Jason's face bending over me and feel his hand behind my head. A cup was pressed to my lips and I heard him say, "Drink, Miriam, dearest, you must get strong and well for my sake."

Finally the fever left me and I returned to the consciousness of a bright, sunshiny day. It hadn't been a hallucination. Outside the windows of my room in the palace the trees were in full blossom. But my chamber had the untidiness of a sick room. I crawled from beneath the covers and looked at myself in the steel mirror. It was a thin, drawn face that looked back at me. I rang for the serving maid, but she did not come.

Finally, trembling and pausing to rest at frequent intervals, I managed to wash myself and dress in clean clothes. Then, supporting myself with a hand against the wall, I faltered out into the corridors. There was a littered, deserted look to the halls. The serving women, in untidy dress, gossiped in slatternly clusters. When I talked to them their looks were bold and insolent and their words just barely courteous. They told me that Herod and the entire court had returned to Jerusalem to celebrate the holidays.

I returned to my room to find one of the lesser servants—a girl about as old as I am—putting my gold hairpins in her hair. When she saw me, she made a guilty movement and knocked over the alabaster lamp—the one that Jason had given me. It smashed upon the floor.

I was so angry I snatched a girdle from the wardrobe and began to whip her with it. She dropped to her knees and whined for mercy.

"Stop sniveling!" I said. "And tell me what has happened. Take me to Jason!"

"He has gone—on the day after the Princess and the women's caravan left for Jerusalem. Enid came back here with a message for Jason."

"And?"

"It seemed to disturb him. He had not left your side since the night of the great storm. He put on his traveling cloak. Then he threw it aside. He walked in the gardens, hour after hour. He called for his chariot, then he returned it to the stables. It was not the first message the Princess had sent to him, but he had rejected all the others with curses. Now after many black looks he called for the chariot again and drove away toward Jerusalem."

"And the message?"

The servant whimpered that she did not know any more. So I ordered her to leave me.

Dear God! Was I never to be sure of him? Had Salome capitulated? Had her message said that she would marry him? And had this last surrender been too great a temptation?

I had to know. I got my faded cloak from the wardrobe. My silver still was secure in the secret pocket of the lining. Hurrying to the beach, I asked for the former tax gatherer, Matthew.

"He isn't here," a surly old fisherman told me. "He and his crowd have gone to Jerusalem for the Passover. Bad luck to them!"

"Why do you say that? Matthew seemed kind."

"Oh, yes," the fisherman grumbled. "Very kind. I took my son, Reuben, to Capernaum to be cured of blindness. But on the night we went there, this Matthew and his Master came to Tiberias. That was the miracle—the evil miracle! We missed each other—for no reason at all!"

"This may have been meant to test you!" I was saying anything in an effort to influence him. "You should follow these Galileans. Take your son to Jerusalem! By boat you can be there for the holidays!"

"By boat?" Such a journey had not occurred to him. I kept on talking and offered him silver. He took the money, but it was his love for his boy that decided him.

My thoughts raced ahead as we left the clear waters of Galilee and rushed through overhanging jungles, made lush and foul by the recent floods of the Jordan.

Despite the skill of the fisherman, the boat sometimes stuck on a sandbar. When this happened, he and I would go over the side. The sand eddied around our feet as we pushed the boat back into deeper current. At last the boat whirled into the shallows and I saw the crested helmets of the Romans at the post house. With the last of my silver I bribed an officer to take me up to Jerusalem on the crupper of his horse. We entered the city by the Double Gate. The streets were filled with people shouting hosannahs and waving palm branches. Through the crowd I caught a glimpse of Matthew in a little group of men. They were gathered around a Man wearing a colored robe, who was seated upon a donkey. And for an instant I thought I saw you, Father, standing on the outer stairs of the Temple, smiling approval toward these men.

But this was just a confused impression. Before I could identify you, the cavalryman turned his horse into one of the side streets leading to Herod's palace.

Galba was the officer in charge at the Portal of the Stairs.

"Where is Jason?" I demanded. "Take me to him at once!"

"I'm afraid I can't do that, ladybird. You see, Jason has been arrested—the King caught him in Salome's boudoir."

My heart was leaden with conflicting sorrows. It was quite clear that Jason had betrayed me. He had left me to go to Salome. But hope dies so hard! I still didn't want him to suffer. There must be some explanation for his contradictory behavior.

Late at night I awakened when I heard someone fumbling at the lock on my door. Salome came in. She was flushed and agitated as she blurted: "That swine! That insufferable swine! My stepfather has condemned Jason to the arena! But you, you can save him—"

I mistrusted her and anything she might tell me. It would be best to question her carefully. I asked: "For what has he been condemned?"

"Herod has charged him with violating the sanctity of the women's quarters—with having gone to your room at night in the palace at Tiberias!"

"You know that is a lie!" I cried.

She made no answer. Her shadow fluttered against the walls like a great moth as she strode up and down past the brazier.

"You have brought him to this!" I burst out angrily. "It is all your doing! He didn't leave Tiberias with the court—he stayed with me—until you lured him away with that wretched note you sent by Enid! What did you say in it?"

"I had no pride—only envy," she said finally. "After I'd seen him in your sick room in Tiberias, nursing you, I knew I had to have him even though he didn't love me. So I sent Enid back to tell him that I'd marry him and run away with him to Alexandria."

I spoke harshly to keep back the tears. "Well, you succeeded! Your bargain must have appealed to him—he abandoned me and went to you!"

"He came to me," her face was averted, "to refuse my offer of marriage." She gave me a quick look from the corner of her eyes. "And to tell me he'd never love anyone but you. That's why he was with me when Herod caught us."

"Then why didn't you intercede for Jason? Why didn't you tell Herod the truth?"

"I did." Her laugh was mirthless. "I begged too hard—I told Herod
that I loved Jason and for that I must be humiliated by being forced to sit
in the arena and see Jason choose between the tiger and the lady *when he
knows that you will be the lady behind one door!*"

"But why will *I* be there?"

"Herod could scarcely accuse the Greek of seducing *me*, his stepdaughter! He has shifted the whole scandal to you. So I shall have to sit there
and watch the man I love being married to my rival—to you!"

"But suppose there isn't any marriage?" I could scarcely pronounce the
words. "Suppose Jason chooses the door that frees the tiger? There is that
terrible chance!"

Salome's smile was sly and determined. "That's why I have come here.
Chance is going to be eliminated. You and I are going to cheat Herod. We
will save Jason."

"Oh, Salome, how?"

"We will save him because we both love him. I am going to give him to
you."

My voice was choking. "Oh, Salome, I have been so wrong about you!"

She brushed my embrace aside. "I'm not doing this for you. I've
thought of a way to save him—because I can't see him die."

It was three nights ago that we had this conversation. We talked far
into the morning. Before she left, I had forgiven Salome all her former
slights and cruelties. For she had shown me how to save Jason. I wonder if
I could be as self-sacrificing as she. Her love for him is so great that she is
willing that he shall marry me—since she says she knows he loves me and
that we will be happy together.

I kissed her as we parted.

Since then I have spent my time writing this long letter to you. I know
that it contains many things that ordinarily a daughter would not write to
a father. But I have tried to be absolutely truthful, because I want you to
know, dearest Father, that in spite of all the doubts and troubles I have
gone through, I have done nothing that was wrong.

It is growing late and I am tired. Soon it will be morning. They will
come and dress me in a bridal gown. My draperies will be arranged with
many golden brooches. They will place flowers in my arms and the flame-
colored veil of a Roman bride over my hair. And they will leave me in that
little room, next to the room where they will have placed the tiger.

As soon as I am alone, I will take one of the golden brooches from my
garment. I will open one of my veins with it and let my blood run from

beneath the crack in the door, out onto the stone pavements of the dark corridor beneath the seats of the arena.

Before Salome takes her seat beside her stepfather, she will slip down into this corridor. She will see the blood and she will know in which room I am waiting. And she will signal to Jason to open my door.

I am happy, Father, despite my dreadful weariness. I hope that you will forgive me everything that has been reckless and foolish. I am a woman now, but still a little girl. How I wish that I could curl up in your lap and go to sleep! I am tired, but so contented and joyful—I must rest and be beautiful for my beloved. All my dreams will come true tomorrow.

Thus ended the letter of Miriam to her father. As I labored over its translation, this Jewish girl of twenty centuries ago became very real to me. I gave all my time to researches concerning Miriam. I had to learn what had happened to her.

The answer was found in the long-sought-for letter of Pontius Pilate to Tiberius. The first paragraph made it obvious that this originally had been dispatched to the Emperor as an explanation of Miriam's manuscript. But during the centuries they had become separated. Pilate's supplement was written in Latin upon two sheets of parchment. The first page read:

"To His Imperial Majesty, Tiberius Caesar, from Pontius Pilate, Procurator of Judea:

"May the Gods preserve Your Majesty! I forward the enclosed document to the Imperial Archives because it has some bearing upon Imperial policy in the Near East.

"As stated in previous reports, the High Priest (to whom the enclosed letter is addressed) has shown great stubbornness in refusing to cooperate in the matter of disposing of a certain Galilean preacher regarded by Your Majesty's Government as a dangerous malcontent. The High Priest was impervious to bribes, and even threats failed to coerce him into making the desired accusations which would enable Rome to crucify the Galilean and still place responsibility for the deed on the Jews.

"But now I am happy to inform Your Majesty that the whole matter has been satisfactorily resolved. Caiphas is a broken man. His will has been completely shattered (indeed, I doubt if he can any longer be considered sane) and is quite incapable of offering any further resistance.

"His transformation was brought about, quite unexpectedly, yesterday, when the Greek, Jason, was forced to choose between the lady and the tiger in Herod's Arena. I watched Caiphas very closely when he made his appearance, as Herod had ordered, in the royal box. His bearing was dignified and aloof. I almost found myself wishing that this well-controlled man was a Roman.

"One of our secret agents had intercepted a letter which the girl, Miriam, had written to her father; so that Caiphas had no way of knowing that his daughter was guiltless of Herod's implications. His trust in her evidently was based upon blind faith.

"Herod looked a trifle embarrassed as he turned to me and asked if I wanted to double my bet on the Greek's chances for survival. Of course, I did. Since I had read Miriam's letter, I felt I was betting on a sure thing. I even smiled to myself as, from the corner of my eye, I saw the Princess make her signal to the Greek to open the right-hand door.

"But I was a fool to trust Salome. The Greek, with his sense of the dramatic, started to pull back the portal very slowly. When it was open about a foot, we saw the sunlight fall on the striped hide and the blinking eyes of the tiger. The Greek seemed doomed. An automatic device made it impossible to push those doors shut, once either of them had started to open.

"But the Greek acted with the speed of lightning. As soon as he glimpsed the tiger, he stepped back and pulled open *both* doors. Now he was protected—wedged in the small space between the two open portals—as secure as if he had a big oak shield on each arm.

"The tiger, a finer specimen than any you'd see in Rome, advanced through the doorway on the right.

"And almost simultaneously, the girl, Miriam, looking pale but smiling beneath her bridal veil, came through the doorway on the left.

"For a few seconds the beast and the woman looked at each other. There was no sound in the amphitheater, except her father's sobbing.

"It was the fastest thinking I had ever seen. I did well to bet on the Greek."

The paper fell from my hand. All the injustice and cruelty of the world seemed summed up in Jason's contemptible stratagem.

I read the second page. Pilate had added the following postscript to his message.

"Despite the Greek's adroitness, I'm sure Your Majesty will agree that this Jason was too clever to be permitted to survive. His plot to marry Salome and seize the throne was a definite menace to Roman policy in Palestine and to Your Majesty's security. Since the man was the son of a slave and was not a Roman citizen, it was not difficult to charge him with the theft of the White Syndicate's horses and to condemn him, along with another thief and the Galilean preacher, to be crucified. He admitted under the torture that he had adopted the name of 'Jason' because of its romantic connotations. His real name was Gestos. He was the last of the three to die, and though his sufferings were excruciating, he did not ask for forgiveness."

Selected Bibliography and Filmography

1. Anthologies by Marvin Kaye

Love, sex and their permutations crop up often in my anthologies. Titles and authors of related pieces in my earlier Doubleday Book and Music Club collections include:

Ghosts "The Castle of the King," Bram Stoker; "The Ensouled Violin," Mme. Blavatsky; "Jane," Barbara Gallow; "The Lady of Finnigan's Hearth," Parke Godwin; "The Midnight Embrace," M. G. Lewis; "Miss Jeromette and the Clergyman," Wilkie Collins; "The Phantom Woman," Anonymous; "The Tale of the German Student," Washington Irving.

Masterpieces of Terror and the Supernatural This collection has a subsection appropriately labeled (what else?) "Lovers and Other Monsters." Its contents include "The Anchor," Jack Snow; "The Black Wedding," Isaac Bashevis Singer; "Carmilla," Sheridan LeFanu; "Eumenides in the Fourth Floor Lavatory," Orson Scott Card; "Graveyard Shift," Richard Matheson; "Hop-Frog," Edgar Allan Poe; "Lenore," Gottfried August Bürger; "Night and Silence," Maurice Level; "Oshidori," Lafcadio Hearn; "Sardonicus," Ray Russell; "Wake Not the Dead," Johann Ludwig Tieck; "When the Clock Strikes," Tanith Lee.

Devils & Demons "A Ballad of Hell," John Davidson; "Daddy," Earl Godwin; "Don Juan's Final Night," Edmond Rostand; "The Demon Lover," Anonymous; "Just a Little Thing," Joan Vander Putten; "Influencing the Hell Out of Time and Teresa Golowitz," Parke Godwin; "The Maze and the Monster," Edward D. Hoch; "Me, Tree," Morgan Llywelyn;

"The Princess and Her Future," Tanith Lee; "The Queen of Sheba's Nightmare," Bertrand Russell; "Rachaela," Poul Anderson; "Seven Come Heaven?," Diane Wnorowska; "The Shadow Watchers," Dick Baldwin; "Ulalume," Edgar Allan Poe.

Weird Tales, The Magazine that Never Dies "The Brotherhood of Blood," Hugh B. Cave; "The Damp Man," Allison V. Harding; "The Dead Smile," F. Marion Crawford; "Eena," Manly Banister; "The House of Ecstasy," Ralph Milne Farley; "In the X-Ray," Fritz Leiber Jr.; "Interim," Ray Bradbury; "The Look," Maurice Level; "Masked Ball," Seabury Quinn; "Men Who Walk Upon the Air," Frank Belknap Long Jr.; "Mr. George," August Derleth; "The Sorcerer's Apprentice," Robert Bloch; "Ti Michel," W. J. Stamper; "Wet Straw," Richard Matheson; "The Woman with the Velvet Collar," Gaston Leroux.

Witches & Warlocks "Doll-Baby," C. H. Sherman; "Emma's Daughter," Alan Rodgers; "Lorelei," Wilhelm Ruland; "The Magic Egg," Frank R. Stockton; "Sanguinarius," Ray Russell; "Seeing Them," Darrell Schweitzer; "St. John's Eve," Nikolai Gogol; "The Witch," Isaac Bashevis Singer.

13 Plays of Ghosts and the Supernatural "Dinny and the Witches," William Gibson; "Madam, Will You Walk?," Sidney Howard; "The Passion of Dracula," Bob Hall and David Richmond; "Teibele and Her Demon," Isaac Bashevis Singer and Eve Friedman.

Haunted America "Dumb Supper," Henderson Starke; "Gibbler's Ghost," William F. Nolan; "The Glove," Fritz Leiber Jr.; "The Girl with the Beckoning Eyes," Bernhardt J. Hurwood; "The Return of the Moresbys," Henry Slesar; "The Rider on the Pale Horse," Helen Eustis; "The Romance of Certain Old Clothes," Henry James; "Slaughter House," Richard Matheson; "The White Old Maid," Nathaniel Hawthorne.

2. Selected Prose

It would be an act of hubris to attempt to enumerate all fiction relevant to the theme of *Lovers & Other Monsters*. The following is merely a list of some of my favorite novels and a few key shorter tales.

A Rose for Emily by William Faulkner, a gently understated shocker, is a justly famous short story about a sexual perversion that most horror writers still consider taboo. It is curiously similar in intent to John Steinbeck's *Johnny Bear* (q.v.).

The Beckoning Fair One by Oliver Onions is a classic novella of ghostly possession that has influenced, consciously or unconsciously, the plots of many modern fantasy tales, especially Parke Godwin's award-winning *The Fire When It Comes* and Richard Matheson's *Slaughter House* (which appeared in my earlier collection, *Haunted America*).

Burning Bright, one of John Steinbeck's least familiar novels (it also exists in play form), is a tale of love, sacrifice and wholly justifiable marital infidelity. Admittedly not one of Steinbeck's most significant works, it still has an undeniable, if somewhat soap opera-ish, fascination. Also worth noting are two tales in this author's short story collection, *The Long Valley:* "The Snake," a singularly unpleasant exercise in morbid sexuality, and "Johnny Bear," which is reminiscent of William Faulkner's *A Rose for Emily,* mentioned above.

Darker Places by Parke Godwin is a nightmarish novel of sadomasochistic murder and revenge. Also worth noting is the same author's above-cited novella, *The Fire When It Comes,* a superb life-affirming ghost story.

The Disappearance by Philip Wylie is a grim sociological science-fiction novel. The inability of modern man and woman to communicate leads to a dimensional rift in which all men are stranded on a world without women and vice versa.

Donovan's Brain by Curt Siodmak is a well-crafted science-fiction novel about the telepathic possession of a scientist by the living brain of a ruthless tycoon, a takeover that incidentally includes the protagonist's beloved.

Ethan Frome, Edith Wharton's stark tragedy of frustrated love on a New England farm, is a once-read, never-forgotten masterpiece.

Four-Sided Triangle by William F. Temple is a novel-length *conte cruelle* about two scientists so in love with the same woman that they clone her, in the mistaken assumption that all four of them can live happily ever after.

How Love Came to Professor Guildea by Robert Hichens is an acclaimed "thinking person's" horror story about the nasty results of a familiarlike entity's adoration of the titular professor.

The Hunger by Charles Beaumont is perhaps the most famous short story by this lamentedly short-lived author. It depicts the gruesome psychological linkage between a rapist and his victim, a theme that is also explored in Ray Bradbury's *The Whole Town's Sleeping* and Michel de Ghelderode's *Lord Halewijn* (both cited below).

Implosion by D. F. Jones is a "doomsday" science-fiction novel in which a minor world power creates a biological weapon capable of destroying the male reproductive system.

The Magus by John Fowles is the ultimate novel of psychological manipulation, in which the protagonist is spiritually and emotionally raped "for his own good." The cynical amorality of Fowles' "godgame" perhaps led the author to rewrite *The Magus*. The revised edition is a more compassionate, emotionally satisfying composition.

The Master of the Day of Judgment by Leo Perutz, a neglected masterpiece, is a labyrinthine maze of sexual obsession and Hellish guilt.

The Moon Pool by A. Merritt is a fantasy novel about a fearful god whose victims suffer in an endless state of mingled ecstasy and horror.

Notre Dame de Paris, Victor Hugo's scathing novel of social injustice (better known as "The Hunchback of Notre Dame"), is rife with love—perverse, unrequited, profane. The crippled bell ringer Quasimodo heads a cast of grotesque, yet sympathetic downtrodden victimized by the corrupt aristocracy and clergy of fifteenth-century France.

The Pledge by Friedrich Duerrenmatt, filmed as *It Happened in Broad Daylight,* is a short novel about a policeman whose vow to avenge a young woman's rape-murder engages him in a quest nearly as repugnant as the crime itself.

Some of Your Blood, a novel by Theodore Sturgeon, attempts to evoke sympathy for consenting participants of a sadomasochistic love affair. Ted Sturgeon is always eminently readable, but variations of this idea have been more skillfully handled by several other authors, including Leopold von Sacher-Masoch, Tennessee Williams and, especially, Guy Endore (see below).

The Sorcerer's Lady by Paula Volsky is a fantasy novel that rings refreshing changes on the old damsel-forced-to-wed plot. Enforced marriage is the medium by which the heroine, like Thackeray's Glencora Palliser, grows in vision and wisdom. *The Sorcerer's Heir* and *The Sorcerer's Curse* continue this witty but essentially tragic trilogy.

Washington Square by Henry James, the tale of a young woman torn between her domineering father and the fortune hunter she falls in love with, was the basis for an excellent play and film, *The Heiress.*

The Werewolf of Paris by Guy Endore is to lycanthropic literature what Bram Stoker's *Dracula* is to the vampire novel. Its vulpine protagonist is ultimately victim of a society riddled with lecherous priests, inhuman scientists and savage soldiery.

The Whole Town's Sleeping by Ray Bradbury is a short story about a rapist known only as The Lonely One. After its initial publications in *McCall's* and *Ellery Queen's Mystery Magazine,* the tale was integrated into Bradbury's novel *Dandelion Wine,* with a brief epilogue that purports to tell "what happened next"—a sequential episode that contradicts Bradbury's own superior sequel, *At Midnight, in the Month of June,* included in his recent story collection, *The Toynbee Convector.*

3. Selected Drama

Angel Street by Patrick Hamilton, a suspenseful melodrama about a vicious murderer trying to drive his wife mad, was the basis for the twice-filmed thriller *Gaslight.*

Before Breakfast, a one-act play by Eugene O'Neill, is a tour de force monologue of a discontented wife whose vicious nagging prompts her husband to commit suicide.

Dance of Death by August Strindberg is actually two plays that span several years of a marriage whose partners both love and loathe one another. Another savage love-hate relationship is depicted in the same author's *The Father.*

The Dybbuk by the pseudonymous S. Anski is the great Jewish poetic tragedy about a young woman possessed by the spirit of a dead scholar whom she loved. A fascinating, unfortunately scarce Polish film circa 1938 is well worth seeing; reportedly, only 16mm prints of it exist in this country.

Edwina Black by William Dinner and William Morum is an atmospheric study of suspicion and guilt engineered by a dead woman to destroy her husband's future romantic happiness.

Francesca da Rimini by George Henry Boker is an important early American tragedy based on the legend of Paola and Francesca, doomed lovers who figure importantly in one of the earlier cantos of Dante's *Inferno.*

Hamlet, King of Denmark is a remarkable tetralogy by Percy MacKaye that, beginning thirty years before Shakespeare's *Hamlet,* develops the love triangle between King Hamlet, Queen Gertrude and Claudius.

Happy Days by Samuel Beckett is a bleak absurdist depiction of the sad final years of a marriage. In the first act, Winnie, the wife, is buried waist-high in sand. Her neglectful mate rarely communicates with her until late in the play, when the symbolic sand has nearly engulfed her.

The Lesson by Eugene Ionesco is a long absurdist one-act comedy that equates tutoring with rape-murder. (An educational TV version exists; it features a splendid performance by Fred Gwynne.) Also worth noting is Ionesco's *Amédee,* in which a dying marriage is represented by a corpse that grows to colossal size.

Lord Halewijn by Michel de Ghelderode is a series of scenes of mounting tension about a nobleman who wants to kill a neighboring princess. In spite of her family's protection and her own common sense, the princess is inexorably drawn to meet the murderer, with unexpected results.

Love from a Stranger, a romantic thriller by Frank Vosper based on an Agatha Christie tale, is an example of the suspect-your-mate school of suspense. Despite its age, it still has effective moments and an ingenious climax.

Murder in the Red Barn, also known as *The Murder of Maria Marten,* is an anonymous "barnstormer" folk drama that, along with George Dibdin Pitt's *Sweeney Todd,* represents the pinnacle of nineteenth-century melodrama. There is an effective English film version starring the aptly named Todd Slaughter, who also did a British movie of Pitt's Sweeney Todd in 1936.

Night Must Fall by Emlyn Williams, twice filmed, is the strangely poetic portrait of a homicidal maniac with a talent for making women who ought to know better fall in love with him.

Salome, a one-act drama by Oscar Wilde that inspired the libretto of Richard Strauss' opera, is a sensuous, sensual study in lust and corruption.

The Shrike by Joseph Kramm was, after Cyrano, one of José Ferrer's most impressive earlier "legit" acting vehicles. This Strindbergian tale of a wife whose tenacious love drives her husband to a nervous breakdown was effectively filmed in 1955 with June Allyson in a change-of-image role as the wife. Though its ending is watered down, the film is culturally significant as one of the first American movie that featured (and publicized) a scene in which a man (Ferrer) cries.

Summer and Smoke is Tennessee Williams' ironic view of physical and spiritual love and their essential incompatibility. The excellent 1961 film stars Geraldine Page and Laurence Harvey.

4. Selected Films

A Safe Place (1971), the first film directed by Henry Jaglom, is a pictorially and emotionally overwhelming stream-of-consciousness fantasy of a young woman (Tuesday Weld) serially betrayed by lovers and ersatz father (Orson Welles, in one of his most appealing performances). Despite its dismissal by America's critical establishment, *A Safe Place* has deservedly become a collegiate cult classic.

The Black Cat (1934), the first teaming of Bela Lugosi and Boris Karloff, contains strong hints of sexual perversion.

Blood and Roses (1961) is loosely based on Sheridan Le Fanu's vampiric *Carmilla*. Though mostly just another Roger Vadim mishmash, the film's climactic "dream" sequence is (arguably) effective enough to make the rest of the picture worth enduring.

The Blue Angel (1930), starring Emil Jannings and Marlene Dietrich, is a masterpiece of sexual domination and humiliation.

The Company of Wolves (1984) is a lycanthropic fantasy with heavily erotic under(and over-)tones. Though too convoluted, and despite a predictable "wimpy" windup, it is still one of the best werewolf films of recent memory, light years ahead of such juvenilia as *The Howling*.

Creature from the Black Lagoon (1954), first and best of the three "creature" movies, features subtly erotic underwater sequences (originally released in 3-D).

Daughters of Darkness (1971), with its heavy burden of homosexuality and sadistic murder, may be the kinkiest vampire film ever made. Yet, far from being exploitational, it boasts a literate script, excellent acting and cinematography. In spite of its hasty, conventional ending, it deserves a high place in the subgenre of serious adult cinema horror.

Dead Ringers (1988) is a shocker that wisely substitutes psychosexual horror for director David Cronenberg's more usual physical gruesomeness. The tale of twin doctors who descend into madness, it is curiously reminiscent of Ingmar Bergman's *Persona* (1966). I agree with film critic Andrew Sarris, who once told me that if the film community had not discounted *Dead Ringers* as "a mere horror movie," Jeremy Irons might have won an Oscar for his dual portrayal of the tormented physicians.

Diabolique (1955), directed by Henri-Georges Clouzot (sometimes called "France's Alfred Hitchcock," though Hitch's darkness seems comparatively healthy compared with Clouzot), is the justly famous tale of two women who plot and kill their respective husband and lover . . . or did they? A good theatrical version, *Monique*, was adapted from the same novel by Pierre Boileau and Thomas Narcejac, who also jointly wrote the book Hitchcock filmed as *Vertigo*.

Dr. Jekyll and Mr. Hyde has been filmed several times, always with unsettling sexual content. The restored 1932 version that won Fredric March an Academy Award for Best Actor is especially effective.

Eye of the Needle (1981), based on Ken Follett's best-selling spy novel, is Follett's first and perhaps best mixture of espionage and politically expedient carnality.

Freaks (1932) is a bizarre tale that stresses the loving familial instincts of a troupe of circus freaks, yet also depicts them as capable of inflicting a grotesque (and totally unbelievable) revenge on a beautiful woman one of them unwisely falls in love with. Yet in spite of its unresolvable thematic contradictions, it is still an engrossing film with a frightening climax reminiscent of German cinematic horror.

Gate of Hell (1954) is a great Japanese film about lust and the shame that follows its fulfillment.

The Innocents (1961), still the best dramatization of Henry James' ghost (?) story, *The Turn of the Screw*, contains an undertone of sexual frustration that, unlike Michael Winner's inept 1972 prequel, *The Nightcomers*, is never prurient.

Laura (1944), Otto Preminger's stylish film of obsessive passion and murder, still holds up well despite a few noticeable excisions necessitated by problems with the music rights.

Love Me or Leave Me (1955), a musical biofilm about singer Ruth Etting (Doris Day), is memorable for its performance by James Cagney of a love-crazed gangster.

Mad Love (1935) is distinguished by a wonderfully repellent "turn" by Peter Lorre as a perverted surgeon.

Monsieur Verdoux (1923) features Charlie Chaplin as a dapper French wife-murderer. Decades ahead of its time, this black comedy is still effective for its humorous moments, but is far more remarkable for its compassion and scathing tragic irony.

Murders in the Rue Morgue (1932) owes less to Poe than the expressionistic German masterpiece, *The Cabinet of Dr. Caligari*. Though dated, it is still worth watching for Bela Lugosi's mad scientist bent on mating a woman with his pet ape.

The Night Porter (1974) is an ugly film about a terminally compulsive love affair between an ex-Nazi (Dirk Bogarde) and a prisoner (Charlotte Rampling) he abused.

Nights of Cabiria (1957) is Federico Fellini's award-winning film about a winsome prostitute (Giuletta Masina) who seeks love but always finds pain.

Once Upon a Time in the West (1969), Sergio Leone's l-o-n-g but enjoyable "spaghetti western," contains many gritty elements, including the heroine's sexual coercion by a particularly loathsome villain (brilliantly portrayed by Henry Fonda).

One of My Wives Is Missing (1976), starring Elizabeth Ashley, James Franciscus and Jack Klugman, is a superb thriller-puzzler full of astonishing plot twists. This made-for-TV movie was almost proclaimed "year's best" by the Mystery Writers of America, but was edged out by *Helter-Skelter*. For the record, I was one of the judges who wanted *One of My Wives Is Missing* to win. I felt that the factual *Helter-Skelter* did not belong in the same category as a fictional film.

Orpheus (1949) is Jean Cocteau's parable of a French poet who falls in love with personified death. Some of the special effects are now familiar because other filmmakers have copied them, yet a few are still startling.

Phantom of the Opera. The 1925 silent is still the recommended version of Gaston Leroux's popular novel. Lon Chaney Sr.'s Erik surely intends to enjoy the intimate favors of heroine Mary Philbin, but in the 1943 color remake, phantom Claude Rains' passion is more spiritual than fleshly.

Play Misty for Me (1971), Clint Eastwood's directorial debut, tells the harrowing tale of a disc jockey (Eastwood) stalked by a psychopathic ex-lover (Jessica Walter). The story is similar to 1987's popular *Fatal Attraction*, but movie buffs generally consider *Misty* superior.

Robin and Marian (1976). In this bleak, moving epilogue to the Robin Hood–Maid Marian legend, James Goldman's existential script is strikingly complemented by director Richard Lester's sweeping landscapes that repeatedly dwarf the aging heroes. Magnificent performances by Robert Shaw, Sean Connery, Richard Harris, Audrey Hepburn and Nicol Williamson distinguish this splendidly autumnal film.

Sawdust and Tinsel (1953), an early Ingmar Bergman film (also called *The Naked Night*), is a tale of infidelity set at a traveling circus. In a list of memorable moments of cinematic horror, Ivan Butler's intelligent book *The Horror Film* (A. Zwemmer Ltd., London, 1967) properly includes the scene in which the circus owner is beaten in his own ring by his wife's lover.

Scarface (1932). Time has scarcely blunted the fury of Paul Muni's unnatural love for his own sister (Ann Dvorak) in this raw gangster feature.

Seven Beauties (1976) is notable for Giancarlo Giannini's harrowing portrayal of a concentration camp prisoner determined to survive at any cost, even if it means becoming the lover of the grossly unappealing commandant.

Tales of Hoffman (1951), conducted by Thomas Beecham and starring Robert Rounseville as "the definitive Hoffman," is an imaginative, spirited English-language version of the Jacques Offenbach opera. Three weird love stories—one science-fictional and the others supernatural—

derive from the fantasy fiction of E. T. A. Hoffman. My late friend Bob Rounseville told me he was especially proud of the final scene of the opera, which the producers excised after the initial release. One hopes some film historian will unearth the missing footage and issue a restored version.

The Virgin Spring (1959) is Ingmar Bergman's ostensibly simple but broodingly complex fable of a rape-murder and the revenge its perpetrators suffer.

Acknowledgments